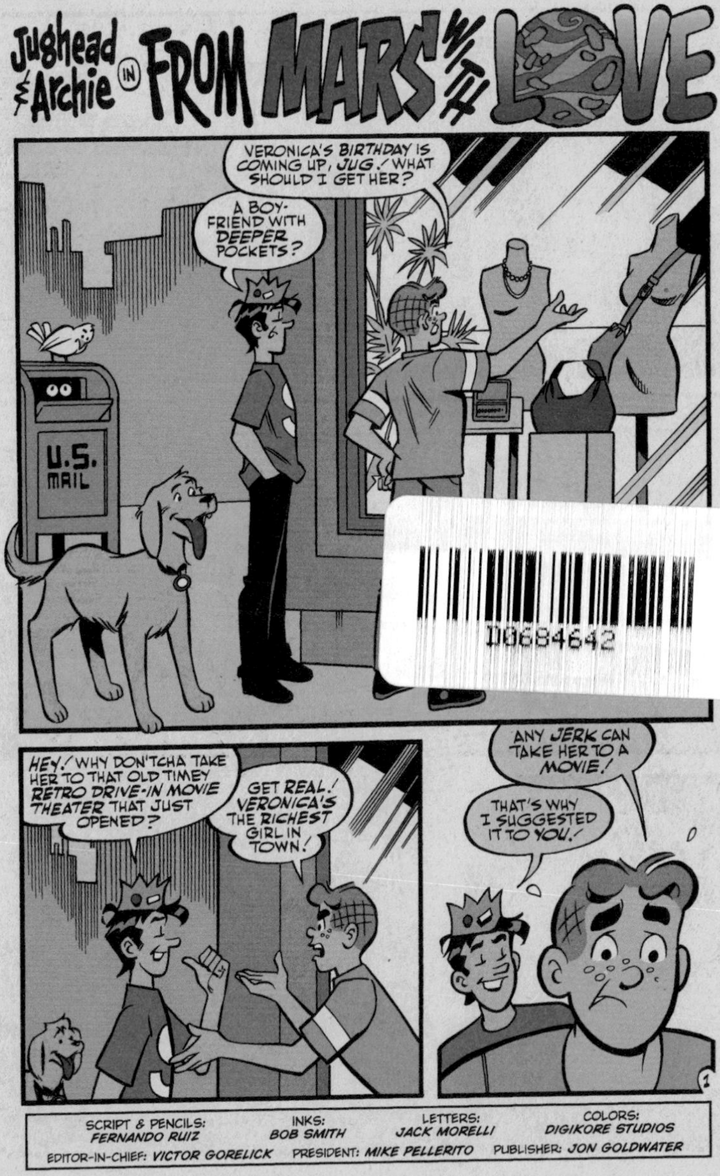
Jughead & Archie in FROM MARS WITH LOVE
VERONICA'S BIRTHDAY IS COMING UP, JUG! WHAT SHOULD I GET HER?
A BOY-FRIEND WITH DEEPER POCKETS?
U.S. MAIL
HEY! WHY DON'TCHA TAKE HER TO THAT OLD TIMEY RETRO DRIVE-IN MOVIE THEATER THAT JUST OPENED?
GET REAL! VERONICA'S THE RICHEST GIRL IN TOWN!
ANY JERK CAN TAKE HER TO A MOVIE!
THAT'S WHY I SUGGESTED IT TO YOU!
1

SCRIPT & PENCILS: FERNANDO RUIZ
INKS: BOB SMITH
LETTERS: JACK MORELLI
COLORS: DIGIKORE STUDIOS
EDITOR-IN-CHIEF: VICTOR GORELICK PRESIDENT: MIKE PELLERITO PUBLISHER: JON GOLDWATER

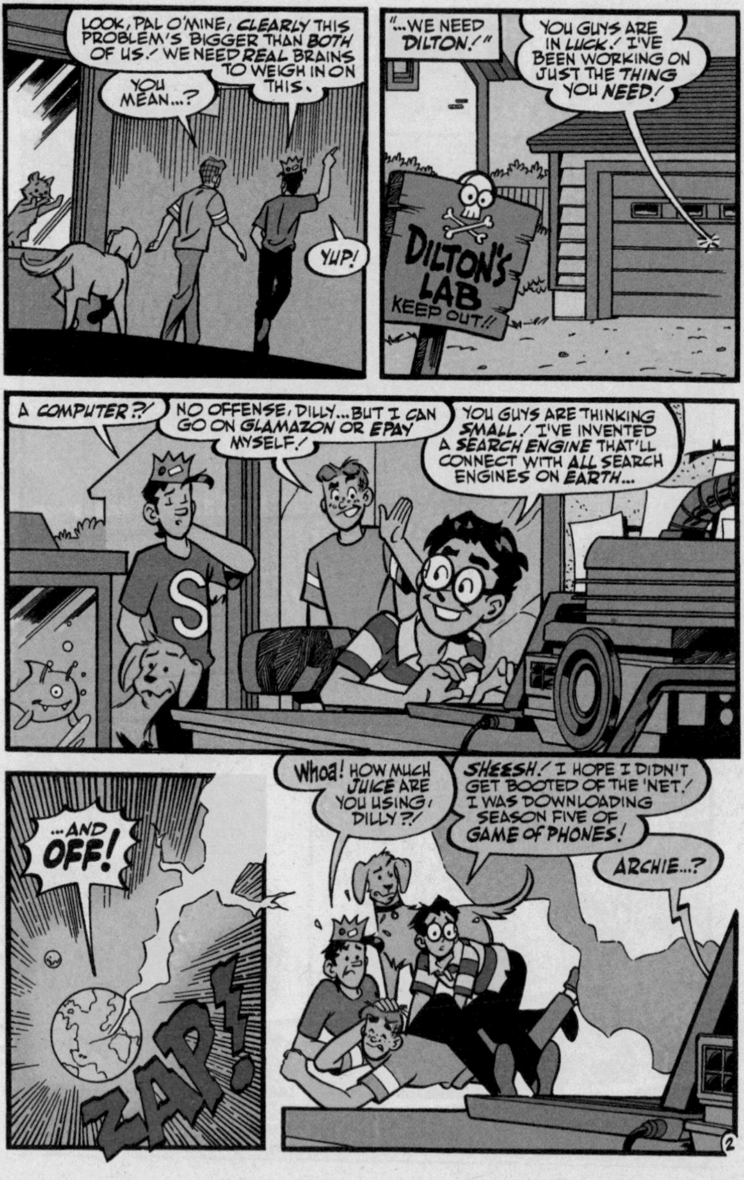
LOOK, PAL O'MINE, CLEARLY THIS PROBLEM'S BIGGER THAN BOTH OF US! WE NEED REAL BRAINS TO WEIGH IN ON THIS.
YOU MEAN...?
YUP!
"...WE NEED DILTON!"
YOU GUYS ARE IN LUCK! I'VE BEEN WORKING ON JUST THE THING YOU NEED!
DILTON'S LAB
KEEP OUT!!
A COMPUTER?!
NO OFFENSE, DILLY...BUT I CAN GO ON GLAMAZON OR EPAY MYSELF!
YOU GUYS ARE THINKING SMALL! I'VE INVENTED A SEARCH ENGINE THAT'LL CONNECT WITH ALL SEARCH ENGINES ON EARTH...
...AND OFF!
ZAP!
Whoa! HOW MUCH JUICE ARE YOU USING, DILLY?!
SHEESH! I HOPE I DIDN'T GET BOOTED OF THE 'NET! I WAS DOWNLOADING SEASON FIVE OF GAME OF PHONES!
ARCHIE...?

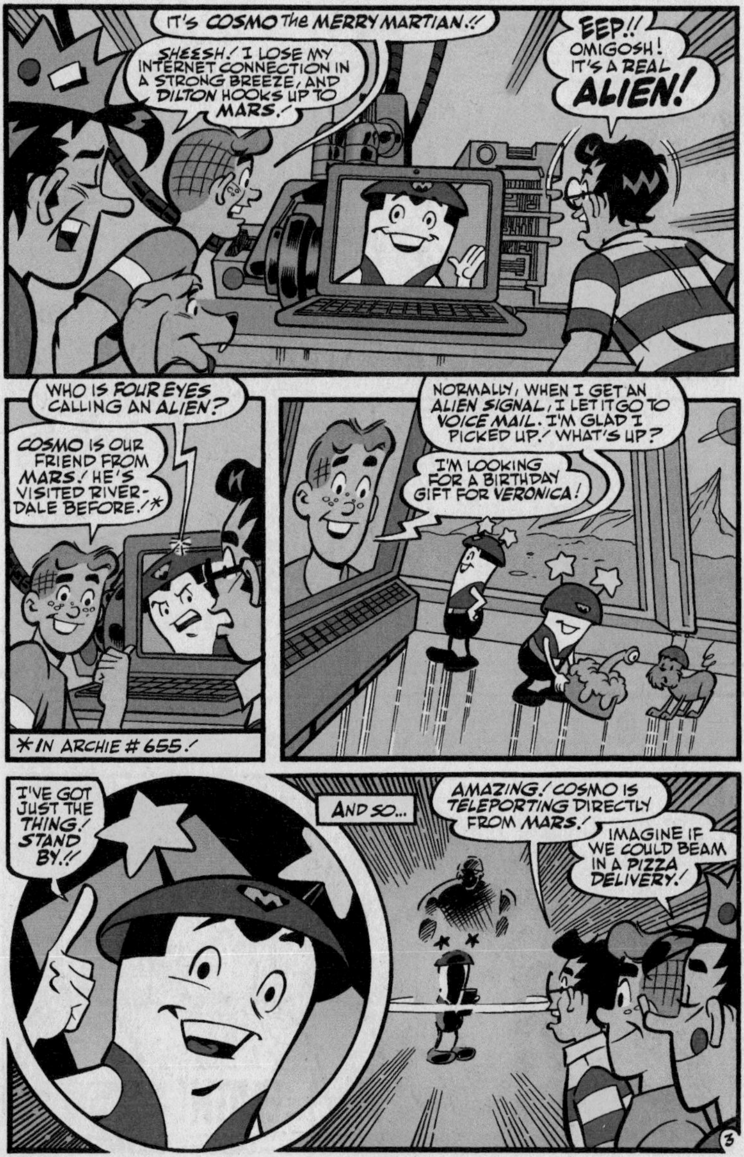
IT'S COSMO THE MERRY MARTIAN!!
SHEESH! I LOSE MY INTERNET CONNECTION IN A STRONG BREEZE, AND DILTON HOOKS UP TO MARS!
EEP!! OMIGOSH! IT'S A REAL ALIEN!
WHO IS FOUR EYES CALLING AN ALIEN?
COSMO IS OUR FRIEND FROM MARS! HE'S VISITED RIVERDALE BEFORE!*
*IN ARCHIE # 655!
NORMALLY, WHEN I GET AN ALIEN SIGNAL, I LET IT GO TO VOICE MAIL. I'M GLAD I PICKED UP! WHAT'S UP?
I'M LOOKING FOR A BIRTHDAY GIFT FOR VERONICA!
I'VE GOT JUST THE THING! STAND BY!!
AND SO...
AMAZING! COSMO IS TELEPORTING DIRECTLY FROM MARS!
IMAGINE IF WE COULD BEAM IN A PIZZA DELIVERY!
3

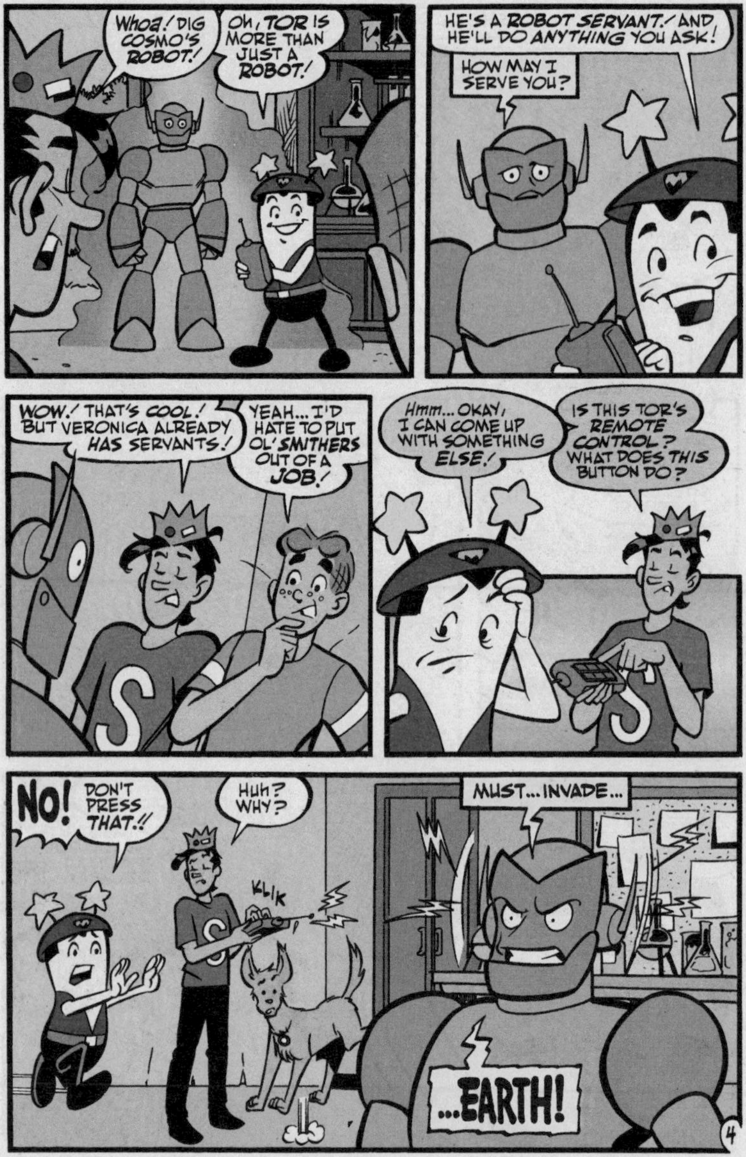
Whoa! DIG COSMO'S ROBOT!
Oh, TOR IS MORE THAN JUST A ROBOT!
HE'S A ROBOT SERVANT! AND HE'LL DO ANYTHING YOU ASK!
HOW MAY I SERVE YOU?
WOW! THAT'S COOL! BUT VERONICA ALREADY HAS SERVANTS!
YEAH... I'D HATE TO PUT OL' SMITHERS OUT OF A JOB!
Hmm... OKAY, I CAN COME UP WITH SOMETHING ELSE!
IS THIS TOR'S REMOTE CONTROL? WHAT DOES THIS BUTTON DO?
NO! DON'T PRESS THAT!!
Huh? WHY?
KLIK
MUST... INVADE...
...EARTH!
4

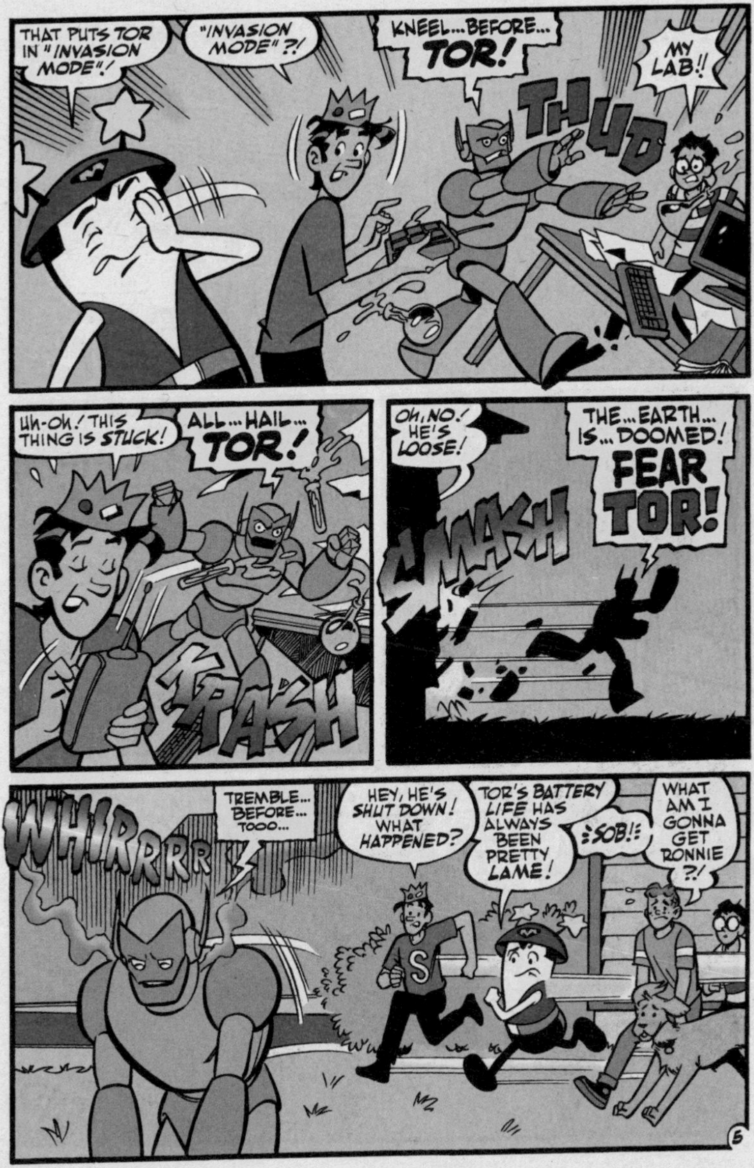
THAT PUTS TOR IN "INVASION MODE"!
"INVASION MODE"?!
KNEEL... BEFORE... TOR!
MY LAB!!
THUD
UH-OH! THIS THING IS STUCK!
ALL... HAIL... TOR!
KRASH
OH, NO! HE'S LOOSE!
THE... EARTH... IS... DOOMED! FEAR TOR!
SMASH
WHIRRRRR
TREMBLE... BEFORE... TOOO...
HEY, HE'S SHUT DOWN! WHAT HAPPENED?
TOR'S BATTERY LIFE HAS ALWAYS BEEN PRETTY LAME!
SOB!
WHAT AM I GONNA GET RONNIE?!
5

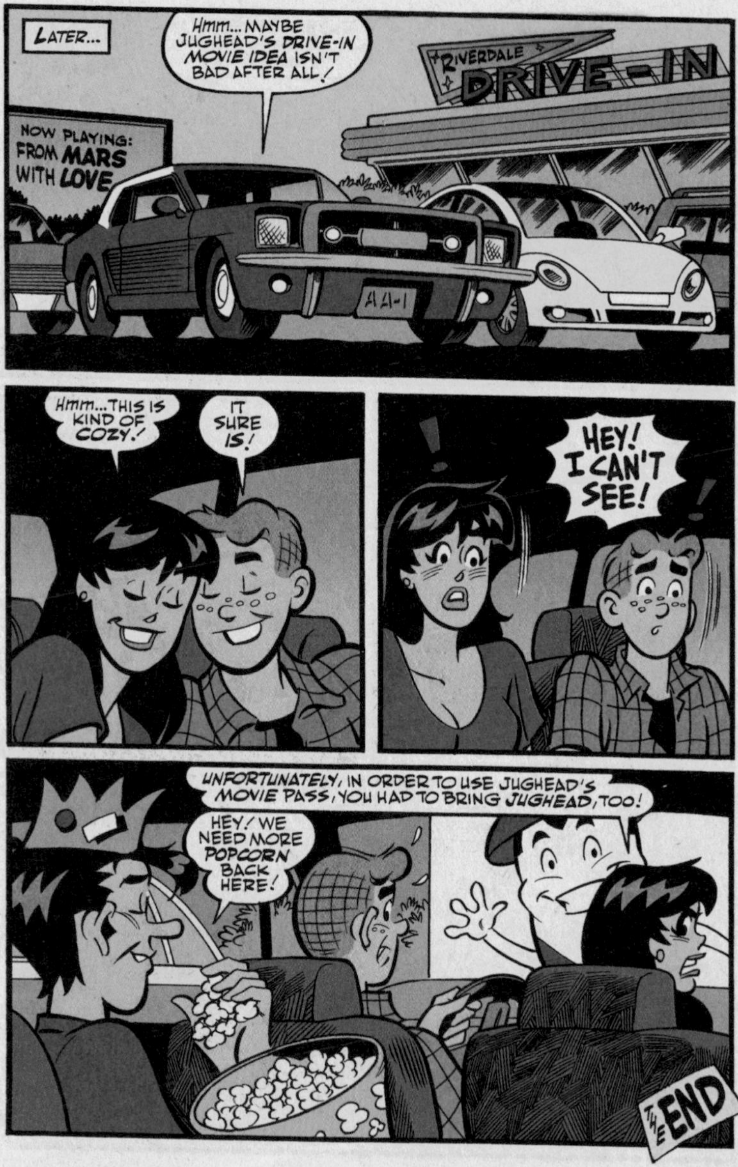
LATER...
Hmm... MAYBE JUGHEAD'S DRIVE-IN MOVIE IDEA ISN'T BAD AFTER ALL!
RIVERDALE DRIVE-IN
NOW PLAYING: FROM MARS WITH LOVE
AA-1
Hmm... THIS IS KIND OF COZY!
IT SURE IS!
HEY! I CAN'T SEE!
UNFORTUNATELY, IN ORDER TO USE JUGHEAD'S MOVIE PASS, YOU HAD TO BRING JUGHEAD, TOO!
HEY! WE NEED MORE POPCORN BACK HERE!
THE END

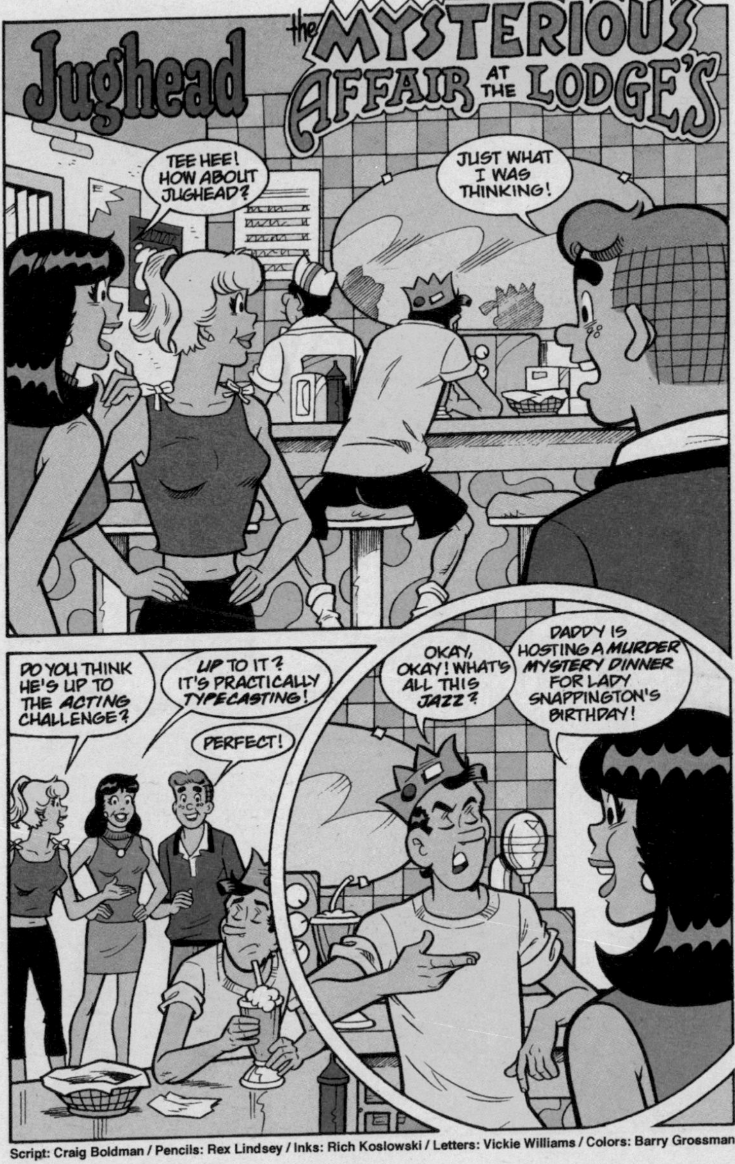
Jughead
the MYSTERIOUS AFFAIR AT THE LODGE'S
TEE HEE! HOW ABOUT JUGHEAD?
JUST WHAT I WAS THINKING!
DO YOU THINK HE'S UP TO THE ACTING CHALLENGE?
UP TO IT? IT'S PRACTICALLY TYPECASTING!
PERFECT!
OKAY, OKAY! WHAT'S ALL THIS JAZZ?
DADDY IS HOSTING A MURDER MYSTERY DINNER FOR LADY SNAPPINGTON'S BIRTHDAY!

Script: Craig Boldman / Pencils: Rex Lindsey / Inks: Rich Koslowski / Letters: Vickie Williams / Colors: Barry Grossman

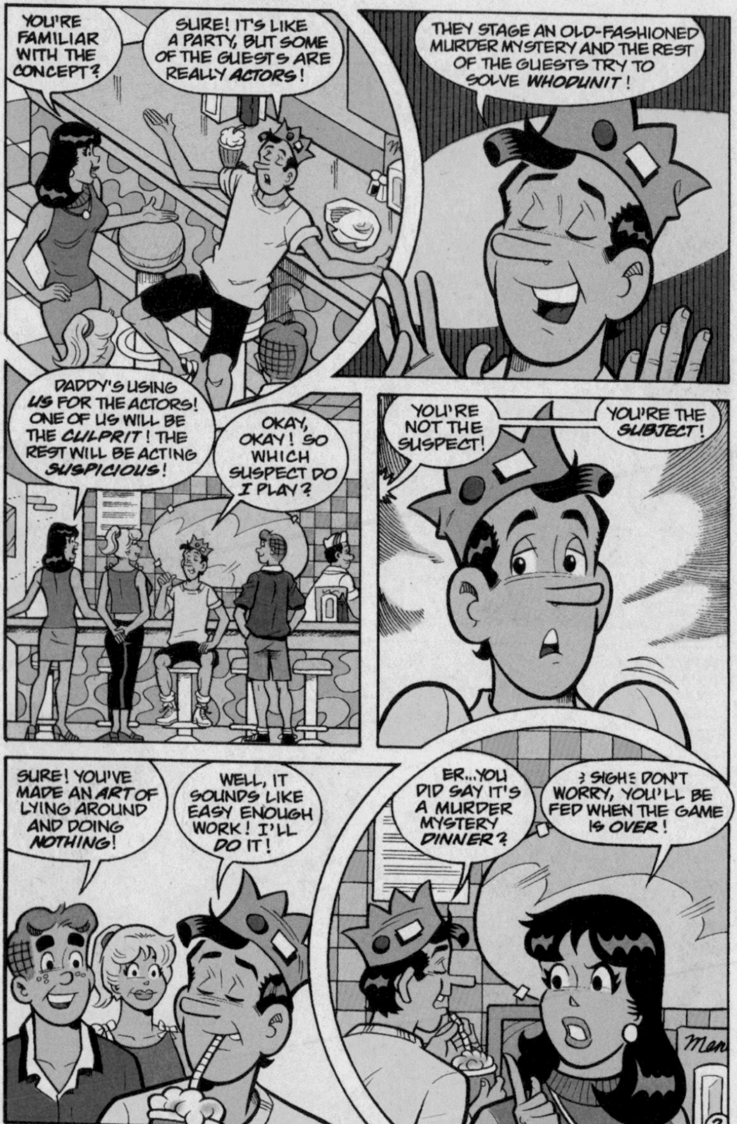
YOU'RE FAMILIAR WITH THE CONCEPT?
SURE! IT'S LIKE A PARTY, BUT SOME OF THE GUESTS ARE REALLY ACTORS!
THEY STAGE AN OLD-FASHIONED MURDER MYSTERY AND THE REST OF THE GUESTS TRY TO SOLVE WHODUNIT!
DADDY'S USING US FOR THE ACTORS! ONE OF US WILL BE THE CULPRIT! THE REST WILL BE ACTING SUSPICIOUS!
OKAY, OKAY! SO WHICH SUSPECT DO I PLAY?
YOU'RE NOT THE SUSPECT!
YOU'RE THE SUBJECT!
SURE! YOU'VE MADE AN ART OF LYING AROUND AND DOING NOTHING!
WELL, IT SOUNDS LIKE EASY ENOUGH WORK! I'LL DO IT!
ER...YOU DID SAY IT'S A MURDER MYSTERY DINNER?
SIGH DON'T WORRY, YOU'LL BE FED WHEN THE GAME IS OVER!
2

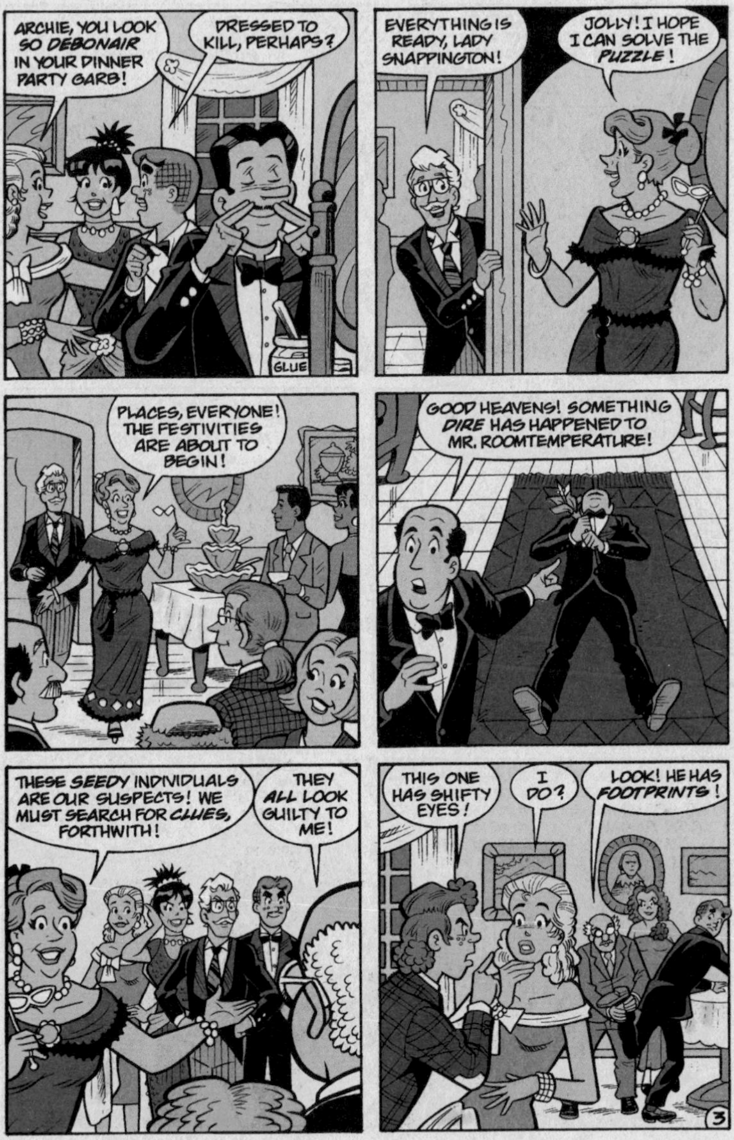
ARCHIE, YOU LOOK SO DEBONAIR IN YOUR DINNER PARTY GARB!
DRESSED TO KILL, PERHAPS?
GLUE
EVERYTHING IS READY, LADY SNAPPINGTON!
JOLLY! I HOPE I CAN SOLVE THE PUZZLE!
PLACES, EVERYONE! THE FESTIVITIES ARE ABOUT TO BEGIN!
GOOD HEAVENS! SOMETHING DIRE HAS HAPPENED TO MR. ROOMTEMPERATURE!
THESE SEEDY INDIVIDUALS ARE OUR SUSPECTS! WE MUST SEARCH FOR CLUES, FORTHWITH!
THEY ALL LOOK GUILTY TO ME!
THIS ONE HAS SHIFTY EYES!
I DO?
LOOK! HE HAS FOOTPRINTS!

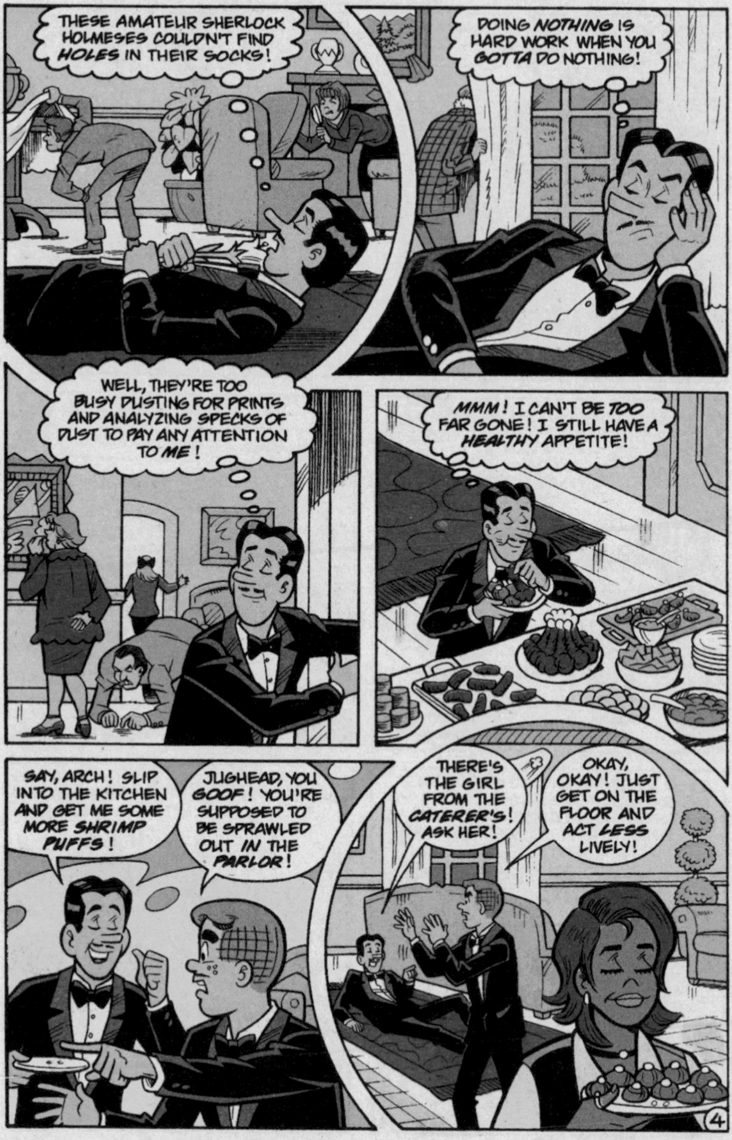
THESE AMATEUR SHERLOCK HOLMESES COULDN'T FIND HOLES IN THEIR SOCKS!
DOING NOTHING IS HARD WORK WHEN YOU GOTTA DO NOTHING!
WELL, THEY'RE TOO BUSY DUSTING FOR PRINTS AND ANALYZING SPECKS OF DUST TO PAY ANY ATTENTION TO ME!
MMM! I CAN'T BE TOO FAR GONE! I STILL HAVE A HEALTHY APPETITE!
SAY, ARCH! SLIP INTO THE KITCHEN AND GET ME SOME MORE SHRIMP PUFFS!
JUGHEAD, YOU GOOF! YOU'RE SUPPOSED TO BE SPRAWLED OUT IN THE PARLOR!
THERE'S THE GIRL FROM THE CATERER'S! ASK HER!
OKAY, OKAY! JUST GET ON THE FLOOR AND ACT LESS LIVELY!
4

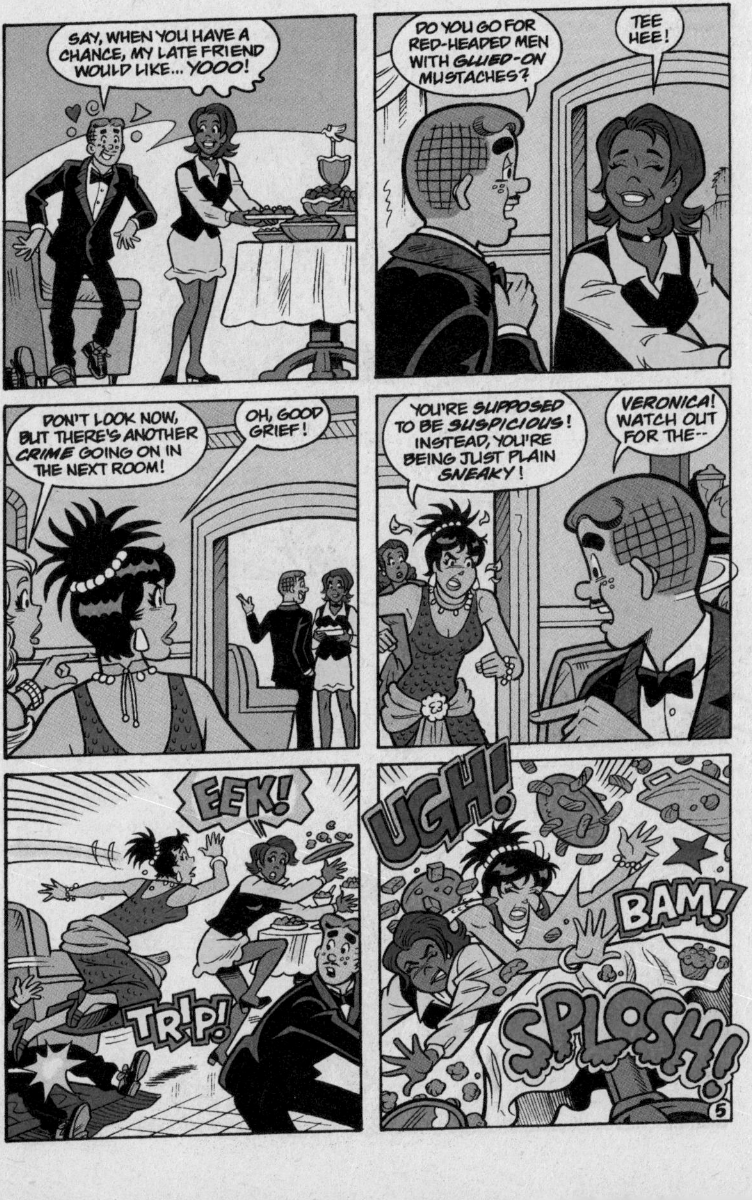

SAY, WHEN YOU HAVE A CHANCE, MY LATE FRIEND WOULD LIKE... YOOO!
DO YOU GO FOR RED-HEADED MEN WITH GLUED-ON MUSTACHES?
TEE HEE!
DON'T LOOK NOW, BUT THERE'S ANOTHER CRIME GOING ON IN THE NEXT ROOM!
OH, GOOD GRIEF!
YOU'RE SUPPOSED TO BE SUSPICIOUS! INSTEAD, YOU'RE BEING JUST PLAIN SNEAKY!
VERONICA! WATCH OUT FOR THE--
EEK!
TRIP!
UGH!
BAM!
SPLOSH!

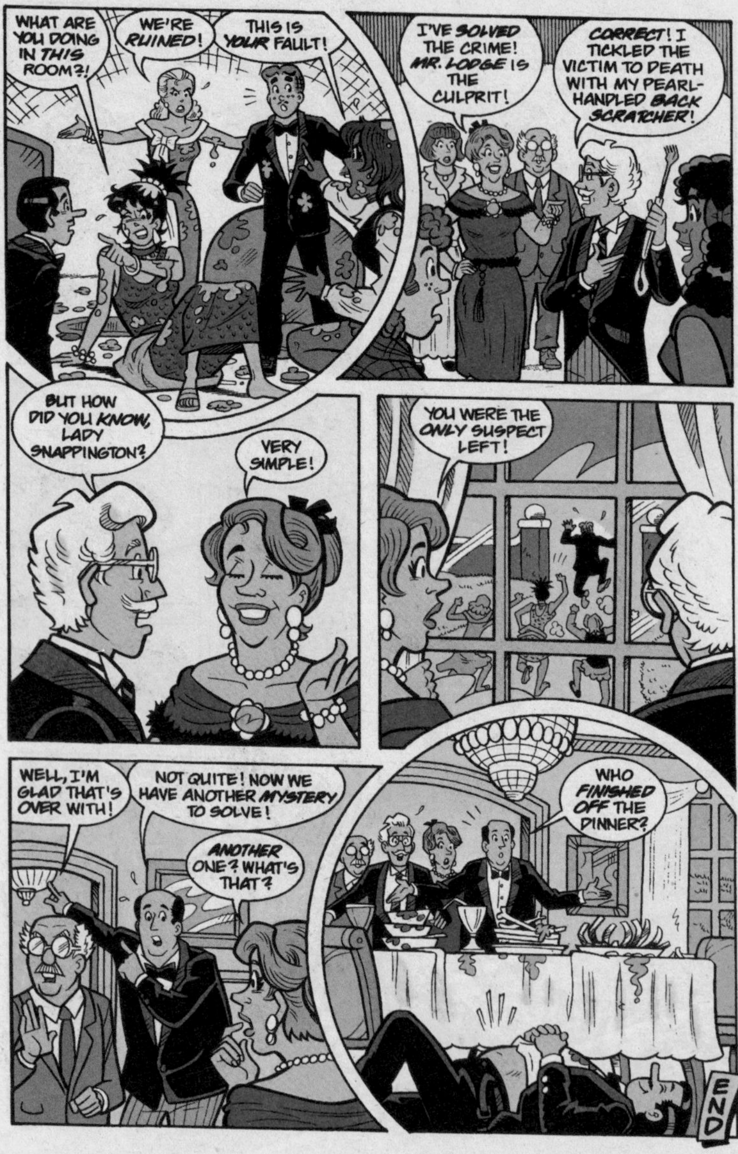
WHAT ARE YOU DOING IN THIS ROOM?!
WE'RE RUINED!
THIS IS YOUR FAULT!
I'VE SOLVED THE CRIME! MR. LODGE IS THE CULPRIT!
CORRECT! I TICKLED THE VICTIM TO DEATH WITH MY PEARL-HANDLED BACK SCRATCHER!
BUT HOW DID YOU KNOW, LADY SNAPPINGTON?
VERY SIMPLE!
YOU WERE THE ONLY SUSPECT LEFT!
WELL, I'M GLAD THAT'S OVER WITH!
NOT QUITE! NOW WE HAVE ANOTHER MYSTERY TO SOLVE!
ANOTHER ONE? WHAT'S THAT?
WHO FINISHED OFF THE DINNER?
END

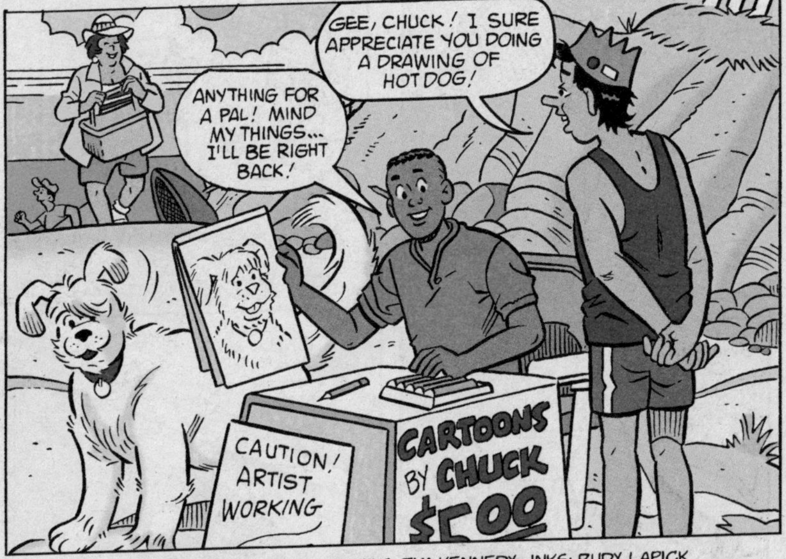
GEE, CHUCK! I SURE APPRECIATE YOU DOING A DRAWING OF HOT DOG!
ANYTHING FOR A PAL! MIND MY THINGS... I'LL BE RIGHT BACK!
CAUTION! ARTIST WORKING
CARTOONS BY CHUCK $5.00

SCRIPT: GEORGE GLADIR PENCILS: TIM KENNEDY INKS: RUDY LAPICK
COLORS: BARRY GROSSMAN LETTERS: BILL YOSHIDA

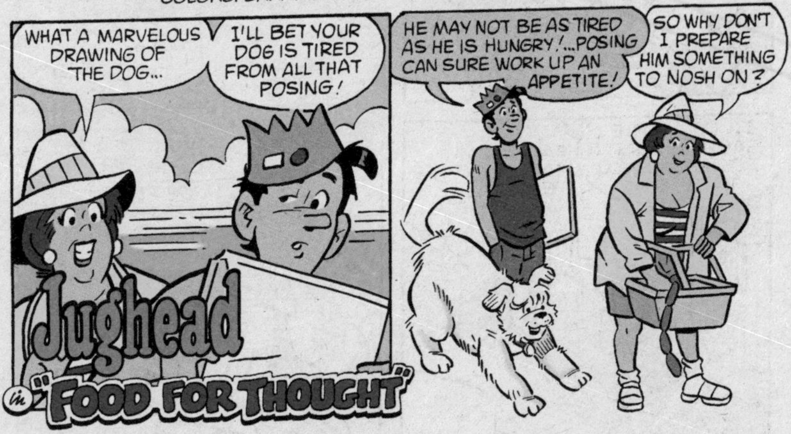
WHAT A MARVELOUS DRAWING OF THE DOG...
I'LL BET YOUR DOG IS TIRED FROM ALL THAT POSING!
HE MAY NOT BE AS TIRED AS HE IS HUNGRY!...POSING CAN SURE WORK UP AN APPETITE!
SO WHY DON'T I PREPARE HIM SOMETHING TO NOSH ON?
Jughead
in "FOOD FOR THOUGHT"

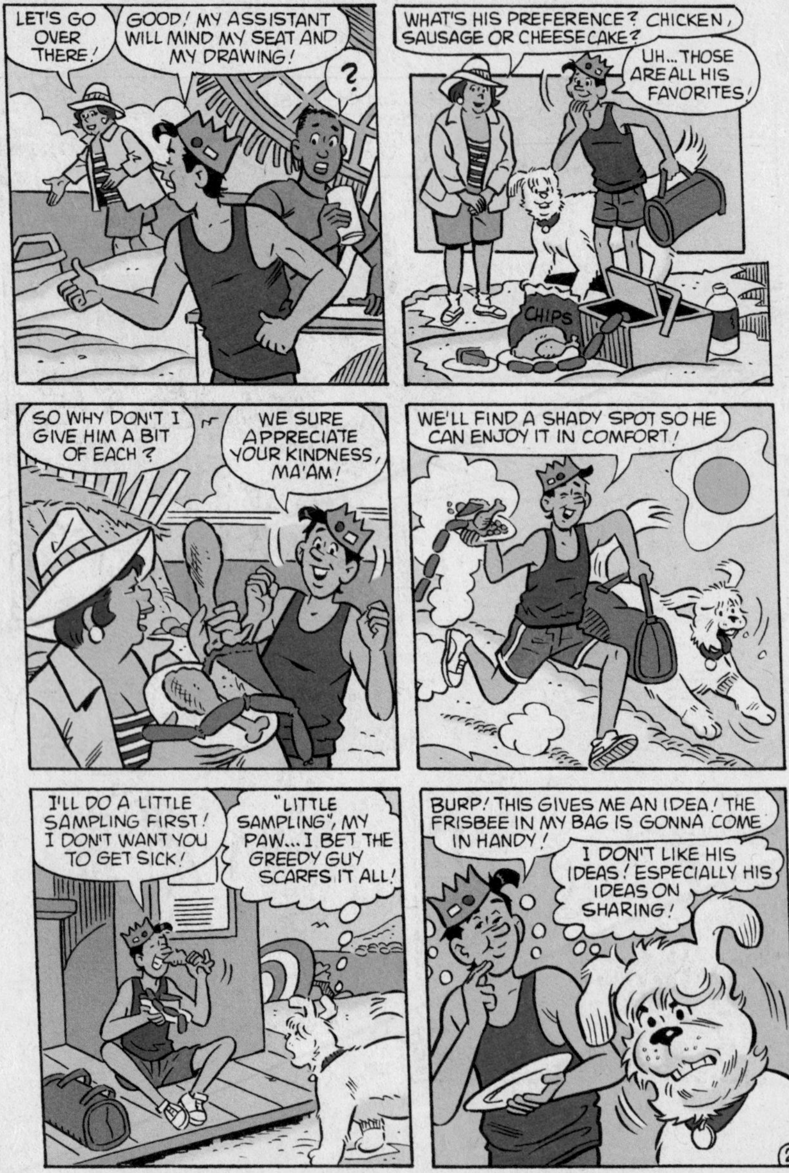
LET'S GO OVER THERE!
GOOD! MY ASSISTANT WILL MIND MY SEAT AND MY DRAWING!
?
WHAT'S HIS PREFERENCE? CHICKEN, SAUSAGE OR CHEESE CAKE?
UH... THOSE ARE ALL HIS FAVORITES!
CHIPS
SO WHY DON'T I GIVE HIM A BIT OF EACH?
WE SURE APPRECIATE YOUR KINDNESS, MA'AM!
WE'LL FIND A SHADY SPOT SO HE CAN ENJOY IT IN COMFORT!
I'LL DO A LITTLE SAMPLING FIRST! I DON'T WANT YOU TO GET SICK!
"LITTLE SAMPLING", MY PAW... I BET THE GREEDY GUY SCARFS IT ALL!
BURP! THIS GIVES ME AN IDEA! THE FRISBEE IN MY BAG IS GONNA COME IN HANDY!
I DON'T LIKE HIS IDEAS! ESPECIALLY HIS IDEAS ON SHARING!
2

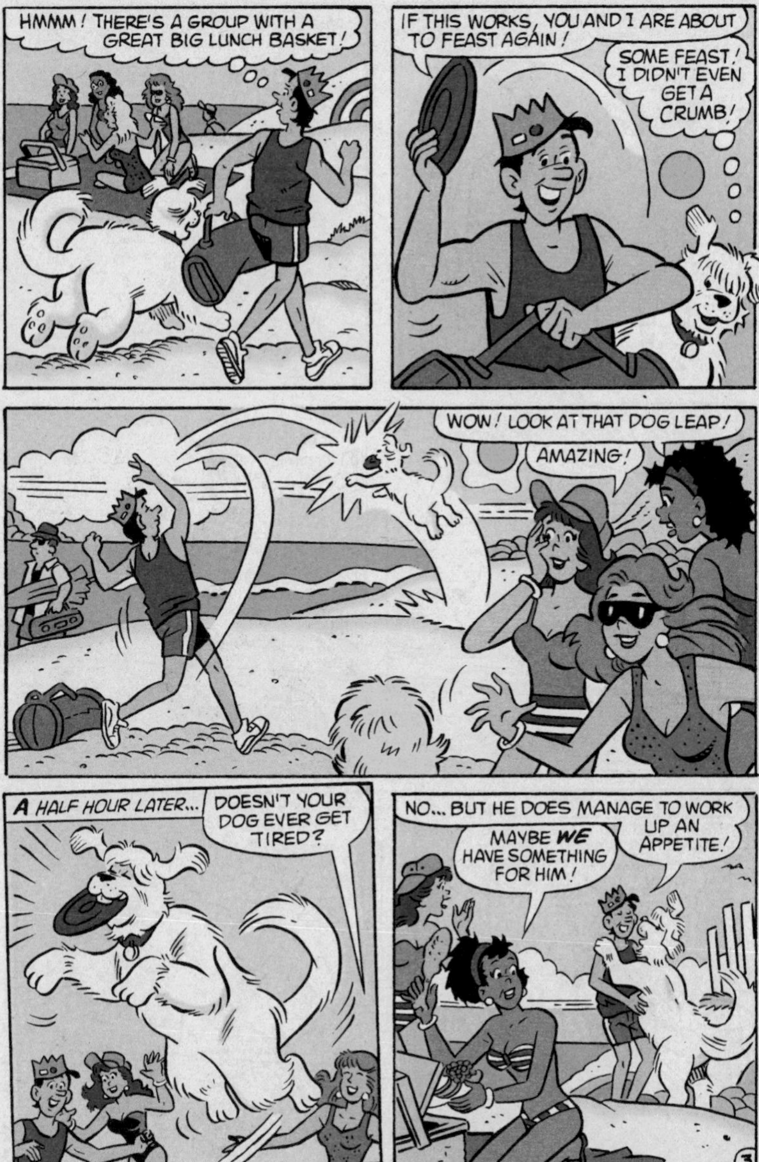
HMMM! THERE'S A GROUP WITH A GREAT BIG LUNCH BASKET!
IF THIS WORKS, YOU AND I ARE ABOUT TO FEAST AGAIN!
SOME FEAST! I DIDN'T EVEN GET A CRUMB!
WOW! LOOK AT THAT DOG LEAP!
AMAZING!
A HALF HOUR LATER...
DOESN'T YOUR DOG EVER GET TIRED?
NO... BUT HE DOES MANAGE TO WORK UP AN APPETITE!
MAYBE WE HAVE SOMETHING FOR HIM!
3

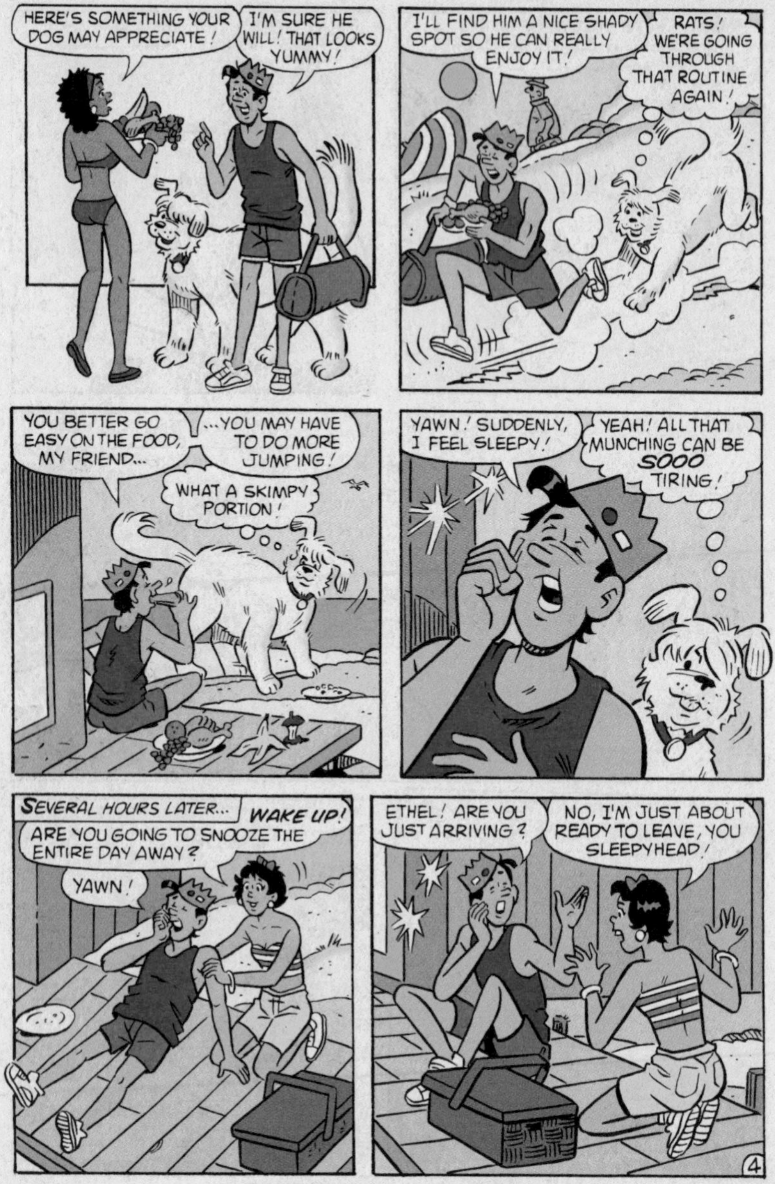
HERE'S SOMETHING YOUR DOG MAY APPRECIATE!
I'M SURE HE WILL! THAT LOOKS YUMMY!
I'LL FIND HIM A NICE SHADY SPOT SO HE CAN REALLY ENJOY IT!
RATS! WE'RE GOING THROUGH THAT ROUTINE AGAIN!
YOU BETTER GO EASY ON THE FOOD, MY FRIEND...
...YOU MAY HAVE TO DO MORE JUMPING!
WHAT A SKIMPY PORTION!
YAWN! SUDDENLY, I FEEL SLEEPY!
YEAH! ALL THAT MUNCHING CAN BE SOOO TIRING!
SEVERAL HOURS LATER...
WAKE UP!
ARE YOU GOING TO SNOOZE THE ENTIRE DAY AWAY?
YAWN!
ETHEL! ARE YOU JUST ARRIVING?
NO, I'M JUST ABOUT READY TO LEAVE, YOU SLEEPYHEAD!
4

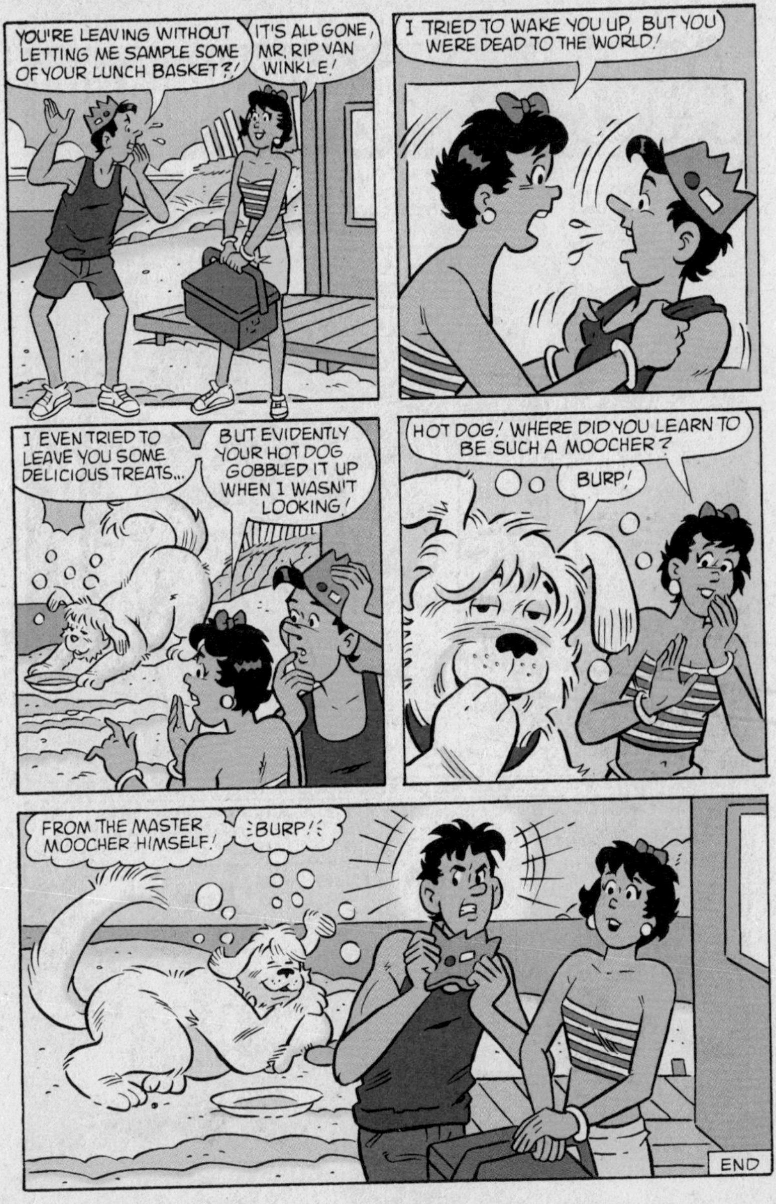

YOU'RE LEAVING WITHOUT LETTING ME SAMPLE SOME OF YOUR LUNCH BASKET?!
IT'S ALL GONE, MR. RIP VAN WINKLE!
I TRIED TO WAKE YOU UP, BUT YOU WERE DEAD TO THE WORLD!
I EVEN TRIED TO LEAVE YOU SOME DELICIOUS TREATS...
BUT EVIDENTLY YOUR HOT DOG GOBBLED IT UP WHEN I WASN'T LOOKING!
HOT DOG! WHERE DID YOU LEARN TO BE SUCH A MOOCHER?
BURP!
FROM THE MASTER MOOCHER HIMSELF!
BURP!
END

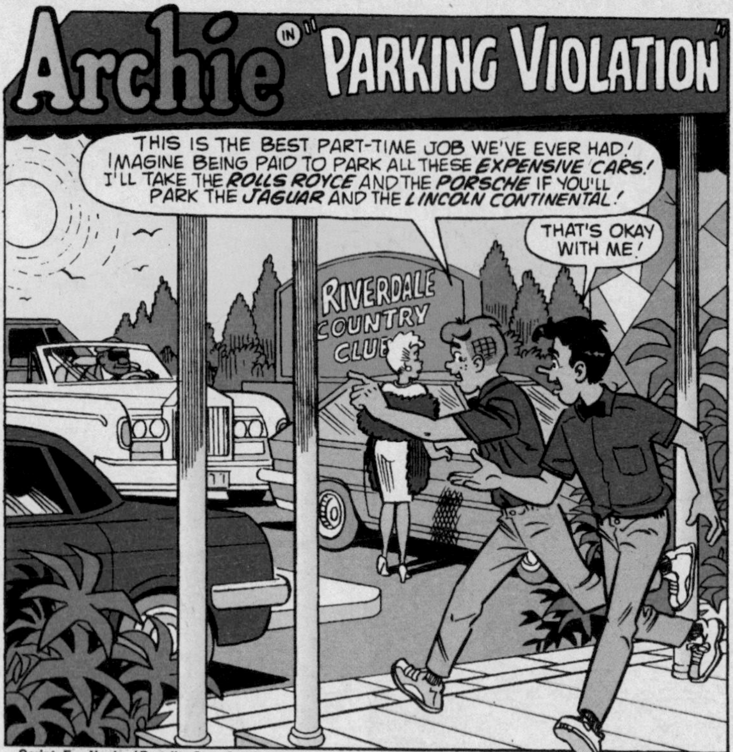
Archie in "PARKING VIOLATION"
THIS IS THE BEST PART-TIME JOB WE'VE EVER HAD! IMAGINE BEING PAID TO PARK ALL THESE EXPENSIVE CARS! I'LL TAKE THE ROLLS ROYCE AND THE PORSCHE IF YOU'LL PARK THE JAGUAR AND THE LINCOLN CONTINENTAL!
THAT'S OKAY WITH ME!
RIVERDALE COUNTRY CLUB

Script: Eve Nagler / Pencils: Stan Goldberg / Inks: Mike Esposito / Letters: Bill Yoshida / Colors: Barry Grossman

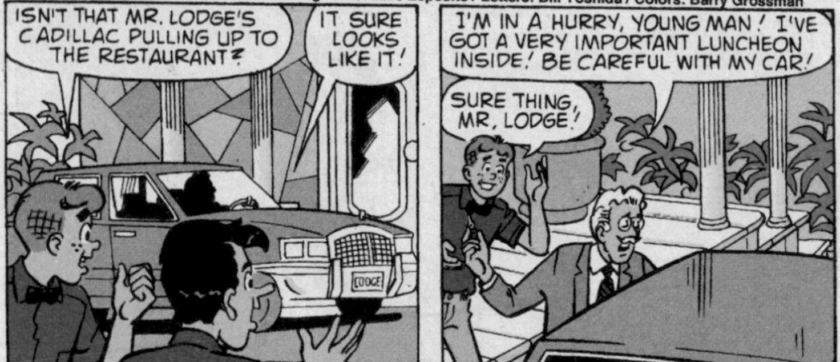
ISN'T THAT MR. LODGE'S CADILLAC PULLING UP TO THE RESTAURANT?
IT SURE LOOKS LIKE IT!
LODGE
I'M IN A HURRY, YOUNG MAN! I'VE GOT A VERY IMPORTANT LUNCHEON INSIDE! BE CAREFUL WITH MY CAR!
SURE THING, MR. LODGE!
1

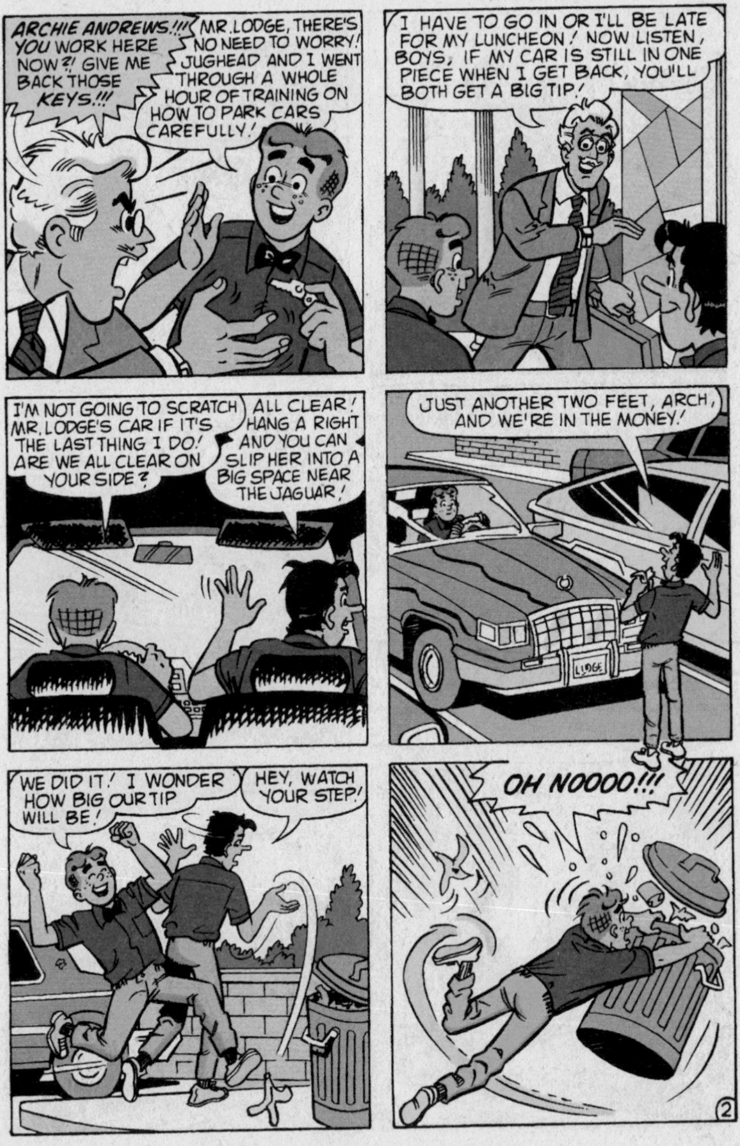
ARCHIE ANDREWS!!! YOU WORK HERE NOW?! GIVE ME BACK THOSE KEYS!!!
MR. LODGE, THERE'S NO NEED TO WORRY! JUGHEAD AND I WENT THROUGH A WHOLE HOUR OF TRAINING ON HOW TO PARK CARS CAREFULLY!
I HAVE TO GO IN OR I'LL BE LATE FOR MY LUNCHEON! NOW LISTEN, BOYS, IF MY CAR IS STILL IN ONE PIECE WHEN I GET BACK, YOU'LL BOTH GET A BIG TIP!
I'M NOT GOING TO SCRATCH MR. LODGE'S CAR IF IT'S THE LAST THING I DO! ARE WE ALL CLEAR ON YOUR SIDE?
ALL CLEAR! HANG A RIGHT AND YOU CAN SLIP HER INTO A BIG SPACE NEAR THE JAGUAR!
JUST ANOTHER TWO FEET, ARCH, AND WE'RE IN THE MONEY!
LODGE
WE DID IT! I WONDER HOW BIG OUR TIP WILL BE!
HEY, WATCH YOUR STEP!
OH NOOOO!!!
2

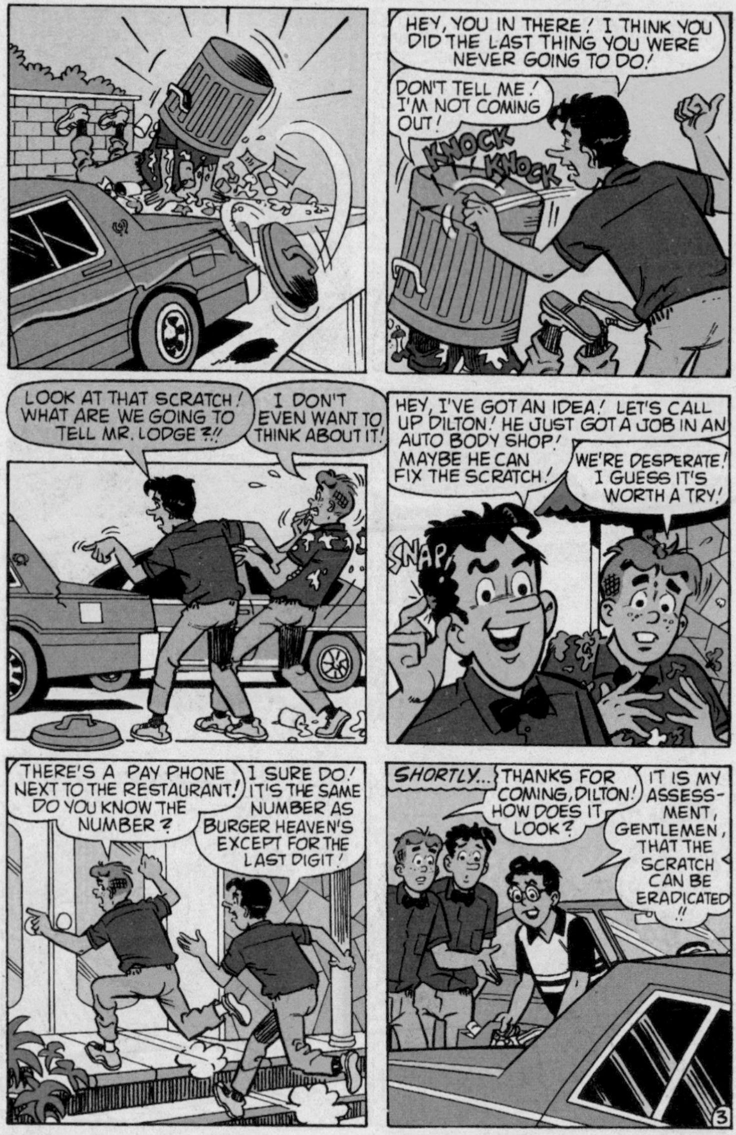

HEY, YOU IN THERE! I THINK YOU DID THE LAST THING YOU WERE NEVER GOING TO DO!
DON'T TELL ME! I'M NOT COMING OUT!
KNOCK KNOCK
LOOK AT THAT SCRATCH! WHAT ARE WE GOING TO TELL MR. LODGE ?!!
I DON'T EVEN WANT TO THINK ABOUT IT!
HEY, I'VE GOT AN IDEA! LET'S CALL UP DILTON! HE JUST GOT A JOB IN AN AUTO BODY SHOP! MAYBE HE CAN FIX THE SCRATCH!
WE'RE DESPERATE! I GUESS IT'S WORTH A TRY!
SNAP!
THERE'S A PAY PHONE NEXT TO THE RESTAURANT! DO YOU KNOW THE NUMBER ?
I SURE DO! IT'S THE SAME NUMBER AS BURGER HEAVEN'S EXCEPT FOR THE LAST DIGIT!
SHORTLY...
THANKS FOR COMING, DILTON! HOW DOES IT LOOK?
IT IS MY ASSESSMENT, GENTLEMEN, THAT THE SCRATCH CAN BE ERADICATED !!

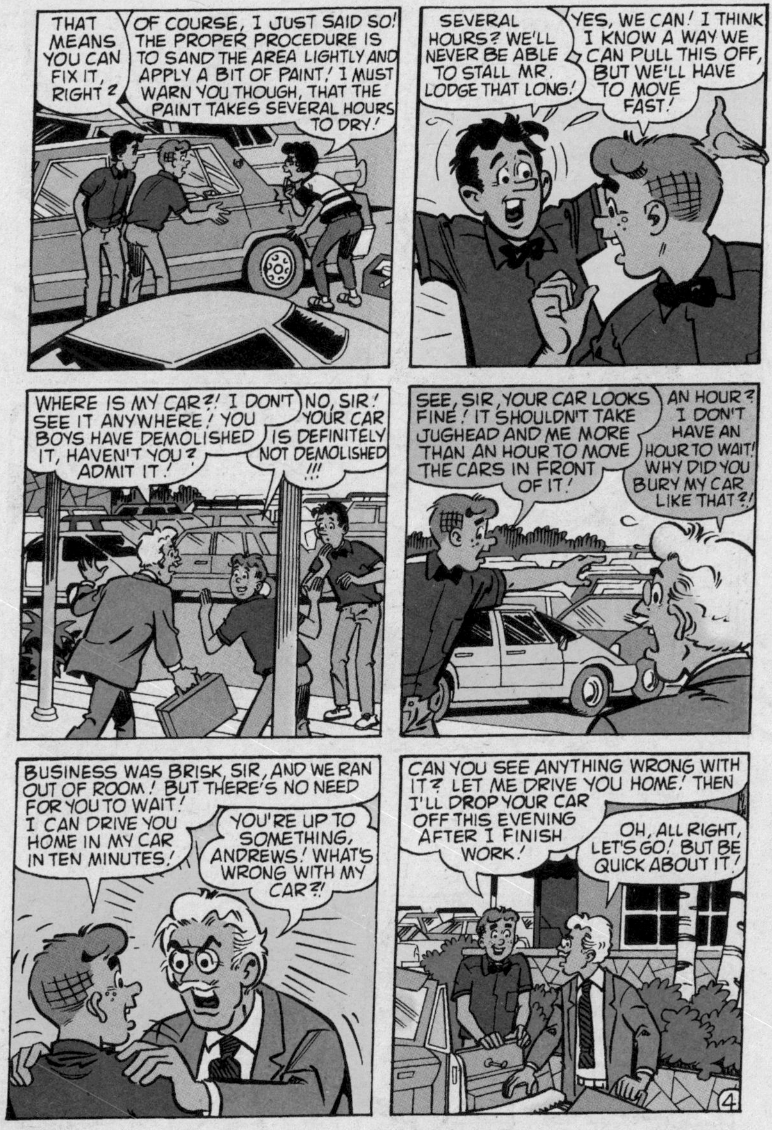
THAT MEANS YOU CAN FIX IT, RIGHT?
OF COURSE, I JUST SAID SO! THE PROPER PROCEDURE IS TO SAND THE AREA LIGHTLY AND APPLY A BIT OF PAINT! I MUST WARN YOU THOUGH, THAT THE PAINT TAKES SEVERAL HOURS TO DRY!
SEVERAL HOURS? WE'LL NEVER BE ABLE TO STALL MR. LODGE THAT LONG!
YES, WE CAN! I THINK I KNOW A WAY WE CAN PULL THIS OFF, BUT WE'LL HAVE TO MOVE FAST!
WHERE IS MY CAR?! I DON'T SEE IT ANYWHERE! YOU BOYS HAVE DEMOLISHED IT, HAVEN'T YOU? ADMIT IT!
NO, SIR! YOUR CAR IS DEFINITELY NOT DEMOLISHED!!!
SEE, SIR, YOUR CAR LOOKS FINE! IT SHOULDN'T TAKE JUGHEAD AND ME MORE THAN AN HOUR TO MOVE THE CARS IN FRONT OF IT!
AN HOUR? I DON'T HAVE AN HOUR TO WAIT! WHY DID YOU BURY MY CAR LIKE THAT?!
BUSINESS WAS BRISK, SIR, AND WE RAN OUT OF ROOM! BUT THERE'S NO NEED FOR YOU TO WAIT! I CAN DRIVE YOU HOME IN MY CAR IN TEN MINUTES!
YOU'RE UP TO SOMETHING, ANDREWS! WHAT'S WRONG WITH MY CAR?!
CAN YOU SEE ANYTHING WRONG WITH IT? LET ME DRIVE YOU HOME! THEN I'LL DROP YOUR CAR OFF THIS EVENING AFTER I FINISH WORK!
OH, ALL RIGHT, LET'S GO! BUT BE QUICK ABOUT IT!
4

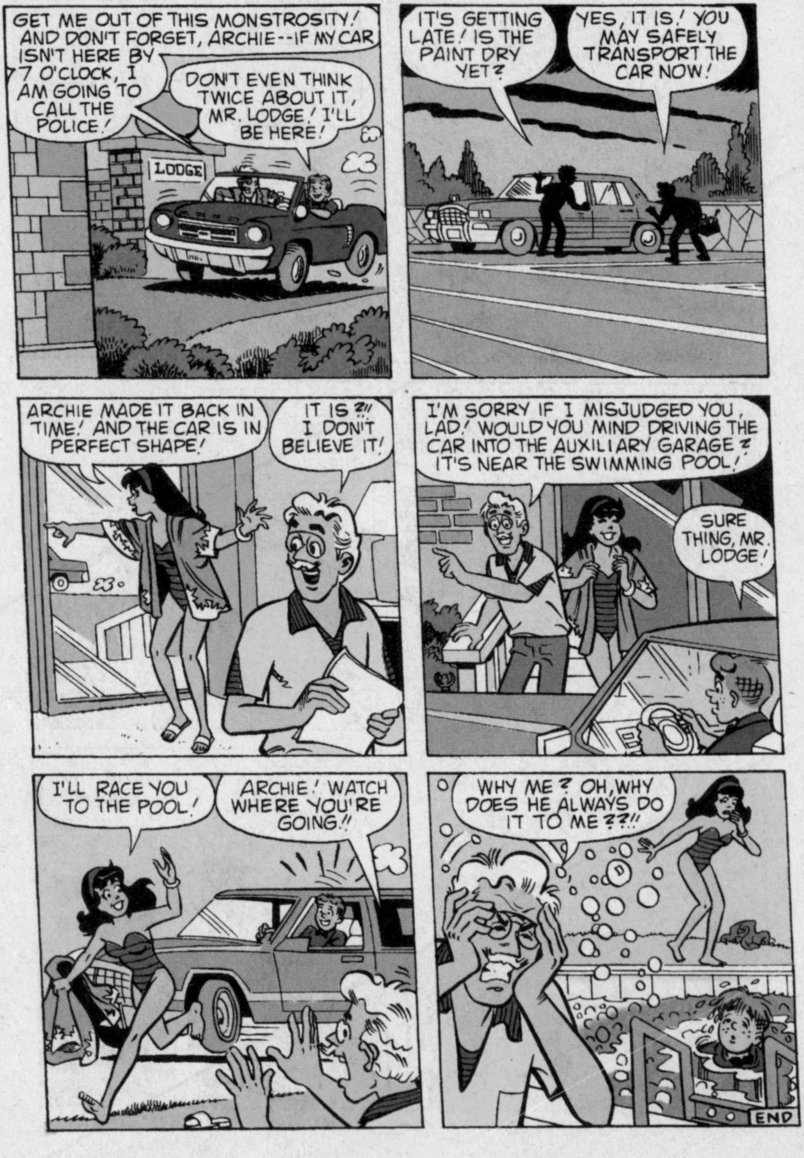
GET ME OUT OF THIS MONSTROSITY! AND DON'T FORGET, ARCHIE--IF MY CAR ISN'T HERE BY 7 O'CLOCK, I AM GOING TO CALL THE POLICE!
DON'T EVEN THINK TWICE ABOUT IT, MR. LODGE! I'LL BE HERE!
LODGE
IT'S GETTING LATE! IS THE PAINT DRY YET?
YES, IT IS! YOU MAY SAFELY TRANSPORT THE CAR NOW!
ARCHIE MADE IT BACK IN TIME! AND THE CAR IS IN PERFECT SHAPE!
IT IS?!! I DON'T BELIEVE IT!
I'M SORRY IF I MISJUDGED YOU, LAD! WOULD YOU MIND DRIVING THE CAR INTO THE AUXILIARY GARAGE? IT'S NEAR THE SWIMMING POOL!
SURE THING, MR. LODGE!
I'LL RACE YOU TO THE POOL!
ARCHIE! WATCH WHERE YOU'RE GOING!!
WHY ME? OH, WHY DOES HE ALWAYS DO IT TO ME??!!
END

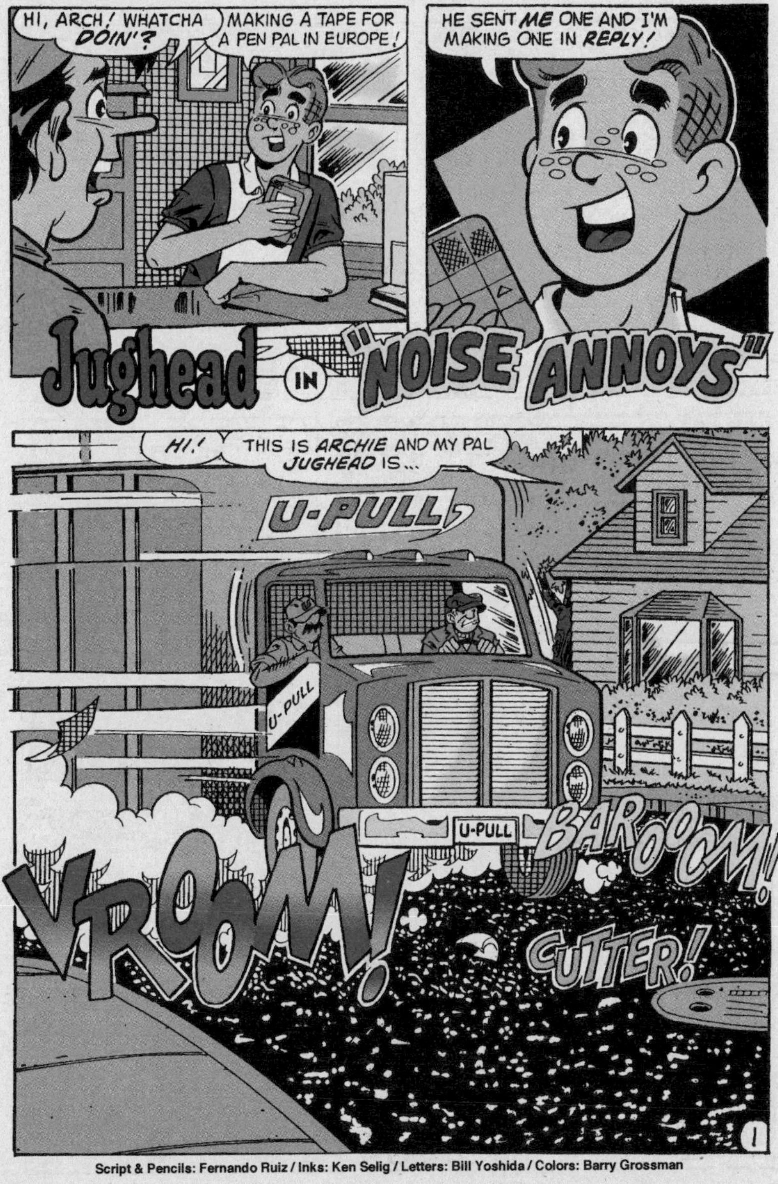
HI, ARCH! WHATCHA DOIN'?
MAKING A TAPE FOR A PEN PAL IN EUROPE!
HE SENT ME ONE AND I'M MAKING ONE IN REPLY!
Jughead IN "NOISE ANNOYS"
HI!
THIS IS ARCHIE AND MY PAL JUGHEAD IS...
U-PULL
U-PULL
U-PULL
BAROOOOM!
VROOM!
CUTTER!
1

Script & Pencils: Fernando Ruiz / Inks: Ken Selig / Letters: Bill Yoshida / Colors: Barry Grossman

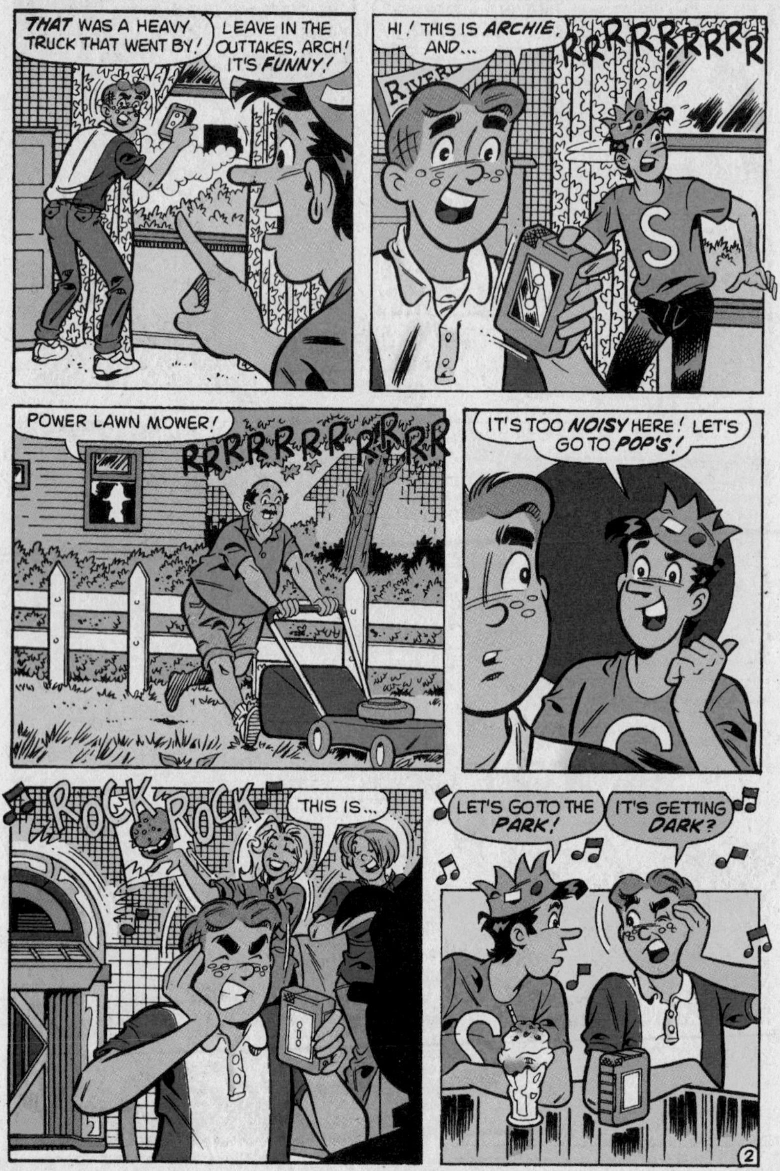
THAT WAS A HEAVY TRUCK THAT WENT BY!
LEAVE IN THE OUTTAKES, ARCH! IT'S FUNNY!
HI! THIS IS ARCHIE, AND...
RRRRRRRRRR
POWER LAWN MOWER!
RRRRRRRRRRR
IT'S TOO NOISY HERE! LET'S GO TO POP'S!
ROCK ROCK
THIS IS...
LET'S GO TO THE PARK!
IT'S GETTING DARK?
2

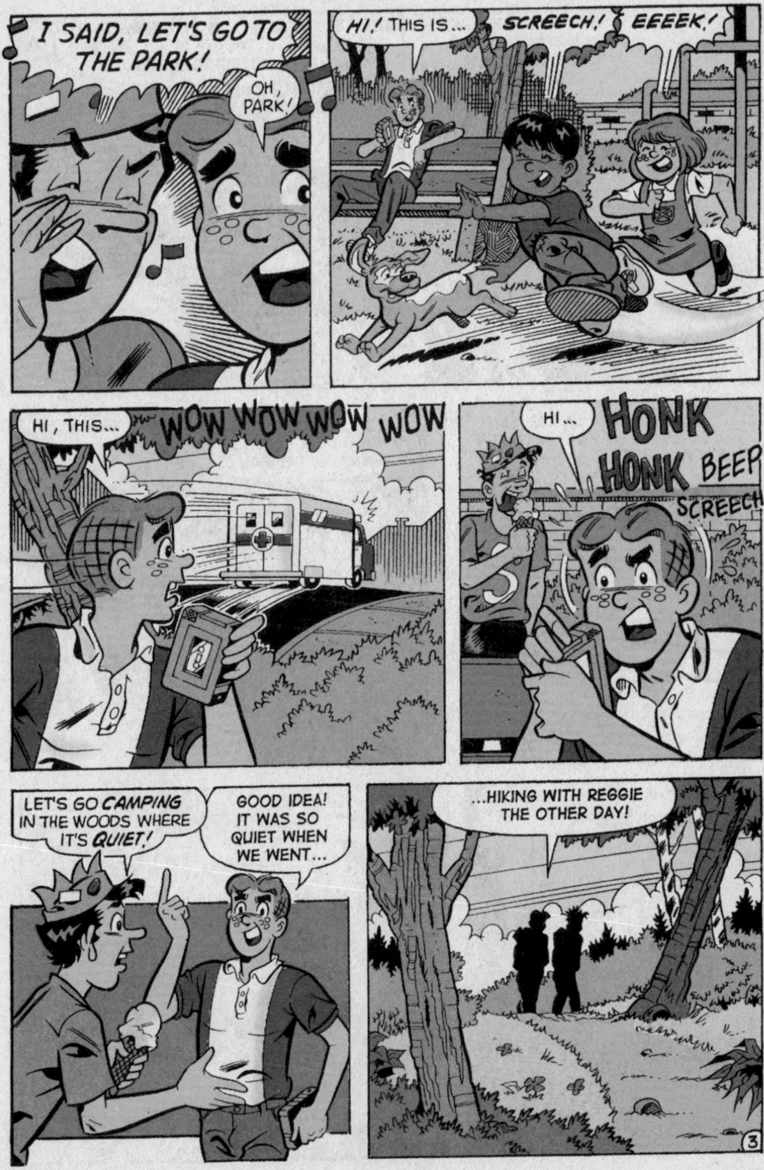
I SAID, LET'S GO TO THE PARK!
OH, PARK!
HI! THIS IS...
SCREECH! EEEEK!
HI, THIS...
WOW WOW WOW WOW
HI...
HONK HONK BEEP
SCREECH!
LET'S GO CAMPING IN THE WOODS WHERE IT'S QUIET!
GOOD IDEA! IT WAS SO QUIET WHEN WE WENT...
...HIKING WITH REGGIE THE OTHER DAY!
3

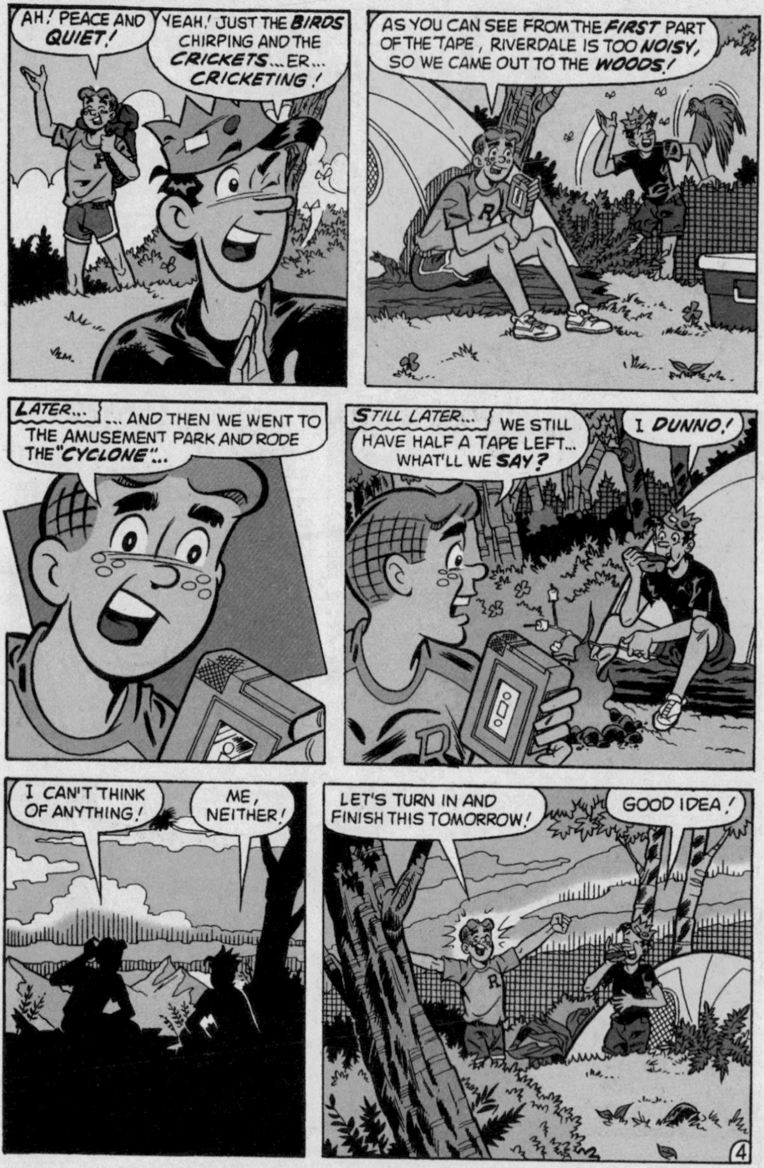
AH! PEACE AND QUIET!
YEAH! JUST THE BIRDS CHIRPING AND THE CRICKETS... ER... CRICKETING!
AS YOU CAN SEE FROM THE FIRST PART OF THE TAPE, RIVERDALE IS TOO NOISY, SO WE CAME OUT TO THE WOODS!
LATER...
...AND THEN WE WENT TO THE AMUSEMENT PARK AND RODE THE "CYCLONE"...
STILL LATER...
WE STILL HAVE HALF A TAPE LEFT... WHAT'LL WE SAY?
I DUNNO!
I CAN'T THINK OF ANYTHING!
ME, NEITHER!
LET'S TURN IN AND FINISH THIS TOMORROW!
GOOD IDEA!
4

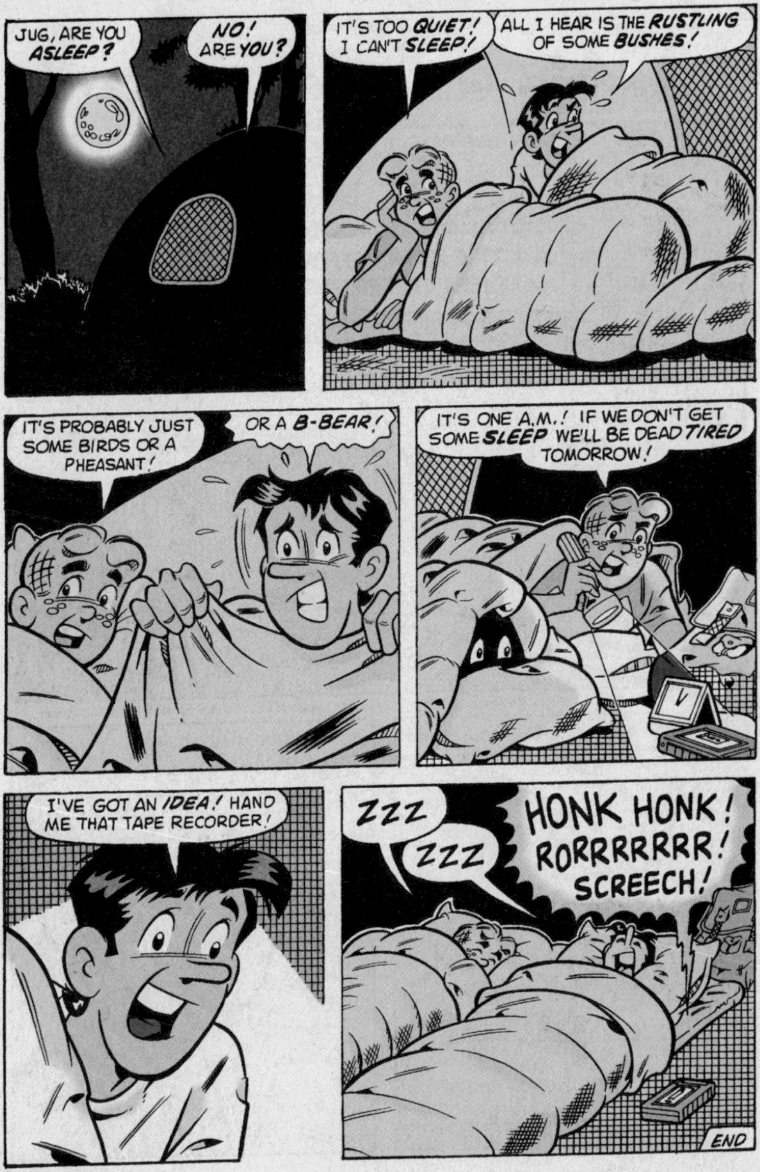
JUG, ARE YOU ASLEEP?
NO! ARE YOU?
IT'S TOO QUIET! I CAN'T SLEEP!
ALL I HEAR IS THE RUSTLING OF SOME BUSHES!
IT'S PROBABLY JUST SOME BIRDS OR A PHEASANT!
OR A B-BEAR!
IT'S ONE A.M.! IF WE DON'T GET SOME SLEEP WE'LL BE DEAD TIRED TOMORROW!
I'VE GOT AN IDEA! HAND ME THAT TAPE RECORDER!
ZZZ
ZZZ
HONK HONK! RORRRRRRR! SCREECH!
END

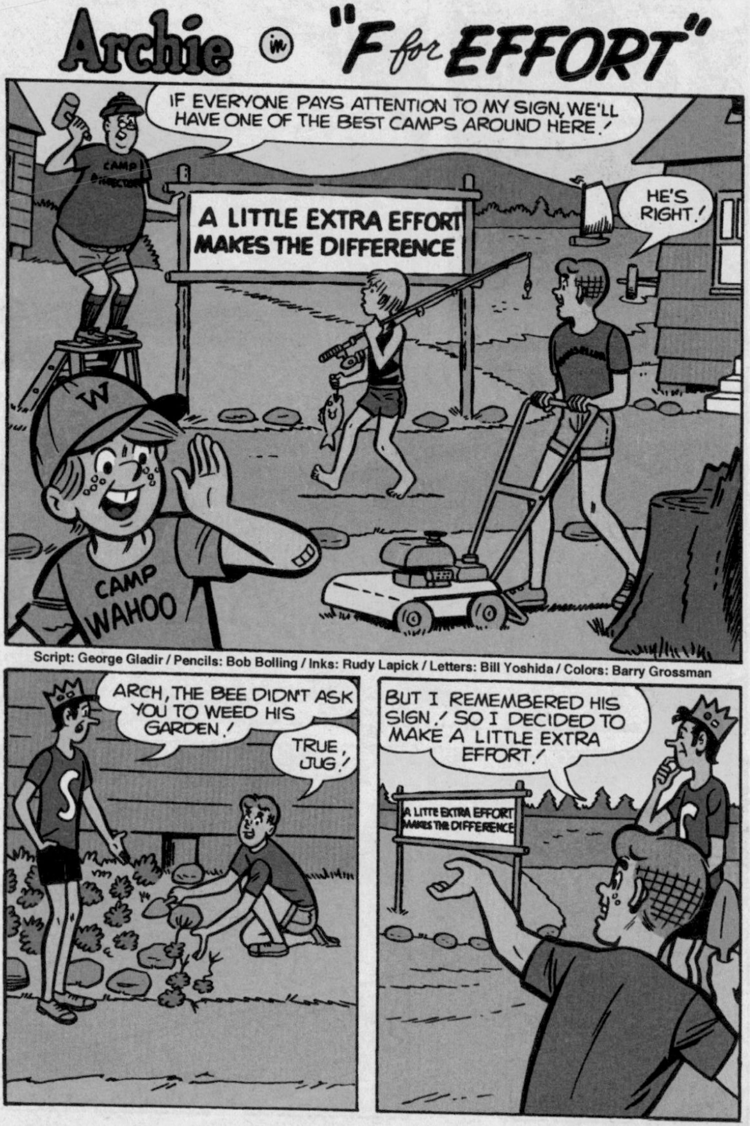

Archie in "F for EFFORT"
IF EVERYONE PAYS ATTENTION TO MY SIGN, WE'LL HAVE ONE OF THE BEST CAMPS AROUND HERE!
A LITTLE EXTRA EFFORT MAKES THE DIFFERENCE
HE'S RIGHT!
CAMP WAHOO
Script: George Gladir / Pencils: Bob Bolling / Inks: Rudy Lapick / Letters: Bill Yoshida / Colors: Barry Grossman
ARCH, THE BEE DIDN'T ASK YOU TO WEED HIS GARDEN!
TRUE, JUG!
BUT I REMEMBERED HIS SIGN! SO I DECIDED TO MAKE A LITTLE EXTRA EFFORT!
A LITTE EXTRA EFFORT MAKES THE DIFFERENCE

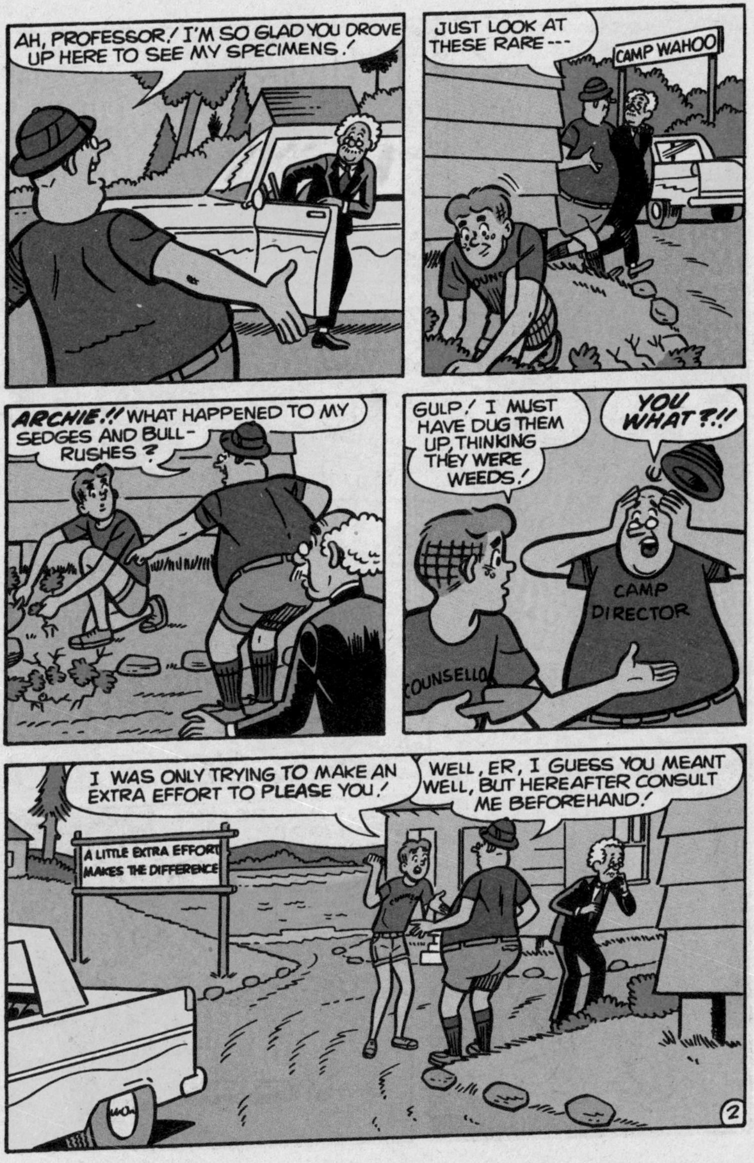
AH, PROFESSOR! I'M SO GLAD YOU DROVE UP HERE TO SEE MY SPECIMENS!
JUST LOOK AT THESE RARE---
CAMP WAHOO
ARCHIE!! WHAT HAPPENED TO MY SEDGES AND BULL-RUSHES?
GULP! I MUST HAVE DUG THEM UP, THINKING THEY WERE WEEDS!
YOU WHAT?!!
CAMP DIRECTOR
COUNSELLO
I WAS ONLY TRYING TO MAKE AN EXTRA EFFORT TO PLEASE YOU!
WELL, ER, I GUESS YOU MEANT WELL, BUT HEREAFTER CONSULT ME BEFOREHAND!
A LITTLE EXTRA EFFORT MAKES THE DIFFERENCE
2

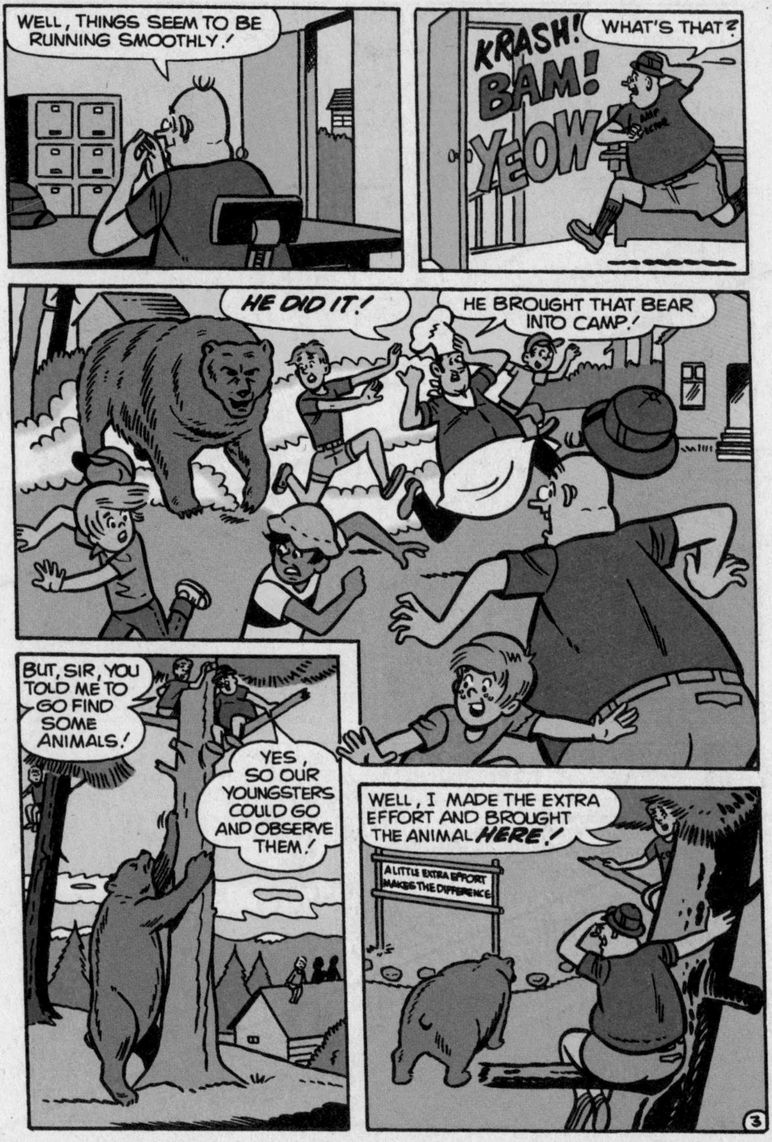

WELL, THINGS SEEM TO BE RUNNING SMOOTHLY!
KRASH!
BAM!
YEOW!
WHAT'S THAT?
HE DID IT!
HE BROUGHT THAT BEAR INTO CAMP!
BUT, SIR, YOU TOLD ME TO GO FIND SOME ANIMALS!
YES, SO OUR YOUNGSTERS COULD GO AND OBSERVE THEM!
WELL, I MADE THE EXTRA EFFORT AND BROUGHT THE ANIMAL HERE!
A LITTLE EXTRA EFFORT MAKES THE DIFFERENCE

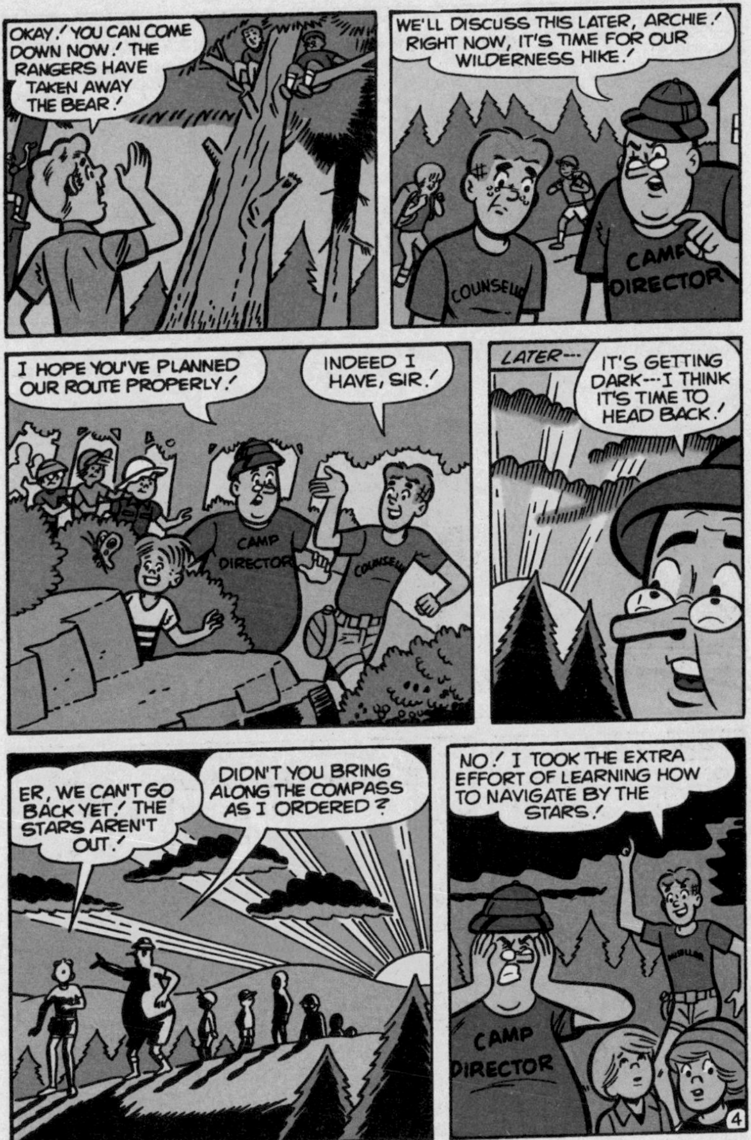
OKAY! YOU CAN COME DOWN NOW! THE RANGERS HAVE TAKEN AWAY THE BEAR!
WE'LL DISCUSS THIS LATER, ARCHIE! RIGHT NOW, IT'S TIME FOR OUR WILDERNESS HIKE!
COUNSELLO
CAMP DIRECTOR
I HOPE YOU'VE PLANNED OUR ROUTE PROPERLY!
INDEED I HAVE, SIR!
CAMP DIRECTOR
COUNSELLO
LATER---
IT'S GETTING DARK---I THINK IT'S TIME TO HEAD BACK!
ER, WE CAN'T GO BACK YET! THE STARS AREN'T OUT!
DIDN'T YOU BRING ALONG THE COMPASS AS I ORDERED?
NO! I TOOK THE EXTRA EFFORT OF LEARNING HOW TO NAVIGATE BY THE STARS!
CAMP DIRECTOR
4

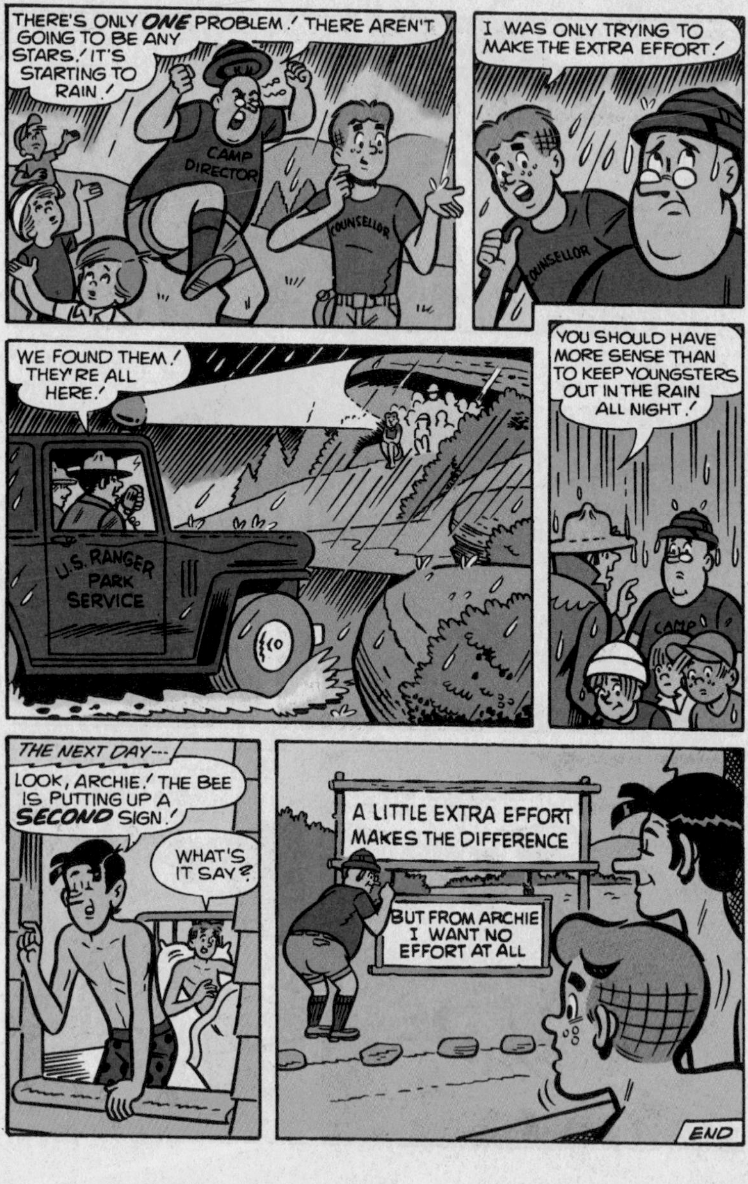
THERE'S ONLY ONE PROBLEM.' THERE AREN'T GOING TO BE ANY STARS.' IT'S STARTING TO RAIN.'
CAMP DIRECTOR
COUNSELLOR
I WAS ONLY TRYING TO MAKE THE EXTRA EFFORT.'
COUNSELLOR
WE FOUND THEM.' THEY'RE ALL HERE.'
U.S. RANGER PARK SERVICE
YOU SHOULD HAVE MORE SENSE THAN TO KEEP YOUNGSTERS OUT IN THE RAIN ALL NIGHT.'
CAMP
THE NEXT DAY---
LOOK, ARCHIE.' THE BEE IS PUTTING UP A SECOND SIGN.'
WHAT'S IT SAY?
A LITTLE EXTRA EFFORT MAKES THE DIFFERENCE
BUT FROM ARCHIE I WANT NO EFFORT AT ALL
END

Betty and Veronica in NICE ADVICE

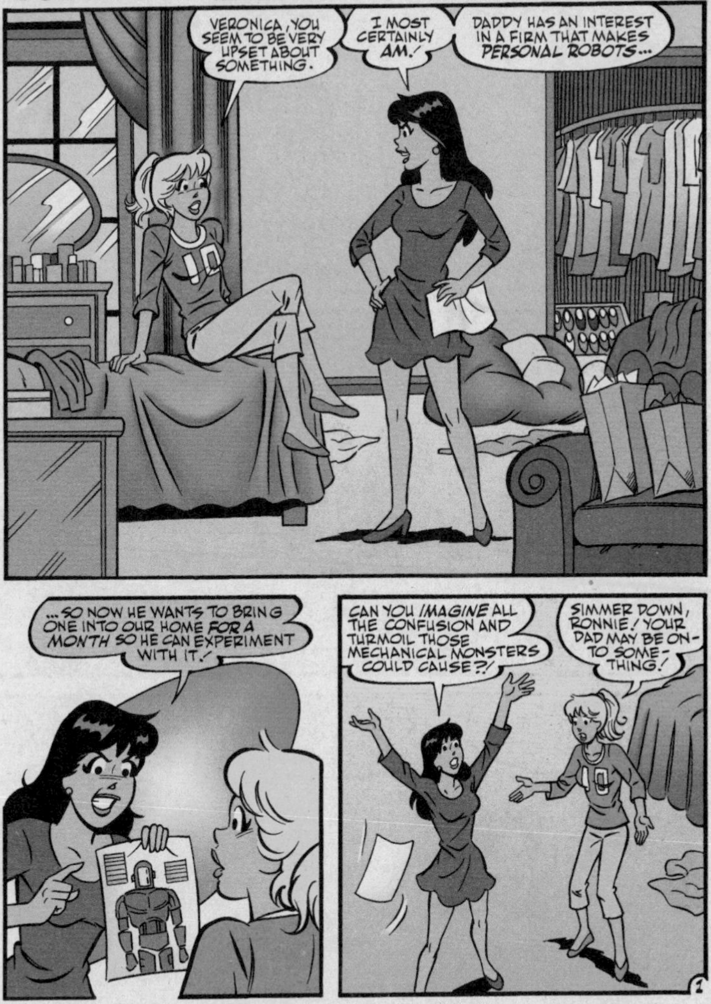

VERONICA, YOU SEEM TO BE VERY UPSET ABOUT SOMETHING.
I MOST CERTAINLY AM.!
DADDY HAS AN INTEREST IN A FIRM THAT MAKES PERSONAL ROBOTS...
...SO NOW HE WANTS TO BRING ONE INTO OUR HOME FOR A MONTH SO HE CAN EXPERIMENT WITH IT.!
CAN YOU IMAGINE ALL THE CONFUSION AND TURMOIL THOSE MECHANICAL MONSTERS COULD CAUSE?!
SIMMER DOWN, RONNIE! YOUR DAD MAY BE ON-TO SOME-THING!
1

SCRIPT: GEORGE GLADIR PENCILS: BILL GALVAN INKS: BOB SMITH LETTERS: JACK MORELLI COLORS: DIGIKORE STUDIOS

EDITOR-IN-CHIEF: VICTOR GORELICK PRESIDENT: MIKE PELLERITO PUBLISHER: JON GOLDWATER

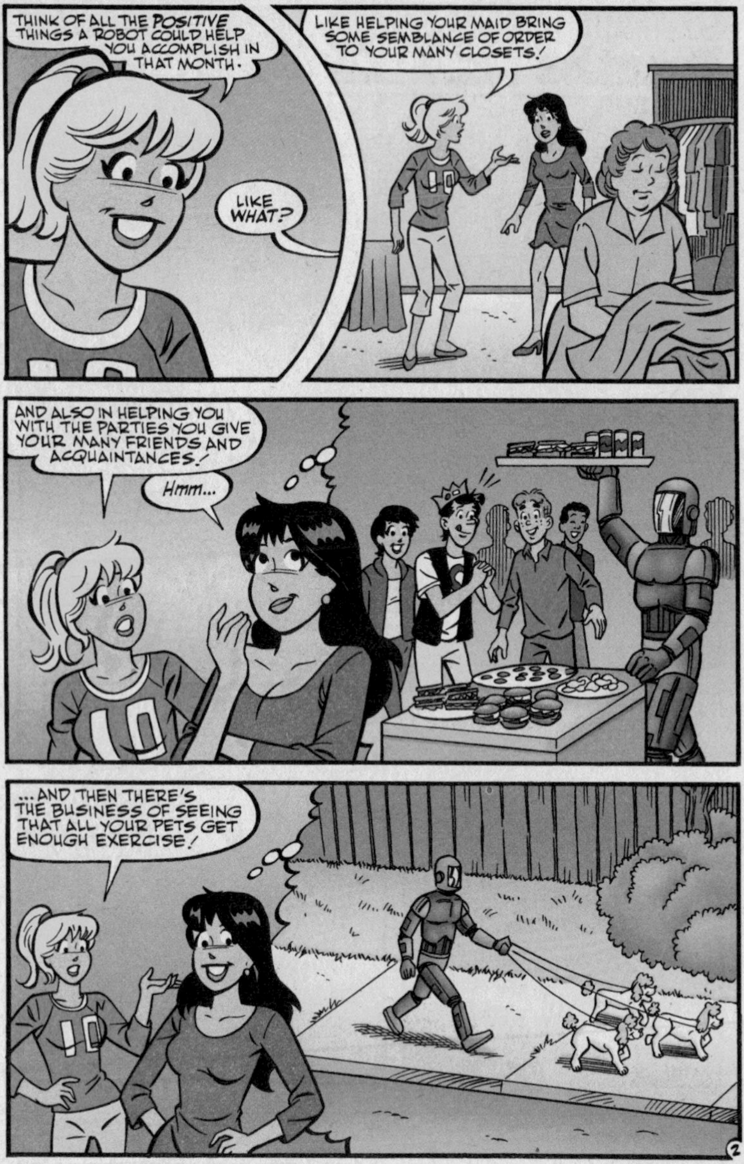
THINK OF ALL THE POSITIVE THINGS A ROBOT COULD HELP YOU ACCOMPLISH IN THAT MONTH.
LIKE WHAT?
LIKE HELPING YOUR MAID BRING SOME SEMBLANCE OF ORDER TO YOUR MANY CLOSETS!
AND ALSO IN HELPING YOU WITH THE PARTIES YOU GIVE YOUR MANY FRIENDS AND ACQUAINTANCES!
Hmm...
...AND THEN THERE'S THE BUSINESS OF SEEING THAT ALL YOUR PETS GET ENOUGH EXERCISE!
2

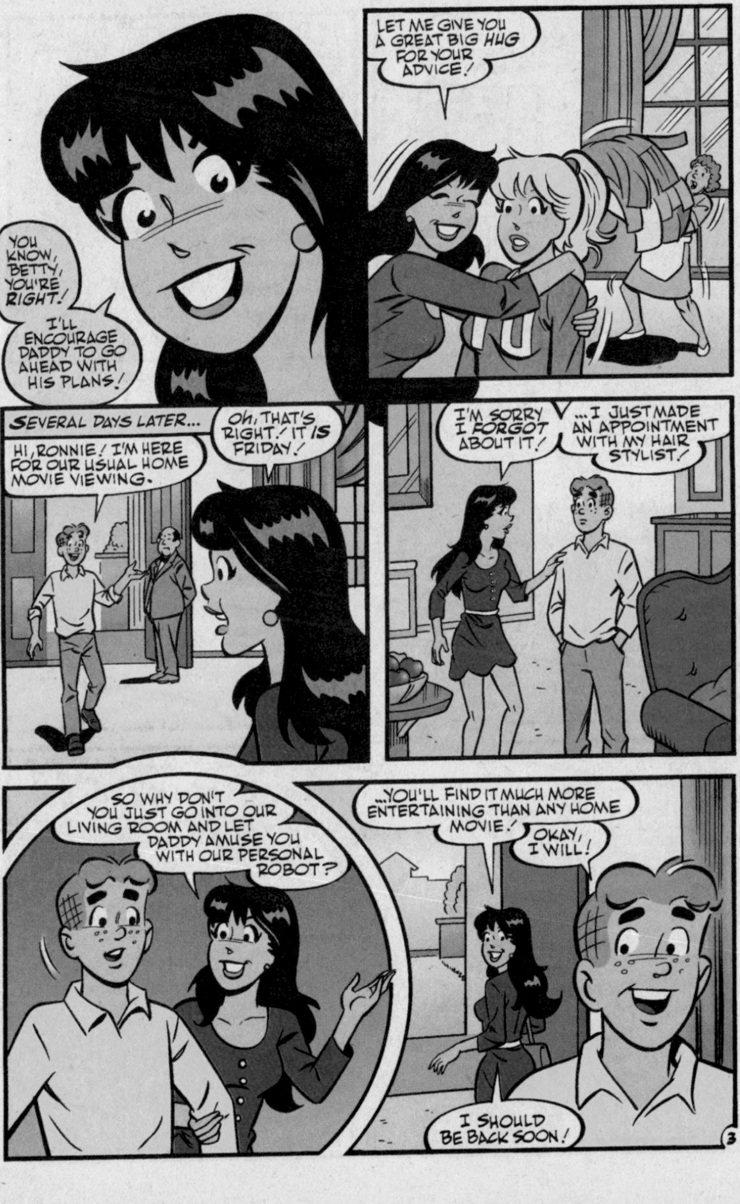
YOU KNOW, BETTY, YOU'RE RIGHT!
I'LL ENCOURAGE DADDY TO GO AHEAD WITH HIS PLANS!
LET ME GIVE YOU A GREAT BIG HUG FOR YOUR ADVICE!
SEVERAL DAYS LATER...
HI, RONNIE! I'M HERE FOR OUR USUAL HOME MOVIE VIEWING.
Oh, THAT'S RIGHT! IT IS FRIDAY!
I'M SORRY I FORGOT ABOUT IT!
...I JUST MADE AN APPOINTMENT WITH MY HAIR STYLIST!
SO WHY DON'T YOU JUST GO INTO OUR LIVING ROOM AND LET DADDY AMUSE YOU WITH OUR PERSONAL ROBOT?
...YOU'LL FIND IT MUCH MORE ENTERTAINING THAN ANY HOME MOVIE!
OKAY, I WILL!
I SHOULD BE BACK SOON!
3

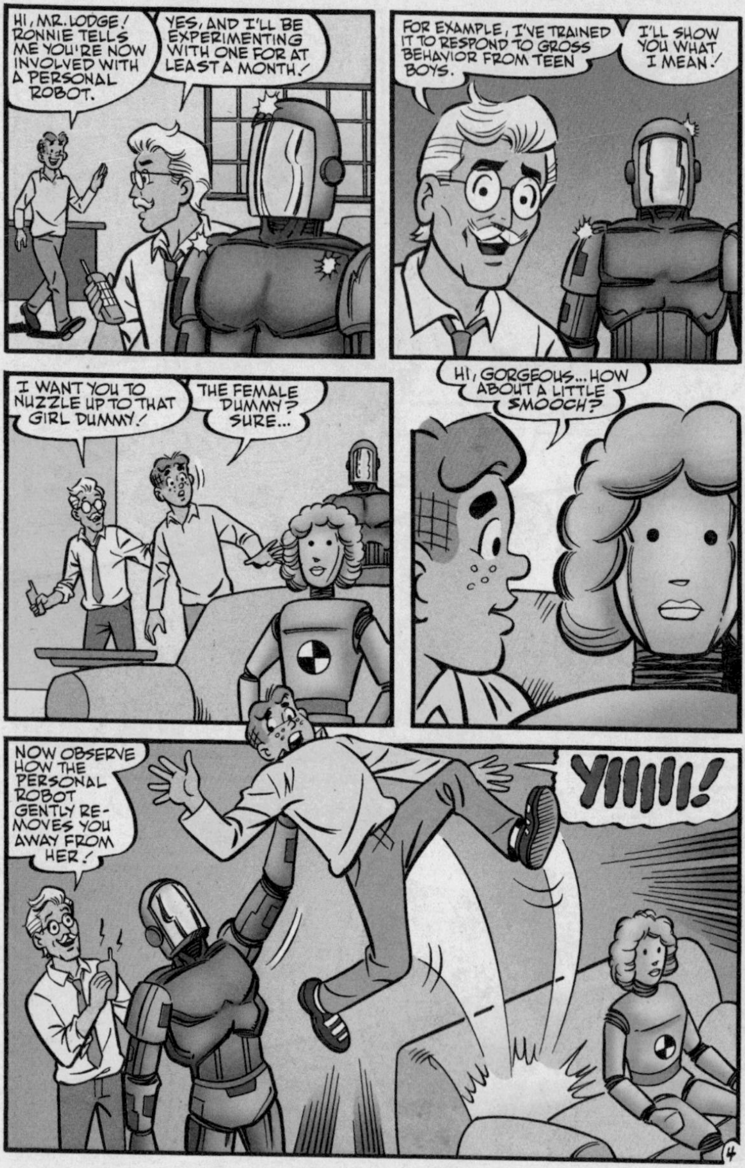

HI, MR. LODGE! RONNIE TELLS ME YOU'RE NOW INVOLVED WITH A PERSONAL ROBOT.
YES, AND I'LL BE EXPERIMENTING WITH ONE FOR AT LEAST A MONTH!
FOR EXAMPLE, I'VE TRAINED IT TO RESPOND TO GROSS BEHAVIOR FROM TEEN BOYS.
I'LL SHOW YOU WHAT I MEAN!
I WANT YOU TO NUZZLE UP TO THAT GIRL DUMMY!
THE FEMALE DUMMY? SURE...
HI, GORGEOUS... HOW ABOUT A LITTLE SMOOCH?
NOW OBSERVE HOW THE PERSONAL ROBOT GENTLY RE-MOVES YOU AWAY FROM HER!
YIIIII!

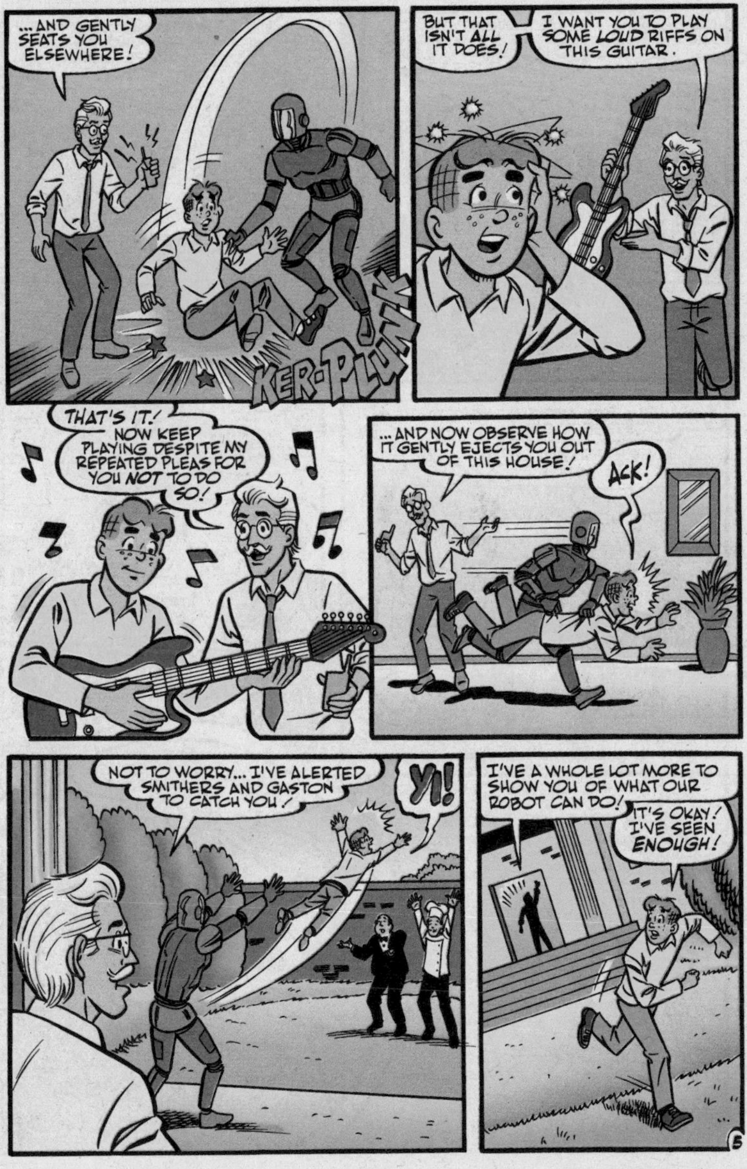

...AND GENTLY SEATS YOU ELSEWHERE!
KER-PLUNK
BUT THAT ISN'T ALL IT DOES!
I WANT YOU TO PLAY SOME LOUD RIFFS ON THIS GUITAR.
THAT'S IT! NOW KEEP PLAYING DESPITE MY REPEATED PLEAS FOR YOU NOT TO DO SO!
...AND NOW OBSERVE HOW IT GENTLY EJECTS YOU OUT OF THIS HOUSE!
ACK!
NOT TO WORRY... I'VE ALERTED SMITHERS AND GASTON TO CATCH YOU!
YI!
I'VE A WHOLE LOT MORE TO SHOW YOU OF WHAT OUR ROBOT CAN DO!
IT'S OKAY! I'VE SEEN ENOUGH!

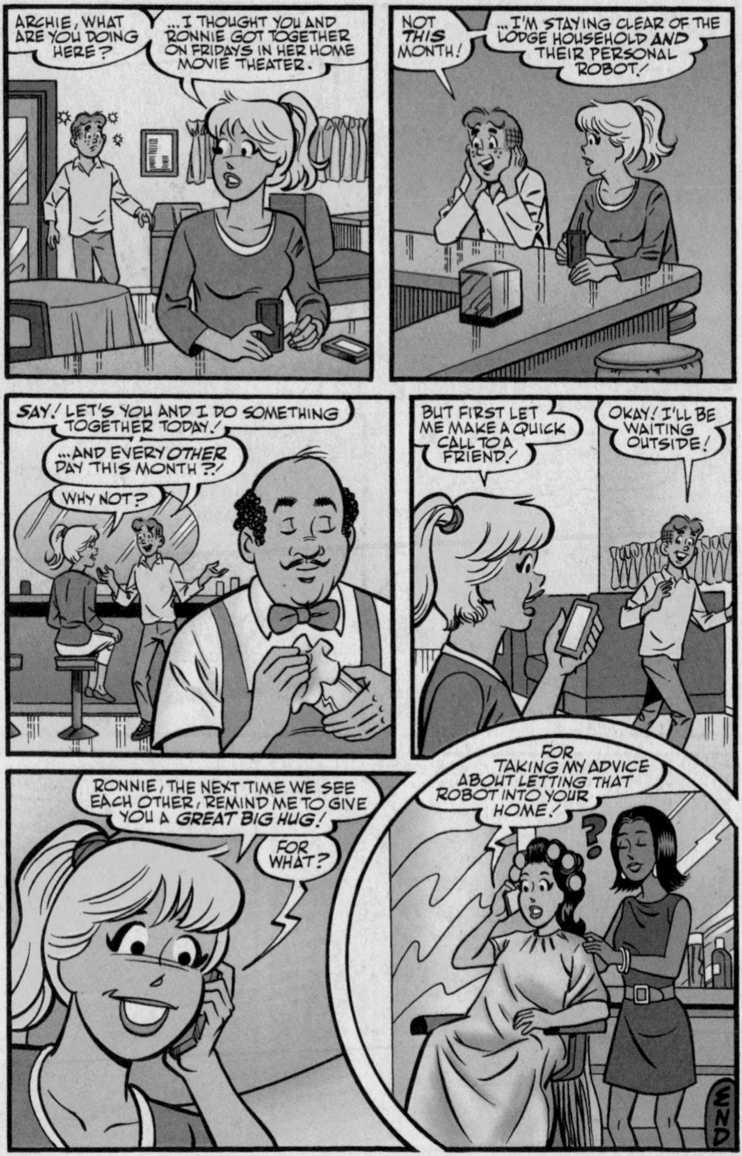
ARCHIE, WHAT ARE YOU DOING HERE?
...I THOUGHT YOU AND RONNIE GOT TOGETHER ON FRIDAYS IN HER HOME MOVIE THEATER.
NOT THIS MONTH!
...I'M STAYING CLEAR OF THE LODGE HOUSEHOLD AND THEIR PERSONAL ROBOT!
SAY! LET'S YOU AND I DO SOMETHING TOGETHER TODAY!
...AND EVERY OTHER DAY THIS MONTH?!
WHY NOT?
BUT FIRST LET ME MAKE A QUICK CALL TO A FRIEND!
OKAY! I'LL BE WAITING OUTSIDE!
RONNIE, THE NEXT TIME WE SEE EACH OTHER, REMIND ME TO GIVE YOU A GREAT BIG HUG!
FOR WHAT?
FOR TAKING MY ADVICE ABOUT LETTING THAT ROBOT INTO YOUR HOME!
?
END

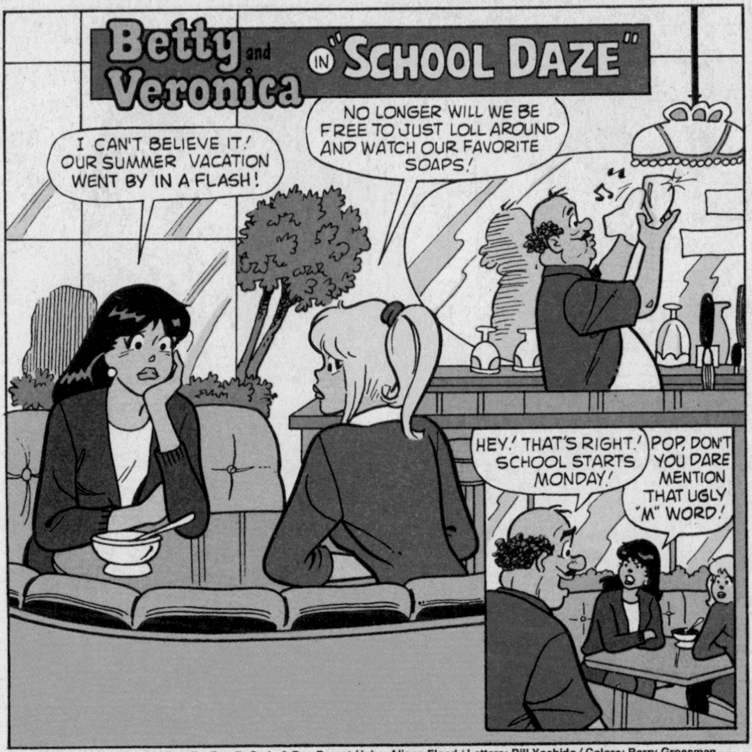
Betty and Veronica IN "SCHOOL DAZE"
I CAN'T BELIEVE IT! OUR SUMMER VACATION WENT BY IN A FLASH!
NO LONGER WILL WE BE FREE TO JUST LOLL AROUND AND WATCH OUR FAVORITE SOAPS!
HEY! THAT'S RIGHT! SCHOOL STARTS MONDAY!
POP, DON'T YOU DARE MENTION THAT UGLY "M" WORD!

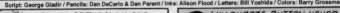

Script: George Gladir / Pencils: Dan DeCarlo & Dan Parent / Inks: Alison Flood / Letters: Bill Yoshida / Colors: Barry Grossman

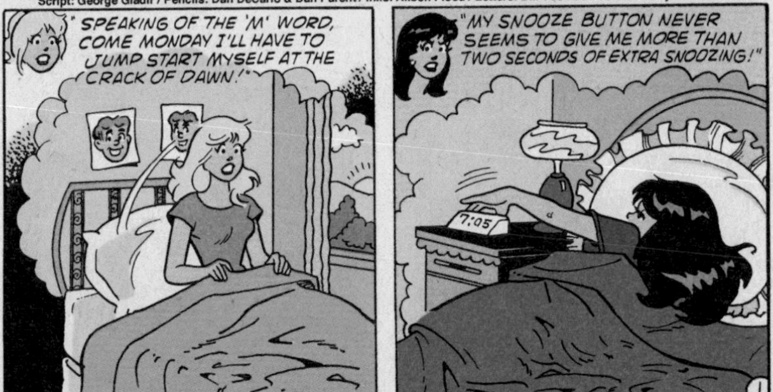
"SPEAKING OF THE 'M' WORD, COME MONDAY I'LL HAVE TO JUMP START MYSELF AT THE CRACK OF DAWN!"
"MY SNOOZE BUTTON NEVER SEEMS TO GIVE ME MORE THAN TWO SECONDS OF EXTRA SNOOZING!"
7:05

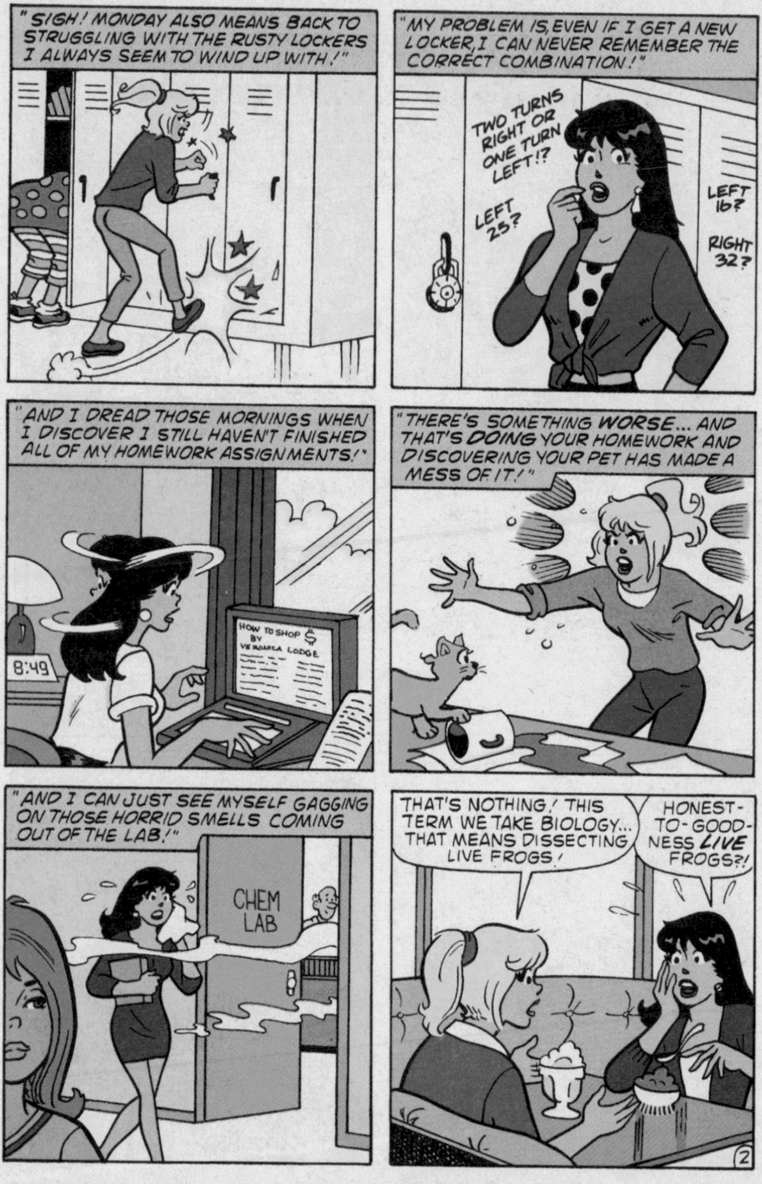
"SIGH! MONDAY ALSO MEANS BACK TO STRUGGLING WITH THE RUSTY LOCKERS I ALWAYS SEEM TO WIND UP WITH!"
"MY PROBLEM IS, EVEN IF I GET A NEW LOCKER, I CAN NEVER REMEMBER THE CORRECT COMBINATION!"
TWO TURNS RIGHT OR ONE TURN LEFT!?
LEFT 25?
LEFT 16?
RIGHT 32?
"AND I DREAD THOSE MORNINGS WHEN I DISCOVER I STILL HAVEN'T FINISHED ALL OF MY HOMEWORK ASSIGNMENTS!"
HOW TO SHOP $ BY VERONICA LODGE
8:49
"THERE'S SOMETHING WORSE... AND THAT'S DOING YOUR HOMEWORK AND DISCOVERING YOUR PET HAS MADE A MESS OF IT!"
"AND I CAN JUST SEE MYSELF GAGGING ON THOSE HORRID SMELLS COMING OUT OF THE LAB!"
CHEM LAB
THAT'S NOTHING! THIS TERM WE TAKE BIOLOGY... THAT MEANS DISSECTING LIVE FROGS!
HONEST-TO-GOODNESS LIVE FROGS?!
2

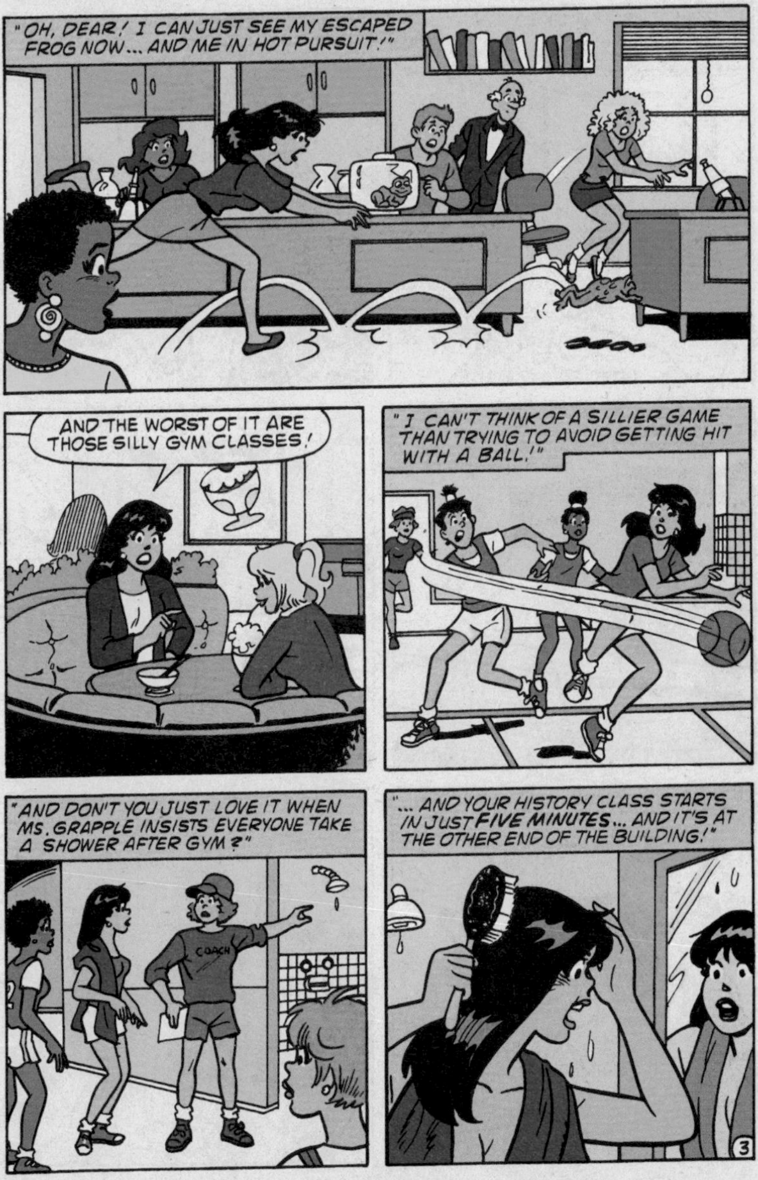
"OH, DEAR! I CAN JUST SEE MY ESCAPED FROG NOW... AND ME IN HOT PURSUIT!"
AND THE WORST OF IT ARE THOSE SILLY GYM CLASSES!
"I CAN'T THINK OF A SILLIER GAME THAN TRYING TO AVOID GETTING HIT WITH A BALL!"
"AND DON'T YOU JUST LOVE IT WHEN MS. GRAPPLE INSISTS EVERYONE TAKE A SHOWER AFTER GYM?"
COACH
"... AND YOUR HISTORY CLASS STARTS IN JUST FIVE MINUTES... AND IT'S AT THE OTHER END OF THE BUILDING!"
3

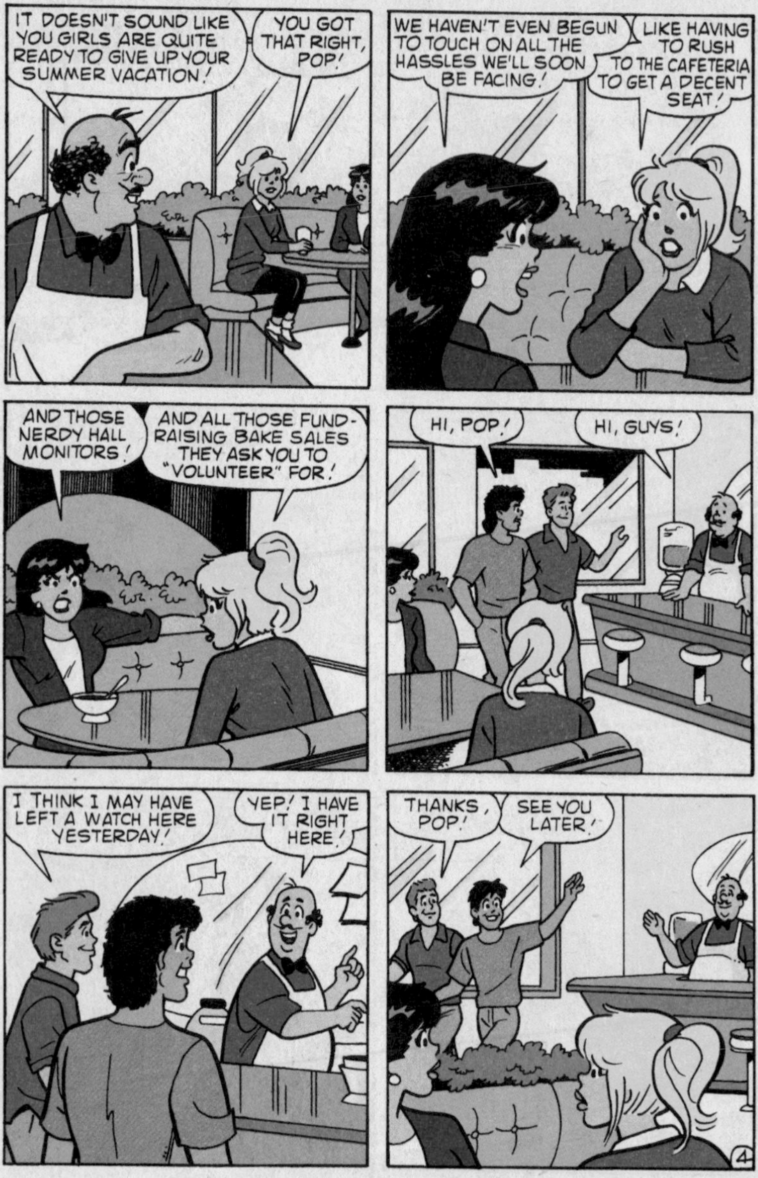
IT DOESN'T SOUND LIKE YOU GIRLS ARE QUITE READY TO GIVE UP YOUR SUMMER VACATION!
YOU GOT THAT RIGHT, POP!
WE HAVEN'T EVEN BEGUN TO TOUCH ON ALL THE HASSLES WE'LL SOON BE FACING!
LIKE HAVING TO RUSH TO THE CAFETERIA TO GET A DECENT SEAT!
AND THOSE NERDY HALL MONITORS!
AND ALL THOSE FUND-RAISING BAKE SALES THEY ASK YOU TO "VOLUNTEER" FOR!
HI, POP!
HI, GUYS!
I THINK I MAY HAVE LEFT A WATCH HERE YESTERDAY!
YEP! I HAVE IT RIGHT HERE!
THANKS, POP!
SEE YOU LATER!
4

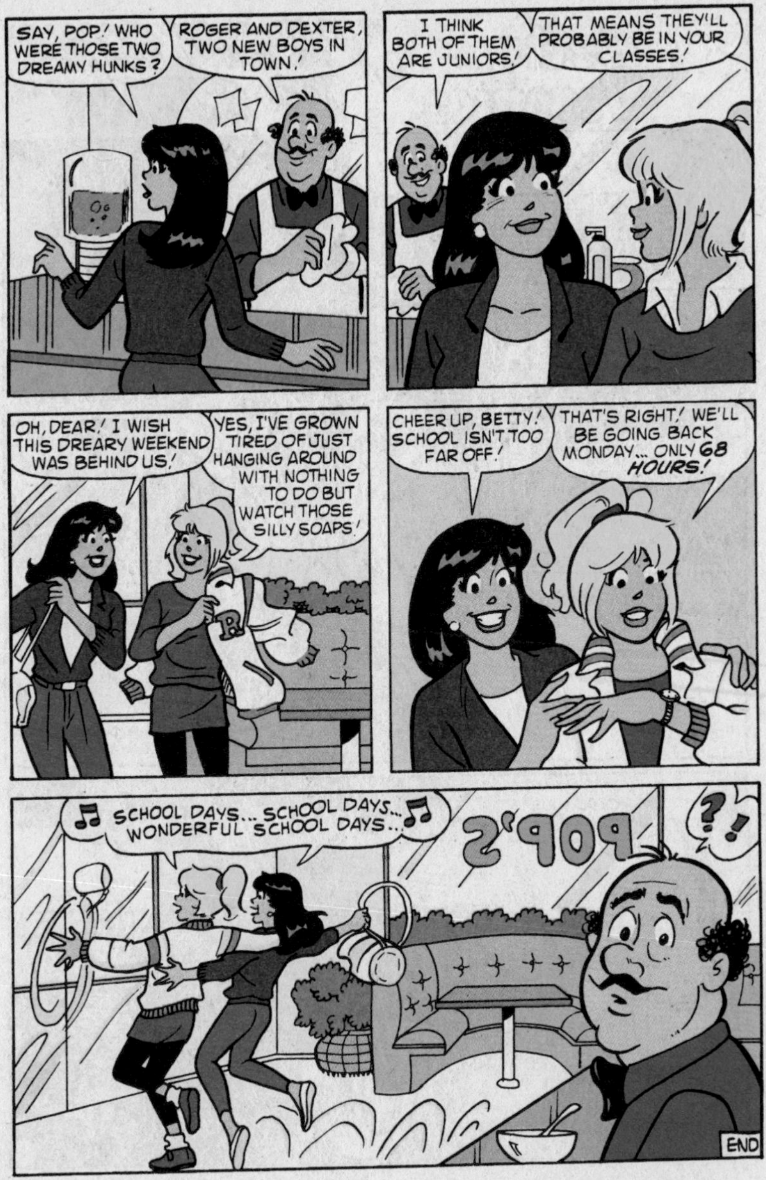
SAY, POP! WHO WERE THOSE TWO DREAMY HUNKS?
ROGER AND DEXTER, TWO NEW BOYS IN TOWN!
I THINK BOTH OF THEM ARE JUNIORS!
THAT MEANS THEY'LL PROBABLY BE IN YOUR CLASSES!
OH, DEAR! I WISH THIS DREARY WEEKEND WAS BEHIND US!
YES, I'VE GROWN TIRED OF JUST HANGING AROUND WITH NOTHING TO DO BUT WATCH THOSE SILLY SOAPS!
CHEER UP, BETTY! SCHOOL ISN'T TOO FAR OFF!
THAT'S RIGHT! WE'LL BE GOING BACK MONDAY... ONLY 68 HOURS!
SCHOOL DAYS... SCHOOL DAYS... WONDERFUL SCHOOL DAYS...
POP'S
?!
END

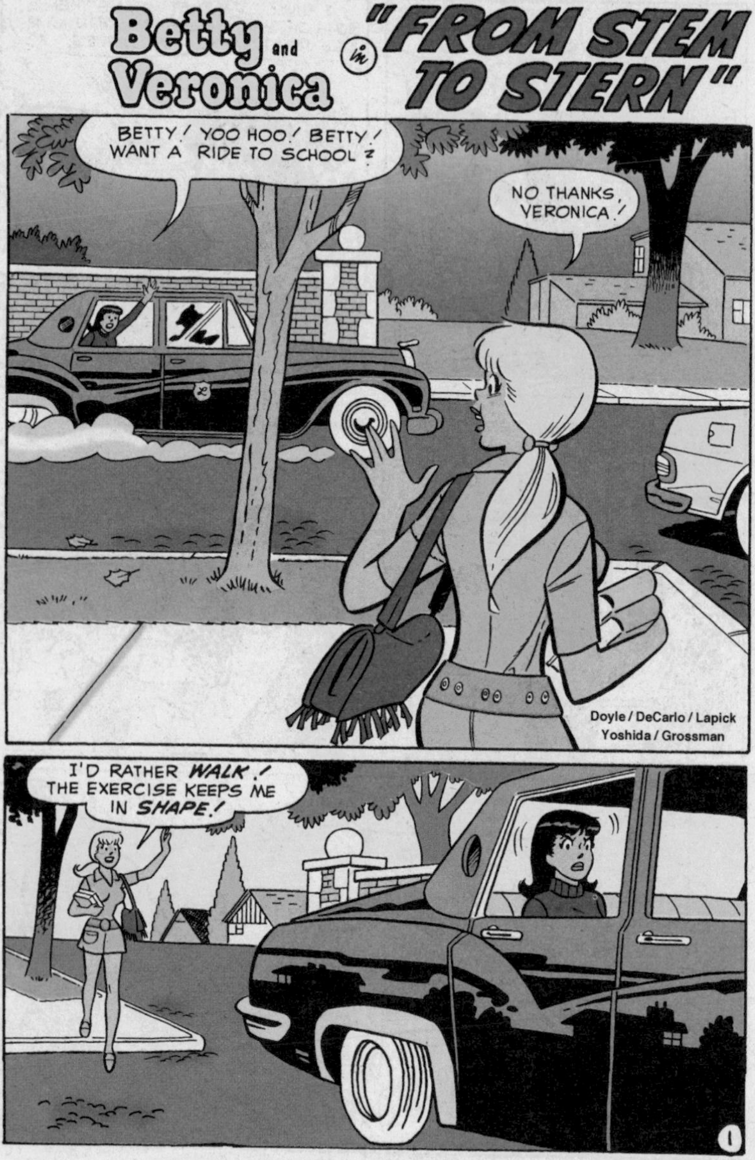
Betty and Veronica in "FROM STEM TO STERN"
BETTY! YOO HOO! BETTY! WANT A RIDE TO SCHOOL?
NO THANKS, VERONICA!
Doyle / DeCarlo / Lapick
Yoshida / Grossman
I'D RATHER WALK! THE EXERCISE KEEPS ME IN SHAPE!
1

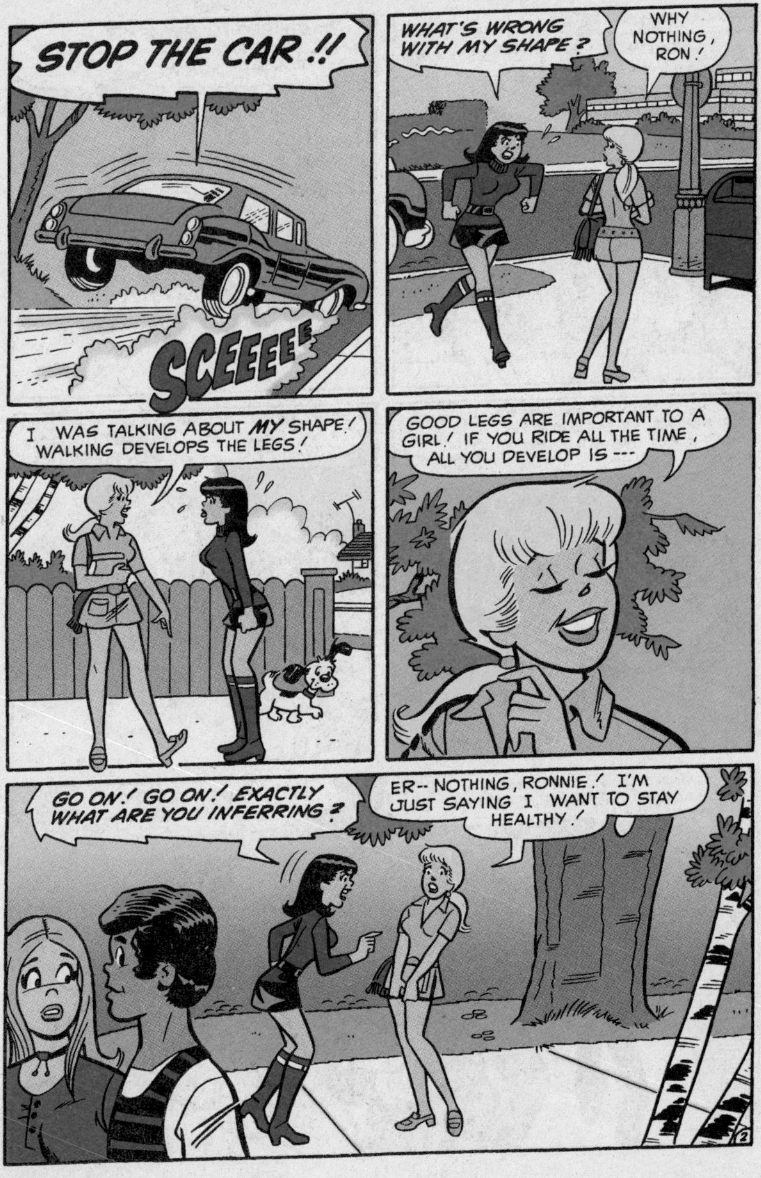
STOP THE CAR !!
SCEEEEEE
WHAT'S WRONG WITH MY SHAPE ?
WHY NOTHING, RON !
I WAS TALKING ABOUT MY SHAPE! WALKING DEVELOPS THE LEGS!
GOOD LEGS ARE IMPORTANT TO A GIRL! IF YOU RIDE ALL THE TIME, ALL YOU DEVELOP IS ---
GO ON! GO ON! EXACTLY WHAT ARE YOU INFERRING ?
ER-- NOTHING, RONNIE! I'M JUST SAYING I WANT TO STAY HEALTHY!
2

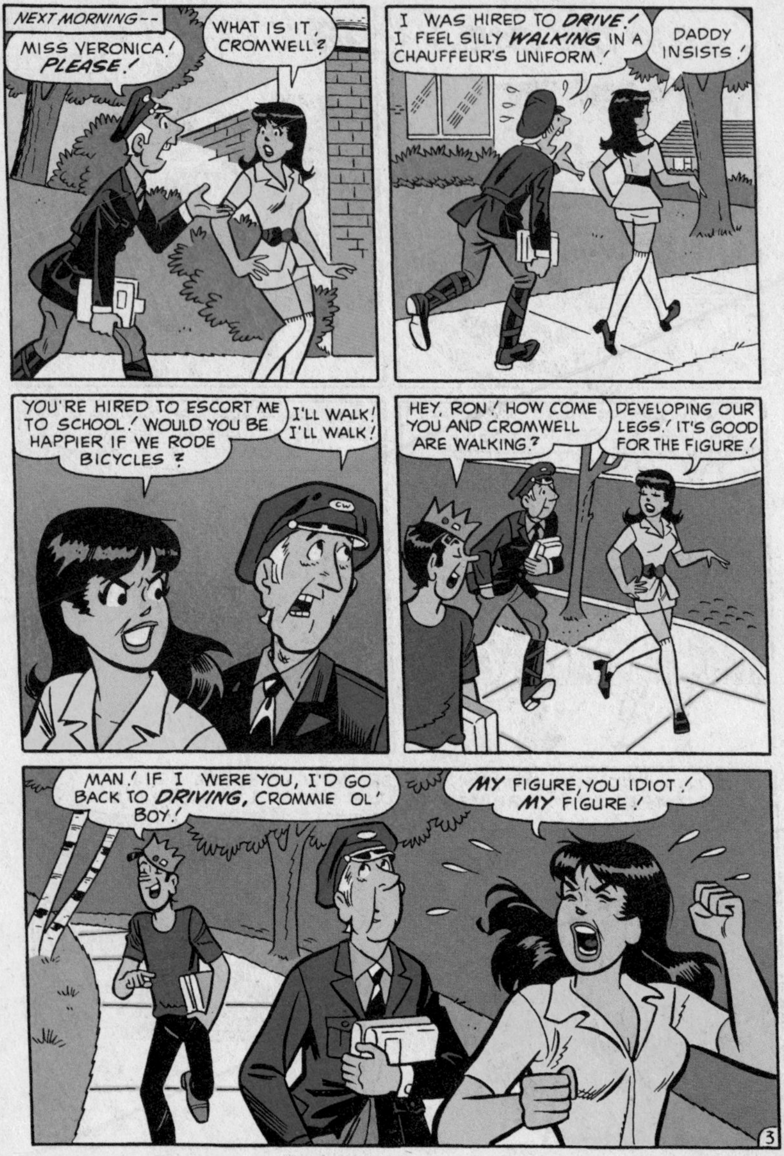
NEXT MORNING--
MISS VERONICA! PLEASE!
WHAT IS IT, CROMWELL?
I WAS HIRED TO DRIVE! I FEEL SILLY WALKING IN A CHAUFFEUR'S UNIFORM!
DADDY INSISTS!
YOU'RE HIRED TO ESCORT ME TO SCHOOL! WOULD YOU BE HAPPIER IF WE RODE BICYCLES?
I'LL WALK! I'LL WALK!
HEY, RON! HOW COME YOU AND CROMWELL ARE WALKING?
DEVELOPING OUR LEGS! IT'S GOOD FOR THE FIGURE!
MAN! IF I WERE YOU, I'D GO BACK TO DRIVING, CROMMIE OL' BOY!
MY FIGURE, YOU IDIOT! MY FIGURE!
3

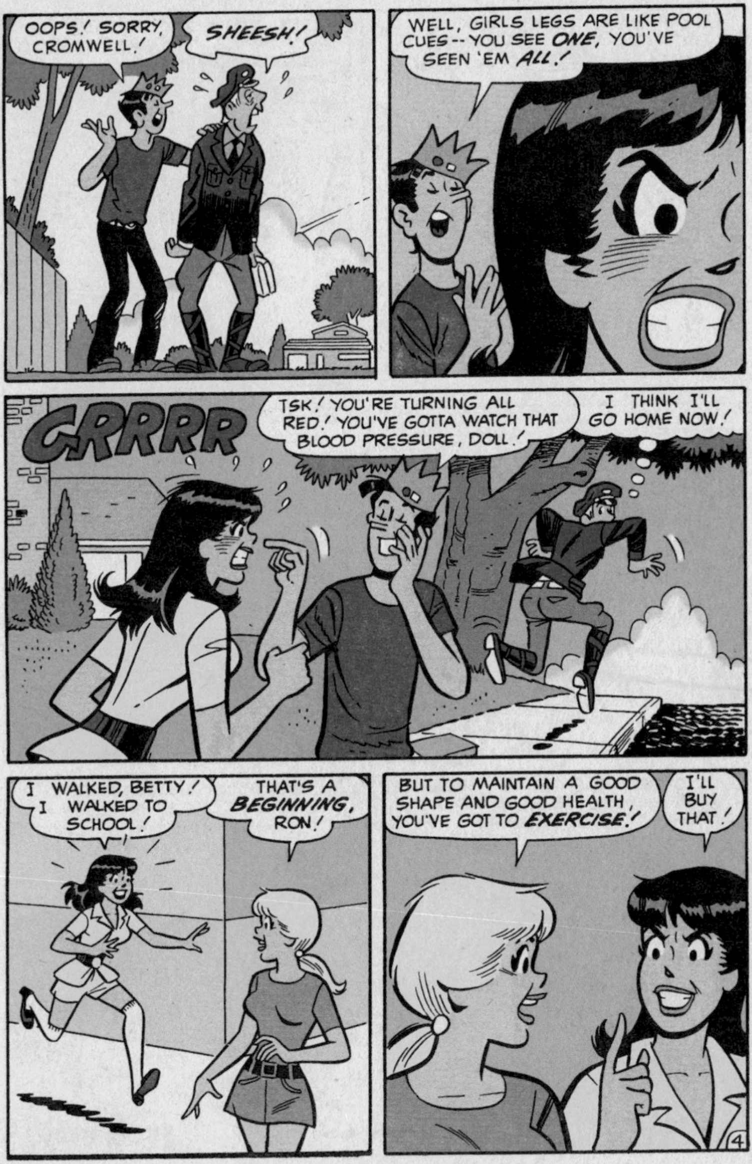

OOPS! SORRY, CROMWELL!
SHEESH!
WELL, GIRLS LEGS ARE LIKE POOL CUES -- YOU SEE ONE, YOU'VE SEEN 'EM ALL!
GRRRR
TSK! YOU'RE TURNING ALL RED! YOU'VE GOTTA WATCH THAT BLOOD PRESSURE, DOLL!
I THINK I'LL GO HOME NOW!
I WALKED, BETTY! I WALKED TO SCHOOL!
THAT'S A BEGINNING, RON!
BUT TO MAINTAIN A GOOD SHAPE AND GOOD HEALTH, YOU'VE GOT TO EXERCISE!
I'LL BUY THAT!
4

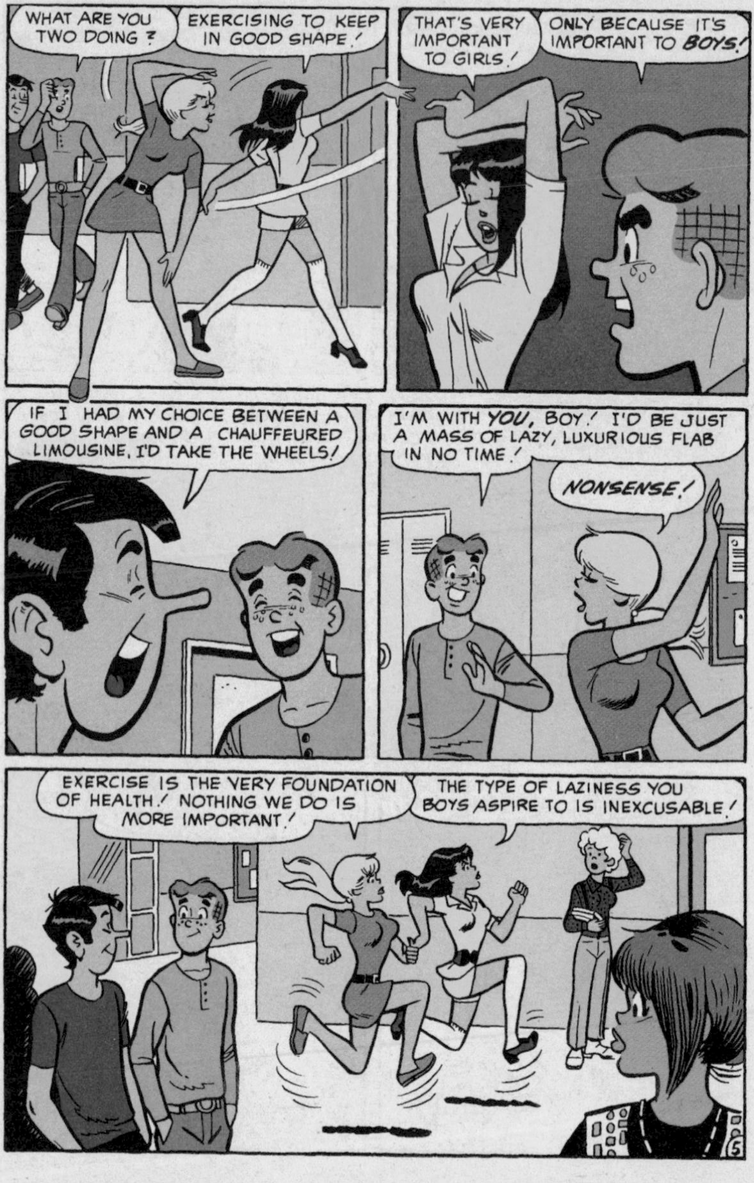
WHAT ARE YOU TWO DOING ?
EXERCISING TO KEEP IN GOOD SHAPE!
THAT'S VERY IMPORTANT TO GIRLS!
ONLY BECAUSE IT'S IMPORTANT TO BOYS!
IF I HAD MY CHOICE BETWEEN A GOOD SHAPE AND A CHAUFFEURED LIMOUSINE, I'D TAKE THE WHEELS!
I'M WITH YOU, BOY! I'D BE JUST A MASS OF LAZY, LUXURIOUS FLAB IN NO TIME!
NONSENSE!
EXERCISE IS THE VERY FOUNDATION OF HEALTH! NOTHING WE DO IS MORE IMPORTANT!
THE TYPE OF LAZINESS YOU BOYS ASPIRE TO IS INEXCUSABLE!
5

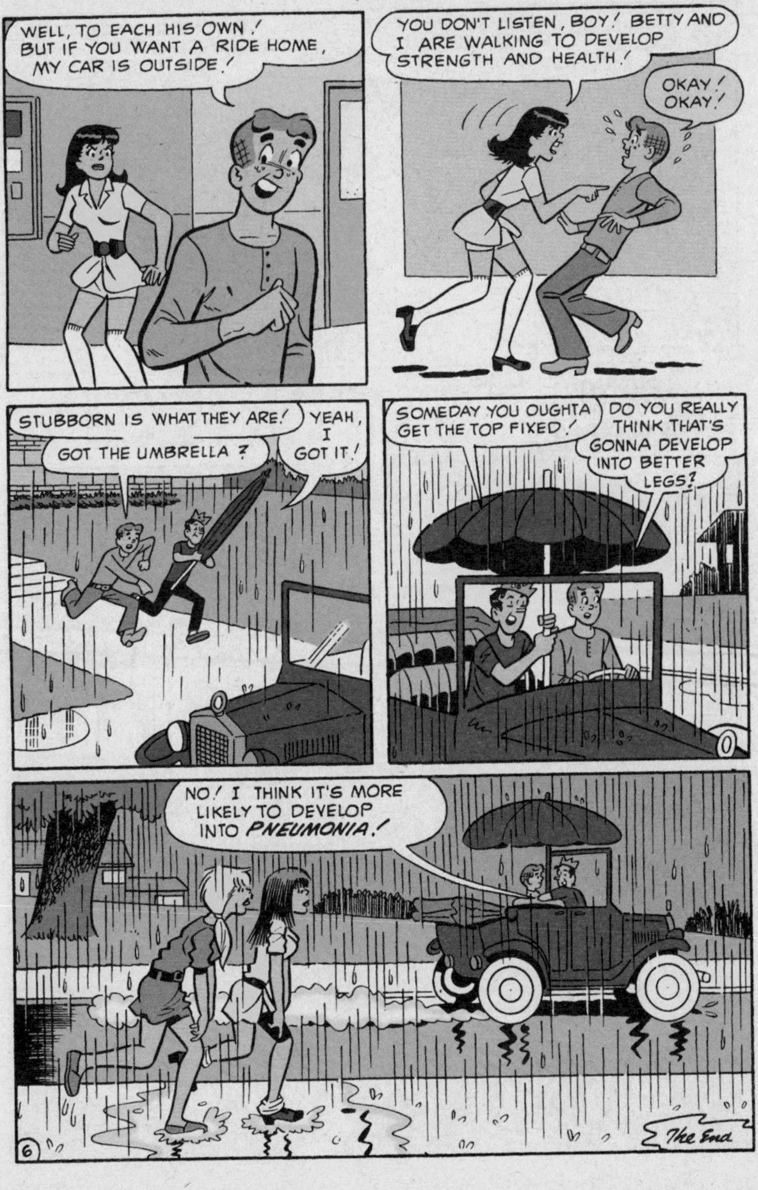

WELL, TO EACH HIS OWN! BUT IF YOU WANT A RIDE HOME, MY CAR IS OUTSIDE!
YOU DON'T LISTEN, BOY! BETTY AND I ARE WALKING TO DEVELOP STRENGTH AND HEALTH!
OKAY! OKAY!
STUBBORN IS WHAT THEY ARE!
YEAH, I GOT IT!
GOT THE UMBRELLA ?
SOMEDAY YOU OUGHTA GET THE TOP FIXED!
DO YOU REALLY THINK THAT'S GONNA DEVELOP INTO BETTER LEGS?
NO! I THINK IT'S MORE LIKELY TO DEVELOP INTO PNEUMONIA!
The End
6

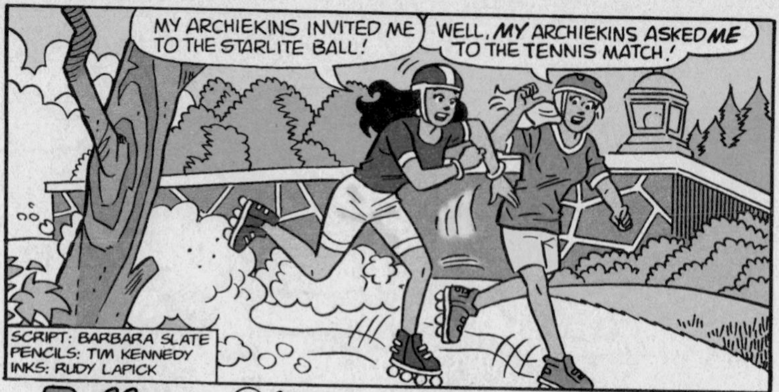
MY ARCHIEKINS INVITED ME TO THE STARLITE BALL!
WELL, MY ARCHIEKINS ASKED ME TO THE TENNIS MATCH!
SCRIPT: BARBARA SLATE
PENCILS: TIM KENNEDY
INKS: RUDY LAPICK

Betty and Veronica in "SPLIT DECISION"

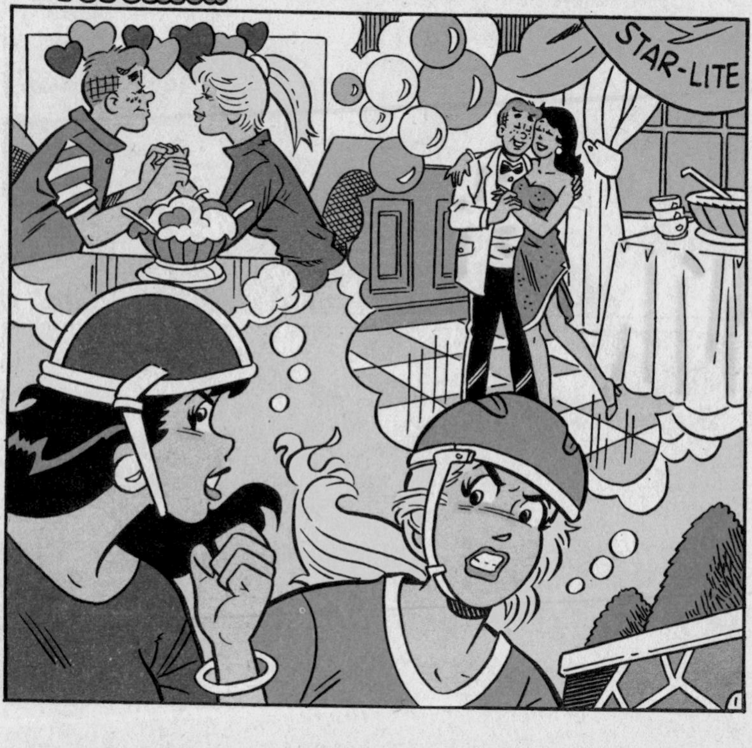
STAR-LITE

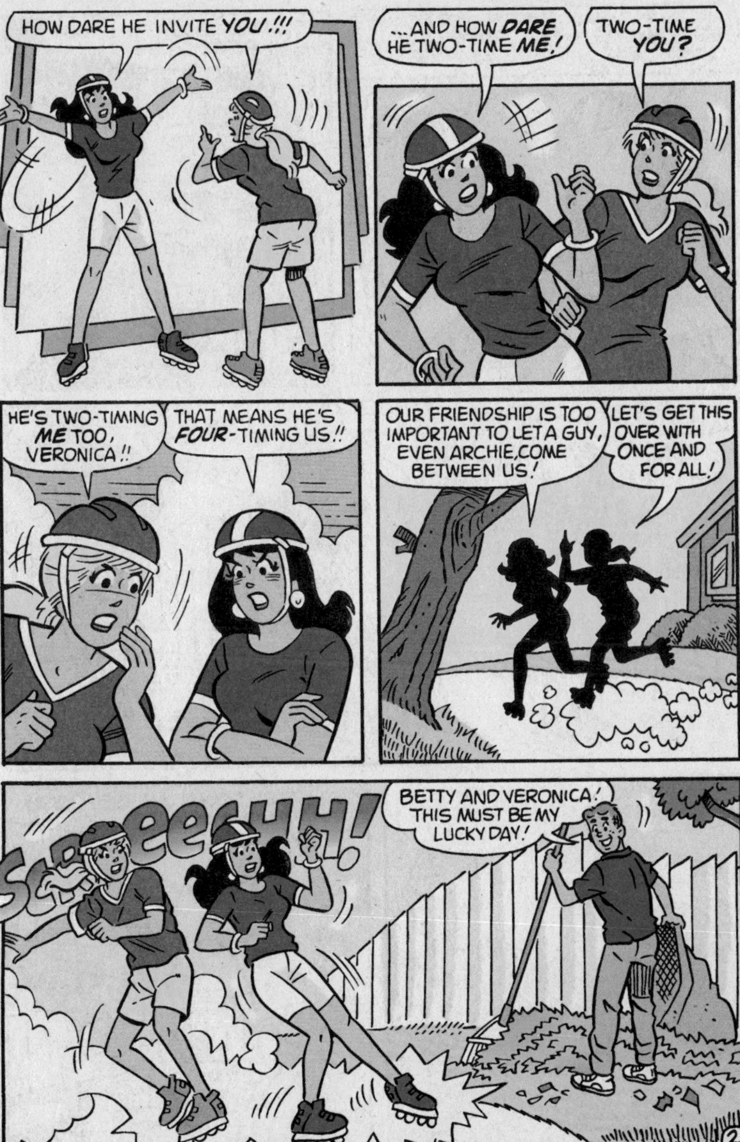

HOW DARE HE INVITE YOU!!!
...AND HOW DARE HE TWO-TIME ME!
TWO-TIME YOU?
HE'S TWO-TIMING ME TOO, VERONICA!!
THAT MEANS HE'S FOUR-TIMING US!!
OUR FRIENDSHIP IS TOO IMPORTANT TO LET A GUY, EVEN ARCHIE, COME BETWEEN US!
LET'S GET THIS OVER WITH ONCE AND FOR ALL!
SCREEECHH!
BETTY AND VERONICA! THIS MUST BE MY LUCKY DAY!
2

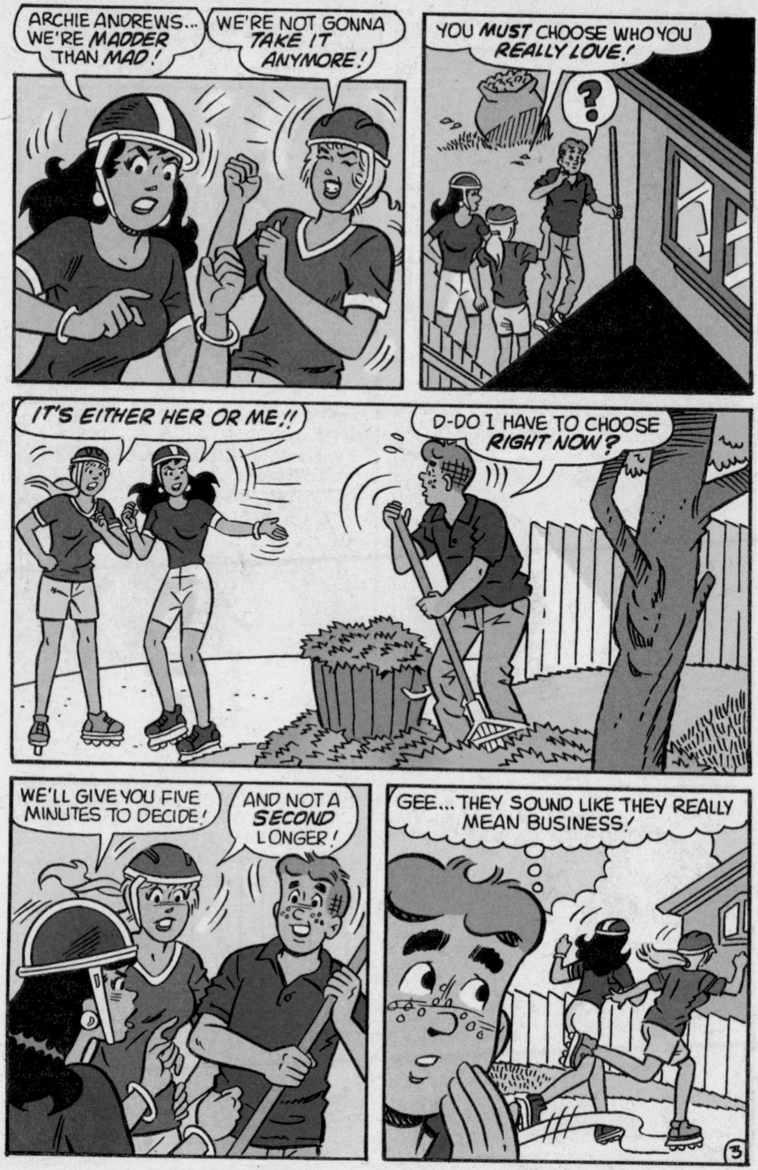
ARCHIE ANDREWS... WE'RE MADDER THAN MAD!
WE'RE NOT GONNA TAKE IT ANYMORE!
YOU MUST CHOOSE WHO YOU REALLY LOVE!
?
IT'S EITHER HER OR ME!!
D-DO I HAVE TO CHOOSE RIGHT NOW?
WE'LL GIVE YOU FIVE MINUTES TO DECIDE!
AND NOT A SECOND LONGER!
GEE... THEY SOUND LIKE THEY REALLY MEAN BUSINESS!
3

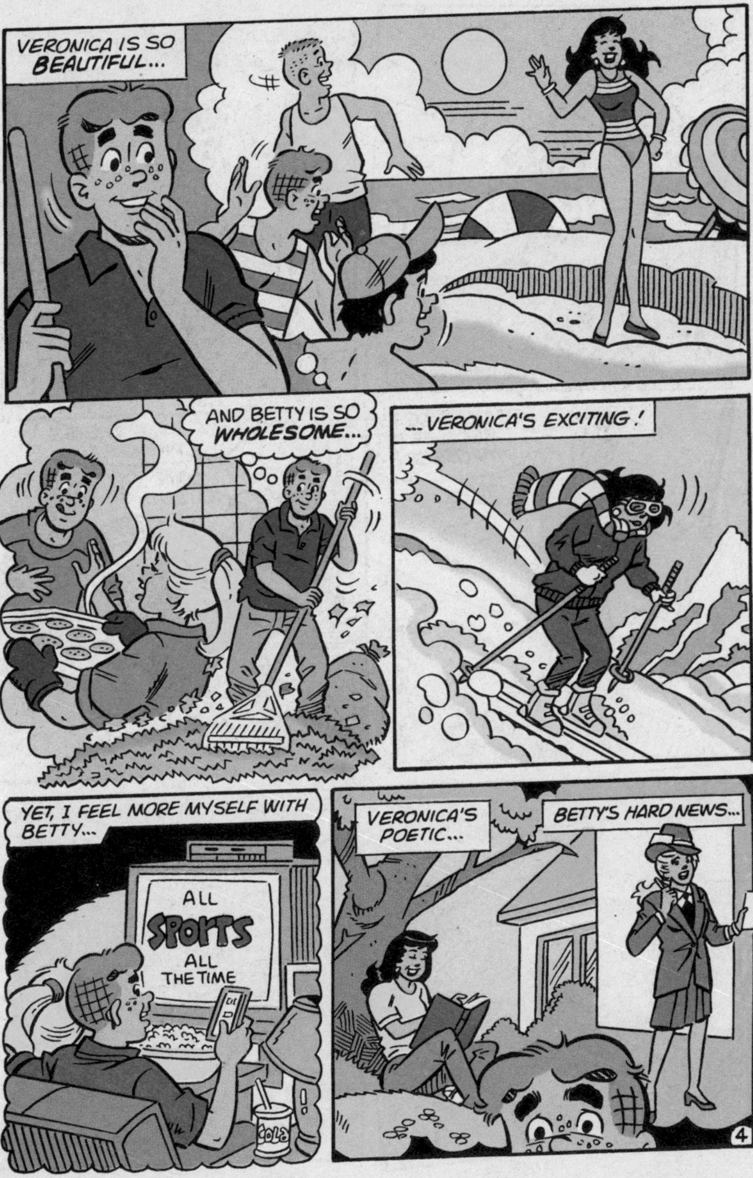

VERONICA IS SO BEAUTIFUL...
AND BETTY IS SO WHOLESOME...
...VERONICA'S EXCITING!
YET, I FEEL MORE MYSELF WITH BETTY...
ALL SPORTS ALL THE TIME
VERONICA'S POETIC...
BETTY'S HARD NEWS...
4

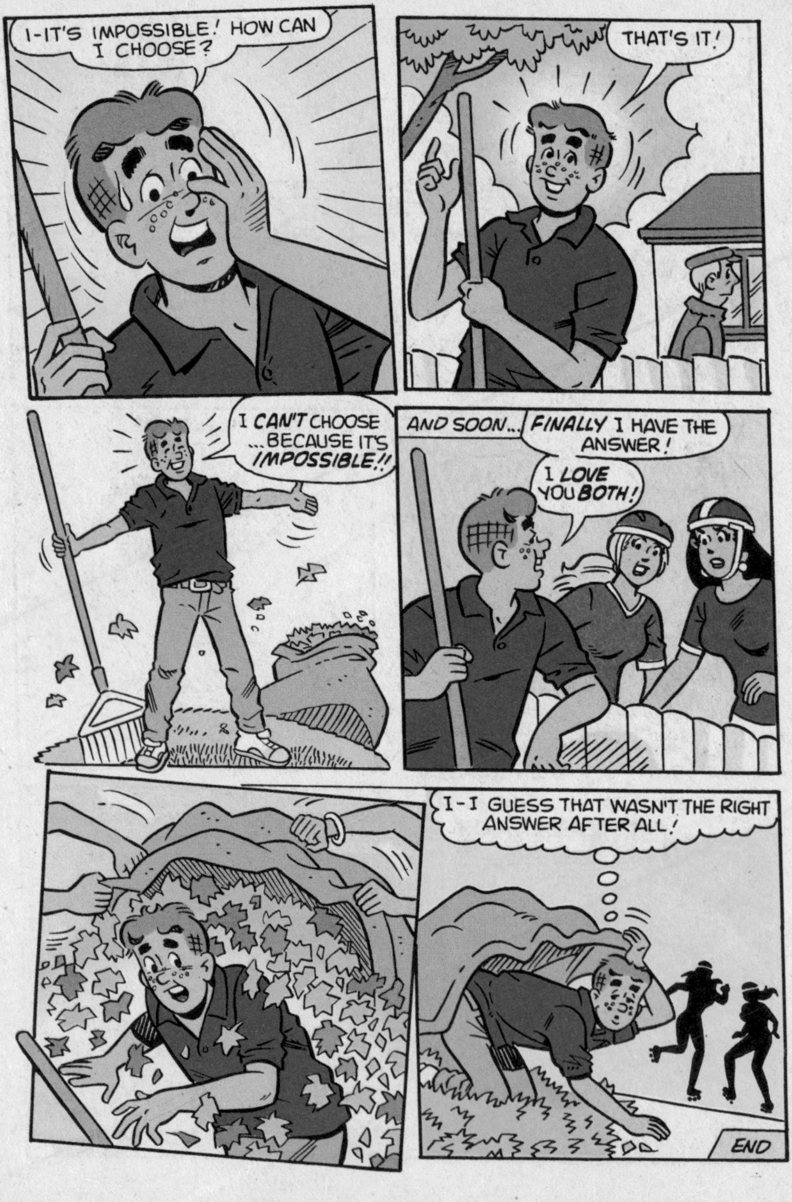

I-IT'S IMPOSSIBLE! HOW CAN I CHOOSE?
THAT'S IT!
I CAN'T CHOOSE ...BECAUSE IT'S IMPOSSIBLE!!
AND SOON...
FINALLY I HAVE THE ANSWER!
I LOVE YOU BOTH!
I-I GUESS THAT WASN'T THE RIGHT ANSWER AFTER ALL!
END

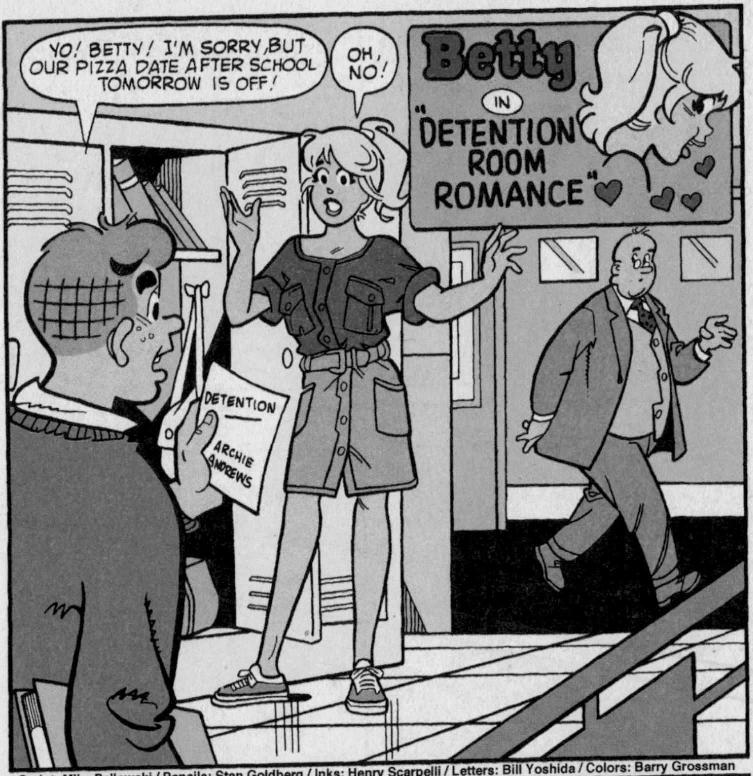
YO! BETTY! I'M SORRY, BUT OUR PIZZA DATE AFTER SCHOOL TOMORROW IS OFF!
OH, NO!
Betty
IN
"DETENTION ROOM ROMANCE"
DETENTION
ARCHIE ANDREWS

Script: Mike Pellowski / Pencils: Stan Goldberg / Inks: Henry Scarpelli / Letters: Bill Yoshida / Colors: Barry Grossman

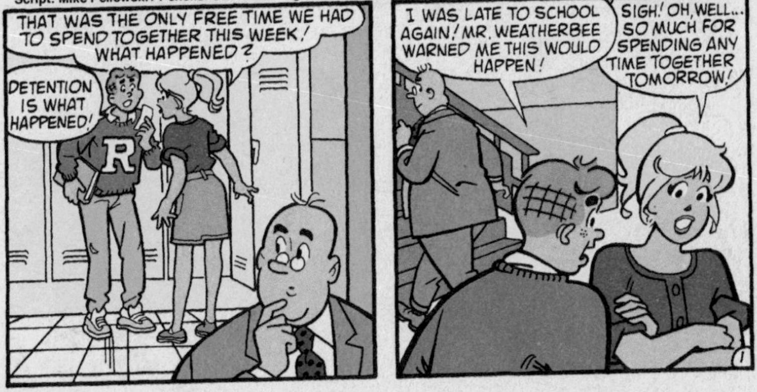
THAT WAS THE ONLY FREE TIME WE HAD TO SPEND TOGETHER THIS WEEK! WHAT HAPPENED?
DETENTION IS WHAT HAPPENED!
R
I WAS LATE TO SCHOOL AGAIN! MR. WEATHERBEE WARNED ME THIS WOULD HAPPEN!
SIGH! OH, WELL... SO MUCH FOR SPENDING ANY TIME TOGETHER TOMORROW!
1

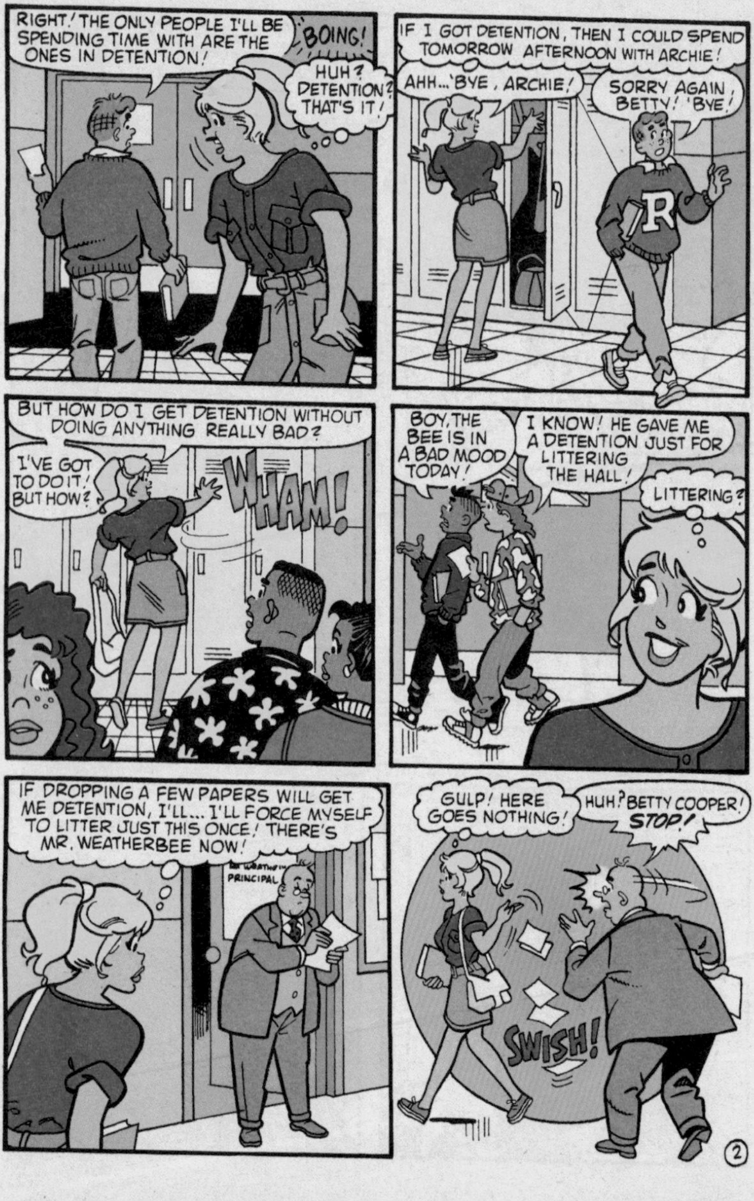

RIGHT! THE ONLY PEOPLE I'LL BE SPENDING TIME WITH ARE THE ONES IN DETENTION!
BOING!
HUH? DETENTION? THAT'S IT!
IF I GOT DETENTION, THEN I COULD SPEND TOMORROW AFTERNOON WITH ARCHIE!
AHH...'BYE, ARCHIE!
SORRY AGAIN, BETTY! 'BYE!
R
BUT HOW DO I GET DETENTION WITHOUT DOING ANYTHING REALLY BAD?
I'VE GOT TO DO IT! BUT HOW?
WHAM!
BOY, THE BEE IS IN A BAD MOOD TODAY!
I KNOW! HE GAVE ME A DETENTION JUST FOR LITTERING THE HALL!
LITTERING?
IF DROPPING A FEW PAPERS WILL GET ME DETENTION, I'LL... I'LL FORCE MYSELF TO LITTER JUST THIS ONCE! THERE'S MR. WEATHERBEE NOW!
PRINCIPAL
GULP! HERE GOES NOTHING!
HUH? BETTY COOPER! STOP!
SWISH!

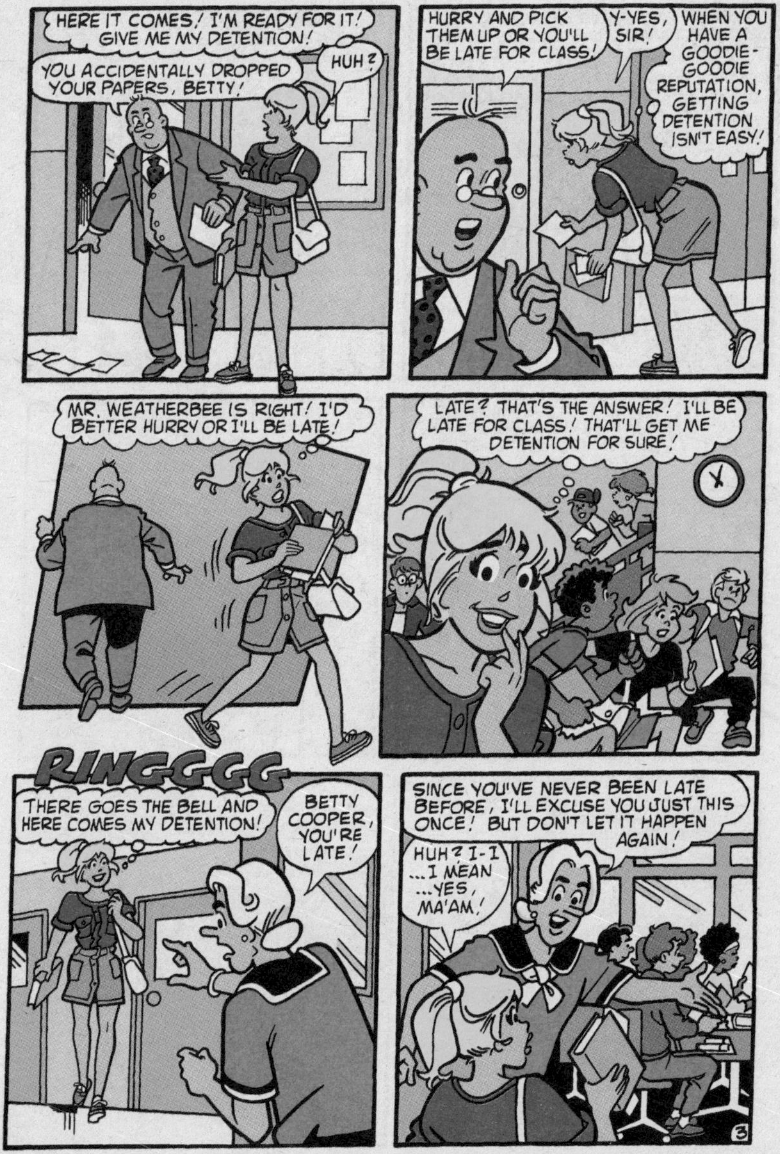
HERE IT COMES! I'M READY FOR IT! GIVE ME MY DETENTION!
YOU ACCIDENTALLY DROPPED YOUR PAPERS, BETTY!
HUH?
HURRY AND PICK THEM UP OR YOU'LL BE LATE FOR CLASS!
Y-YES, SIR!
WHEN YOU HAVE A GOODIE-GOODIE REPUTATION, GETTING DETENTION ISN'T EASY!
MR. WEATHERBEE IS RIGHT! I'D BETTER HURRY OR I'LL BE LATE!
LATE? THAT'S THE ANSWER! I'LL BE LATE FOR CLASS! THAT'LL GET ME DETENTION FOR SURE!
RINGGGG
THERE GOES THE BELL AND HERE COMES MY DETENTION!
BETTY COOPER, YOU'RE LATE!
SINCE YOU'VE NEVER BEEN LATE BEFORE, I'LL EXCUSE YOU JUST THIS ONCE! BUT DON'T LET IT HAPPEN AGAIN!
HUH? I-I ...I MEAN ...YES, MA'AM!
3

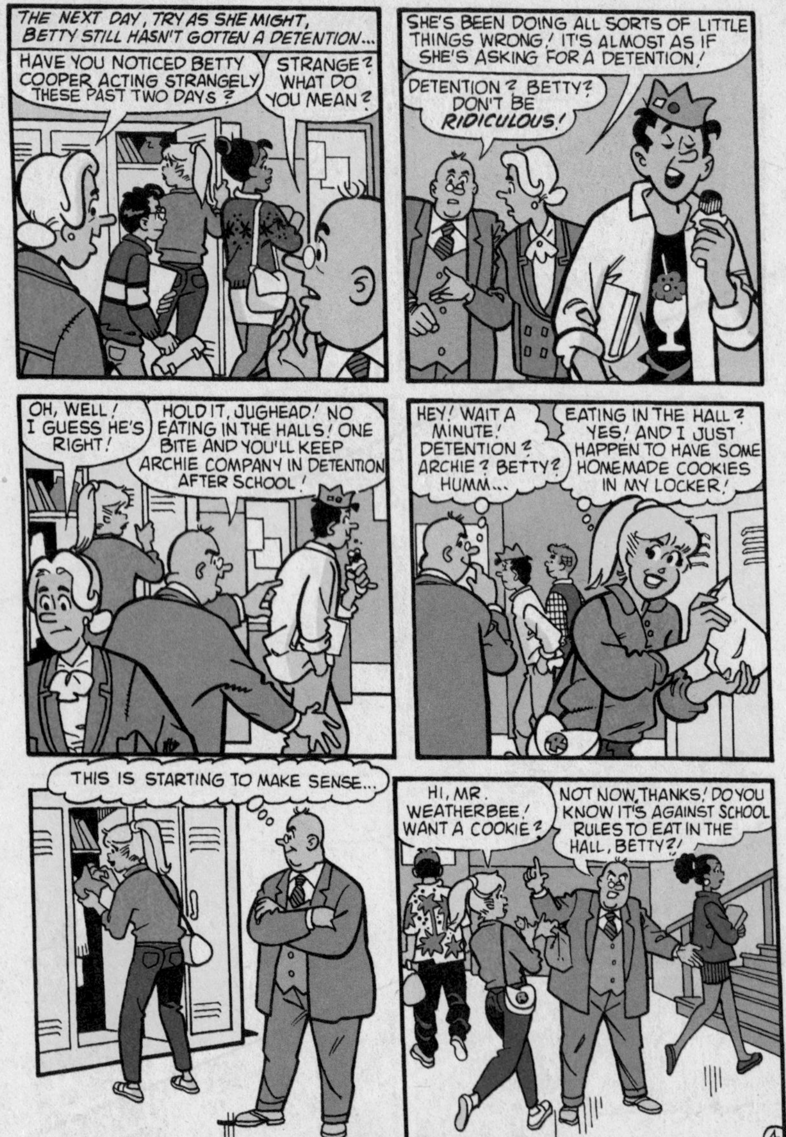
THE NEXT DAY, TRY AS SHE MIGHT, BETTY STILL HASN'T GOTTEN A DETENTION...
HAVE YOU NOTICED BETTY COOPER ACTING STRANGELY THESE PAST TWO DAYS?
STRANGE? WHAT DO YOU MEAN?
SHE'S BEEN DOING ALL SORTS OF LITTLE THINGS WRONG! IT'S ALMOST AS IF SHE'S ASKING FOR A DETENTION!
DETENTION? BETTY? DON'T BE RIDICULOUS!
OH, WELL! I GUESS HE'S RIGHT!
HOLD IT, JUGHEAD! NO EATING IN THE HALLS! ONE BITE AND YOU'LL KEEP ARCHIE COMPANY IN DETENTION AFTER SCHOOL!
HEY! WAIT A MINUTE! DETENTION? ARCHIE? BETTY? HUMM...
EATING IN THE HALL? YES! AND I JUST HAPPEN TO HAVE SOME HOMEMADE COOKIES IN MY LOCKER!
THIS IS STARTING TO MAKE SENSE...
HI, MR. WEATHERBEE! WANT A COOKIE?
NOT NOW, THANKS! DO YOU KNOW IT'S AGAINST SCHOOL RULES TO EAT IN THE HALL, BETTY?!
4

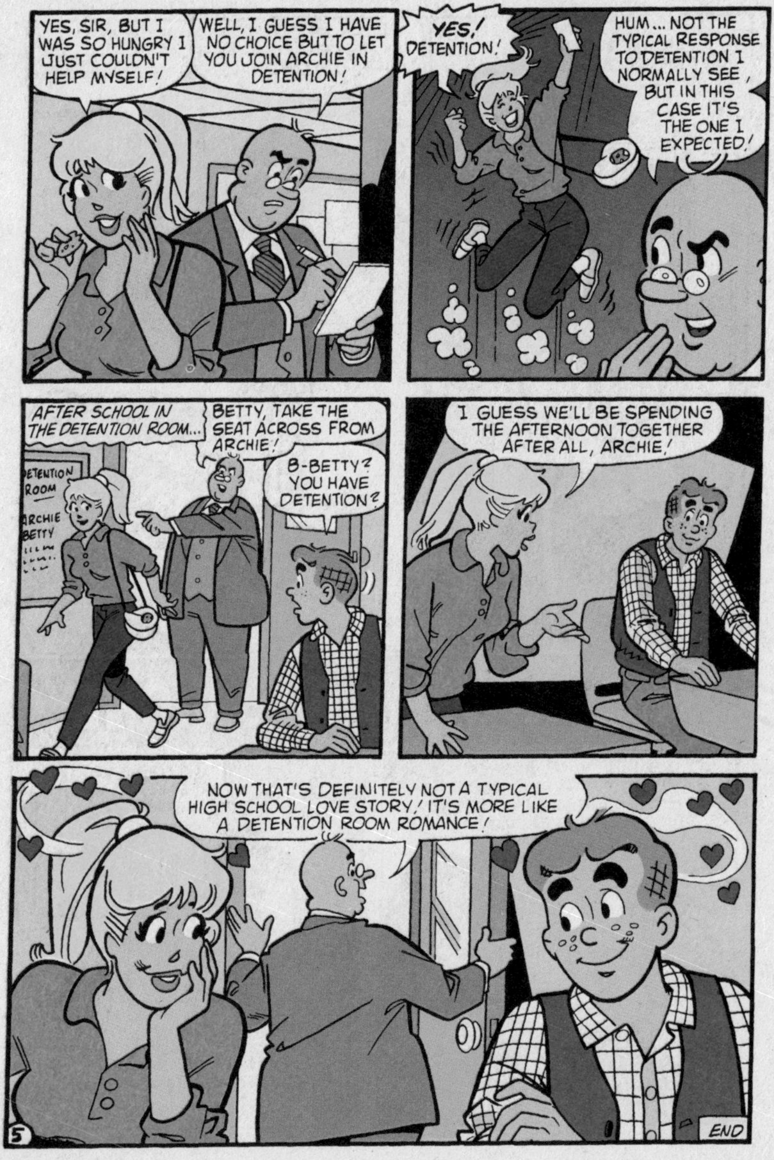
YES, SIR, BUT I WAS SO HUNGRY I JUST COULDN'T HELP MYSELF!
WELL, I GUESS I HAVE NO CHOICE BUT TO LET YOU JOIN ARCHIE IN DETENTION!
YES! DETENTION!
HUM... NOT THE TYPICAL RESPONSE TO DETENTION I NORMALLY SEE, BUT IN THIS CASE IT'S THE ONE I EXPECTED!
AFTER SCHOOL IN THE DETENTION ROOM...
BETTY, TAKE THE SEAT ACROSS FROM ARCHIE!
DETENTION ROOM
ARCHIE
BETTY
B-BETTY? YOU HAVE DETENTION?
I GUESS WE'LL BE SPENDING THE AFTERNOON TOGETHER AFTER ALL, ARCHIE!
NOW THAT'S DEFINITELY NOT A TYPICAL HIGH SCHOOL LOVE STORY! IT'S MORE LIKE A DETENTION ROOM ROMANCE!
5
END

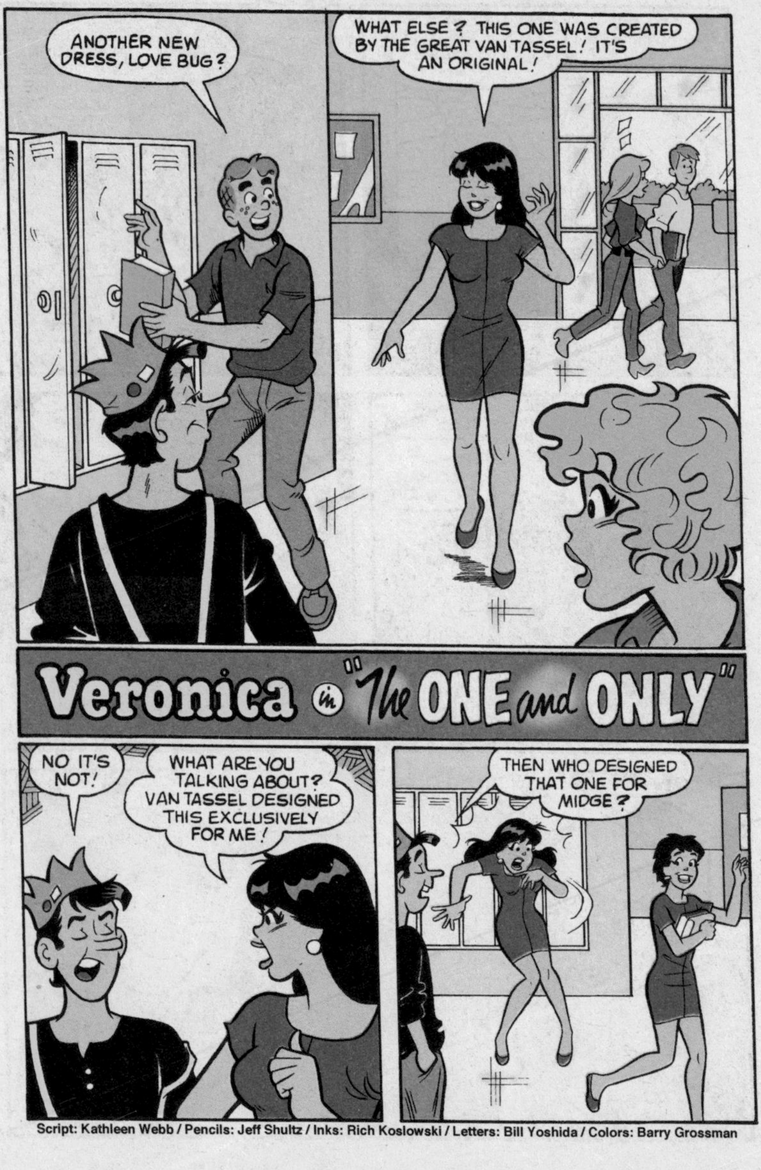
ANOTHER NEW DRESS, LOVE BUG?
WHAT ELSE? THIS ONE WAS CREATED BY THE GREAT VAN TASSEL! IT'S AN ORIGINAL!
Veronica in "The ONE and ONLY"
NO IT'S NOT!
WHAT ARE YOU TALKING ABOUT? VAN TASSEL DESIGNED THIS EXCLUSIVELY FOR ME!
THEN WHO DESIGNED THAT ONE FOR MIDGE?

Script: Kathleen Webb / Pencils: Jeff Shultz / Inks: Rich Koslowski / Letters: Bill Yoshida / Colors: Barry Grossman

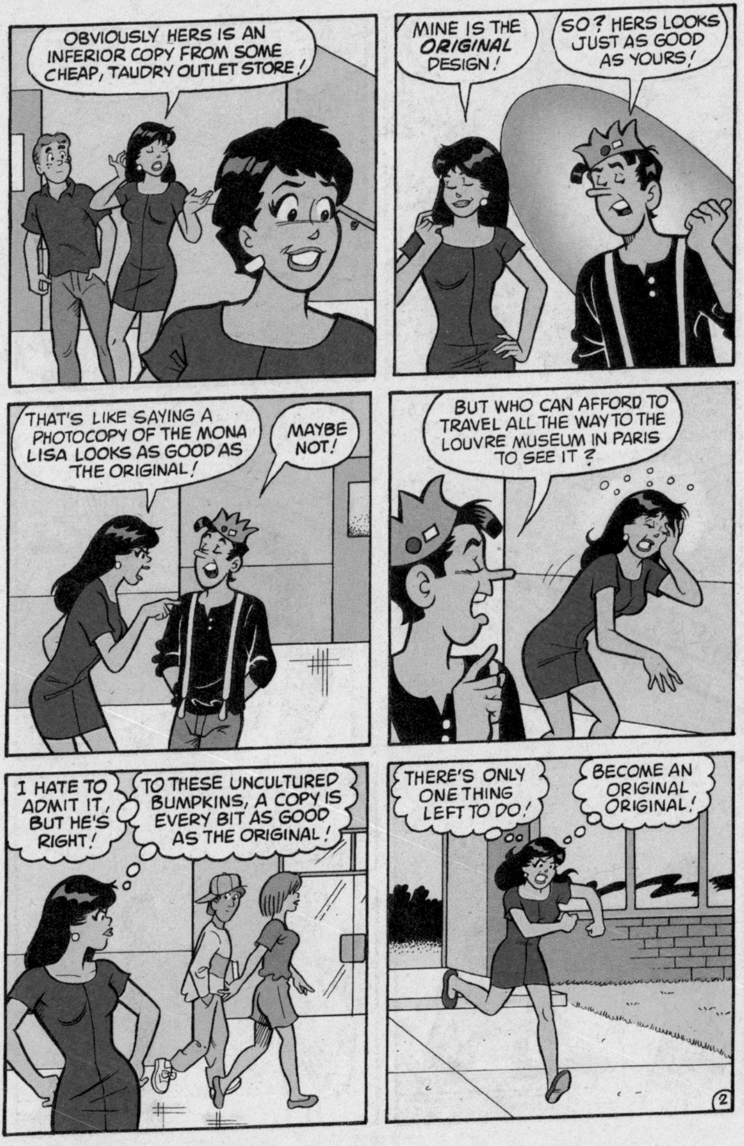
OBVIOUSLY HERS IS AN INFERIOR COPY FROM SOME CHEAP, TAUDRY OUTLET STORE!
MINE IS THE ORIGINAL DESIGN!
SO? HERS LOOKS JUST AS GOOD AS YOURS!
THAT'S LIKE SAYING A PHOTOCOPY OF THE MONA LISA LOOKS AS GOOD AS THE ORIGINAL!
MAYBE NOT!
BUT WHO CAN AFFORD TO TRAVEL ALL THE WAY TO THE LOUVRE MUSEUM IN PARIS TO SEE IT?
I HATE TO ADMIT IT, BUT HE'S RIGHT!
TO THESE UNCULTURED BUMPKINS, A COPY IS EVERY BIT AS GOOD AS THE ORIGINAL!
THERE'S ONLY ONE THING LEFT TO DO!
BECOME AN ORIGINAL ORIGINAL!

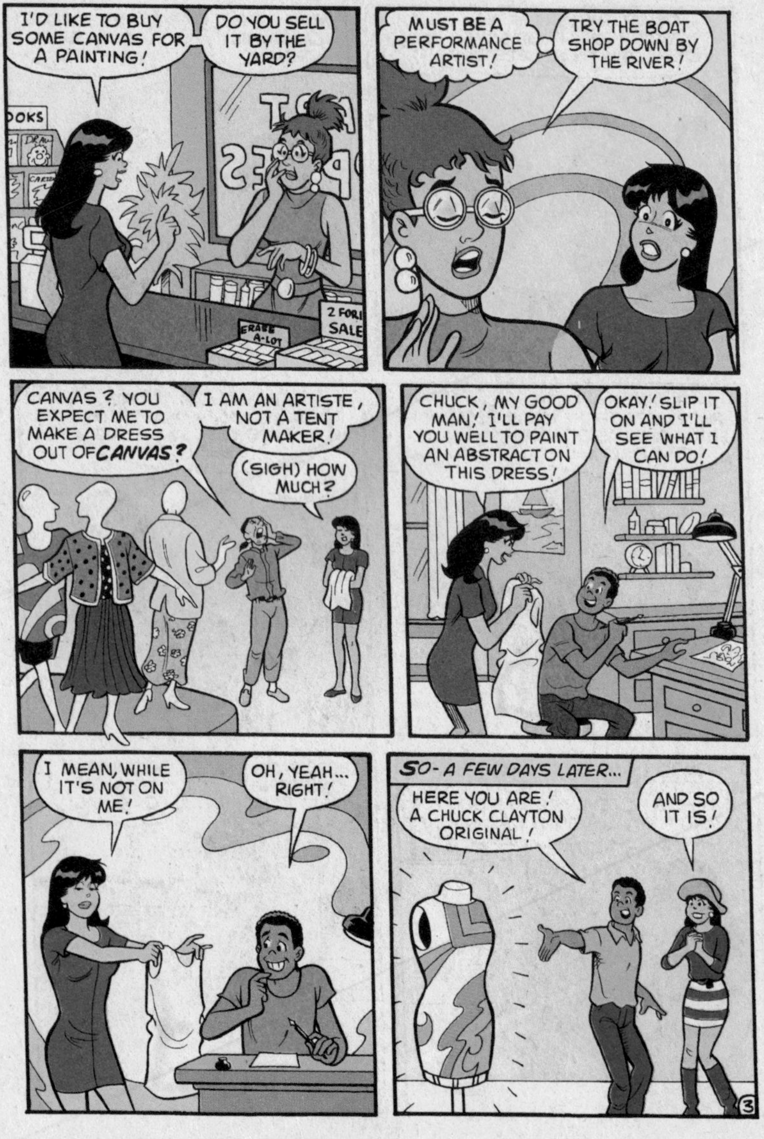
I'D LIKE TO BUY SOME CANVAS FOR A PAINTING!
DO YOU SELL IT BY THE YARD?
OOKS
2 FOR 1 SALE
ERASE A-LOT
MUST BE A PERFORMANCE ARTIST!
TRY THE BOAT SHOP DOWN BY THE RIVER!
CANVAS? YOU EXPECT ME TO MAKE A DRESS OUT OF CANVAS?
I AM AN ARTISTE, NOT A TENT MAKER!
(SIGH) HOW MUCH?
CHUCK, MY GOOD MAN! I'LL PAY YOU WELL TO PAINT AN ABSTRACT ON THIS DRESS!
OKAY! SLIP IT ON AND I'LL SEE WHAT I CAN DO!
I MEAN, WHILE IT'S NOT ON ME!
OH, YEAH... RIGHT!
SO- A FEW DAYS LATER...
HERE YOU ARE! A CHUCK CLAYTON ORIGINAL!
AND SO IT IS!
3

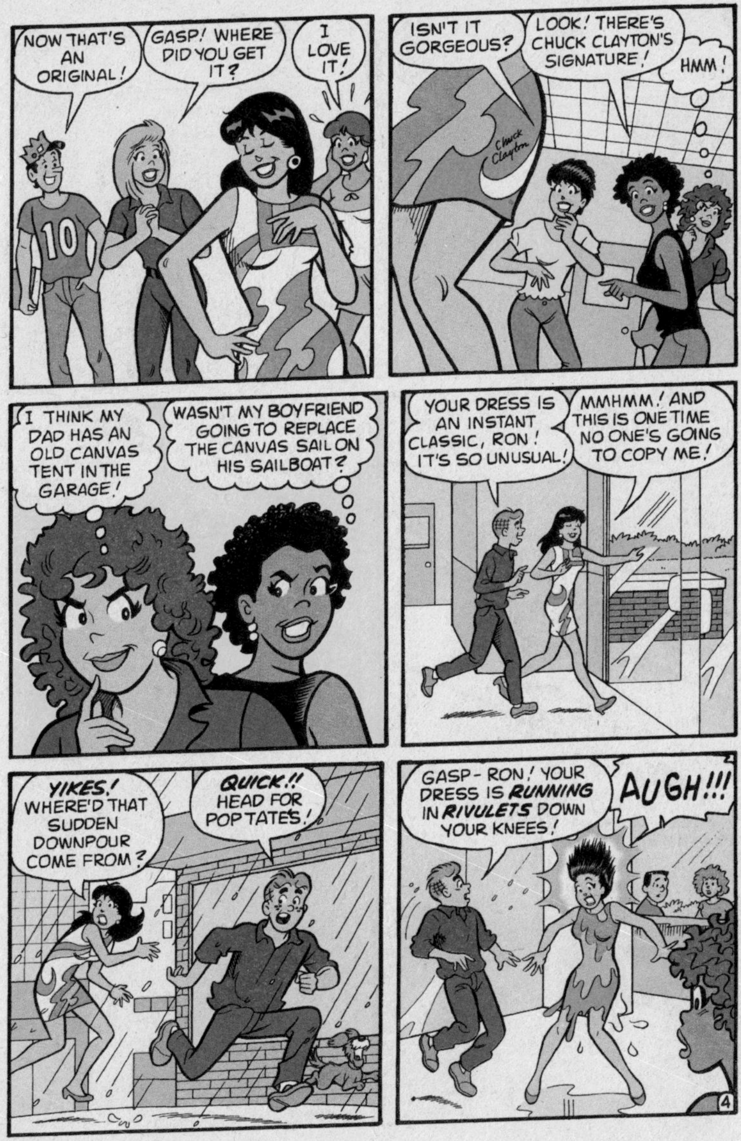

NOW THAT'S AN ORIGINAL!
GASP! WHERE DID YOU GET IT?
I LOVE IT!
ISN'T IT GORGEOUS?
LOOK! THERE'S CHUCK CLAYTON'S SIGNATURE!
HMM!
Chuck Clayton
I THINK MY DAD HAS AN OLD CANVAS TENT IN THE GARAGE!
WASN'T MY BOYFRIEND GOING TO REPLACE THE CANVAS SAIL ON HIS SAILBOAT?
YOUR DRESS IS AN INSTANT CLASSIC, RON! IT'S SO UNUSUAL!
MMHMM! AND THIS IS ONE TIME NO ONE'S GOING TO COPY ME!
YIKES! WHERE'D THAT SUDDEN DOWNPOUR COME FROM?
QUICK!! HEAD FOR POP TATE'S!
GASP - RON! YOUR DRESS IS RUNNING IN RIVULETS DOWN YOUR KNEES!
AUGH!!!

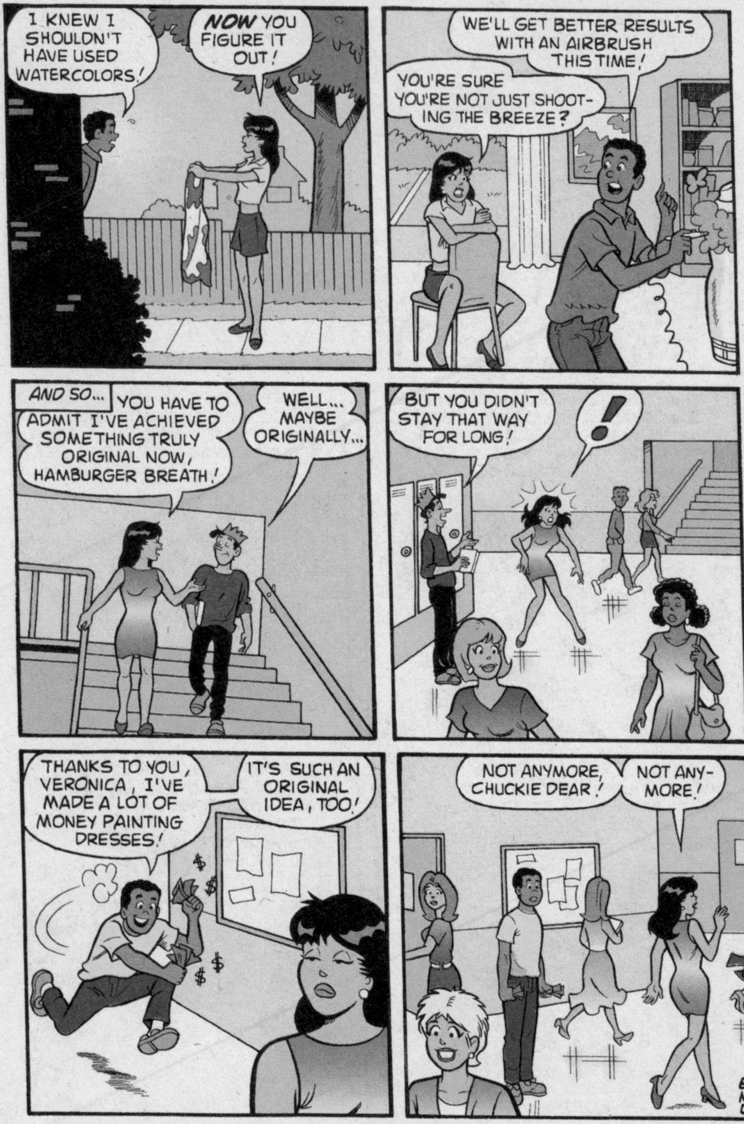
I KNEW I SHOULDN'T HAVE USED WATERCOLORS!
NOW YOU FIGURE IT OUT!
WE'LL GET BETTER RESULTS WITH AN AIRBRUSH THIS TIME!
YOU'RE SURE YOU'RE NOT JUST SHOOTING THE BREEZE?
AND SO...
YOU HAVE TO ADMIT I'VE ACHIEVED SOMETHING TRULY ORIGINAL NOW, HAMBURGER BREATH!
WELL... MAYBE ORIGINALLY...
BUT YOU DIDN'T STAY THAT WAY FOR LONG!
!
THANKS TO YOU, VERONICA, I'VE MADE A LOT OF MONEY PAINTING DRESSES!
IT'S SUCH AN ORIGINAL IDEA, TOO!
NOT ANYMORE, CHUCKIE DEAR!
NOT ANYMORE!
END

Welcome to this special
COLLECTOR'S EDITION _featuring_
THE BEST OF ARCHIE
STARRING BETTY & VERONICA!

You are holding a MUST-HAVE, JUMBO issue—chock-full of the BEST stories ever told! All from the pages of the best-selling series ***THE BEST OF ARCHIE COMICS!*** This collection also includes story introductions by CELEBRITY fans, top WRITERS, awesome ARTISTS and other insights into some of the HILARIOUS and most POPULAR tales from Archie Comics' 75-year history!

In this SPECTACULAR collection, you'll experience FAVORITE, laugh-out-loud moments that make **Archie, Jughead, Betty and Veronica, plus Cheryl Blossom, Sabrina the Teenage Witch, and more ICONS!** Get ready for your BEST and most JUMBO laugh, ever!

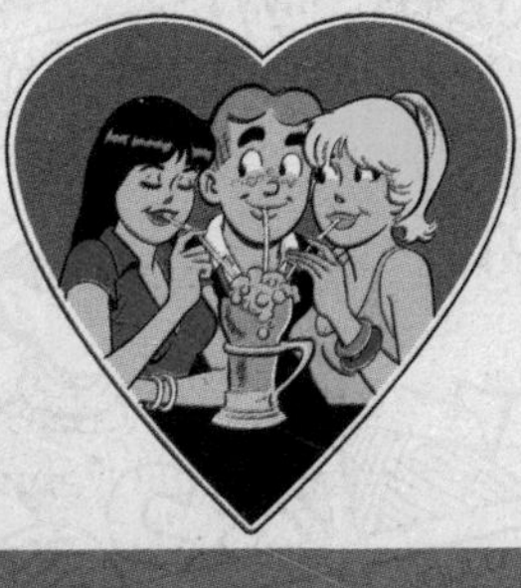

The stories, characters and incidents in this collection are entirely fictional. This book contains some material that was originally created in a less socially sensitive time in our society and reflects attitudes that may be interpreted as being unacceptable today. The stories are reprinted here without alteration for historical reference.

Summer Help

Veronica #128, 2002

by Dan Parent, Jim Amash, Bill Yoshida and Barry Grossman

Betty and Veronica shouldn't need an introduction. They've been around for so long that they're practically family to a lot of us, young and old. These two girls have stood the test of time, and for good reasons. They were designed to be love interests for Archie, and they served that purpose well (very well) but they had such dynamic personalities, readers wanted to see more. And more they got!

They were the original frenemies, and it's this intriguing relationship that keeps us following their adventures. Oh, and such adventures! Their stories are funny, fast-paced, full of heart, and NEVER boring. And it doesn't hurt that the art really makes their stories shine.

If you're discovering Betty and Veronica for the first time, all I can say is that you're holding in your hands some of the most fun stories ever written. If you've been away from Betty and Veronica, and want to rekindle your old friendship, this is the perfect place to start. You'll relive some of their greatest moments, and be reminded how these girls taught you the importance of friendship and how to earn it.

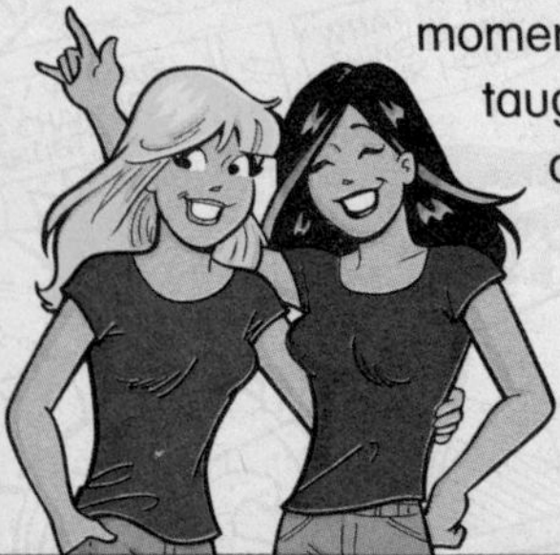

Now go read, the girls are waiting!

Gisele
Artist, Archie Comics

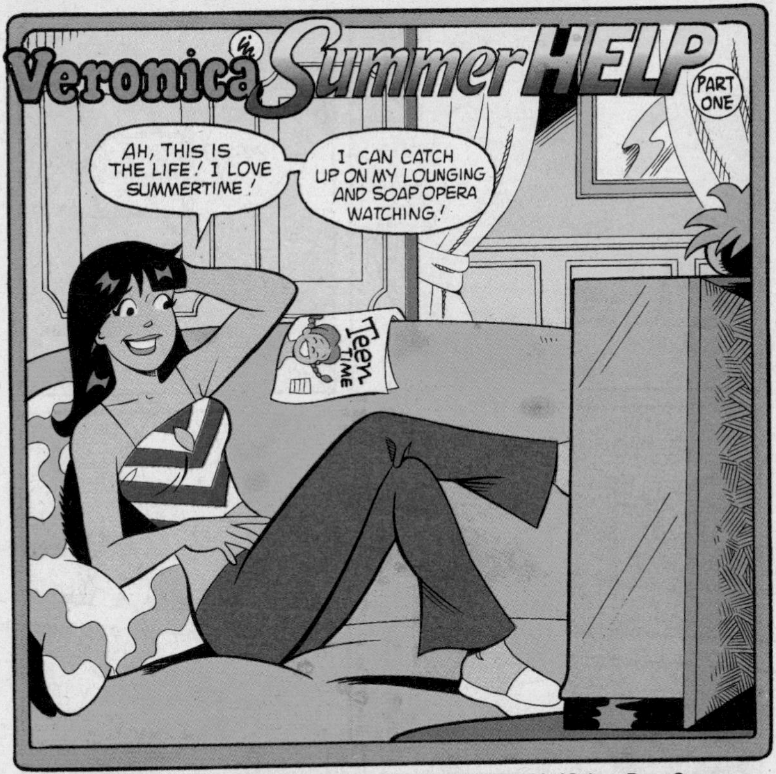
Veronica in Summer HELP
PART ONE
AH, THIS IS THE LIFE! I LOVE SUMMERTIME!
I CAN CATCH UP ON MY LOUNGING AND SOAP OPERA WATCHING!
Teen TIME

Script & Pencils: Dan Parent / Inks: Jim Amash / Letters: Bill Yoshida / Colors: Barry Grossman

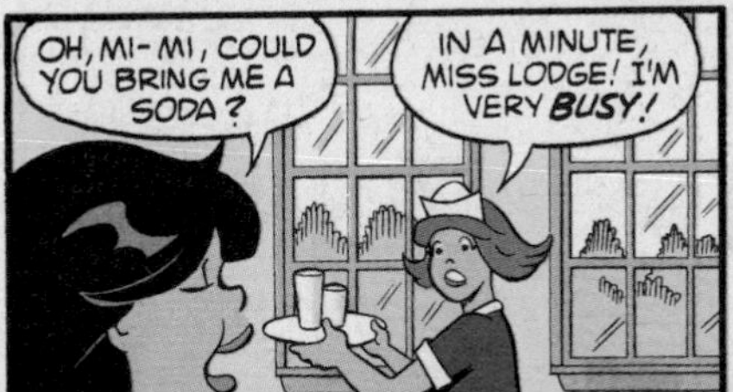
OH, MI-MI, COULD YOU BRING ME A SODA?
IN A MINUTE, MISS LODGE! I'M VERY **BUSY**!

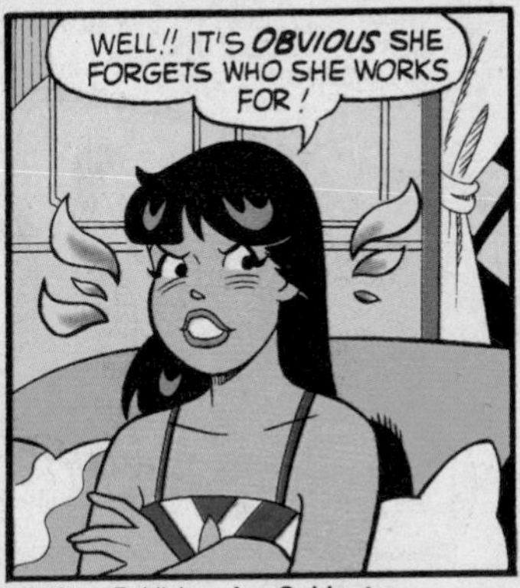
WELL!! IT'S ***OBVIOUS*** SHE FORGETS WHO SHE WORKS FOR!

Editor-In-Chief: **Victor Gorelick** President: **Mike Pellerito** Publisher: **Jon Goldwater**

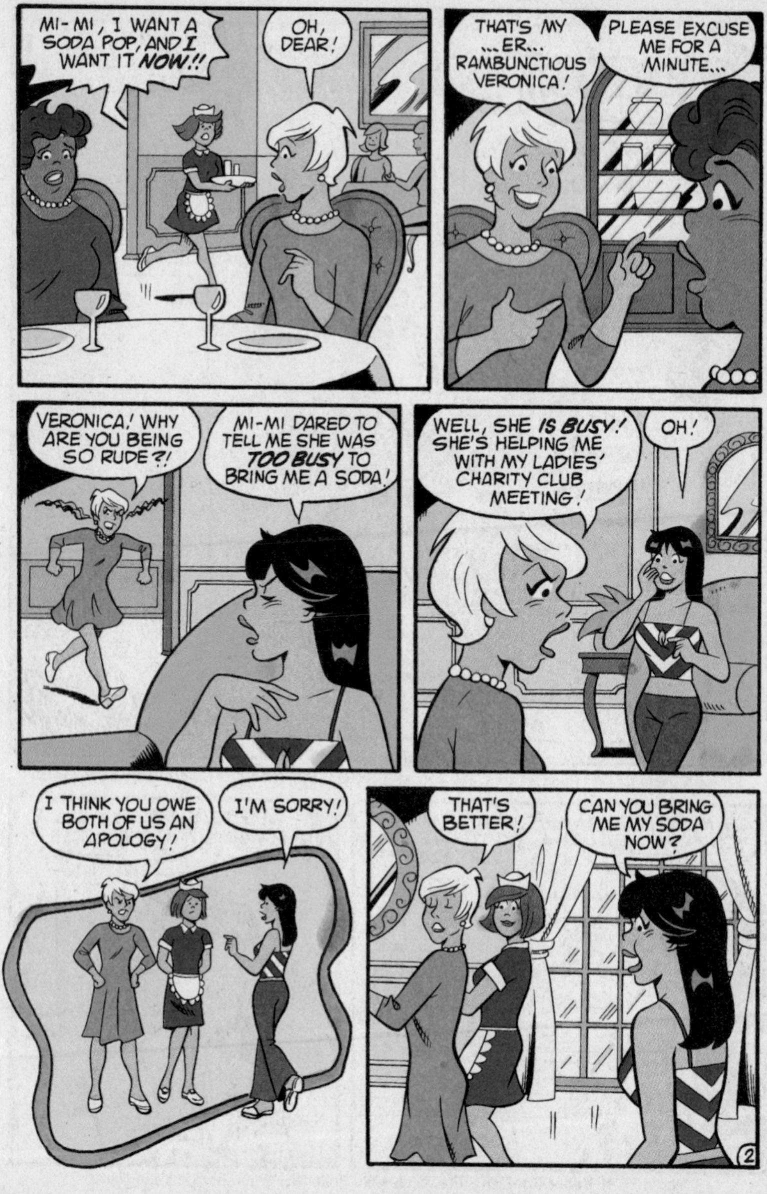
MI-MI, I WANT A SODA POP, AND I WANT IT NOW!!
OH, DEAR!
THAT'S MY ...ER... RAMBUNCTIOUS VERONICA!
PLEASE EXCUSE ME FOR A MINUTE...
VERONICA! WHY ARE YOU BEING SO RUDE?!
MI-MI DARED TO TELL ME SHE WAS TOO BUSY TO BRING ME A SODA!
WELL, SHE IS BUSY! SHE'S HELPING ME WITH MY LADIES' CHARITY CLUB MEETING!
OH!
I THINK YOU OWE BOTH OF US AN APOLOGY!
I'M SORRY!
THAT'S BETTER!
CAN YOU BRING ME MY SODA NOW?
2

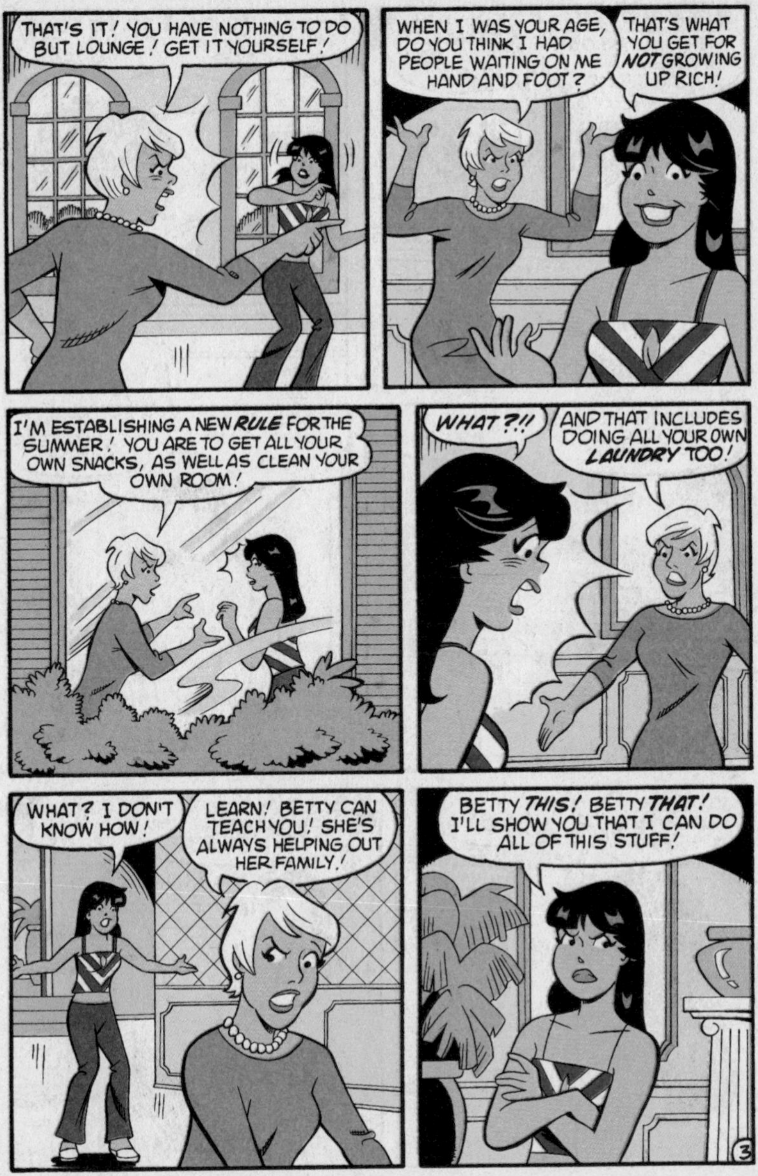
THAT'S IT! YOU HAVE NOTHING TO DO BUT LOUNGE! GET IT YOURSELF!
WHEN I WAS YOUR AGE, DO YOU THINK I HAD PEOPLE WAITING ON ME HAND AND FOOT?
THAT'S WHAT YOU GET FOR NOT GROWING UP RICH!
I'M ESTABLISHING A NEW RULE FOR THE SUMMER! YOU ARE TO GET ALL YOUR OWN SNACKS, AS WELL AS CLEAN YOUR OWN ROOM!
WHAT?!!
AND THAT INCLUDES DOING ALL YOUR OWN LAUNDRY TOO!
WHAT? I DON'T KNOW HOW!
LEARN! BETTY CAN TEACH YOU! SHE'S ALWAYS HELPING OUT HER FAMILY!
BETTY THIS! BETTY THAT! I'LL SHOW YOU THAT I CAN DO ALL OF THIS STUFF!
3

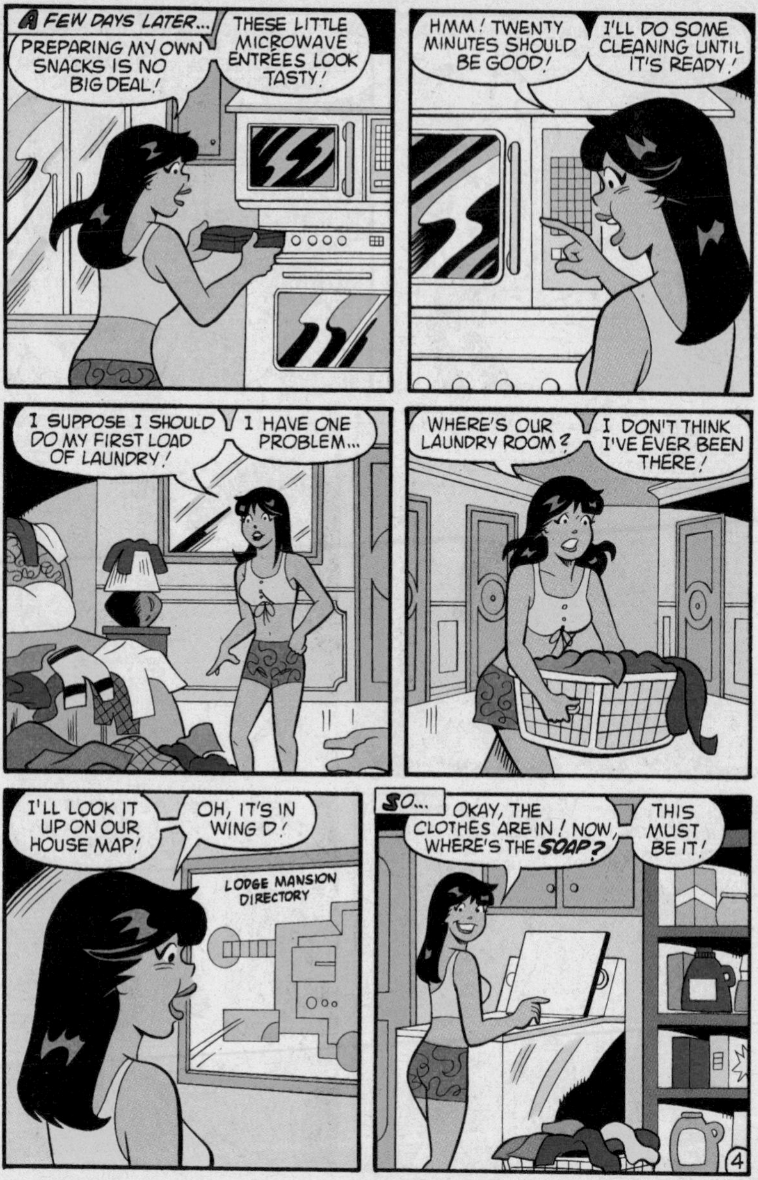

A FEW DAYS LATER...
PREPARING MY OWN SNACKS IS NO BIG DEAL!
THESE LITTLE MICROWAVE ENTRÉES LOOK TASTY!
HMM! TWENTY MINUTES SHOULD BE GOOD!
I'LL DO SOME CLEANING UNTIL IT'S READY!
I SUPPOSE I SHOULD DO MY FIRST LOAD OF LAUNDRY!
I HAVE ONE PROBLEM...
WHERE'S OUR LAUNDRY ROOM?
I DON'T THINK I'VE EVER BEEN THERE!
I'LL LOOK IT UP ON OUR HOUSE MAP!
OH, IT'S IN WING D!
LODGE MANSION DIRECTORY
SO...
OKAY, THE CLOTHES ARE IN! NOW, WHERE'S THE SOAP?
THIS MUST BE IT!
4

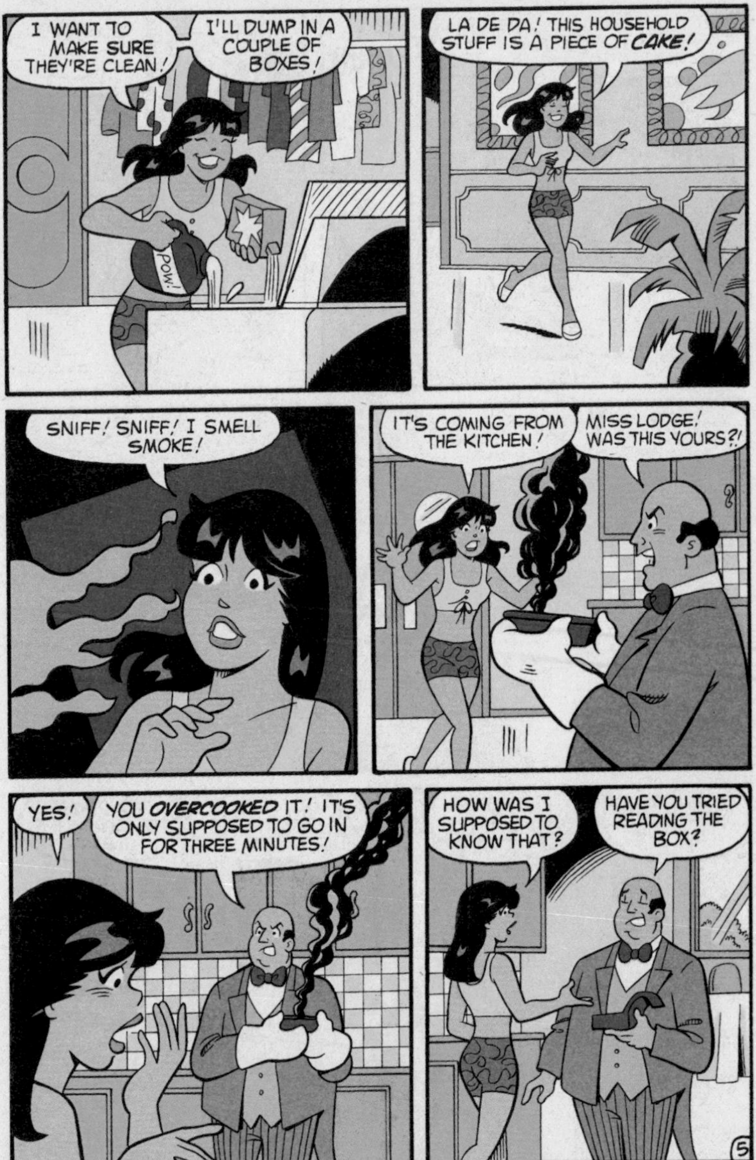
I WANT TO MAKE SURE THEY'RE CLEAN!
I'LL DUMP IN A COUPLE OF BOXES!
POW!
LA DE DA! THIS HOUSEHOLD STUFF IS A PIECE OF CAKE!
SNIFF! SNIFF! I SMELL SMOKE!
IT'S COMING FROM THE KITCHEN!
MISS LODGE! WAS THIS YOURS?!
YES!
YOU OVERCOOKED IT! IT'S ONLY SUPPOSED TO GO IN FOR THREE MINUTES!
HOW WAS I SUPPOSED TO KNOW THAT?
HAVE YOU TRIED READING THE BOX?
5

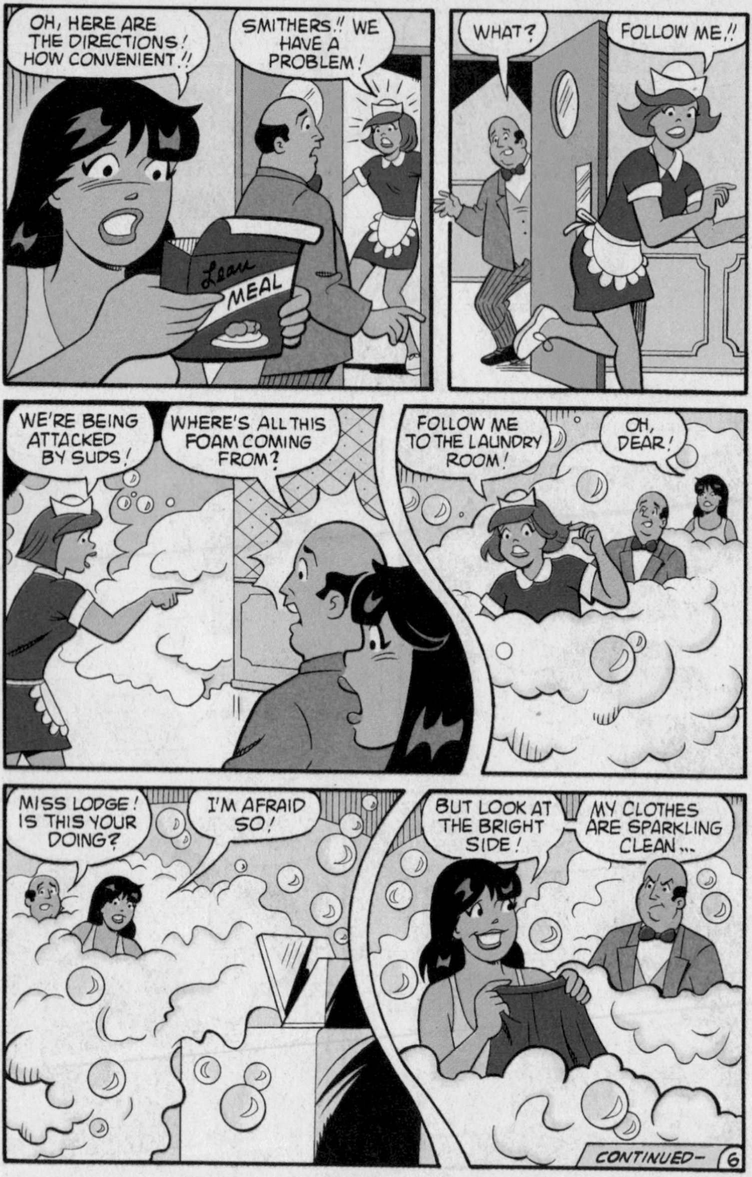

OH, HERE ARE THE DIRECTIONS! HOW CONVENIENT!!
SMITHERS!! WE HAVE A PROBLEM!
MEAL
WHAT?
FOLLOW ME!!
WE'RE BEING ATTACKED BY SUDS!
WHERE'S ALL THIS FOAM COMING FROM?
FOLLOW ME TO THE LAUNDRY ROOM!
OH, DEAR!
MISS LODGE! IS THIS YOUR DOING?
I'M AFRAID SO!
BUT LOOK AT THE BRIGHT SIDE!
MY CLOTHES ARE SPARKLING CLEAN...
CONTINUED–

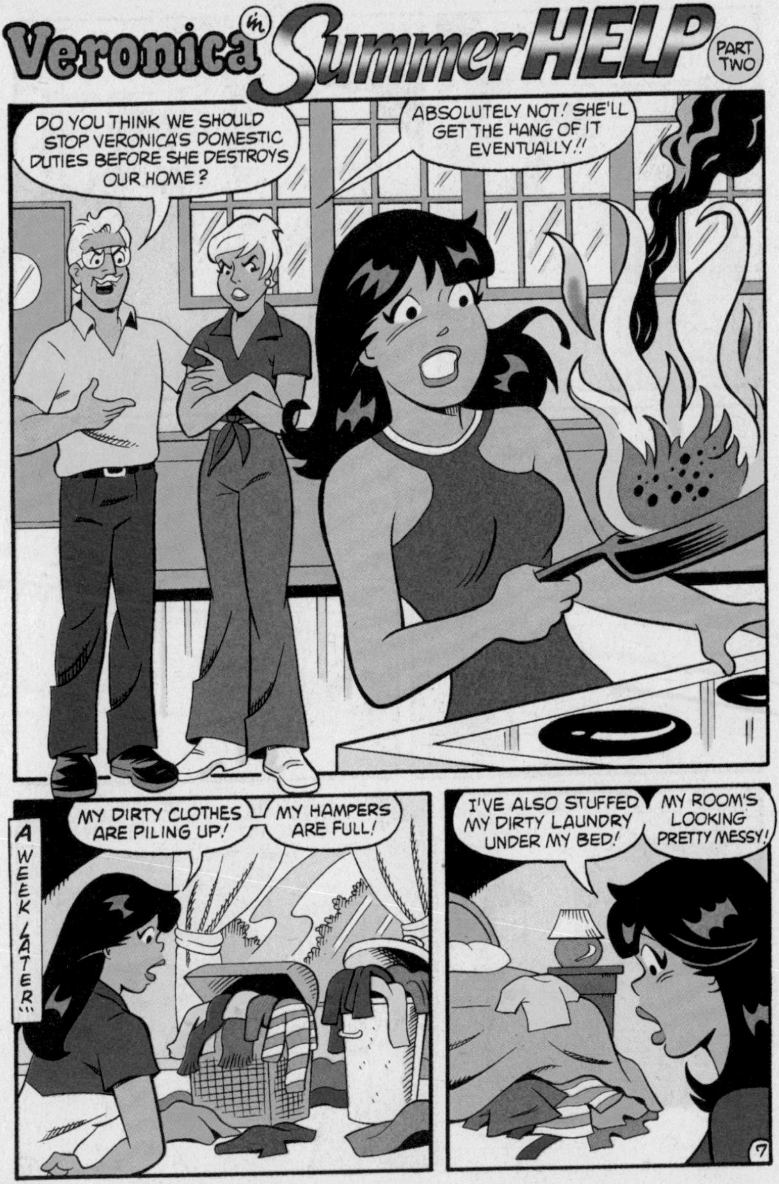

Veronica in Summer HELP
PART TWO
DO YOU THINK WE SHOULD STOP VERONICA'S DOMESTIC DUTIES BEFORE SHE DESTROYS OUR HOME?
ABSOLUTELY NOT! SHE'LL GET THE HANG OF IT EVENTUALLY!!
A WEEK LATER...
MY DIRTY CLOTHES ARE PILING UP!
MY HAMPERS ARE FULL!
I'VE ALSO STUFFED MY DIRTY LAUNDRY UNDER MY BED!
MY ROOM'S LOOKING PRETTY MESSY!
7

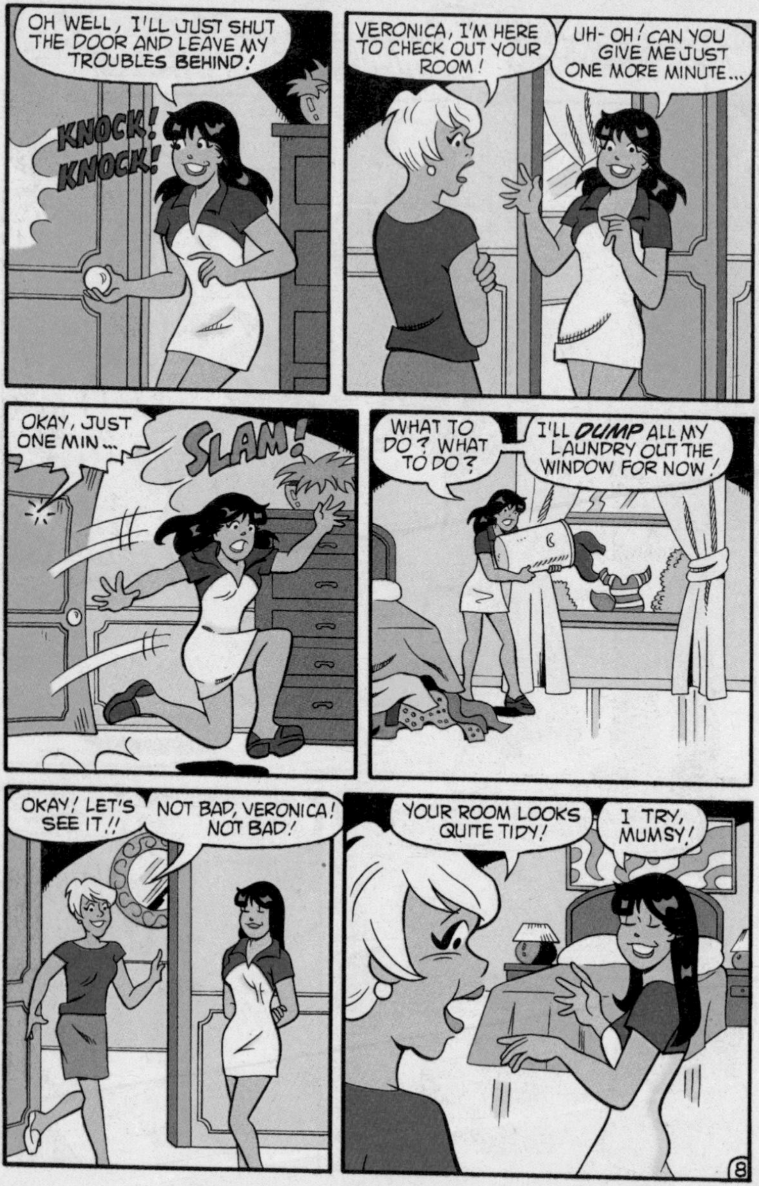
OH WELL, I'LL JUST SHUT THE DOOR AND LEAVE MY TROUBLES BEHIND!
KNOCK! KNOCK!
VERONICA, I'M HERE TO CHECK OUT YOUR ROOM!
UH- OH! CAN YOU GIVE ME JUST ONE MORE MINUTE...
OKAY, JUST ONE MIN...
SLAM!
WHAT TO DO? WHAT TO DO?
I'LL DUMP ALL MY LAUNDRY OUT THE WINDOW FOR NOW!
OKAY! LET'S SEE IT!!
NOT BAD, VERONICA! NOT BAD!
YOUR ROOM LOOKS QUITE TIDY!
I TRY, MUMSY!
8

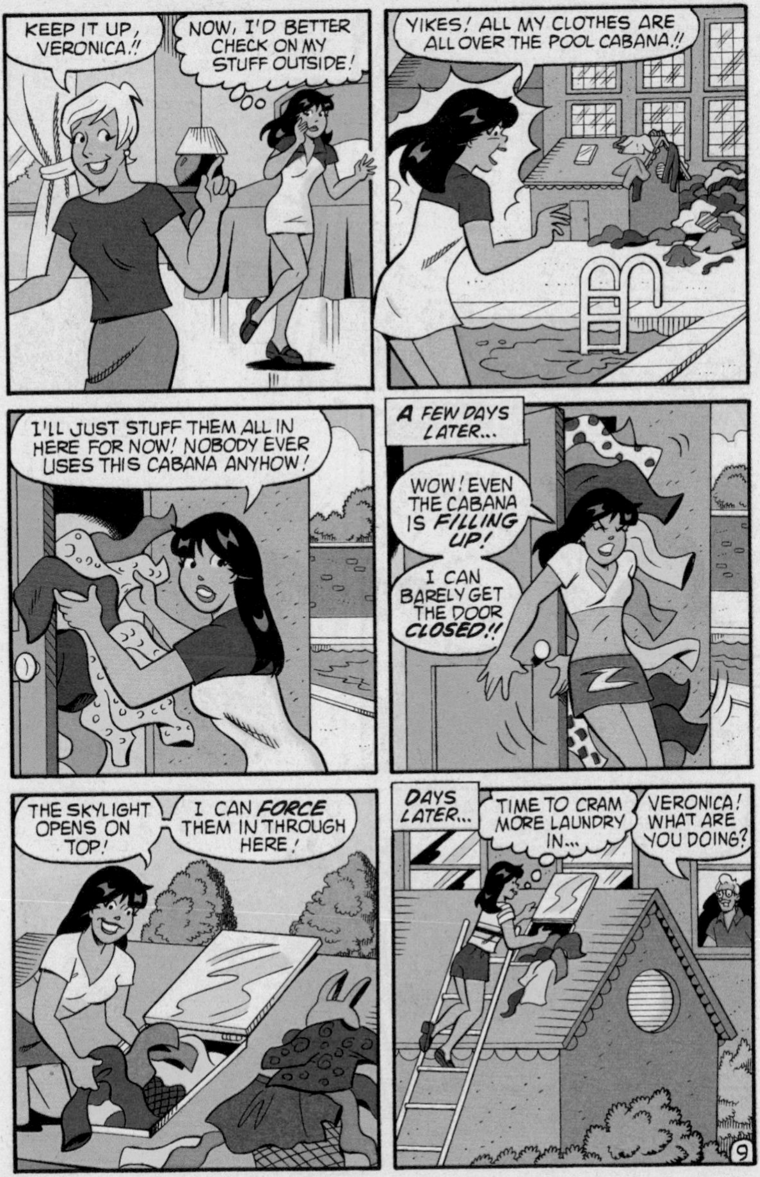
KEEP IT UP, VERONICA.!!
NOW, I'D BETTER CHECK ON MY STUFF OUTSIDE!
YIKES! ALL MY CLOTHES ARE ALL OVER THE POOL CABANA.!!
I'LL JUST STUFF THEM ALL IN HERE FOR NOW! NOBODY EVER USES THIS CABANA ANYHOW!
A FEW DAYS LATER...
WOW! EVEN THE CABANA IS FILLING UP!
I CAN BARELY GET THE DOOR CLOSED!!
THE SKYLIGHT OPENS ON TOP!
I CAN FORCE THEM IN THROUGH HERE!
DAYS LATER...
TIME TO CRAM MORE LAUNDRY IN...
VERONICA! WHAT ARE YOU DOING?
9

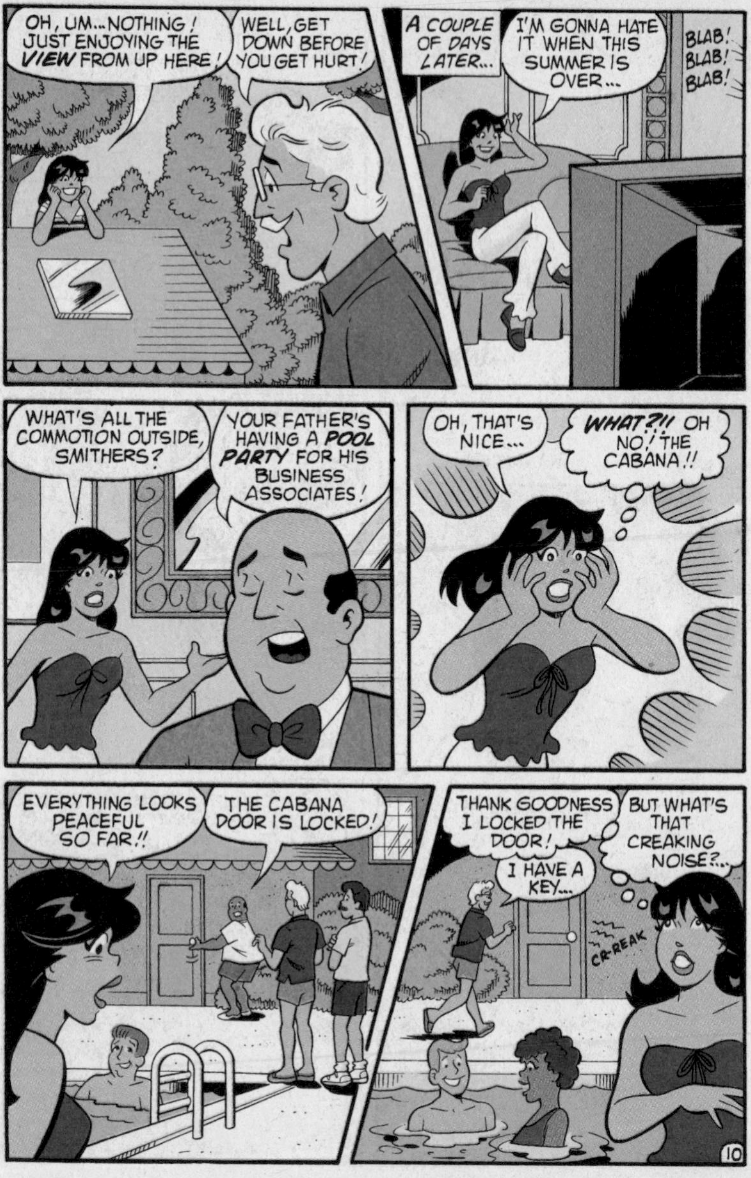

OH, UM...NOTHING! JUST ENJOYING THE VIEW FROM UP HERE!
WELL, GET DOWN BEFORE YOU GET HURT!
A COUPLE OF DAYS LATER...
I'M GONNA HATE IT WHEN THIS SUMMER IS OVER...
BLAB! BLAB! BLAB!
WHAT'S ALL THE COMMOTION OUTSIDE, SMITHERS?
YOUR FATHER'S HAVING A POOL PARTY FOR HIS BUSINESS ASSOCIATES!
OH, THAT'S NICE...
WHAT?!! OH NO! THE CABANA!!
EVERYTHING LOOKS PEACEFUL SO FAR!!
THE CABANA DOOR IS LOCKED!
THANK GOODNESS I LOCKED THE DOOR!
BUT WHAT'S THAT CREAKING NOISE?...
I HAVE A KEY...
CR-REAK
10

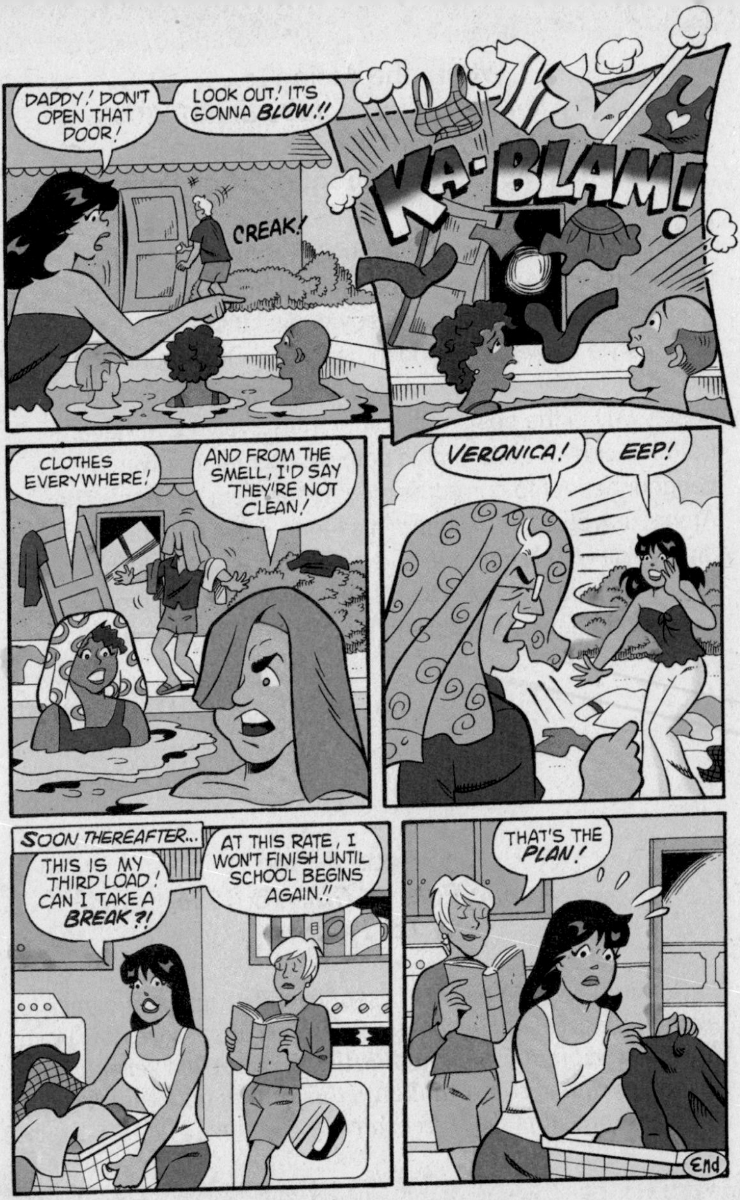
DADDY! DON'T OPEN THAT DOOR!
LOOK OUT! IT'S GONNA BLOW!!
CREAK!
KA-BLAM!
CLOTHES EVERYWHERE!
AND FROM THE SMELL, I'D SAY THEY'RE NOT CLEAN!
VERONICA!
EEP!
SOON THEREAFTER...
THIS IS MY THIRD LOAD! CAN I TAKE A BREAK?!
AT THIS RATE, I WON'T FINISH UNTIL SCHOOL BEGINS AGAIN!!
THAT'S THE PLAN!
End

Where the Action Is...
Betty & Veronica Spectacular #87, 2008
by Dan Parent, Rich Koslowski,
Jack Morelli and Rosario "Tito" Peña

We all love spy-style action movies, another genre ripe for the picking when it comes to Betty and Veronica. Plus the girls look so cool in their slick spy outfits! It's always fun to do action-style stories, bringing in new characters... and some old. In this story we are revisited from a character from the past... way in the past: none other than Evelyn Evernever from the classic Little Archie comics. She returns with a vengeance, out to correct some wrongs from her past. The Archie universe is so big that it's fun to delve into the past and revisit old characters, and give them a new twist here and there! This was one of a few B&V spy girl-themed stories, and I'm already getting the feeling that we need to do more.

Dan Parent
Writer and Artist,
Archie Comics

The Rose Achoo
Archie Pals 'n' Gals #5, 1956
by Tom Moore

Betty and Veronica are the best of friends... unless it comes to Archie! Showcasing gorgeous art from Tom Moore, this yarn finds the original frenemies battling it out. After Veronica causes Archie to stand-up Betty, the usually good-natured blonde soon sniffs the sweet smell of revenge.

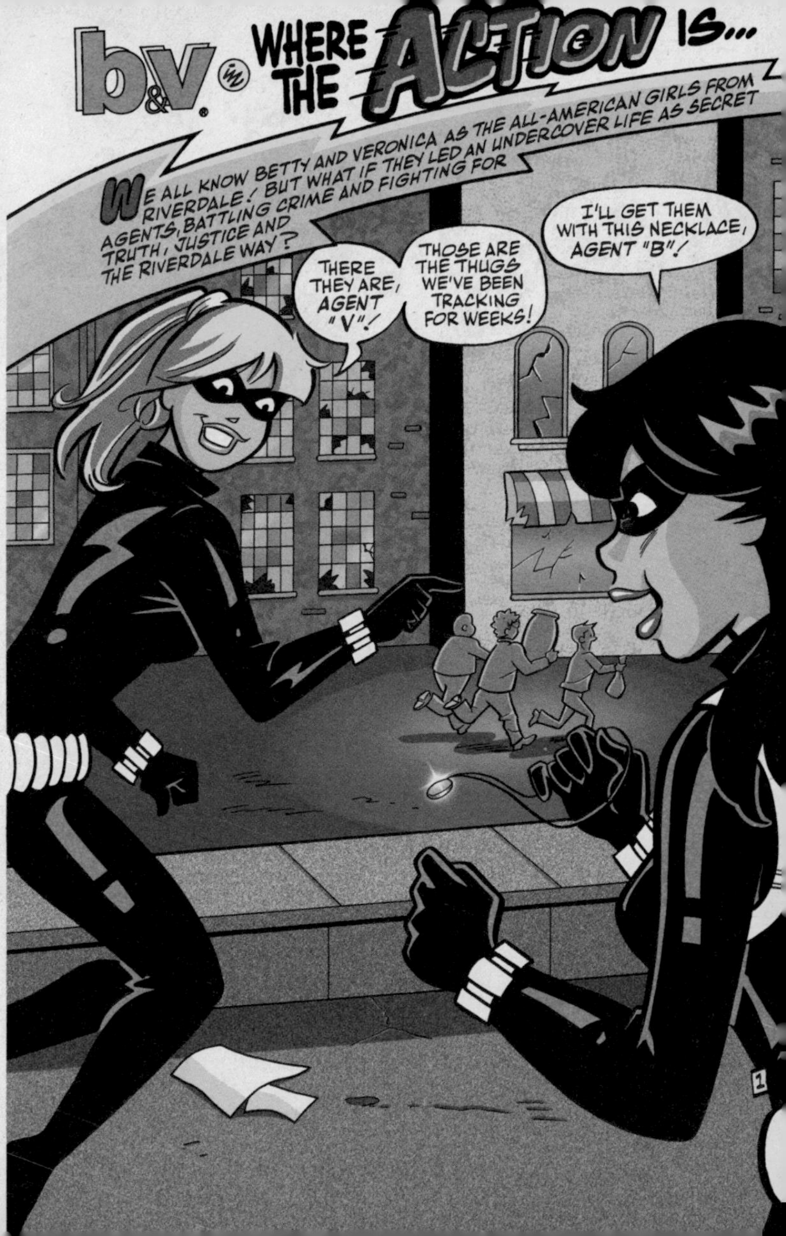
b&V in WHERE THE ACTION IS...
WE ALL KNOW BETTY AND VERONICA AS THE ALL-AMERICAN GIRLS FROM RIVERDALE! BUT WHAT IF THEY LED AN UNDERCOVER LIFE AS SECRET AGENTS, BATTLING CRIME AND FIGHTING FOR TRUTH, JUSTICE AND THE RIVERDALE WAY?
THERE THEY ARE, AGENT "V"!
THOSE ARE THE THUGS WE'VE BEEN TRACKING FOR WEEKS!
I'LL GET THEM WITH THIS NECKLACE, AGENT "B"!
1

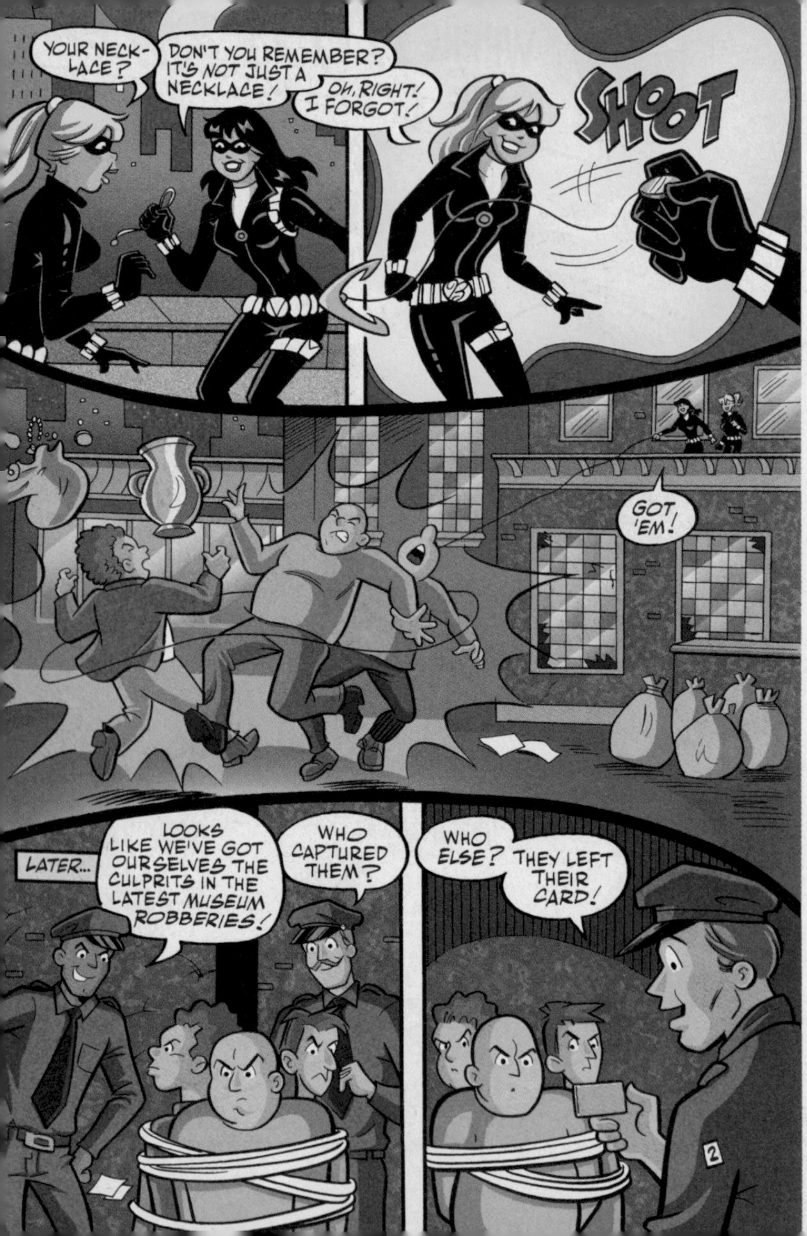
YOUR NECK-LACE?
DON'T YOU REMEMBER? IT'S NOT JUST A NECKLACE!
OH, RIGHT! I FORGOT!
SHOOT
GOT 'EM!
LATER...
LOOKS LIKE WE'VE GOT OURSELVES THE CULPRITS IN THE LATEST MUSEUM ROBBERIES!
WHO CAPTURED THEM?
WHO ELSE?
THEY LEFT THEIR CARD!
2

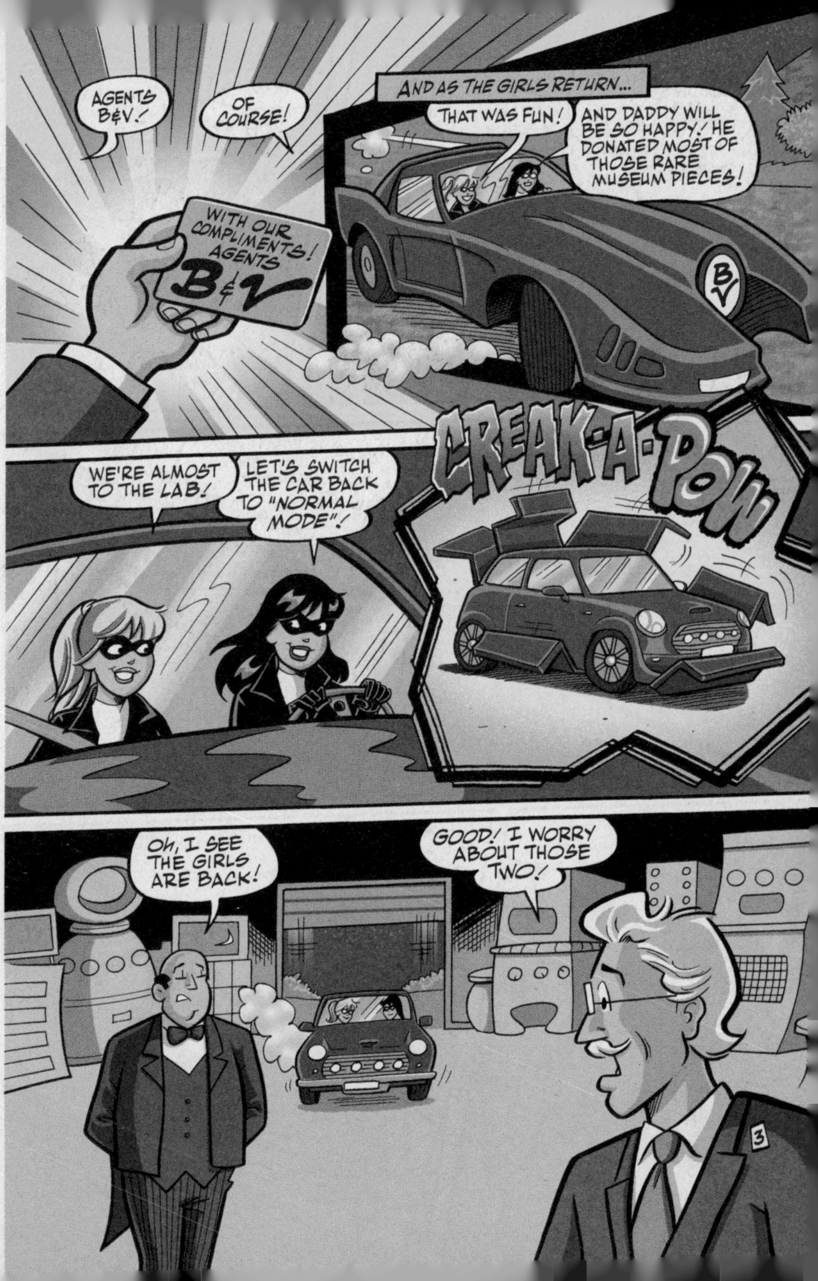
AGENTS B&V!
OF COURSE!
WITH OUR COMPLIMENTS! AGENTS B&V
AND AS THE GIRLS RETURN...
THAT WAS FUN!
AND DADDY WILL BE SO HAPPY! HE DONATED MOST OF THOSE RARE MUSEUM PIECES!
BV
WE'RE ALMOST TO THE LAB!
LET'S SWITCH THE CAR BACK TO "NORMAL MODE"!
CREAK-A-POW
OH, I SEE THE GIRLS ARE BACK!
GOOD! I WORRY ABOUT THOSE TWO!
3

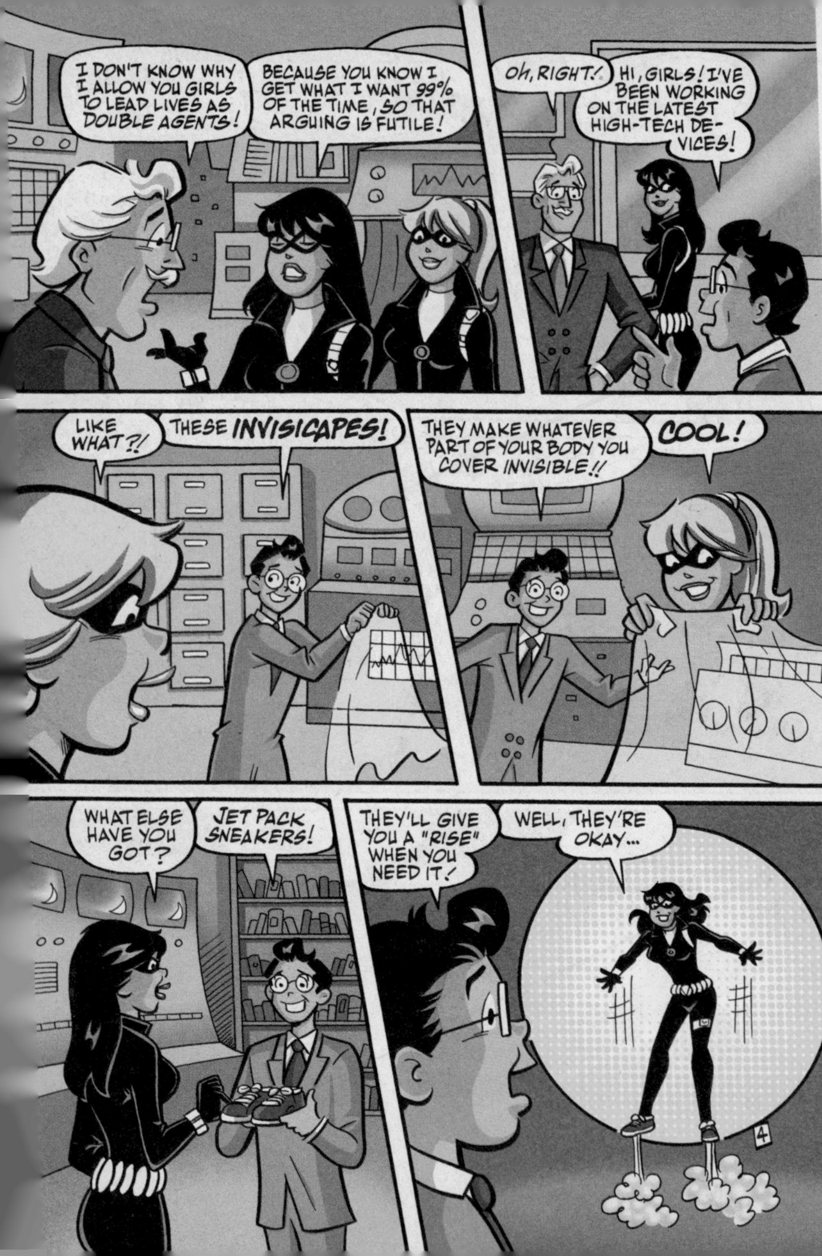
I DON'T KNOW WHY I ALLOW YOU GIRLS TO LEAD LIVES AS DOUBLE AGENTS!
BECAUSE YOU KNOW I GET WHAT I WANT 99% OF THE TIME, SO THAT ARGUING IS FUTILE!
Oh, RIGHT!
HI, GIRLS! I'VE BEEN WORKING ON THE LATEST HIGH-TECH DE-VICES!
LIKE WHAT?!
THESE INVISICAPES!
THEY MAKE WHATEVER PART OF YOUR BODY YOU COVER INVISIBLE!!
COOL!
WHAT ELSE HAVE YOU GOT?
JET PACK SNEAKERS!
THEY'LL GIVE YOU A "RISE" WHEN YOU NEED IT!
WELL, THEY'RE OKAY...
4

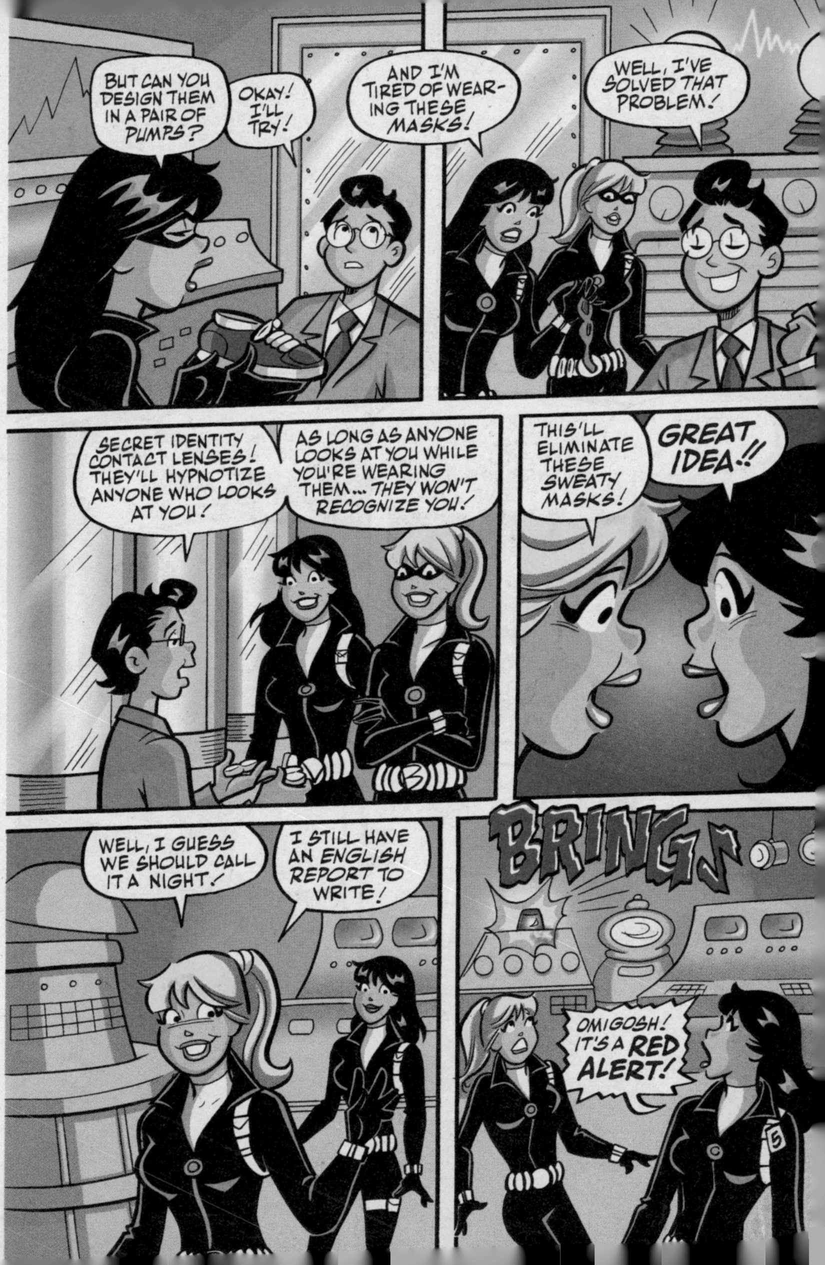

BUT CAN YOU DESIGN THEM IN A PAIR OF PUMPS?
OKAY! I'LL TRY!
AND I'M TIRED OF WEARING THESE MASKS!
WELL, I'VE SOLVED THAT PROBLEM!
SECRET IDENTITY CONTACT LENSES! THEY'LL HYPNOTIZE ANYONE WHO LOOKS AT YOU!
AS LONG AS ANYONE LOOKS AT YOU WHILE YOU'RE WEARING THEM... THEY WON'T RECOGNIZE YOU!
THIS'LL ELIMINATE THESE SWEATY MASKS!
GREAT IDEA!!
WELL, I GUESS WE SHOULD CALL IT A NIGHT!
I STILL HAVE AN ENGLISH REPORT TO WRITE!
BRINGG
OMIGOSH! IT'S A RED ALERT!

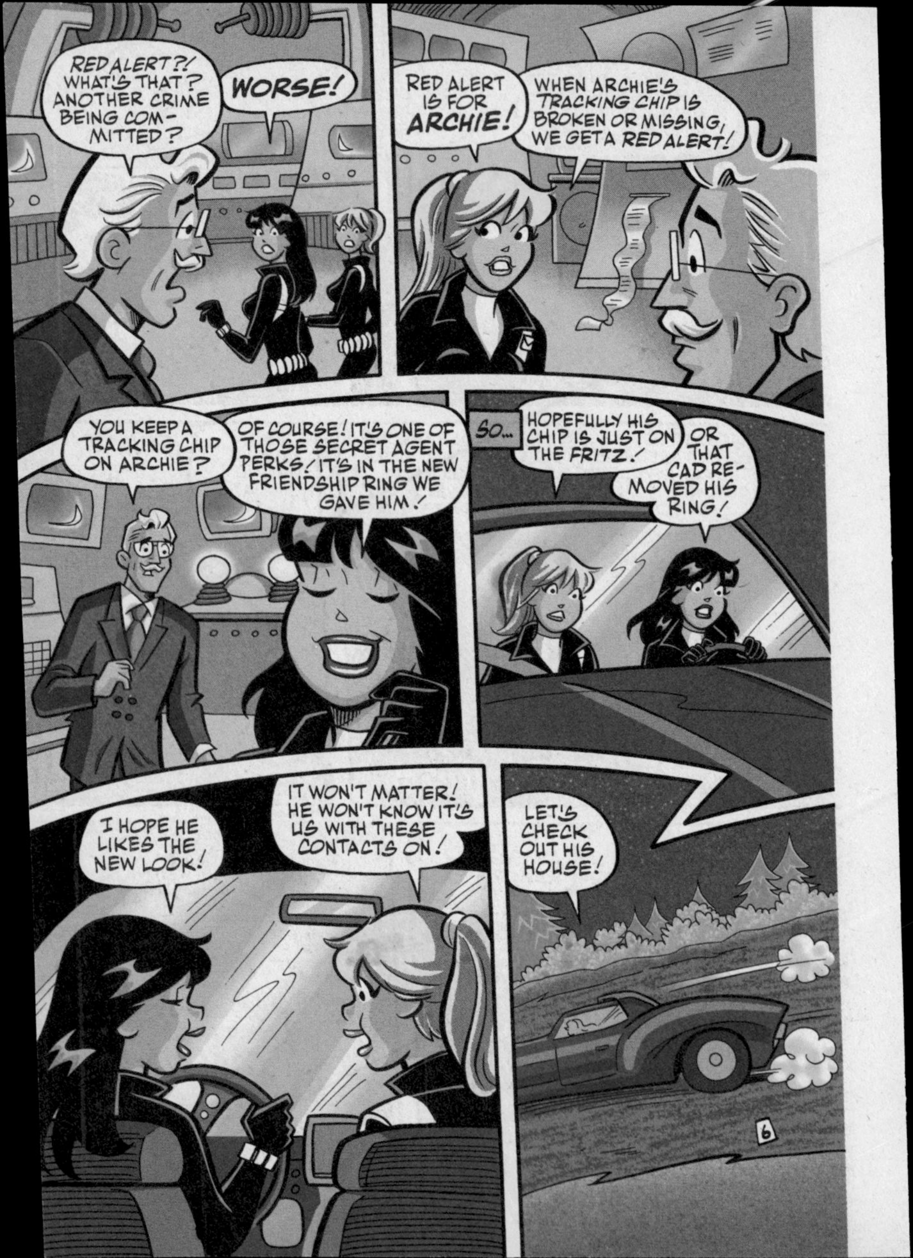

RED ALERT?! WHAT'S THAT? ANOTHER CRIME BEING COM-MITTED?
WORSE!
RED ALERT IS FOR ARCHIE!
WHEN ARCHIE'S TRACKING CHIP IS BROKEN OR MISSING, WE GET A RED ALERT!
YOU KEEP A TRACKING CHIP ON ARCHIE?
OF COURSE! IT'S ONE OF THOSE SECRET AGENT PERKS! IT'S IN THE NEW FRIENDSHIP RING WE GAVE HIM!
SO...
HOPEFULLY HIS CHIP IS JUST ON THE FRITZ!
OR THAT CAD RE-MOVED HIS RING!
I HOPE HE LIKES THE NEW LOOK!
IT WON'T MATTER! HE WON'T KNOW IT'S US WITH THESE CONTACTS ON!
LET'S CHECK OUT HIS HOUSE!
6

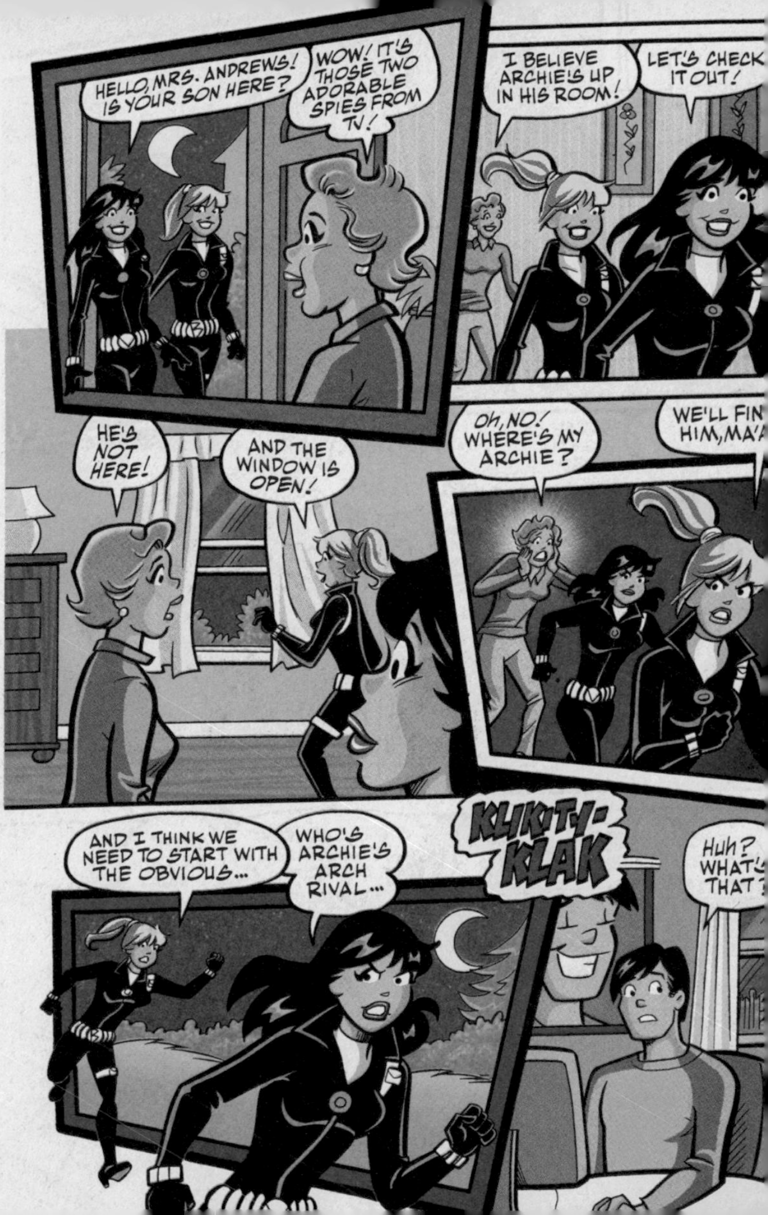
HELLO, MRS. ANDREWS! IS YOUR SON HERE?
WOW! IT'S THOSE TWO ADORABLE SPIES FROM TV!
I BELIEVE ARCHIE'S UP IN HIS ROOM!
LET'S CHECK IT OUT!
HE'S NOT HERE!
AND THE WINDOW IS OPEN!
Oh, NO! WHERE'S MY ARCHIE?
WE'LL FIN HIM, MA'
AND I THINK WE NEED TO START WITH THE OBVIOUS...
WHO'S ARCHIE'S ARCH RIVAL...
KLIKITY-KLAK
Huh? WHAT' THAT

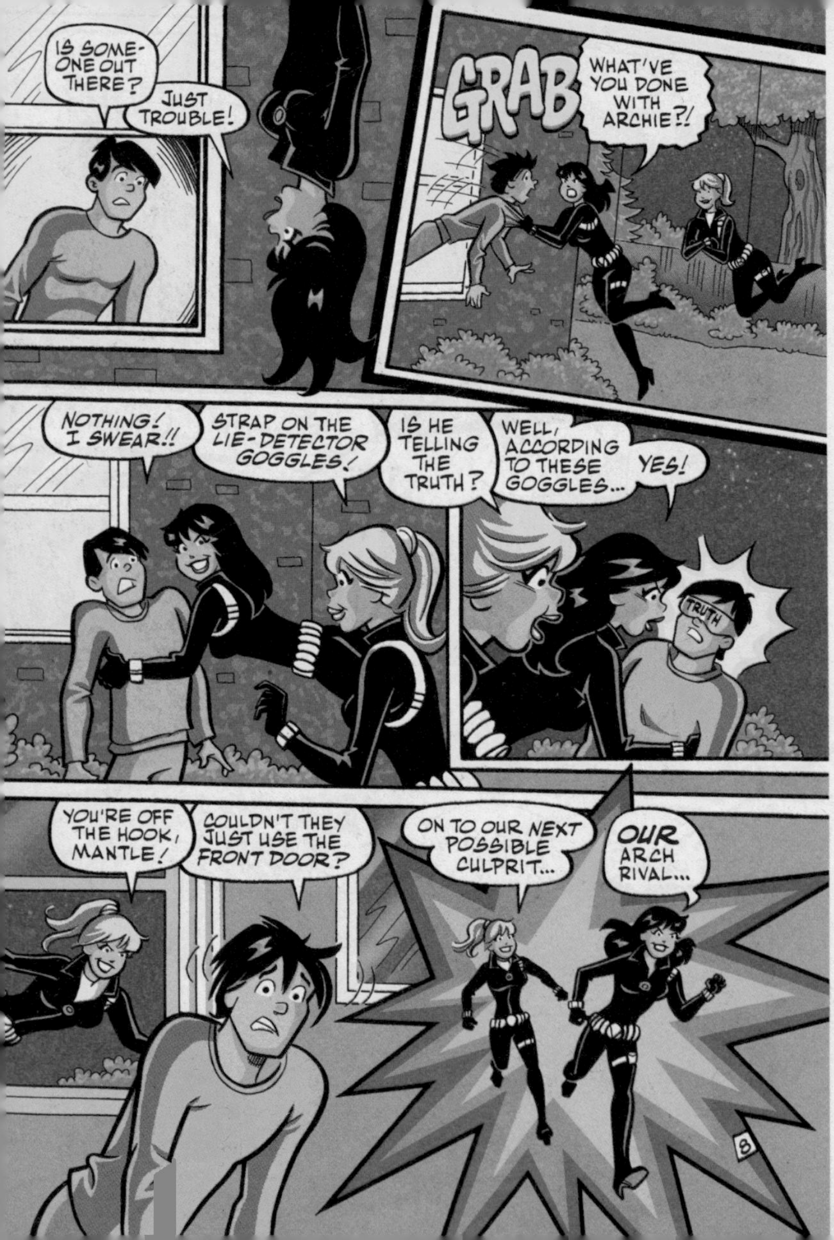
IS SOME-ONE OUT THERE?
JUST TROUBLE!
GRAB
WHAT'VE YOU DONE WITH ARCHIE?!
NOTHING! I SWEAR!!
STRAP ON THE LIE-DETECTOR GOGGLES!
IS HE TELLING THE TRUTH?
WELL, ACCORDING TO THESE GOGGLES...
YES!
TRUTH
YOU'RE OFF THE HOOK, MANTLE!
COULDN'T THEY JUST USE THE FRONT DOOR?
ON TO OUR NEXT POSSIBLE CULPRIT...
OUR ARCH RIVAL...
8

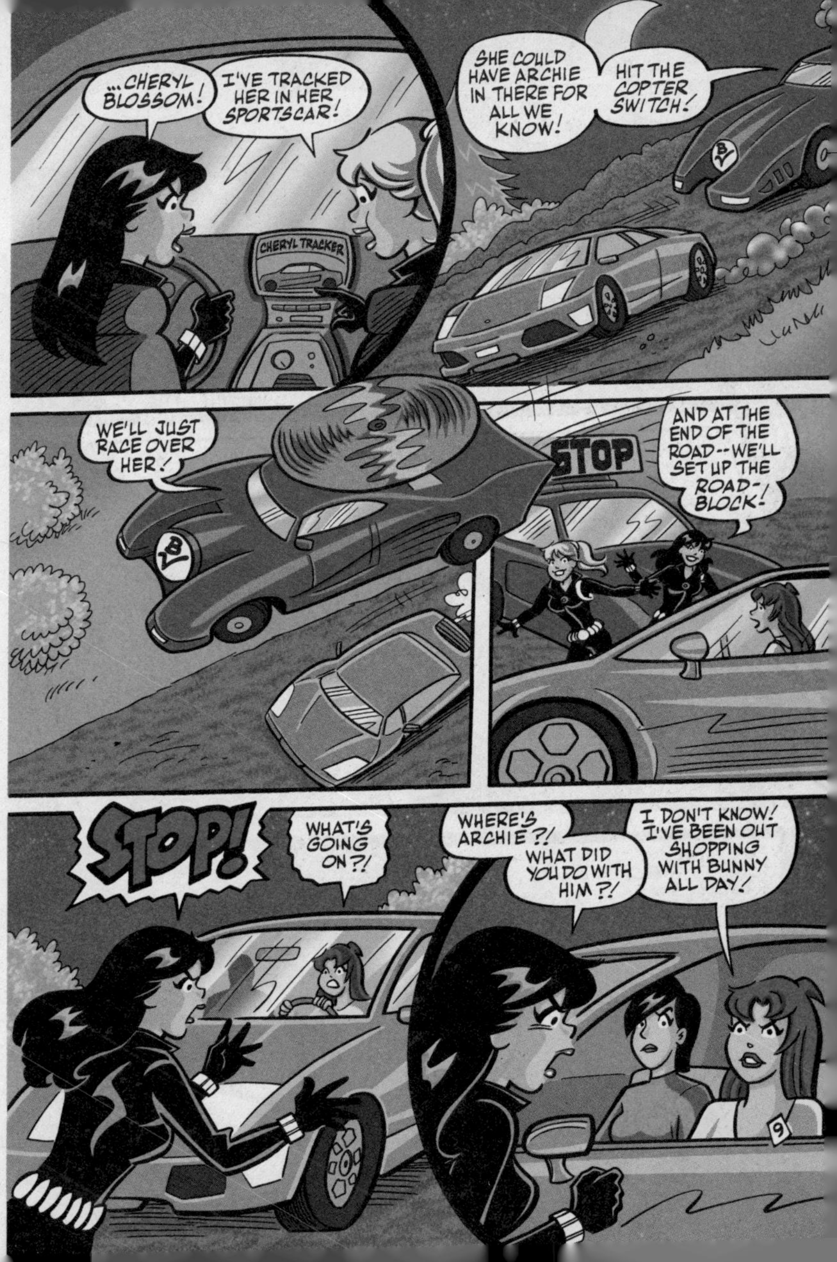
...CHERYL BLOSSOM!
I'VE TRACKED HER IN HER SPORTSCAR!
CHERYL TRACKER
SHE COULD HAVE ARCHIE IN THERE FOR ALL WE KNOW!
HIT THE COPTER SWITCH!
WE'LL JUST RACE OVER HER!
STOP
AND AT THE END OF THE ROAD--WE'LL SET UP THE ROAD-BLOCK!
STOP!
WHAT'S GOING ON?!
WHERE'S ARCHIE?!
WHAT DID YOU DO WITH HIM?!
I DON'T KNOW! I'VE BEEN OUT SHOPPING WITH BUNNY ALL DAY!
9

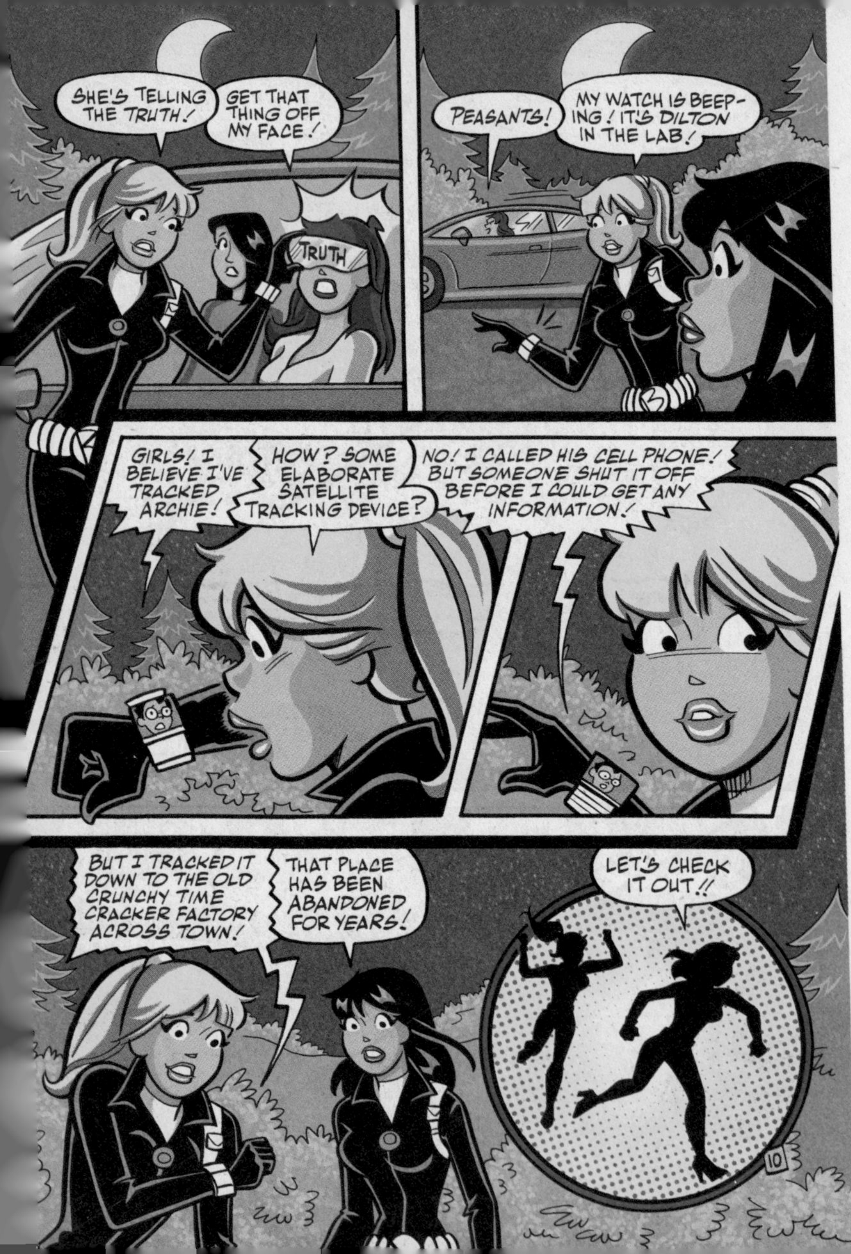
SHE'S TELLING THE TRUTH!
GET THAT THING OFF MY FACE!
TRUTH
PEASANTS!
MY WATCH IS BEEPING! IT'S DILTON IN THE LAB!
GIRLS! I BELIEVE I'VE TRACKED ARCHIE!
HOW? SOME ELABORATE SATELLITE TRACKING DEVICE?
NO! I CALLED HIS CELL PHONE! BUT SOMEONE SHUT IT OFF BEFORE I COULD GET ANY INFORMATION!
BUT I TRACKED IT DOWN TO THE OLD CRUNCHY TIME CRACKER FACTORY ACROSS TOWN!
THAT PLACE HAS BEEN ABANDONED FOR YEARS!
LET'S CHECK IT OUT!!
10

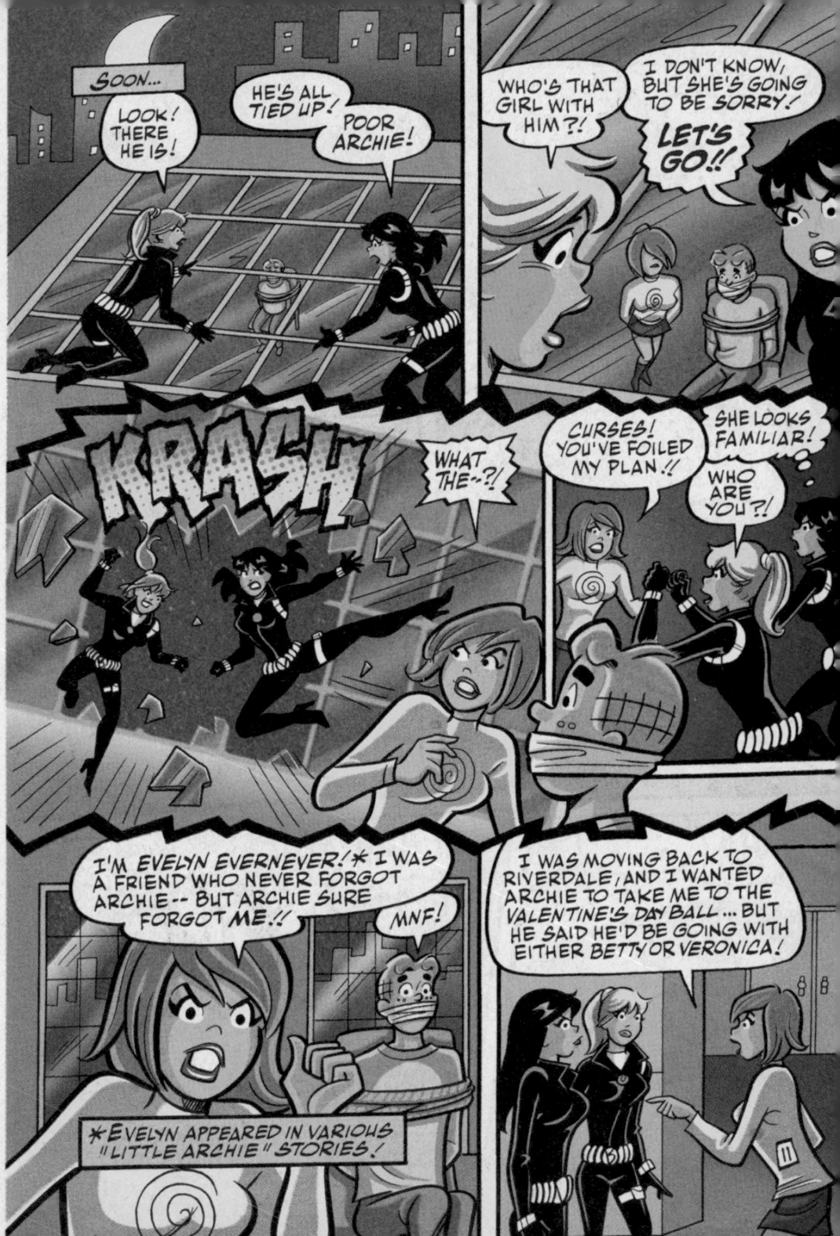
SOON...
LOOK! THERE HE IS!
HE'S ALL TIED UP!
POOR ARCHIE!
WHO'S THAT GIRL WITH HIM?!
I DON'T KNOW, BUT SHE'S GOING TO BE SORRY!
LET'S GO!!
KRASH
WHAT THE--?!
CURSES! YOU'VE FOILED MY PLAN!!
SHE LOOKS FAMILIAR!
WHO ARE YOU?!
I'M EVELYN EVERNEVER!* I WAS A FRIEND WHO NEVER FORGOT ARCHIE-- BUT ARCHIE SURE FORGOT ME!!
MNF!
*EVELYN APPEARED IN VARIOUS "LITTLE ARCHIE" STORIES!
I WAS MOVING BACK TO RIVERDALE, AND I WANTED ARCHIE TO TAKE ME TO THE VALENTINE'S DAY BALL ... BUT HE SAID HE'D BE GOING WITH EITHER BETTY OR VERONICA!

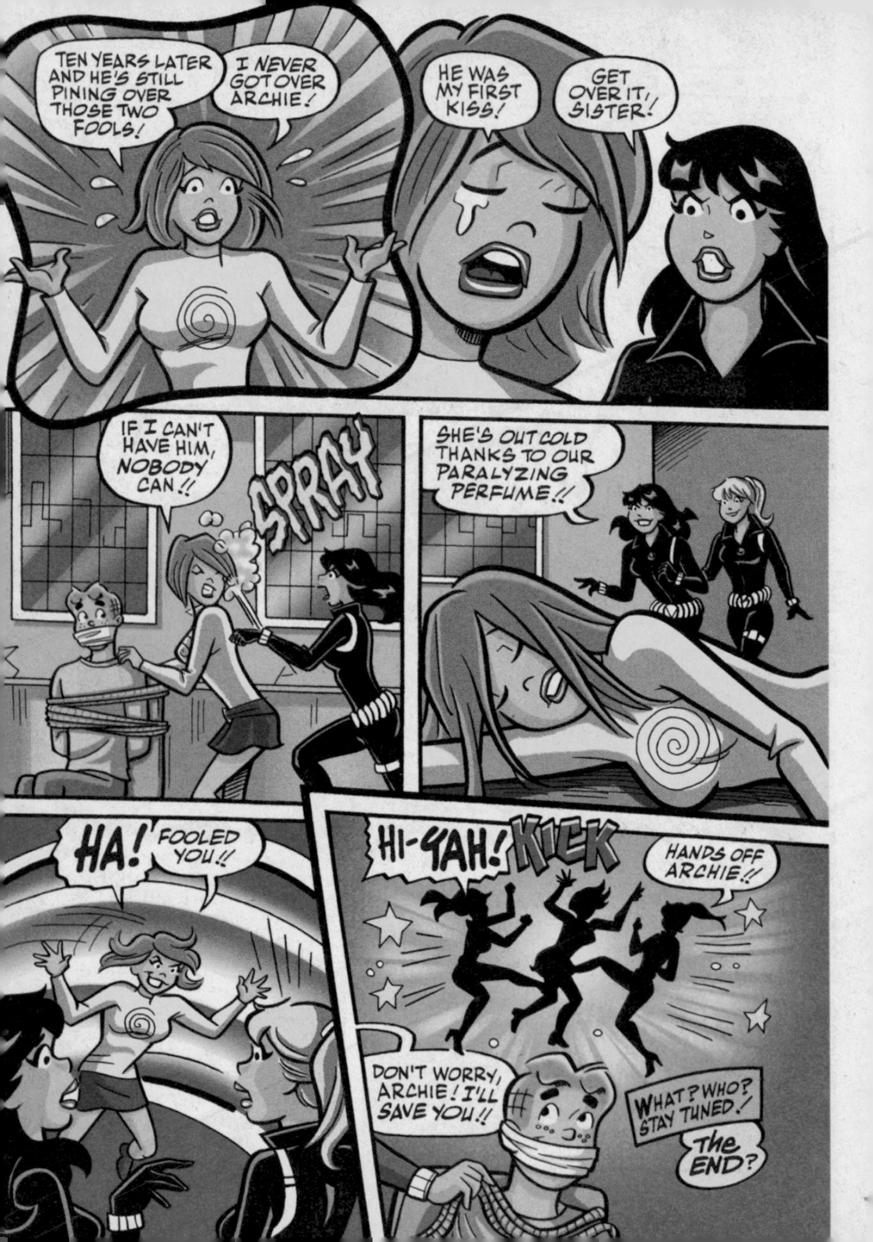
TEN YEARS LATER AND HE'S STILL PINING OVER THOSE TWO FOOLS!
I NEVER GOT OVER ARCHIE!
HE WAS MY FIRST KISS!
GET OVER IT, SISTER!
IF I CAN'T HAVE HIM, NOBODY CAN!!
SPRAY
SHE'S OUT COLD THANKS TO OUR PARALYZING PERFUME!!
HA!
FOOLED YOU!!
HI-YAH!
KICK
HANDS OFF ARCHIE!!
DON'T WORRY, ARCHIE! I'LL SAVE YOU!!
WHAT? WHO? STAY TUNED!
The END?

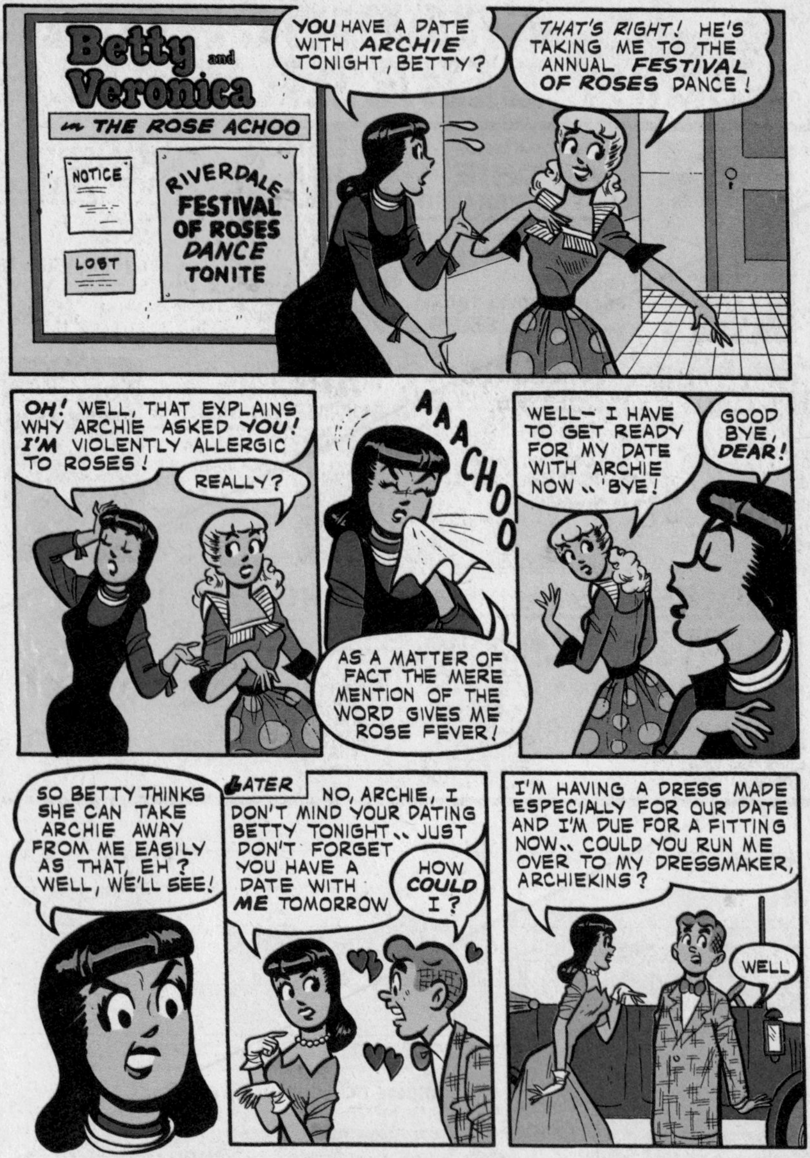

Betty and Veronica
in THE ROSE ACHOO
NOTICE
LOST
RIVERDALE FESTIVAL OF ROSES DANCE TONITE
YOU HAVE A DATE WITH ARCHIE TONIGHT, BETTY?
THAT'S RIGHT! HE'S TAKING ME TO THE ANNUAL FESTIVAL OF ROSES DANCE!
OH! WELL, THAT EXPLAINS WHY ARCHIE ASKED YOU! I'M VIOLENTLY ALLERGIC TO ROSES!
REALLY?
AAAACHOOO
AS A MATTER OF FACT THE MERE MENTION OF THE WORD GIVES ME ROSE FEVER!
WELL– I HAVE TO GET READY FOR MY DATE WITH ARCHIE NOW .. 'BYE!
GOOD BYE, DEAR!
SO BETTY THINKS SHE CAN TAKE ARCHIE AWAY FROM ME EASILY AS THAT, EH? WELL, WE'LL SEE!
LATER
NO, ARCHIE, I DON'T MIND YOUR DATING BETTY TONIGHT .. JUST DON'T FORGET YOU HAVE A DATE WITH ME TOMORROW
HOW COULD I?
I'M HAVING A DRESS MADE ESPECIALLY FOR OUR DATE AND I'M DUE FOR A FITTING NOW .. COULD YOU RUN ME OVER TO MY DRESSMAKER, ARCHIEKINS?
WELL

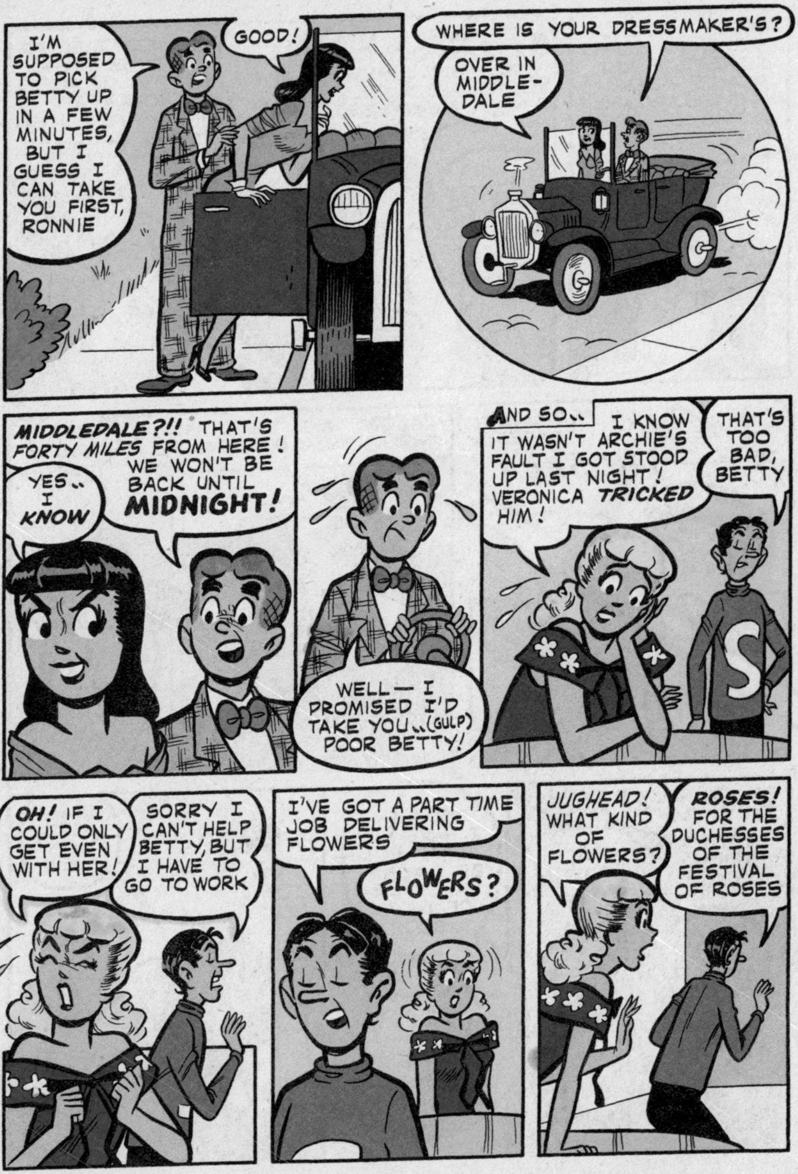
I'M SUPPOSED TO PICK BETTY UP IN A FEW MINUTES, BUT I GUESS I CAN TAKE YOU FIRST, RONNIE
GOOD!
WHERE IS YOUR DRESSMAKER'S?
OVER IN MIDDLE-DALE
MIDDLEDALE?!! THAT'S FORTY MILES FROM HERE! WE WON'T BE BACK UNTIL MIDNIGHT!
YES.. I KNOW
WELL— I PROMISED I'D TAKE YOU..(GULP) POOR BETTY!
AND SO..
I KNOW IT WASN'T ARCHIE'S FAULT I GOT STOOD UP LAST NIGHT! VERONICA TRICKED HIM!
THAT'S TOO BAD, BETTY
OH! IF I COULD ONLY GET EVEN WITH HER!
SORRY I CAN'T HELP BETTY, BUT I HAVE TO GO TO WORK
I'VE GOT A PART TIME JOB DELIVERING FLOWERS
FLOWERS?
JUGHEAD! WHAT KIND OF FLOWERS?
ROSES! FOR THE DUCHESSES OF THE FESTIVAL OF ROSES

Panel 1: THAT'S IT! I'LL BUY A DOZEN ROSES, AND JUGHEAD, IF YOU REALLY MEANT WHAT YOU SAID ABOUT HELPING ME HERE'S WHAT YOU CAN DO..

Panel 2: Bzzz Bzzz GAD! WHAT A FIENDISH PLAN! GIRLS ARE ABSOLUTELY MERCILESS!

Panel 3: JUG-HEAD! WHAT? YOU WERE ELECTED A DUCHESS OF THE FESTIVAL OF ROSES, VERONICA, AND THESE ARE FOR YOU

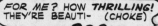

Panel 4: FOR ME? HOW THRILLING! THEY'RE BEAUTI- (CHOKE) ROSES!

Panel 5: JASON! TAKE THESE AND THROW THEM OUT! QUICK! YES, MISS

Panel 6: DID YOU DELIVER THEM, JUG? YEAH..

Panel 7: STAND BY.. I HAVE AN IDEA YOU'LL BE MAKING ANOTHER DELIVERY SOON!

Panel 8: YEAH— HERE THEY COME!

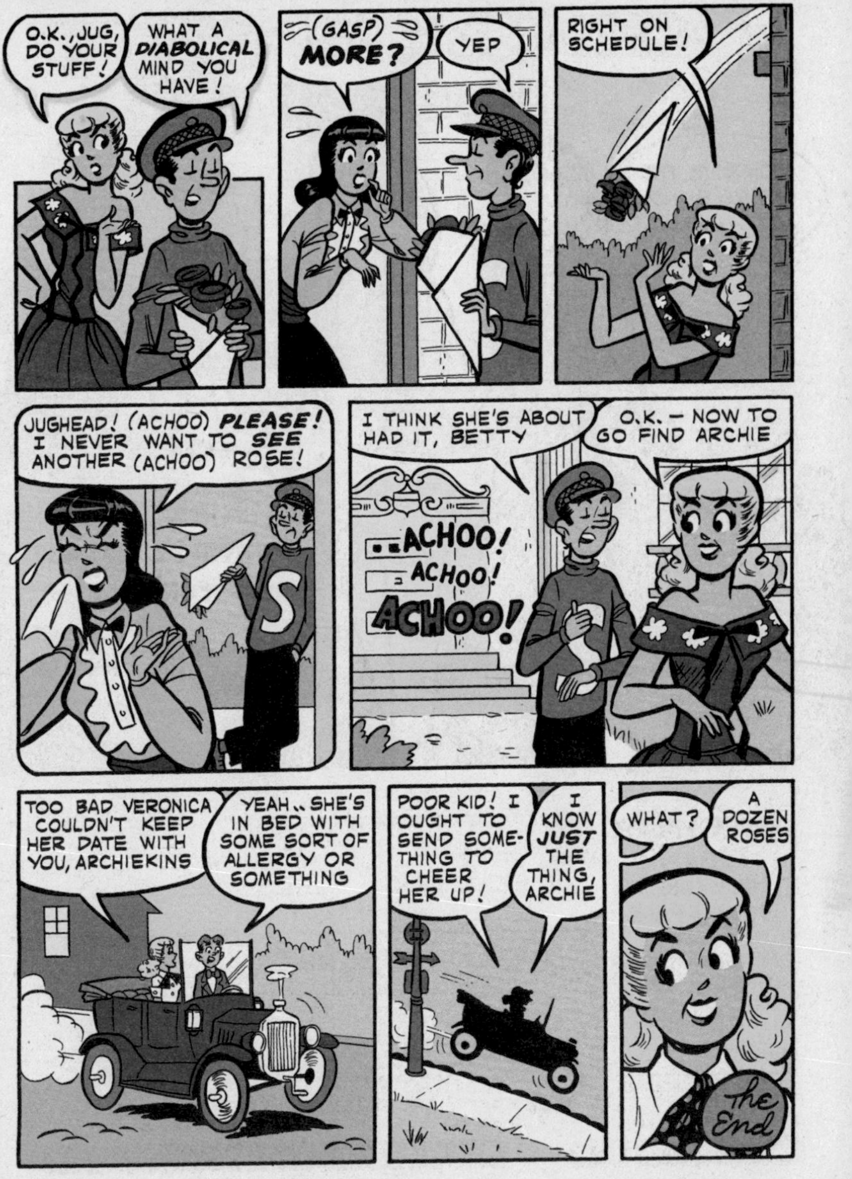
O.K., JUG, DO YOUR STUFF!
WHAT A DIABOLICAL MIND YOU HAVE!
(GASP) MORE?
YEP
RIGHT ON SCHEDULE!
JUGHEAD! (ACHOO) PLEASE! I NEVER WANT TO SEE ANOTHER (ACHOO) ROSE!
I THINK SHE'S ABOUT HAD IT, BETTY
O.K. — NOW TO GO FIND ARCHIE
ACHOO! ACHOO! ACHOO!
TOO BAD VERONICA COULDN'T KEEP HER DATE WITH YOU, ARCHIEKINS
YEAH .. SHE'S IN BED WITH SOME SORT OF ALLERGY OR SOMETHING
POOR KID! I OUGHT TO SEND SOME-THING TO CHEER HER UP!
I KNOW JUST THE THING, ARCHIE
WHAT?
A DOZEN ROSES
The End

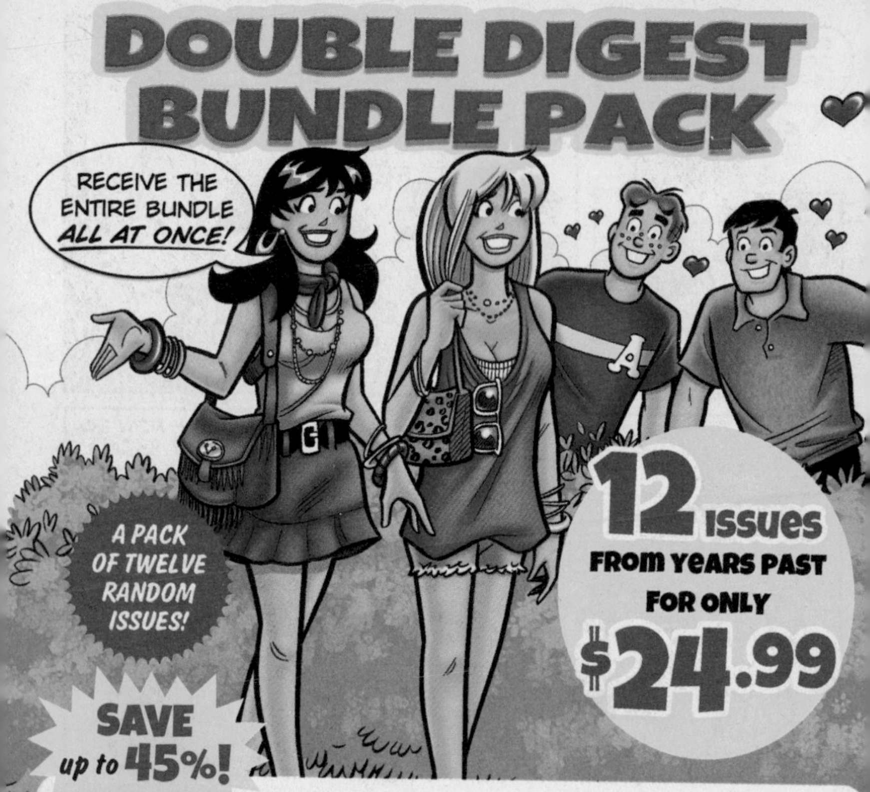
DOUBLE DIGEST BUNDLE PACK
RECEIVE THE ENTIRE BUNDLE ALL AT ONCE!
A PACK OF TWELVE RANDOM ISSUES!
12 issues FROM YEARS PAST FOR ONLY $24.99
SAVE up to 45%!

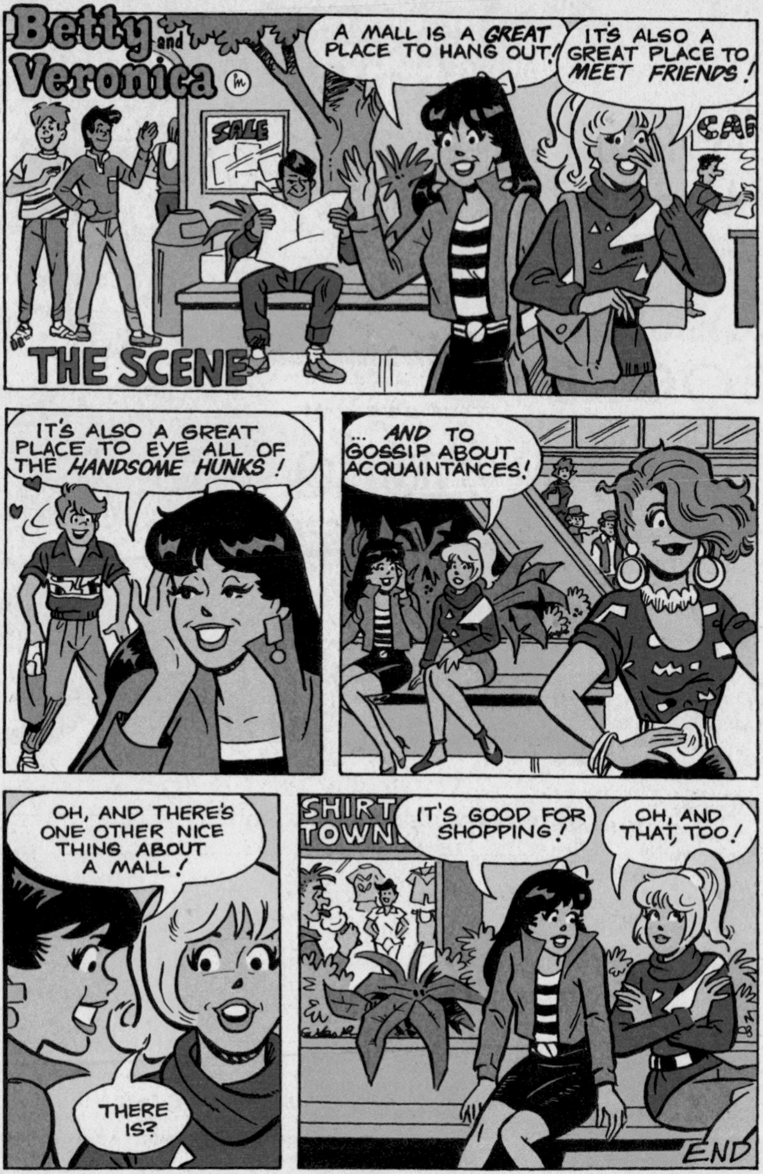
Betty and Veronica
THE SCENE
A MALL IS A GREAT PLACE TO HANG OUT!
IT'S ALSO A GREAT PLACE TO MEET FRIENDS!
SALE
IT'S ALSO A GREAT PLACE TO EYE ALL OF THE HANDSOME HUNKS!
... AND TO GOSSIP ABOUT ACQUAINTANCES!
OH, AND THERE'S ONE OTHER NICE THING ABOUT A MALL!
THERE IS?
SHIRT TOWN
IT'S GOOD FOR SHOPPING!
OH, AND THAT, TOO!
END

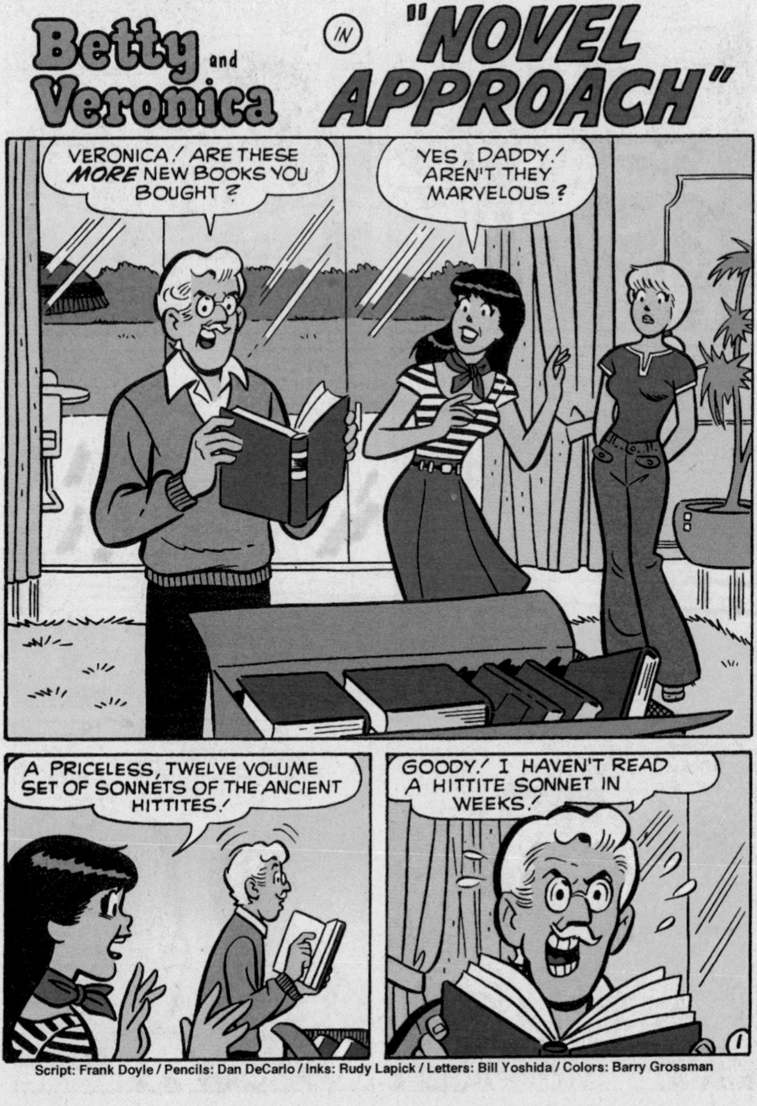
Betty and Veronica
IN
"NOVEL APPROACH"
VERONICA! ARE THESE MORE NEW BOOKS YOU BOUGHT?
YES, DADDY! AREN'T THEY MARVELOUS?
A PRICELESS, TWELVE VOLUME SET OF SONNETS OF THE ANCIENT HITTITES!
GOODY! I HAVEN'T READ A HITTITE SONNET IN WEEKS!
1

Script: Frank Doyle / Pencils: Dan DeCarlo / Inks: Rudy Lapick / Letters: Bill Yoshida / Colors: Barry Grossman

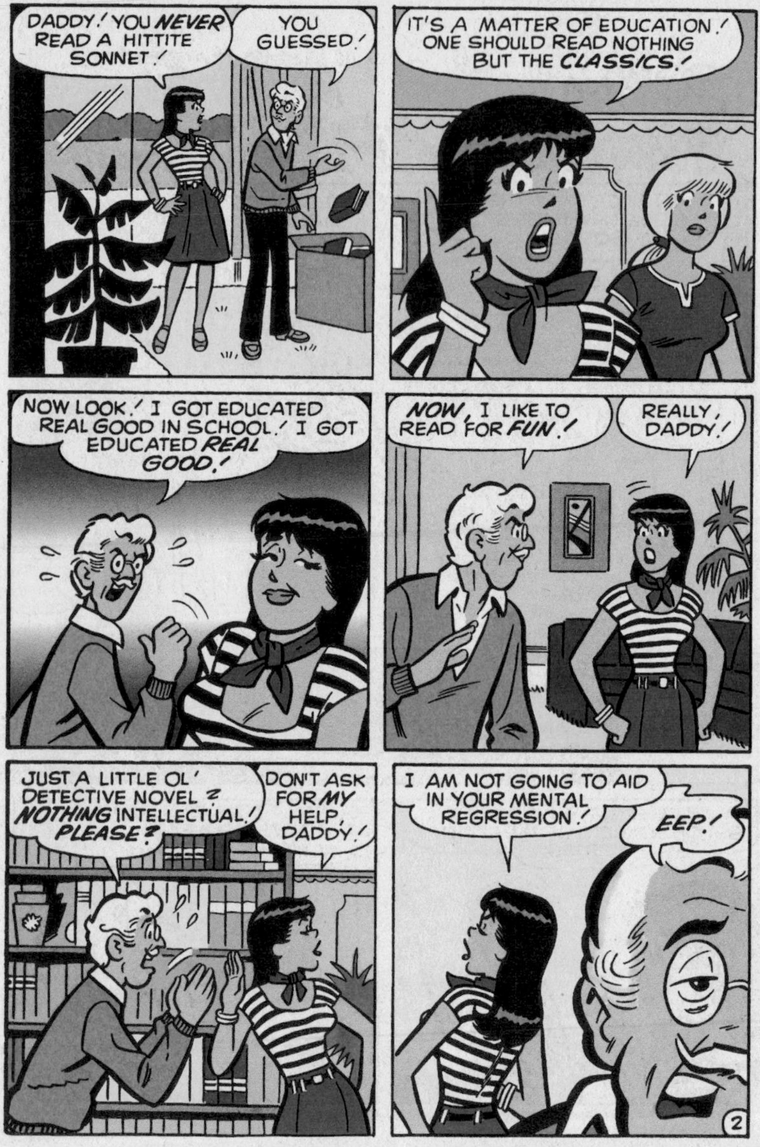
DADDY! YOU NEVER READ A HITTITE SONNET!
YOU GUESSED!
IT'S A MATTER OF EDUCATION! ONE SHOULD READ NOTHING BUT THE CLASSICS!
NOW LOOK! I GOT EDUCATED REAL GOOD IN SCHOOL! I GOT EDUCATED REAL GOOD!
NOW, I LIKE TO READ FOR FUN!
REALLY, DADDY!
JUST A LITTLE OL' DETECTIVE NOVEL? NOTHING INTELLECTUAL! PLEASE?
DON'T ASK FOR MY HELP, DADDY!
I AM NOT GOING TO AID IN YOUR MENTAL REGRESSION!
EEP!
2

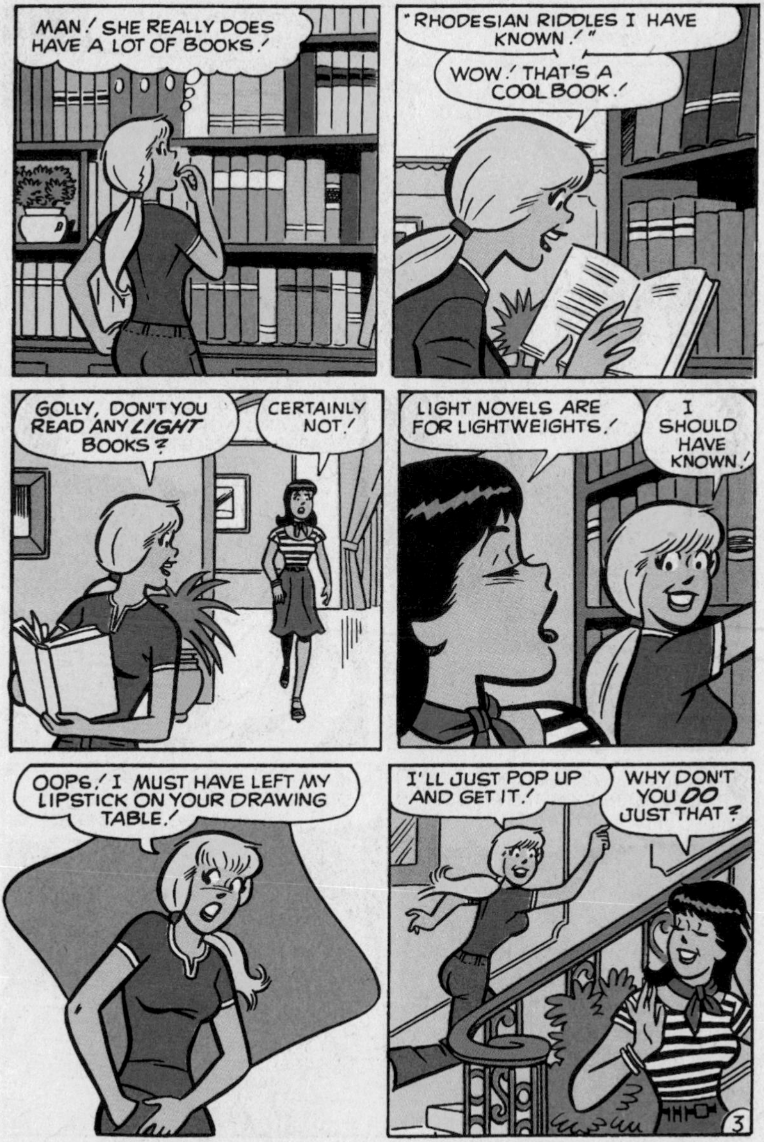
MAN! SHE REALLY DOES HAVE A LOT OF BOOKS!
"RHODESIAN RIDDLES I HAVE KNOWN!"
WOW! THAT'S A COOL BOOK!
GOLLY, DON'T YOU READ ANY *LIGHT* BOOKS?
CERTAINLY NOT!
LIGHT NOVELS ARE FOR LIGHTWEIGHTS!
I SHOULD HAVE KNOWN!
OOPS! I MUST HAVE LEFT MY LIPSTICK ON YOUR DRAWING TABLE!
I'LL JUST POP UP AND GET IT!
WHY DON'T YOU *DO* JUST THAT?
3

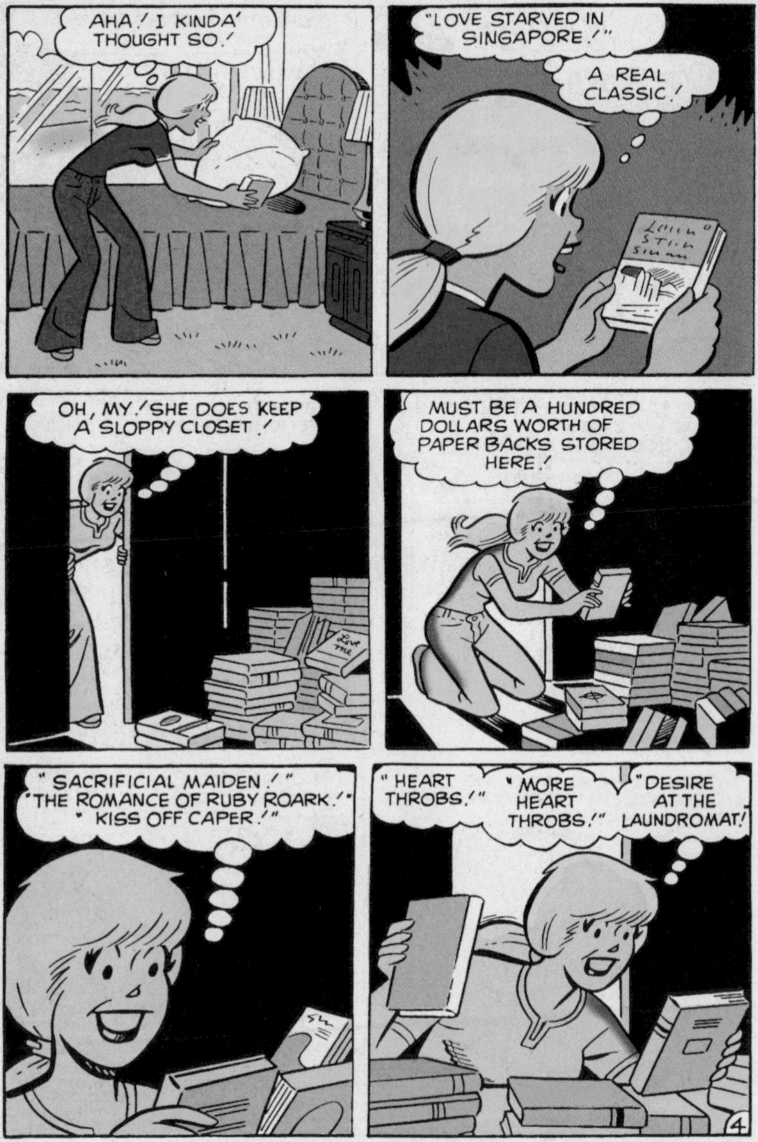
AHA! I KINDA' THOUGHT SO!
"LOVE STARVED IN SINGAPORE!"
A REAL CLASSIC!
OH, MY! SHE DOES KEEP A SLOPPY CLOSET!
MUST BE A HUNDRED DOLLARS WORTH OF PAPER BACKS STORED HERE!
"SACRIFICIAL MAIDEN!" "THE ROMANCE OF RUBY ROARK!" "KISS OFF CAPER!"
"HEART THROBS!"
"MORE HEART THROBS!"
"DESIRE AT THE LAUNDROMAT!"

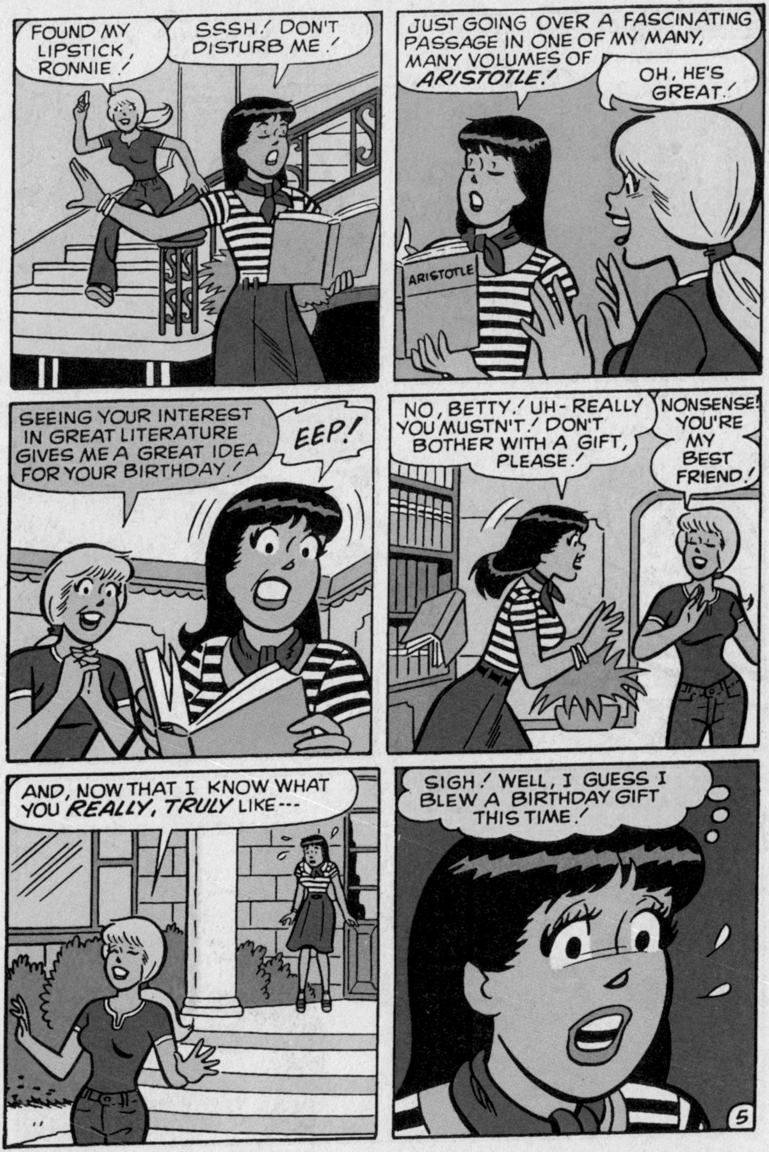
FOUND MY LIPSTICK, RONNIE!
SSSH! DON'T DISTURB ME!
JUST GOING OVER A FASCINATING PASSAGE IN ONE OF MY MANY, MANY VOLUMES OF ARISTOTLE!
OH, HE'S GREAT!
ARISTOTLE
SEEING YOUR INTEREST IN GREAT LITERATURE GIVES ME A GREAT IDEA FOR YOUR BIRTHDAY!
EEP!
NO, BETTY! UH- REALLY YOU MUSTN'T! DON'T BOTHER WITH A GIFT, PLEASE!
NONSENSE! YOU'RE MY BEST FRIEND!
AND, NOW THAT I KNOW WHAT YOU REALLY, TRULY LIKE---
SIGH! WELL, I GUESS I BLEW A BIRTHDAY GIFT THIS TIME!
5

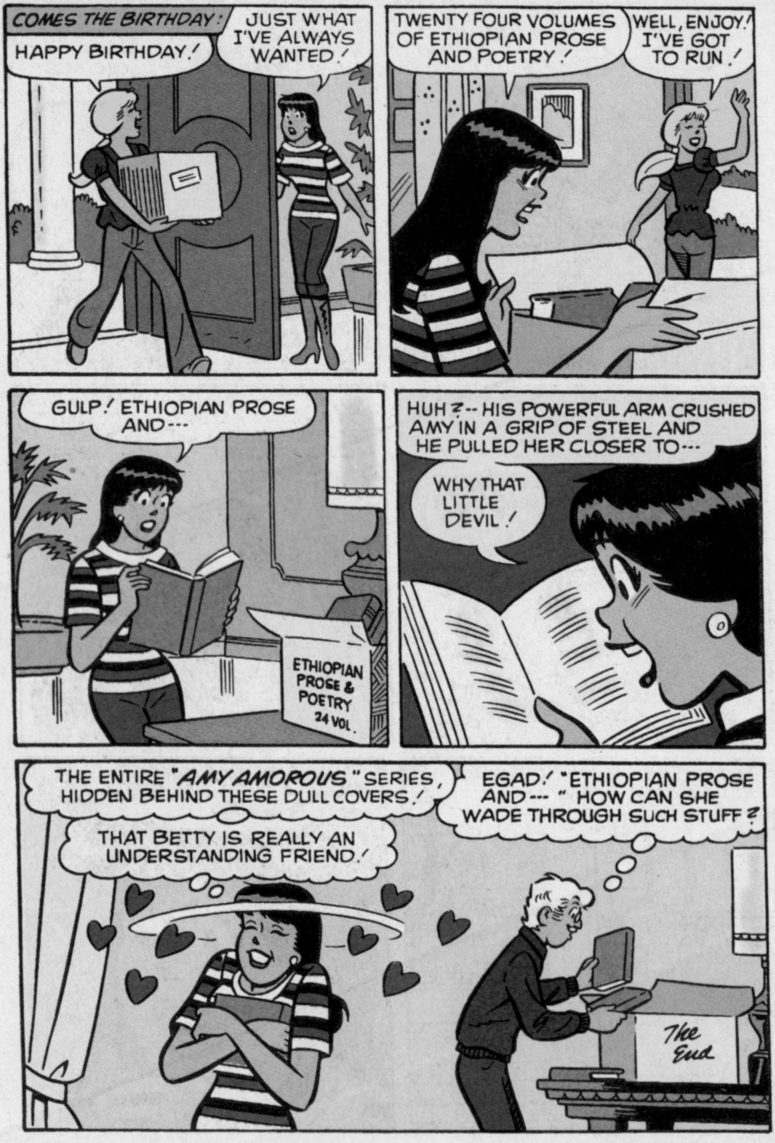
COMES THE BIRTHDAY:
HAPPY BIRTHDAY!
JUST WHAT I'VE ALWAYS WANTED!
TWENTY FOUR VOLUMES OF ETHIOPIAN PROSE AND POETRY!
WELL, ENJOY! I'VE GOT TO RUN!
GULP! ETHIOPIAN PROSE AND---
ETHIOPIAN PROSE & POETRY 24 VOL.
HUH?-- HIS POWERFUL ARM CRUSHED AMY IN A GRIP OF STEEL AND HE PULLED HER CLOSER TO---
WHY THAT LITTLE DEVIL!
THE ENTIRE "AMY AMOROUS" SERIES, HIDDEN BEHIND THESE DULL COVERS!
THAT BETTY IS REALLY AN UNDERSTANDING FRIEND!
EGAD! "ETHIOPIAN PROSE AND---" HOW CAN SHE WADE THROUGH SUCH STUFF?
The End

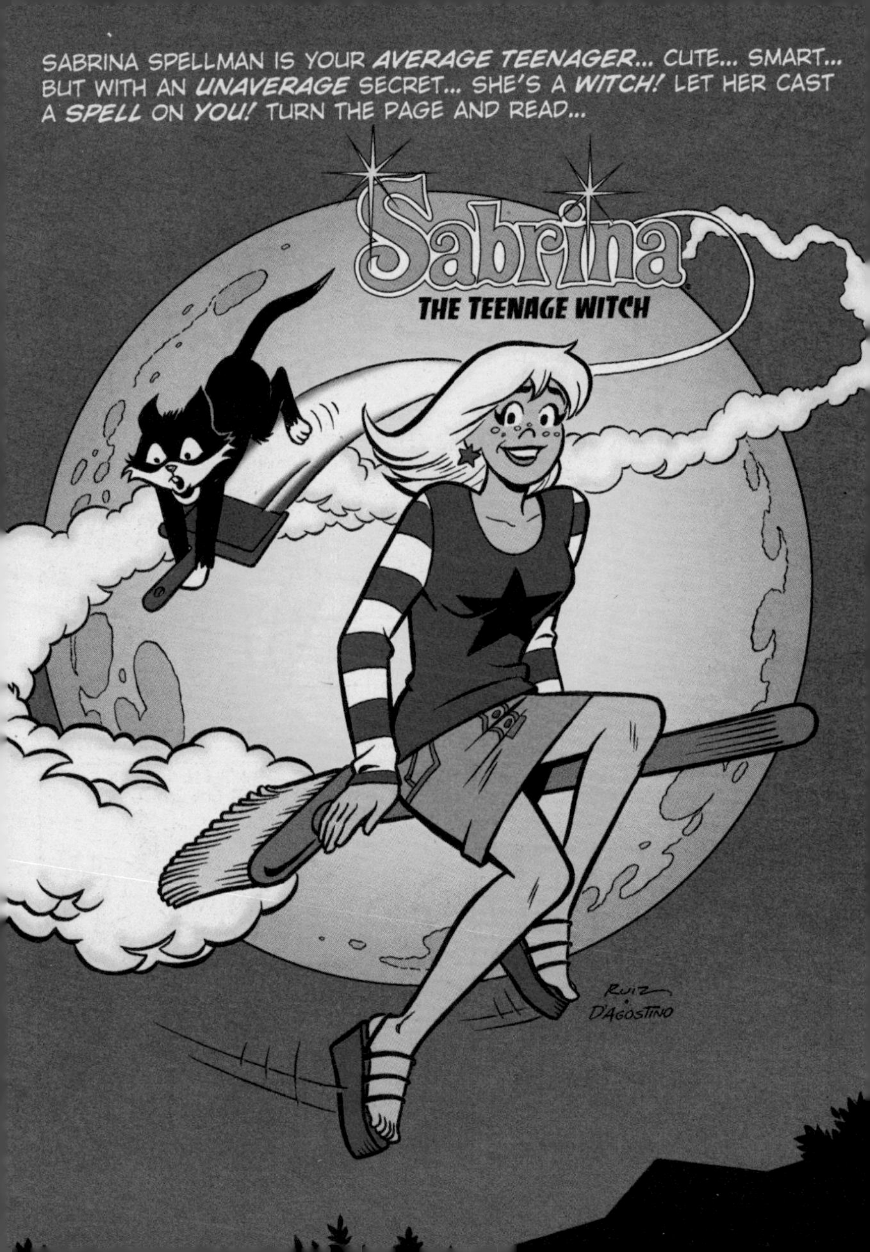
SABRINA SPELLMAN IS YOUR AVERAGE TEENAGER... CUTE... SMART... BUT WITH AN UNAVERAGE SECRET... SHE'S A WITCH! LET HER CAST A SPELL ON YOU! TURN THE PAGE AND READ...
Sabrina
THE TEENAGE WITCH
RUIZ & D'AGOSTINO

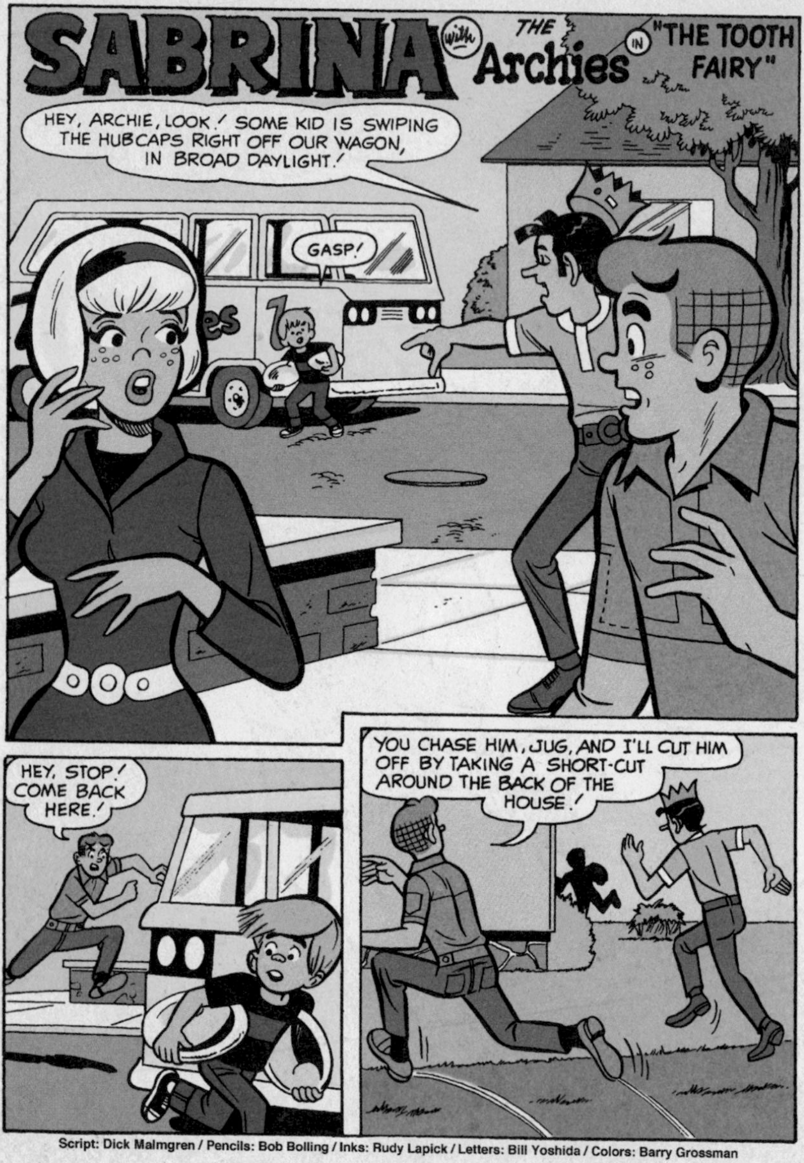
SABRINA with THE Archies IN "THE TOOTH FAIRY"
HEY, ARCHIE, LOOK! SOME KID IS SWIPING THE HUBCAPS RIGHT OFF OUR WAGON, IN BROAD DAYLIGHT!
GASP!
HEY, STOP! COME BACK HERE!
YOU CHASE HIM, JUG, AND I'LL CUT HIM OFF BY TAKING A SHORT-CUT AROUND THE BACK OF THE HOUSE!

Script: Dick Malmgren / Pencils: Bob Bolling / Inks: Rudy Lapick / Letters: Bill Yoshida / Colors: Barry Grossman

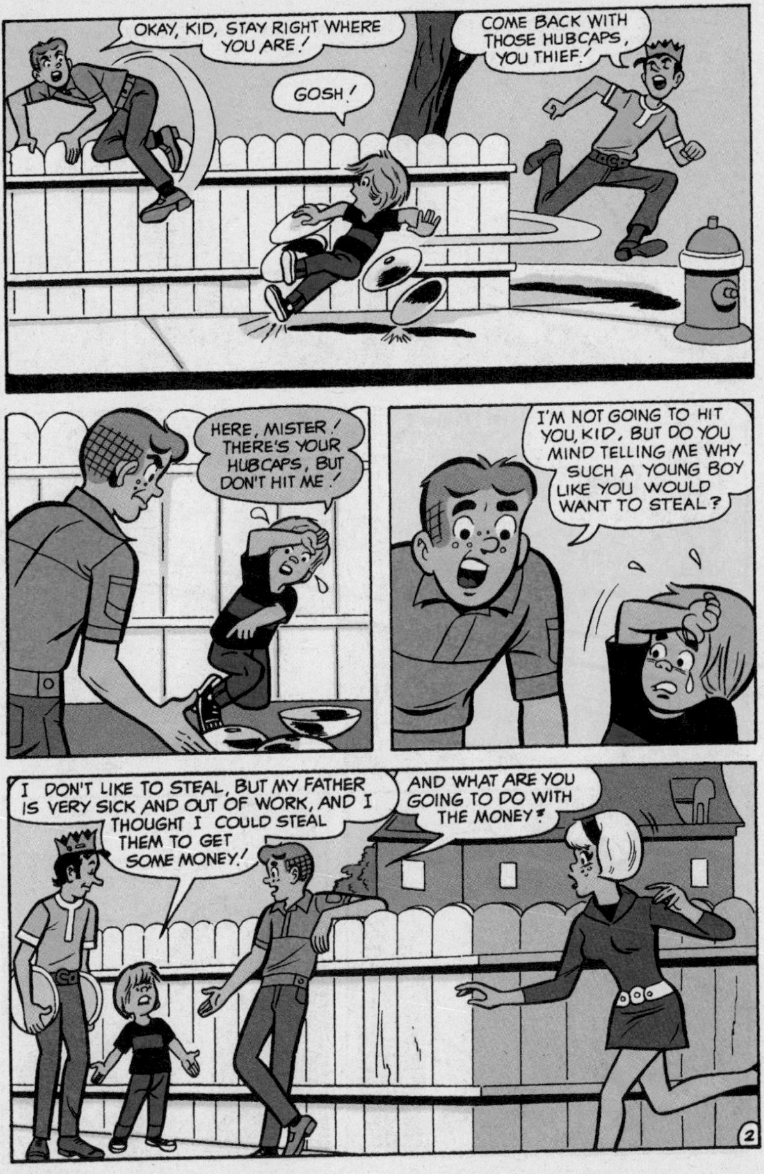
OKAY, KID, STAY RIGHT WHERE YOU ARE!
COME BACK WITH THOSE HUBCAPS, YOU THIEF!
GOSH!
HERE, MISTER! THERE'S YOUR HUBCAPS, BUT DON'T HIT ME!
I'M NOT GOING TO HIT YOU, KID, BUT DO YOU MIND TELLING ME WHY SUCH A YOUNG BOY LIKE YOU WOULD WANT TO STEAL?
I DON'T LIKE TO STEAL, BUT MY FATHER IS VERY SICK AND OUT OF WORK, AND I THOUGHT I COULD STEAL THEM TO GET SOME MONEY!
AND WHAT ARE YOU GOING TO DO WITH THE MONEY?
2

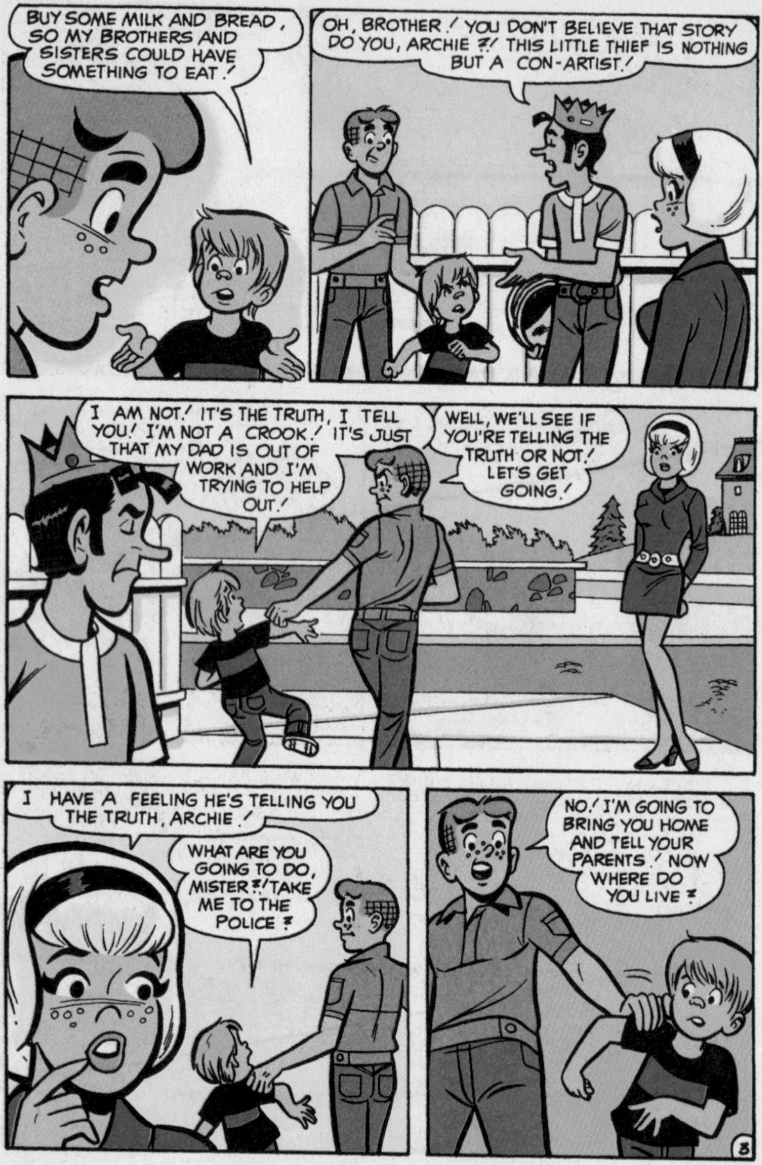

BUY SOME MILK AND BREAD, SO MY BROTHERS AND SISTERS COULD HAVE SOMETHING TO EAT!
OH, BROTHER! YOU DON'T BELIEVE THAT STORY DO YOU, ARCHIE ?! THIS LITTLE THIEF IS NOTHING BUT A CON-ARTIST!
I AM NOT! IT'S THE TRUTH, I TELL YOU! I'M NOT A CROOK! IT'S JUST THAT MY DAD IS OUT OF WORK AND I'M TRYING TO HELP OUT!
WELL, WE'LL SEE IF YOU'RE TELLING THE TRUTH OR NOT! LET'S GET GOING!
I HAVE A FEELING HE'S TELLING YOU THE TRUTH, ARCHIE!
WHAT ARE YOU GOING TO DO, MISTER ?! TAKE ME TO THE POLICE ?
NO! I'M GOING TO BRING YOU HOME AND TELL YOUR PARENTS! NOW WHERE DO YOU LIVE ?
8

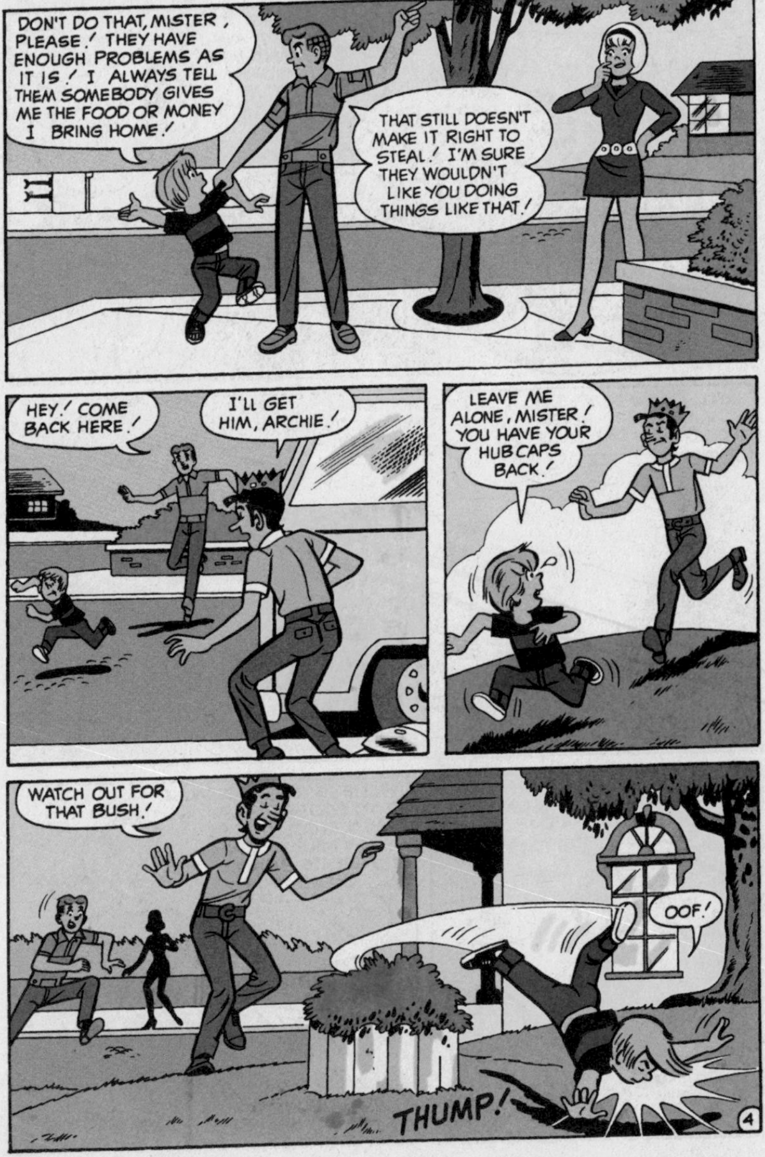
DON'T DO THAT, MISTER, PLEASE! THEY HAVE ENOUGH PROBLEMS AS IT IS! I ALWAYS TELL THEM SOMEBODY GIVES ME THE FOOD OR MONEY I BRING HOME!
THAT STILL DOESN'T MAKE IT RIGHT TO STEAL! I'M SURE THEY WOULDN'T LIKE YOU DOING THINGS LIKE THAT!
HEY! COME BACK HERE!
I'LL GET HIM, ARCHIE!
LEAVE ME ALONE, MISTER! YOU HAVE YOUR HUB CAPS BACK!
WATCH OUT FOR THAT BUSH!
OOF!
THUMP!
4

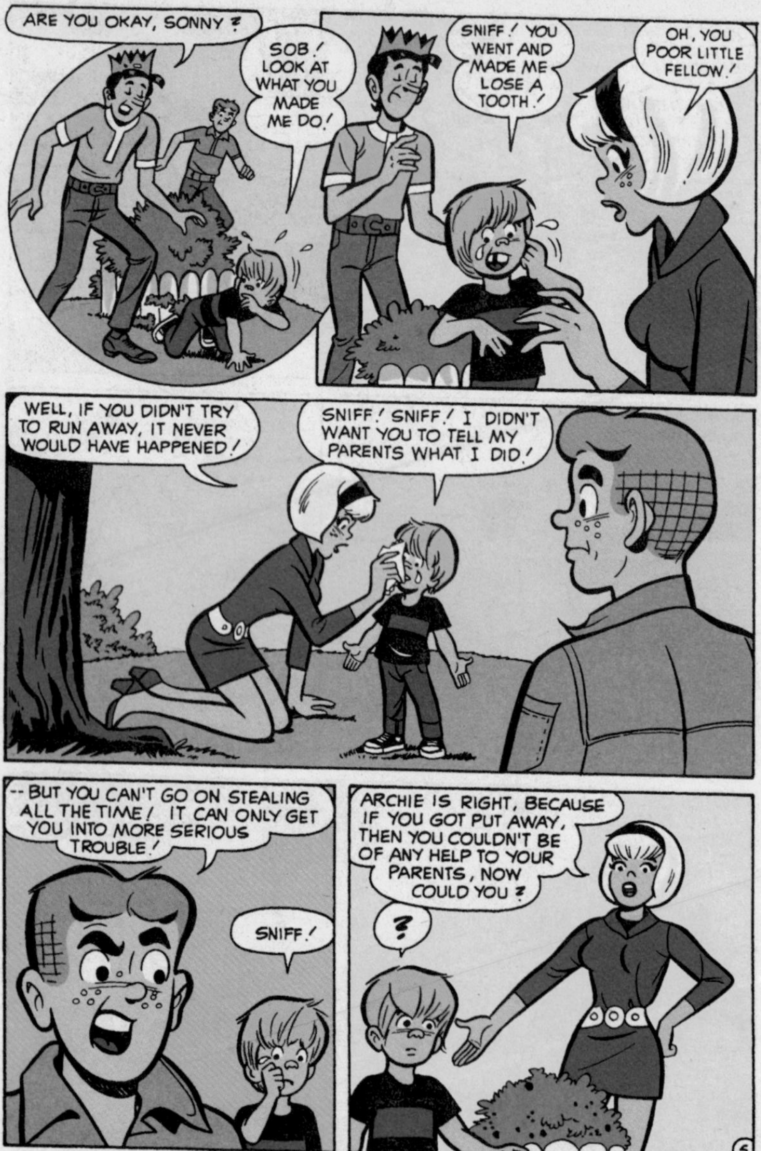

ARE YOU OKAY, SONNY ?
SOB! LOOK AT WHAT YOU MADE ME DO!
SNIFF! YOU WENT AND MADE ME LOSE A TOOTH!
OH, YOU POOR LITTLE FELLOW!
WELL, IF YOU DIDN'T TRY TO RUN AWAY, IT NEVER WOULD HAVE HAPPENED!
SNIFF! SNIFF! I DIDN'T WANT YOU TO TELL MY PARENTS WHAT I DID!
-- BUT YOU CAN'T GO ON STEALING ALL THE TIME! IT CAN ONLY GET YOU INTO MORE SERIOUS TROUBLE!
SNIFF!
ARCHIE IS RIGHT, BECAUSE IF YOU GOT PUT AWAY, THEN YOU COULDN'T BE OF ANY HELP TO YOUR PARENTS, NOW COULD YOU ?
?
5

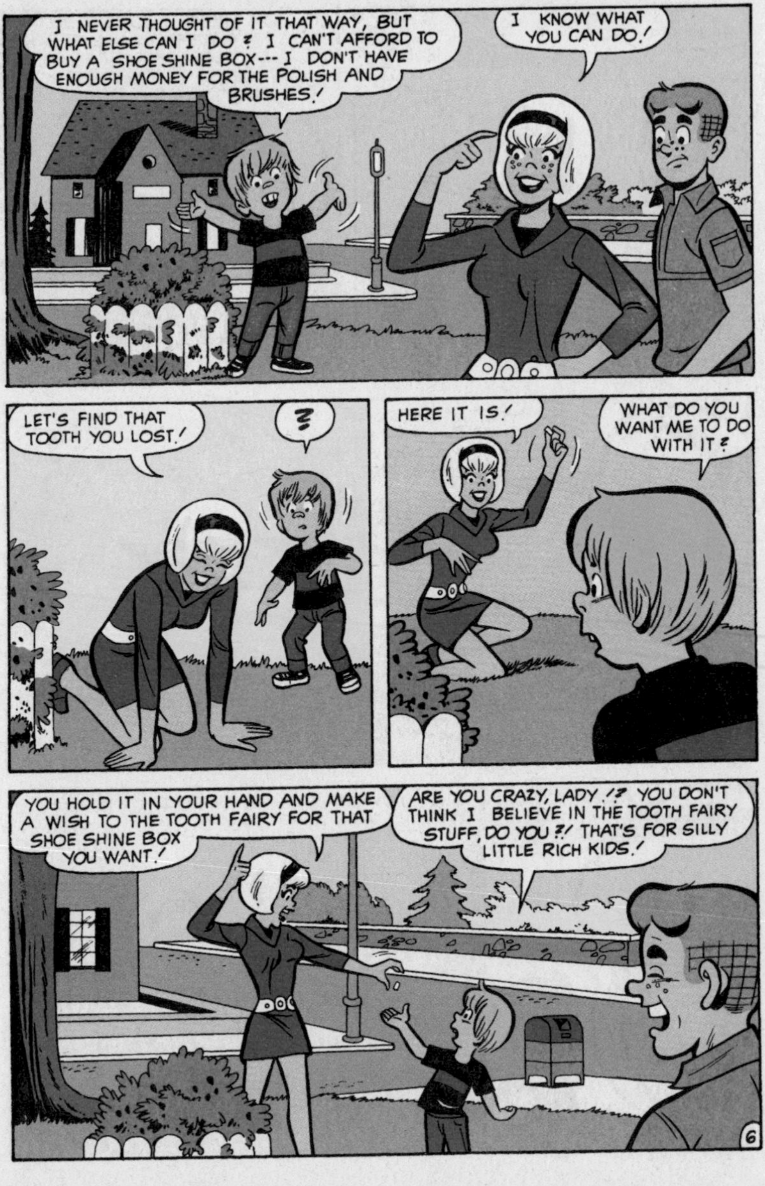
I NEVER THOUGHT OF IT THAT WAY, BUT WHAT ELSE CAN I DO? I CAN'T AFFORD TO BUY A SHOE SHINE BOX--- I DON'T HAVE ENOUGH MONEY FOR THE POLISH AND BRUSHES!
I KNOW WHAT YOU CAN DO!
LET'S FIND THAT TOOTH YOU LOST!
?
HERE IT IS!
WHAT DO YOU WANT ME TO DO WITH IT?
YOU HOLD IT IN YOUR HAND AND MAKE A WISH TO THE TOOTH FAIRY FOR THAT SHOE SHINE BOX YOU WANT!
ARE YOU CRAZY, LADY!? YOU DON'T THINK I BELIEVE IN THE TOOTH FAIRY STUFF, DO YOU?! THAT'S FOR SILLY LITTLE RICH KIDS!
6

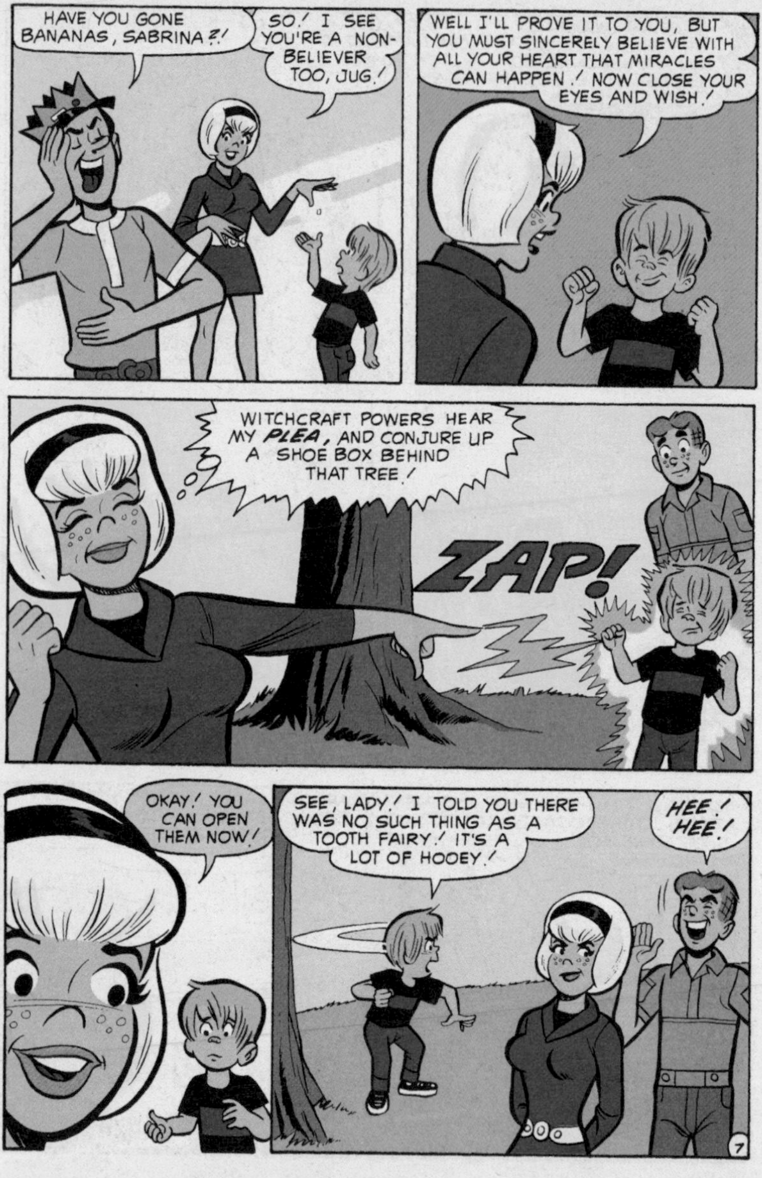
HAVE YOU GONE BANANAS, SABRINA ?!
SO! I SEE YOU'RE A NON-BELIEVER TOO, JUG!
WELL I'LL PROVE IT TO YOU, BUT YOU MUST SINCERELY BELIEVE WITH ALL YOUR HEART THAT MIRACLES CAN HAPPEN! NOW CLOSE YOUR EYES AND WISH!
WITCHCRAFT POWERS HEAR MY *PLEA*, AND CONJURE UP A SHOE BOX BEHIND THAT TREE!
ZAP!
OKAY! YOU CAN OPEN THEM NOW!
SEE, LADY! I TOLD YOU THERE WAS NO SUCH THING AS A TOOTH FAIRY! IT'S A LOT OF HOOEY!
HEE! HEE!
7

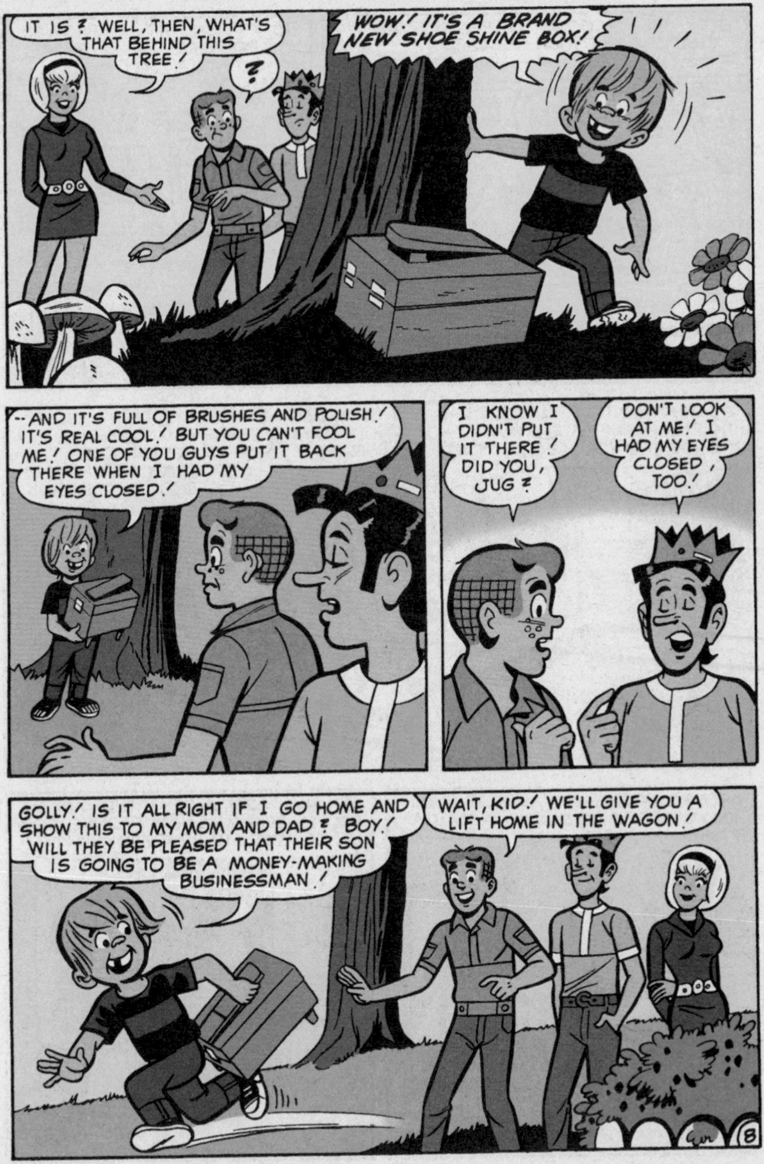
IT IS ? WELL, THEN, WHAT'S THAT BEHIND THIS TREE!
?
WOW! IT'S A BRAND NEW SHOE SHINE BOX!
--AND IT'S FULL OF BRUSHES AND POLISH! IT'S REAL COOL! BUT YOU CAN'T FOOL ME! ONE OF YOU GUYS PUT IT BACK THERE WHEN I HAD MY EYES CLOSED!
I KNOW I DIDN'T PUT IT THERE! DID YOU, JUG ?
DON'T LOOK AT ME! I HAD MY EYES CLOSED, TOO!
GOLLY! IS IT ALL RIGHT IF I GO HOME AND SHOW THIS TO MY MOM AND DAD ? BOY! WILL THEY BE PLEASED THAT THEIR SON IS GOING TO BE A MONEY-MAKING BUSINESSMAN!
WAIT, KID! WE'LL GIVE YOU A LIFT HOME IN THE WAGON!
8

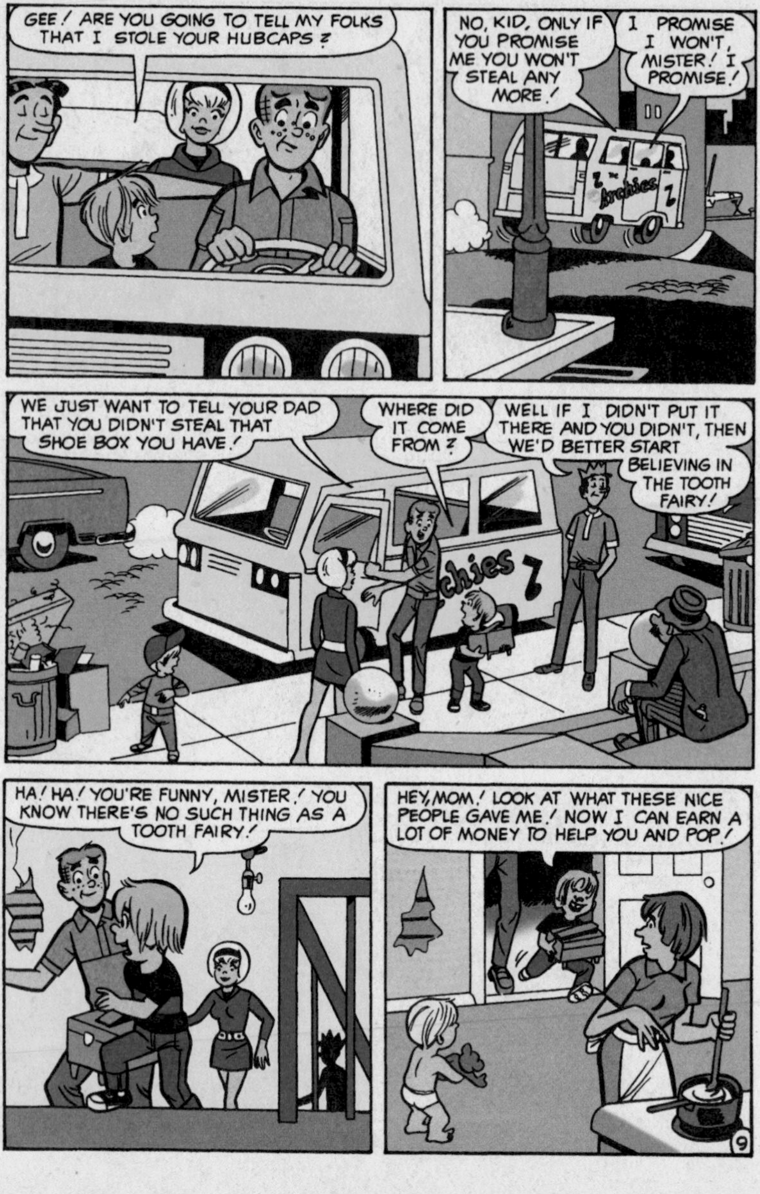

GEE! ARE YOU GOING TO TELL MY FOLKS THAT I STOLE YOUR HUBCAPS?
NO, KID, ONLY IF YOU PROMISE ME YOU WON'T STEAL ANY MORE!
I PROMISE I WON'T, MISTER! I PROMISE!
THE Archies
WE JUST WANT TO TELL YOUR DAD THAT YOU DIDN'T STEAL THAT SHOE BOX YOU HAVE!
WHERE DID IT COME FROM?
WELL IF I DIDN'T PUT IT THERE AND YOU DIDN'T, THEN WE'D BETTER START BELIEVING IN THE TOOTH FAIRY!
HA! HA! YOU'RE FUNNY, MISTER! YOU KNOW THERE'S NO SUCH THING AS A TOOTH FAIRY!
HEY, MOM! LOOK AT WHAT THESE NICE PEOPLE GAVE ME! NOW I CAN EARN A LOT OF MONEY TO HELP YOU AND POP!

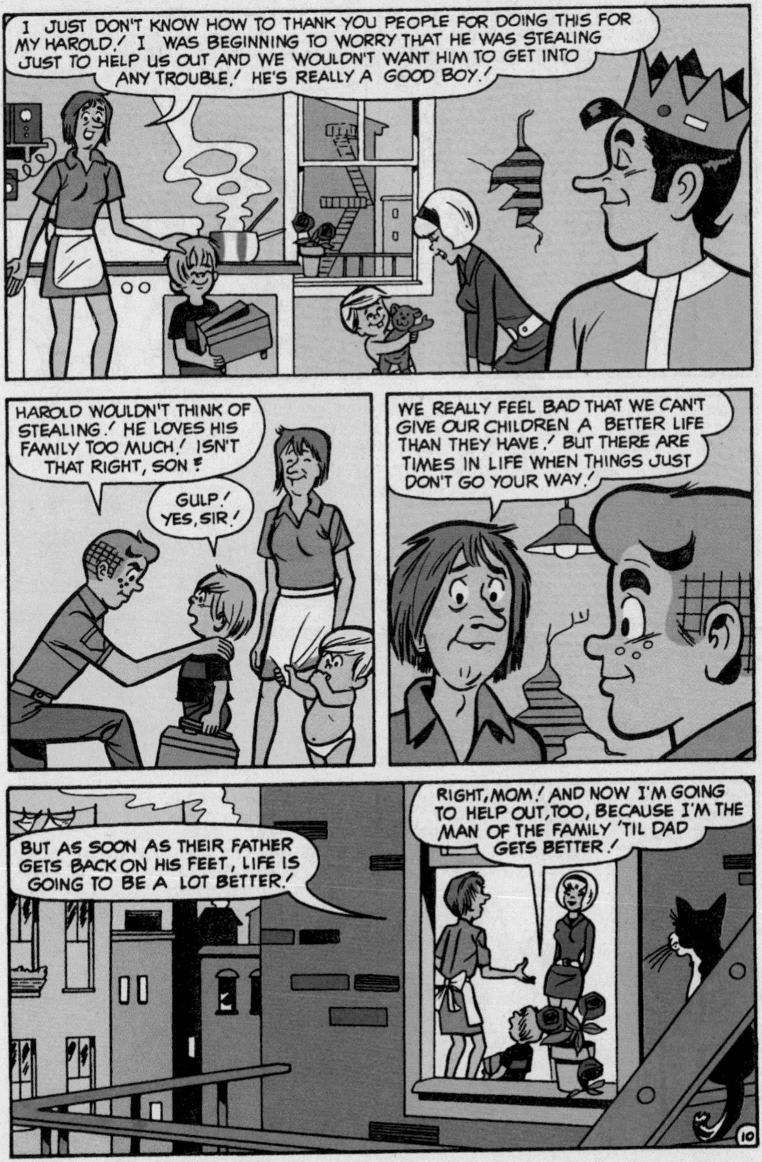
I JUST DON'T KNOW HOW TO THANK YOU PEOPLE FOR DOING THIS FOR MY HAROLD! I WAS BEGINNING TO WORRY THAT HE WAS STEALING JUST TO HELP US OUT AND WE WOULDN'T WANT HIM TO GET INTO ANY TROUBLE! HE'S REALLY A GOOD BOY!
HAROLD WOULDN'T THINK OF STEALING! HE LOVES HIS FAMILY TOO MUCH! ISN'T THAT RIGHT, SON?
GULP! YES, SIR!
WE REALLY FEEL BAD THAT WE CAN'T GIVE OUR CHILDREN A BETTER LIFE THAN THEY HAVE! BUT THERE ARE TIMES IN LIFE WHEN THINGS JUST DON'T GO YOUR WAY!
BUT AS SOON AS THEIR FATHER GETS BACK ON HIS FEET, LIFE IS GOING TO BE A LOT BETTER!
RIGHT, MOM! AND NOW I'M GOING TO HELP OUT, TOO, BECAUSE I'M THE MAN OF THE FAMILY 'TIL DAD GETS BETTER!
10

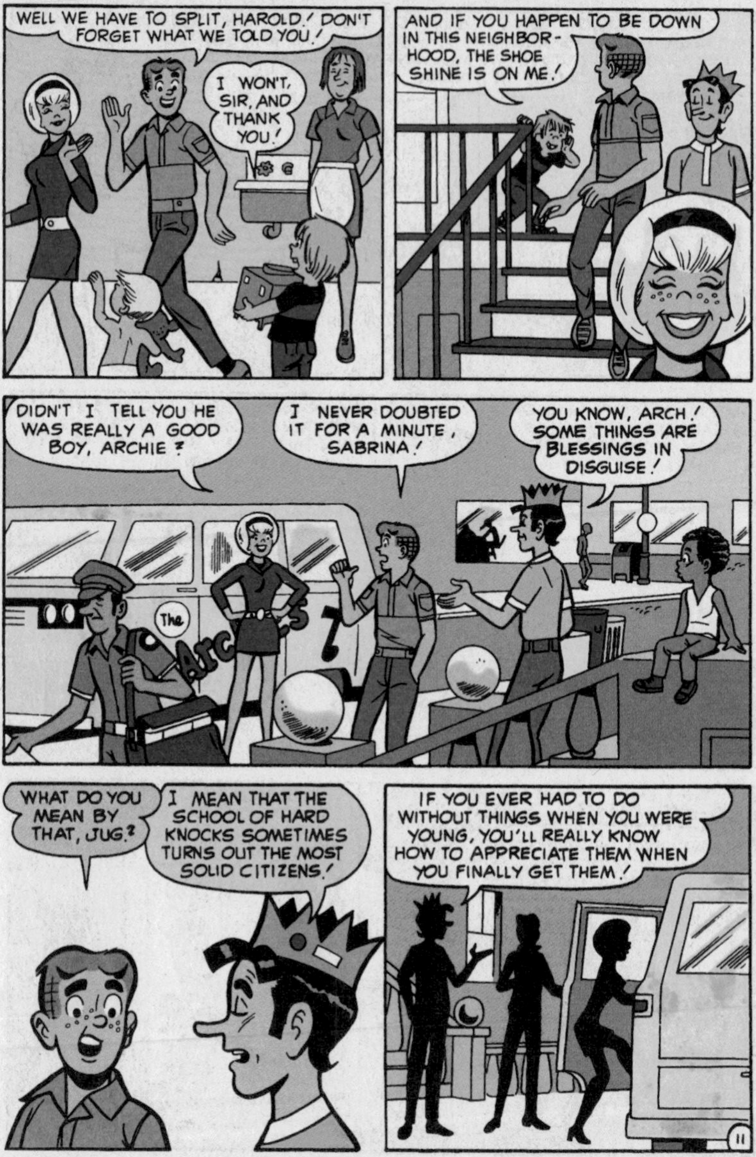
WELL WE HAVE TO SPLIT, HAROLD! DON'T FORGET WHAT WE TOLD YOU!
I WON'T, SIR, AND THANK YOU!
AND IF YOU HAPPEN TO BE DOWN IN THIS NEIGHBOR-HOOD, THE SHOE SHINE IS ON ME!
DIDN'T I TELL YOU HE WAS REALLY A GOOD BOY, ARCHIE?
I NEVER DOUBTED IT FOR A MINUTE, SABRINA!
YOU KNOW, ARCH! SOME THINGS ARE BLESSINGS IN DISGUISE!
The Arc
WHAT DO YOU MEAN BY THAT, JUG?
I MEAN THAT THE SCHOOL OF HARD KNOCKS SOMETIMES TURNS OUT THE MOST SOLID CITIZENS!
IF YOU EVER HAD TO DO WITHOUT THINGS WHEN YOU WERE YOUNG, YOU'LL REALLY KNOW HOW TO APPRECIATE THEM WHEN YOU FINALLY GET THEM!
11

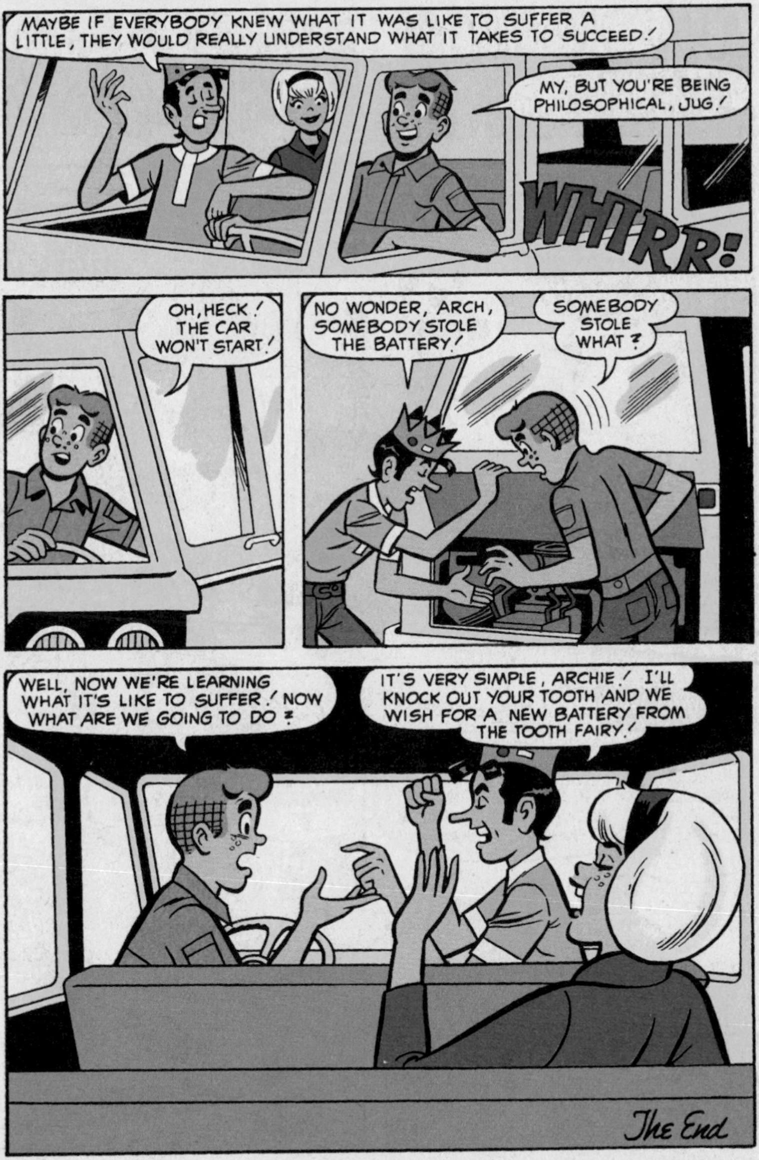
MAYBE IF EVERYBODY KNEW WHAT IT WAS LIKE TO SUFFER A LITTLE, THEY WOULD REALLY UNDERSTAND WHAT IT TAKES TO SUCCEED!
MY, BUT YOU'RE BEING PHILOSOPHICAL, JUG!
WHIRR!
OH, HECK! THE CAR WON'T START!
NO WONDER, ARCH, SOMEBODY STOLE THE BATTERY!
SOMEBODY STOLE WHAT?
WELL, NOW WE'RE LEARNING WHAT IT'S LIKE TO SUFFER! NOW WHAT ARE WE GOING TO DO?
IT'S VERY SIMPLE, ARCHIE! I'LL KNOCK OUT YOUR TOOTH AND WE WISH FOR A NEW BATTERY FROM THE TOOTH FAIRY!
The End

SABRINA -in- AUNTIE CLIMAX

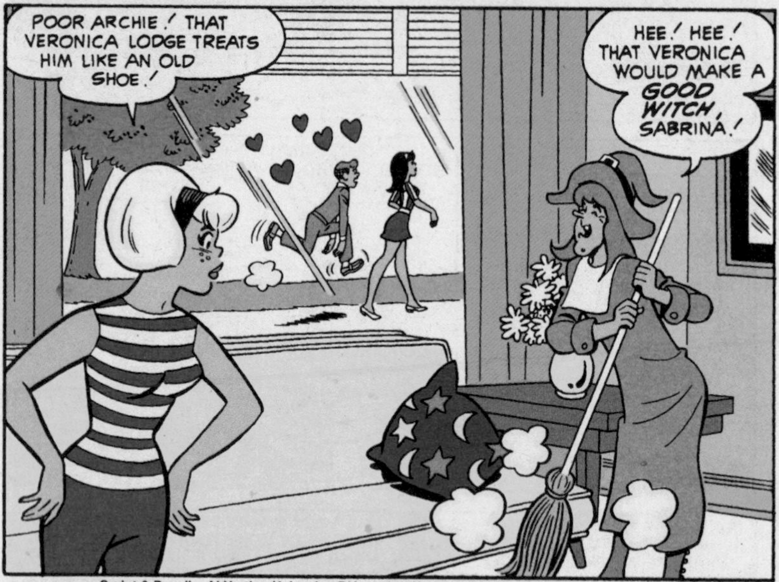

POOR ARCHIE! THAT VERONICA LODGE TREATS HIM LIKE AN OLD SHOE!
HEE! HEE! THAT VERONICA WOULD MAKE A GOOD WITCH, SABRINA!

Script & Pencils: Al Hartley / Inks: Jon D'Agostino / Letters: Bill Yoshida / Colors: Barry Grossman

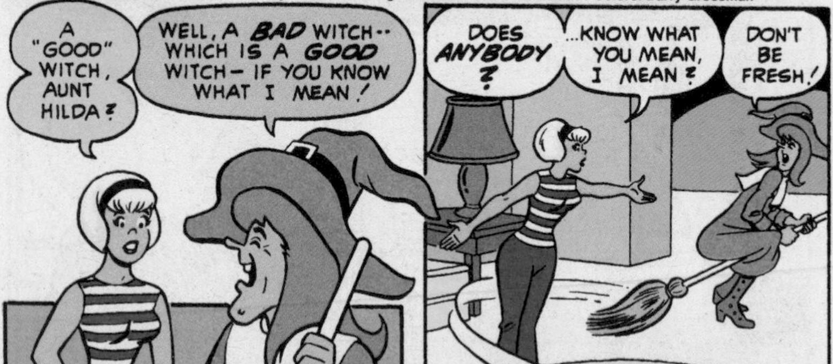

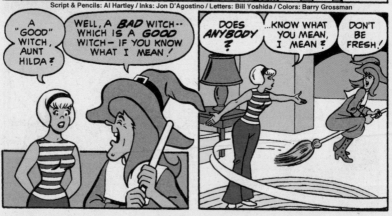

A "GOOD" WITCH, AUNT HILDA?
WELL, A BAD WITCH-- WHICH IS A GOOD WITCH- IF YOU KNOW WHAT I MEAN!
DOES ANYBODY ?
...KNOW WHAT YOU MEAN, I MEAN?
DON'T BE FRESH!

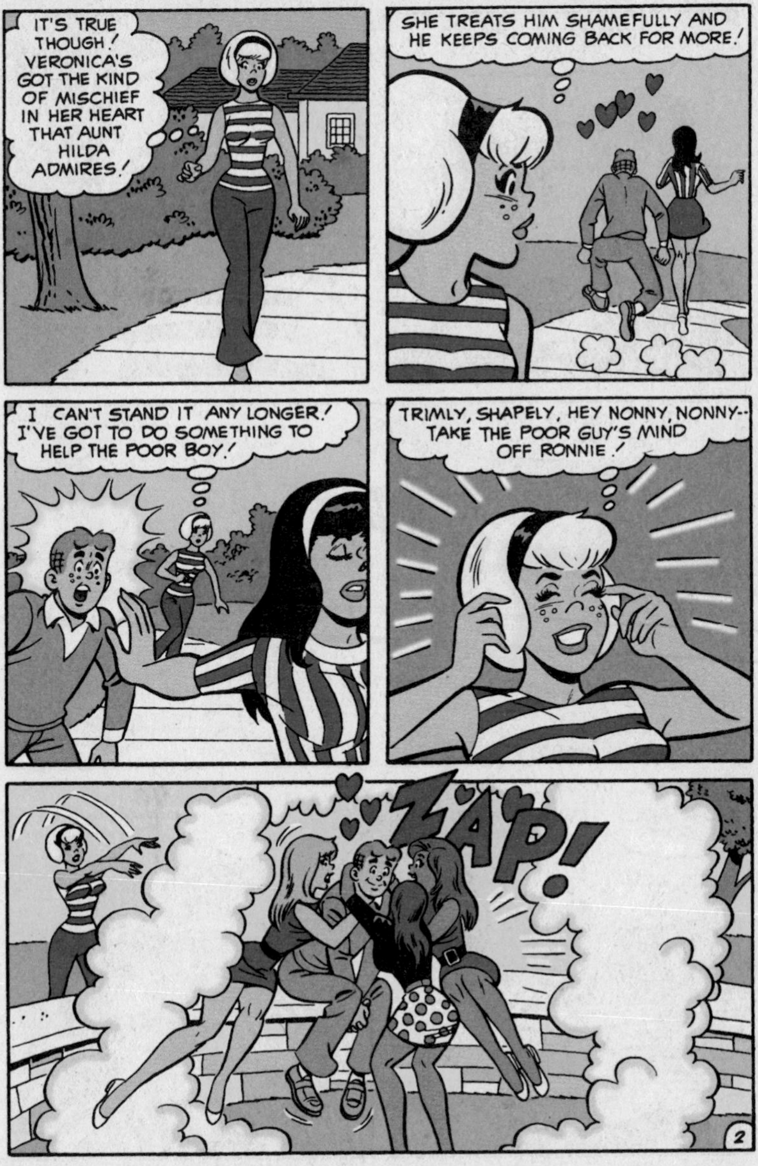
IT'S TRUE THOUGH! VERONICA'S GOT THE KIND OF MISCHIEF IN HER HEART THAT AUNT HILDA ADMIRES!
SHE TREATS HIM SHAMEFULLY AND HE KEEPS COMING BACK FOR MORE!
I CAN'T STAND IT ANY LONGER! I'VE GOT TO DO SOMETHING TO HELP THE POOR BOY!
TRIMLY, SHAPELY, HEY NONNY, NONNY-- TAKE THE POOR GUY'S MIND OFF RONNIE!
ZAP!
2

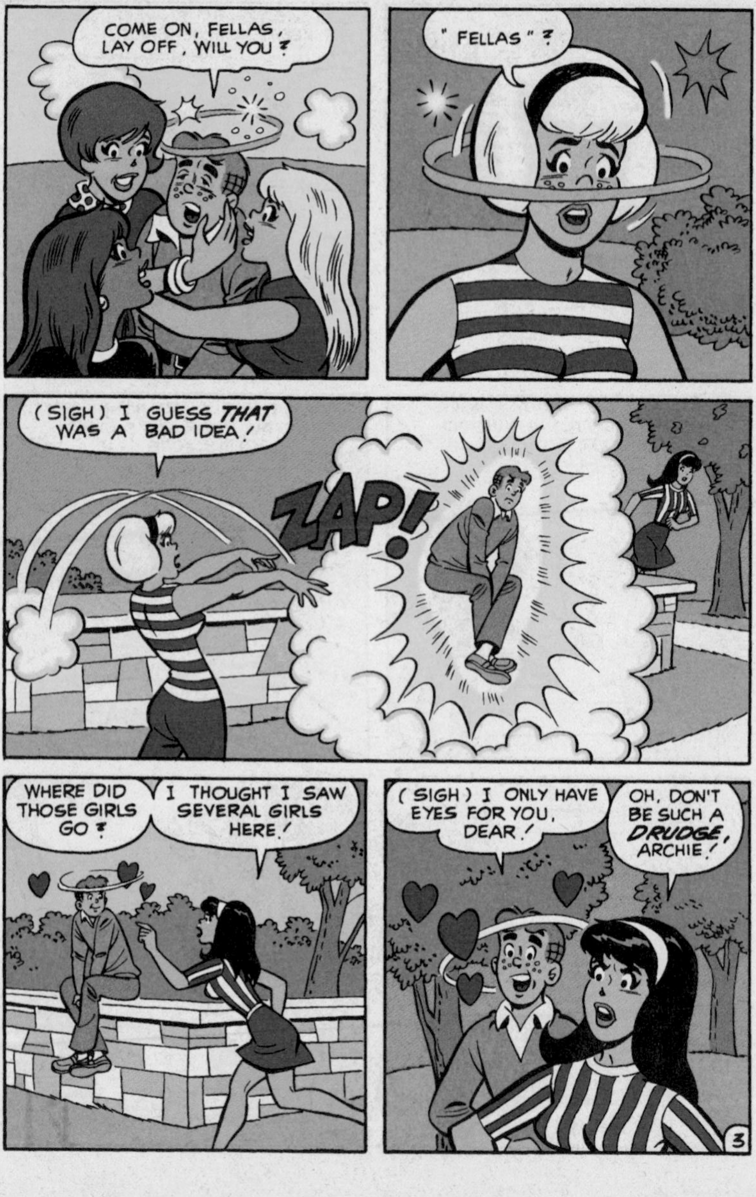
COME ON, FELLAS, LAY OFF, WILL YOU ?
" FELLAS " ?
(SIGH) I GUESS THAT WAS A BAD IDEA!
ZAP!
WHERE DID THOSE GIRLS GO ?
I THOUGHT I SAW SEVERAL GIRLS HERE!
(SIGH) I ONLY HAVE EYES FOR YOU, DEAR!
OH, DON'T BE SUCH A DRUDGE, ARCHIE!
3

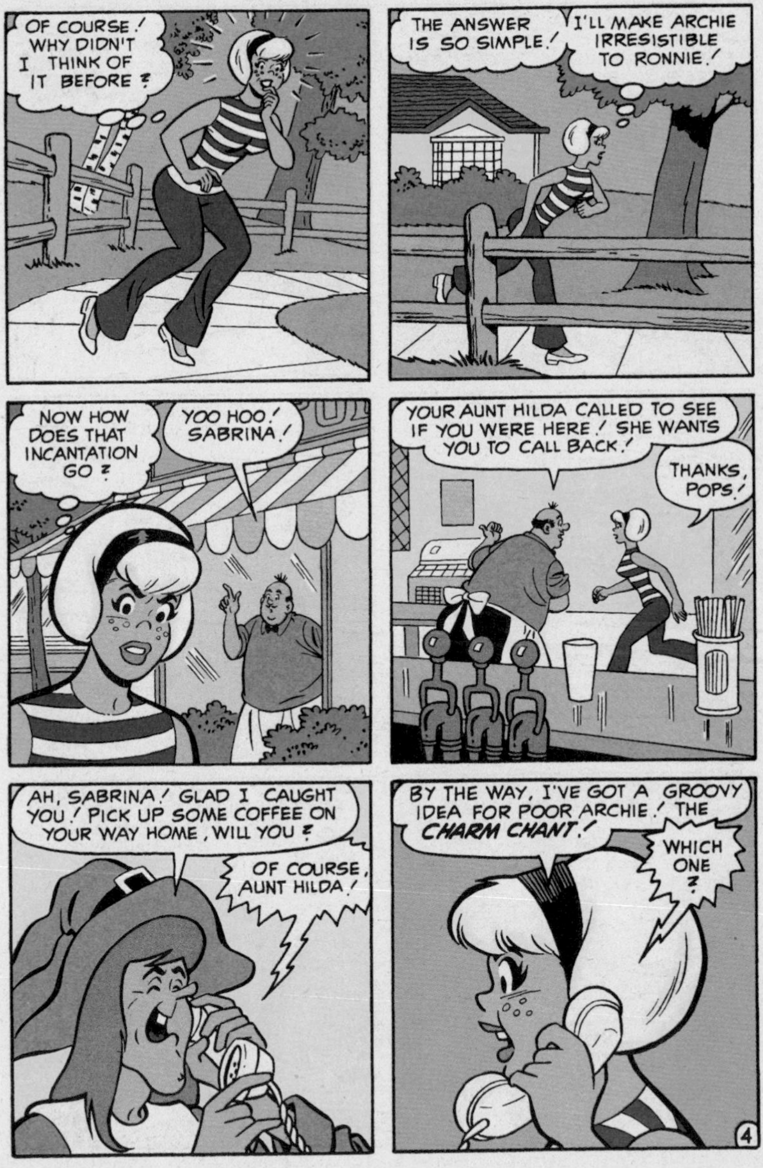
OF COURSE! WHY DIDN'T I THINK OF IT BEFORE?
THE ANSWER IS SO SIMPLE!
I'LL MAKE ARCHIE IRRESISTIBLE TO RONNIE!
NOW HOW DOES THAT INCANTATION GO?
YOO HOO! SABRINA!
YOUR AUNT HILDA CALLED TO SEE IF YOU WERE HERE! SHE WANTS YOU TO CALL BACK!
THANKS, POPS!
AH, SABRINA! GLAD I CAUGHT YOU! PICK UP SOME COFFEE ON YOUR WAY HOME, WILL YOU?
OF COURSE, AUNT HILDA!
BY THE WAY, I'VE GOT A GROOVY IDEA FOR POOR ARCHIE! THE *CHARM CHANT*!
WHICH ONE?

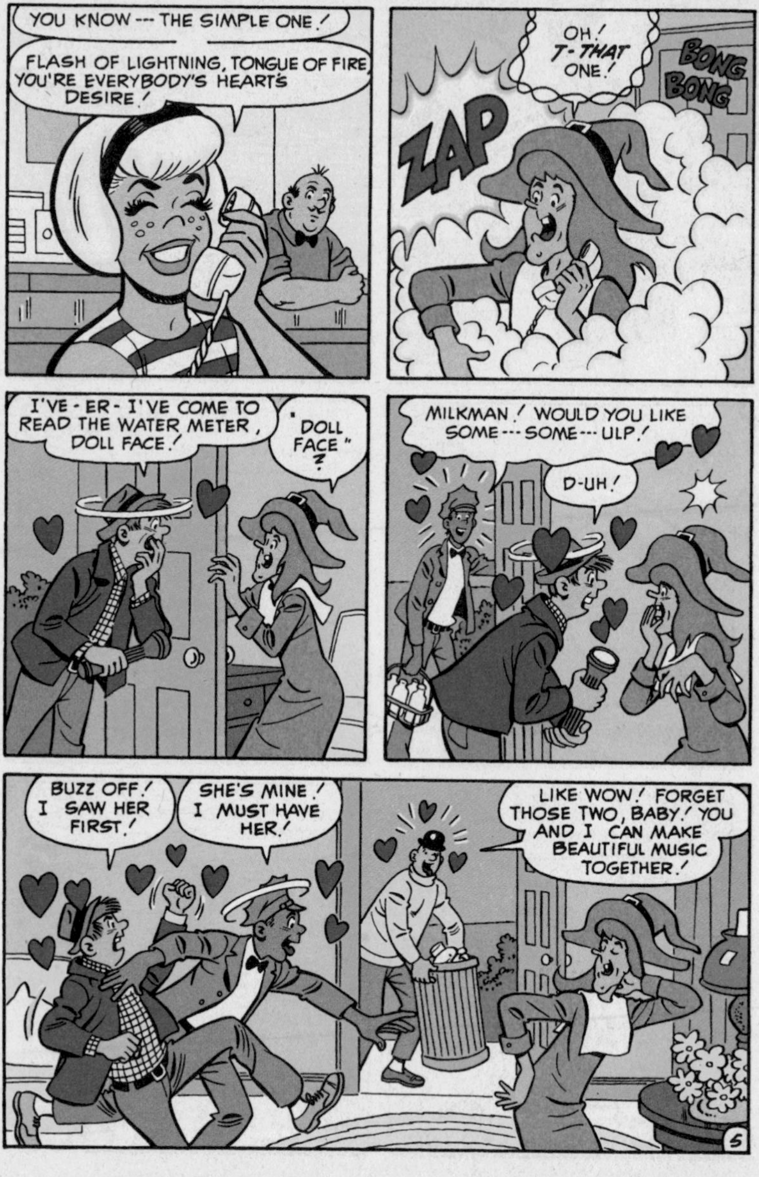

YOU KNOW --- THE SIMPLE ONE!
FLASH OF LIGHTNING, TONGUE OF FIRE, YOU'RE EVERYBODY'S HEART'S DESIRE!
OH! T-THAT ONE!
BONG BONG
ZAP
I'VE - ER - I'VE COME TO READ THE WATER METER, DOLL FACE!
"DOLL FACE"?
MILKMAN! WOULD YOU LIKE SOME --- SOME --- ULP!
D-UH!
BUZZ OFF! I SAW HER FIRST!
SHE'S MINE! I MUST HAVE HER!
LIKE WOW! FORGET THOSE TWO, BABY! YOU AND I CAN MAKE BEAUTIFUL MUSIC TOGETHER!
5

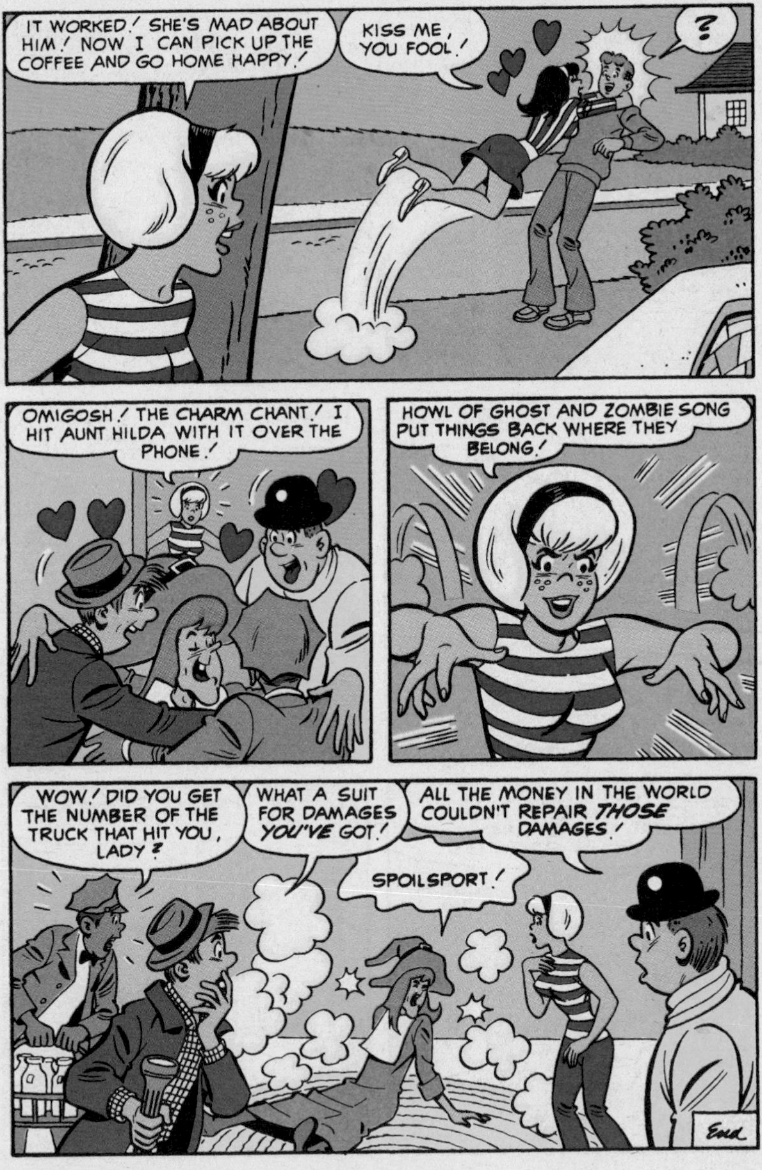
IT WORKED! SHE'S MAD ABOUT HIM! NOW I CAN PICK UP THE COFFEE AND GO HOME HAPPY!
KISS ME, YOU FOOL!
?
OMIGOSH! THE CHARM CHANT! I HIT AUNT HILDA WITH IT OVER THE PHONE!
HOWL OF GHOST AND ZOMBIE SONG PUT THINGS BACK WHERE THEY BELONG!
WOW! DID YOU GET THE NUMBER OF THE TRUCK THAT HIT YOU, LADY?
WHAT A SUIT FOR DAMAGES *YOU'VE* GOT!
ALL THE MONEY IN THE WORLD COULDN'T REPAIR *THOSE* DAMAGES!
SPOILSPORT!
End

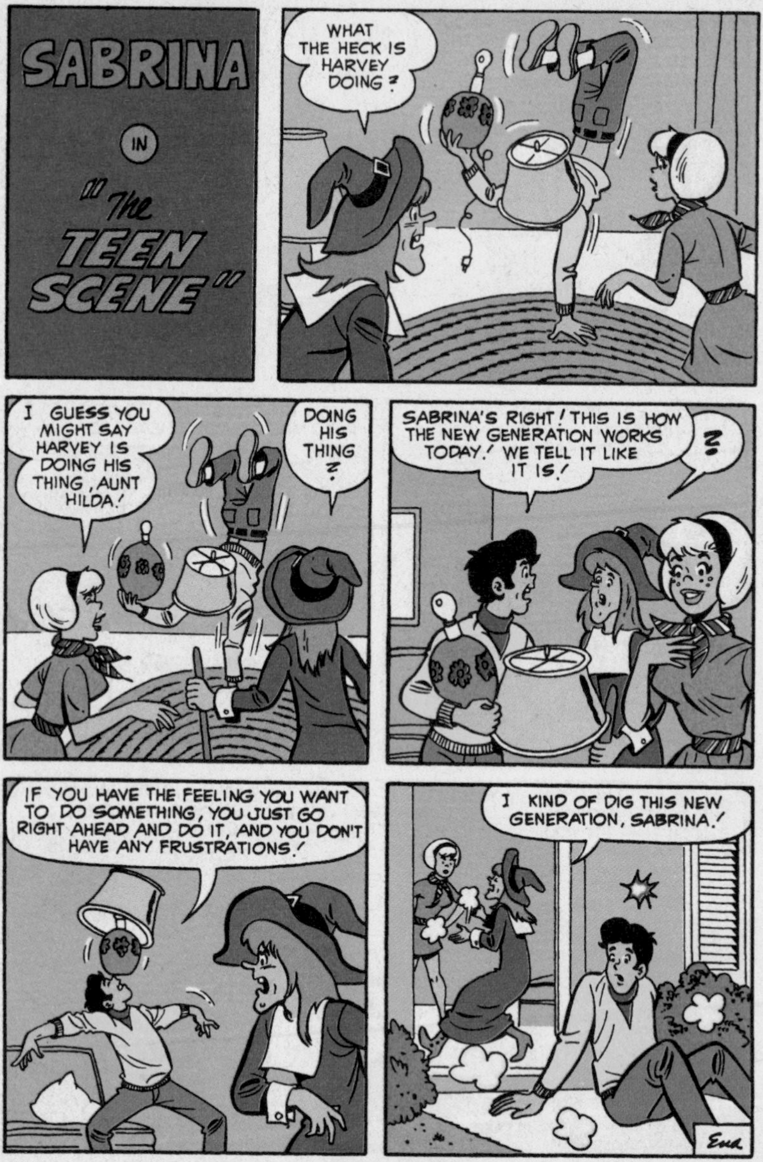
SABRINA
IN
"The TEEN SCENE"
WHAT THE HECK IS HARVEY DOING ?
I GUESS YOU MIGHT SAY HARVEY IS DOING HIS THING, AUNT HILDA!
DOING HIS THING ?
SABRINA'S RIGHT! THIS IS HOW THE NEW GENERATION WORKS TODAY! WE TELL IT LIKE IT IS!
?
IF YOU HAVE THE FEELING YOU WANT TO DO SOMETHING, YOU JUST GO RIGHT AHEAD AND DO IT, AND YOU DON'T HAVE ANY FRUSTRATIONS!
I KIND OF DIG THIS NEW GENERATION, SABRINA!
End

ALL HAIL.

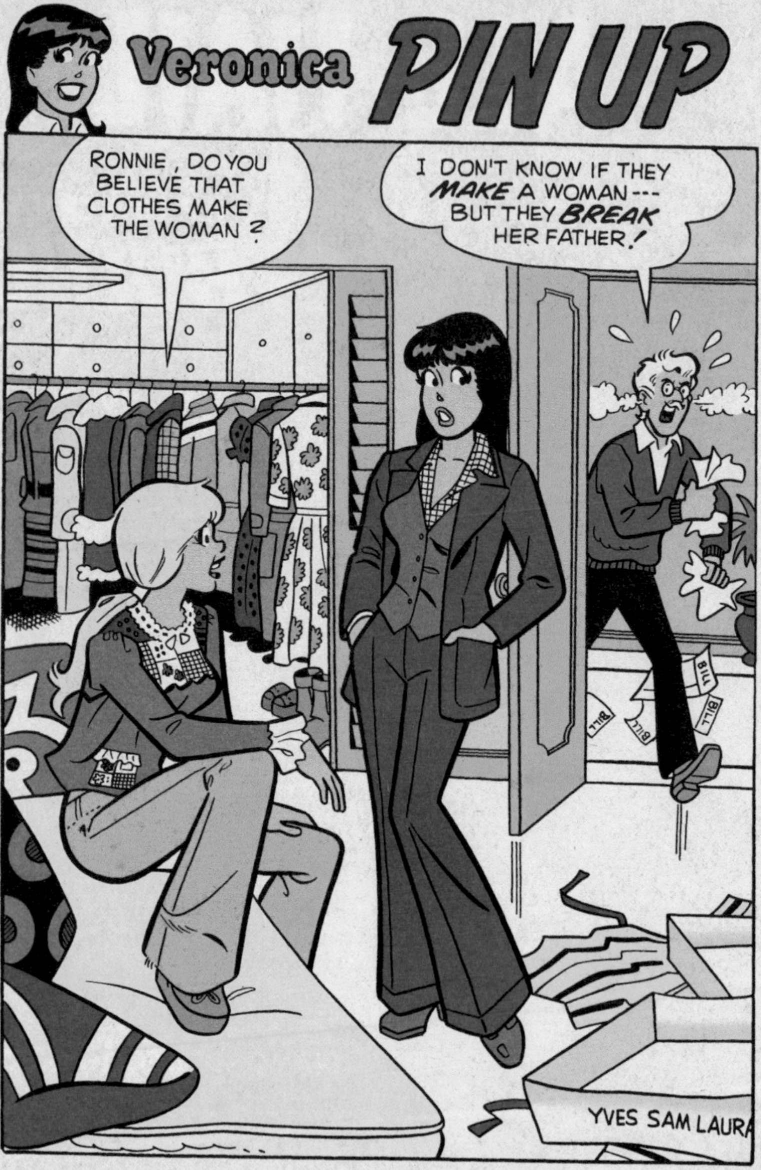
Veronica PIN UP
RONNIE, DO YOU BELIEVE THAT CLOTHES MAKE THE WOMAN?
I DON'T KNOW IF THEY MAKE A WOMAN--- BUT THEY BREAK HER FATHER!
BILL
BILL
BILL
BILL
YVES SAM LAURA

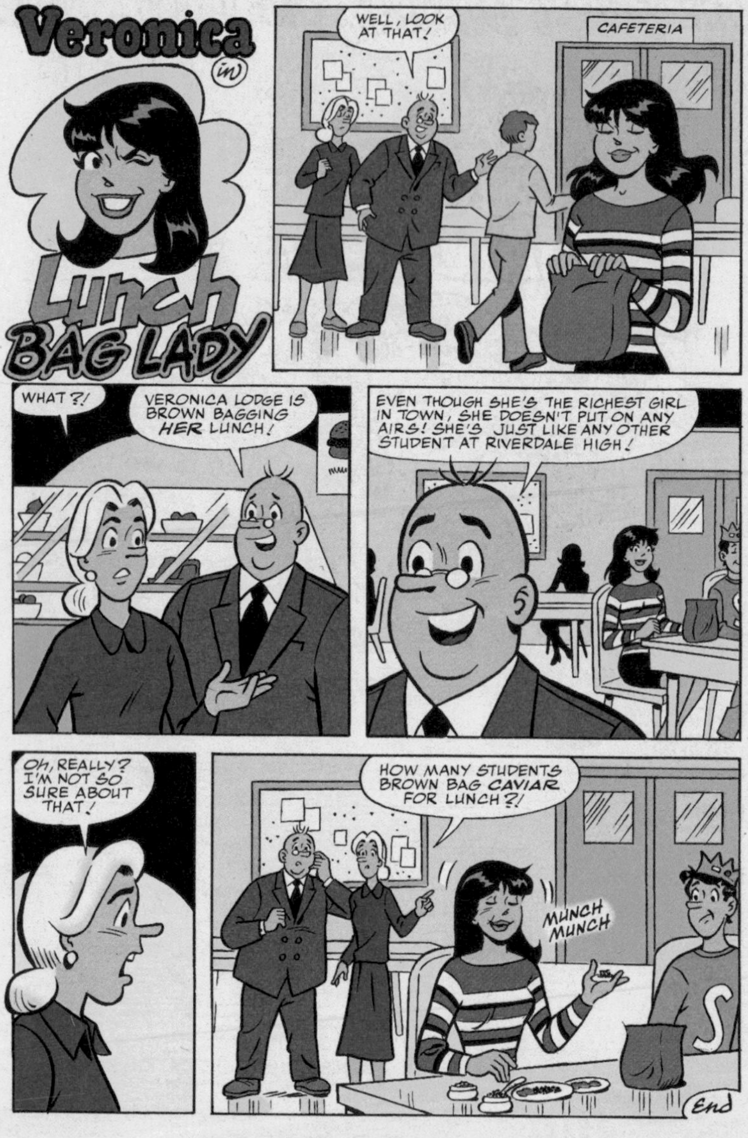
Veronica
in
Lunch BAG LADY
CAFETERIA
WELL, LOOK AT THAT!
WHAT?!
VERONICA LODGE IS BROWN BAGGING HER LUNCH!
EVEN THOUGH SHE'S THE RICHEST GIRL IN TOWN, SHE DOESN'T PUT ON ANY AIRS! SHE'S JUST LIKE ANY OTHER STUDENT AT RIVERDALE HIGH!
OH, REALLY? I'M NOT SO SURE ABOUT THAT!
HOW MANY STUDENTS BROWN BAG CAVIAR FOR LUNCH?!
MUNCH MUNCH
End

Star Struck
Laugh #267, 1973
by Stan Goldberg and Jon D'Agostino

Archie Comics were probably put in my hand at a very young age because they were definitely the first comics I ever read and pretty much the only ones I had access to as a child. You really have to go out of your way to get into superhero comics or anything like that, and you can only really buy them at specialty comic shops, which is not the case with Archie, obviously; it sold at every grocery store and gas station. My parents just gave them to me and my brother and I've read them for my whole life.

Fiona Staples
Eisner Award-winning Artist,
Artist for the new Archie series

The Me-ning of Life
Veronica #42, 1995
by Angelo DeCesare, Stan Goldberg,
Henry Scarpelli and Bill Yoshida

When vast wealth is mixed together with the emotional rollercoaster that comes from being a teen, trouble will almost certainly occur. "The Me-ning of Life" focuses on a dream that has Veronica indulging her most selfish whims and acting as spoiled as can be. Ladies and gentlemen, welcome to Veronicaville!

Archie in STAR STRUCK

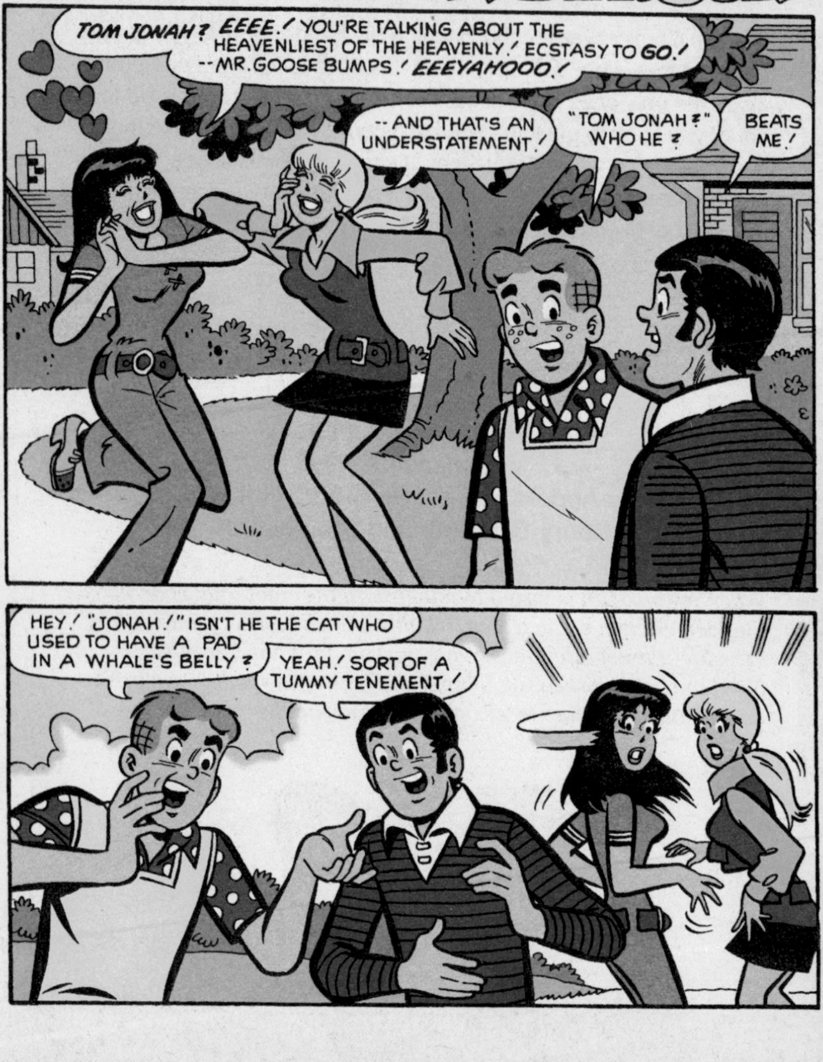
TOM JONAH? EEEE.! YOU'RE TALKING ABOUT THE HEAVENLIEST OF THE HEAVENLY.! ECSTASY TO GO.! --MR. GOOSE BUMPS.! EEEYAHOOO.!
-- AND THAT'S AN UNDERSTATEMENT.!
"TOM JONAH?" WHO HE?
BEATS ME.!
HEY.! "JONAH.!" ISN'T HE THE CAT WHO USED TO HAVE A PAD IN A WHALE'S BELLY?
YEAH.! SORT OF A TUMMY TENEMENT.!

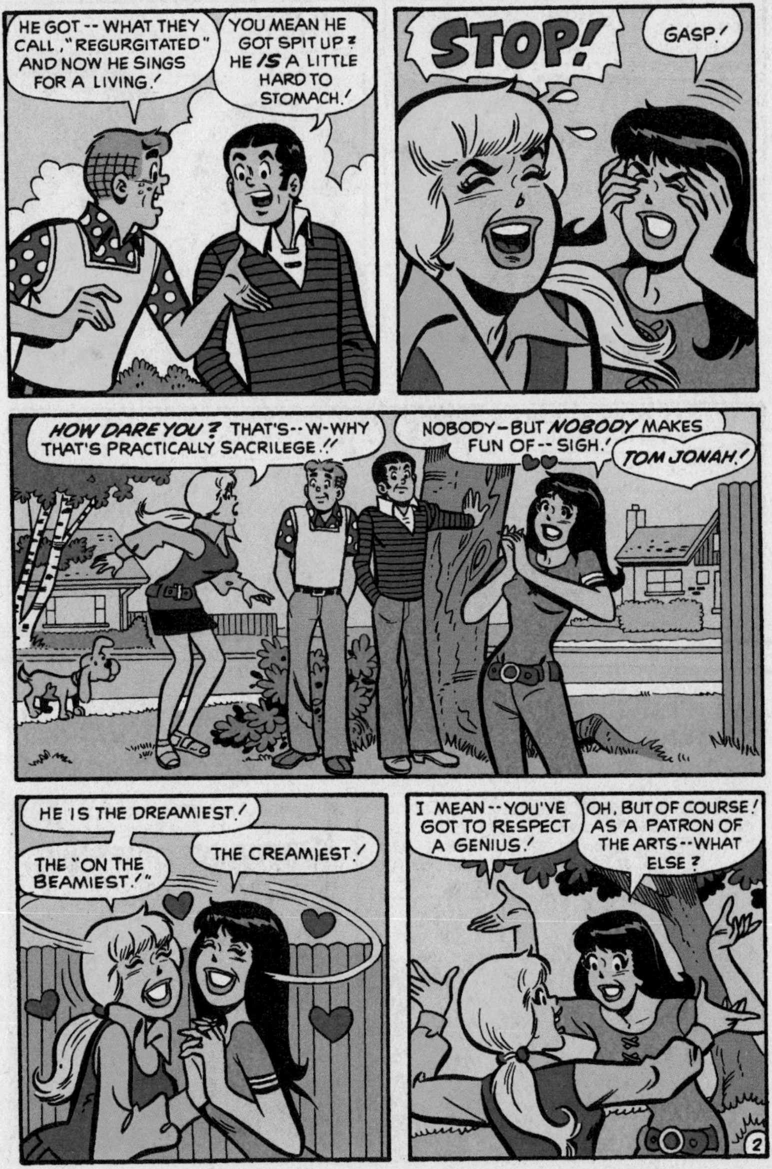
HE GOT -- WHAT THEY CALL, "REGURGITATED" AND NOW HE SINGS FOR A LIVING!
YOU MEAN HE GOT SPIT UP? HE IS A LITTLE HARD TO STOMACH!
STOP!
GASP!
HOW DARE YOU? THAT'S -- W-WHY THAT'S PRACTICALLY SACRILEGE!!
NOBODY -- BUT NOBODY MAKES FUN OF -- SIGH!
TOM JONAH!
HE IS THE DREAMIEST!
THE "ON THE BEAMIEST!"
THE CREAMIEST!
I MEAN -- YOU'VE GOT TO RESPECT A GENIUS!
OH, BUT OF COURSE! AS A PATRON OF THE ARTS -- WHAT ELSE?
2

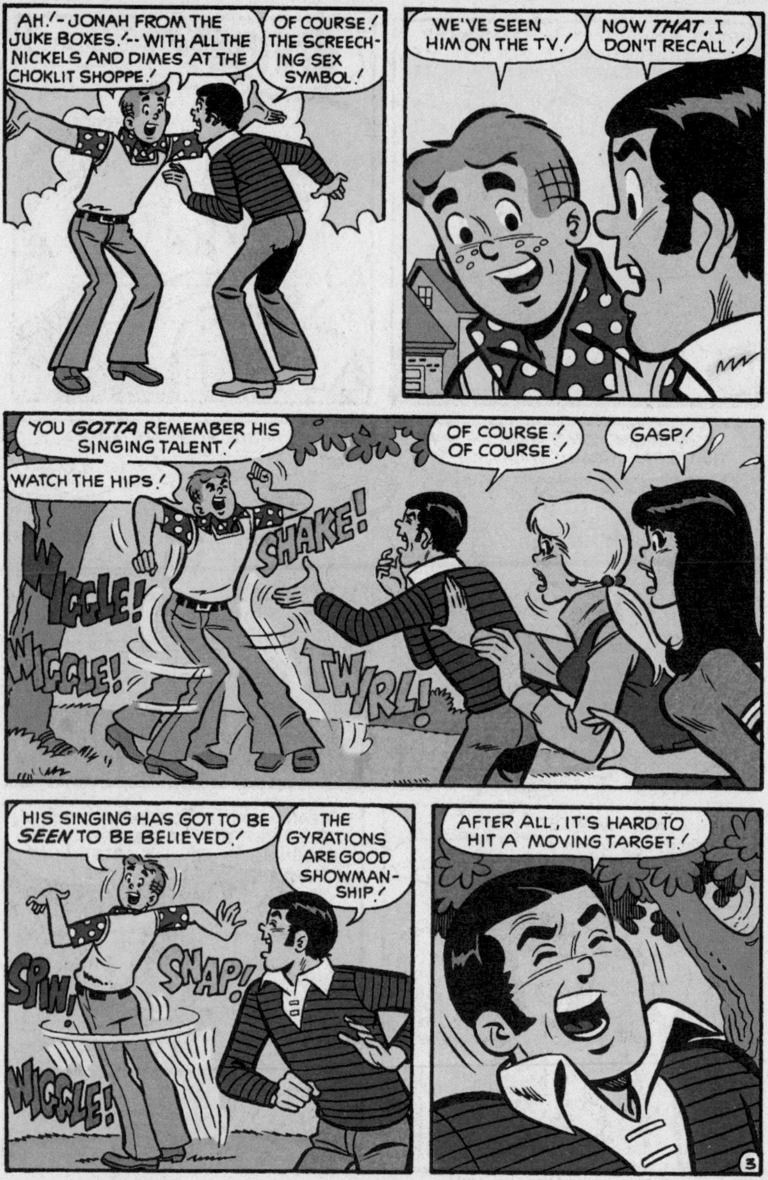
AH.! - JONAH FROM THE JUKE BOXES.! -- WITH ALL THE NICKELS AND DIMES AT THE CHOKLIT SHOPPE.!
OF COURSE.! THE SCREECHING SEX SYMBOL.!
WE'VE SEEN HIM ON THE TV.!
NOW *THAT*, I DON'T RECALL.!
YOU *GOTTA* REMEMBER HIS SINGING TALENT.!
WATCH THE HIPS.!
WIGGLE!
WIGGLE!
SHAKE!
TWIRL!
OF COURSE.! OF COURSE.!
GASP.!
HIS SINGING HAS GOT TO BE *SEEN* TO BE BELIEVED.!
THE GYRATIONS ARE GOOD SHOWMANSHIP.!
SPIN!
SNAP!
WIGGLE!
AFTER ALL, IT'S HARD TO HIT A MOVING TARGET.!
3

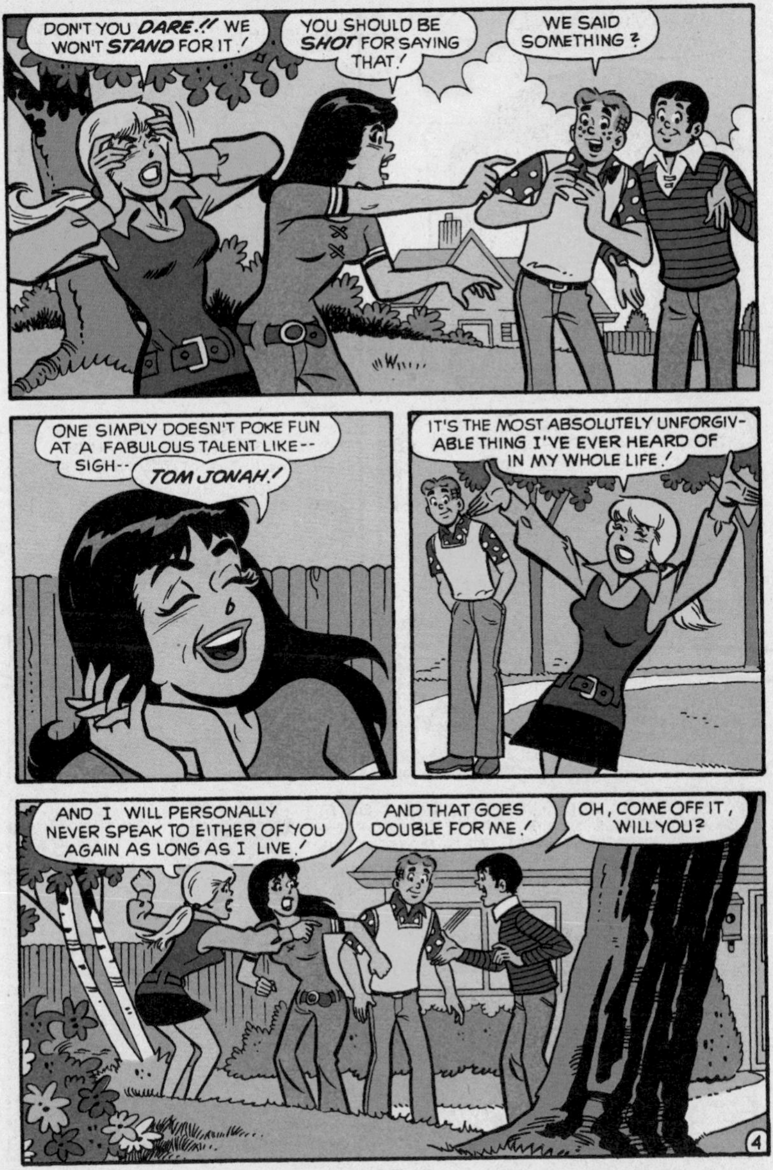
DON'T YOU DARE.!! WE WON'T STAND FOR IT!
YOU SHOULD BE SHOT FOR SAYING THAT!
WE SAID SOMETHING?
ONE SIMPLY DOESN'T POKE FUN AT A FABULOUS TALENT LIKE-- SIGH--
TOM JONAH!
IT'S THE MOST ABSOLUTELY UNFORGIV-ABLE THING I'VE EVER HEARD OF IN MY WHOLE LIFE!
AND I WILL PERSONALLY NEVER SPEAK TO EITHER OF YOU AGAIN AS LONG AS I LIVE!
AND THAT GOES DOUBLE FOR ME!
OH, COME OFF IT, WILL YOU?
4

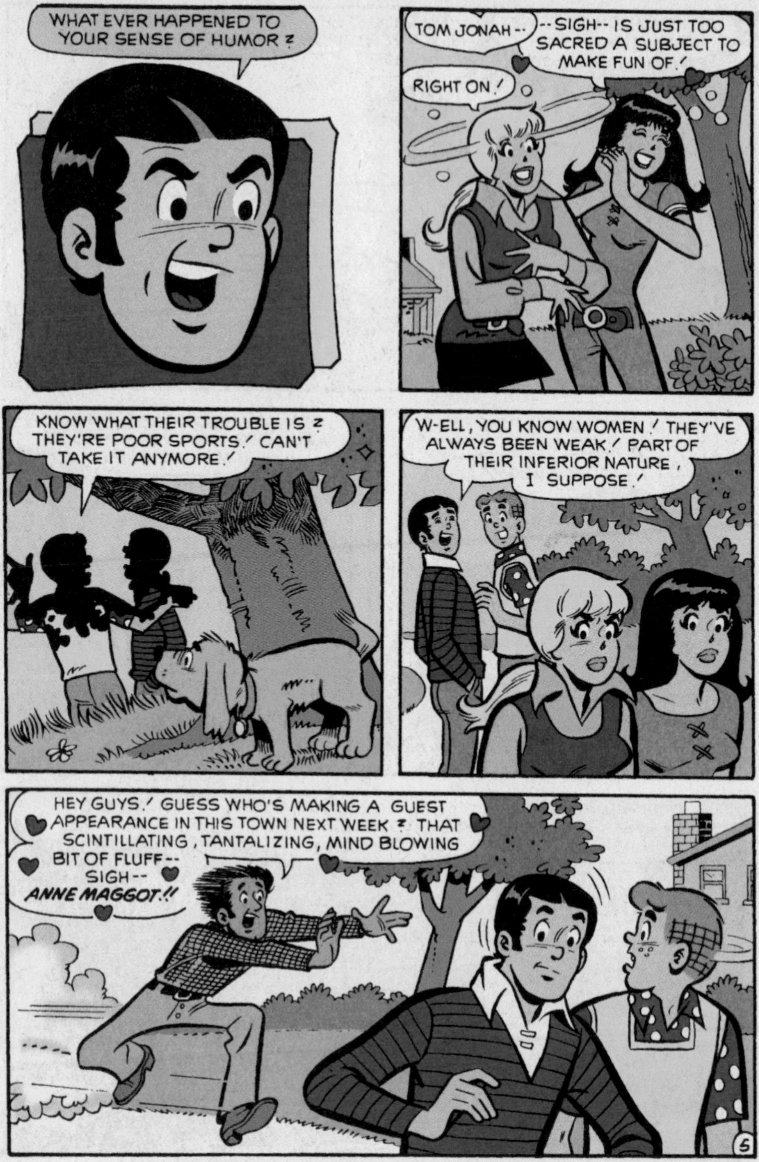
WHAT EVER HAPPENED TO YOUR SENSE OF HUMOR ?
TOM JONAH --
-- SIGH -- IS JUST TOO SACRED A SUBJECT TO MAKE FUN OF!
RIGHT ON!
KNOW WHAT THEIR TROUBLE IS ? THEY'RE POOR SPORTS! CAN'T TAKE IT ANYMORE!
W-ELL, YOU KNOW WOMEN! THEY'VE ALWAYS BEEN WEAK! PART OF THEIR INFERIOR NATURE, I SUPPOSE!
HEY GUYS! GUESS WHO'S MAKING A GUEST APPEARANCE IN THIS TOWN NEXT WEEK ? THAT SCINTILLATING, TANTALIZING, MIND BLOWING BIT OF FLUFF -- SIGH -- ANNE MAGGOT!!
5

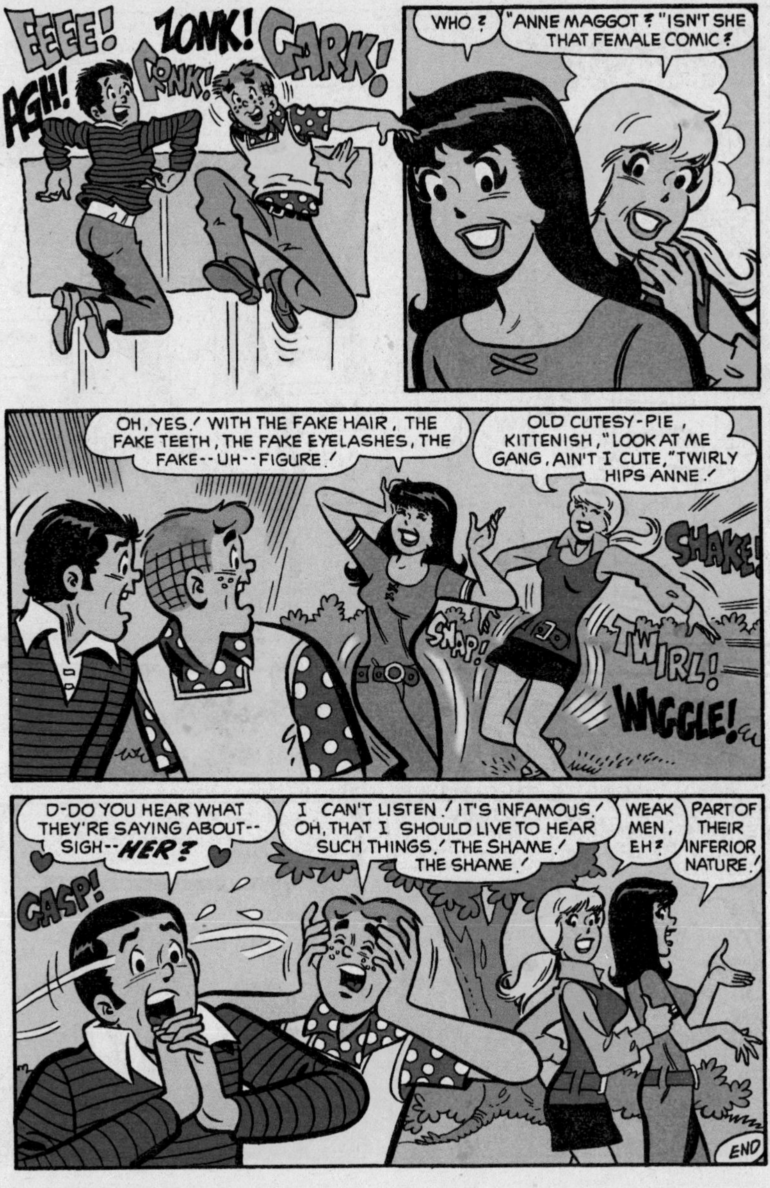
EEEE!
AGH!
ZONK!
CONK!
GARK!
WHO?
"ANNE MAGGOT?" ISN'T SHE THAT FEMALE COMIC?
OH, YES! WITH THE FAKE HAIR, THE FAKE TEETH, THE FAKE EYELASHES, THE FAKE--UH--FIGURE!
OLD CUTESY-PIE, KITTENISH, "LOOK AT ME GANG, AIN'T I CUTE," TWIRLY HIPS ANNE!
SHAKE!
SNAP!
TWIRL!
WIGGLE!
D-DO YOU HEAR WHAT THEY'RE SAYING ABOUT-- SIGH--HER?
GASP!
I CAN'T LISTEN! IT'S INFAMOUS! OH, THAT I SHOULD LIVE TO HEAR SUCH THINGS! THE SHAME! THE SHAME!
WEAK MEN, EH?
PART OF THEIR INFERIOR NATURE!
END

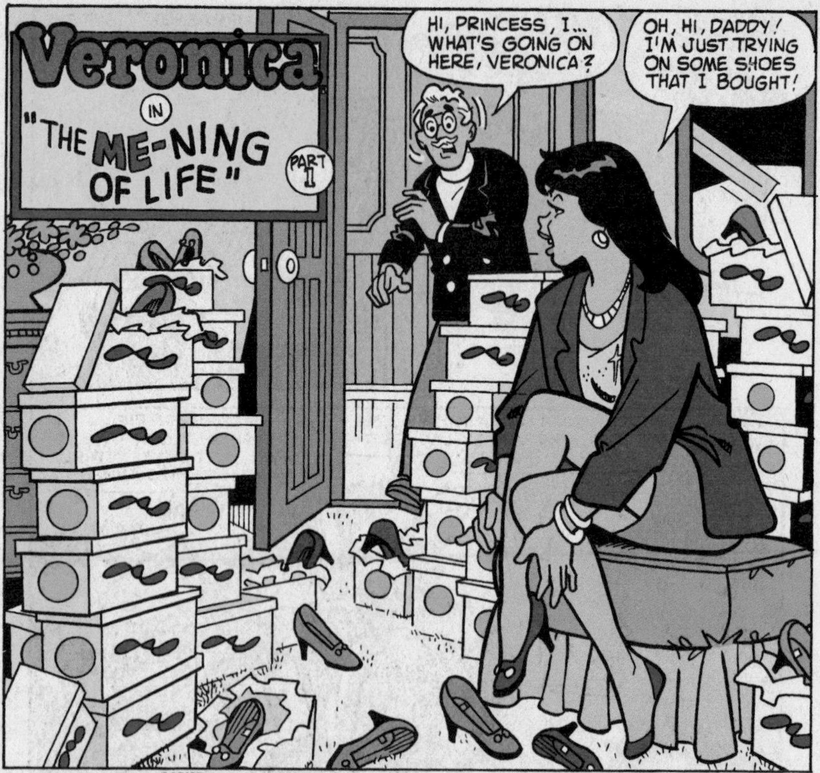
Veronica
IN
"THE ME-NING OF LIFE"
PART 1
HI, PRINCESS, I... WHAT'S GOING ON HERE, VERONICA?
OH, HI, DADDY! I'M JUST TRYING ON SOME SHOES THAT I BOUGHT!

SCRIPT: ANGELO DECESARE   PENCILS: STAN GOLDBERG   INKS: HENRY SCARPELLI   LETTERING: BILL YOSHIDA   COLORING: BARRY GROSSMAN

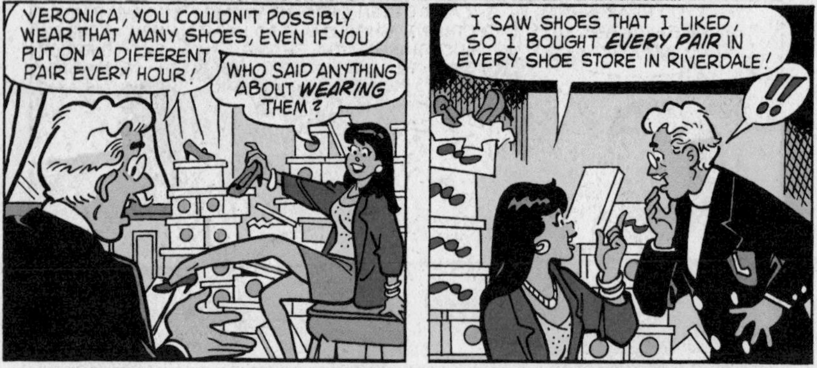
VERONICA, YOU COULDN'T POSSIBLY WEAR THAT MANY SHOES, EVEN IF YOU PUT ON A DIFFERENT PAIR EVERY HOUR!
WHO SAID ANYTHING ABOUT *WEARING* THEM?
I SAW SHOES THAT I LIKED, SO I BOUGHT *EVERY PAIR* IN EVERY SHOE STORE IN RIVERDALE!
!!

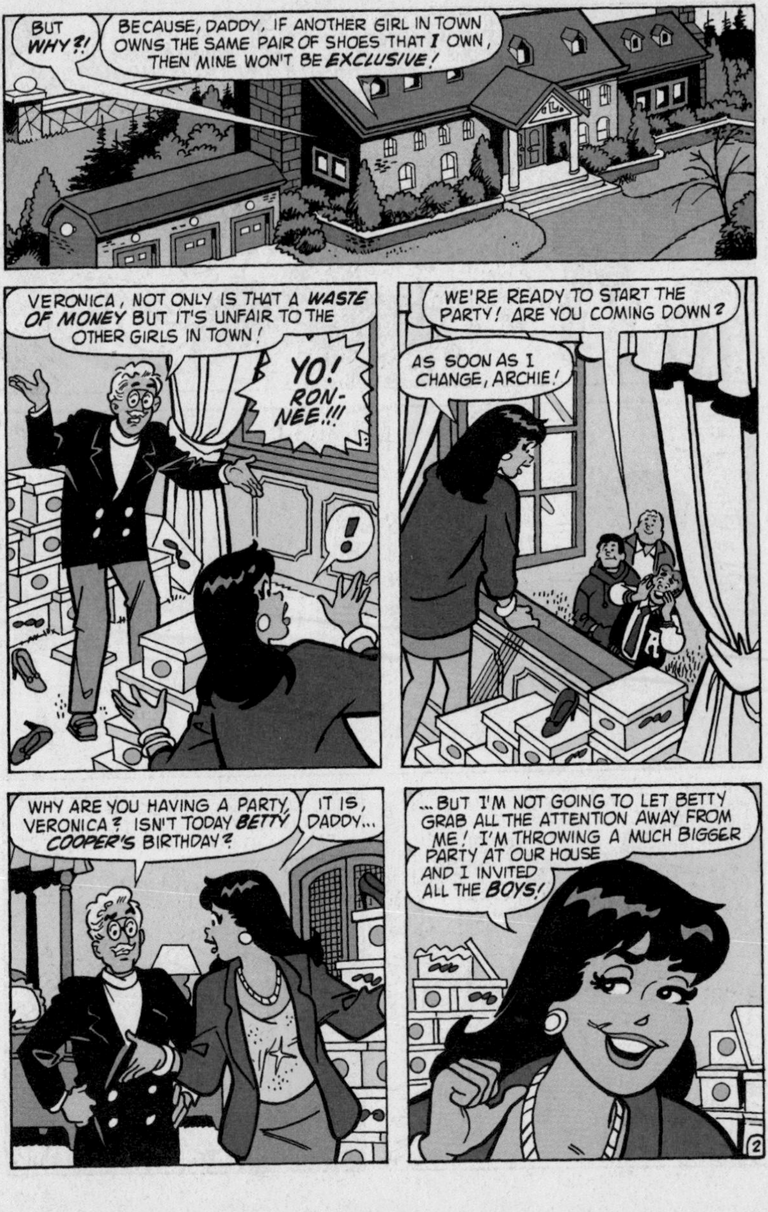
BUT WHY?!
BECAUSE, DADDY, IF ANOTHER GIRL IN TOWN OWNS THE SAME PAIR OF SHOES THAT I OWN, THEN MINE WON'T BE EXCLUSIVE!
VERONICA, NOT ONLY IS THAT A WASTE OF MONEY BUT IT'S UNFAIR TO THE OTHER GIRLS IN TOWN!
YO! RON-NEE!!!
!
WE'RE READY TO START THE PARTY! ARE YOU COMING DOWN?
AS SOON AS I CHANGE, ARCHIE!
WHY ARE YOU HAVING A PARTY, VERONICA? ISN'T TODAY BETTY COOPER'S BIRTHDAY?
IT IS, DADDY...
...BUT I'M NOT GOING TO LET BETTY GRAB ALL THE ATTENTION AWAY FROM ME! I'M THROWING A MUCH BIGGER PARTY AT OUR HOUSE AND I INVITED ALL THE BOYS!
2

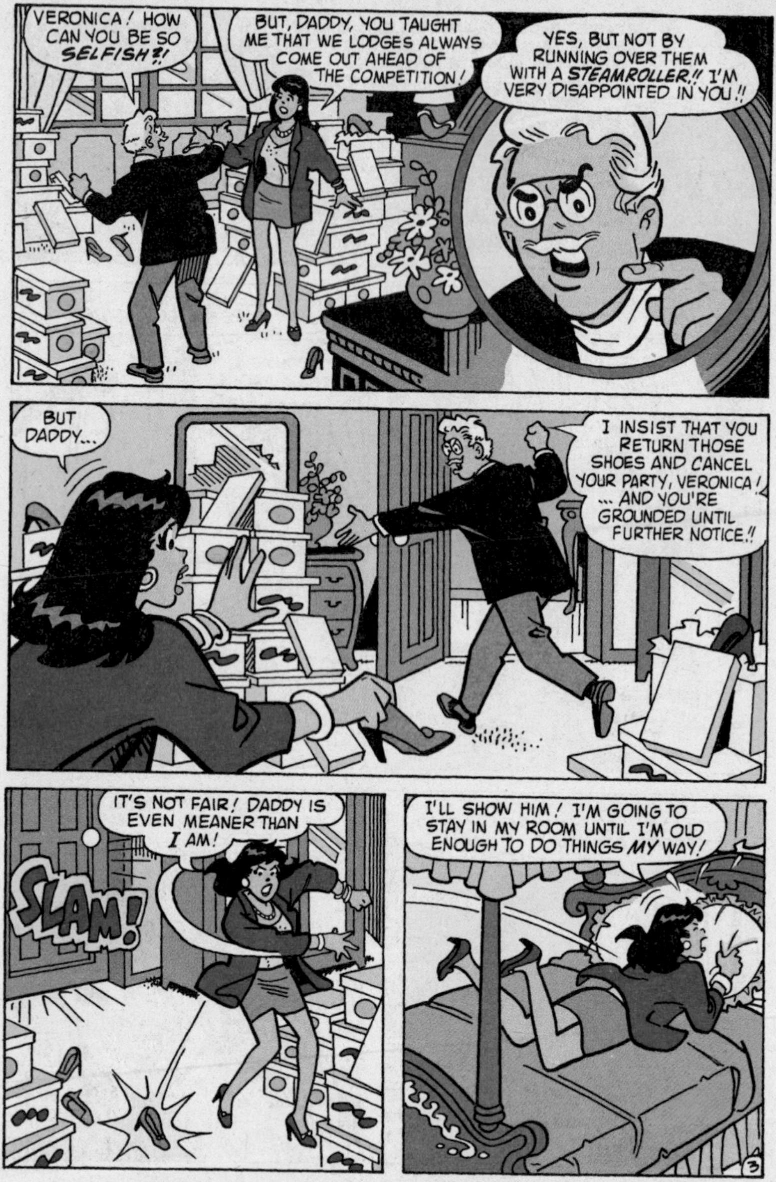
VERONICA! HOW CAN YOU BE SO SELFISH?!
BUT, DADDY, YOU TAUGHT ME THAT WE LODGES ALWAYS COME OUT AHEAD OF THE COMPETITION!
YES, BUT NOT BY RUNNING OVER THEM WITH A STEAMROLLER!! I'M VERY DISAPPOINTED IN YOU!!
BUT DADDY...
I INSIST THAT YOU RETURN THOSE SHOES AND CANCEL YOUR PARTY, VERONICA! ... AND YOU'RE GROUNDED UNTIL FURTHER NOTICE!!
IT'S NOT FAIR! DADDY IS EVEN MEANER THAN I AM!
SLAM!
I'LL SHOW HIM! I'M GOING TO STAY IN MY ROOM UNTIL I'M OLD ENOUGH TO DO THINGS MY WAY!
3

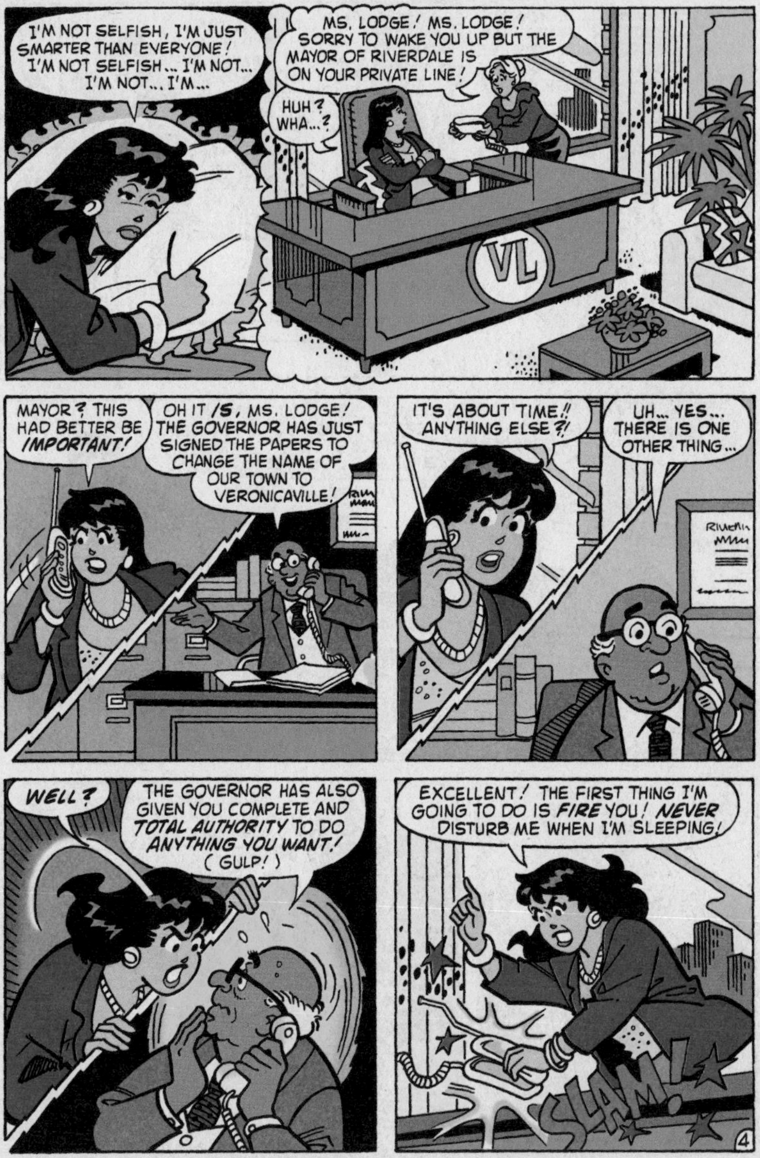
I'M NOT SELFISH, I'M JUST SMARTER THAN EVERYONE! I'M NOT SELFISH... I'M NOT... I'M NOT... I'M...
MS. LODGE! MS. LODGE! SORRY TO WAKE YOU UP BUT THE MAYOR OF RIVERDALE IS ON YOUR PRIVATE LINE!
HUH? WHA...?
VL
MAYOR? THIS HAD BETTER BE IMPORTANT!
OH IT IS, MS. LODGE! THE GOVERNOR HAS JUST SIGNED THE PAPERS TO CHANGE THE NAME OF OUR TOWN TO VERONICAVILLE!
IT'S ABOUT TIME!! ANYTHING ELSE?!
UH... YES... THERE IS ONE OTHER THING...
WELL?
THE GOVERNOR HAS ALSO GIVEN YOU COMPLETE AND TOTAL AUTHORITY TO DO ANYTHING YOU WANT! (GULP!)
EXCELLENT! THE FIRST THING I'M GOING TO DO IS FIRE YOU! NEVER DISTURB ME WHEN I'M SLEEPING!
SLAM!
4

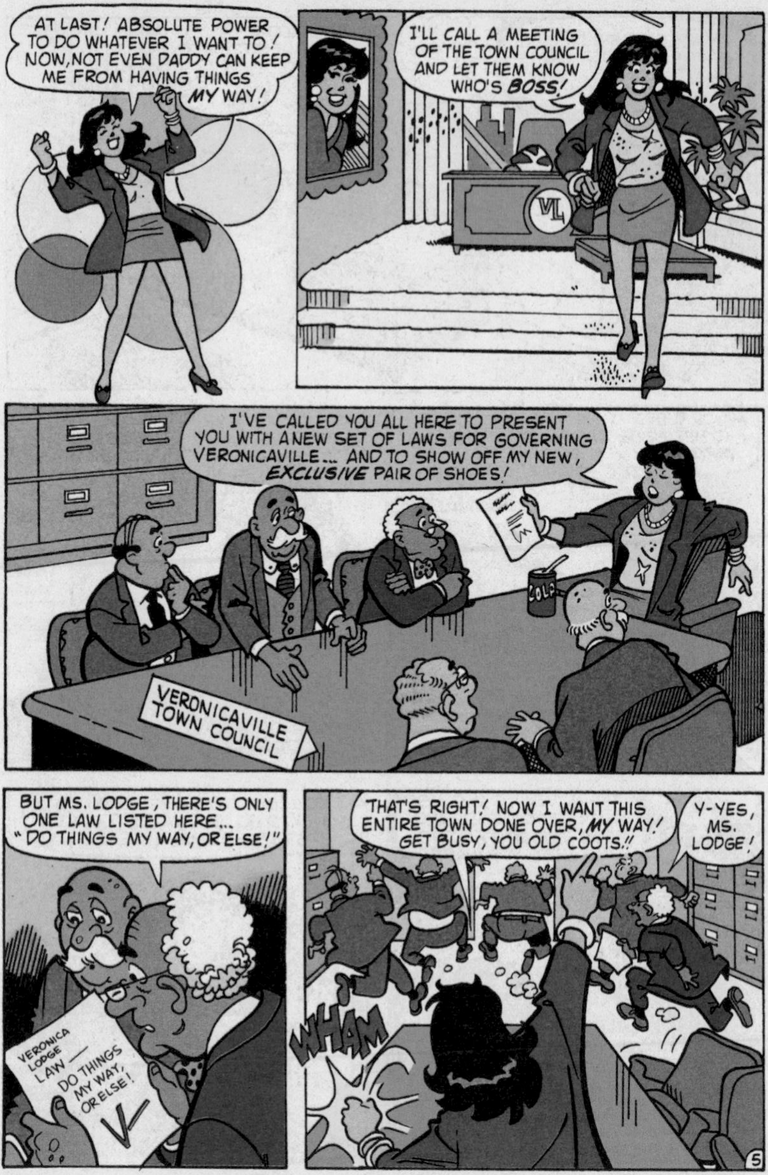
AT LAST! ABSOLUTE POWER TO DO WHATEVER I WANT TO! NOW, NOT EVEN DADDY CAN KEEP ME FROM HAVING THINGS MY WAY!
I'LL CALL A MEETING OF THE TOWN COUNCIL AND LET THEM KNOW WHO'S BOSS!
VL
I'VE CALLED YOU ALL HERE TO PRESENT YOU WITH A NEW SET OF LAWS FOR GOVERNING VERONICAVILLE... AND TO SHOW OFF MY NEW, EXCLUSIVE PAIR OF SHOES!
COLA
VERONICAVILLE TOWN COUNCIL
BUT MS. LODGE, THERE'S ONLY ONE LAW LISTED HERE... "DO THINGS MY WAY, OR ELSE!"
VERONICA LODGE LAW — DO THINGS MY WAY, OR ELSE!
V
THAT'S RIGHT! NOW I WANT THIS ENTIRE TOWN DONE OVER, MY WAY! GET BUSY, YOU OLD COOTS!!
Y-YES, MS. LODGE!
WHAM

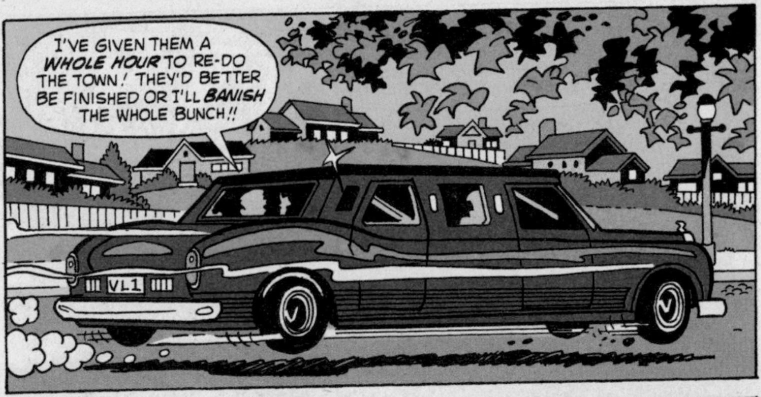
I'VE GIVEN THEM A WHOLE HOUR TO RE-DO THE TOWN! THEY'D BETTER BE FINISHED OR I'LL BANISH THE WHOLE BUNCH!!
VL1

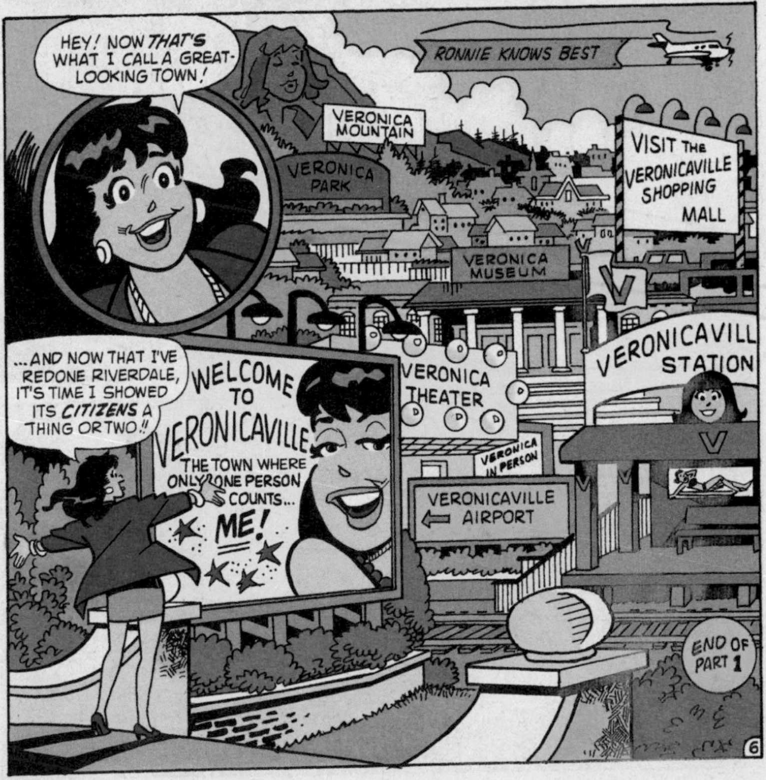
HEY! NOW THAT'S WHAT I CALL A GREAT-LOOKING TOWN!
RONNIE KNOWS BEST
VERONICA MOUNTAIN
VERONICA PARK
VISIT THE VERONICAVILLE SHOPPING MALL
VERONICA MUSEUM
...AND NOW THAT I'VE REDONE RIVERDALE, IT'S TIME I SHOWED ITS CITIZENS A THING OR TWO!!
WELCOME TO VERONICAVILLE THE TOWN WHERE ONLY ONE PERSON COUNTS... ME!
VERONICA THEATER
VERONICAVILL STATION
VERONICA IN PERSON
VERONICAVILLE AIRPORT
END OF PART 1
6

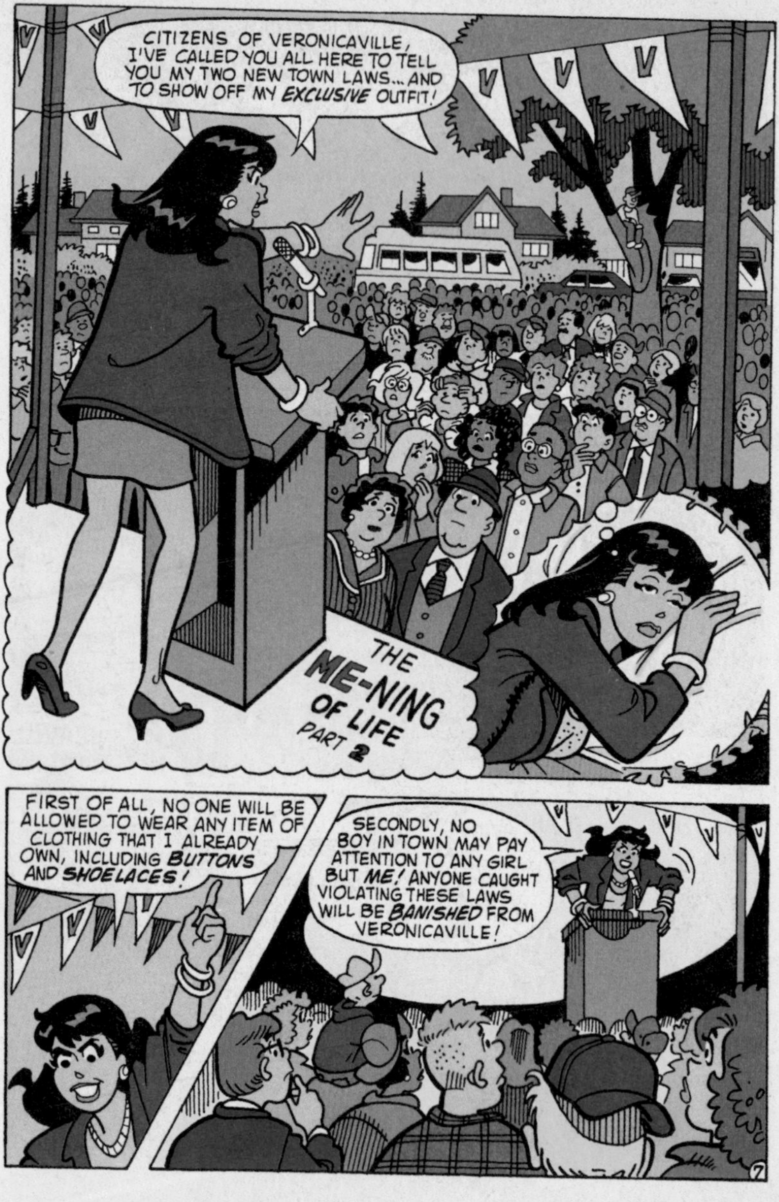
CITIZENS OF VERONICAVILLE, I'VE CALLED YOU ALL HERE TO TELL YOU MY TWO NEW TOWN LAWS... AND TO SHOW OFF MY EXCLUSIVE OUTFIT!
THE ME-NING OF LIFE PART 2
FIRST OF ALL, NO ONE WILL BE ALLOWED TO WEAR ANY ITEM OF CLOTHING THAT I ALREADY OWN, INCLUDING BUTTONS AND SHOELACES!
SECONDLY, NO BOY IN TOWN MAY PAY ATTENTION TO ANY GIRL BUT ME! ANYONE CAUGHT VIOLATING THESE LAWS WILL BE BANISHED FROM VERONICAVILLE!
7

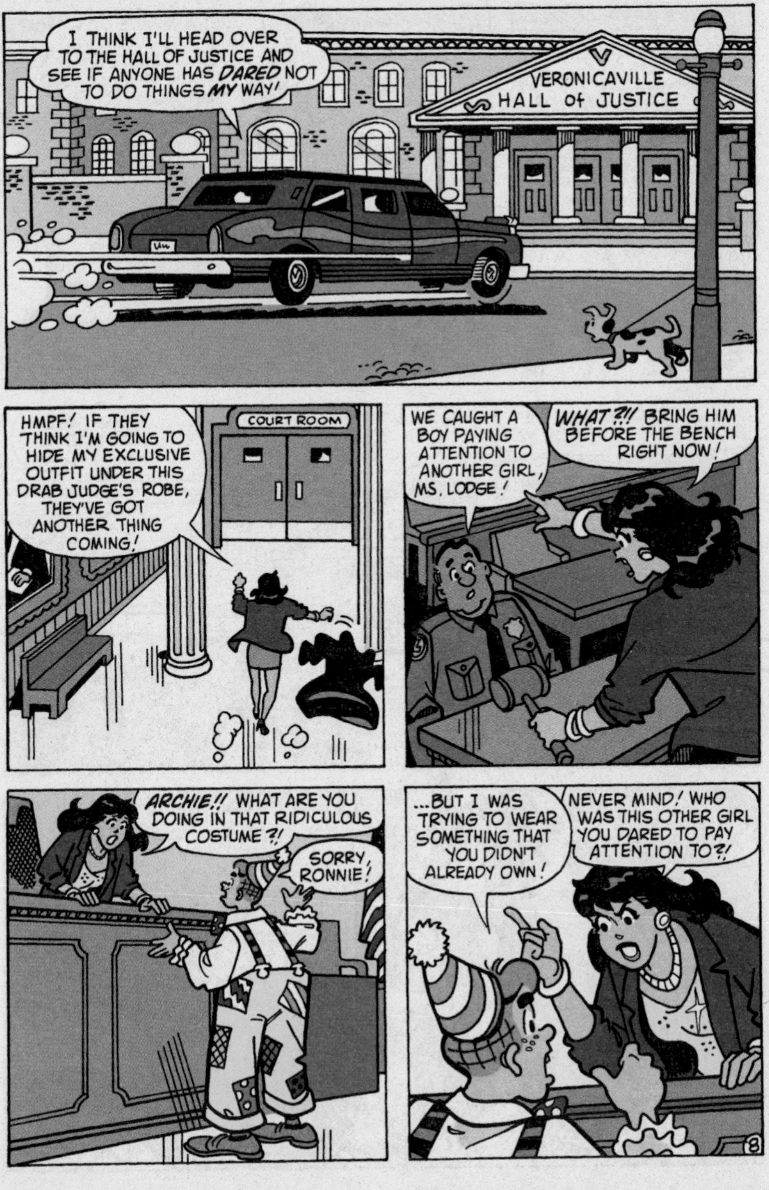

I THINK I'LL HEAD OVER TO THE HALL OF JUSTICE AND SEE IF ANYONE HAS DARED NOT TO DO THINGS MY WAY!
VERONICAVILLE HALL of JUSTICE
HMPF! IF THEY THINK I'M GOING TO HIDE MY EXCLUSIVE OUTFIT UNDER THIS DRAB JUDGE'S ROBE, THEY'VE GOT ANOTHER THING COMING!
COURT ROOM
WE CAUGHT A BOY PAYING ATTENTION TO ANOTHER GIRL, MS. LODGE!
WHAT?!! BRING HIM BEFORE THE BENCH RIGHT NOW!
ARCHIE!! WHAT ARE YOU DOING IN THAT RIDICULOUS COSTUME?!
SORRY, RONNIE!
...BUT I WAS TRYING TO WEAR SOMETHING THAT YOU DIDN'T ALREADY OWN!
NEVER MIND! WHO WAS THIS OTHER GIRL YOU DARED TO PAY ATTENTION TO?!
8

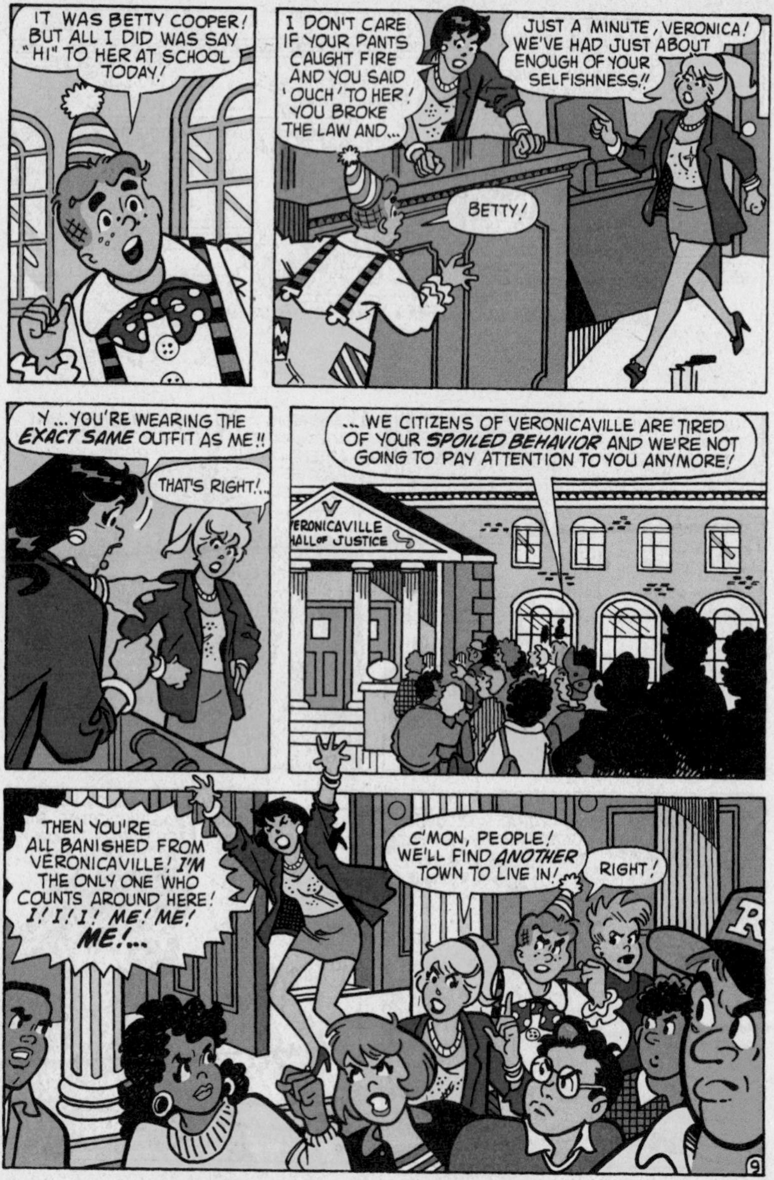
IT WAS BETTY COOPER! BUT ALL I DID WAS SAY "HI" TO HER AT SCHOOL TODAY!
I DON'T CARE IF YOUR PANTS CAUGHT FIRE AND YOU SAID 'OUCH' TO HER! YOU BROKE THE LAW AND...
JUST A MINUTE, VERONICA! WE'VE HAD JUST ABOUT ENOUGH OF YOUR SELFISHNESS!!
BETTY!
Y... YOU'RE WEARING THE EXACT SAME OUTFIT AS ME!!
THAT'S RIGHT!...
... WE CITIZENS OF VERONICAVILLE ARE TIRED OF YOUR SPOILED BEHAVIOR AND WE'RE NOT GOING TO PAY ATTENTION TO YOU ANYMORE!
V
VERONICAVILLE HALL OF JUSTICE
THEN YOU'RE ALL BANISHED FROM VERONICAVILLE! I'M THE ONLY ONE WHO COUNTS AROUND HERE! I! I! I! ME! ME! ME!...
C'MON, PEOPLE! WE'LL FIND ANOTHER TOWN TO LIVE IN!
RIGHT!
9

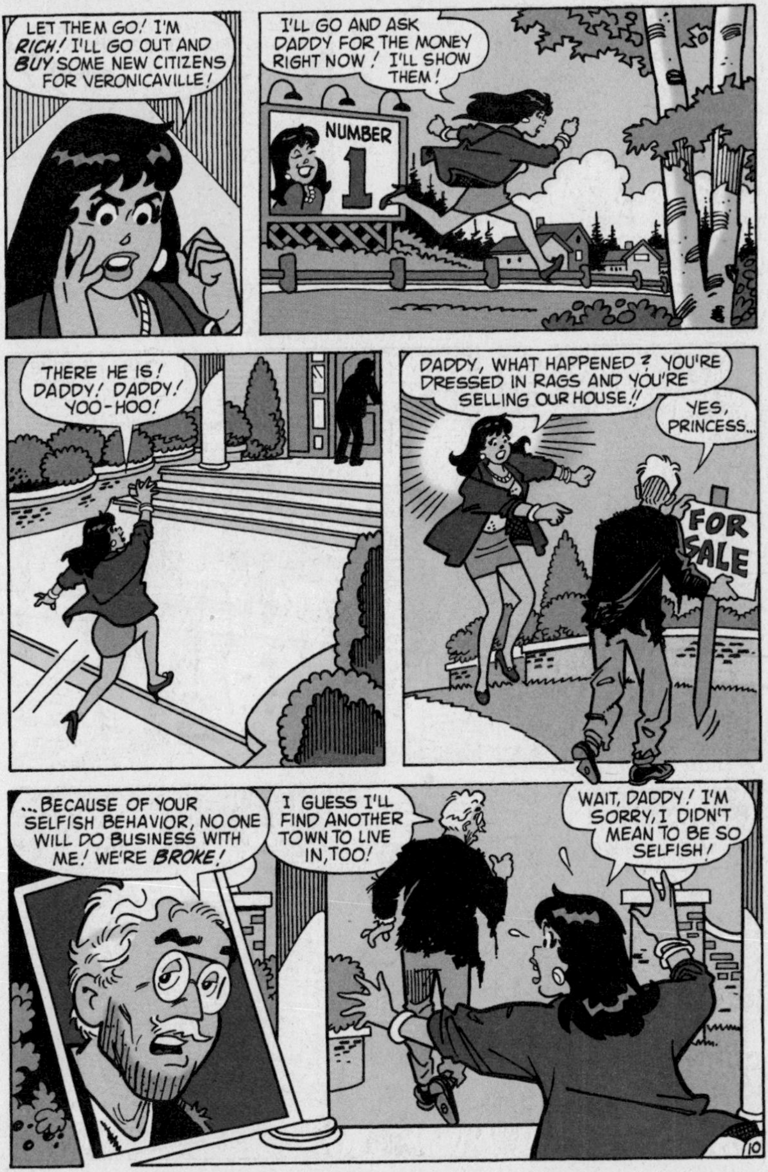
LET THEM GO! I'M RICH! I'LL GO OUT AND BUY SOME NEW CITIZENS FOR VERONICAVILLE!
I'LL GO AND ASK DADDY FOR THE MONEY RIGHT NOW! I'LL SHOW THEM!
NUMBER 1
THERE HE IS! DADDY! DADDY! YOO-HOO!
DADDY, WHAT HAPPENED? YOU'RE DRESSED IN RAGS AND YOU'RE SELLING OUR HOUSE!!
YES, PRINCESS...
FOR SALE
...BECAUSE OF YOUR SELFISH BEHAVIOR, NO ONE WILL DO BUSINESS WITH ME! WE'RE BROKE!
I GUESS I'LL FIND ANOTHER TOWN TO LIVE IN, TOO!
WAIT, DADDY! I'M SORRY, I DIDN'T MEAN TO BE SO SELFISH!
10

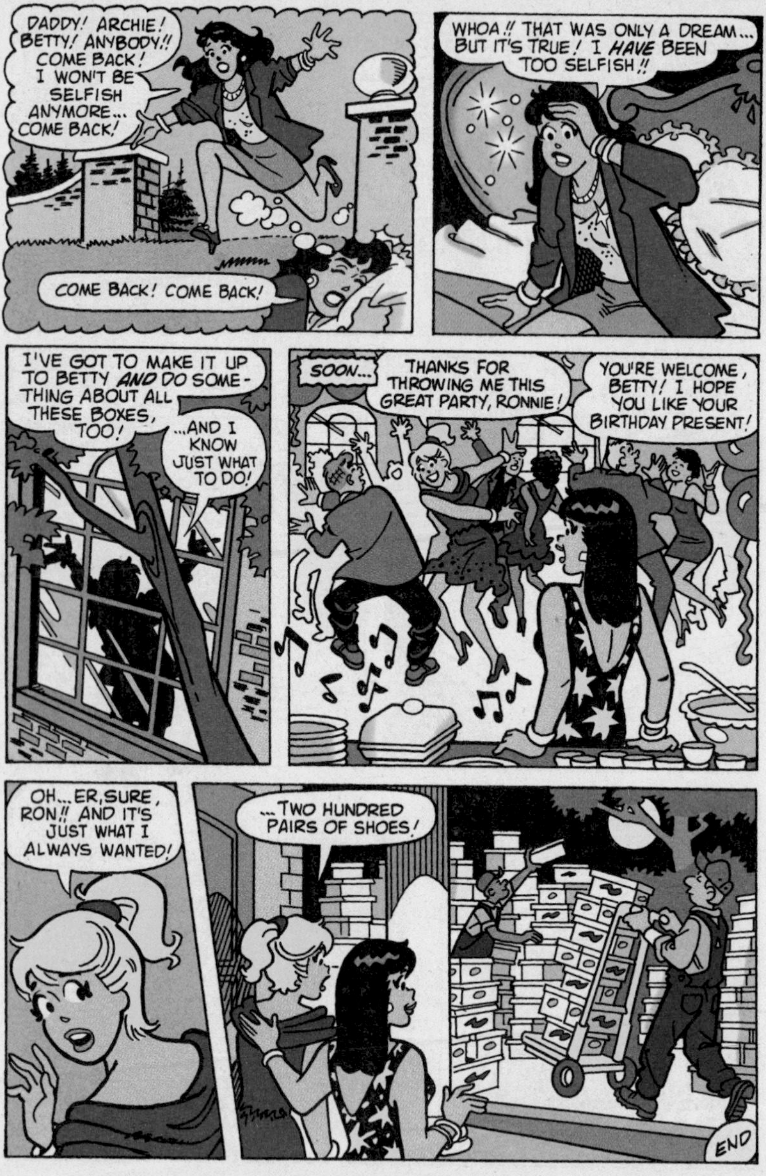
DADDY! ARCHIE! BETTY! ANYBODY!! COME BACK! I WON'T BE SELFISH ANYMORE... COME BACK!
COME BACK! COME BACK!
WHOA!! THAT WAS ONLY A DREAM... BUT IT'S TRUE! I HAVE BEEN TOO SELFISH!!
I'VE GOT TO MAKE IT UP TO BETTY AND DO SOME-THING ABOUT ALL THESE BOXES, TOO!
...AND I KNOW JUST WHAT TO DO!
SOON...
THANKS FOR THROWING ME THIS GREAT PARTY, RONNIE!
YOU'RE WELCOME, BETTY! I HOPE YOU LIKE YOUR BIRTHDAY PRESENT!
OH... ER, SURE, RON!! AND IT'S JUST WHAT I ALWAYS WANTED!
...TWO HUNDRED PAIRS OF SHOES!
END

Guess Again
Laugh #142, 1963
by Frank Doyle, Harry Lucey and Terry Szenics

"Guess Again" features Archie and Reggie trying to get an impartial person to choose which of them will take Veronica to their dance, and to me it spotlights some of my favorite drawings of Betty and Veronica. I think it's the combination of fashion and hairstyles and drawing and storytelling as well as the simple and fun stories that still hold up today.

Jill Thompson
Award-winning Artist,
Scary Godmother

Art Smart
Betty's Diary #1, 1987
by Kathleen Webb, Dan DeCarlo,
Jim DeCarlo and Bill Yoshida

During a trip to the Riverdale Museum of Modern Art, Betty and Veronica swoon over a work that Archie and Jughead find to be absolutely ridiculous. To mock the girls, Jughead creates his own unique piece of modern art in a story that illustrates how beauty may be in the eye of the beholder, but comedy is apparent to everyone.

~BONUS COVER~
Archie's Girls Betty & Veronica #15, November 1954

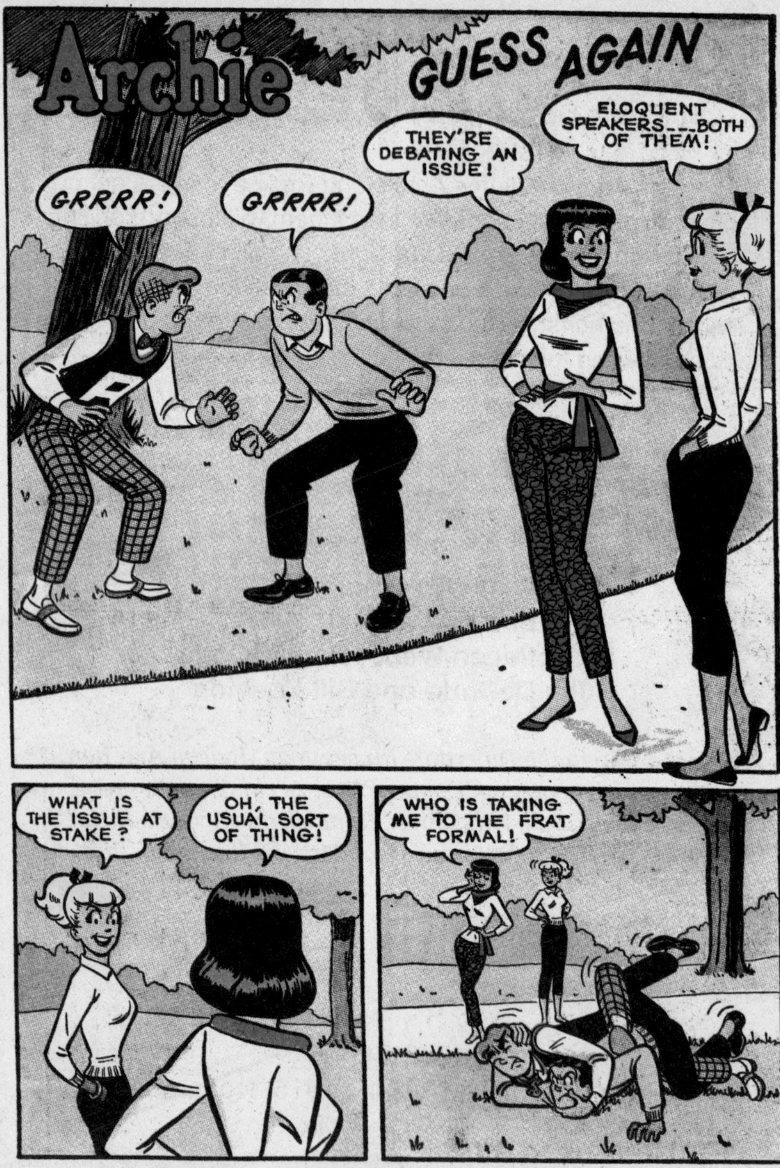
Archie
GUESS AGAIN
GRRRR!
GRRRR!
THEY'RE DEBATING AN ISSUE!
ELOQUENT SPEAKERS---BOTH OF THEM!
WHAT IS THE ISSUE AT STAKE?
OH, THE USUAL SORT OF THING!
WHO IS TAKING ME TO THE FRAT FORMAL!

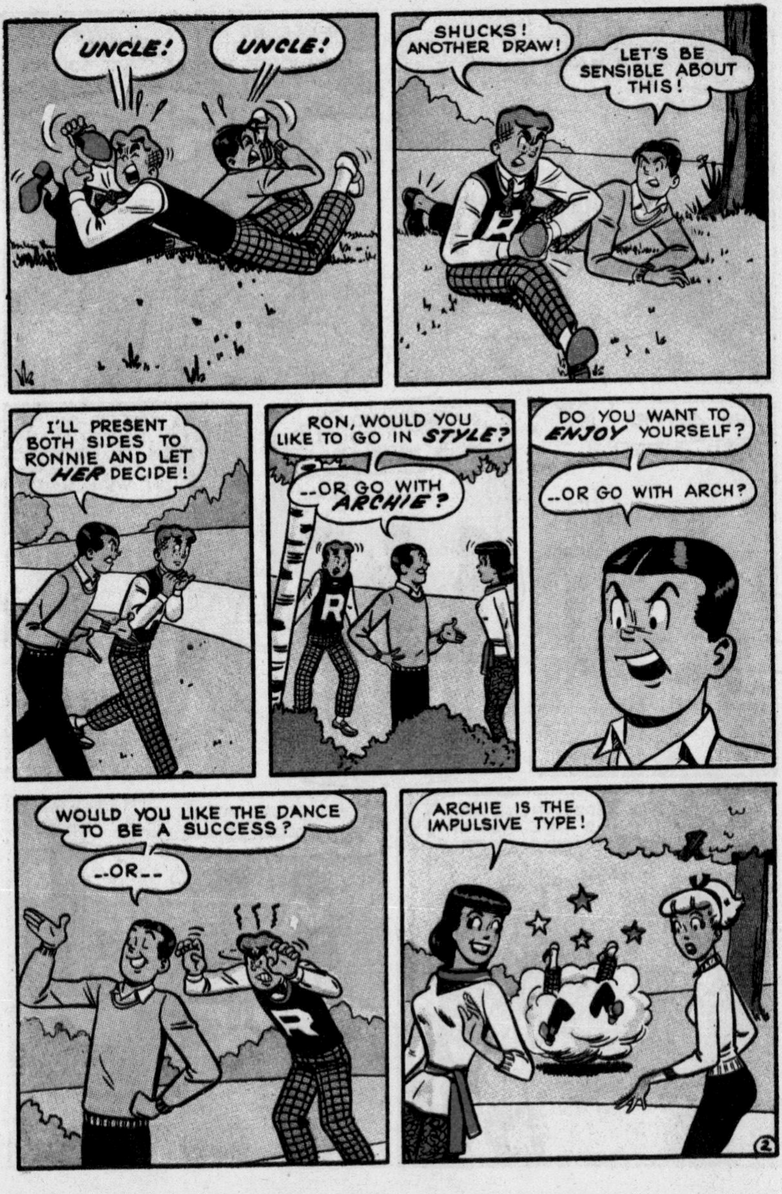
UNCLE!
UNCLE!
SHUCKS! ANOTHER DRAW!
LET'S BE SENSIBLE ABOUT THIS!
I'LL PRESENT BOTH SIDES TO RONNIE AND LET HER DECIDE!
RON, WOULD YOU LIKE TO GO IN STYLE?
--OR GO WITH ARCHIE?
DO YOU WANT TO ENJOY YOURSELF?
--OR GO WITH ARCH?
WOULD YOU LIKE THE DANCE TO BE A SUCCESS?
--OR--
ARCHIE IS THE IMPULSIVE TYPE!
2

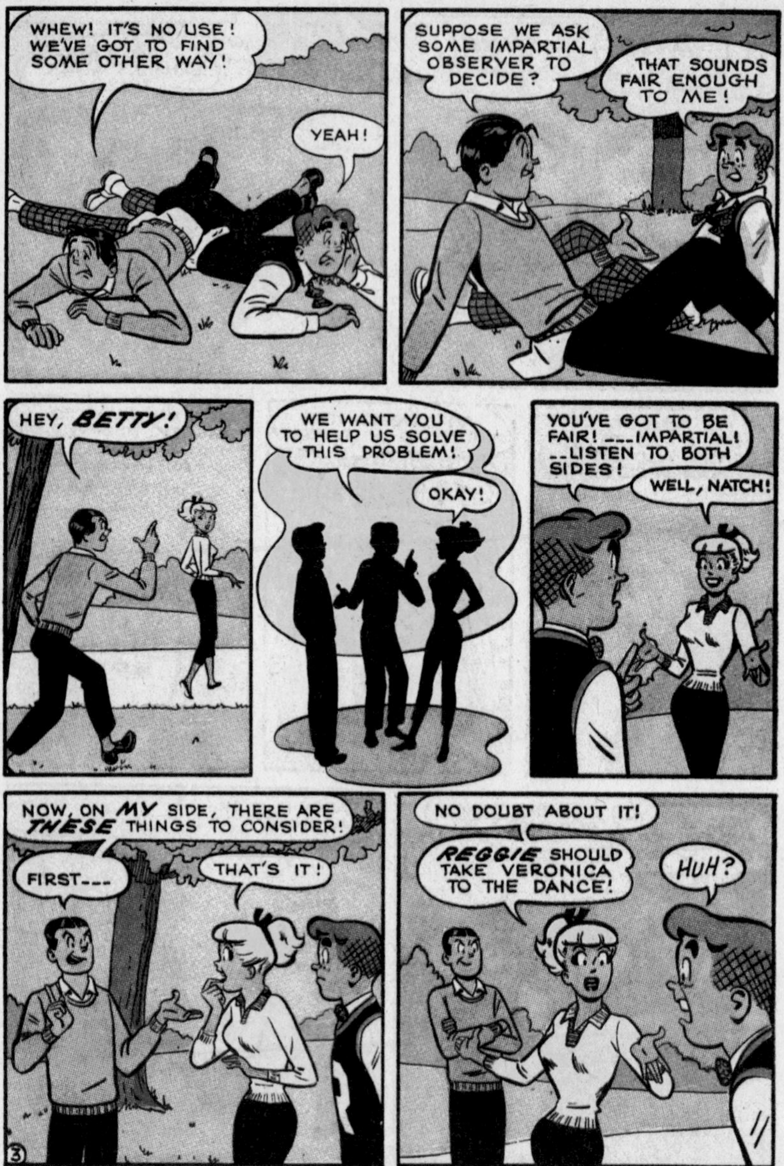
WHEW! IT'S NO USE! WE'VE GOT TO FIND SOME OTHER WAY!
YEAH!
SUPPOSE WE ASK SOME IMPARTIAL OBSERVER TO DECIDE?
THAT SOUNDS FAIR ENOUGH TO ME!
HEY, BETTY!
WE WANT YOU TO HELP US SOLVE THIS PROBLEM!
OKAY!
YOU'VE GOT TO BE FAIR! ---IMPARTIAL! --LISTEN TO BOTH SIDES!
WELL, NATCH!
NOW, ON MY SIDE, THERE ARE THESE THINGS TO CONSIDER!
FIRST---
THAT'S IT!
NO DOUBT ABOUT IT!
REGGIE SHOULD TAKE VERONICA TO THE DANCE!
HUH?
3

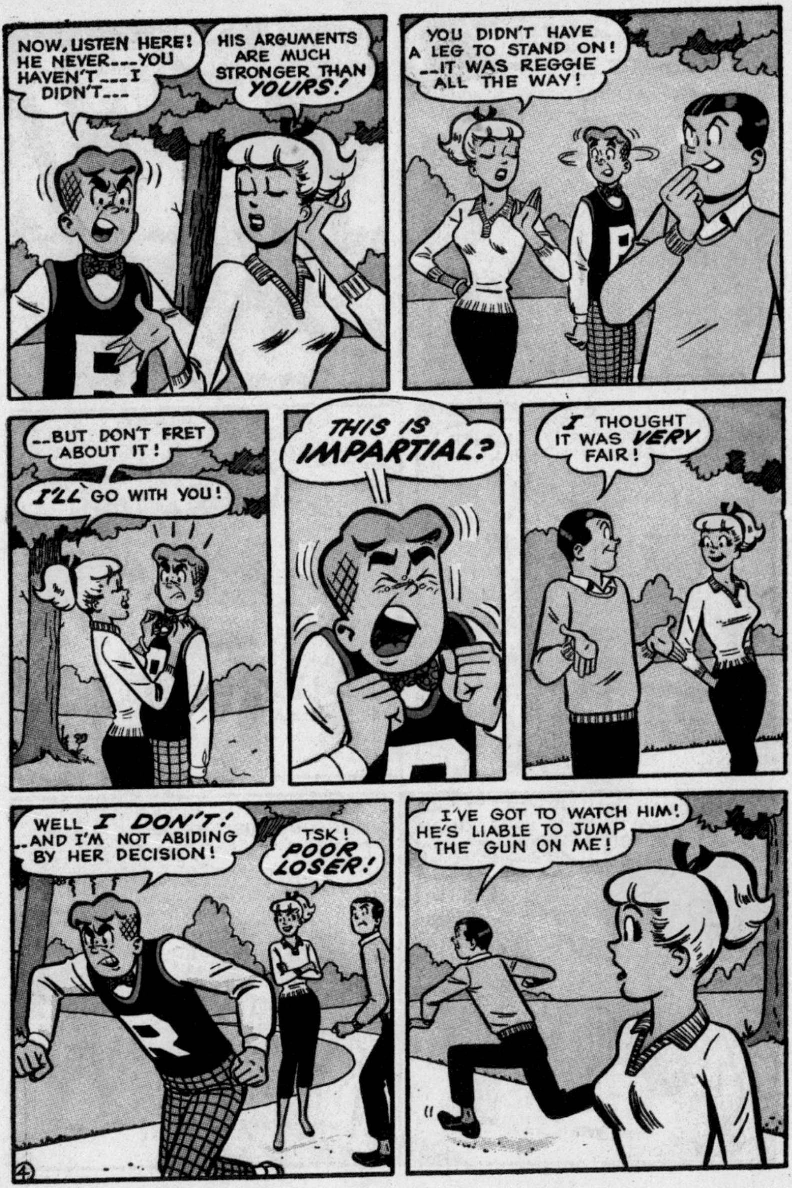
NOW, LISTEN HERE! HE NEVER---YOU HAVEN'T---I DIDN'T---
HIS ARGUMENTS ARE MUCH STRONGER THAN YOURS!
YOU DIDN'T HAVE A LEG TO STAND ON! --IT WAS REGGIE ALL THE WAY!
--BUT DON'T FRET ABOUT IT!
I'LL GO WITH YOU!
THIS IS IMPARTIAL?
I THOUGHT IT WAS VERY FAIR!
WELL I DON'T! --AND I'M NOT ABIDING BY HER DECISION!
TSK! POOR LOSER!
I'VE GOT TO WATCH HIM! HE'S LIABLE TO JUMP THE GUN ON ME!
4

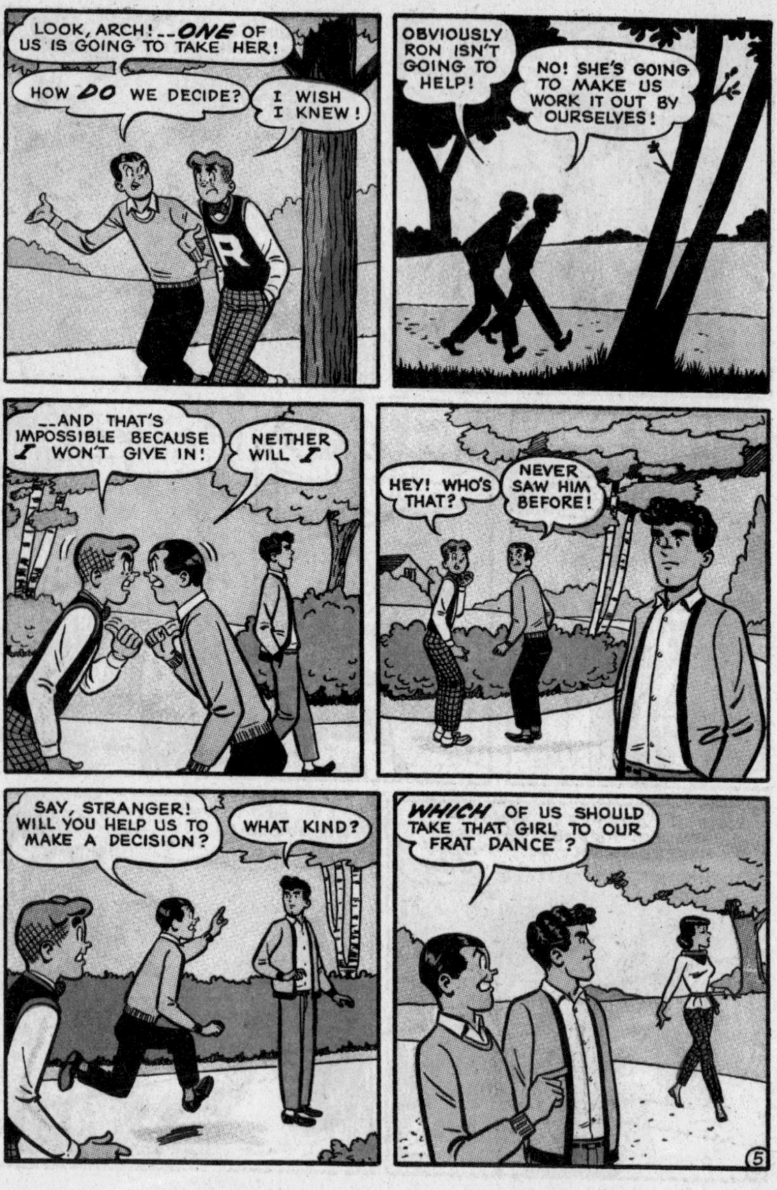
LOOK, ARCH! --ONE OF US IS GOING TO TAKE HER!
HOW DO WE DECIDE?
I WISH I KNEW!
OBVIOUSLY RON ISN'T GOING TO HELP!
NO! SHE'S GOING TO MAKE US WORK IT OUT BY OURSELVES!
--AND THAT'S IMPOSSIBLE BECAUSE I WON'T GIVE IN!
NEITHER WILL I
HEY! WHO'S THAT?
NEVER SAW HIM BEFORE!
SAY, STRANGER! WILL YOU HELP US TO MAKE A DECISION?
WHAT KIND?
WHICH OF US SHOULD TAKE THAT GIRL TO OUR FRAT DANCE?
5

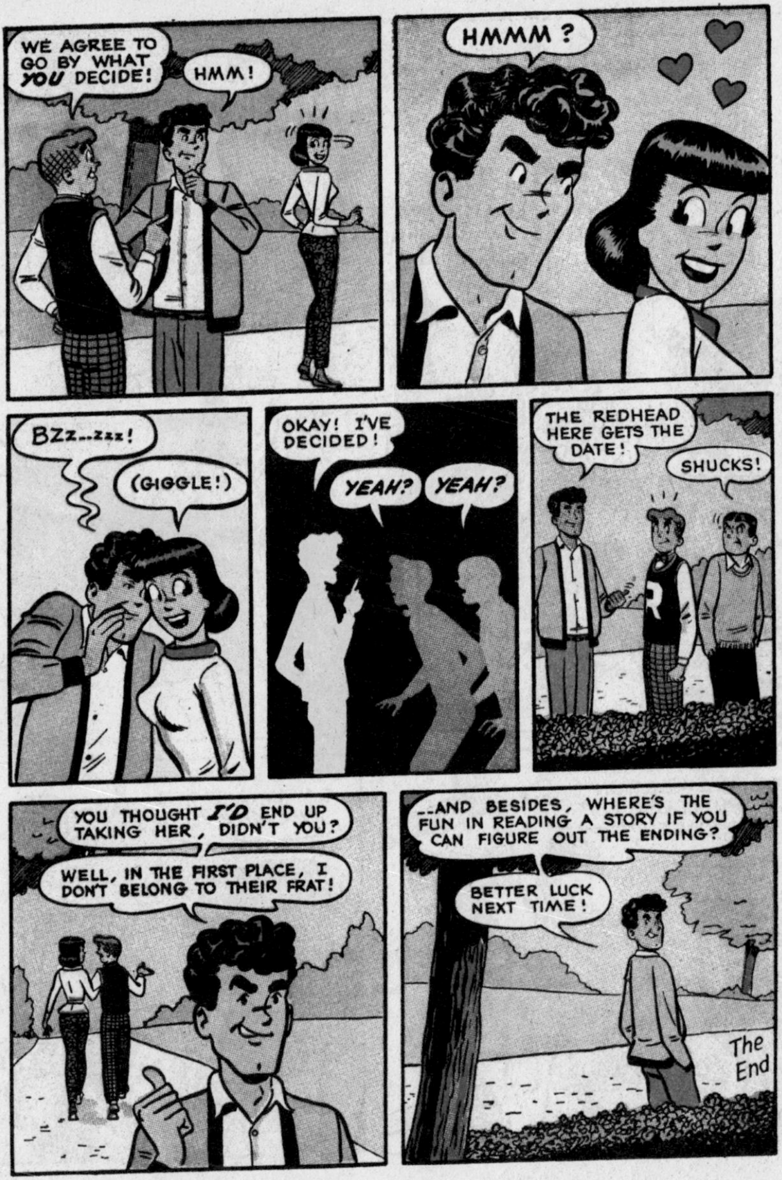
WE AGREE TO GO BY WHAT *YOU* DECIDE!
HMM!
HMMM?
BZz..zzz!
(GIGGLE!)
OKAY! I'VE DECIDED!
YEAH?
YEAH?
THE REDHEAD HERE GETS THE DATE!
SHUCKS!
YOU THOUGHT *I'D* END UP TAKING HER, DIDN'T YOU?
WELL, IN THE FIRST PLACE, I DON'T BELONG TO THEIR FRAT!
..AND BESIDES, WHERE'S THE FUN IN READING A STORY IF YOU CAN FIGURE OUT THE ENDING?
BETTER LUCK NEXT TIME!
The End

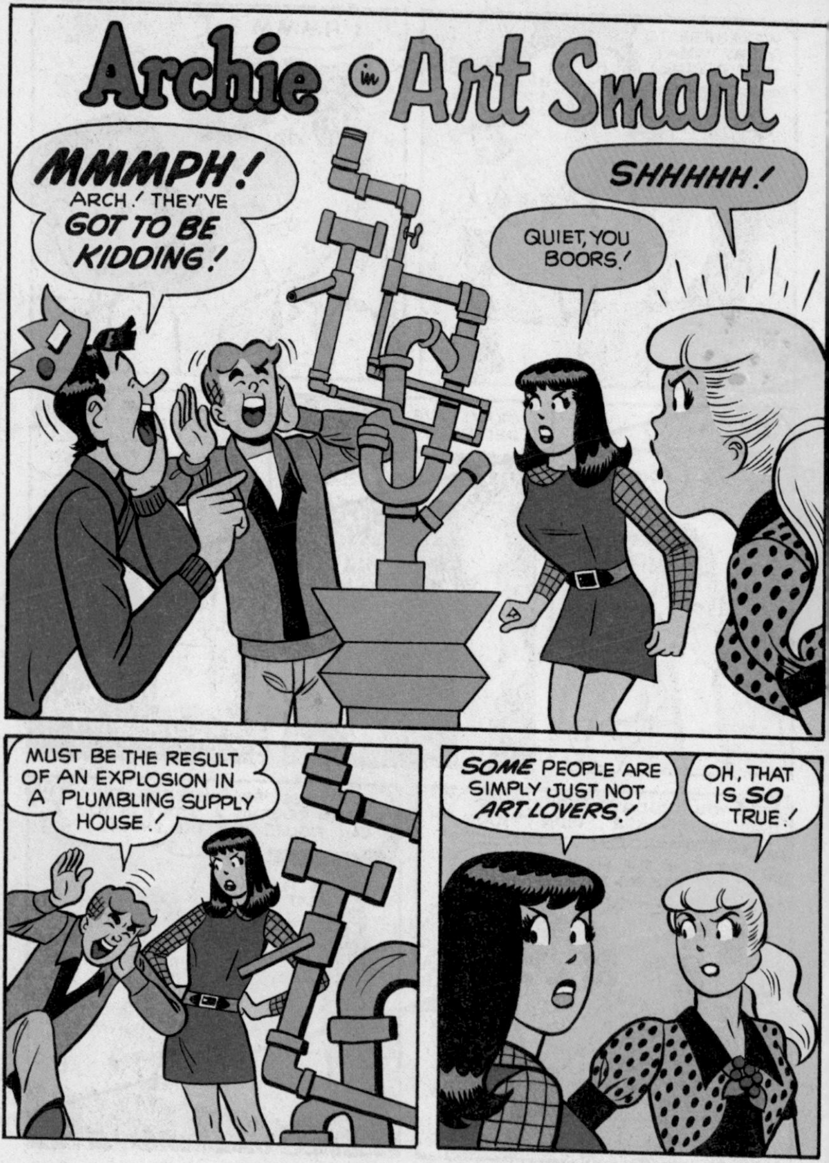

Archie in Art Smart
MMMMPH! ARCH! THEY'VE GOT TO BE KIDDING!
SHHHHH!
QUIET, YOU BOORS!
MUST BE THE RESULT OF AN EXPLOSION IN A PLUMBLING SUPPLY HOUSE!
SOME PEOPLE ARE SIMPLY JUST NOT ART LOVERS!
OH, THAT IS SO TRUE!

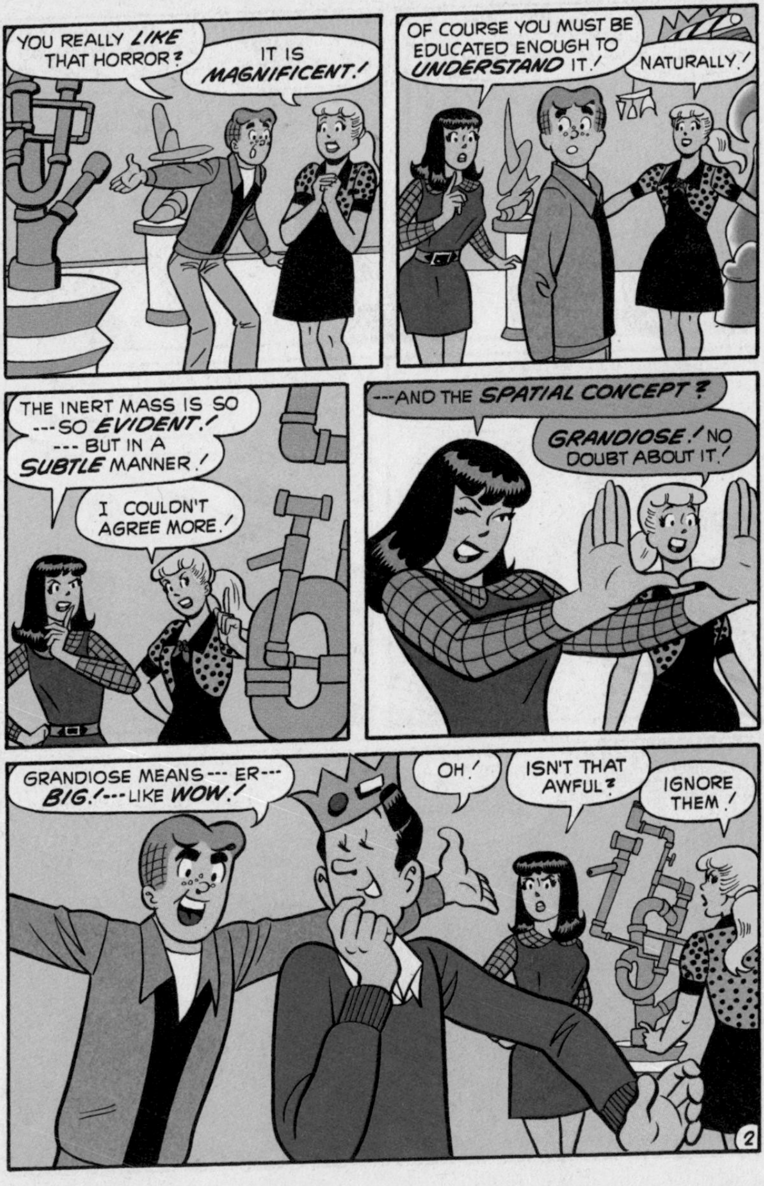
YOU REALLY LIKE THAT HORROR?
IT IS MAGNIFICENT!
OF COURSE YOU MUST BE EDUCATED ENOUGH TO UNDERSTAND IT!
NATURALLY!
THE INERT MASS IS SO ---SO EVIDENT! ---BUT IN A SUBTLE MANNER!
I COULDN'T AGREE MORE!
---AND THE SPATIAL CONCEPT?
GRANDIOSE! NO DOUBT ABOUT IT!
GRANDIOSE MEANS--- ER--- BIG!---LIKE WOW!
OH!
ISN'T THAT AWFUL?
IGNORE THEM!
2

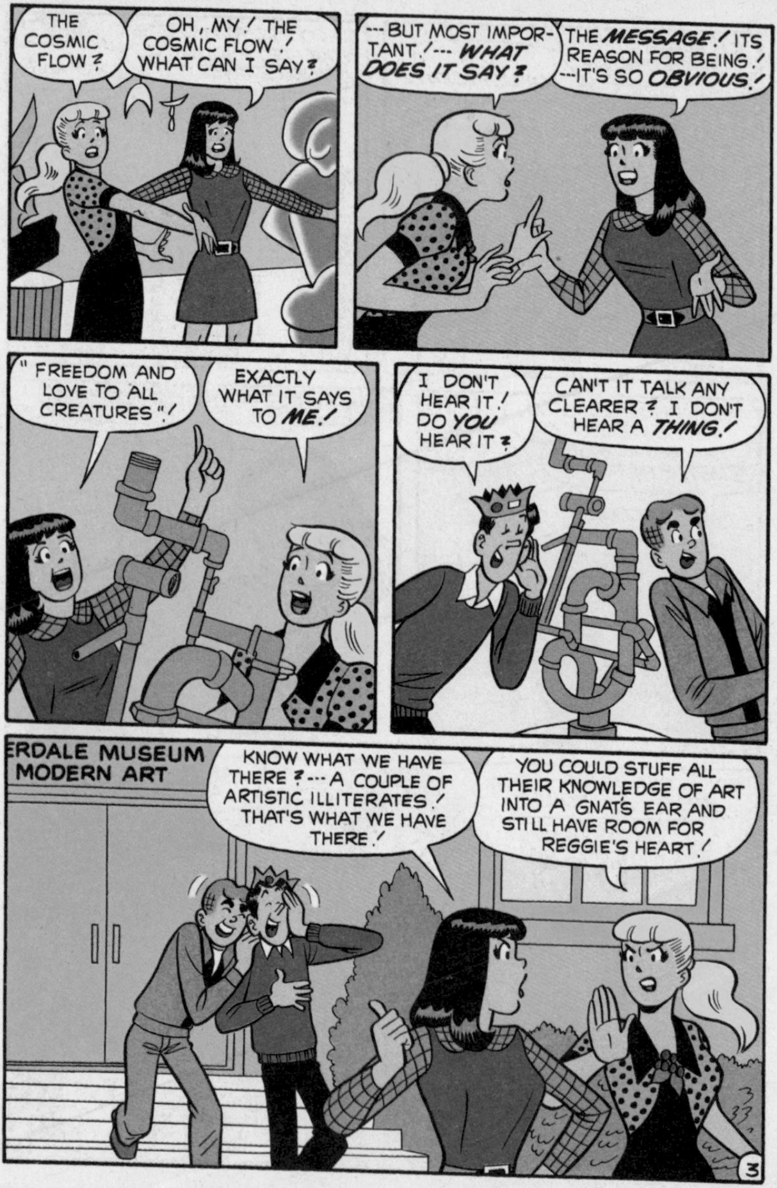
THE COSMIC FLOW?
OH, MY! THE COSMIC FLOW! WHAT CAN I SAY?
--- BUT MOST IMPORTANT! --- WHAT DOES IT SAY?
THE MESSAGE! ITS REASON FOR BEING! --- IT'S SO OBVIOUS!
" FREEDOM AND LOVE TO ALL CREATURES "!
EXACTLY WHAT IT SAYS TO ME!
I DON'T HEAR IT! DO YOU HEAR IT?
CAN'T IT TALK ANY CLEARER? I DON'T HEAR A THING!
ERDALE MUSEUM MODERN ART
KNOW WHAT WE HAVE THERE? --- A COUPLE OF ARTISTIC ILLITERATES! THAT'S WHAT WE HAVE THERE!
YOU COULD STUFF ALL THEIR KNOWLEDGE OF ART INTO A GNAT'S EAR AND STILL HAVE ROOM FOR REGGIE'S HEART!
3

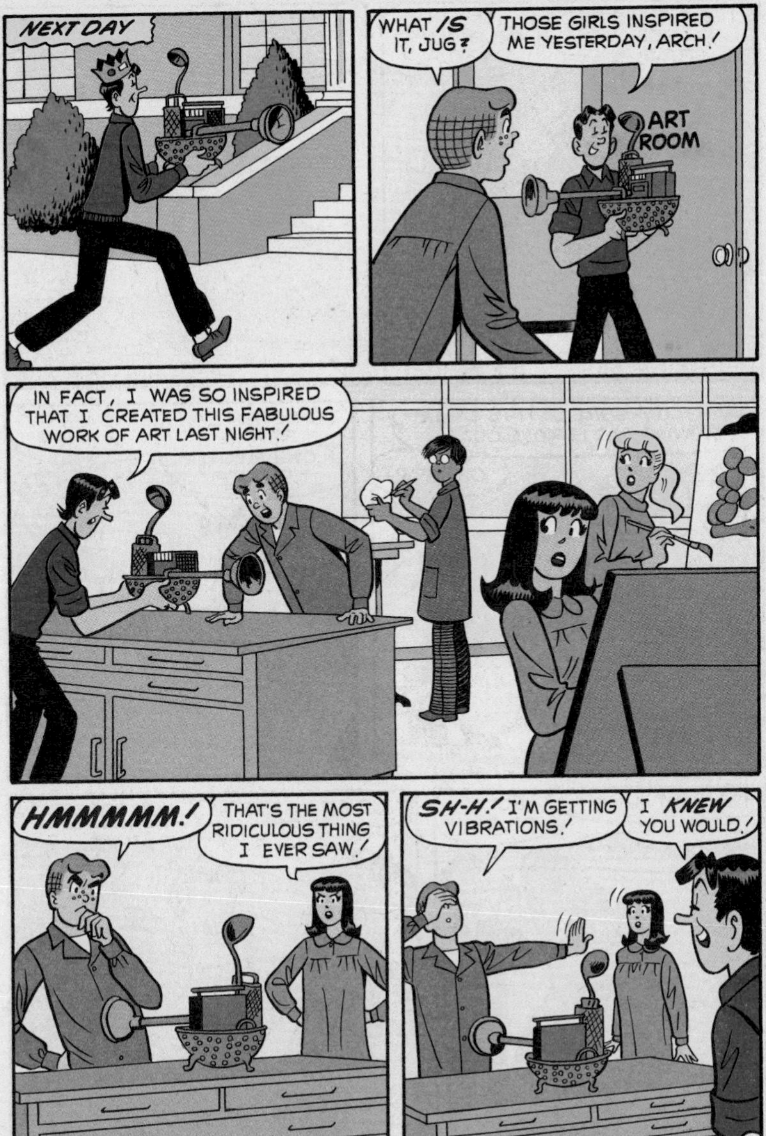
NEXT DAY
WHAT IS IT, JUG?
THOSE GIRLS INSPIRED ME YESTERDAY, ARCH!
ART ROOM
IN FACT, I WAS SO INSPIRED THAT I CREATED THIS FABULOUS WORK OF ART LAST NIGHT!
HMMMMMM!
THAT'S THE MOST RIDICULOUS THING I EVER SAW!
SH-H! I'M GETTING VIBRATIONS!
I KNEW YOU WOULD!
4

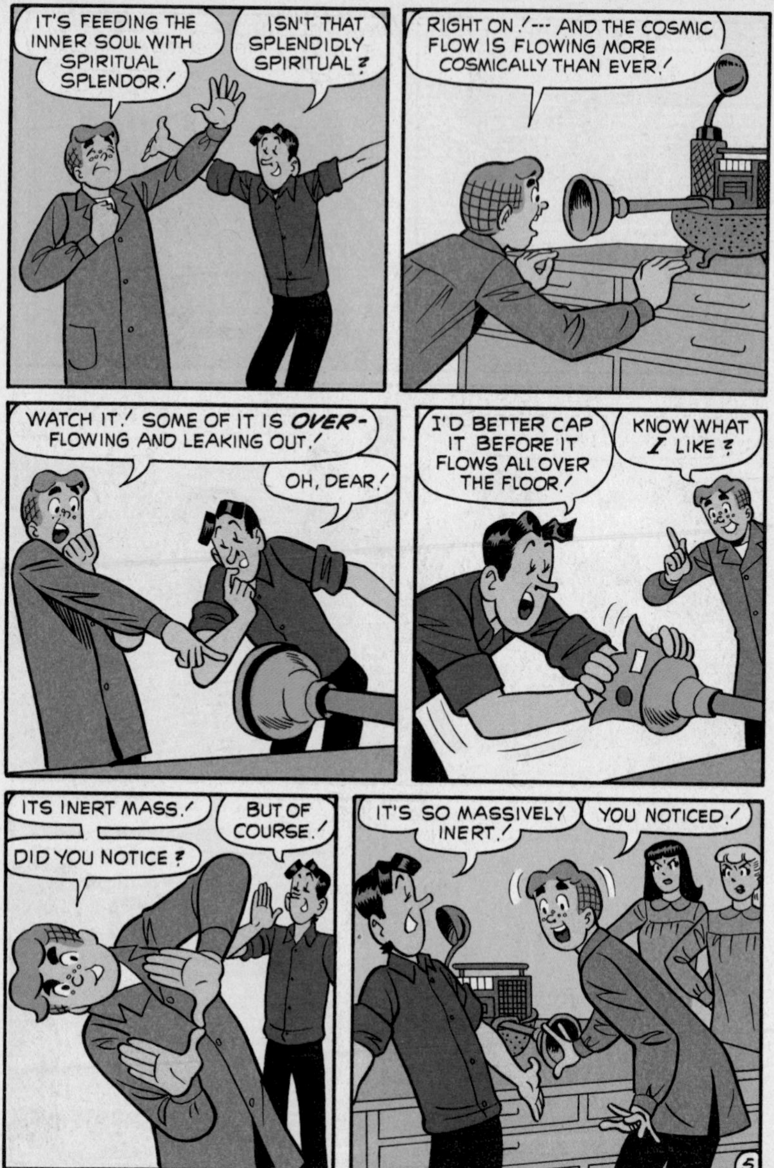
IT'S FEEDING THE INNER SOUL WITH SPIRITUAL SPLENDOR!
ISN'T THAT SPLENDIDLY SPIRITUAL?
RIGHT ON!--- AND THE COSMIC FLOW IS FLOWING MORE COSMICALLY THAN EVER!
WATCH IT! SOME OF IT IS OVER-FLOWING AND LEAKING OUT!
OH, DEAR!
I'D BETTER CAP IT BEFORE IT FLOWS ALL OVER THE FLOOR!
KNOW WHAT I LIKE?
ITS INERT MASS!
DID YOU NOTICE?
BUT OF COURSE!
IT'S SO MASSIVELY INERT!
YOU NOTICED!
5

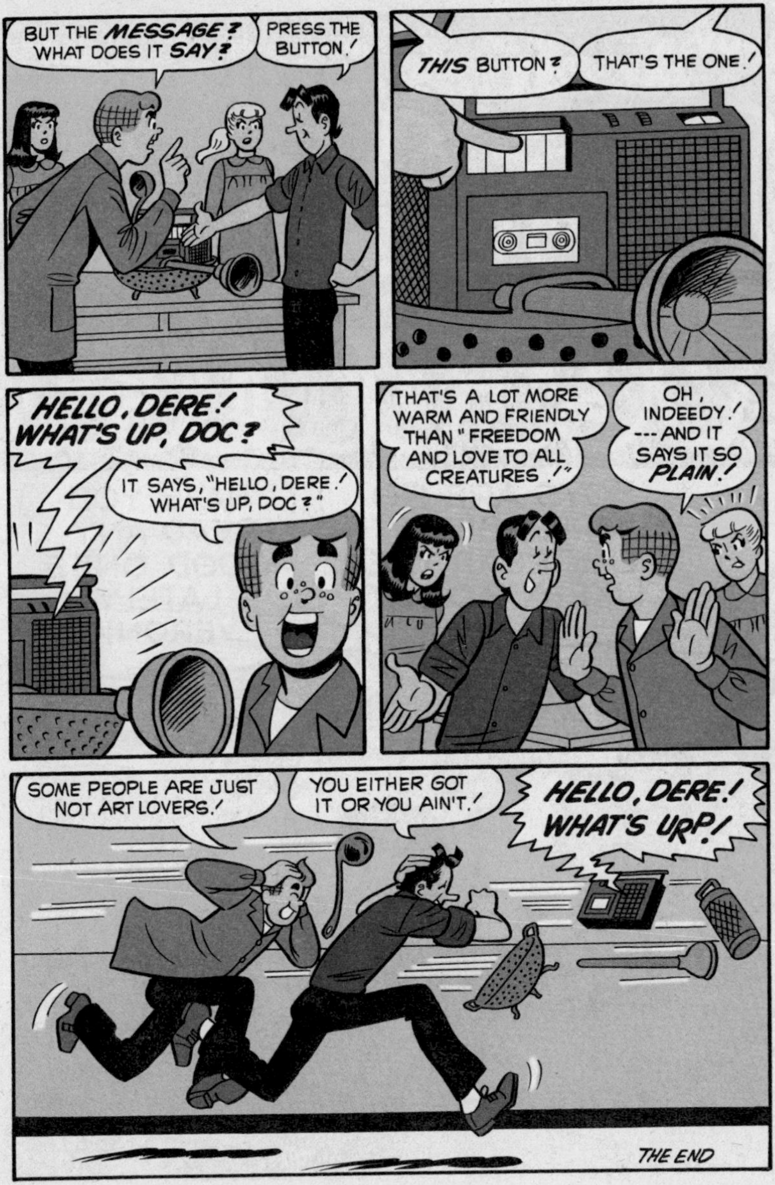
BUT THE MESSAGE? WHAT DOES IT SAY?
PRESS THE BUTTON!
THIS BUTTON?
THAT'S THE ONE!
HELLO, DERE! WHAT'S UP, DOC?
IT SAYS, "HELLO, DERE! WHAT'S UP, DOC?"
THAT'S A LOT MORE WARM AND FRIENDLY THAN "FREEDOM AND LOVE TO ALL CREATURES!"
OH, INDEEDY! --- AND IT SAYS IT SO PLAIN!
SOME PEOPLE ARE JUST NOT ART LOVERS!
YOU EITHER GOT IT OR YOU AIN'T!
HELLO, DERE! WHAT'S UP!
THE END

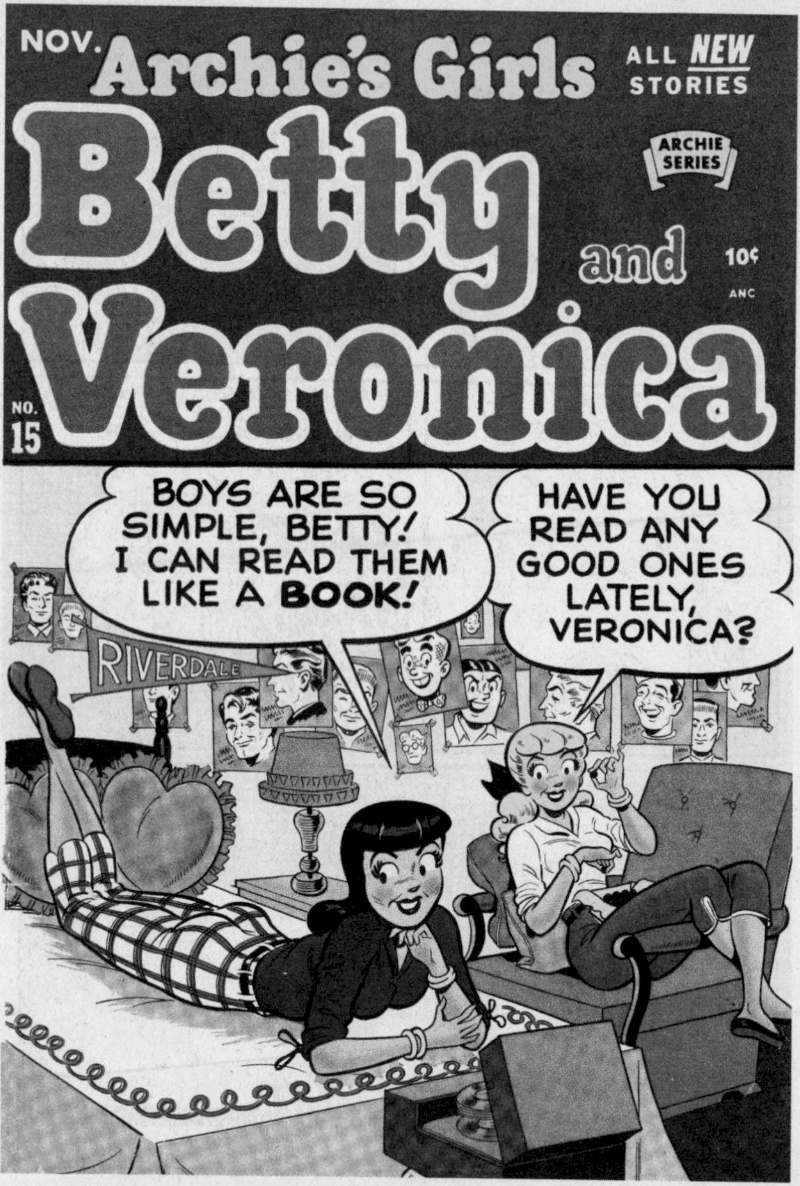
NOV.
Archie's Girls
ALL NEW STORIES
ARCHIE SERIES
Betty and Veronica
10¢
ANC
NO. 15
BOYS ARE SO SIMPLE, BETTY! I CAN READ THEM LIKE A BOOK!
HAVE YOU READ ANY GOOD ONES LATELY, VERONICA?
RIVERDALE

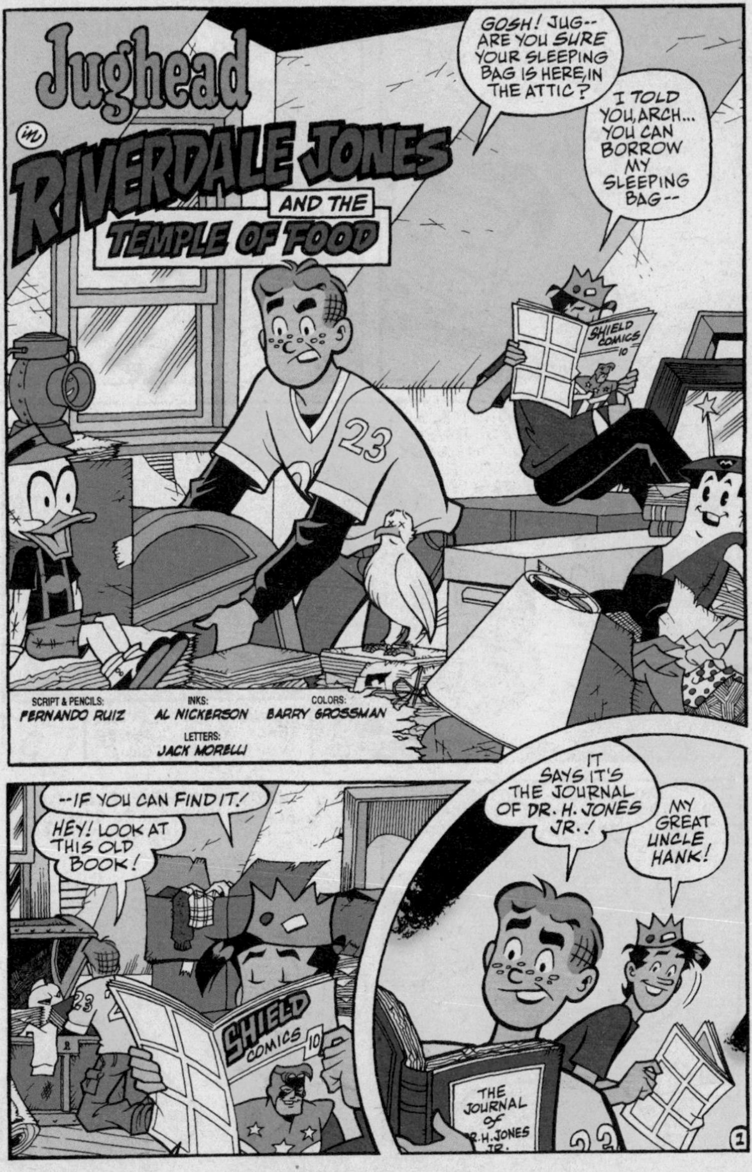

Jughead
in
RIVERDALE JONES
AND THE
TEMPLE OF FOOD
GOSH! JUG-- ARE YOU SURE YOUR SLEEPING BAG IS HERE, IN THE ATTIC?
I TOLD YOU, ARCH... YOU CAN BORROW MY SLEEPING BAG--
SHIELD COMICS 10
SCRIPT & PENCILS: FERNANDO RUIZ
INKS: AL NICKERSON
COLORS: BARRY GROSSMAN
LETTERS: JACK MORELLI
--IF YOU CAN FIND IT!
HEY! LOOK AT THIS OLD BOOK!
SHIELD COMICS 10
IT SAYS IT'S THE JOURNAL OF DR. H. JONES JR.!
MY GREAT UNCLE HANK!
THE JOURNAL OF DR. H. JONES JR.
1

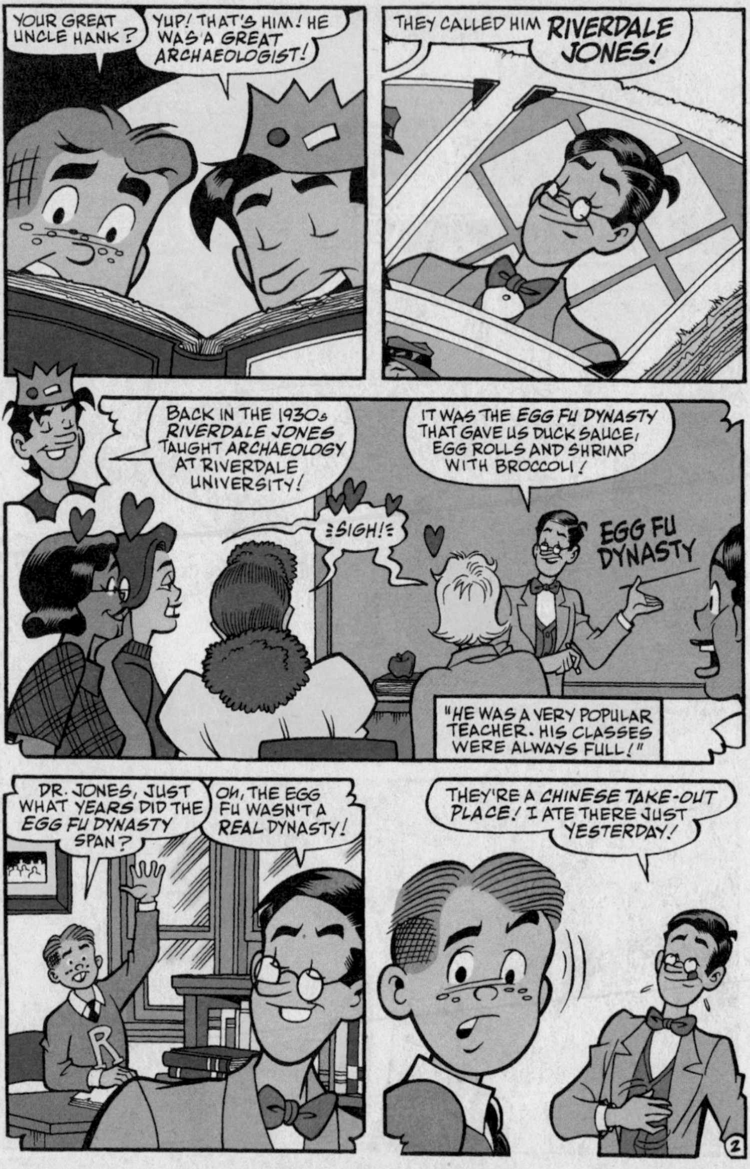
YOUR GREAT UNCLE HANK?
YUP! THAT'S HIM! HE WAS A GREAT ARCHAEOLOGIST!
THEY CALLED HIM RIVERDALE JONES!
BACK IN THE 1930s RIVERDALE JONES TAUGHT ARCHAEOLOGY AT RIVERDALE UNIVERSITY!
IT WAS THE EGG FU DYNASTY THAT GAVE US DUCK SAUCE, EGG ROLLS AND SHRIMP WITH BROCCOLI!
SIGH!
EGG FU DYNASTY
"HE WAS A VERY POPULAR TEACHER. HIS CLASSES WERE ALWAYS FULL!"
DR. JONES, JUST WHAT YEARS DID THE EGG FU DYNASTY SPAN?
OH, THE EGG FU WASN'T A REAL DYNASTY!
THEY'RE A CHINESE TAKE-OUT PLACE! I ATE THERE JUST YESTERDAY!
2

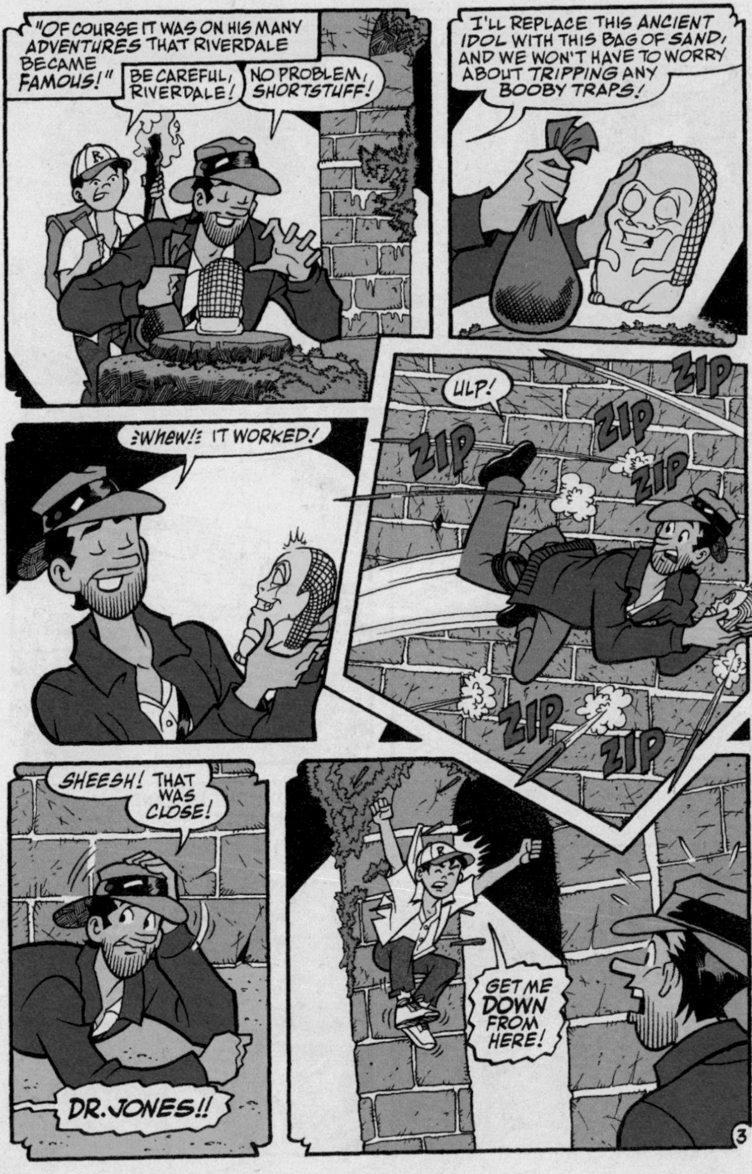
"OF COURSE IT WAS ON HIS MANY ADVENTURES THAT RIVERDALE BECAME FAMOUS!"
BE CAREFUL, RIVERDALE!
NO PROBLEM, SHORTSTUFF!
I'LL REPLACE THIS ANCIENT IDOL WITH THIS BAG OF SAND, AND WE WON'T HAVE TO WORRY ABOUT TRIPPING ANY BOOBY TRAPS!
WHEW!! IT WORKED!
ULP!
ZIP
ZIP
ZIP
ZIP
ZIP
ZIP
ZIP
SHEESH! THAT WAS CLOSE!
DR. JONES!!
GET ME DOWN FROM HERE!
3

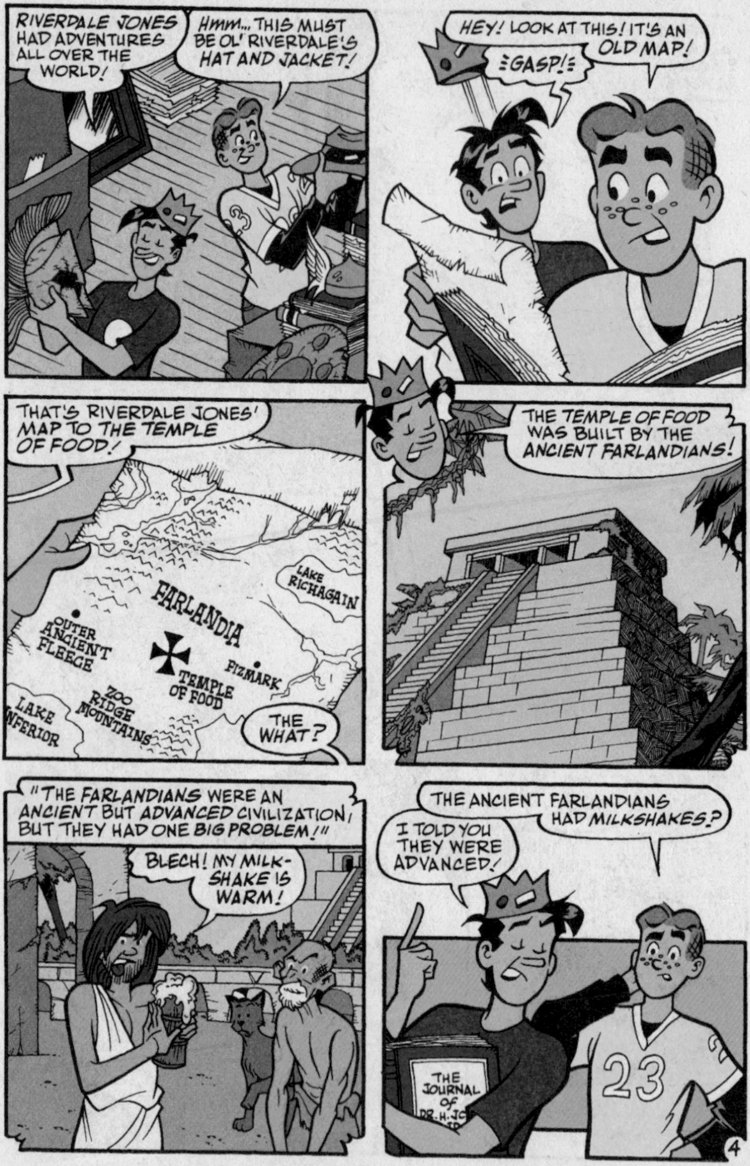
RIVERDALE JONES HAD ADVENTURES ALL OVER THE WORLD!
HMM... THIS MUST BE OL' RIVERDALE'S HAT AND JACKET!
HEY! LOOK AT THIS! IT'S AN OLD MAP!
GASP!
THAT'S RIVERDALE JONES' MAP TO THE TEMPLE OF FOOD!
FARLANDIA
LAKE RICHAGAIN
OUTER ANCIENT FLEECE
FIZMARK
TEMPLE OF FOOD
ZOO RIDGE MOUNTAINS
LAKE INFERIOR
THE WHAT?
THE TEMPLE OF FOOD WAS BUILT BY THE ANCIENT FARLANDIANS!
"THE FARLANDIANS WERE AN ANCIENT BUT ADVANCED CIVILIZATION, BUT THEY HAD ONE BIG PROBLEM!"
BLECH! MY MILK-SHAKE IS WARM!
THE ANCIENT FARLANDIANS HAD MILKSHAKES?
I TOLD YOU THEY WERE ADVANCED!
THE JOURNAL OF
23
4

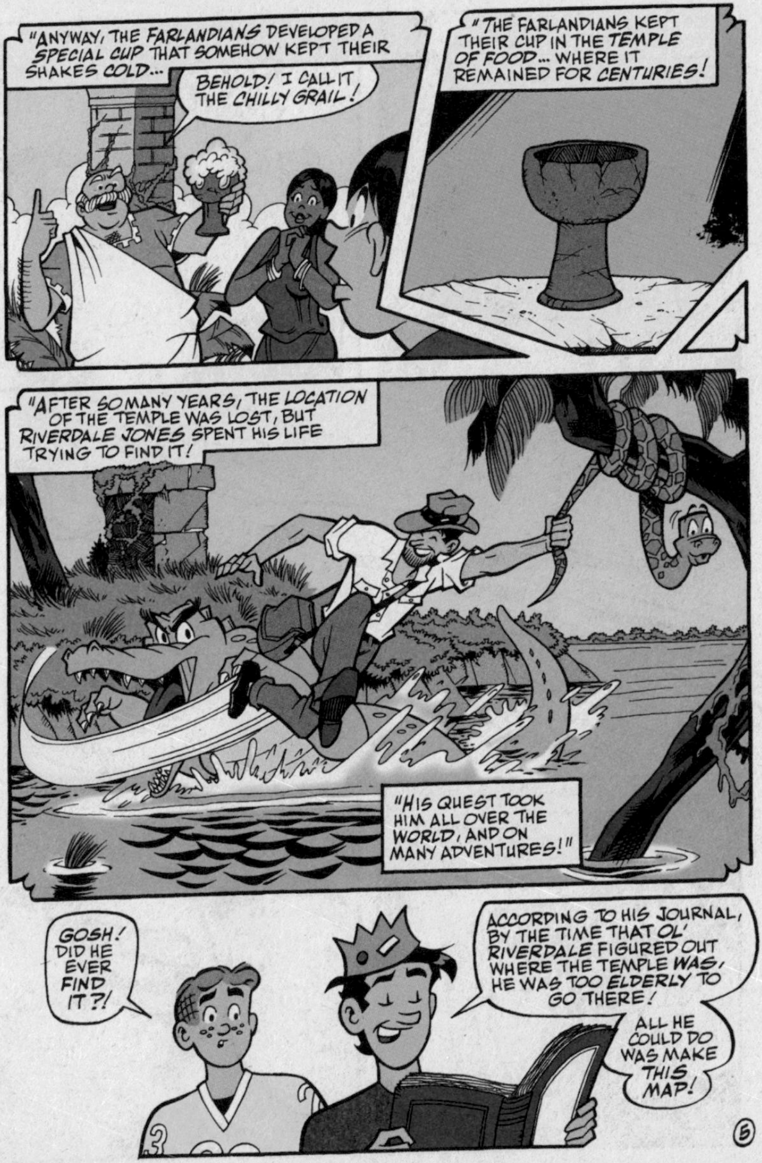
"ANYWAY, THE FARLANDIANS DEVELOPED A SPECIAL CUP THAT SOMEHOW KEPT THEIR SHAKES COLD...
BEHOLD! I CALL IT THE CHILLY GRAIL!
"THE FARLANDIANS KEPT THEIR CUP IN THE TEMPLE OF FOOD... WHERE IT REMAINED FOR CENTURIES!
"AFTER SO MANY YEARS, THE LOCATION OF THE TEMPLE WAS LOST, BUT RIVERDALE JONES SPENT HIS LIFE TRYING TO FIND IT!
"HIS QUEST TOOK HIM ALL OVER THE WORLD, AND ON MANY ADVENTURES!"
GOSH! DID HE EVER FIND IT?!
ACCORDING TO HIS JOURNAL, BY THE TIME THAT OL' RIVERDALE FIGURED OUT WHERE THE TEMPLE WAS, HE WAS TOO ELDERLY TO GO THERE!
ALL HE COULD DO WAS MAKE THIS MAP!

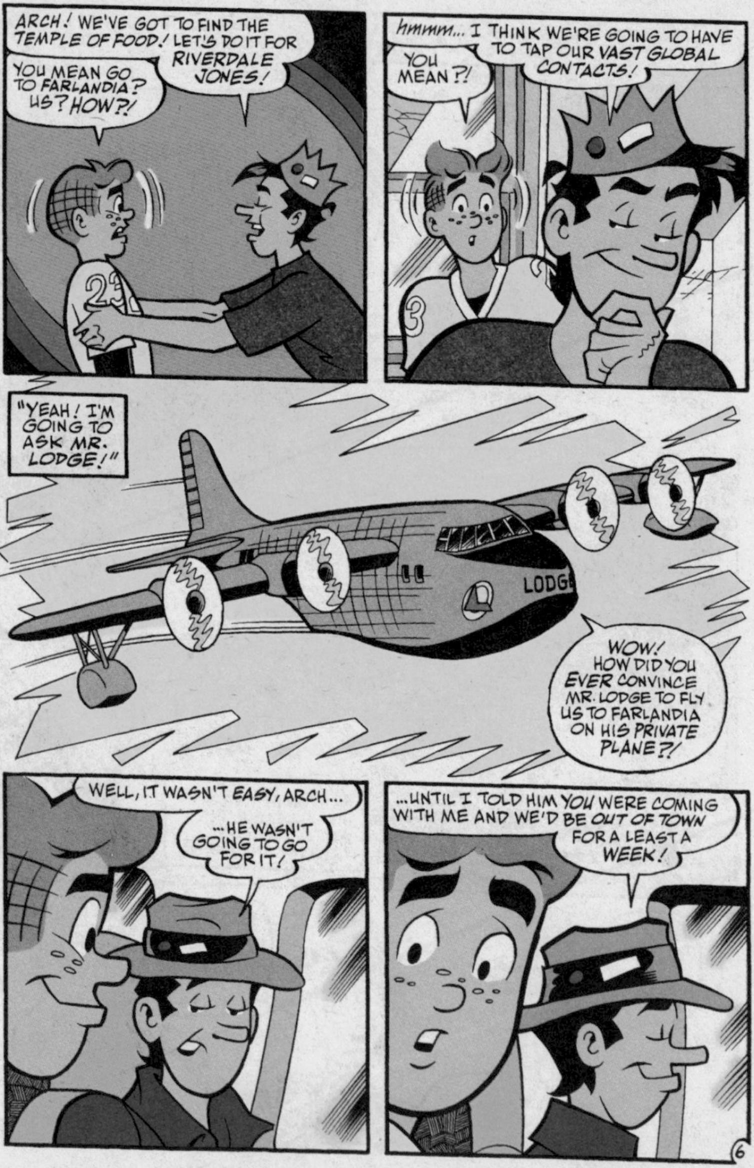
ARCH! WE'VE GOT TO FIND THE TEMPLE OF FOOD! LET'S DO IT FOR RIVERDALE JONES!
YOU MEAN GO TO FARLANDIA? US? HOW?!
hmmm... I THINK WE'RE GOING TO HAVE TO TAP OUR VAST GLOBAL CONTACTS!
YOU MEAN?!
"YEAH! I'M GOING TO ASK MR. LODGE!"
LODGE
WOW! HOW DID YOU EVER CONVINCE MR. LODGE TO FLY US TO FARLANDIA ON HIS PRIVATE PLANE?!
WELL, IT WASN'T EASY, ARCH...
...HE WASN'T GOING TO GO FOR IT!
...UNTIL I TOLD HIM YOU WERE COMING WITH ME AND WE'D BE OUT OF TOWN FOR A LEAST A WEEK!
6

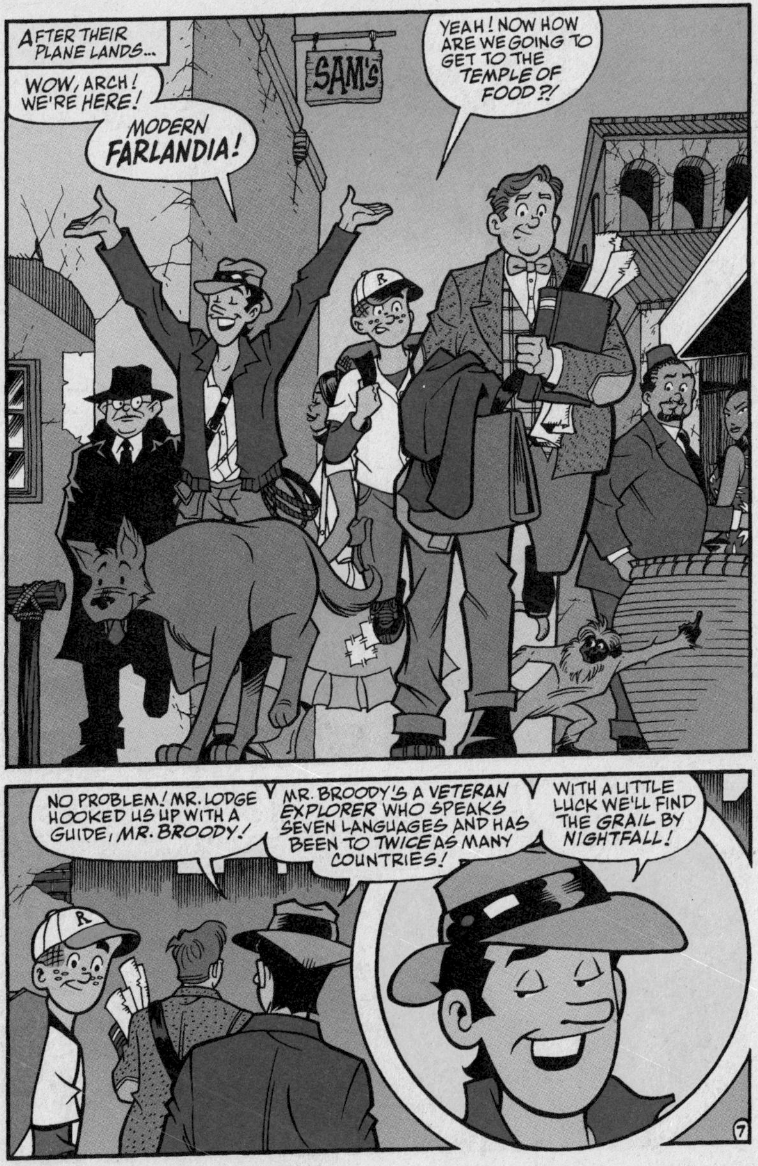

AFTER THEIR PLANE LANDS...
WOW, ARCH! WE'RE HERE!
MODERN FARLANDIA!
SAM'S
YEAH! NOW HOW ARE WE GOING TO GET TO THE TEMPLE OF FOOD?!
NO PROBLEM! MR. LODGE HOOKED US UP WITH A GUIDE, MR. BROODY!
MR. BROODY'S A VETERAN EXPLORER WHO SPEAKS SEVEN LANGUAGES AND HAS BEEN TO TWICE AS MANY COUNTRIES!
WITH A LITTLE LUCK WE'LL FIND THE GRAIL BY NIGHTFALL!

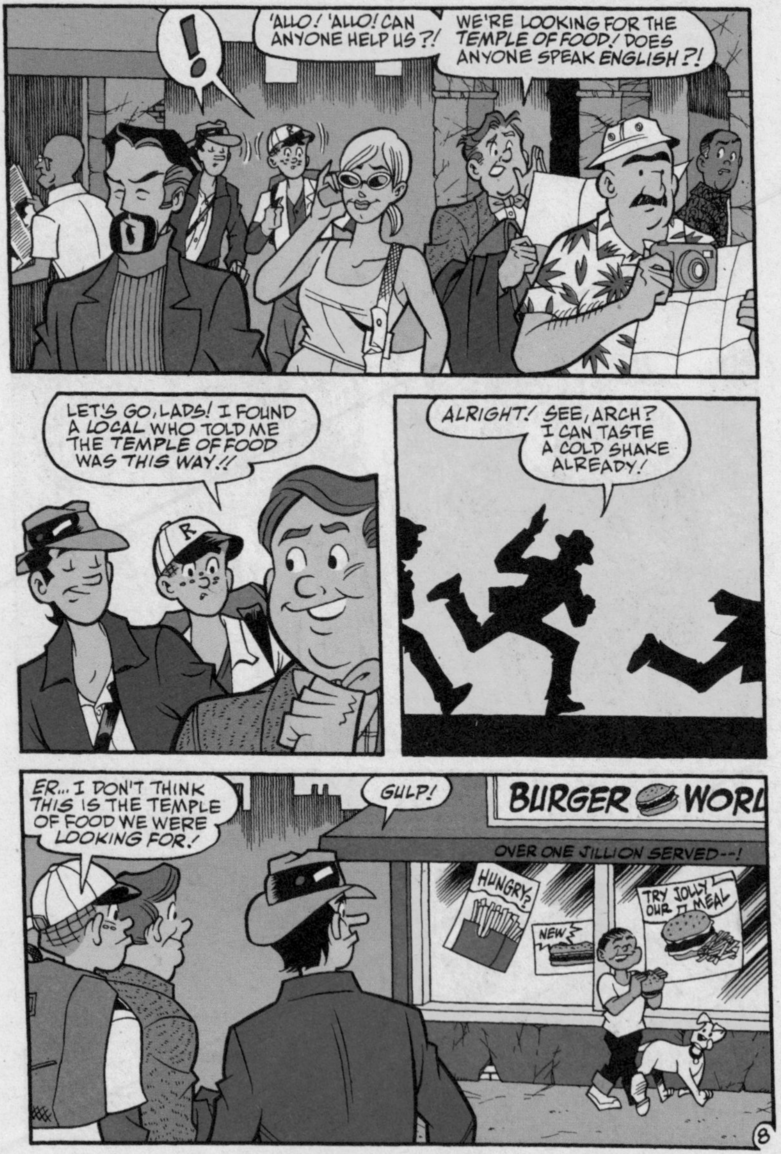
!
'ALLO! 'ALLO! CAN ANYONE HELP US?!
WE'RE LOOKING FOR THE TEMPLE OF FOOD! DOES ANYONE SPEAK ENGLISH?!
LET'S GO, LADS! I FOUND A LOCAL WHO TOLD ME THE TEMPLE OF FOOD WAS THIS WAY!!
ALRIGHT! SEE, ARCH? I CAN TASTE A COLD SHAKE ALREADY!
ER... I DON'T THINK THIS IS THE TEMPLE OF FOOD WE WERE LOOKING FOR!
GULP!
BURGER WORL
OVER ONE JILLION SERVED--!
HUNGRY?
NEW
TRY OUR JOLLY MEAL

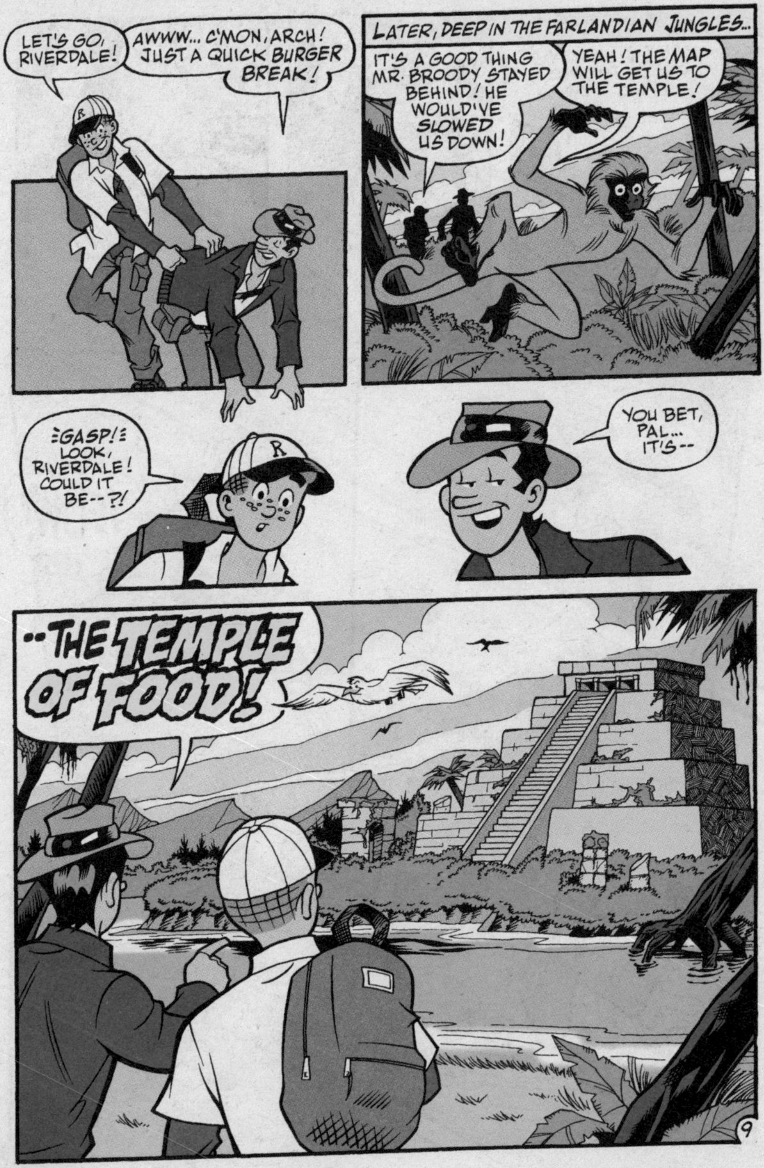
LET'S GO, RIVERDALE!
AWWW... C'MON, ARCH! JUST A QUICK BURGER BREAK!
LATER, DEEP IN THE FARLANDIAN JUNGLES...
IT'S A GOOD THING MR. BROODY STAYED BEHIND! HE WOULD'VE SLOWED US DOWN!
YEAH! THE MAP WILL GET US TO THE TEMPLE!
GASP! LOOK, RIVERDALE! COULD IT BE--?!
YOU BET, PAL... IT'S--
--THE TEMPLE OF FOOD!
9

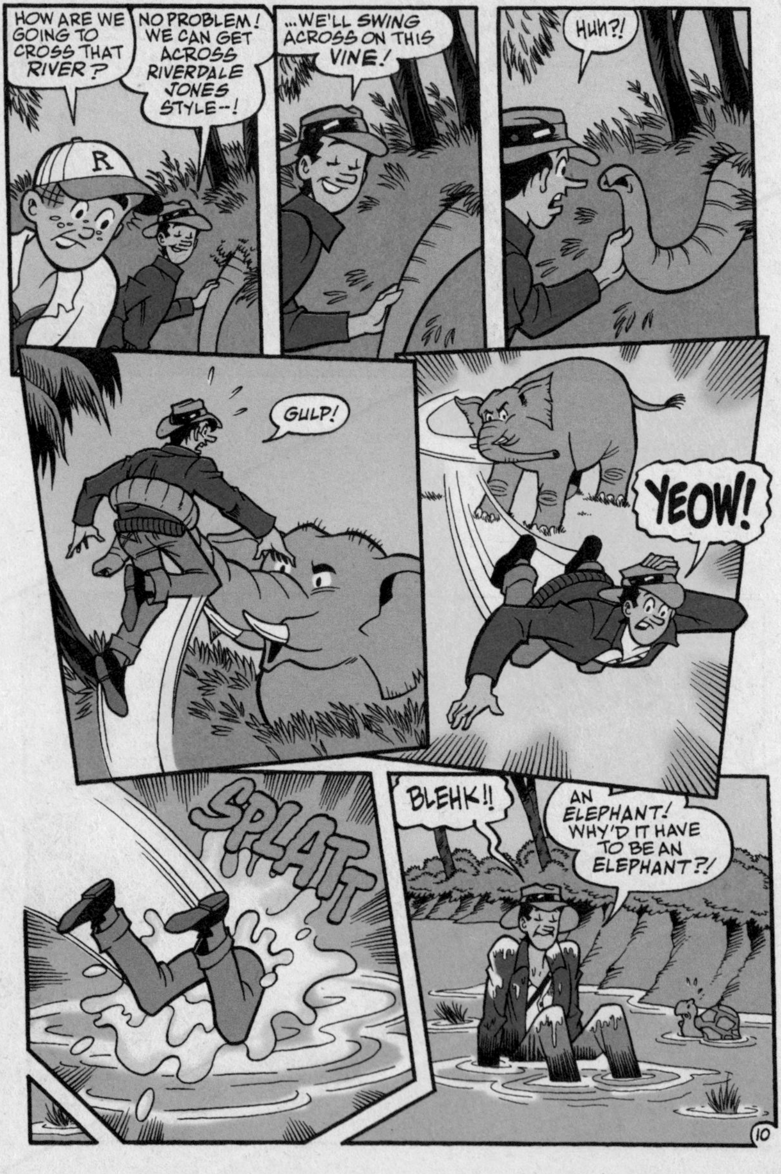
HOW ARE WE GOING TO CROSS THAT RIVER?
NO PROBLEM! WE CAN GET ACROSS RIVERDALE JONES STYLE--!
...WE'LL SWING ACROSS ON THIS VINE!
HUH?!
GULP!
YEOW!
SPLATT
BLEHK!!
AN ELEPHANT! WHY'D IT HAVE TO BE AN ELEPHANT?!

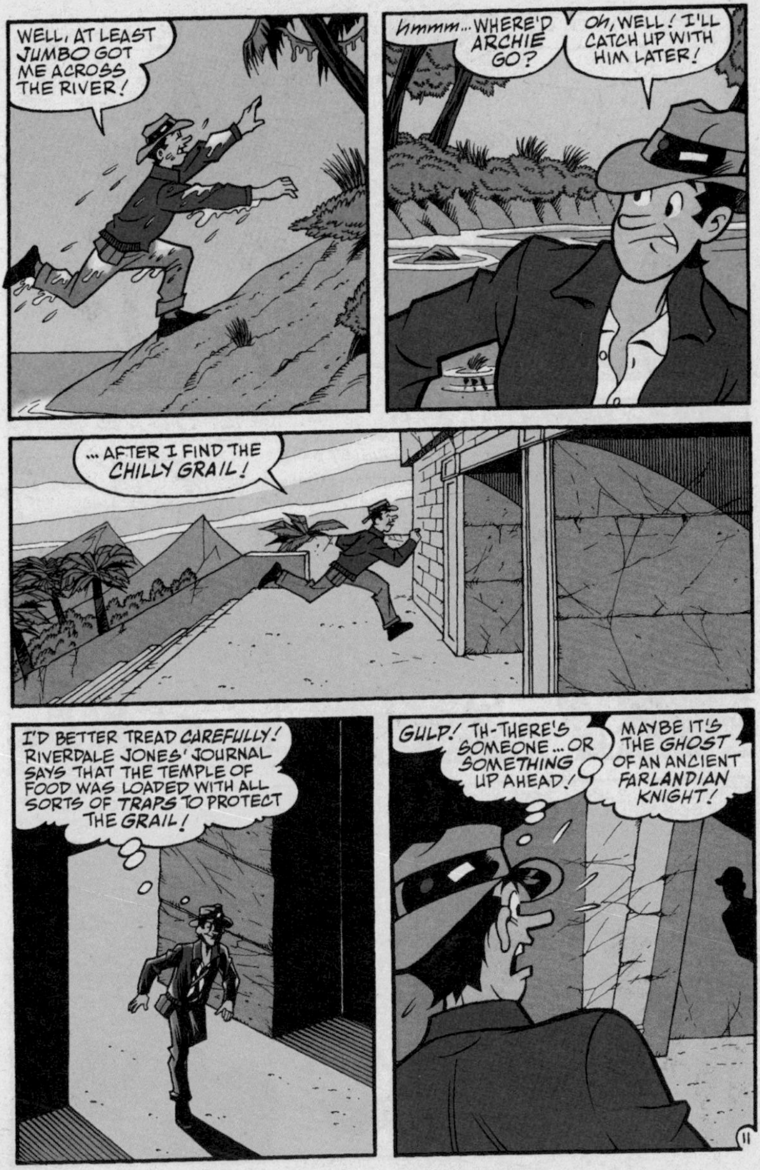
WELL, AT LEAST JUMBO GOT ME ACROSS THE RIVER!
hmmm... WHERE'D ARCHIE GO?
OH, WELL! I'LL CATCH UP WITH HIM LATER!
...AFTER I FIND THE CHILLY GRAIL!
I'D BETTER TREAD CAREFULLY! RIVERDALE JONES' JOURNAL SAYS THAT THE TEMPLE OF FOOD WAS LOADED WITH ALL SORTS OF TRAPS TO PROTECT THE GRAIL!
GULP! TH-THERE'S SOMEONE ... OR SOMETHING UP AHEAD!
MAYBE IT'S THE GHOST OF AN ANCIENT FARLANDIAN KNIGHT!
11

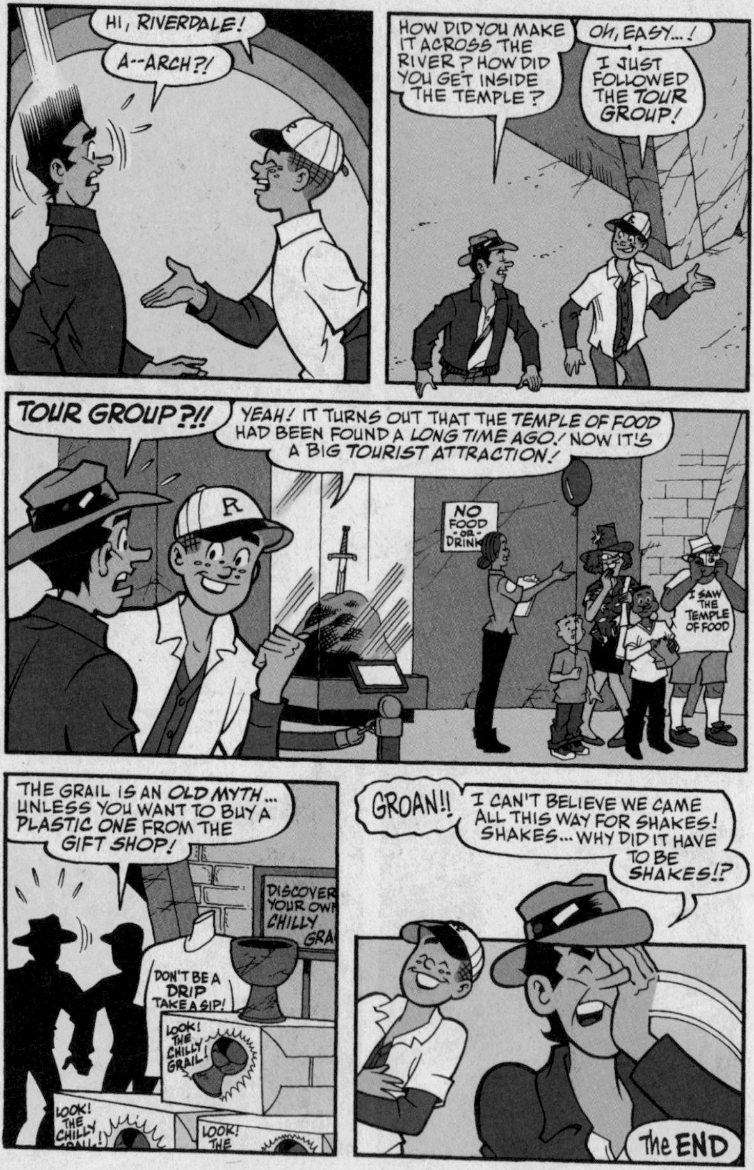
HI, RIVERDALE!
A--ARCH?!
HOW DID YOU MAKE IT ACROSS THE RIVER? HOW DID YOU GET INSIDE THE TEMPLE?
OH, EASY...!
I JUST FOLLOWED THE TOUR GROUP!
TOUR GROUP?!!
YEAH! IT TURNS OUT THAT THE TEMPLE OF FOOD HAD BEEN FOUND A LONG TIME AGO! NOW IT'S A BIG TOURIST ATTRACTION!
NO FOOD -OR- DRINK
I SAW THE TEMPLE OF FOOD
THE GRAIL IS AN OLD MYTH... UNLESS YOU WANT TO BUY A PLASTIC ONE FROM THE GIFT SHOP!
DISCOVER YOUR OWN CHILLY GRA
DON'T BE A DRIP TAKE A SIP!
LOOK! THE CHILLY GRAIL!
GROAN!!
I CAN'T BELIEVE WE CAME ALL THIS WAY FOR SHAKES! SHAKES... WHY DID IT HAVE TO BE SHAKES!?
The END

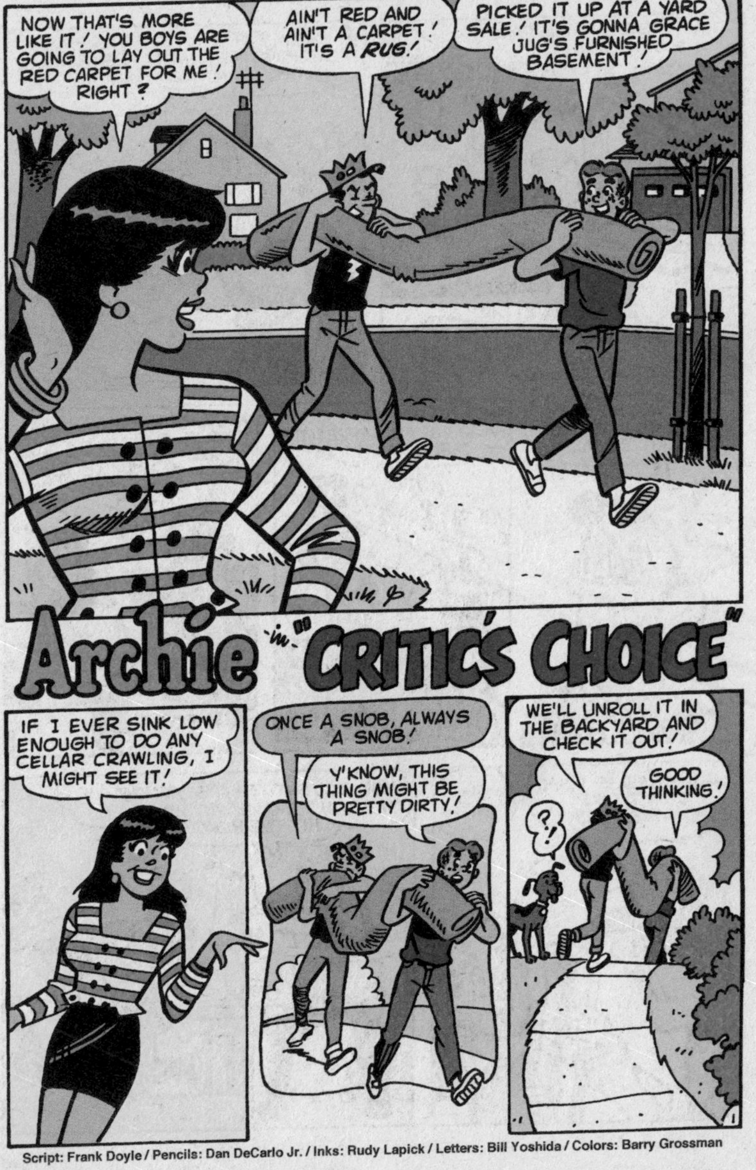

NOW THAT'S MORE LIKE IT! YOU BOYS ARE GOING TO LAY OUT THE RED CARPET FOR ME! RIGHT?
AIN'T RED AND AIN'T A CARPET! IT'S A RUG!
PICKED IT UP AT A YARD SALE! IT'S GONNA GRACE JUG'S FURNISHED BASEMENT!
Archie -in- "CRITIC'S CHOICE"
IF I EVER SINK LOW ENOUGH TO DO ANY CELLAR CRAWLING, I MIGHT SEE IT!
ONCE A SNOB, ALWAYS A SNOB!
Y'KNOW, THIS THING MIGHT BE PRETTY DIRTY!
WE'LL UNROLL IT IN THE BACKYARD AND CHECK IT OUT!
GOOD THINKING!
?!
1

Script: Frank Doyle / Pencils: Dan DeCarlo Jr. / Inks: Rudy Lapick / Letters: Bill Yoshida / Colors: Barry Grossman

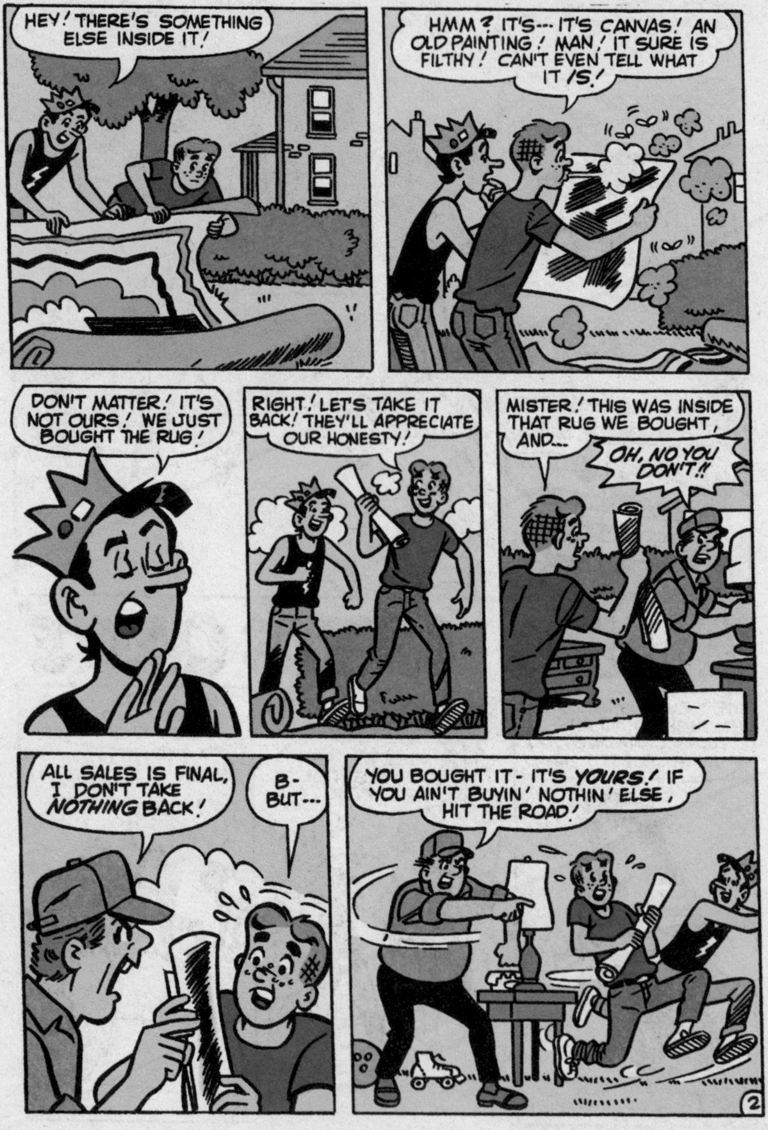

HEY! THERE'S SOMETHING ELSE INSIDE IT!
HMM? IT'S--- IT'S CANVAS! AN OLD PAINTING! MAN! IT SURE IS FILTHY! CAN'T EVEN TELL WHAT IT IS!
DON'T MATTER! IT'S NOT OURS! WE JUST BOUGHT THE RUG!
RIGHT! LET'S TAKE IT BACK! THEY'LL APPRECIATE OUR HONESTY!
MISTER! THIS WAS INSIDE THAT RUG WE BOUGHT, AND...
OH, NO YOU DON'T!!
ALL SALES IS FINAL, I DON'T TAKE NOTHING BACK!
B- BUT---
YOU BOUGHT IT - IT'S YOURS! IF YOU AIN'T BUYIN' NOTHIN' ELSE, HIT THE ROAD!

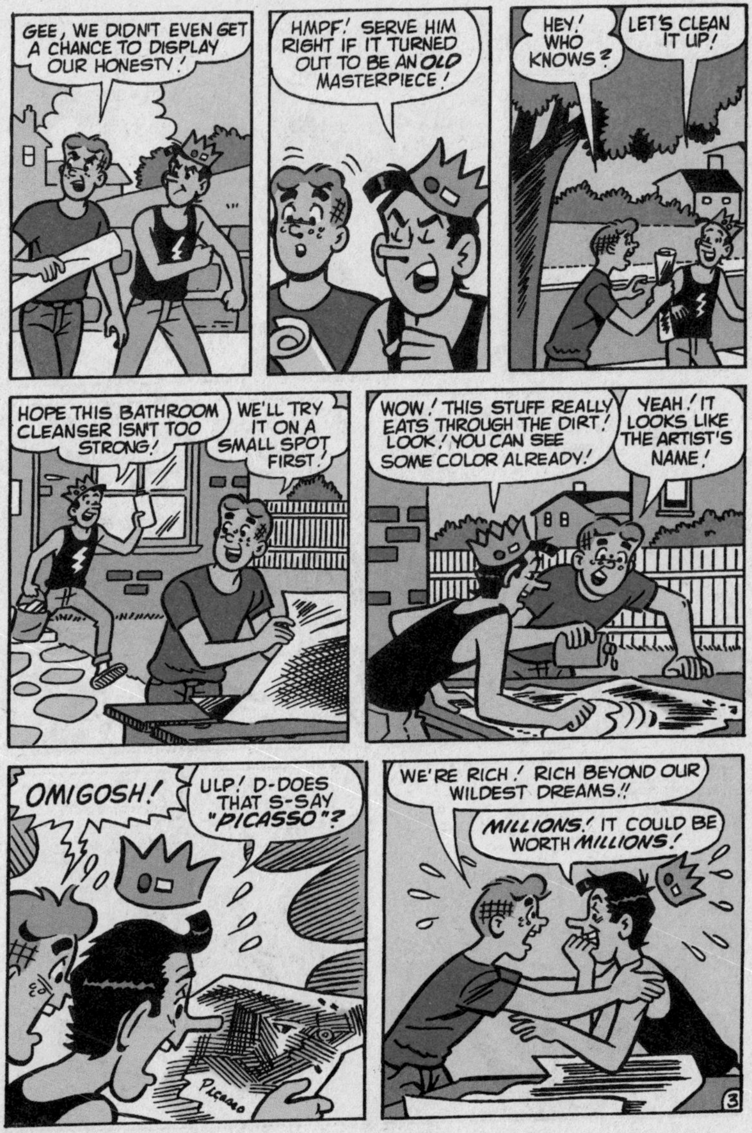
GEE, WE DIDN'T EVEN GET A CHANCE TO DISPLAY OUR HONESTY!
HMPF! SERVE HIM RIGHT IF IT TURNED OUT TO BE AN *OLD* MASTERPIECE!
HEY! WHO KNOWS?
LET'S CLEAN IT UP!
HOPE THIS BATHROOM CLEANSER ISN'T TOO STRONG!
WE'LL TRY IT ON A SMALL SPOT FIRST!
WOW! THIS STUFF REALLY EATS THROUGH THE DIRT! LOOK! YOU CAN SEE SOME COLOR ALREADY!
YEAH! IT LOOKS LIKE THE ARTIST'S NAME!
OMIGOSH!
ULP! D-DOES THAT S-SAY "*PICASSO*"?
PICASSO
WE'RE RICH! RICH BEYOND OUR WILDEST DREAMS!!
MILLIONS! IT COULD BE WORTH *MILLIONS!*
3

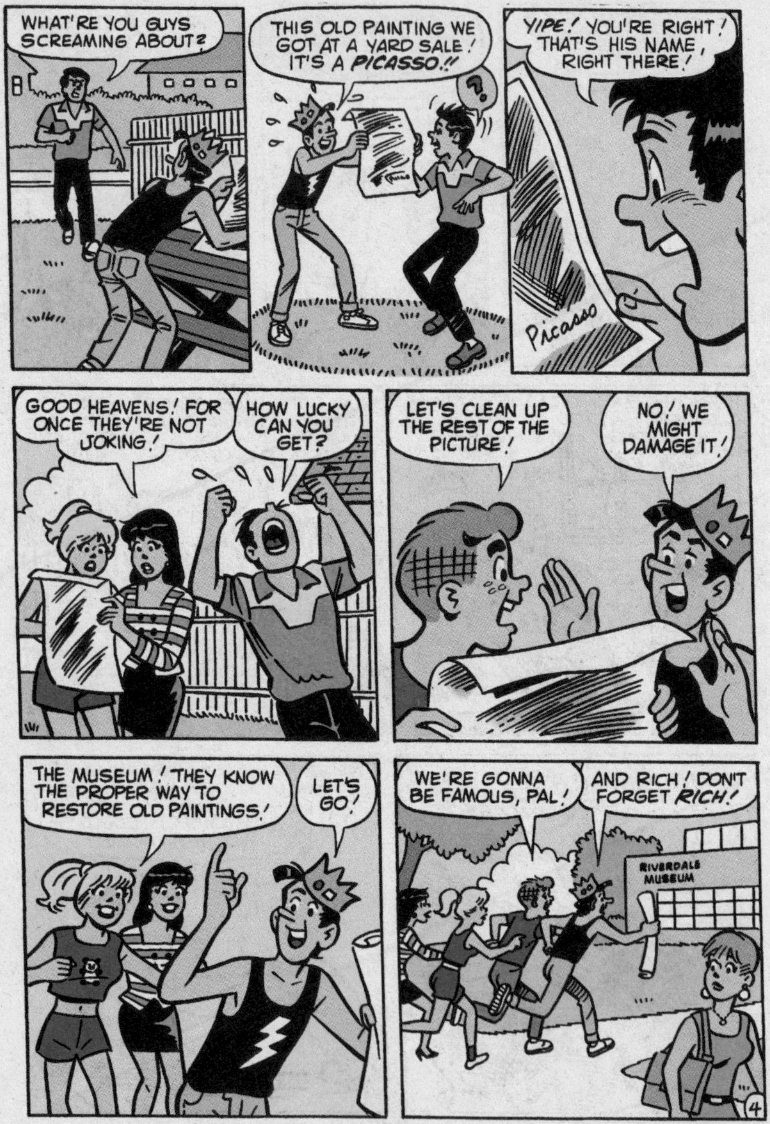
WHAT'RE YOU GUYS SCREAMING ABOUT?
THIS OLD PAINTING WE GOT AT A YARD SALE! IT'S A PICASSO!!
YIPE! YOU'RE RIGHT! THAT'S HIS NAME, RIGHT THERE!
Picasso
GOOD HEAVENS! FOR ONCE THEY'RE NOT JOKING!
HOW LUCKY CAN YOU GET?
LET'S CLEAN UP THE REST OF THE PICTURE!
NO! WE MIGHT DAMAGE IT!
THE MUSEUM! THEY KNOW THE PROPER WAY TO RESTORE OLD PAINTINGS!
LET'S GO!
WE'RE GONNA BE FAMOUS, PAL!
AND RICH! DON'T FORGET RICH!
RIVERDALE MUSEUM

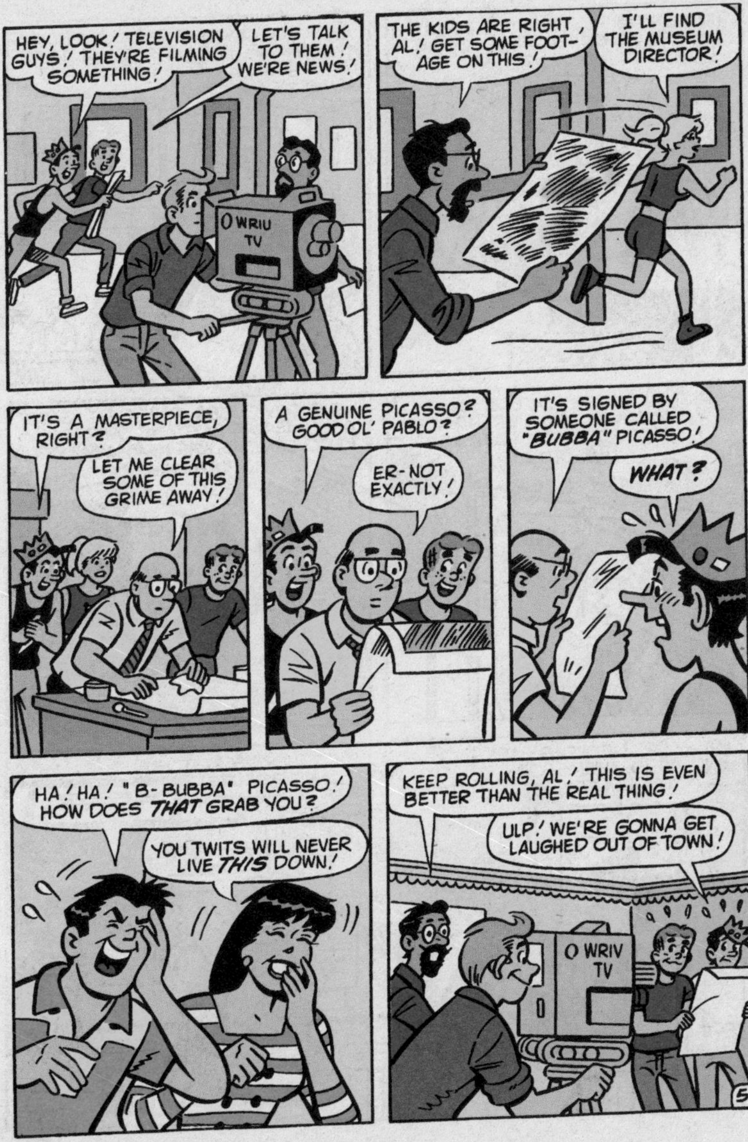

HEY, LOOK! TELEVISION GUYS! THEY'RE FILMING SOMETHING!
LET'S TALK TO THEM! WE'RE NEWS!
O WRIU TV
THE KIDS ARE RIGHT, AL! GET SOME FOOT-AGE ON THIS!
I'LL FIND THE MUSEUM DIRECTOR!
IT'S A MASTERPIECE, RIGHT?
LET ME CLEAR SOME OF THIS GRIME AWAY!
A GENUINE PICASSO? GOOD OL' PABLO?
ER-NOT EXACTLY!
IT'S SIGNED BY SOMEONE CALLED "BUBBA" PICASSO!
WHAT?
HA! HA! "B-BUBBA" PICASSO! HOW DOES THAT GRAB YOU?
YOU TWITS WILL NEVER LIVE THIS DOWN!
KEEP ROLLING, AL! THIS IS EVEN BETTER THAN THE REAL THING!
ULP! WE'RE GONNA GET LAUGHED OUT OF TOWN!
O WRIV TV

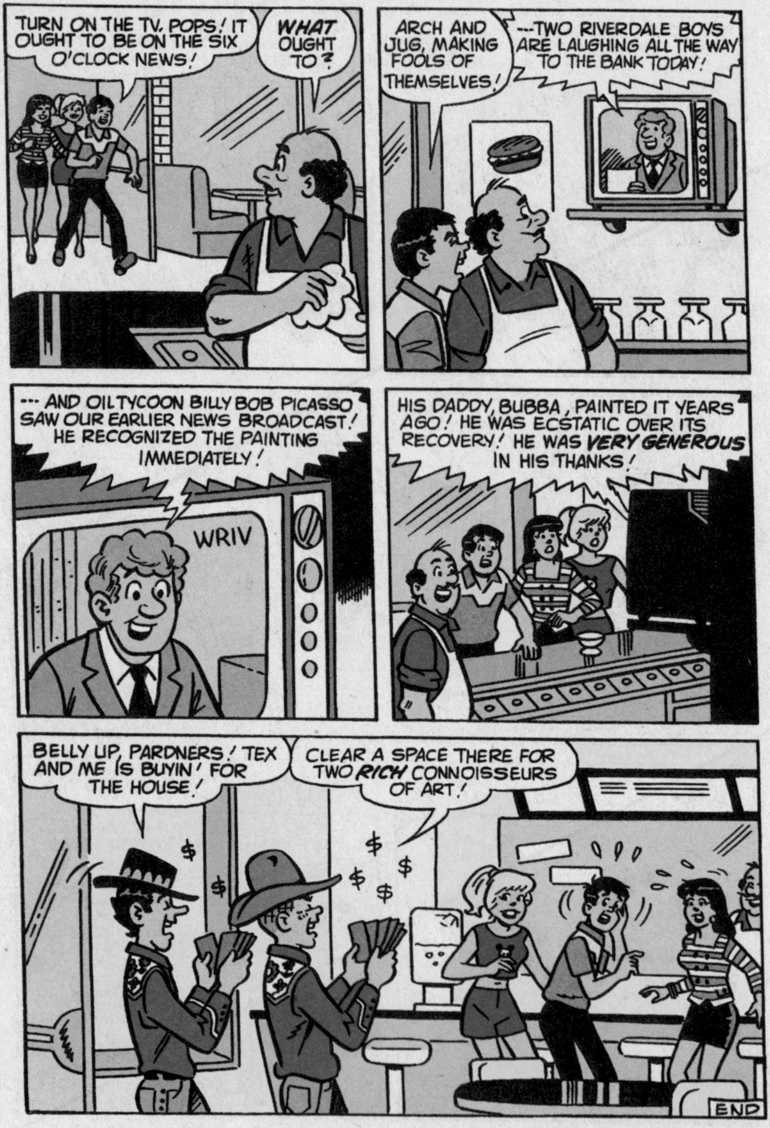
TURN ON THE TV, POPS! IT OUGHT TO BE ON THE SIX O'CLOCK NEWS!
WHAT OUGHT TO?
ARCH AND JUG, MAKING FOOLS OF THEMSELVES!
---TWO RIVERDALE BOYS ARE LAUGHING ALL THE WAY TO THE BANK TODAY!
--- AND OILTYCOON BILLY BOB PICASSO SAW OUR EARLIER NEWS BROADCAST! HE RECOGNIZED THE PAINTING IMMEDIATELY!
WRIV
HIS DADDY, BUBBA, PAINTED IT YEARS AGO! HE WAS ECSTATIC OVER ITS RECOVERY! HE WAS VERY GENEROUS IN HIS THANKS!
BELLY UP, PARDNERS! TEX AND ME IS BUYIN' FOR THE HOUSE!
CLEAR A SPACE THERE FOR TWO RICH CONNOISSEURS OF ART!
END

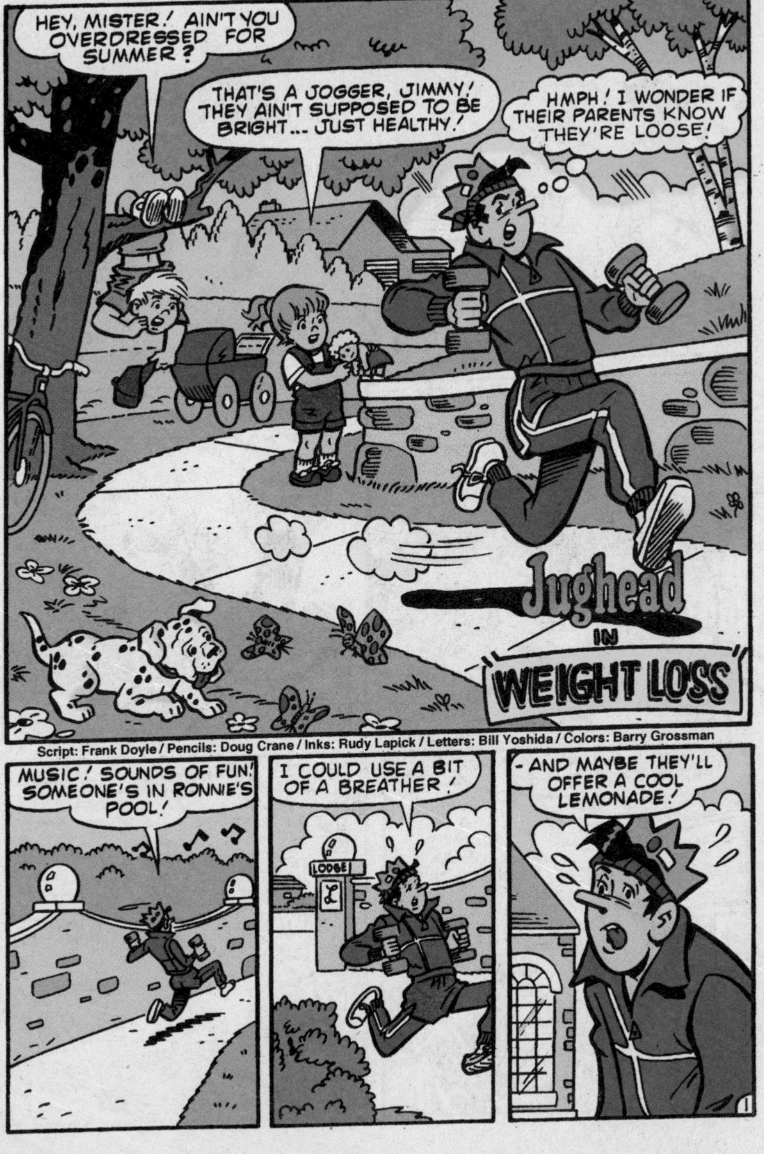
HEY, MISTER! AIN'T YOU OVERDRESSED FOR SUMMER?
THAT'S A JOGGER, JIMMY! THEY AIN'T SUPPOSED TO BE BRIGHT... JUST HEALTHY!
HMPH! I WONDER IF THEIR PARENTS KNOW THEY'RE LOOSE!
Jughead
IN
WEIGHT LOSS
Script: Frank Doyle / Pencils: Doug Crane / Inks: Rudy Lapick / Letters: Bill Yoshida / Colors: Barry Grossman
MUSIC! SOUNDS OF FUN! SOMEONE'S IN RONNIE'S POOL!
I COULD USE A BIT OF A BREATHER!
LODGE
-AND MAYBE THEY'LL OFFER A COOL LEMONADE!
1

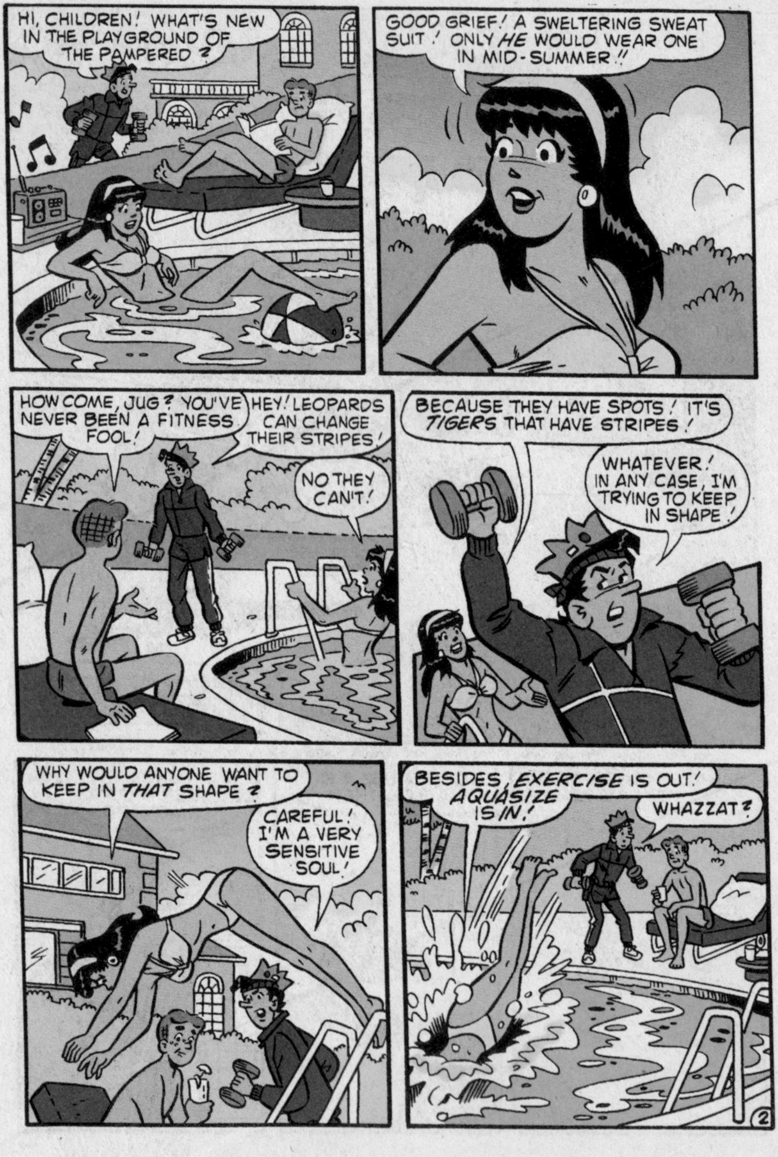
HI, CHILDREN! WHAT'S NEW IN THE PLAYGROUND OF THE PAMPERED?
GOOD GRIEF! A SWELTERING SWEAT SUIT! ONLY HE WOULD WEAR ONE IN MID-SUMMER!!
HOW COME, JUG? YOU'VE NEVER BEEN A FITNESS FOOL!
HEY! LEOPARDS CAN CHANGE THEIR STRIPES!
NO THEY CAN'T!
BECAUSE THEY HAVE SPOTS! IT'S TIGERS THAT HAVE STRIPES!
WHATEVER! IN ANY CASE, I'M TRYING TO KEEP IN SHAPE!
WHY WOULD ANYONE WANT TO KEEP IN THAT SHAPE?
CAREFUL! I'M A VERY SENSITIVE SOUL!
BESIDES, EXERCISE IS OUT! AQUASIZE IS IN!
WHAZZAT?
2

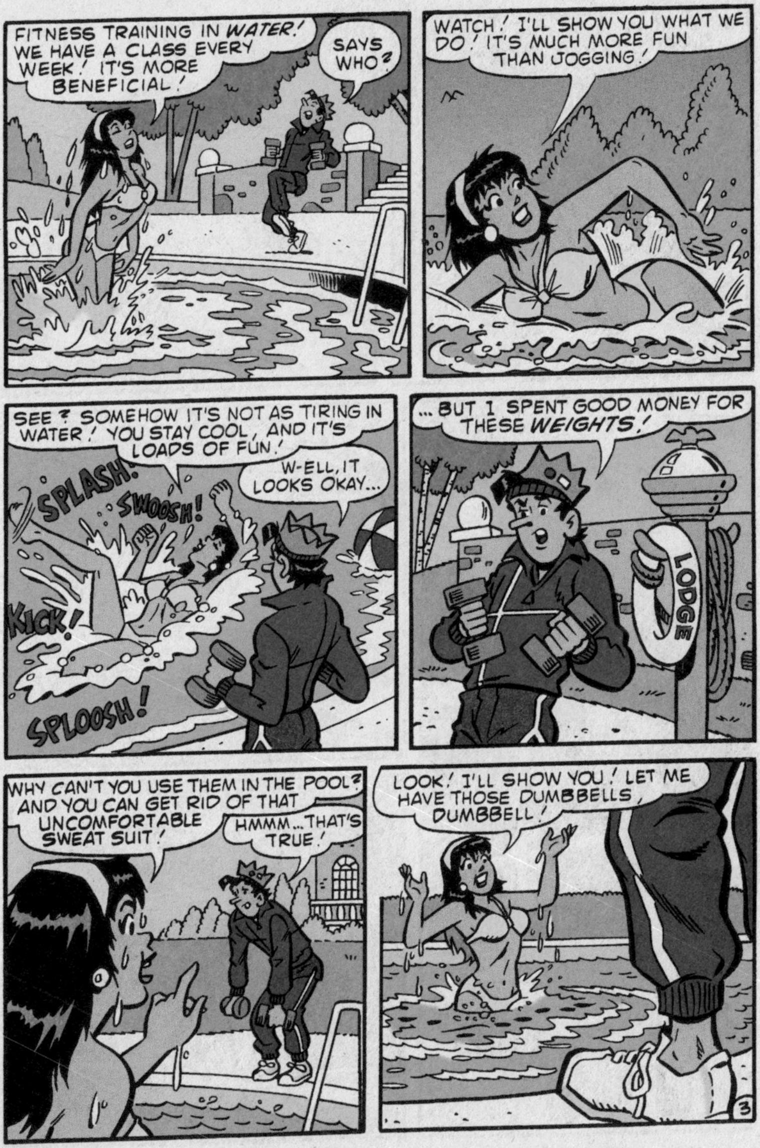
FITNESS TRAINING IN WATER! WE HAVE A CLASS EVERY WEEK! IT'S MORE BENEFICIAL!
SAYS WHO?
WATCH! I'LL SHOW YOU WHAT WE DO! IT'S MUCH MORE FUN THAN JOGGING!
SEE? SOMEHOW IT'S NOT AS TIRING IN WATER! YOU STAY COOL, AND IT'S LOADS OF FUN!
SPLASH!
SWOOSH!
W-ELL, IT LOOKS OKAY...
KICK!
SPLOOSH!
...BUT I SPENT GOOD MONEY FOR THESE WEIGHTS!
LODGE
WHY CAN'T YOU USE THEM IN THE POOL? AND YOU CAN GET RID OF THAT UNCOMFORTABLE SWEAT SUIT!
HMMM...THAT'S TRUE!
LOOK! I'LL SHOW YOU! LET ME HAVE THOSE DUMBBELLS, DUMBBELL!
3

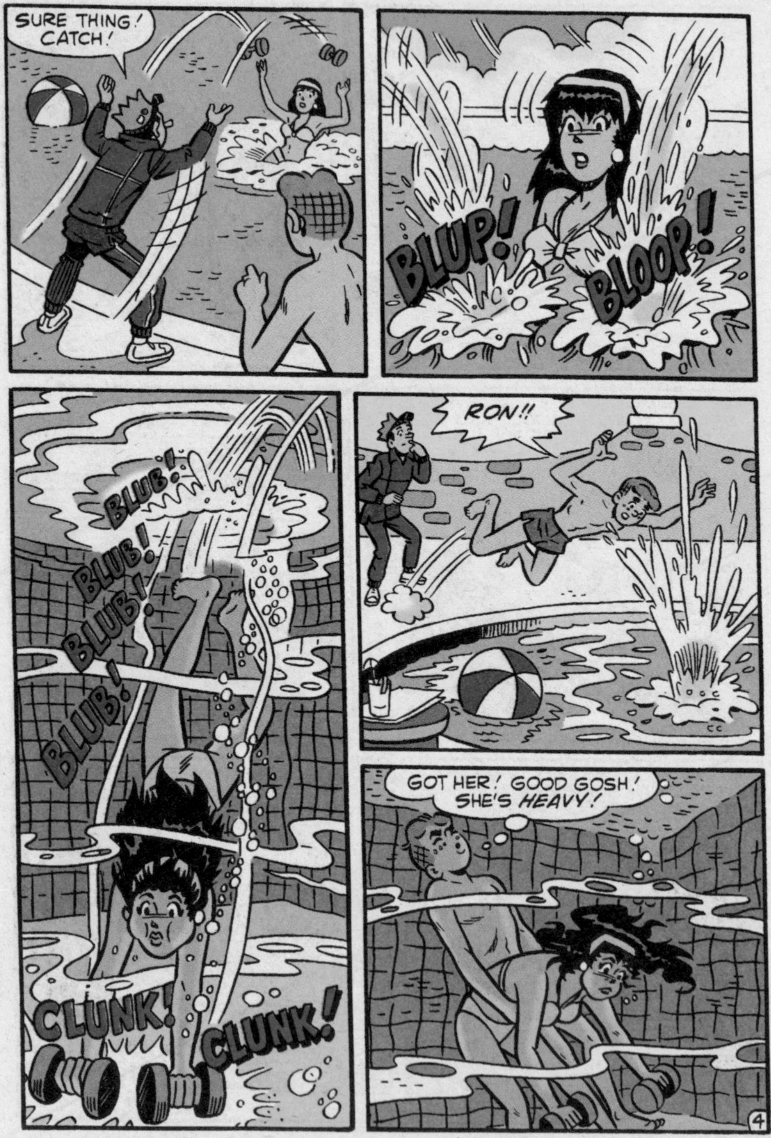
SURE THING! CATCH!
BLUP!
BLOOP!
BLUB!
BLUB!
BLUB!
BLUB!
CLUNK!
CLUNK!
RON!!
GOT HER! GOOD GOSH! SHE'S HEAVY!
4

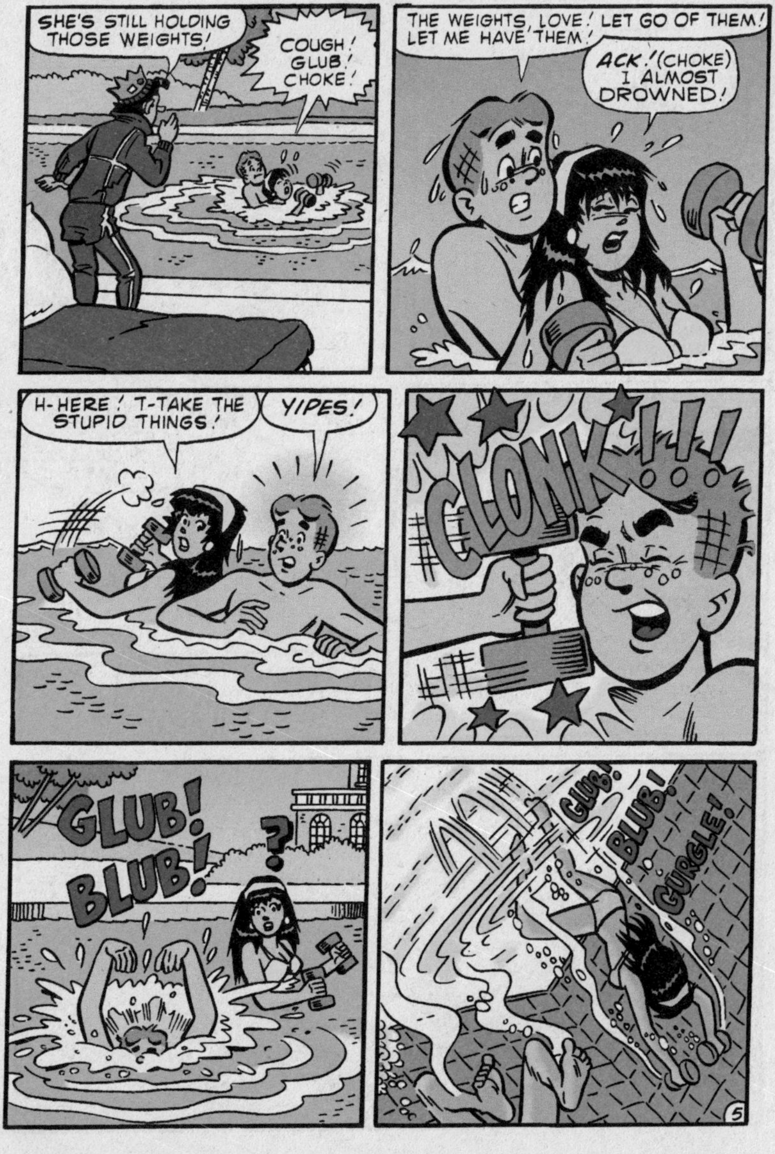
SHE'S STILL HOLDING THOSE WEIGHTS!
COUGH! GLUB! CHOKE!
THE WEIGHTS, LOVE! LET GO OF THEM! LET ME HAVE THEM!
ACK! (CHOKE) I ALMOST DROWNED!
H-HERE! T-TAKE THE STUPID THINGS!
YIPES!
CLONK!!!
GLUB! BLUB!
?
GLUB! BLUB! GURGLE!
5

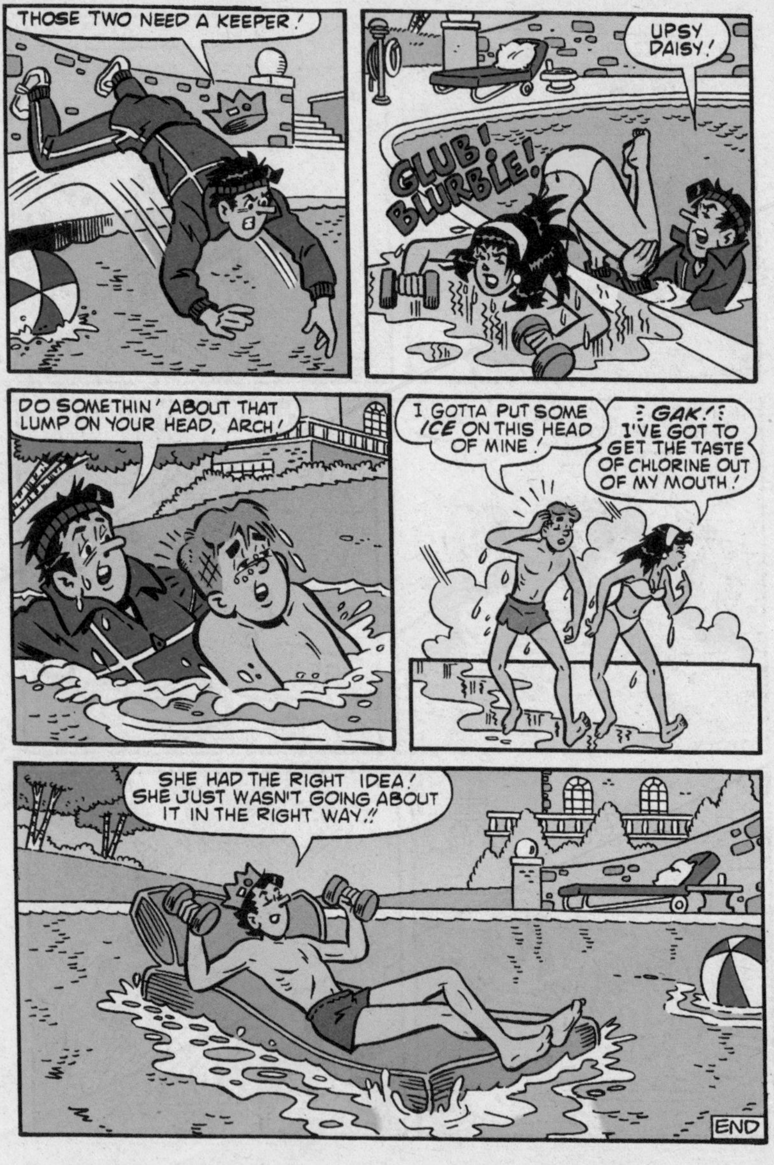
THOSE TWO NEED A KEEPER!
UPSY DAISY!
GLUB! BLURBLE!
DO SOMETHIN' ABOUT THAT LUMP ON YOUR HEAD, ARCH!
I GOTTA PUT SOME ICE ON THIS HEAD OF MINE!
GAK! I'VE GOT TO GET THE TASTE OF CHLORINE OUT OF MY MOUTH!
SHE HAD THE RIGHT IDEA! SHE JUST WASN'T GOING ABOUT IT IN THE RIGHT WAY!!
END

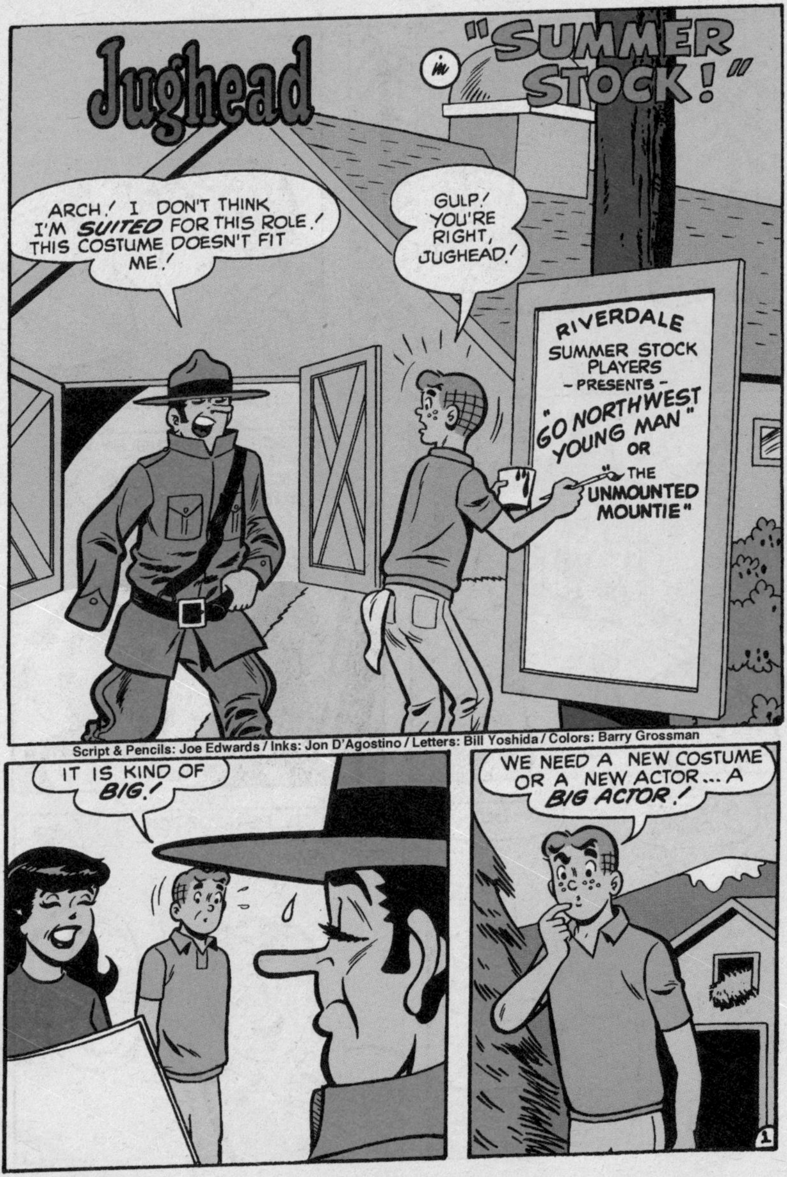
Jughead
in "SUMMER STOCK!"
ARCH! I DON'T THINK I'M SUITED FOR THIS ROLE! THIS COSTUME DOESN'T FIT ME!
GULP! YOU'RE RIGHT, JUGHEAD!
RIVERDALE SUMMER STOCK PLAYERS - PRESENTS - "GO NORTHWEST YOUNG MAN" OR "THE UNMOUNTED MOUNTIE"
Script & Pencils: Joe Edwards / Inks: Jon D'Agostino / Letters: Bill Yoshida / Colors: Barry Grossman
IT IS KIND OF BIG!
WE NEED A NEW COSTUME OR A NEW ACTOR... A BIG ACTOR!
1

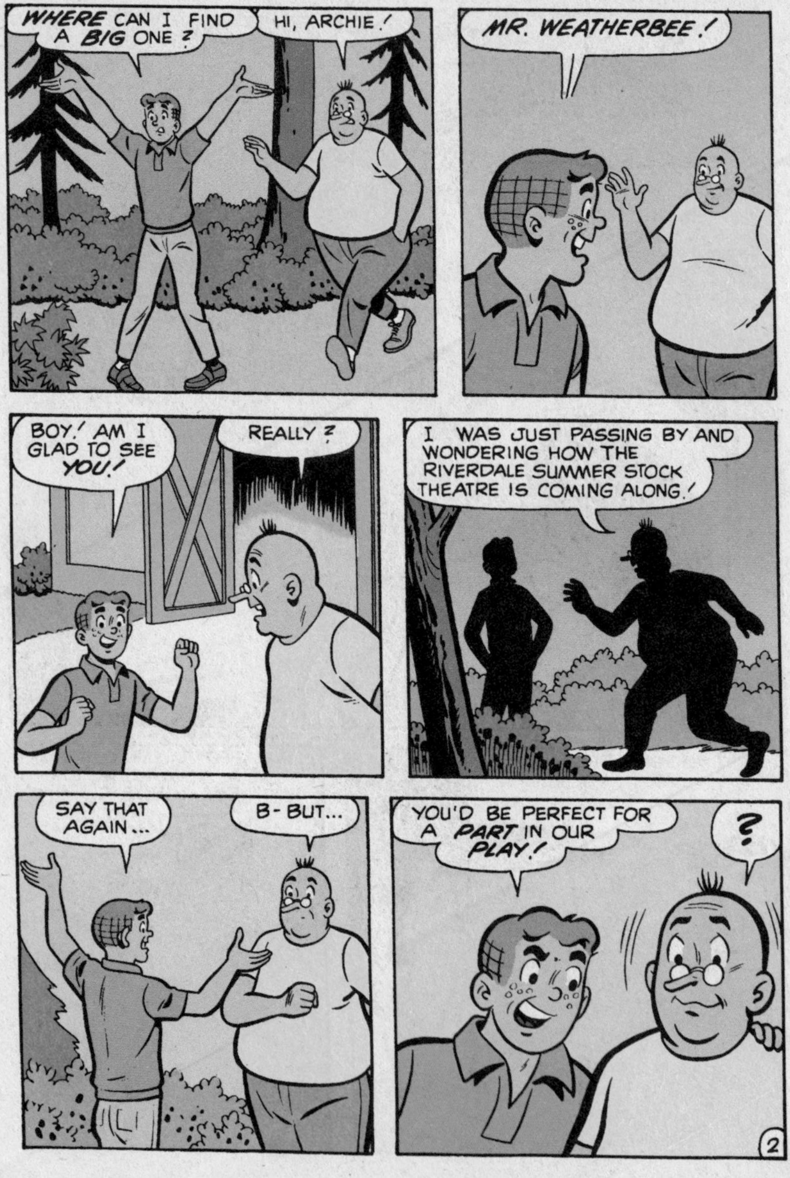
WHERE CAN I FIND A BIG ONE?
HI, ARCHIE!
MR. WEATHERBEE!
BOY! AM I GLAD TO SEE YOU!
REALLY?
I WAS JUST PASSING BY AND WONDERING HOW THE RIVERDALE SUMMER STOCK THEATRE IS COMING ALONG!
SAY THAT AGAIN...
B-BUT...
YOU'D BE PERFECT FOR A PART IN OUR PLAY!
?
2

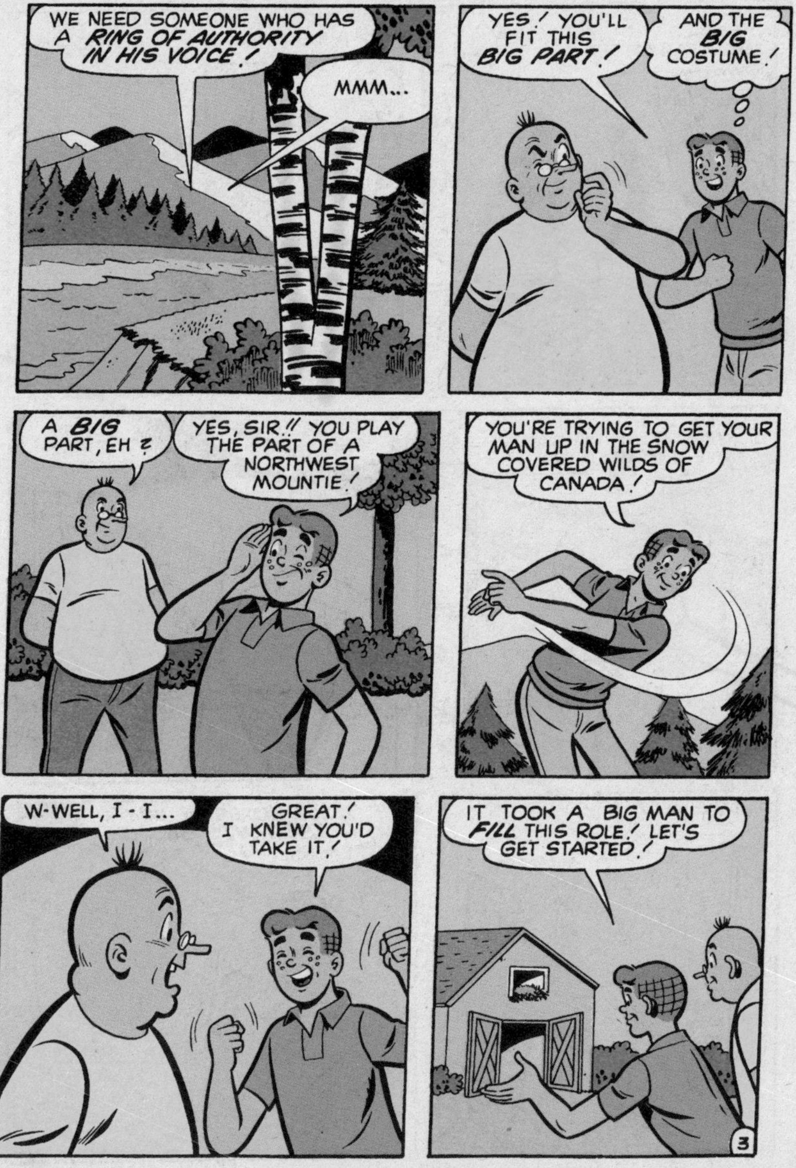
WE NEED SOMEONE WHO HAS A RING OF AUTHORITY IN HIS VOICE!
MMM...
YES! YOU'LL FIT THIS BIG PART!
AND THE BIG COSTUME!
A BIG PART, EH?
YES, SIR!! YOU PLAY THE PART OF A NORTHWEST MOUNTIE!
YOU'RE TRYING TO GET YOUR MAN UP IN THE SNOW COVERED WILDS OF CANADA!
W-WELL, I - I...
GREAT! I KNEW YOU'D TAKE IT!
IT TOOK A BIG MAN TO FILL THIS ROLE! LET'S GET STARTED!
3

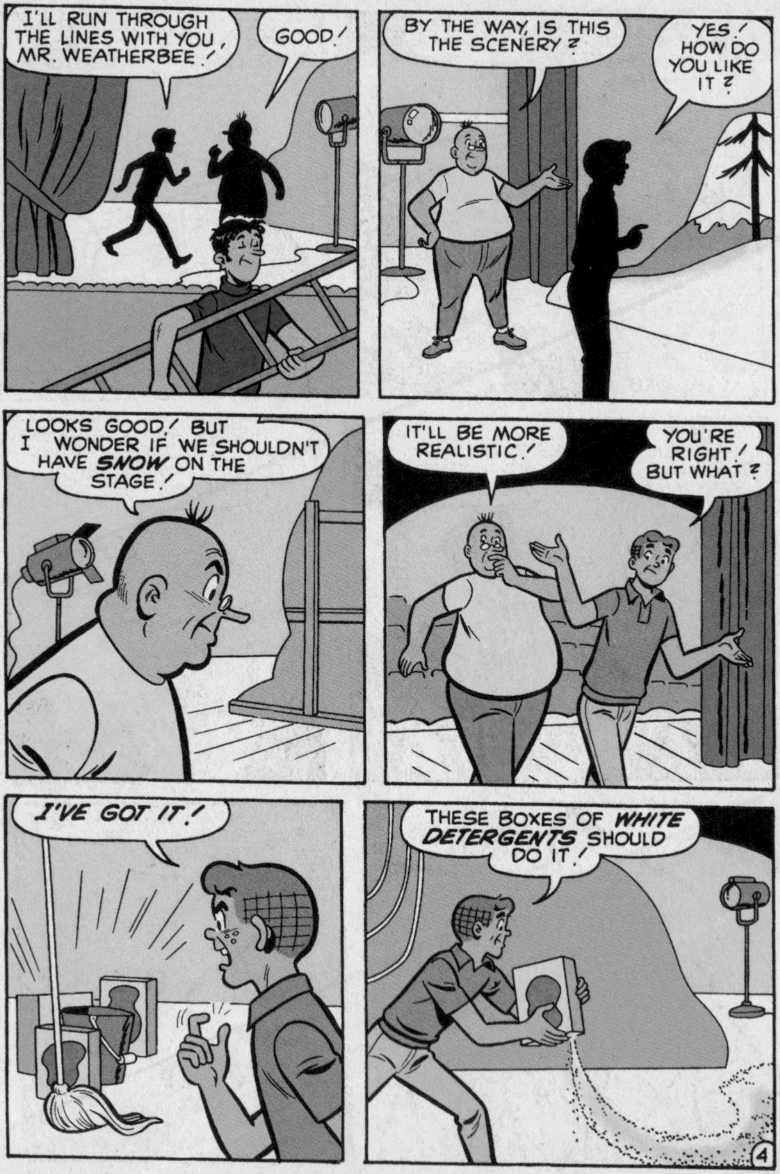

I'LL RUN THROUGH THE LINES WITH YOU, MR. WEATHERBEE!
GOOD!
BY THE WAY, IS THIS THE SCENERY?
YES! HOW DO YOU LIKE IT?
LOOKS GOOD! BUT I WONDER IF WE SHOULDN'T HAVE *SNOW* ON THE STAGE!
IT'LL BE MORE REALISTIC!
YOU'RE RIGHT! BUT WHAT?
I'VE GOT IT!
THESE BOXES OF *WHITE DETERGENTS* SHOULD DO IT!
4

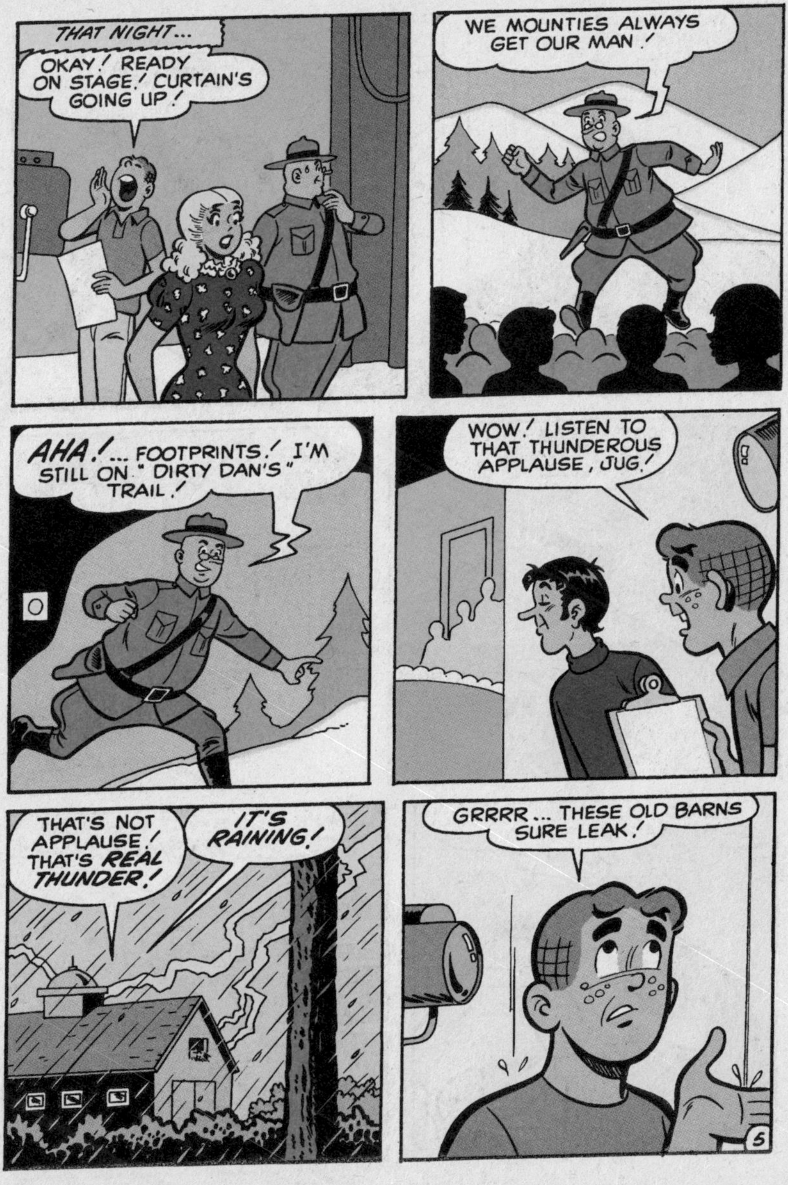
THAT NIGHT...
OKAY! READY ON STAGE! CURTAIN'S GOING UP!
WE MOUNTIES ALWAYS GET OUR MAN!
AHA!... FOOTPRINTS! I'M STILL ON "DIRTY DAN'S" TRAIL!
WOW! LISTEN TO THAT THUNDEROUS APPLAUSE, JUG!
THAT'S NOT APPLAUSE! THAT'S REAL THUNDER!
IT'S RAINING!
GRRRR... THESE OLD BARNS SURE LEAK!
5

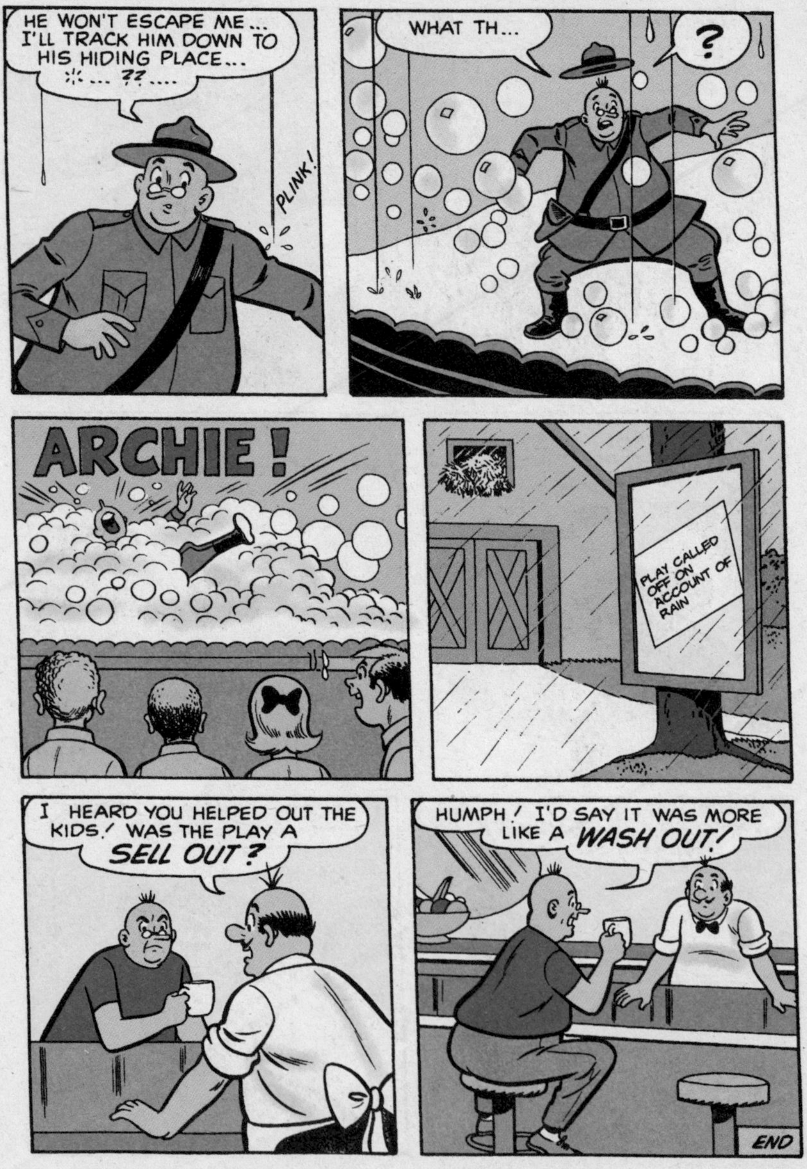
HE WON'T ESCAPE ME... I'LL TRACK HIM DOWN TO HIS HIDING PLACE... ... ??....
PLINK!
WHAT TH...
?
ARCHIE!
PLAY CALLED OFF ON ACCOUNT OF RAIN
I HEARD YOU HELPED OUT THE KIDS! WAS THE PLAY A SELL OUT?
HUMPH! I'D SAY IT WAS MORE LIKE A WASH OUT!
END

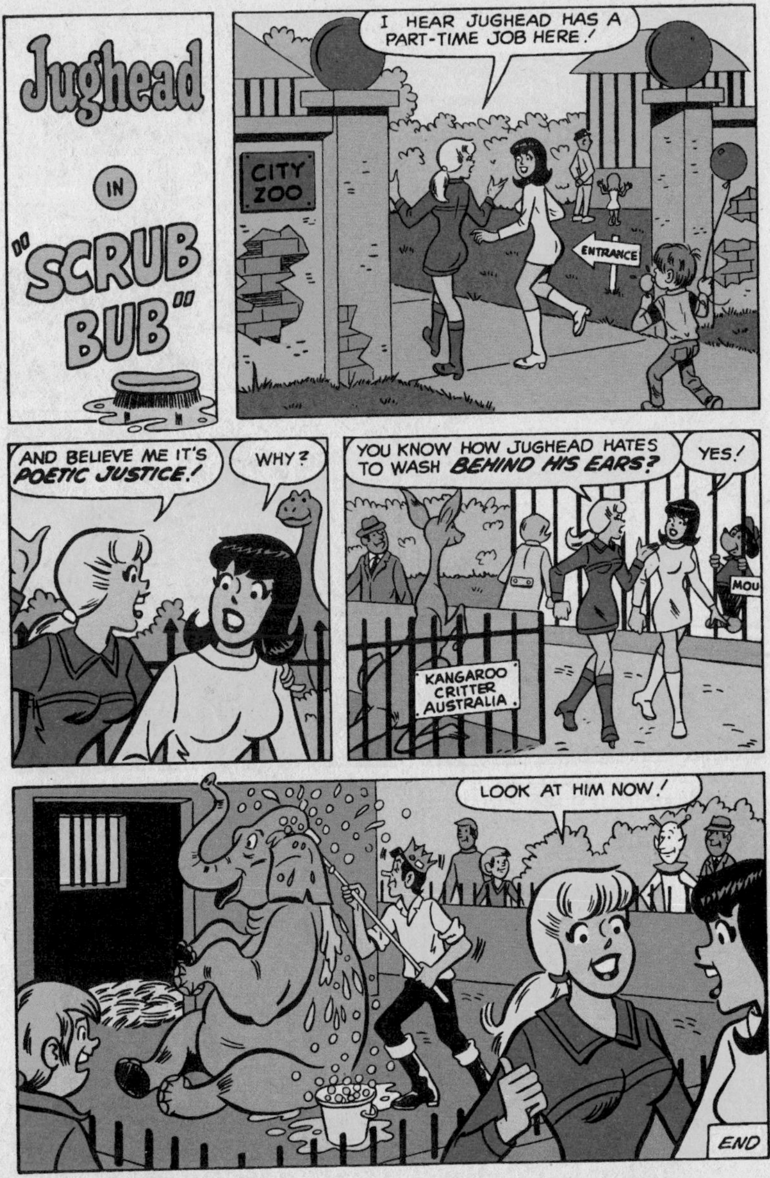
Jughead
IN
"SCRUB BUB"
I HEAR JUGHEAD HAS A PART-TIME JOB HERE!
CITY ZOO
ENTRANCE
AND BELIEVE ME IT'S POETIC JUSTICE!
WHY?
YOU KNOW HOW JUGHEAD HATES TO WASH BEHIND HIS EARS?
YES!
KANGAROO CRITTER AUSTRALIA
LOOK AT HIM NOW!
END

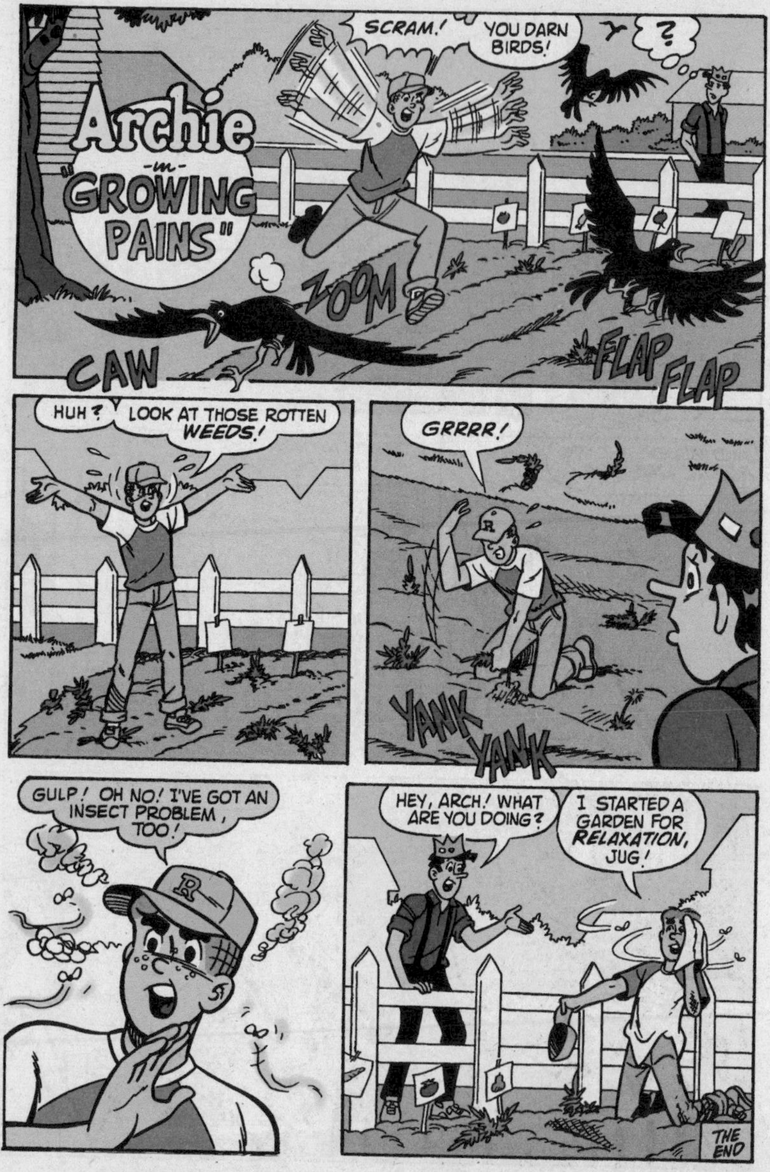
Archie
-in-
"GROWING PAINS"
SCRAM!
YOU DARN BIRDS!
?
ZOOM
CAW
FLAP FLAP
HUH?
LOOK AT THOSE ROTTEN WEEDS!
GRRRR!
YANK YANK
GULP! OH NO! I'VE GOT AN INSECT PROBLEM, TOO!
HEY, ARCH! WHAT ARE YOU DOING?
I STARTED A GARDEN FOR RELAXATION, JUG!
THE END

Vamp It Up
***Betty & Veronica* #261, 2012**
by Dan Parent, Rich Koslowski, Jack Morelli and Tom Chu

This story was so much fun, because drawing the summery beach-type stories are always the best. And this story was twice the fun because I borrowed from the very popular genre of vampires, which we know permeates in pop culture today with everything from *Twilight* to *True Blood*.

For those of us comic geeks, Vampirella was another popular vampire character. So with a few tweaks, we have Vampironica! And we all know Buffy the Vampire Slayer, so why not make the plunge and go for Betty the Vampire Slayer? This was another one of those fun stories that just sort of writes itself. Because when you have vampire teen beach parties, vampire slayers and mad vampire scientists, what else do you need?

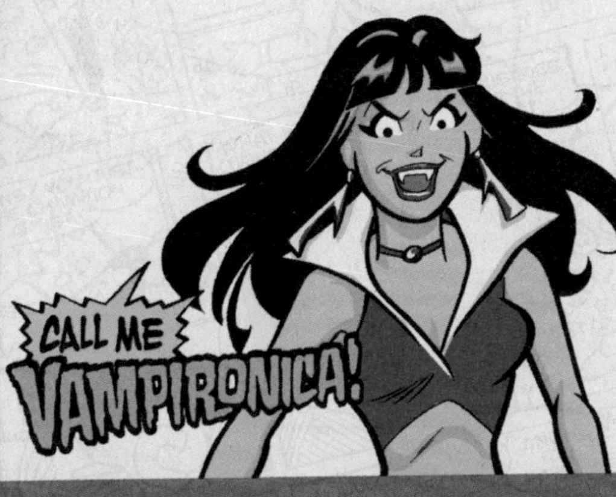
CALL ME
VAMPIRONICA!

Dan Parent
Writer and Artist,
Archie Comics

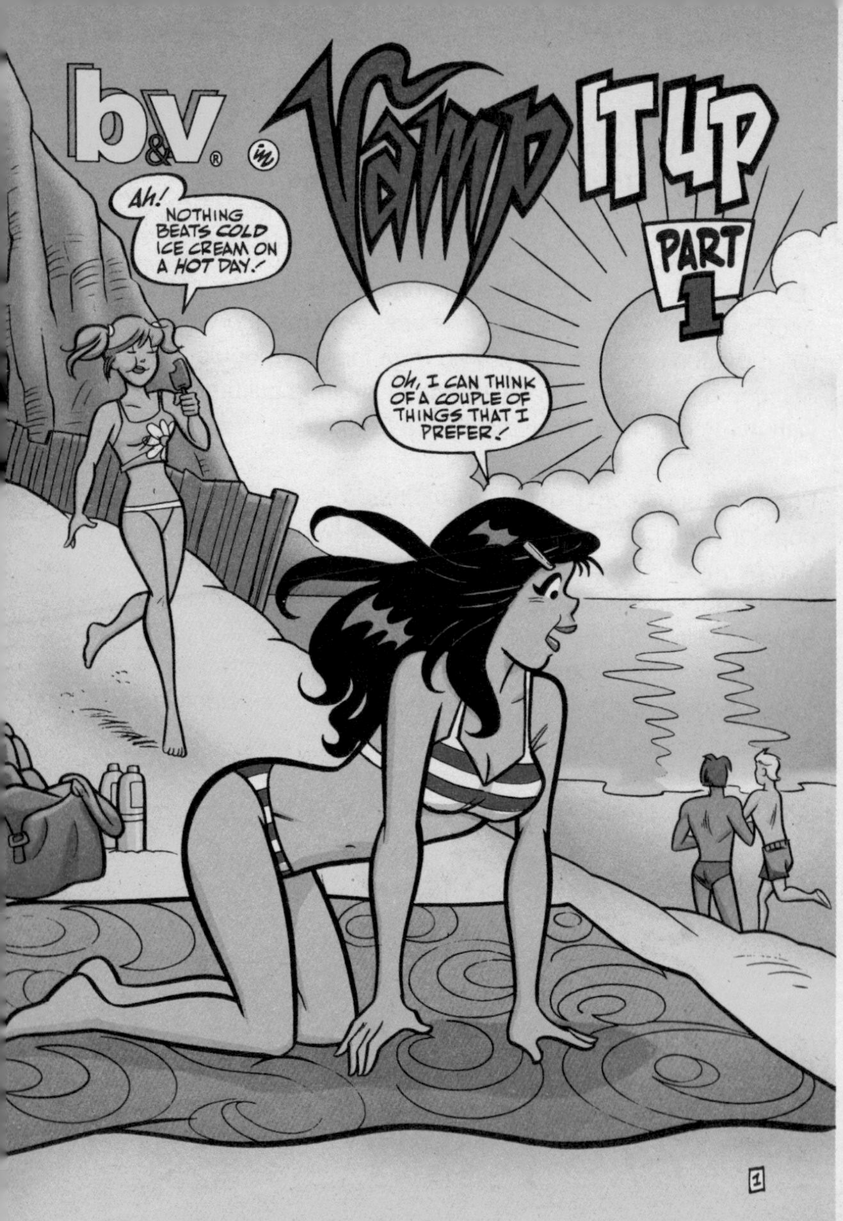
b&v®
in
Vamp It Up
Part 1
Ah! Nothing beats cold ice cream on a hot day!
Oh, I can think of a couple of things that I prefer!
1

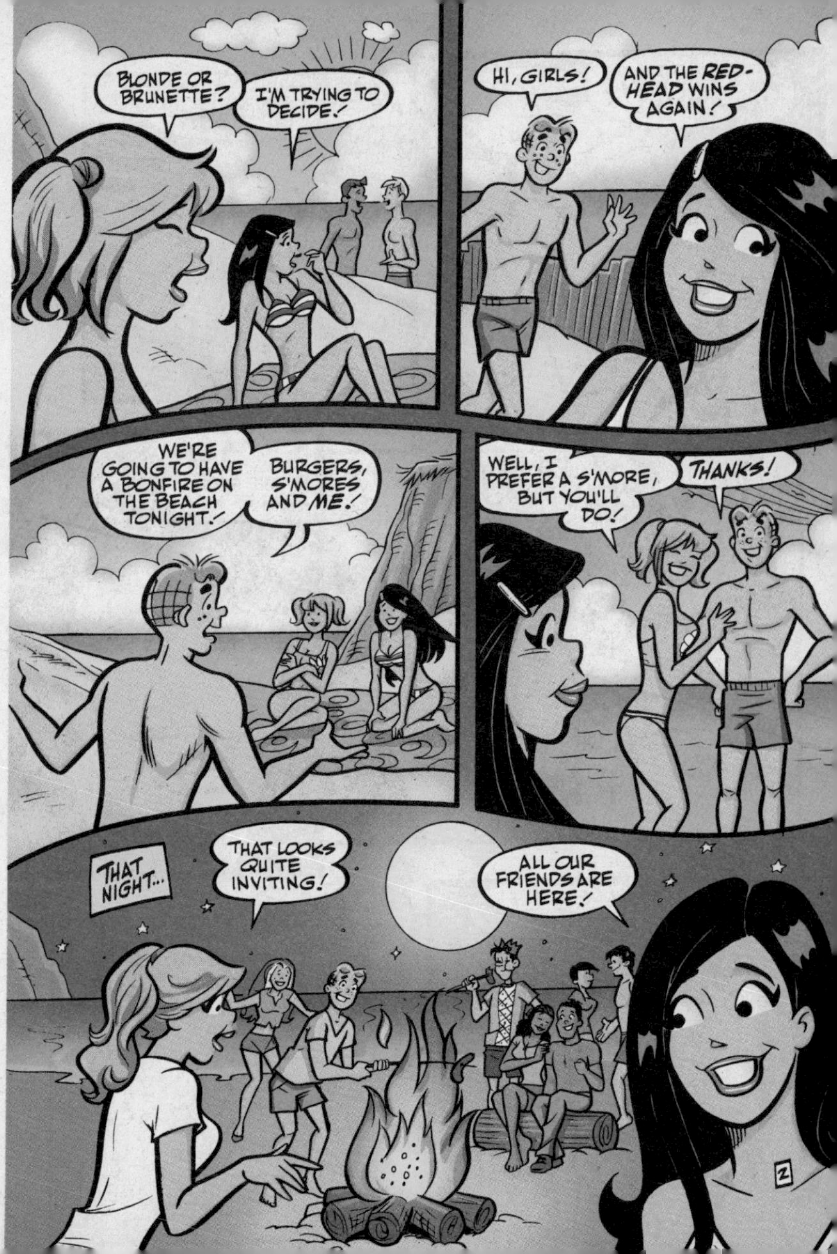
BLONDE OR BRUNETTE?
I'M TRYING TO DECIDE!
HI, GIRLS!
AND THE RED-HEAD WINS AGAIN!
WE'RE GOING TO HAVE A BONFIRE ON THE BEACH TONIGHT!
BURGERS, S'MORES AND ME!
WELL, I PREFER A S'MORE, BUT YOU'LL DO!
THANKS!
THAT NIGHT...
THAT LOOKS QUITE INVITING!
ALL OUR FRIENDS ARE HERE!
2

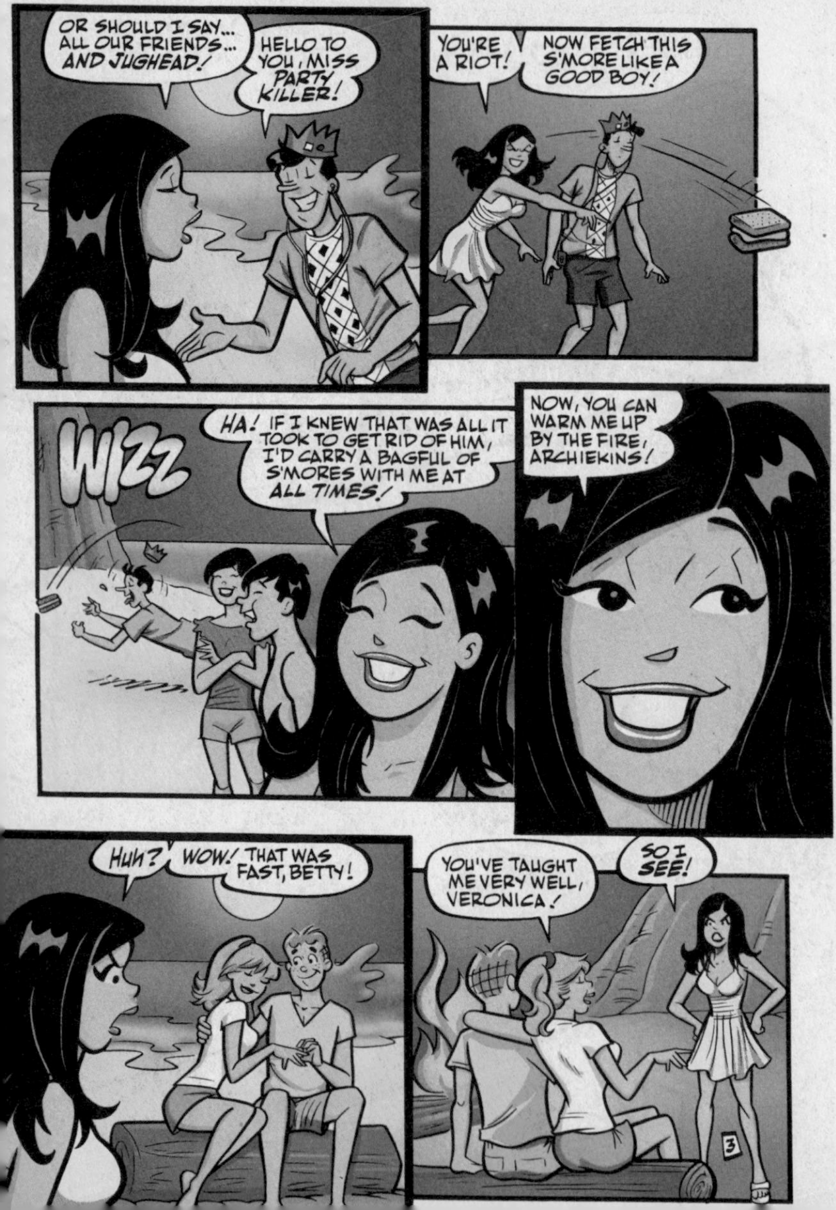

OR SHOULD I SAY... ALL OUR FRIENDS... AND JUGHEAD!
HELLO TO YOU, MISS PARTY KILLER!
YOU'RE A RIOT!
NOW FETCH THIS S'MORE LIKE A GOOD BOY!
WIZZ
HA! IF I KNEW THAT WAS ALL IT TOOK TO GET RID OF HIM, I'D CARRY A BAGFUL OF S'MORES WITH ME AT ALL TIMES!
NOW, YOU CAN WARM ME UP BY THE FIRE, ARCHIEKINS!
HUH?
WOW! THAT WAS FAST, BETTY!
YOU'VE TAUGHT ME VERY WELL, VERONICA!
SO I SEE!
3

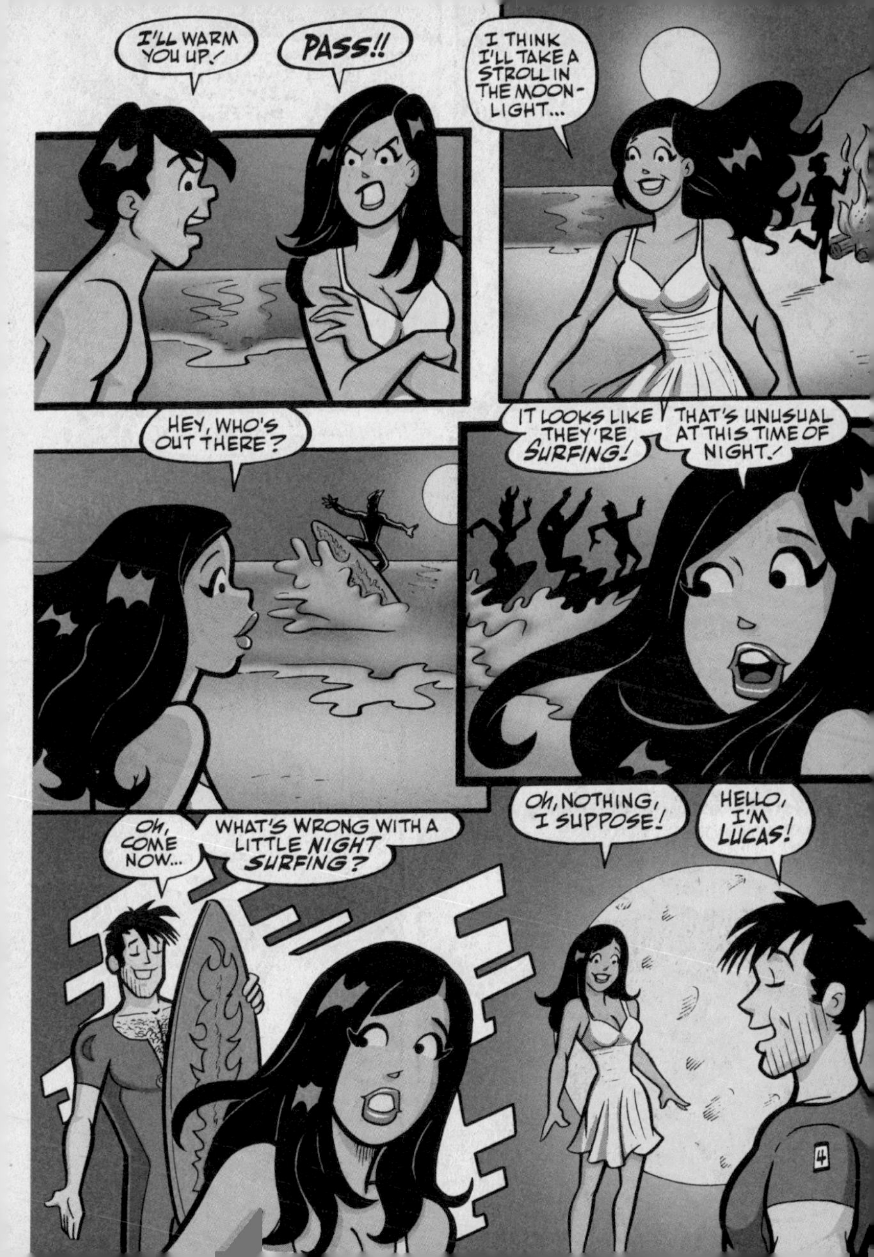

I'LL WARM YOU UP!
PASS!!
I THINK I'LL TAKE A STROLL IN THE MOON-LIGHT...
HEY, WHO'S OUT THERE?
IT LOOKS LIKE THEY'RE SURFING!
THAT'S UNUSUAL AT THIS TIME OF NIGHT!
Oh, COME NOW...
WHAT'S WRONG WITH A LITTLE NIGHT SURFING?
Oh, NOTHING, I SUPPOSE!
HELLO, I'M LUCAS!

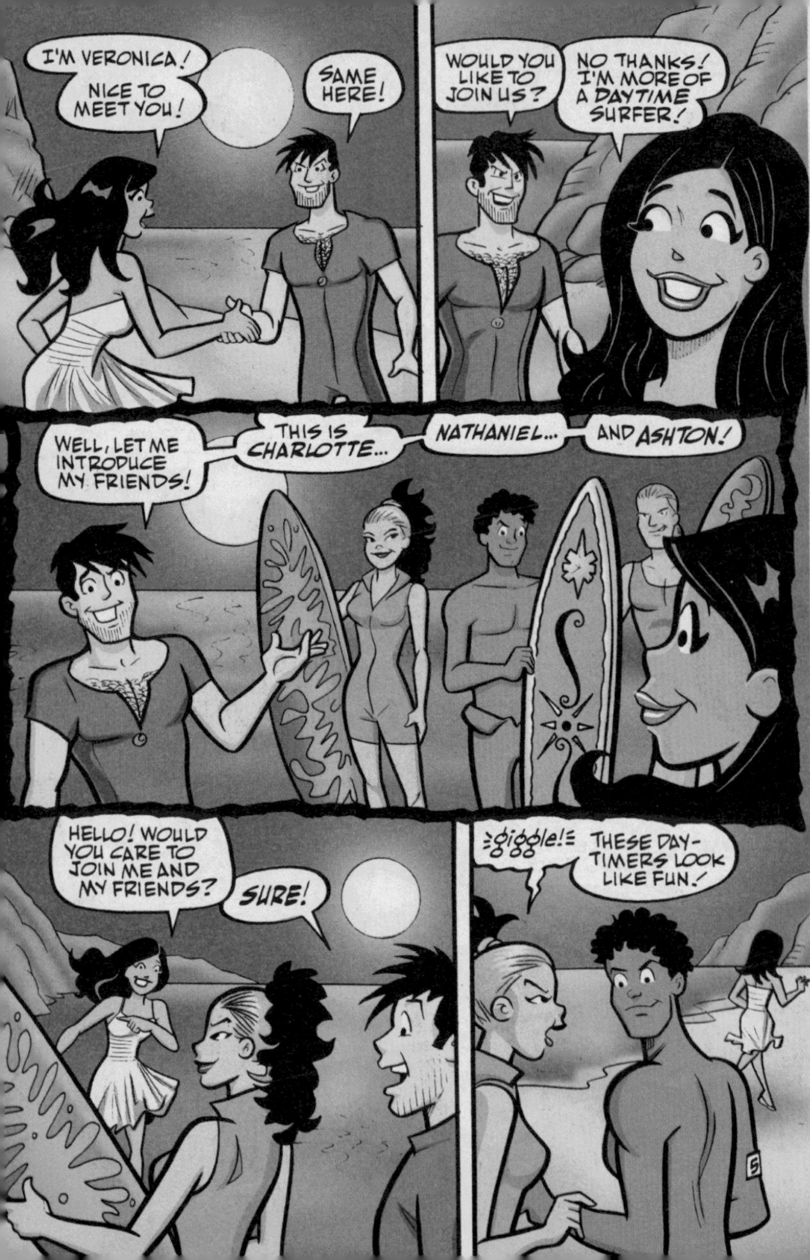
I'M VERONICA!
NICE TO MEET YOU!
SAME HERE!
WOULD YOU LIKE TO JOIN US?
NO THANKS! I'M MORE OF A DAYTIME SURFER!
WELL, LET ME INTRODUCE MY FRIENDS!
THIS IS CHARLOTTE...
NATHANIEL...
AND ASHTON!
HELLO! WOULD YOU CARE TO JOIN ME AND MY FRIENDS?
SURE!
giggle!
THESE DAY-TIMERS LOOK LIKE FUN!
5

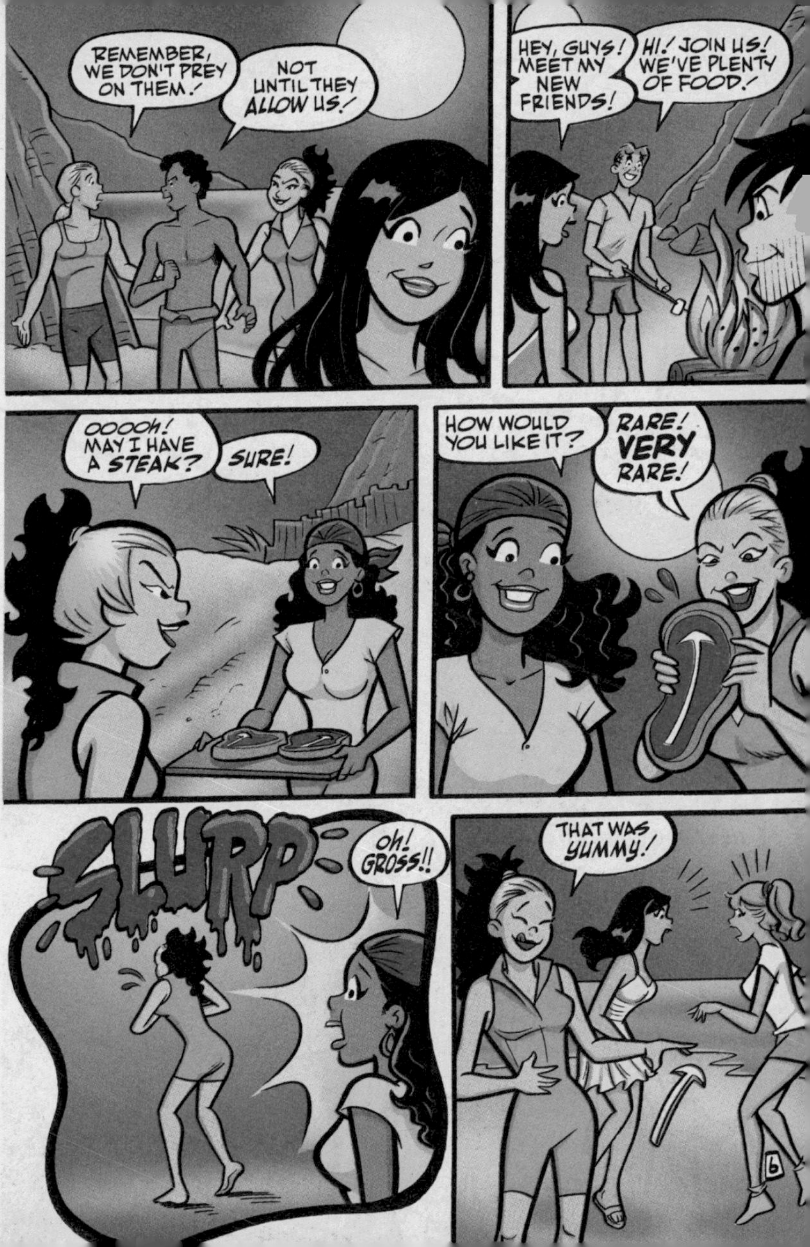
REMEMBER, WE DON'T PREY ON THEM!
NOT UNTIL THEY ALLOW US!
HEY, GUYS! MEET MY NEW FRIENDS!
HI! JOIN US! WE'VE PLENTY OF FOOD!
OOOOH! MAY I HAVE A STEAK?
SURE!
HOW WOULD YOU LIKE IT?
RARE! VERY RARE!
SLURP
OH! GROSS!!
THAT WAS YUMMY!
6

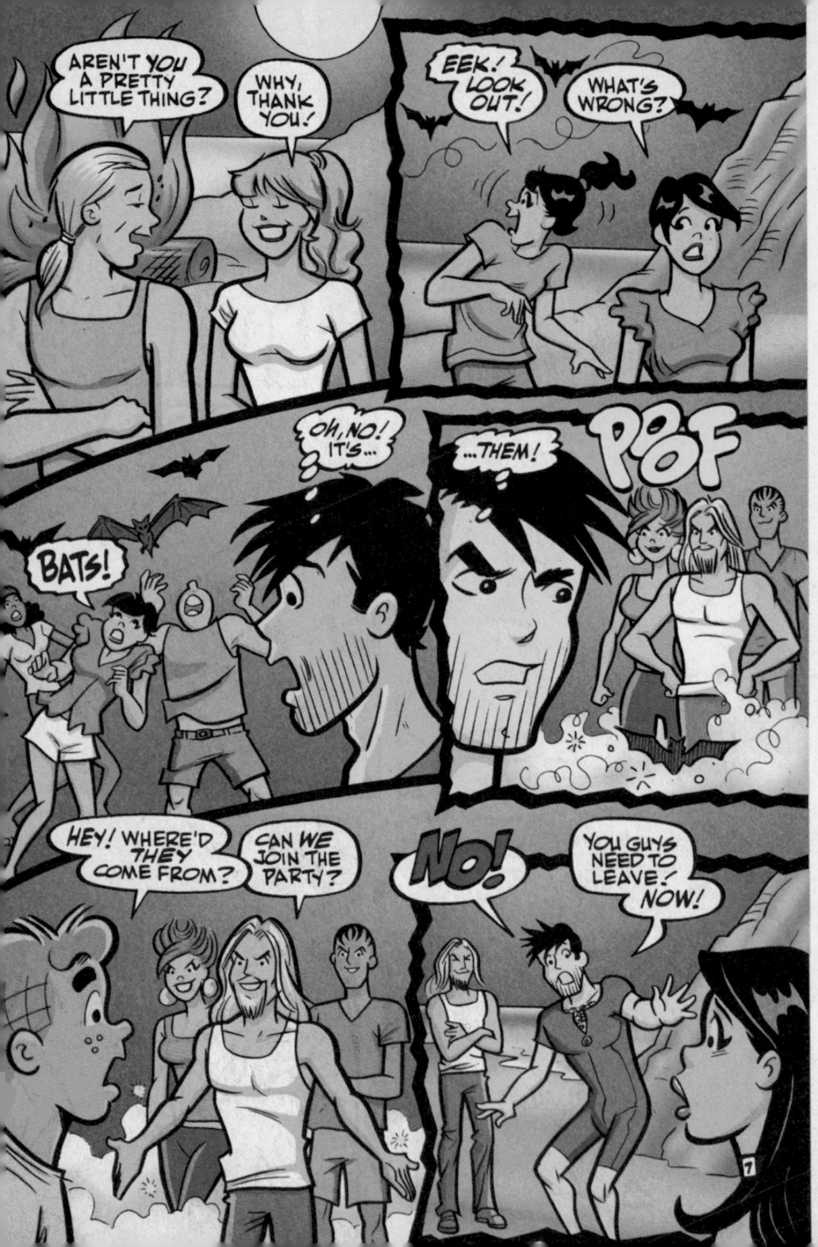

AREN'T YOU A PRETTY LITTLE THING?
WHY, THANK YOU!
EEK! LOOK OUT!
WHAT'S WRONG?
BATS!
Oh, NO! IT'S...
...THEM!
POOF
HEY! WHERE'D THEY COME FROM?
CAN WE JOIN THE PARTY?
NO!
YOU GUYS NEED TO LEAVE! NOW!
7

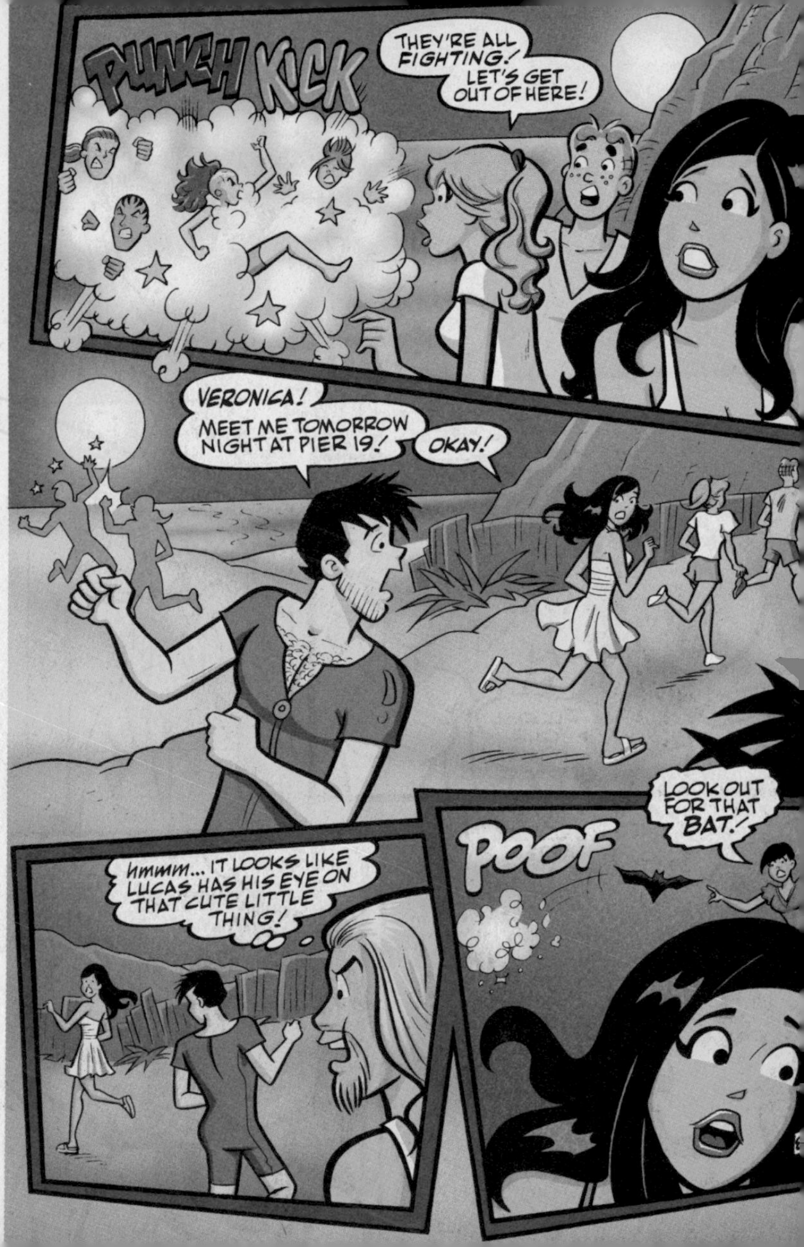
PUNCH
KICK
THEY'RE ALL FIGHTING! LET'S GET OUT OF HERE!
VERONICA! MEET ME TOMORROW NIGHT AT PIER 19!
OKAY!
hmmm... IT LOOKS LIKE LUCAS HAS HIS EYE ON THAT CUTE LITTLE THING!
POOF
LOOK OUT FOR THAT BAT!

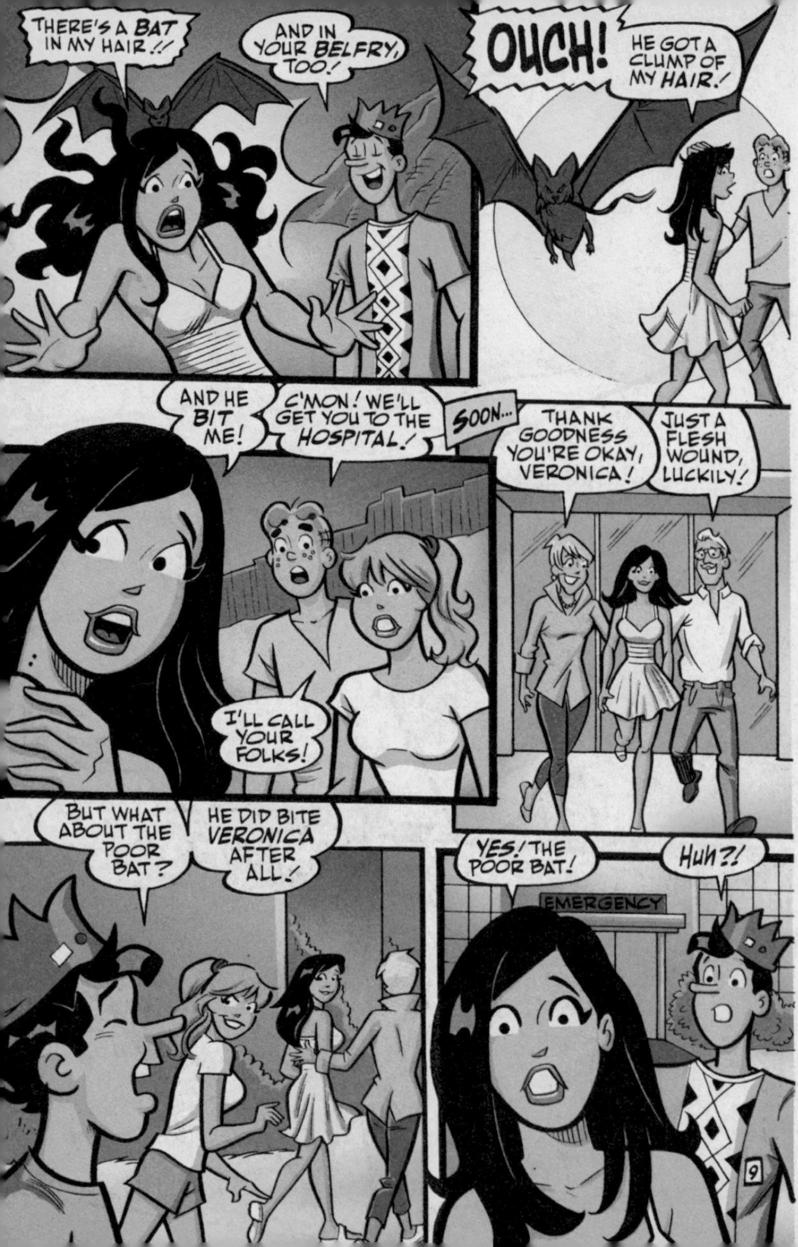
THERE'S A BAT IN MY HAIR!!
AND IN YOUR BELFRY, TOO!
OUCH!
HE GOT A CLUMP OF MY HAIR!
AND HE BIT ME!
C'MON! WE'LL GET YOU TO THE HOSPITAL!
I'LL CALL YOUR FOLKS!
SOON...
THANK GOODNESS YOU'RE OKAY, VERONICA!
JUST A FLESH WOUND, LUCKILY!
BUT WHAT ABOUT THE POOR BAT?
HE DID BITE VERONICA AFTER ALL!
YES! THE POOR BAT!
Huh?!
EMERGENCY
9

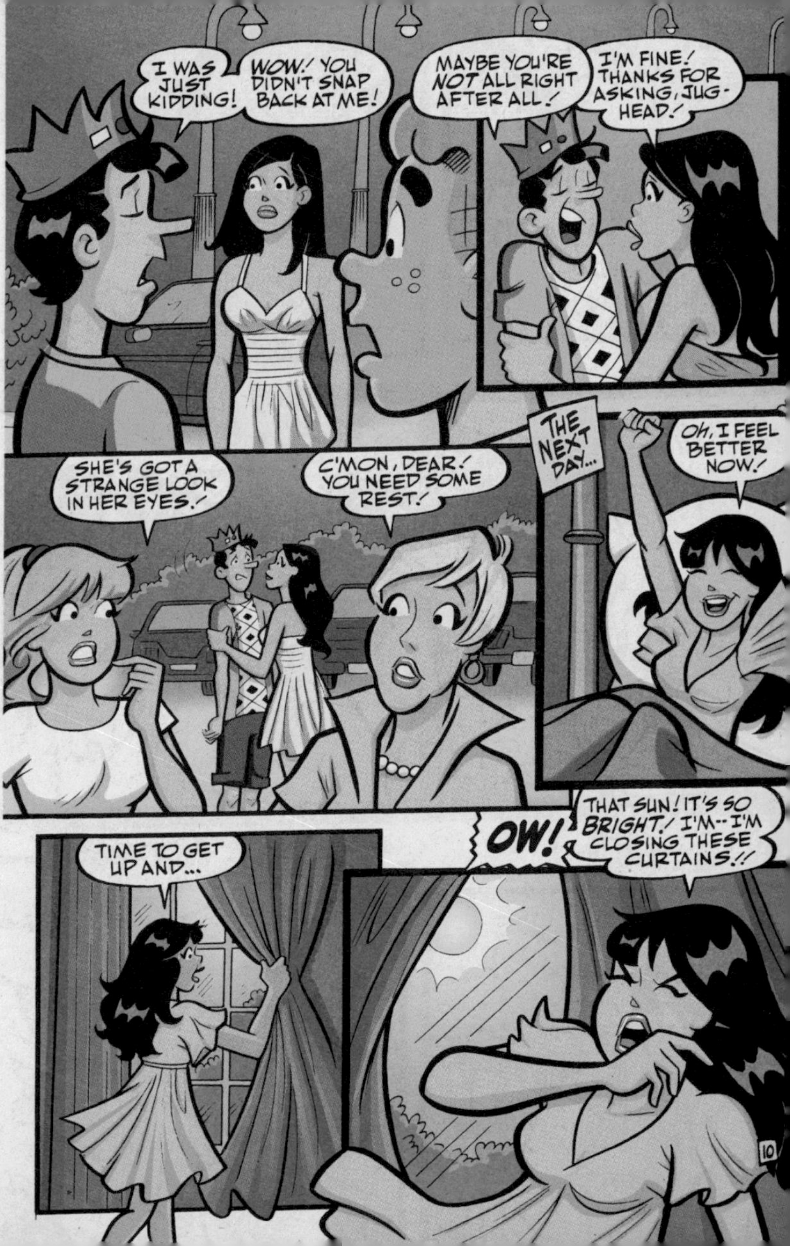
I WAS JUST KIDDING!
WOW! YOU DIDN'T SNAP BACK AT ME!
MAYBE YOU'RE NOT ALL RIGHT AFTER ALL!
I'M FINE! THANKS FOR ASKING, JUG-HEAD!
SHE'S GOT A STRANGE LOOK IN HER EYES!
C'MON, DEAR! YOU NEED SOME REST!
THE NEXT DAY...
Oh, I FEEL BETTER NOW!
TIME TO GET UP AND...
OW!
THAT SUN! IT'S SO BRIGHT! I'M-- I'M CLOSING THESE CURTAINS!!
10

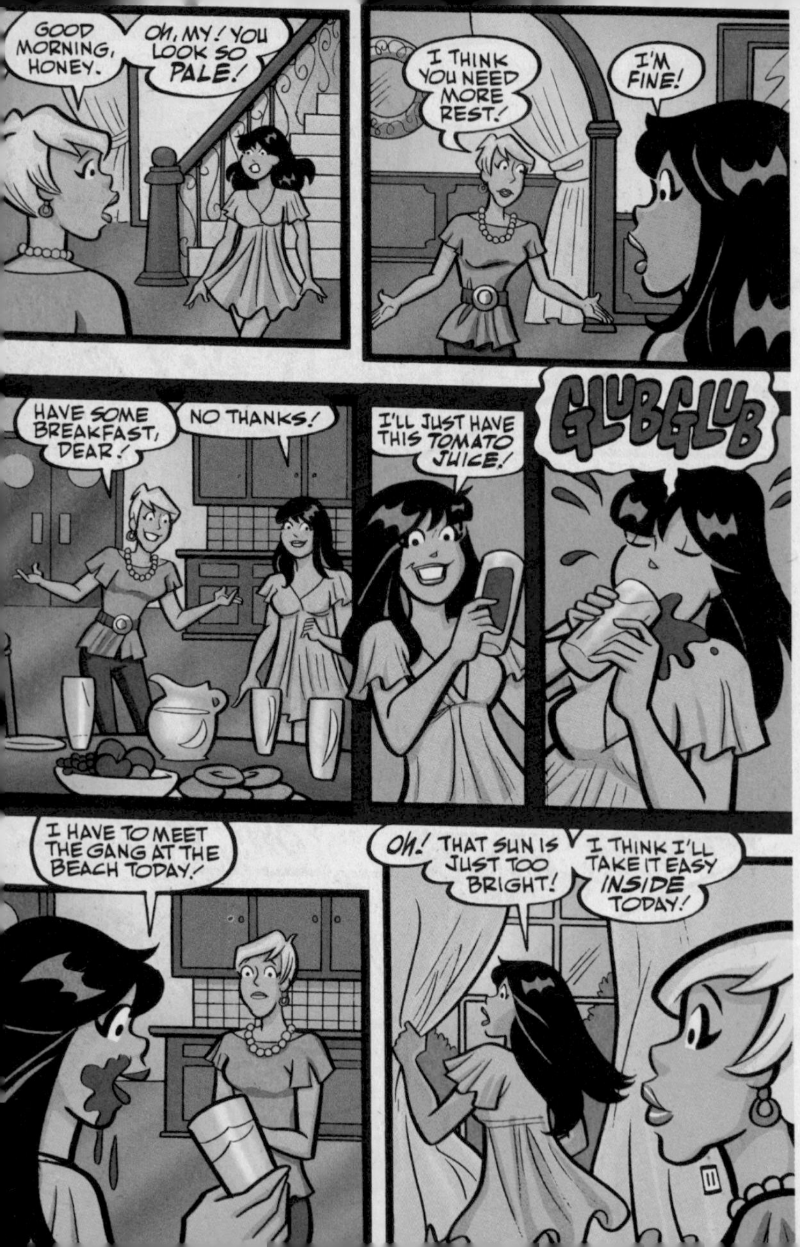
GOOD MORNING, HONEY.
Oh, MY! YOU LOOK SO PALE!
I THINK YOU NEED MORE REST!
I'M FINE!
HAVE SOME BREAKFAST, DEAR!
NO THANKS!
I'LL JUST HAVE THIS TOMATO JUICE!
GLUBGLUB
I HAVE TO MEET THE GANG AT THE BEACH TODAY!
Oh! THAT SUN IS JUST TOO BRIGHT!
I THINK I'LL TAKE IT EASY INSIDE TODAY!

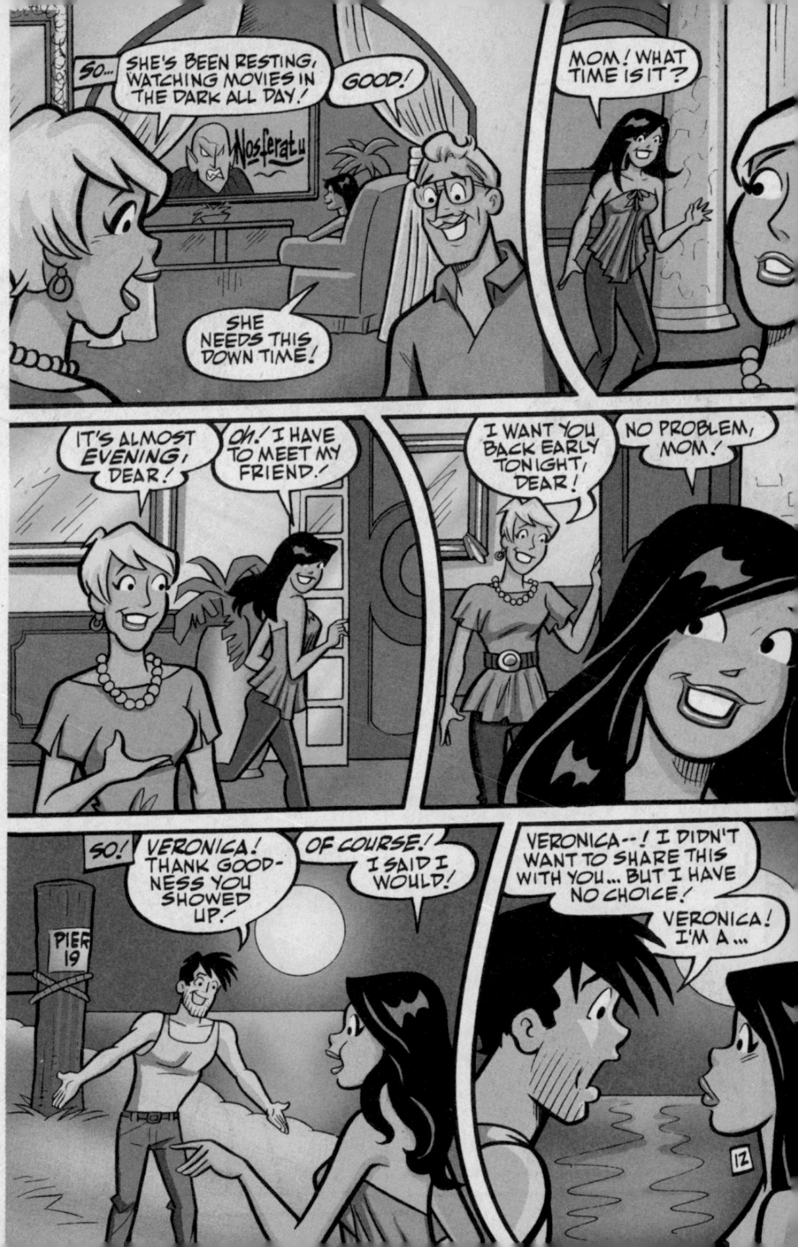
SO...
SHE'S BEEN RESTING, WATCHING MOVIES IN THE DARK ALL DAY!
GOOD!
SHE NEEDS THIS DOWN TIME!
Nosferatu
MOM! WHAT TIME IS IT?
IT'S ALMOST EVENING, DEAR!
Oh! I HAVE TO MEET MY FRIEND!
I WANT YOU BACK EARLY TONIGHT, DEAR!
NO PROBLEM, MOM!
SO!
VERONICA! THANK GOODNESS YOU SHOWED UP!
OF COURSE! I SAID I WOULD!
PIER 19
VERONICA--! I DIDN'T WANT TO SHARE THIS WITH YOU... BUT I HAVE NO CHOICE!
VERONICA! I'M A...
12

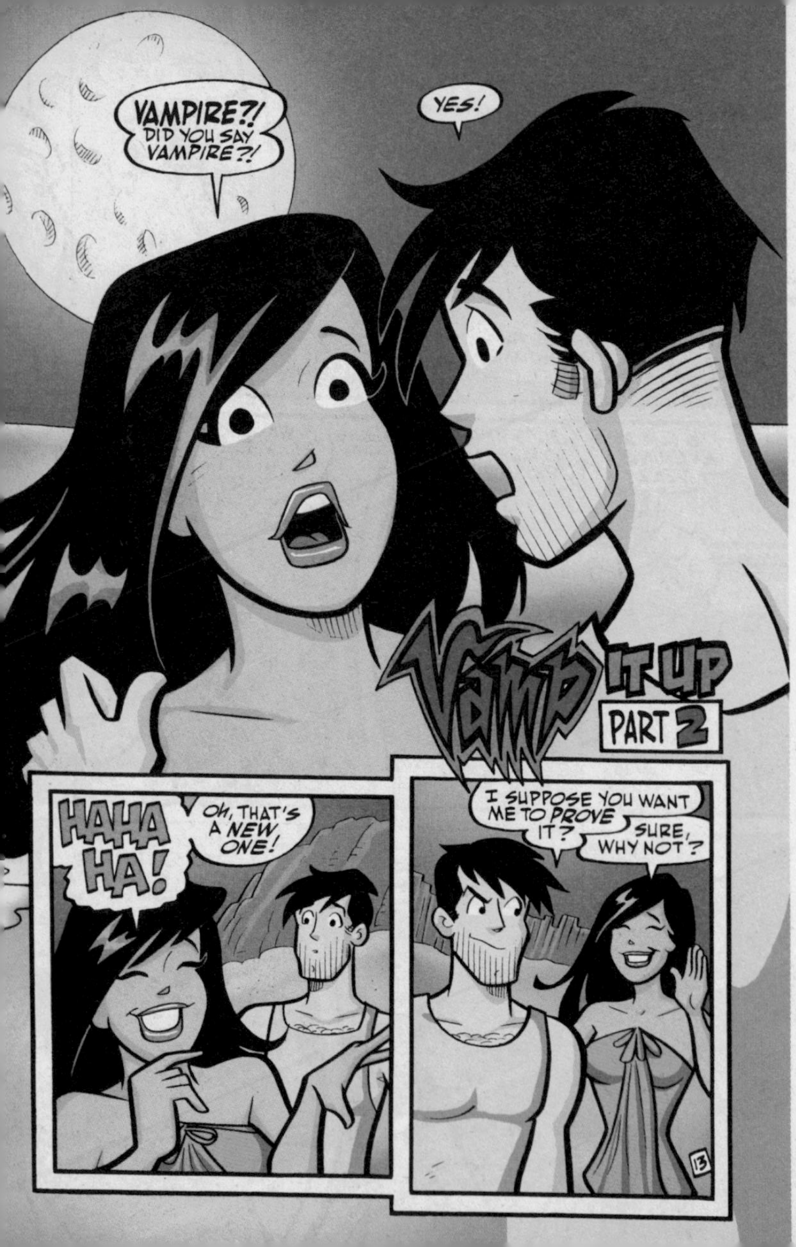
VAMPIRE?! DID YOU SAY VAMPIRE?!
YES!
VAMP IT UP
PART 2
HAHA HA!
Oh, THAT'S A NEW ONE!
I SUPPOSE YOU WANT ME TO PROVE IT?
SURE, WHY NOT?
13

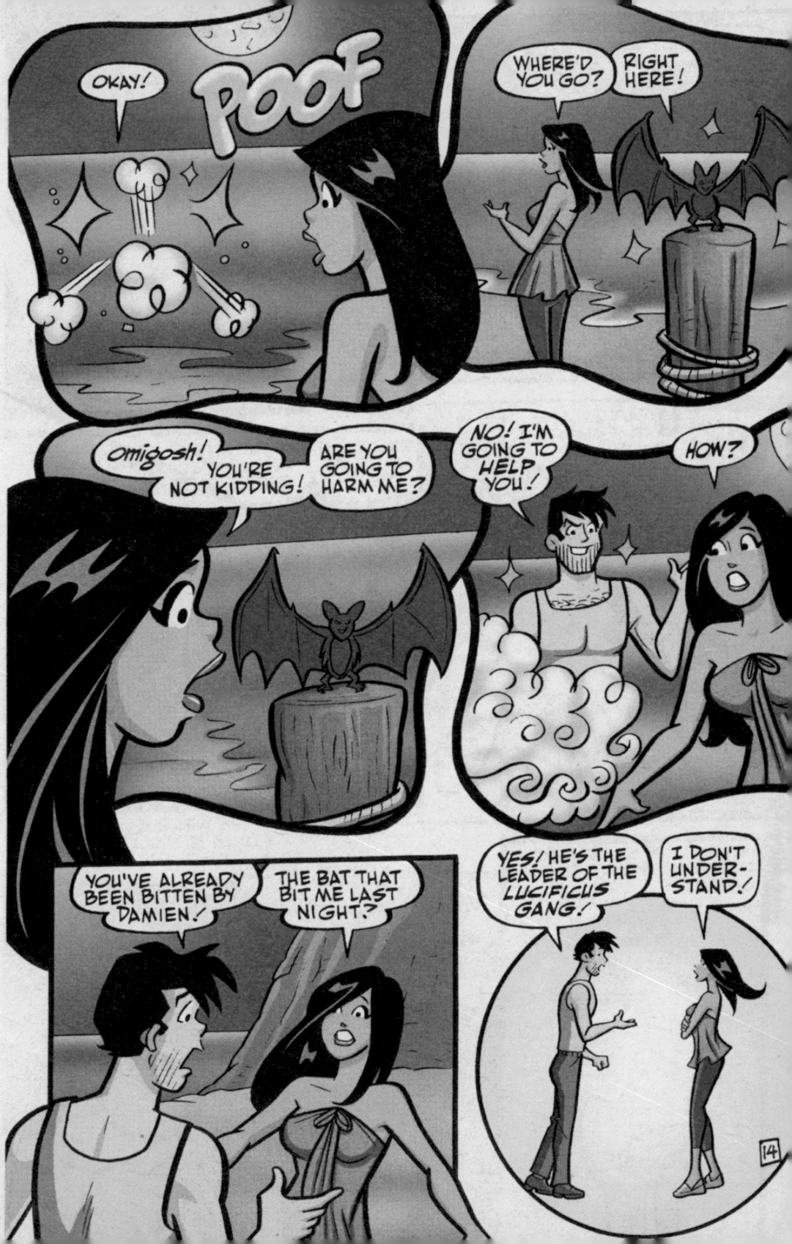
OKAY!
POOF
WHERE'D YOU GO?
RIGHT HERE!
omigosh! YOU'RE NOT KIDDING!
ARE YOU GOING TO HARM ME?
NO! I'M GOING TO HELP YOU!
HOW?
YOU'VE ALREADY BEEN BITTEN BY DAMIEN!
THE BAT THAT BIT ME LAST NIGHT?
YES! HE'S THE LEADER OF THE LUCIFICUS GANG!
I DON'T UNDER-STAND!
14

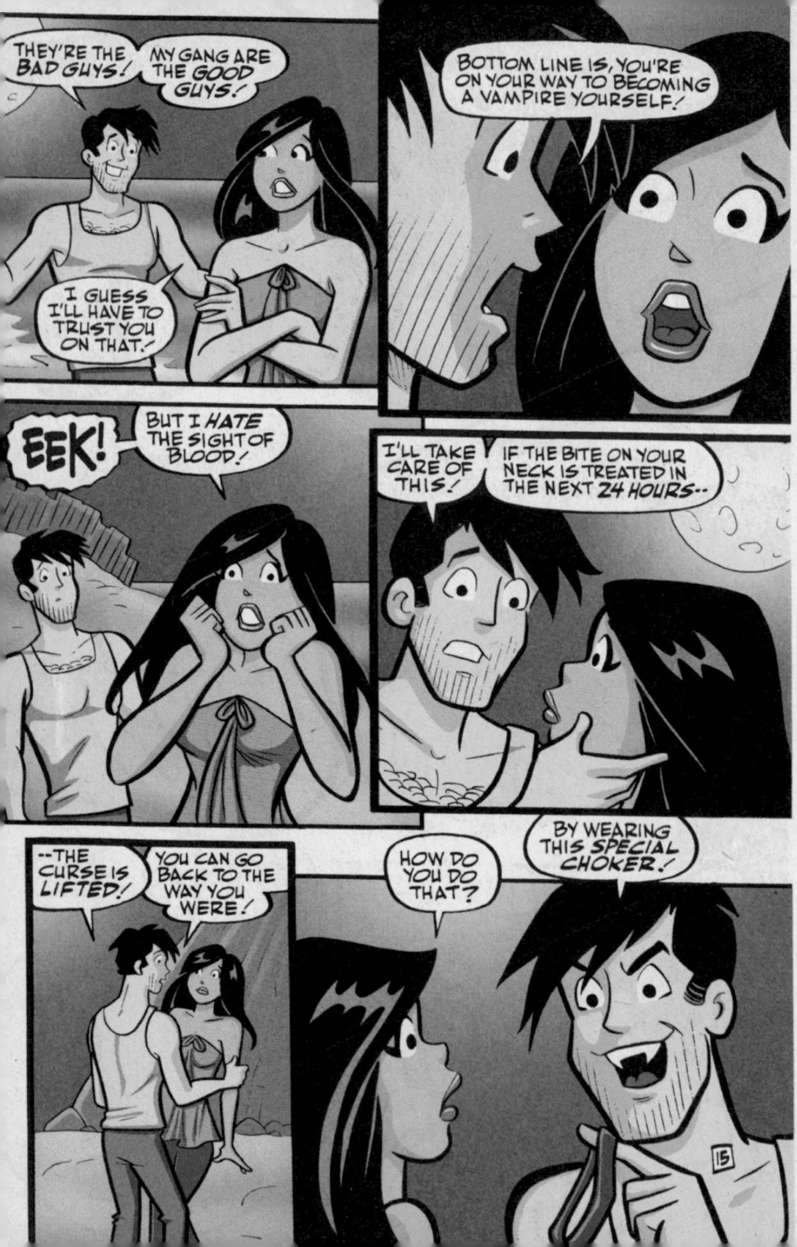
THEY'RE THE BAD GUYS!
MY GANG ARE THE GOOD GUYS!
I GUESS I'LL HAVE TO TRUST YOU ON THAT!
BOTTOM LINE IS, YOU'RE ON YOUR WAY TO BECOMING A VAMPIRE YOURSELF!
EEK!
BUT I HATE THE SIGHT OF BLOOD!
I'LL TAKE CARE OF THIS!
IF THE BITE ON YOUR NECK IS TREATED IN THE NEXT 24 HOURS--
--THE CURSE IS LIFTED!
YOU CAN GO BACK TO THE WAY YOU WERE!
HOW DO YOU DO THAT?
BY WEARING THIS SPECIAL CHOKER!
15

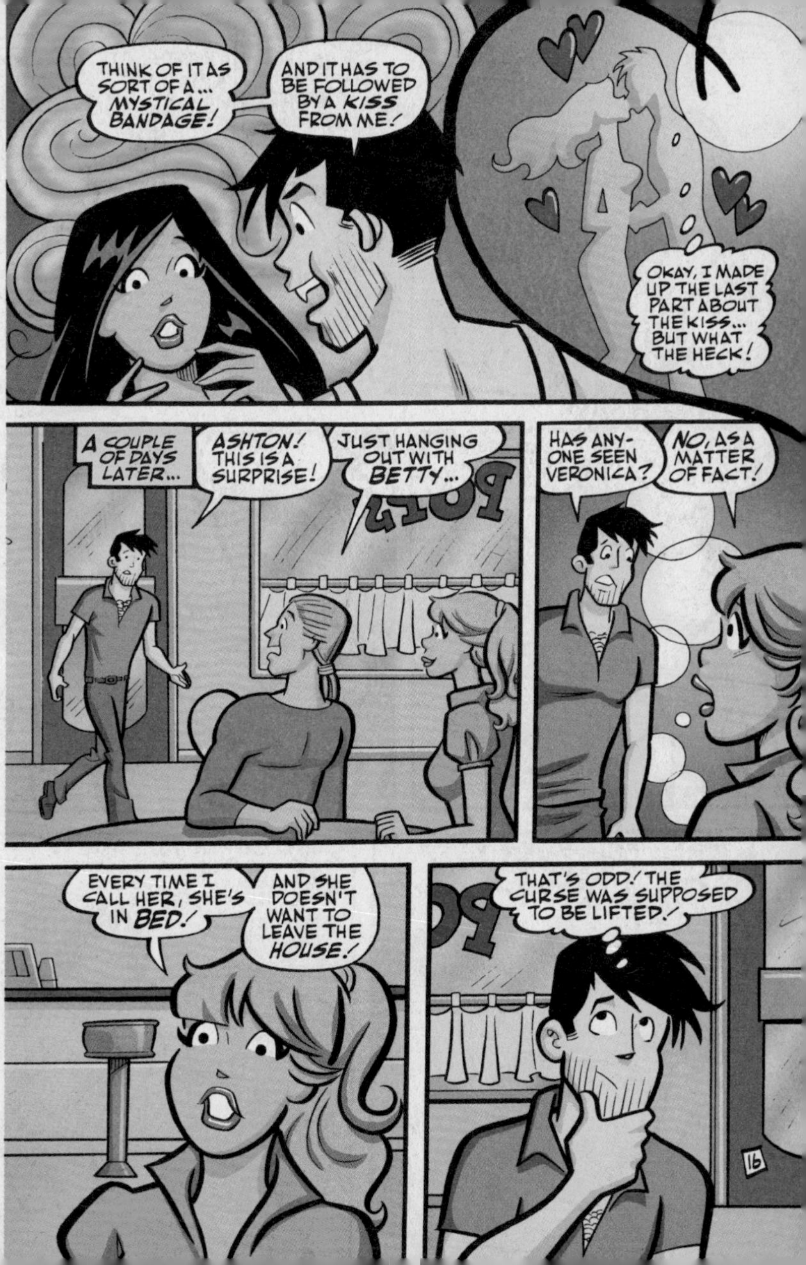
THINK OF IT AS SORT OF A... MYSTICAL BANDAGE!
AND IT HAS TO BE FOLLOWED BY A KISS FROM ME!
OKAY, I MADE UP THE LAST PART ABOUT THE KISS... BUT WHAT THE HECK!
A COUPLE OF DAYS LATER...
ASHTON! THIS IS A SURPRISE!
JUST HANGING OUT WITH BETTY...
POP'S
HAS ANYONE SEEN VERONICA?
NO, AS A MATTER OF FACT!
EVERY TIME I CALL HER, SHE'S IN BED!
AND SHE DOESN'T WANT TO LEAVE THE HOUSE!
THAT'S ODD! THE CURSE WAS SUPPOSED TO BE LIFTED!
16

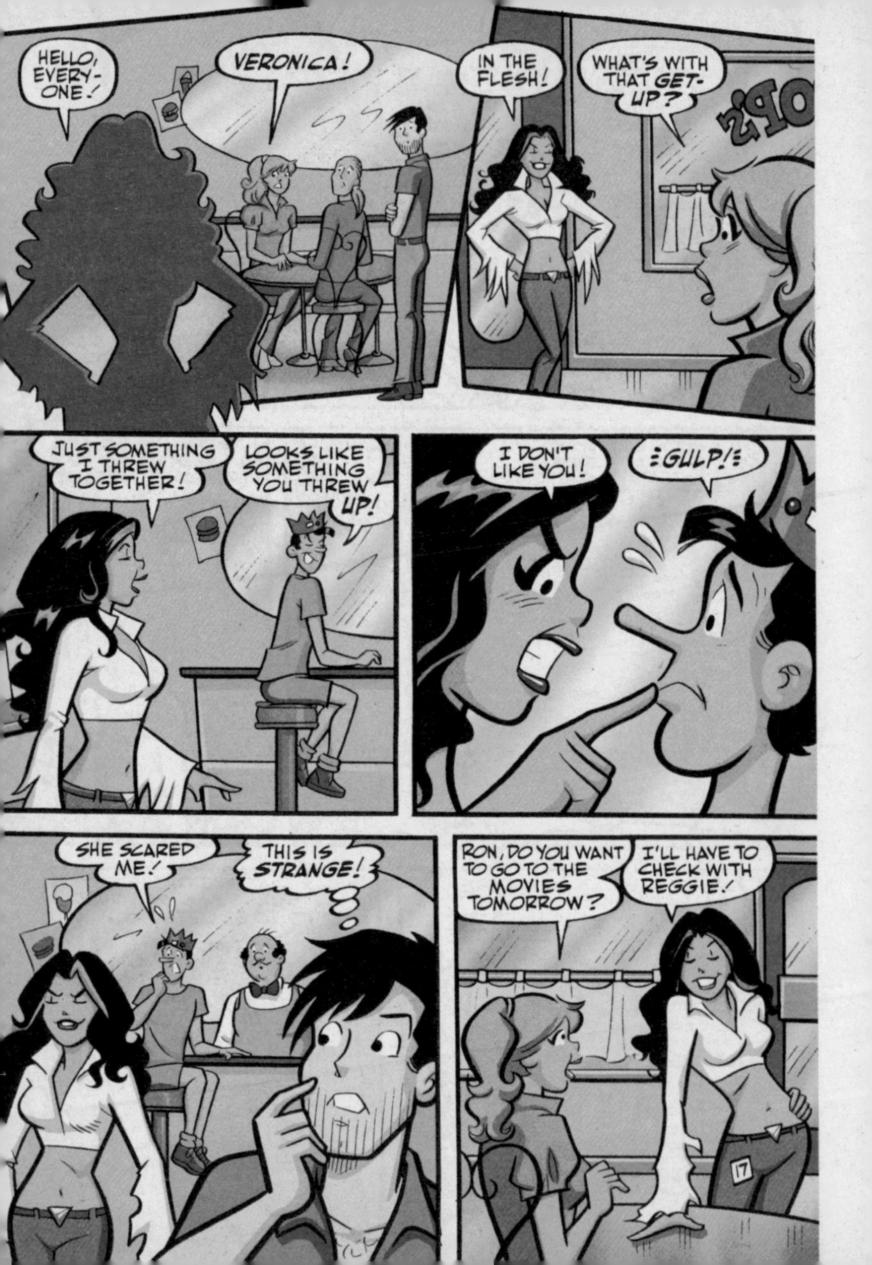
HELLO, EVERY-ONE.!
VERONICA!
IN THE FLESH!
WHAT'S WITH THAT GET-UP?
POP'S
JUST SOMETHING I THREW TOGETHER!
LOOKS LIKE SOMETHING YOU THREW UP!
I DON'T LIKE YOU!
GULP!
SHE SCARED ME!
THIS IS STRANGE!
RON, DO YOU WANT TO GO TO THE MOVIES TOMORROW?
I'LL HAVE TO CHECK WITH REGGIE!
17

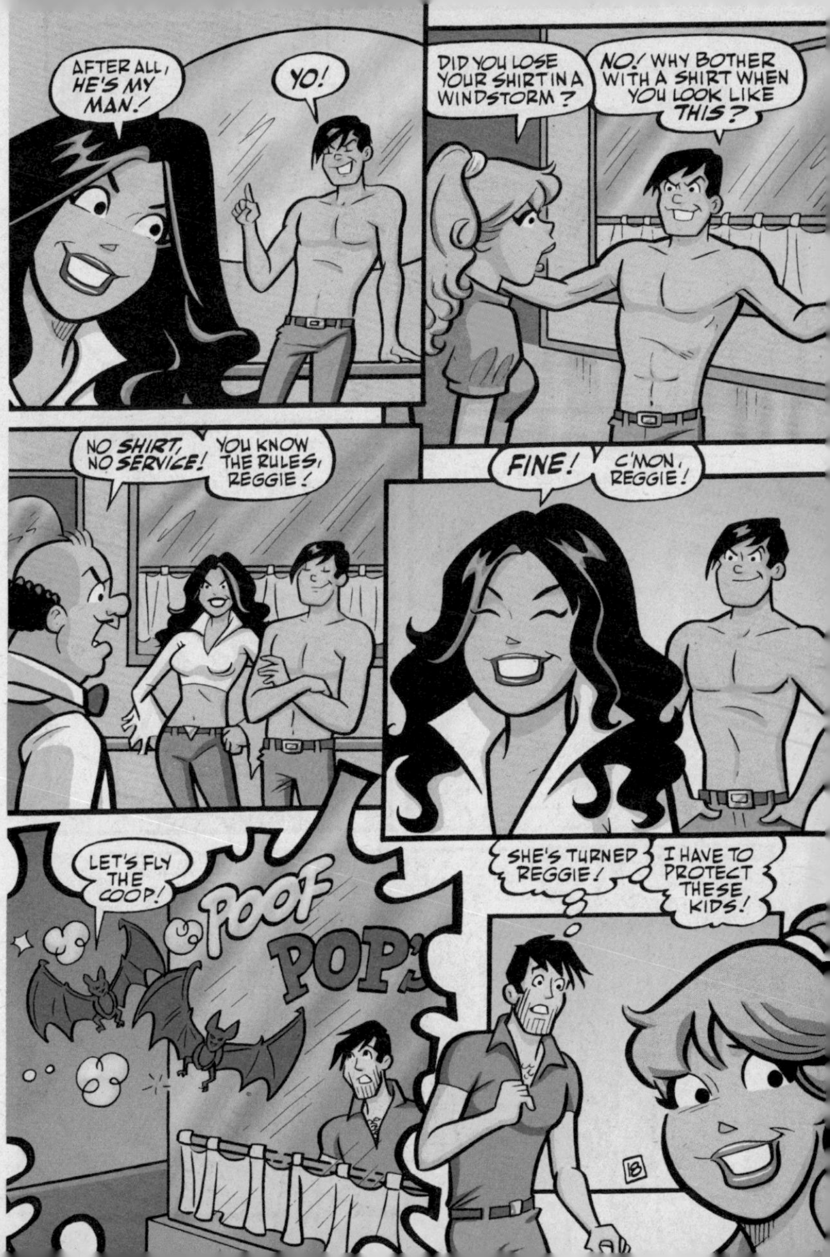
AFTER ALL, HE'S MY MAN!
YO!
DID YOU LOSE YOUR SHIRT IN A WINDSTORM?
NO! WHY BOTHER WITH A SHIRT WHEN YOU LOOK LIKE THIS?
NO SHIRT, NO SERVICE!
YOU KNOW THE RULES, REGGIE!
FINE!
C'MON, REGGIE!
LET'S FLY THE COOP!
POOF
POP'S
SHE'S TURNED REGGIE!
I HAVE TO PROTECT THESE KIDS!
18

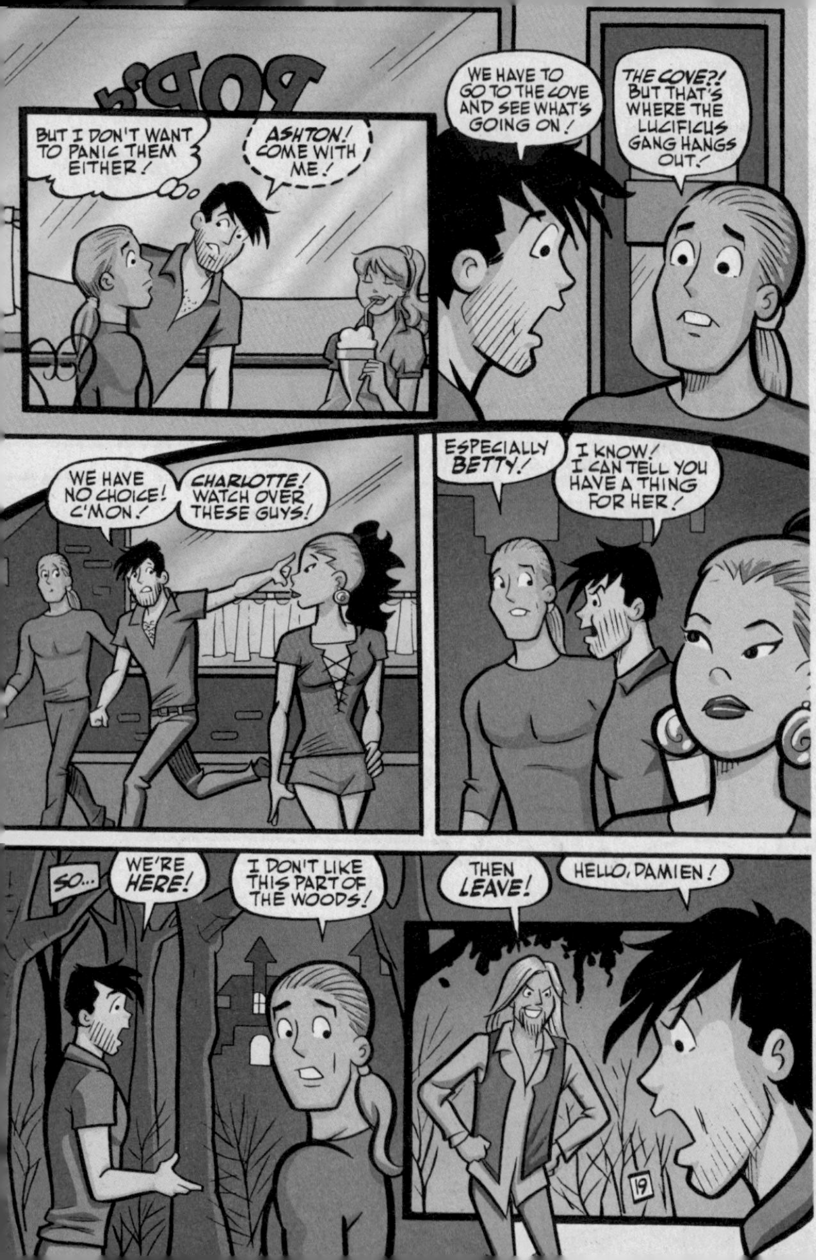
POP'S
BUT I DON'T WANT TO PANIC THEM EITHER!
ASHTON! COME WITH ME!
WE HAVE TO GO TO THE COVE AND SEE WHAT'S GOING ON!
THE COVE?! BUT THAT'S WHERE THE LUCIFICUS GANG HANGS OUT!
WE HAVE NO CHOICE! C'MON!
CHARLOTTE! WATCH OVER THESE GUYS!
ESPECIALLY BETTY!
I KNOW! I CAN TELL YOU HAVE A THING FOR HER!
SO...
WE'RE HERE!
I DON'T LIKE THIS PART OF THE WOODS!
THEN LEAVE!
HELLO, DAMIEN!
19

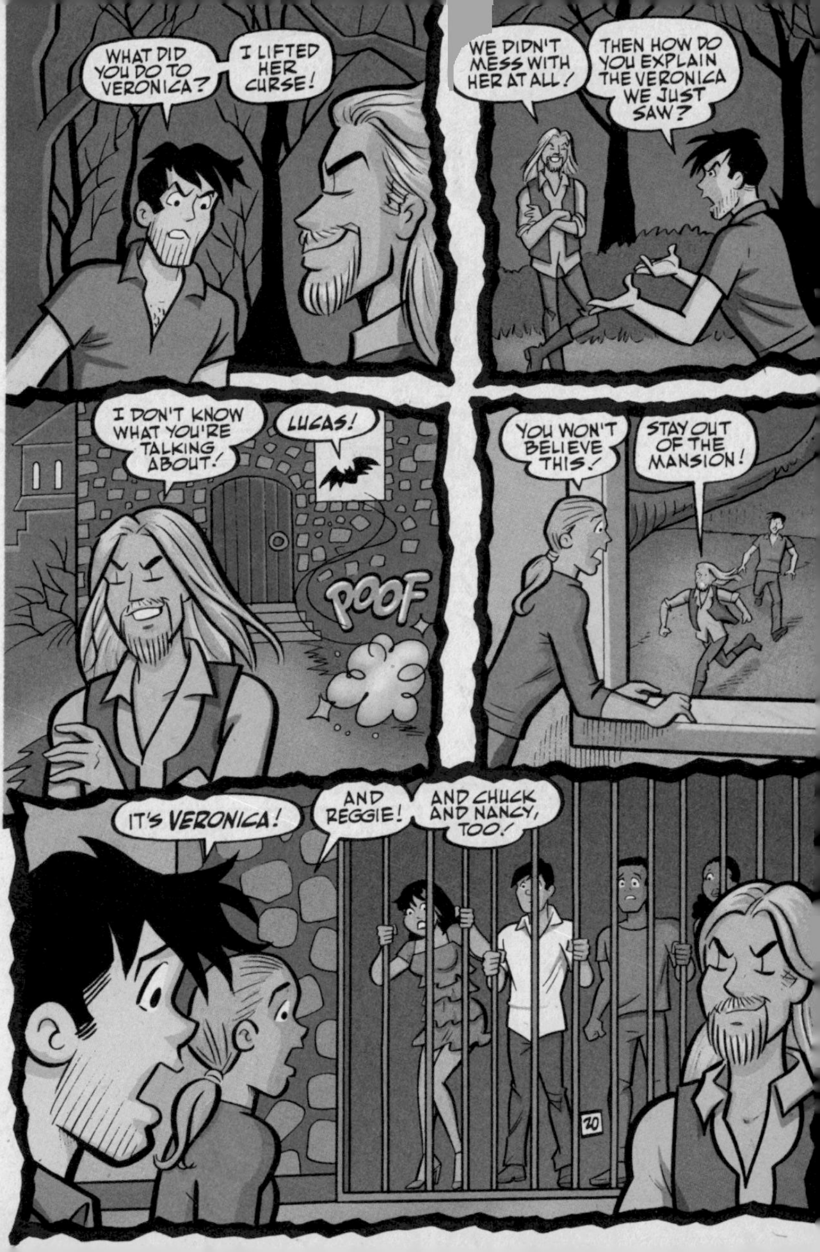
WHAT DID YOU DO TO VERONICA?
I LIFTED HER CURSE!
WE DIDN'T MESS WITH HER AT ALL!
THEN HOW DO YOU EXPLAIN THE VERONICA WE JUST SAW?
I DON'T KNOW WHAT YOU'RE TALKING ABOUT!
LUCAS!
POOF
YOU WON'T BELIEVE THIS!
STAY OUT OF THE MANSION!
IT'S VERONICA!
AND REGGIE!
AND CHUCK AND NANCY, TOO!
20

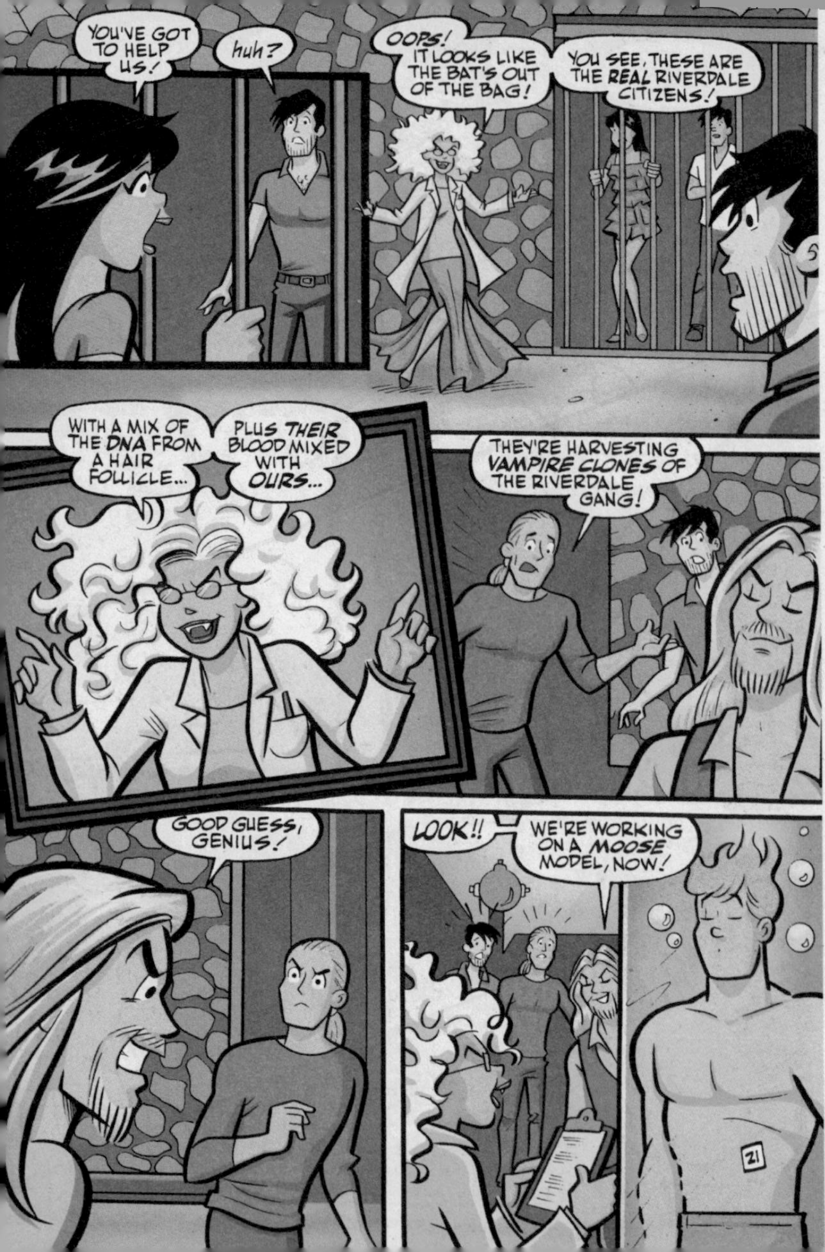
YOU'VE GOT TO HELP US!
huh?
OOPS! IT LOOKS LIKE THE BAT'S OUT OF THE BAG!
YOU SEE, THESE ARE THE REAL RIVERDALE CITIZENS!
WITH A MIX OF THE DNA FROM A HAIR FOLLICLE...
PLUS THEIR BLOOD MIXED WITH OURS...
THEY'RE HARVESTING VAMPIRE CLONES OF THE RIVERDALE GANG!
GOOD GUESS, GENIUS!
LOOK!!
WE'RE WORKING ON A MOOSE MODEL, NOW!
21

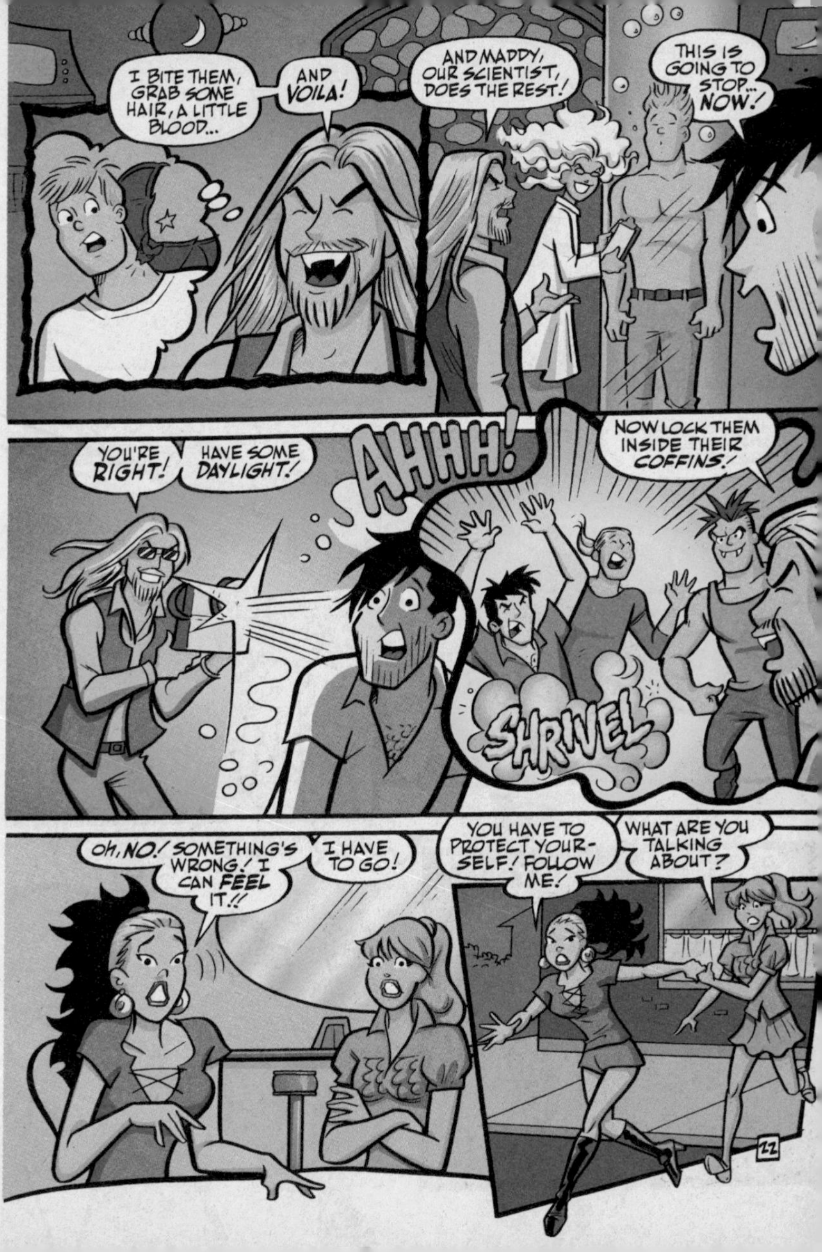

I BITE THEM, GRAB SOME HAIR, A LITTLE BLOOD...
AND VOILA!
AND MADDY, OUR SCIENTIST, DOES THE REST!
THIS IS GOING TO STOP... NOW!
YOU'RE RIGHT!
HAVE SOME DAYLIGHT!
AHHH!
NOW LOCK THEM INSIDE THEIR COFFINS!
SHRIVEL
OH, NO! SOMETHING'S WRONG! I CAN FEEL IT!!
I HAVE TO GO!
YOU HAVE TO PROTECT YOURSELF! FOLLOW ME!
WHAT ARE YOU TALKING ABOUT?
22

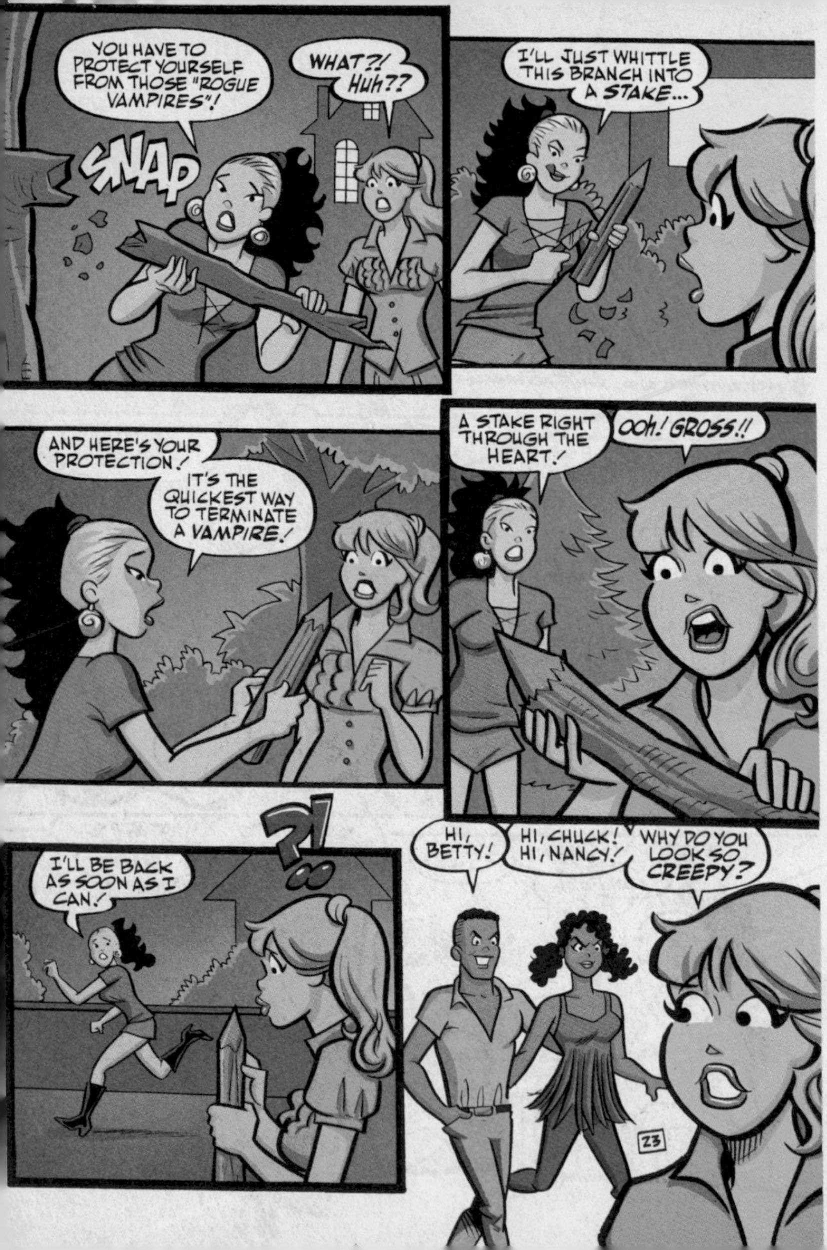

YOU HAVE TO PROTECT YOURSELF FROM THOSE "ROGUE VAMPIRES"!
WHAT?! Huh??
SNAP
I'LL JUST WHITTLE THIS BRANCH INTO A STAKE...
AND HERE'S YOUR PROTECTION!
IT'S THE QUICKEST WAY TO TERMINATE A VAMPIRE!
A STAKE RIGHT THROUGH THE HEART!
OOh! GROSS!!
I'LL BE BACK AS SOON AS I CAN!
?!
HI, BETTY!
HI, CHUCK! HI, NANCY!
WHY DO YOU LOOK SO CREEPY?

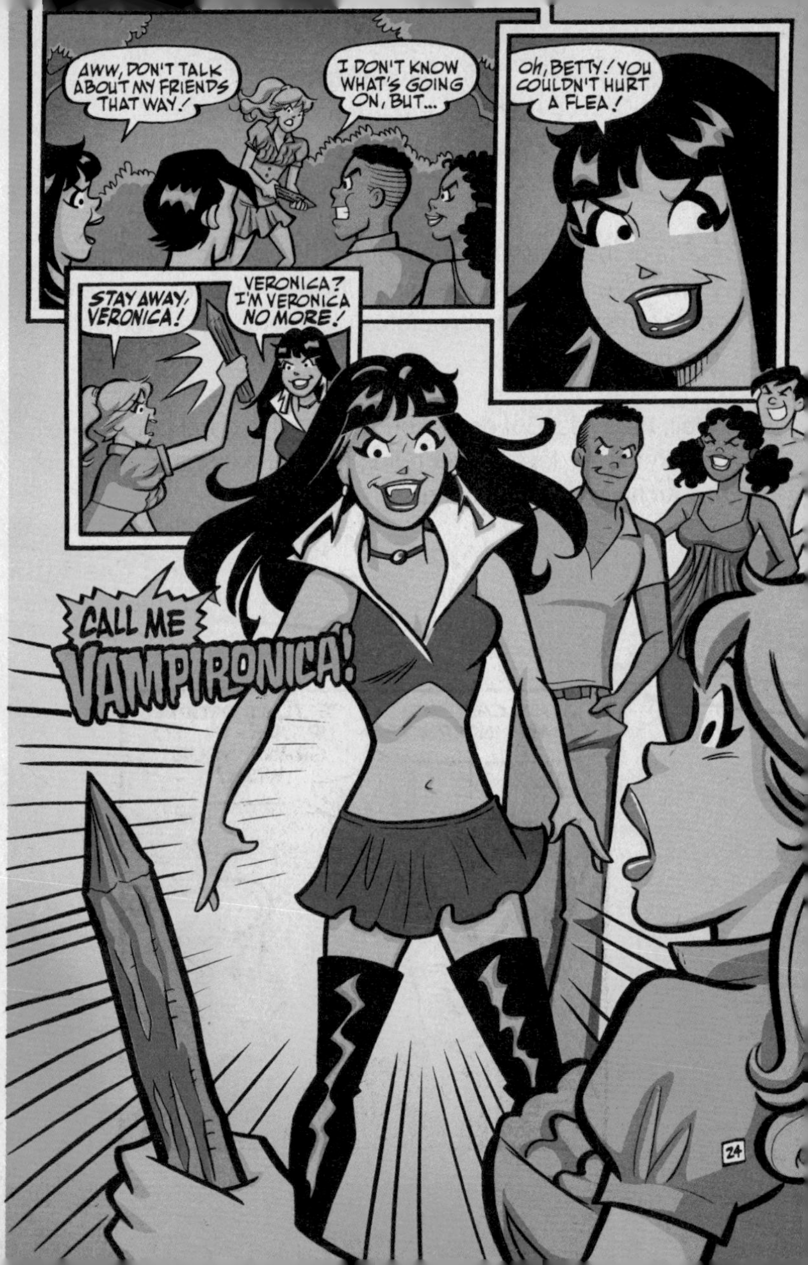

AWW, DON'T TALK ABOUT MY FRIENDS THAT WAY!
I DON'T KNOW WHAT'S GOING ON, BUT...
Oh, BETTY! YOU COULDN'T HURT A FLEA!
STAY AWAY, VERONICA!
VERONICA? I'M VERONICA NO MORE!
CALL ME VAMPIRONICA!
24

Mr. Inferno
Betty & Veronica #75, 1962
by Frank Doyle and Dan DeCarlo

One of the most talked-about Archie Comics stories ever: Betty & Veronica sell their souls to the devil! This one has taken on such legendary status that many don't even believe it exists.

Well, here it is! But don't worry… it's all in good fun. After all, you know no devil is ever going to get the upper cloven hoof on Archie's favorite gal pals!

Paul Castiglia
Writer and Archivist,
Archie Comics

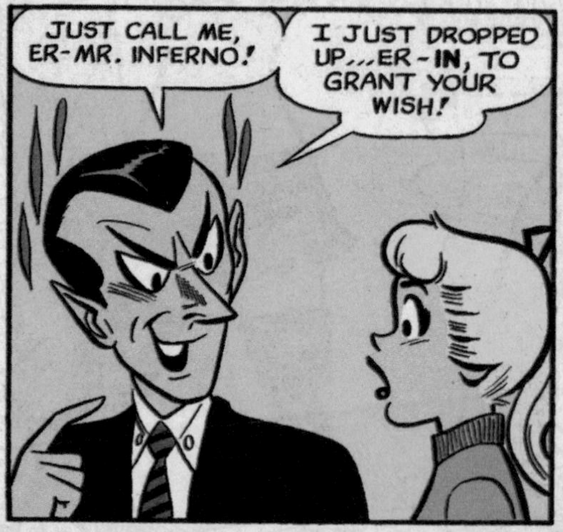
JUST CALL ME, ER-MR. INFERNO!
I JUST DROPPED UP,,,ER-IN, TO GRANT YOUR WISH!

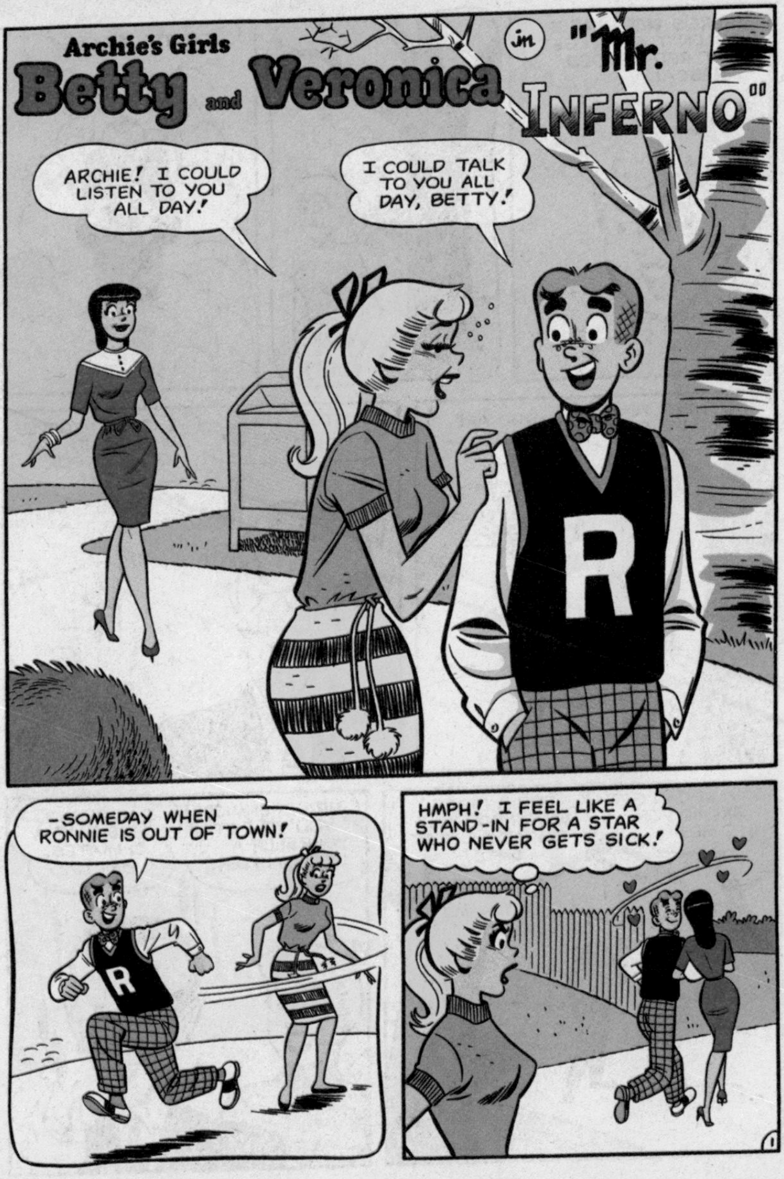
Archie's Girls
Betty and Veronica
in
"Mr. INFERNO"
ARCHIE! I COULD LISTEN TO YOU ALL DAY!
I COULD TALK TO YOU ALL DAY, BETTY!
-SOMEDAY WHEN RONNIE IS OUT OF TOWN!
HMPH! I FEEL LIKE A STAND-IN FOR A STAR WHO NEVER GETS SICK!
1

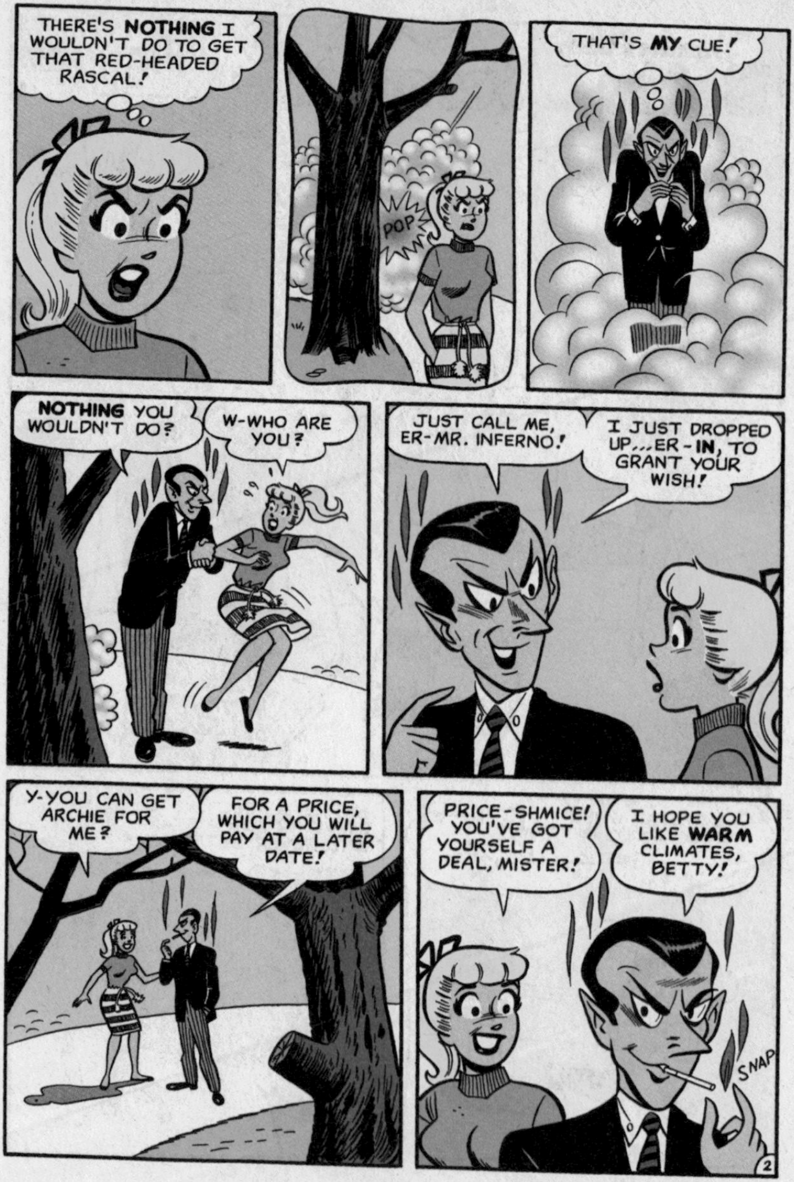

THERE'S NOTHING I WOULDN'T DO TO GET THAT RED-HEADED RASCAL!
POP
THAT'S MY CUE!
NOTHING YOU WOULDN'T DO?
W-WHO ARE YOU?
JUST CALL ME, ER-MR. INFERNO!
I JUST DROPPED UP,...ER-IN, TO GRANT YOUR WISH!
Y-YOU CAN GET ARCHIE FOR ME?
FOR A PRICE, WHICH YOU WILL PAY AT A LATER DATE!
PRICE-SHMICE! YOU'VE GOT YOURSELF A DEAL, MISTER!
I HOPE YOU LIKE WARM CLIMATES, BETTY!
SNAP
2

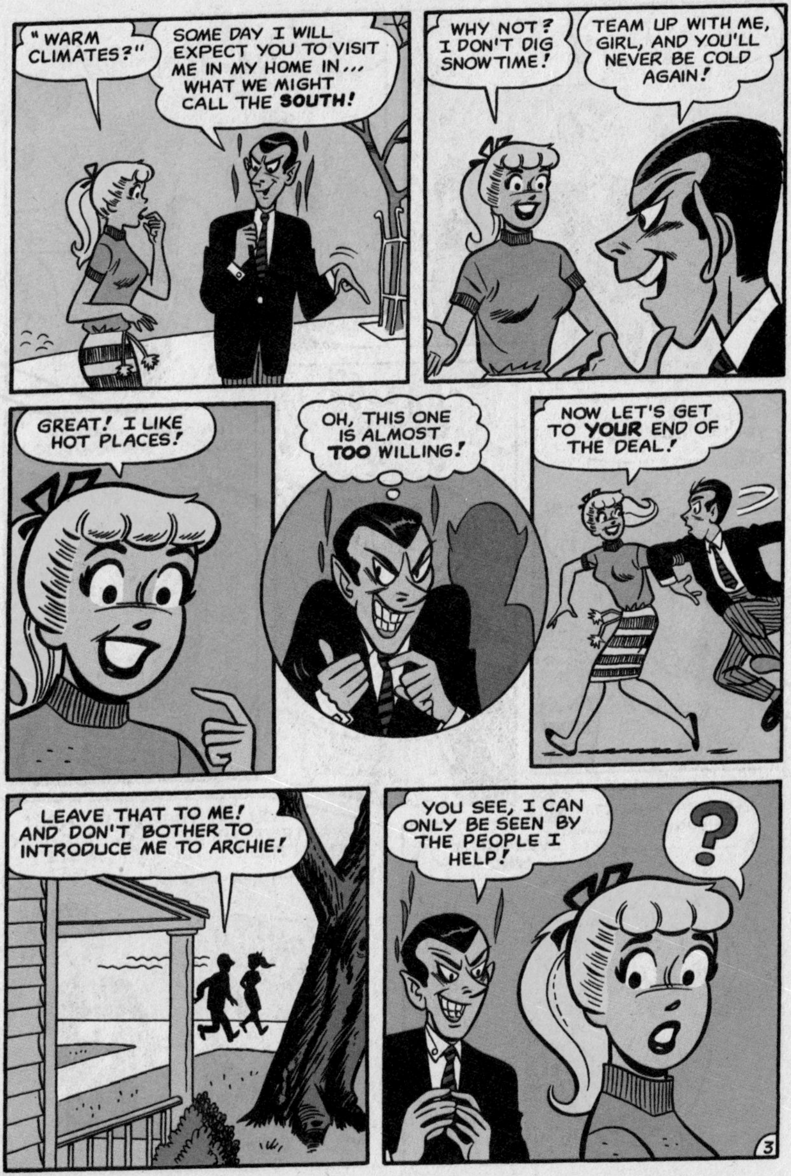
"WARM CLIMATES?"
SOME DAY I WILL EXPECT YOU TO VISIT ME IN MY HOME IN... WHAT WE MIGHT CALL THE **SOUTH**!
WHY NOT? I DON'T DIG SNOWTIME!
TEAM UP WITH ME, GIRL, AND YOU'LL NEVER BE COLD AGAIN!
GREAT! I LIKE HOT PLACES!
OH, THIS ONE IS ALMOST **TOO** WILLING!
NOW LET'S GET TO **YOUR** END OF THE DEAL!
LEAVE THAT TO ME! AND DON'T BOTHER TO INTRODUCE ME TO ARCHIE!
YOU SEE, I CAN ONLY BE SEEN BY THE PEOPLE I HELP!
?
3

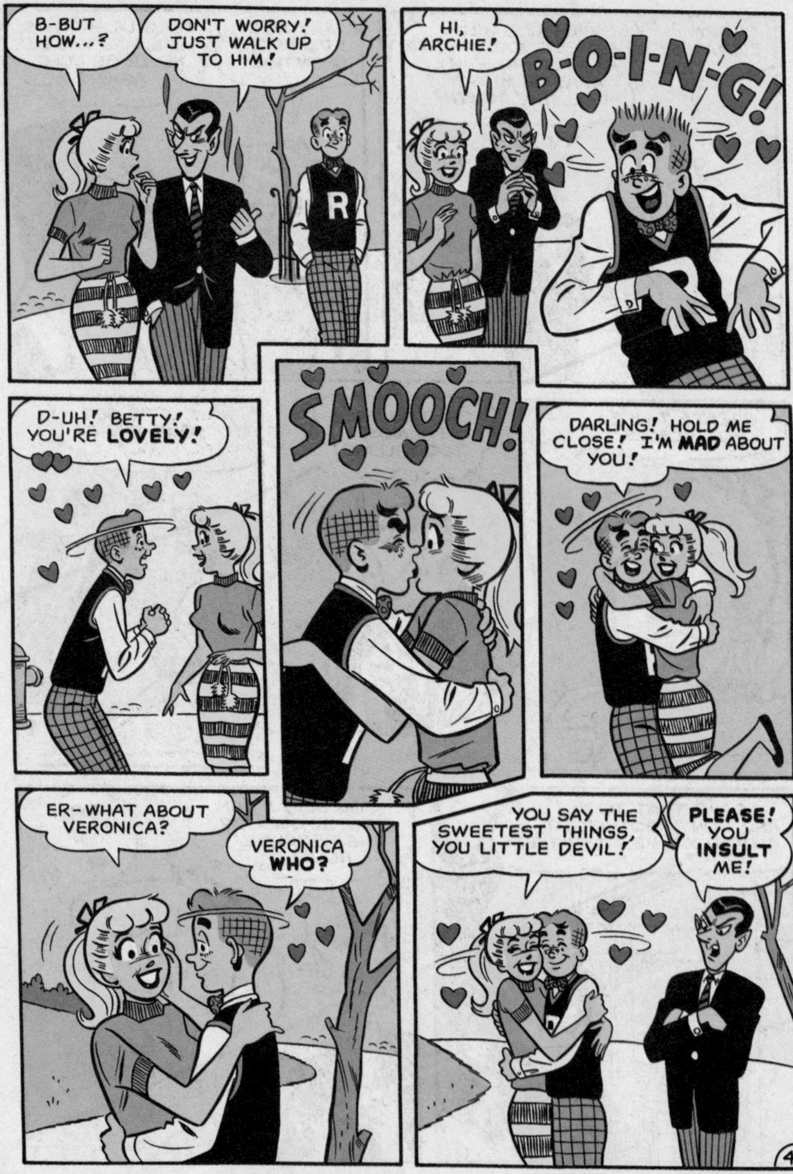

B-BUT HOW...?
DON'T WORRY! JUST WALK UP TO HIM!
HI, ARCHIE!
B-O-I-N-G!
D-UH! BETTY! YOU'RE **LOVELY**!
SMOOCH!
DARLING! HOLD ME CLOSE! I'M **MAD** ABOUT YOU!
ER-WHAT ABOUT VERONICA?
VERONICA **WHO?**
YOU SAY THE SWEETEST THINGS, YOU LITTLE DEVIL!
PLEASE! YOU **INSULT** ME!
4

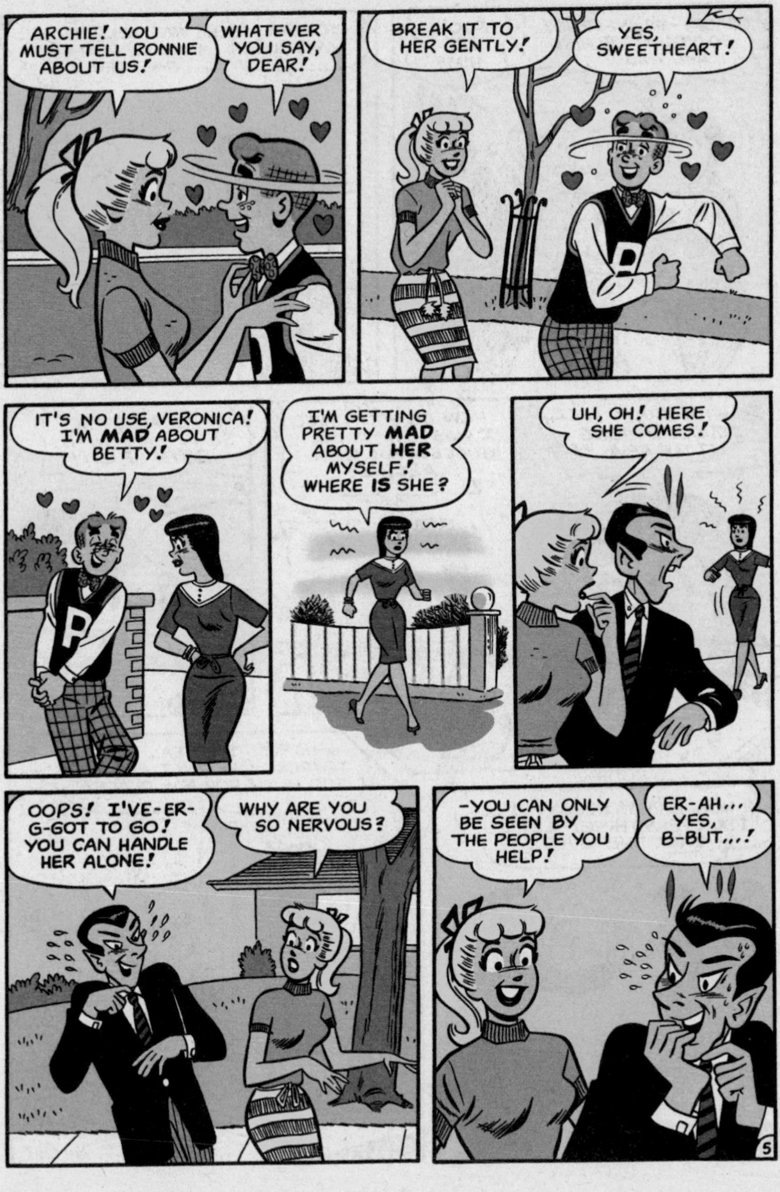
ARCHIE! YOU MUST TELL RONNIE ABOUT US!
WHATEVER YOU SAY, DEAR!
BREAK IT TO HER GENTLY!
YES, SWEETHEART!
IT'S NO USE, VERONICA! I'M **MAD** ABOUT BETTY!
I'M GETTING PRETTY **MAD** ABOUT **HER** MYSELF! WHERE **IS** SHE?
UH, OH! HERE SHE COMES!
OOPS! I'VE-ER-G-GOT TO GO! YOU CAN HANDLE HER ALONE!
WHY ARE YOU SO NERVOUS?
-YOU CAN ONLY BE SEEN BY THE PEOPLE YOU HELP!
ER-AH... YES, B-BUT...!
5

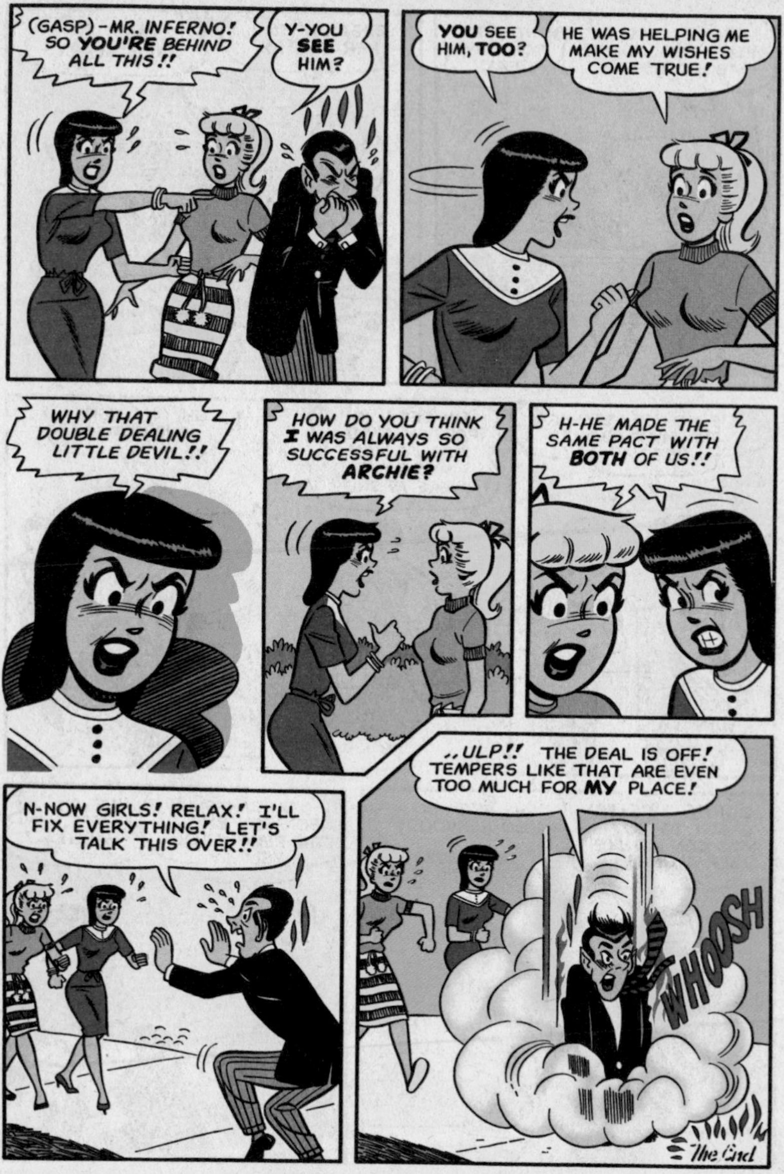
(GASP) – MR. INFERNO! SO YOU'RE BEHIND ALL THIS!!
Y-YOU SEE HIM?
YOU SEE HIM, TOO?
HE WAS HELPING ME MAKE MY WISHES COME TRUE!
WHY THAT DOUBLE DEALING LITTLE DEVIL!!
HOW DO YOU THINK I WAS ALWAYS SO SUCCESSFUL WITH ARCHIE?
H-HE MADE THE SAME PACT WITH BOTH OF US!!
N-NOW GIRLS! RELAX! I'LL FIX EVERYTHING! LET'S TALK THIS OVER!!
..ULP!! THE DEAL IS OFF! TEMPERS LIKE THAT ARE EVEN TOO MUCH FOR MY PLACE!
WHOOSH
The End

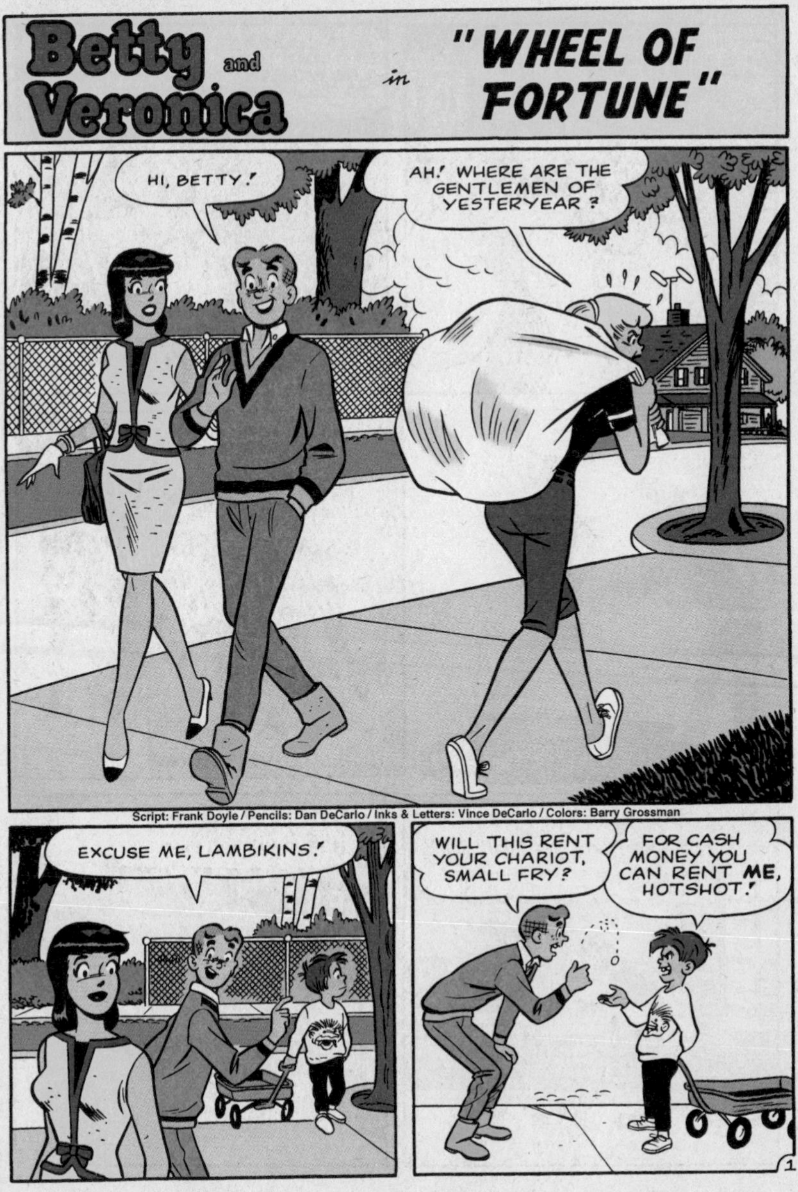
Betty and Veronica in "WHEEL OF FORTUNE"
HI, BETTY!
AH! WHERE ARE THE GENTLEMEN OF YESTERYEAR?
Script: Frank Doyle / Pencils: Dan DeCarlo / Inks & Letters: Vince DeCarlo / Colors: Barry Grossman
EXCUSE ME, LAMBIKINS!
WILL THIS RENT YOUR CHARIOT, SMALL FRY?
FOR CASH MONEY YOU CAN RENT ME, HOTSHOT!
1

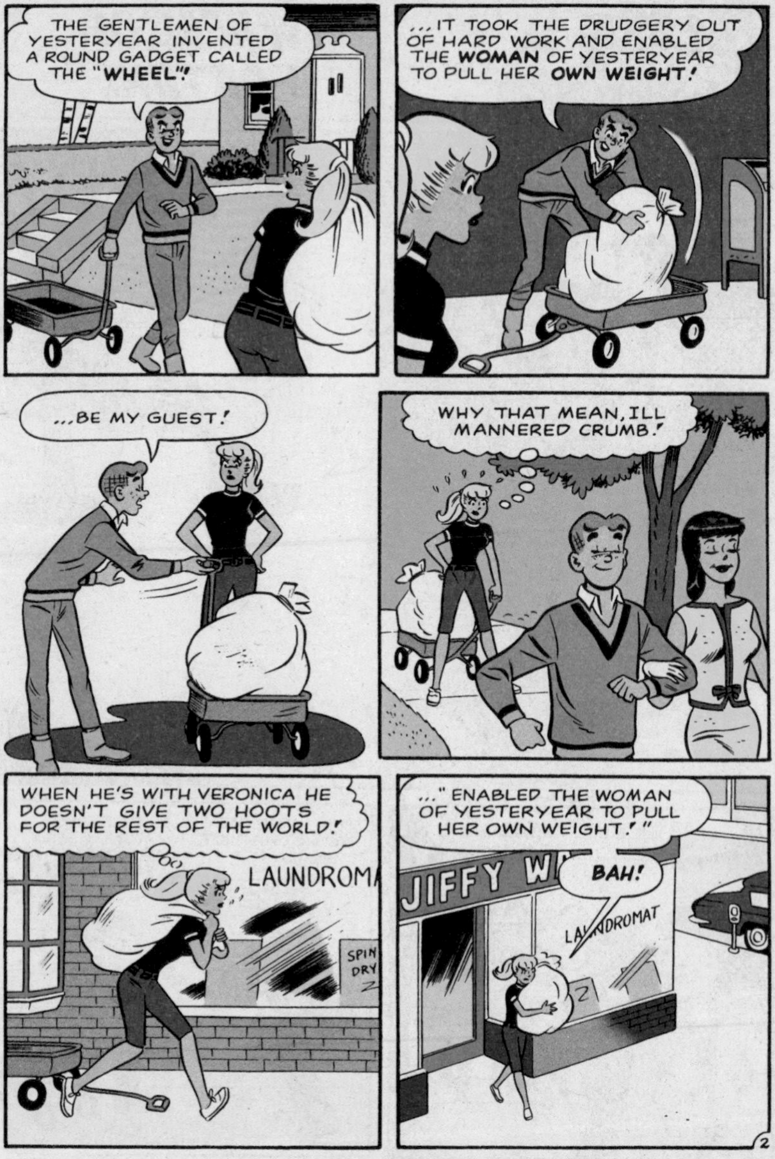
THE GENTLEMEN OF YESTERYEAR INVENTED A ROUND GADGET CALLED THE "WHEEL"!
...IT TOOK THE DRUDGERY OUT OF HARD WORK AND ENABLED THE WOMAN OF YESTERYEAR TO PULL HER OWN WEIGHT!
...BE MY GUEST!
WHY THAT MEAN, ILL MANNERED CRUMB!
WHEN HE'S WITH VERONICA HE DOESN'T GIVE TWO HOOTS FOR THE REST OF THE WORLD!
LAUNDROMA
SPIN DRY
..."ENABLED THE WOMAN OF YESTERYEAR TO PULL HER OWN WEIGHT!"
JIFFY W
BAH!
LAUNDROMAT

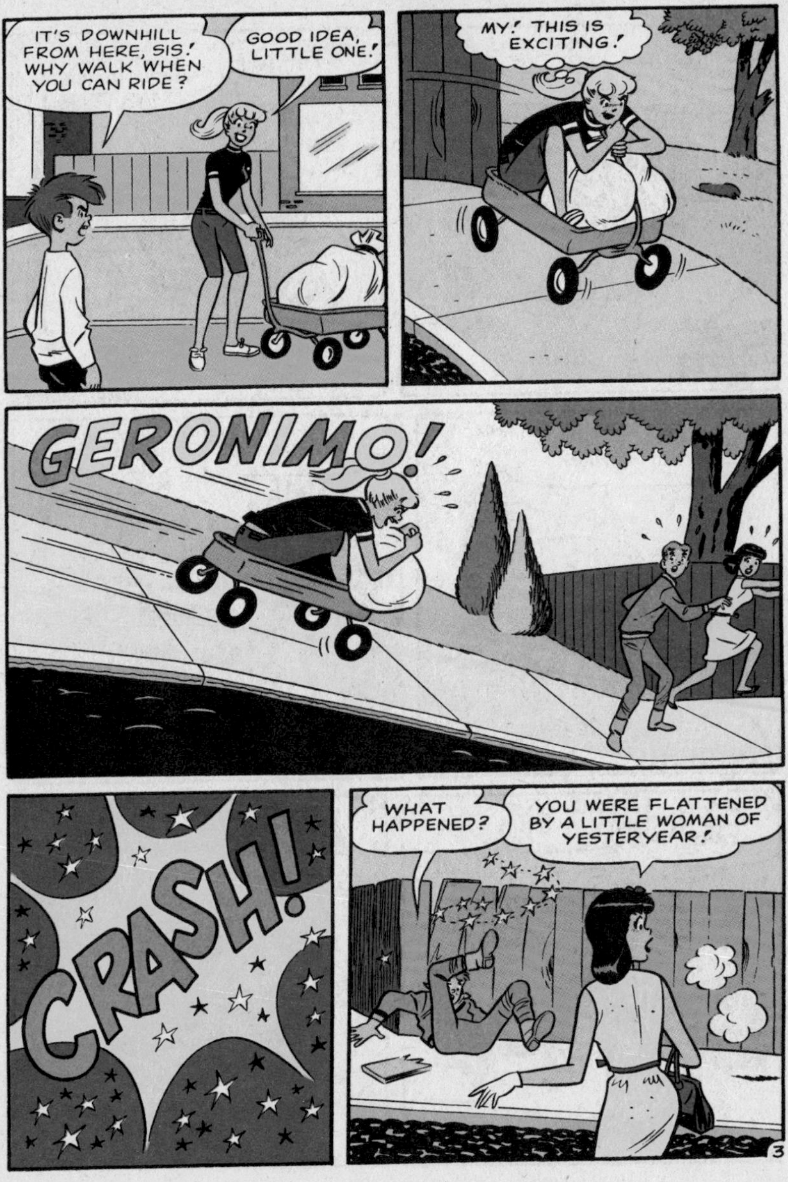

IT'S DOWNHILL FROM HERE, SIS! WHY WALK WHEN YOU CAN RIDE?
GOOD IDEA, LITTLE ONE!
MY! THIS IS EXCITING!
GERONIMO!
CRASH!
WHAT HAPPENED?
YOU WERE FLATTENED BY A LITTLE WOMAN OF YESTERYEAR!

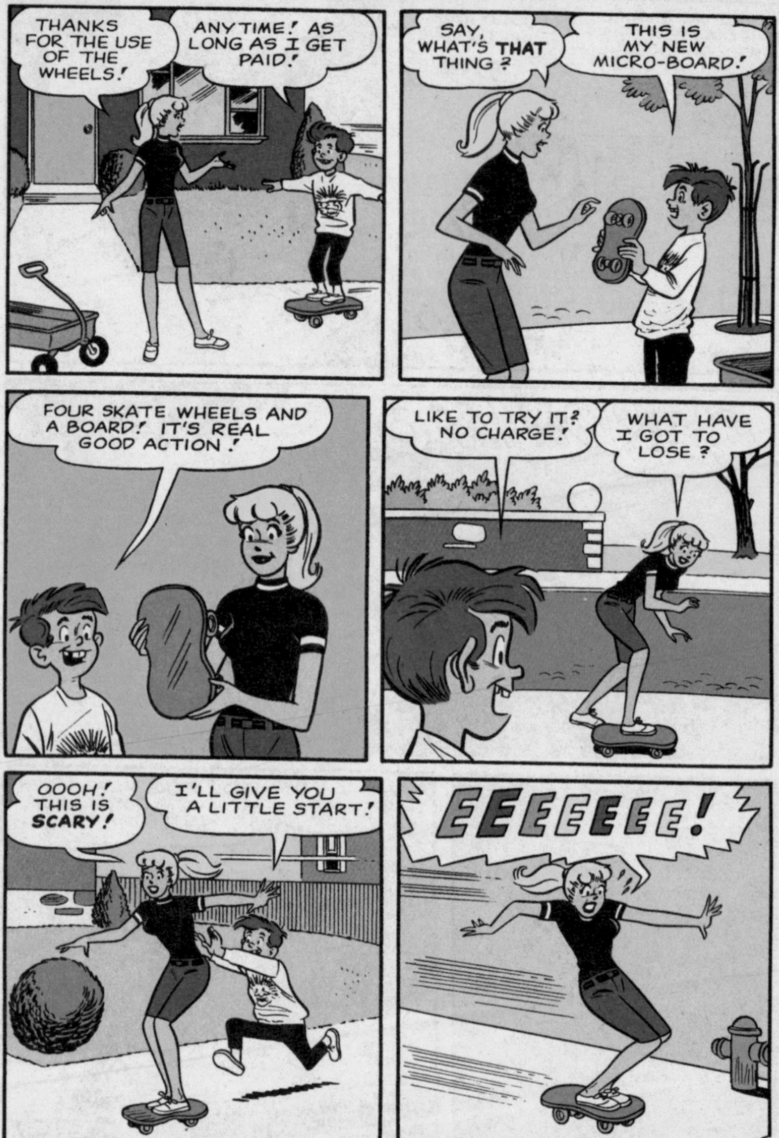
THANKS FOR THE USE OF THE WHEELS!
ANYTIME! AS LONG AS I GET PAID!
SAY, WHAT'S **THAT** THING?
THIS IS MY NEW MICRO-BOARD!
FOUR SKATE WHEELS AND A BOARD! IT'S REAL GOOD ACTION!
LIKE TO TRY IT? NO CHARGE!
WHAT HAVE I GOT TO LOSE?
OOOH! THIS IS **SCARY**!
I'LL GIVE YOU A LITTLE START!
EEEEEEE!
4

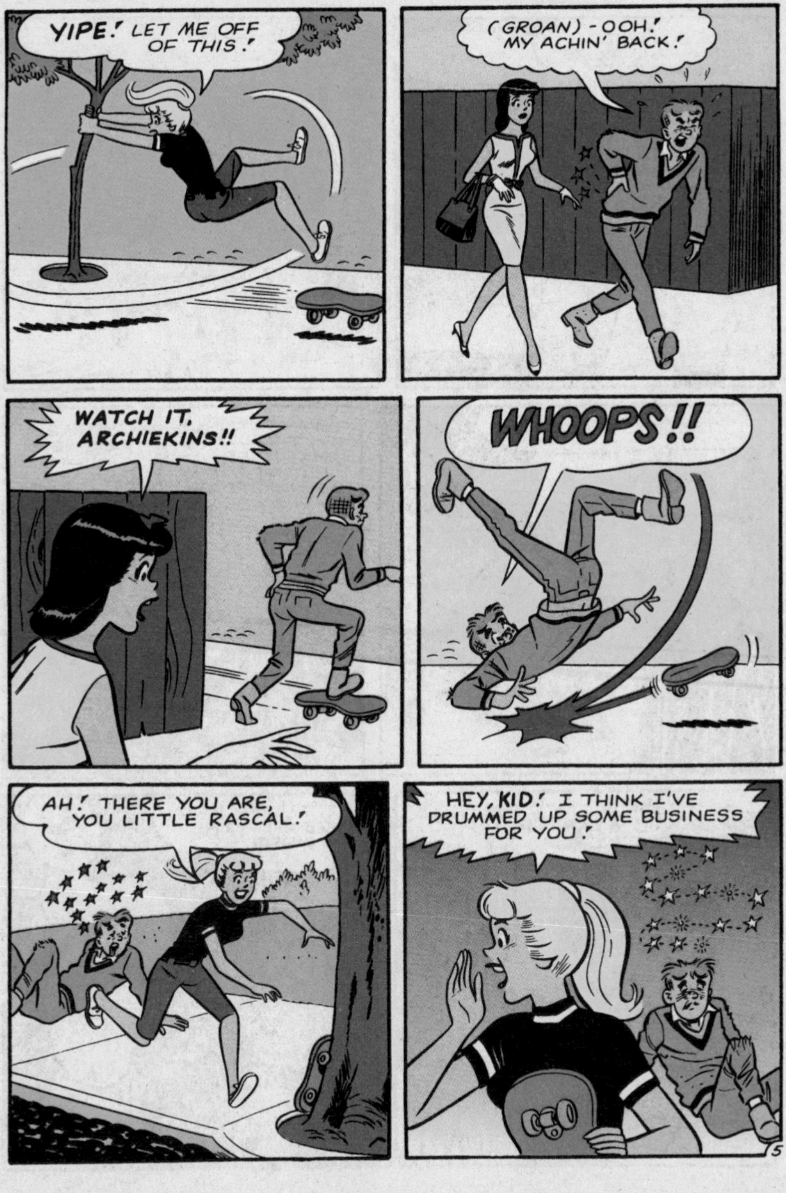
YIPE! LET ME OFF OF THIS!
(GROAN) - OOH! MY ACHIN' BACK!
WATCH IT, ARCHIEKINS!!
WHOOPS!!
AH! THERE YOU ARE, YOU LITTLE RASCAL!
HEY, KID! I THINK I'VE DRUMMED UP SOME BUSINESS FOR YOU!

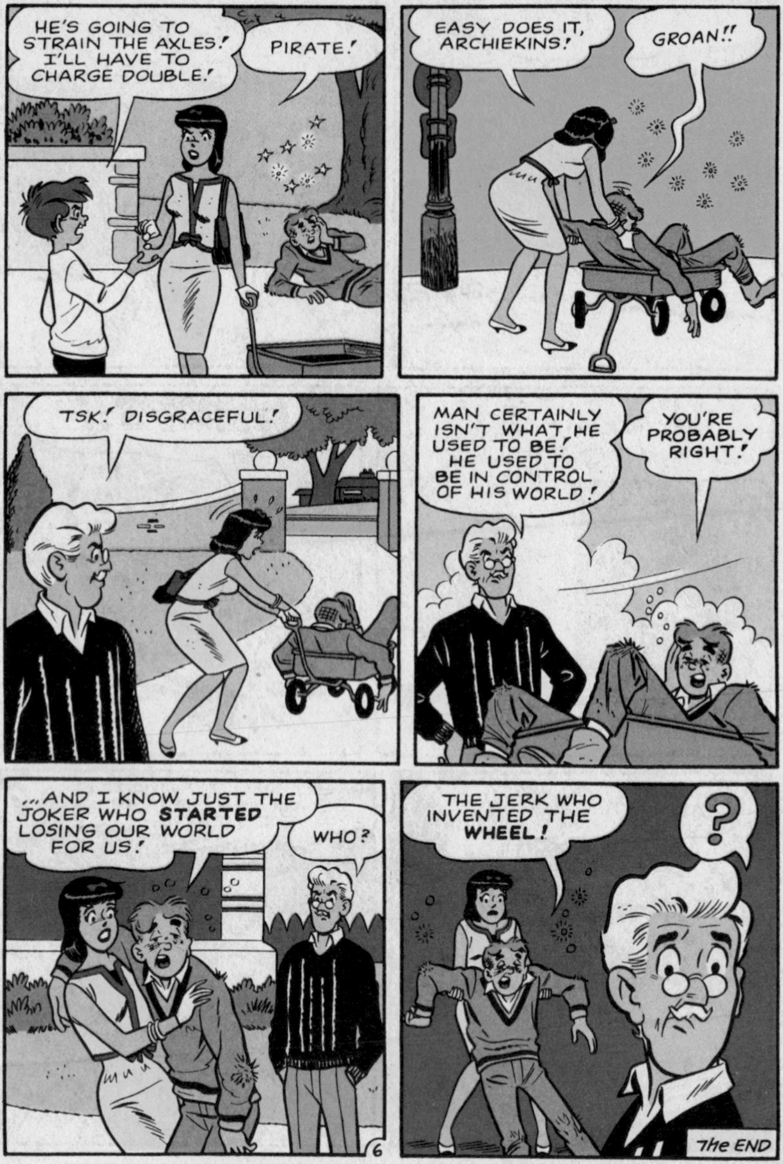

HE'S GOING TO STRAIN THE AXLES! I'LL HAVE TO CHARGE DOUBLE!
PIRATE!
EASY DOES IT, ARCHIEKINS!
GROAN!!
TSK! DISGRACEFUL!
MAN CERTAINLY ISN'T WHAT HE USED TO BE! HE USED TO BE IN CONTROL OF HIS WORLD!
YOU'RE PROBABLY RIGHT!
...AND I KNOW JUST THE JOKER WHO **STARTED** LOSING OUR WORLD FOR US!
WHO?
THE JERK WHO INVENTED THE **WHEEL**!
?
6
The END

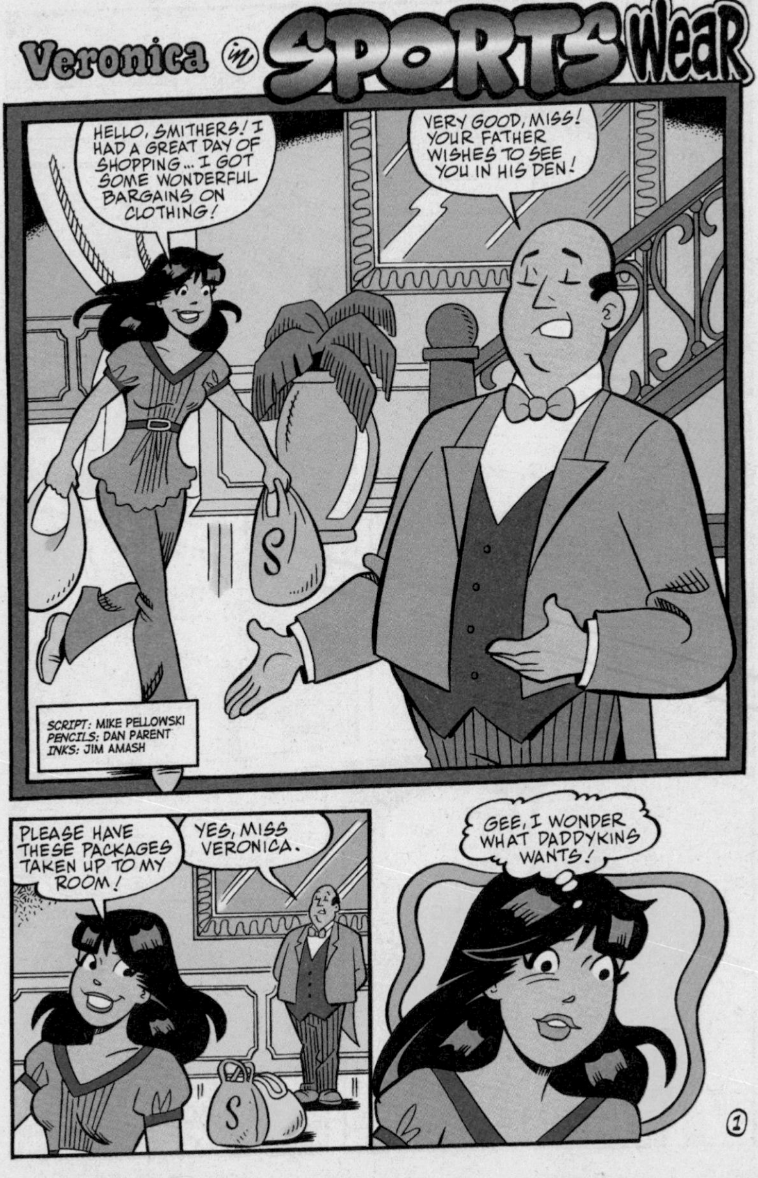
Veronica in SPORTS Wear
HELLO, SMITHERS! I HAD A GREAT DAY OF SHOPPING... I GOT SOME WONDERFUL BARGAINS ON CLOTHING!
VERY GOOD, MISS! YOUR FATHER WISHES TO SEE YOU IN HIS DEN!
SCRIPT: MIKE PELLOWSKI
PENCILS: DAN PARENT
INKS: JIM AMASH
PLEASE HAVE THESE PACKAGES TAKEN UP TO MY ROOM!
YES, MISS VERONICA.
GEE, I WONDER WHAT DADDYKINS WANTS!
1

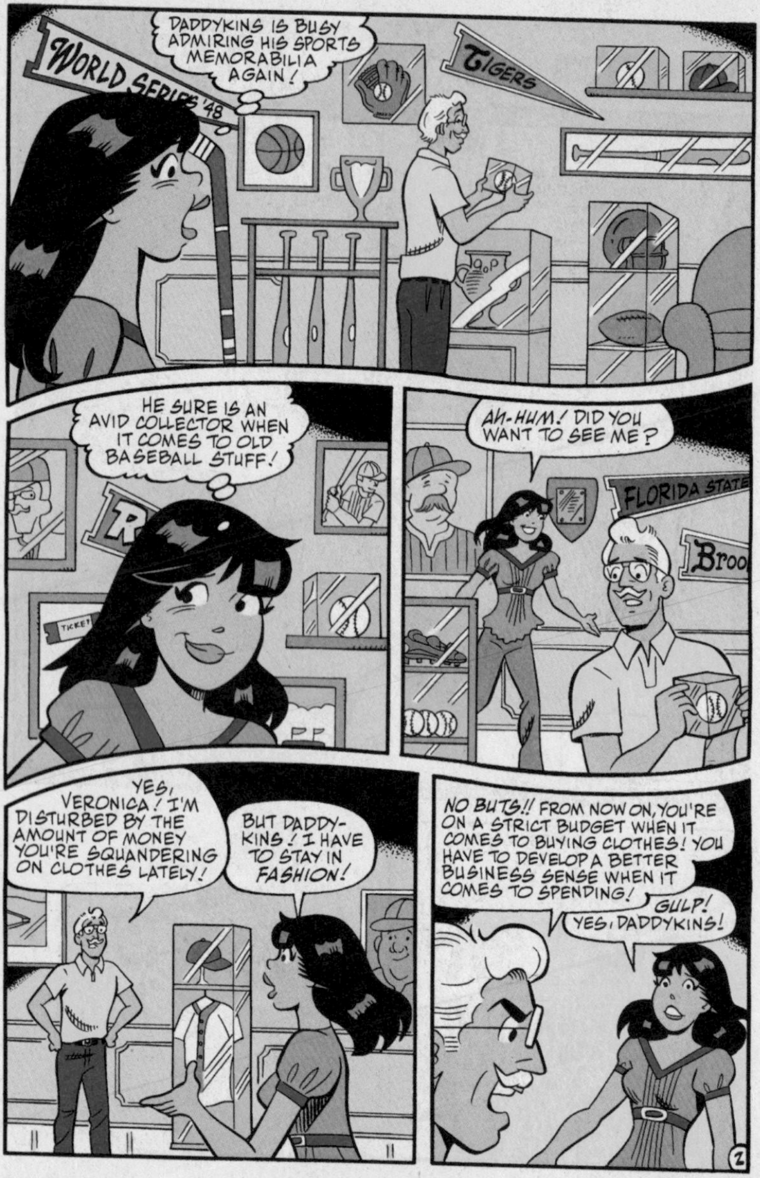
WORLD SERIES '48
DADDYKINS IS BUSY ADMIRING HIS SPORTS MEMORABILIA AGAIN!
TIGERS
HE SURE IS AN AVID COLLECTOR WHEN IT COMES TO OLD BASEBALL STUFF!
AH-HUM! DID YOU WANT TO SEE ME?
FLORIDA STATE
YES, VERONICA! I'M DISTURBED BY THE AMOUNT OF MONEY YOU'RE SQUANDERING ON CLOTHES LATELY!
BUT DADDY-KINS! I HAVE TO STAY IN FASHION!
NO BUTS!! FROM NOW ON, YOU'RE ON A STRICT BUDGET WHEN IT COMES TO BUYING CLOTHES! YOU HAVE TO DEVELOP A BETTER BUSINESS SENSE WHEN IT COMES TO SPENDING!
GULP! YES, DADDYKINS!
2

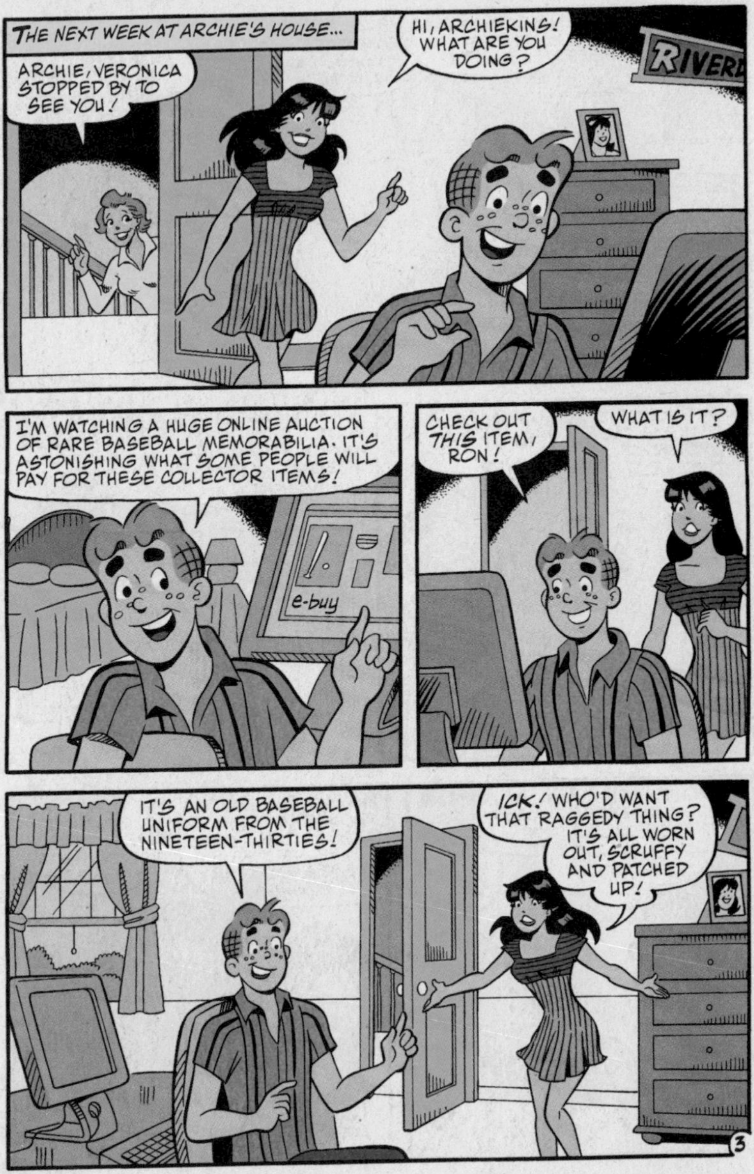
THE NEXT WEEK AT ARCHIE'S HOUSE...
ARCHIE, VERONICA STOPPED BY TO SEE YOU!
HI, ARCHIEKINS! WHAT ARE YOU DOING?
RIVERD
I'M WATCHING A HUGE ONLINE AUCTION OF RARE BASEBALL MEMORABILIA. IT'S ASTONISHING WHAT SOME PEOPLE WILL PAY FOR THESE COLLECTOR ITEMS!
e-buy
CHECK OUT THIS ITEM, RON!
WHAT IS IT?
IT'S AN OLD BASEBALL UNIFORM FROM THE NINETEEN-THIRTIES!
ICK! WHO'D WANT THAT RAGGEDY THING? IT'S ALL WORN OUT, SCRUFFY AND PATCHED UP!
3

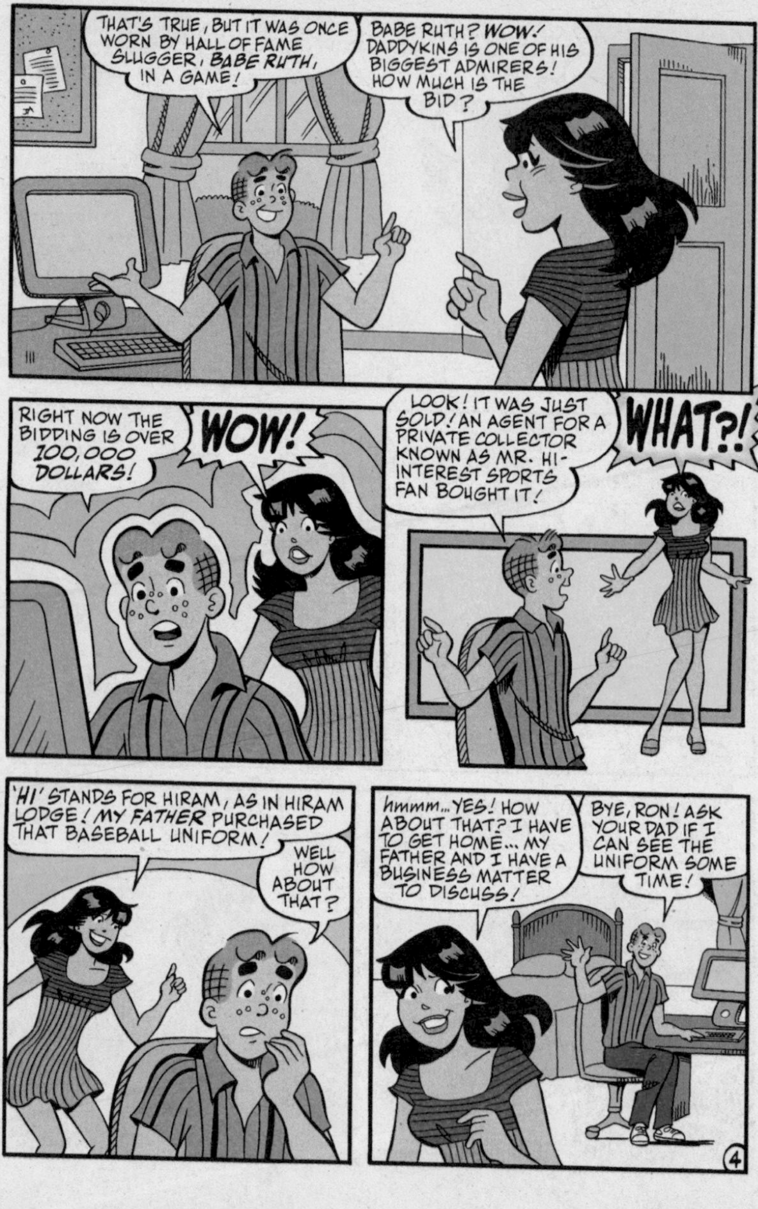
THAT'S TRUE, BUT IT WAS ONCE WORN BY HALL OF FAME SLUGGER, BABE RUTH, IN A GAME!
BABE RUTH? WOW! DADDYKINS IS ONE OF HIS BIGGEST ADMIRERS! HOW MUCH IS THE BID?
RIGHT NOW THE BIDDING IS OVER 100,000 DOLLARS!
WOW!
LOOK! IT WAS JUST SOLD! AN AGENT FOR A PRIVATE COLLECTOR KNOWN AS MR. HI-INTEREST SPORTS FAN BOUGHT IT!
WHAT?!
'HI' STANDS FOR HIRAM, AS IN HIRAM LODGE! MY FATHER PURCHASED THAT BASEBALL UNIFORM!
WELL HOW ABOUT THAT?
hmmm... YES! HOW ABOUT THAT? I HAVE TO GET HOME... MY FATHER AND I HAVE A BUSINESS MATTER TO DISCUSS!
BYE, RON! ASK YOUR DAD IF I CAN SEE THE UNIFORM SOME TIME!
4

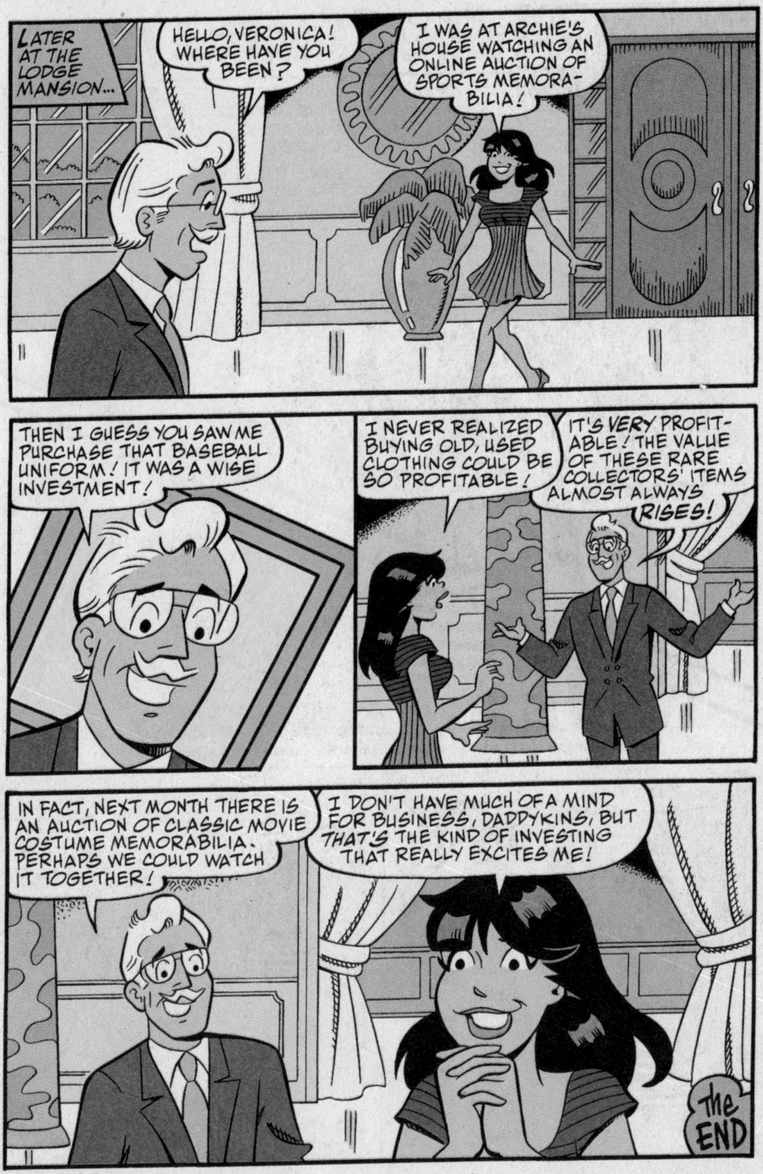
LATER AT THE LODGE MANSION...
HELLO, VERONICA! WHERE HAVE YOU BEEN?
I WAS AT ARCHIE'S HOUSE WATCHING AN ONLINE AUCTION OF SPORTS MEMORA-BILIA!
THEN I GUESS YOU SAW ME PURCHASE THAT BASEBALL UNIFORM! IT WAS A WISE INVESTMENT!
I NEVER REALIZED BUYING OLD, USED CLOTHING COULD BE SO PROFITABLE!
IT'S VERY PROFIT-ABLE! THE VALUE OF THESE RARE COLLECTORS' ITEMS ALMOST ALWAYS RISES!
IN FACT, NEXT MONTH THERE IS AN AUCTION OF CLASSIC MOVIE COSTUME MEMORABILIA. PERHAPS WE COULD WATCH IT TOGETHER!
I DON'T HAVE MUCH OF A MIND FOR BUSINESS, DADDYKINS, BUT THAT'S THE KIND OF INVESTING THAT REALLY EXCITES ME!
THE END

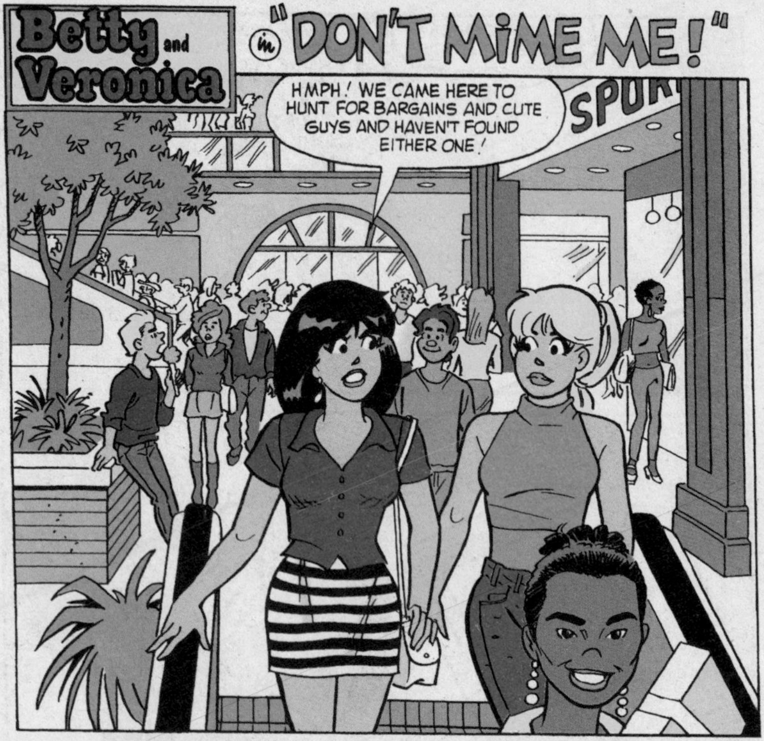
Betty and Veronica
in "DON'T MIME ME!"
HMPH! WE CAME HERE TO HUNT FOR BARGAINS AND CUTE GUYS AND HAVEN'T FOUND EITHER ONE!
SPOR

Script: Mike Pellowski / Art: Dan DeCarlo / Letters: Bill Yoshida / Colors: Barry Grossman

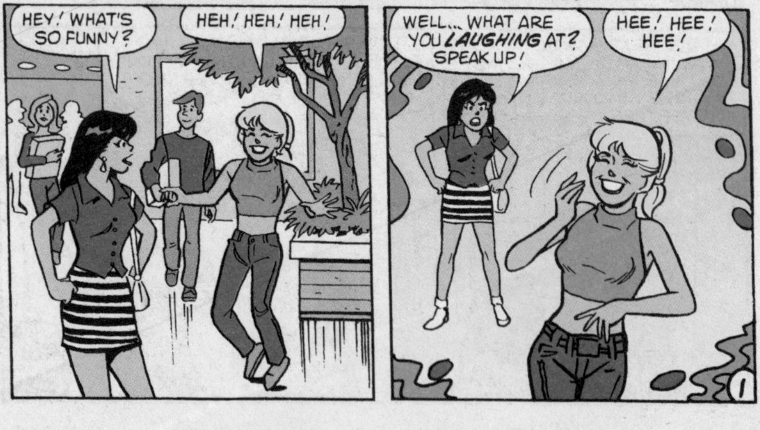
HEY! WHAT'S SO FUNNY?
HEH! HEH! HEH!
WELL... WHAT ARE YOU *LAUGHING* AT? SPEAK UP!
HEE! HEE! HEE!

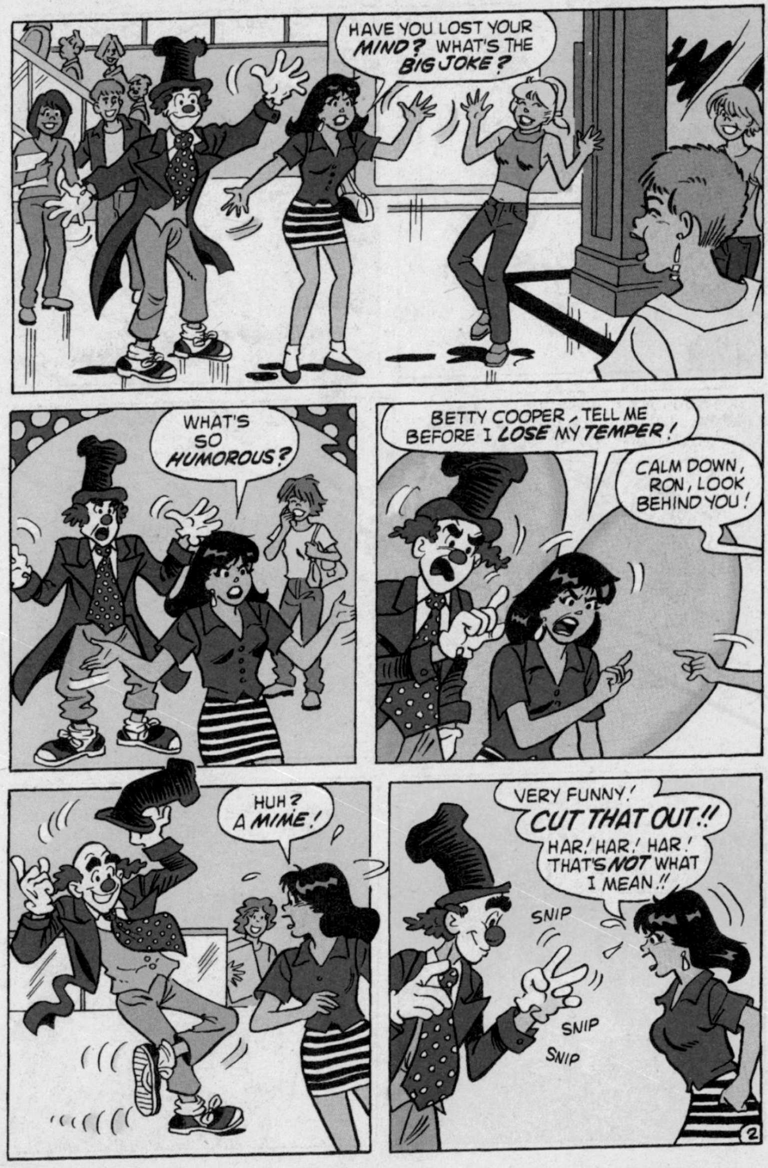

HAVE YOU LOST YOUR MIND? WHAT'S THE BIG JOKE?
WHAT'S SO HUMOROUS?
BETTY COOPER, TELL ME BEFORE I LOSE MY TEMPER!
CALM DOWN, RON, LOOK BEHIND YOU!
HUH? A MIME!
VERY FUNNY! CUT THAT OUT!!
HAR! HAR! HAR! THAT'S NOT WHAT I MEAN!!
SNIP
SNIP
SNIP
2

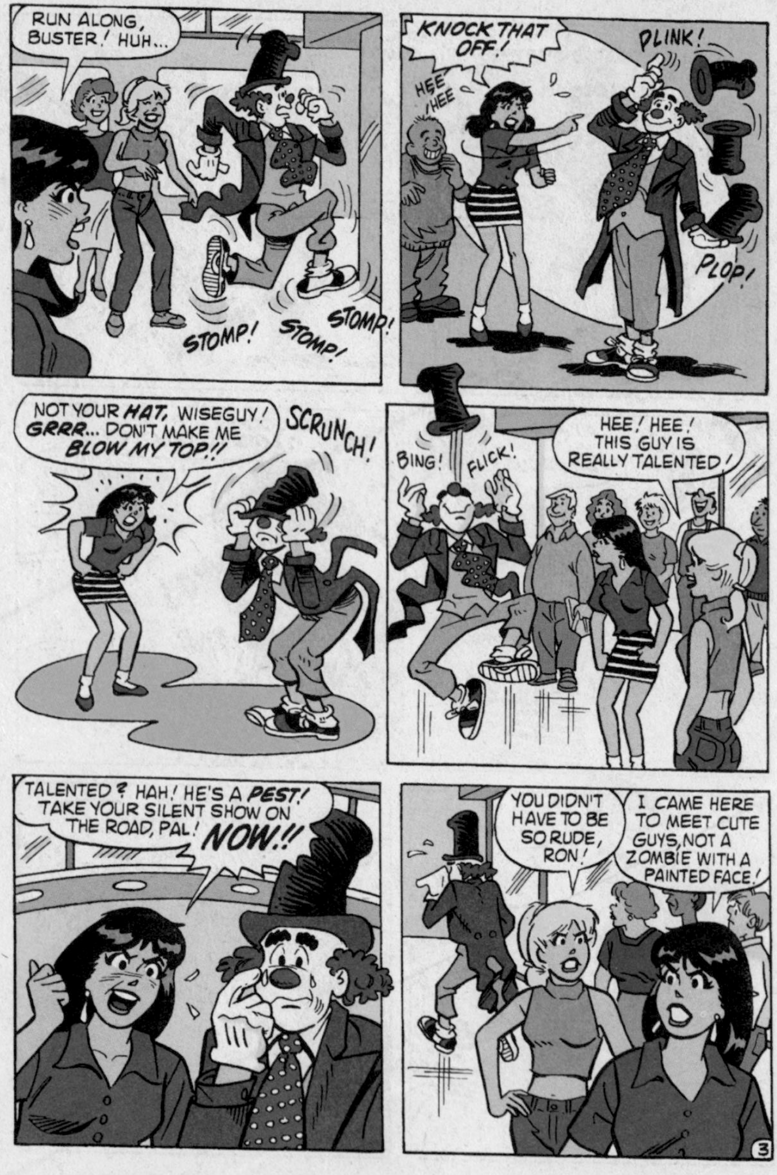
RUN ALONG, BUSTER! HUH...
STOMP! STOMP! STOMP!
KNOCK THAT OFF!
HEE HEE
PLINK!
PLOP!
NOT YOUR HAT, WISEGUY! GRRR... DON'T MAKE ME BLOW MY TOP!!
SCRUNCH!
BING!
FLICK!
HEE! HEE! THIS GUY IS REALLY TALENTED!
TALENTED? HAH! HE'S A PEST! TAKE YOUR SILENT SHOW ON THE ROAD, PAL! NOW!!
YOU DIDN'T HAVE TO BE SO RUDE, RON!
I CAME HERE TO MEET CUTE GUYS, NOT A ZOMBIE WITH A PAINTED FACE!
3

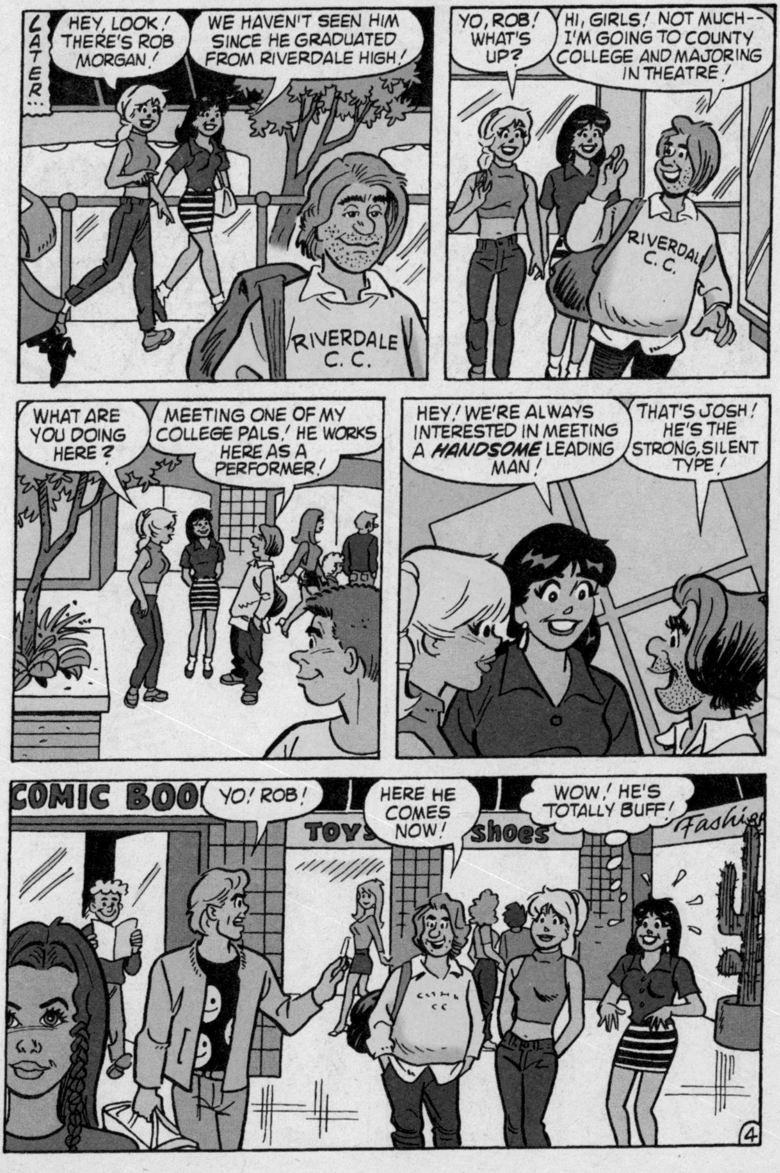
LATER...
HEY, LOOK! THERE'S ROB MORGAN!
WE HAVEN'T SEEN HIM SINCE HE GRADUATED FROM RIVERDALE HIGH!
RIVERDALE C. C.
YO, ROB! WHAT'S UP?
HI, GIRLS! NOT MUCH-- I'M GOING TO COUNTY COLLEGE AND MAJORING IN THEATRE!
RIVERDALE C. C.
WHAT ARE YOU DOING HERE?
MEETING ONE OF MY COLLEGE PALS! HE WORKS HERE AS A PERFORMER!
HEY! WE'RE ALWAYS INTERESTED IN MEETING A *HANDSOME* LEADING MAN!
THAT'S JOSH! HE'S THE STRONG, SILENT TYPE!
COMIC BOO
YO! ROB!
HERE HE COMES NOW!
WOW! HE'S TOTALLY BUFF!
TOYS
shoes
Fashi
4

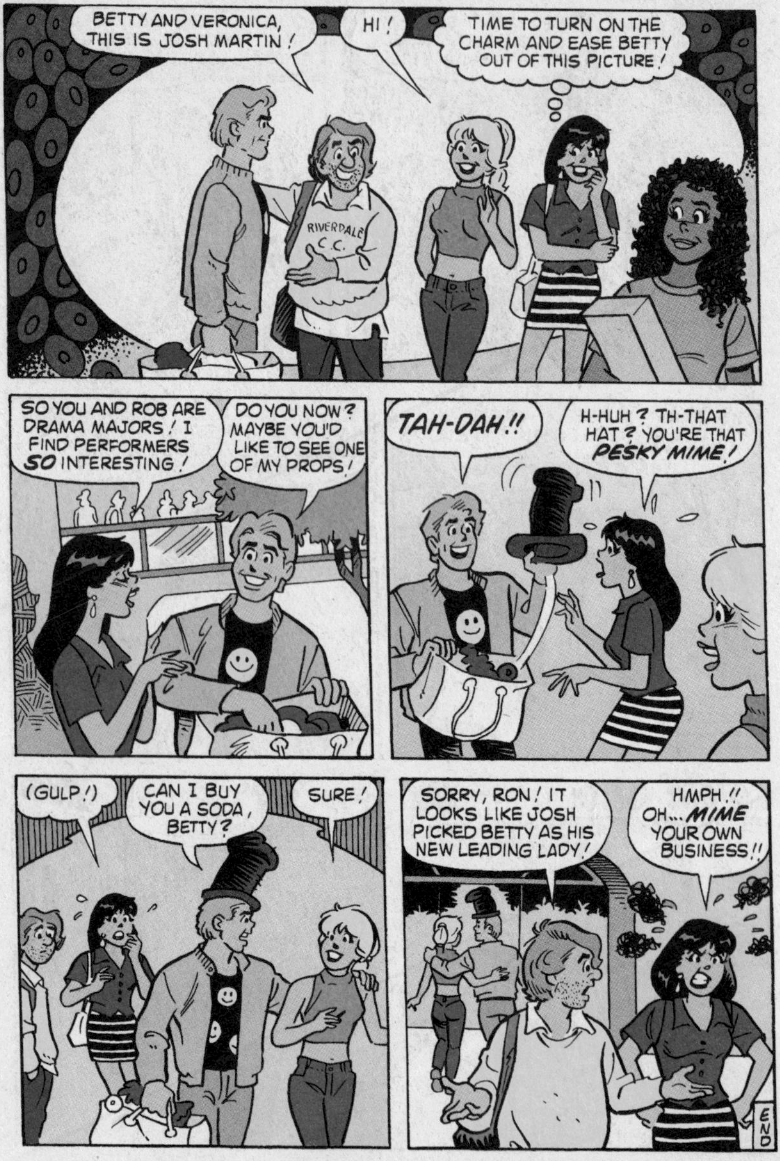
BETTY AND VERONICA, THIS IS JOSH MARTIN!
HI!
TIME TO TURN ON THE CHARM AND EASE BETTY OUT OF THIS PICTURE!
RIVERDALE C.C.
SO YOU AND ROB ARE DRAMA MAJORS! I FIND PERFORMERS SO INTERESTING!
DO YOU NOW? MAYBE YOU'D LIKE TO SEE ONE OF MY PROPS!
TAH-DAH!!
H-HUH? TH-THAT HAT? YOU'RE THAT PESKY MIME!
(GULP!)
CAN I BUY YOU A SODA, BETTY?
SURE!
SORRY, RON! IT LOOKS LIKE JOSH PICKED BETTY AS HIS NEW LEADING LADY!
HMPH!! OH...MIME YOUR OWN BUSINESS!!
END

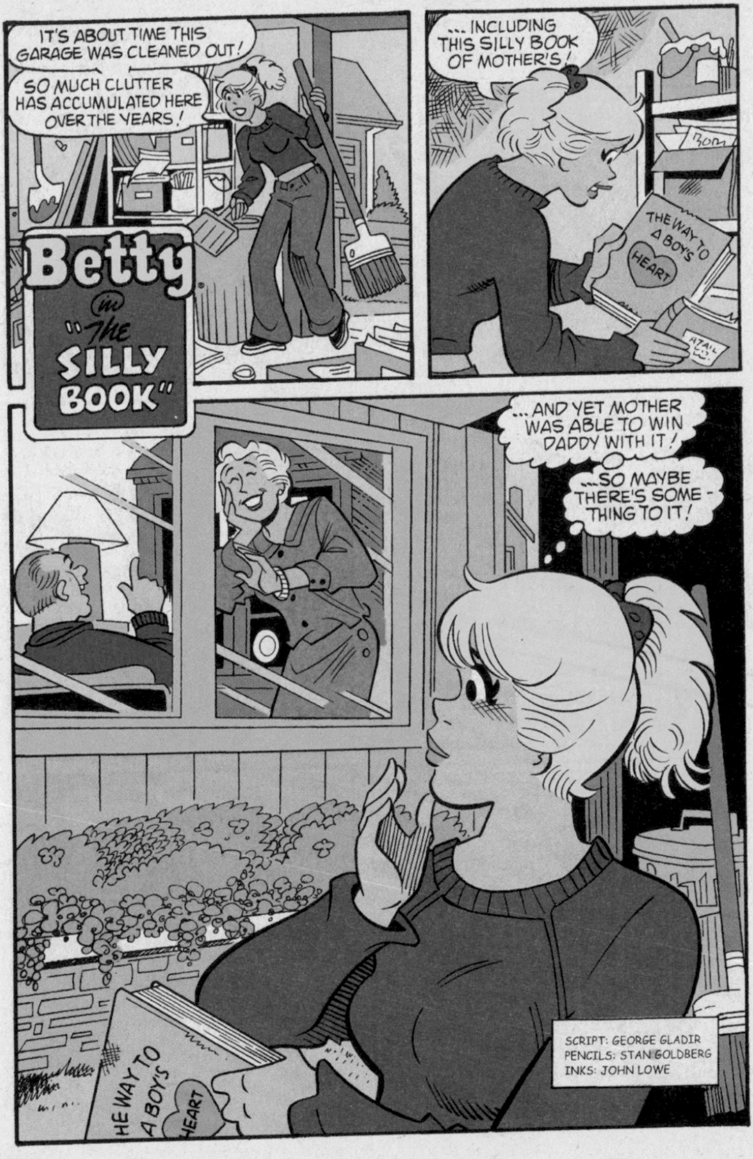
IT'S ABOUT TIME THIS GARAGE WAS CLEANED OUT!
SO MUCH CLUTTER HAS ACCUMULATED HERE OVER THE YEARS!
Betty in "The SILLY BOOK"
... INCLUDING THIS SILLY BOOK OF MOTHER'S!
THE WAY TO A BOY'S HEART
... AND YET MOTHER WAS ABLE TO WIN DADDY WITH IT!
...SO MAYBE THERE'S SOME-THING TO IT!
HE WAY TO A BOY'S HEART
SCRIPT: GEORGE GLADIR
PENCILS: STAN GOLDBERG
INKS: JOHN LOWE

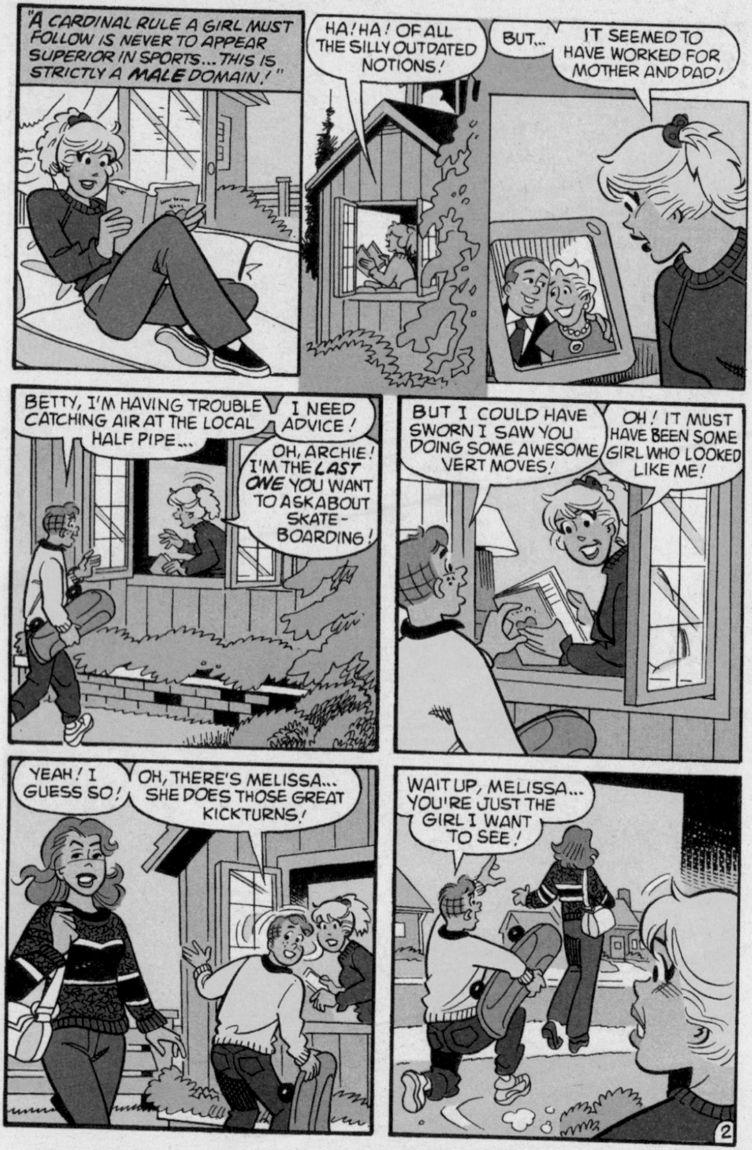
"A CARDINAL RULE A GIRL MUST FOLLOW IS NEVER TO APPEAR SUPERIOR IN SPORTS... THIS IS STRICTLY A MALE DOMAIN!"
HA! HA! OF ALL THE SILLY OUTDATED NOTIONS!
BUT...
IT SEEMED TO HAVE WORKED FOR MOTHER AND DAD!
BETTY, I'M HAVING TROUBLE CATCHING AIR AT THE LOCAL HALF PIPE...
I NEED ADVICE!
OH, ARCHIE! I'M THE LAST ONE YOU WANT TO ASKABOUT SKATE-BOARDING!
BUT I COULD HAVE SWORN I SAW YOU DOING SOME AWESOME VERT MOVES!
OH! IT MUST HAVE BEEN SOME GIRL WHO LOOKED LIKE ME!
YEAH! I GUESS SO!
OH, THERE'S MELISSA... SHE DOES THOSE GREAT KICKTURNS!
WAIT UP, MELISSA... YOU'RE JUST THE GIRL I WANT TO SEE!
2

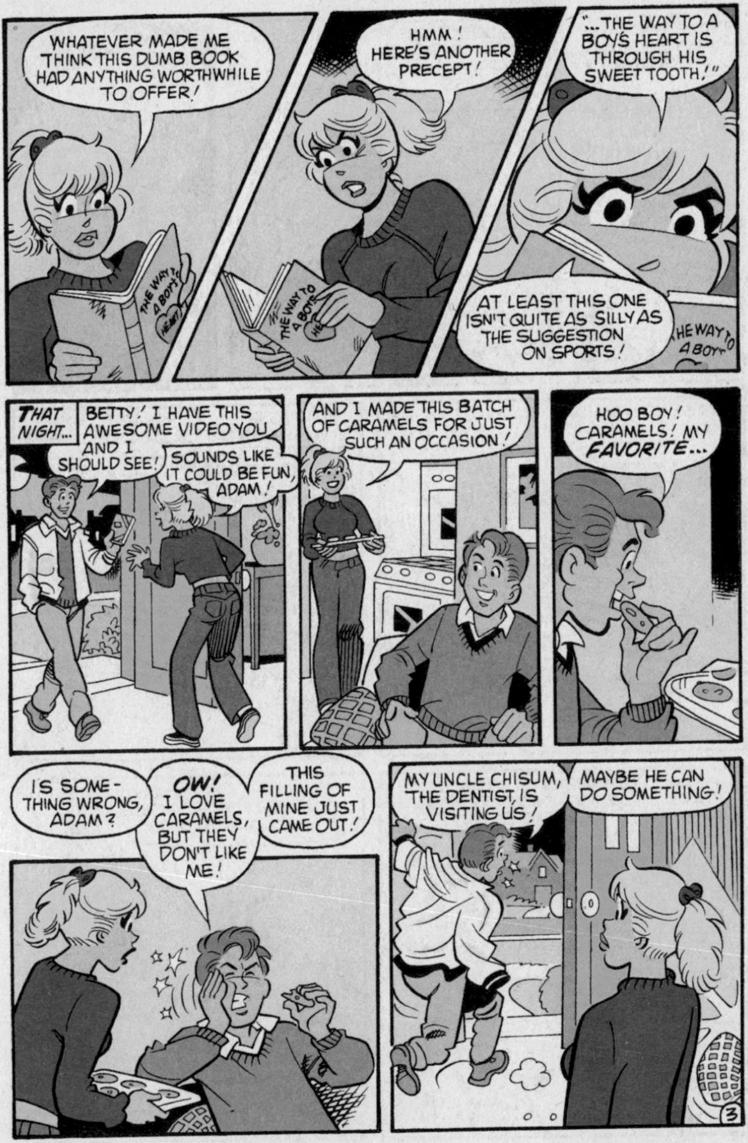
WHATEVER MADE ME THINK THIS DUMB BOOK HAD ANYTHING WORTHWHILE TO OFFER!
THE WAY TO A BOY'S HEART
HMM! HERE'S ANOTHER PRECEPT!
THE WAY TO A BOY'S
"...THE WAY TO A BOY'S HEART IS THROUGH HIS SWEET TOOTH!"
AT LEAST THIS ONE ISN'T QUITE AS SILLY AS THE SUGGESTION ON SPORTS!
THAT NIGHT...
BETTY! I HAVE THIS AWESOME VIDEO YOU AND I SHOULD SEE!
SOUNDS LIKE IT COULD BE FUN, ADAM!
AND I MADE THIS BATCH OF CARAMELS FOR JUST SUCH AN OCCASION!
HOO BOY! CARAMELS! MY FAVORITE...
IS SOME-THING WRONG, ADAM?
OW! I LOVE CARAMELS, BUT THEY DON'T LIKE ME!
THIS FILLING OF MINE JUST CAME OUT!
MY UNCLE CHISUM, THE DENTIST, IS VISITING US!
MAYBE HE CAN DO SOMETHING!
3

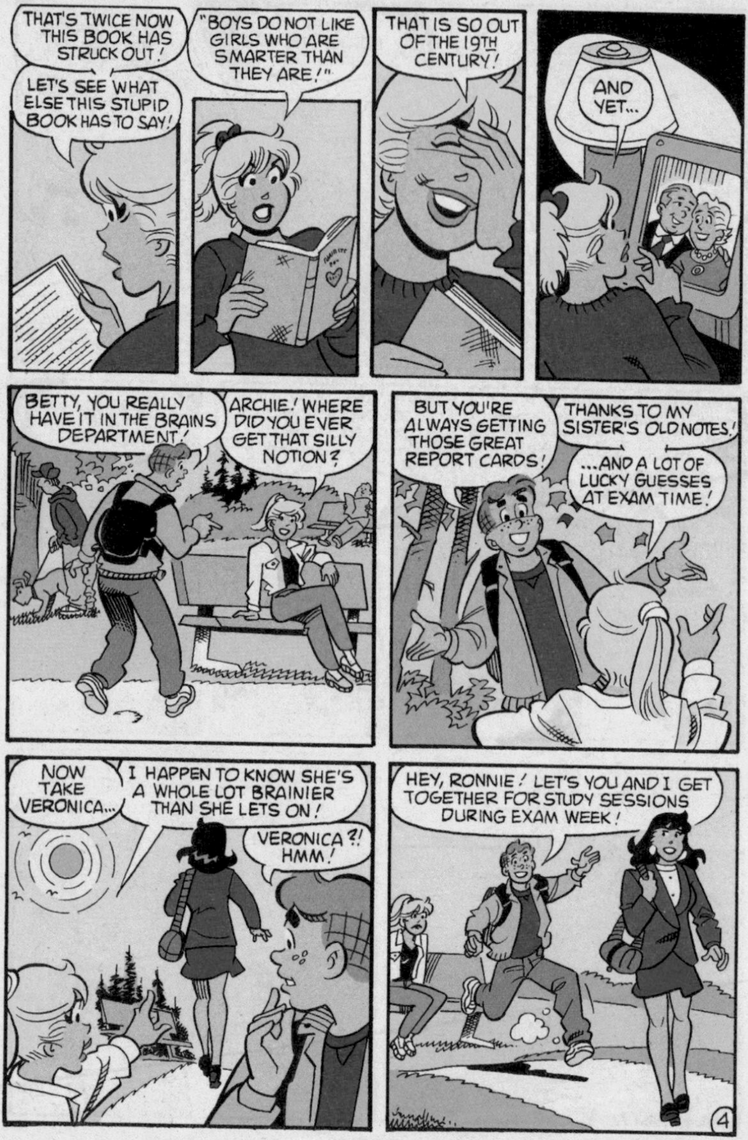
THAT'S TWICE NOW THIS BOOK HAS STRUCK OUT!
LET'S SEE WHAT ELSE THIS STUPID BOOK HAS TO SAY!
"BOYS DO NOT LIKE GIRLS WHO ARE SMARTER THAN THEY ARE!"
THAT IS SO OUT OF THE 19TH CENTURY!
AND YET...
BETTY, YOU REALLY HAVE IT IN THE BRAINS DEPARTMENT!
ARCHIE! WHERE DID YOU EVER GET THAT SILLY NOTION?
BUT YOU'RE ALWAYS GETTING THOSE GREAT REPORT CARDS!
THANKS TO MY SISTER'S OLD NOTES!
...AND A LOT OF LUCKY GUESSES AT EXAM TIME!
NOW TAKE VERONICA...
I HAPPEN TO KNOW SHE'S A WHOLE LOT BRAINIER THAN SHE LETS ON!
VERONICA?! HMM!
HEY, RONNIE! LET'S YOU AND I GET TOGETHER FOR STUDY SESSIONS DURING EXAM WEEK!
4

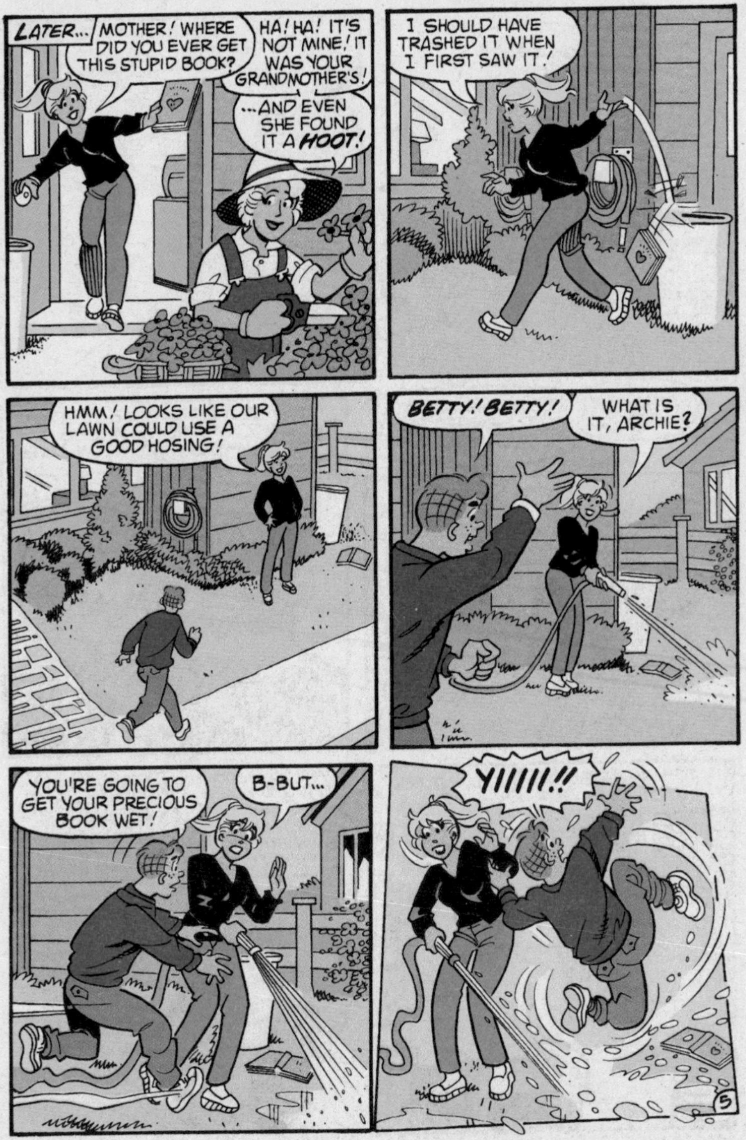
LATER...
MOTHER! WHERE DID YOU EVER GET THIS STUPID BOOK?
HA! HA! IT'S NOT MINE! IT WAS YOUR GRANDMOTHER'S!
...AND EVEN SHE FOUND IT A HOOT!
I SHOULD HAVE TRASHED IT WHEN I FIRST SAW IT!
HMM! LOOKS LIKE OUR LAWN COULD USE A GOOD HOSING!
BETTY! BETTY!
WHAT IS IT, ARCHIE?
YOU'RE GOING TO GET YOUR PRECIOUS BOOK WET!
B-BUT...
YIIIII!!

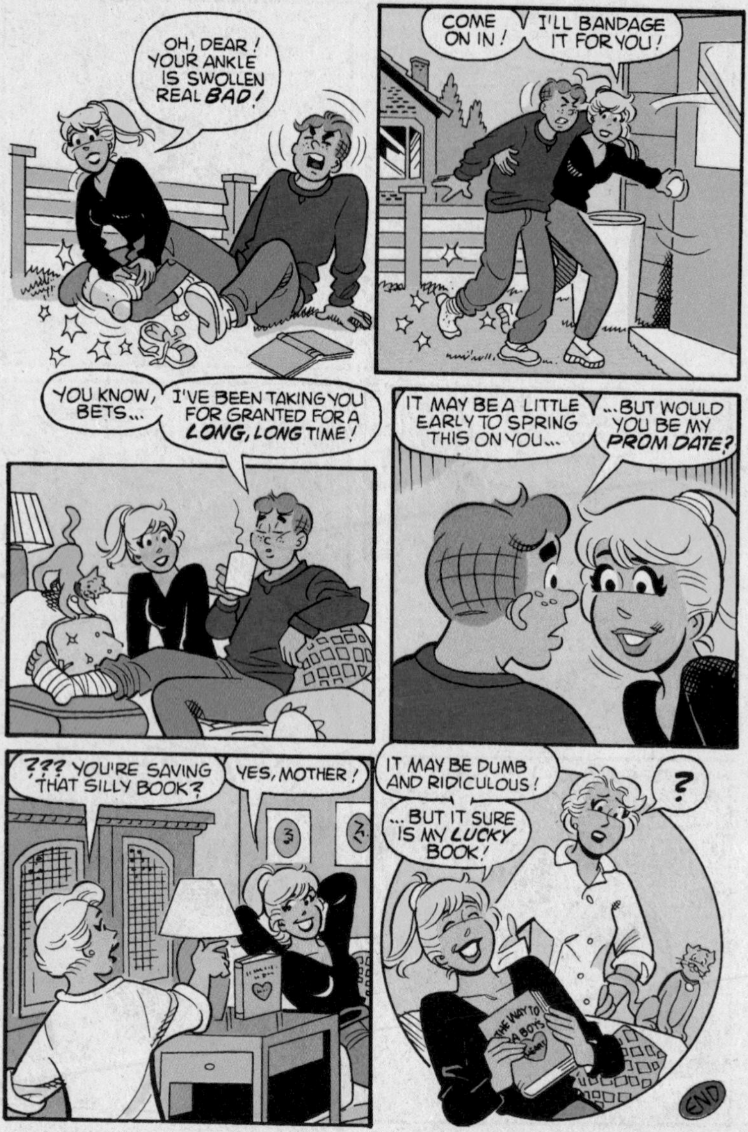
OH, DEAR! YOUR ANKLE IS SWOLLEN REAL BAD!
COME ON IN!
I'LL BANDAGE IT FOR YOU!
YOU KNOW, BETS...
I'VE BEEN TAKING YOU FOR GRANTED FOR A LONG, LONG TIME!
IT MAY BE A LITTLE EARLY TO SPRING THIS ON YOU...
...BUT WOULD YOU BE MY PROM DATE?
??? YOU'RE SAVING THAT SILLY BOOK?
YES, MOTHER!
IT MAY BE DUMB AND RIDICULOUS!
...BUT IT SURE IS MY LUCKY BOOK!
?
THE WAY TO A BOY'S HEART
END

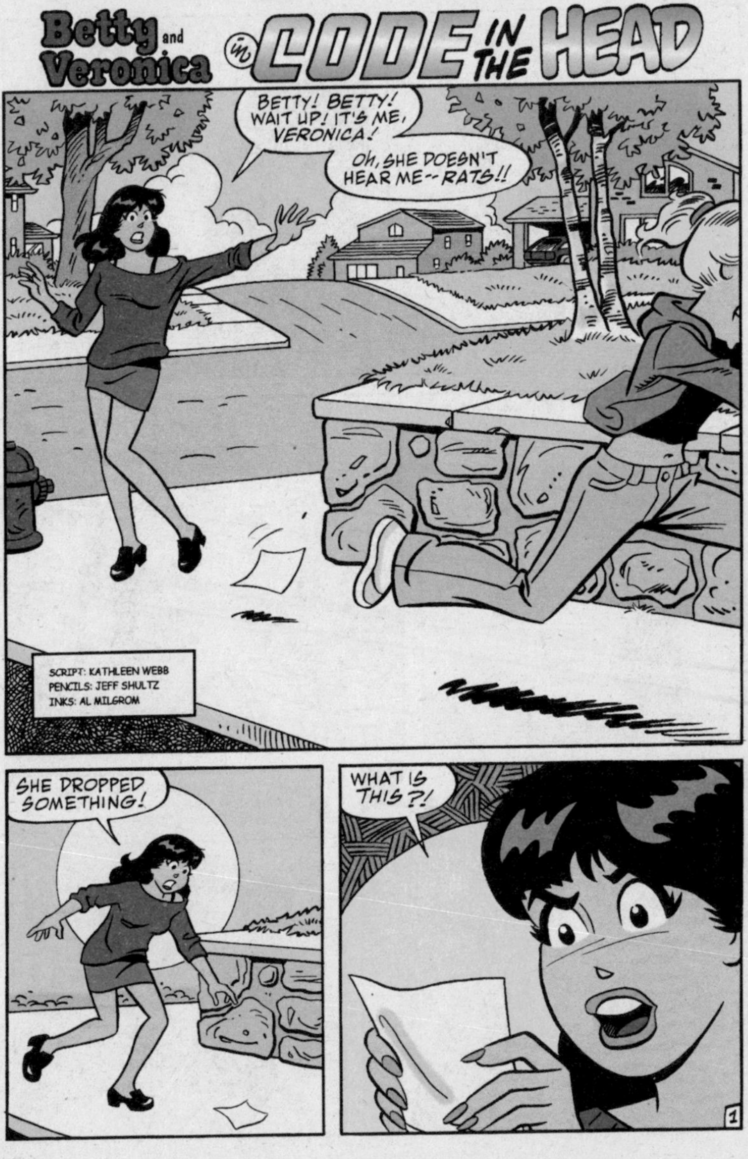
Betty and Veronica in CODE IN THE HEAD
BETTY! BETTY! WAIT UP! IT'S ME, VERONICA!
Oh, SHE DOESN'T HEAR ME-- RATS!!
SCRIPT: KATHLEEN WEBB
PENCILS: JEFF SHULTZ
INKS: AL MILGROM
SHE DROPPED SOMETHING!
WHAT IS THIS?!
1

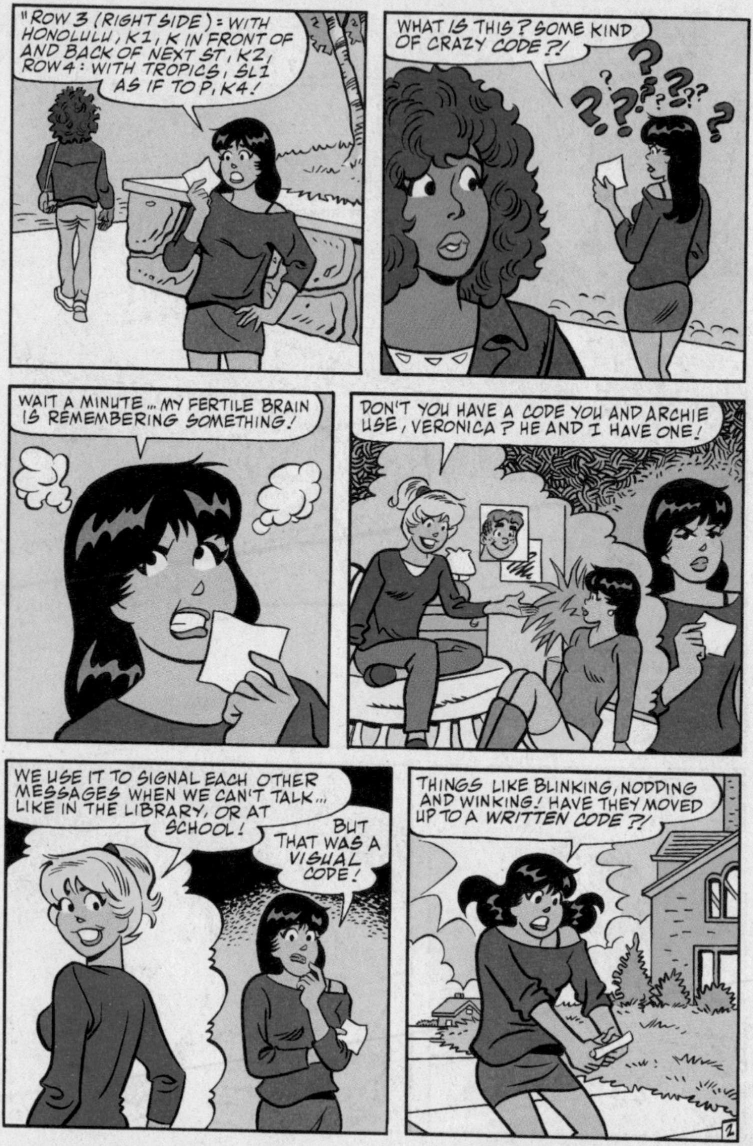

"ROW 3 (RIGHT SIDE) = WITH HONOLULU, K1, K IN FRONT OF AND BACK OF NEXT ST, K2, ROW 4: WITH TROPICS, SL1 AS IF TO P, K4!
WHAT IS THIS? SOME KIND OF CRAZY CODE?!
WAIT A MINUTE... MY FERTILE BRAIN IS REMEMBERING SOMETHING!
DON'T YOU HAVE A CODE YOU AND ARCHIE USE, VERONICA? HE AND I HAVE ONE!
WE USE IT TO SIGNAL EACH OTHER MESSAGES WHEN WE CAN'T TALK... LIKE IN THE LIBRARY, OR AT SCHOOL!
BUT THAT WAS A VISUAL CODE!
THINGS LIKE BLINKING, NODDING AND WINKING! HAVE THEY MOVED UP TO A WRITTEN CODE?!
2

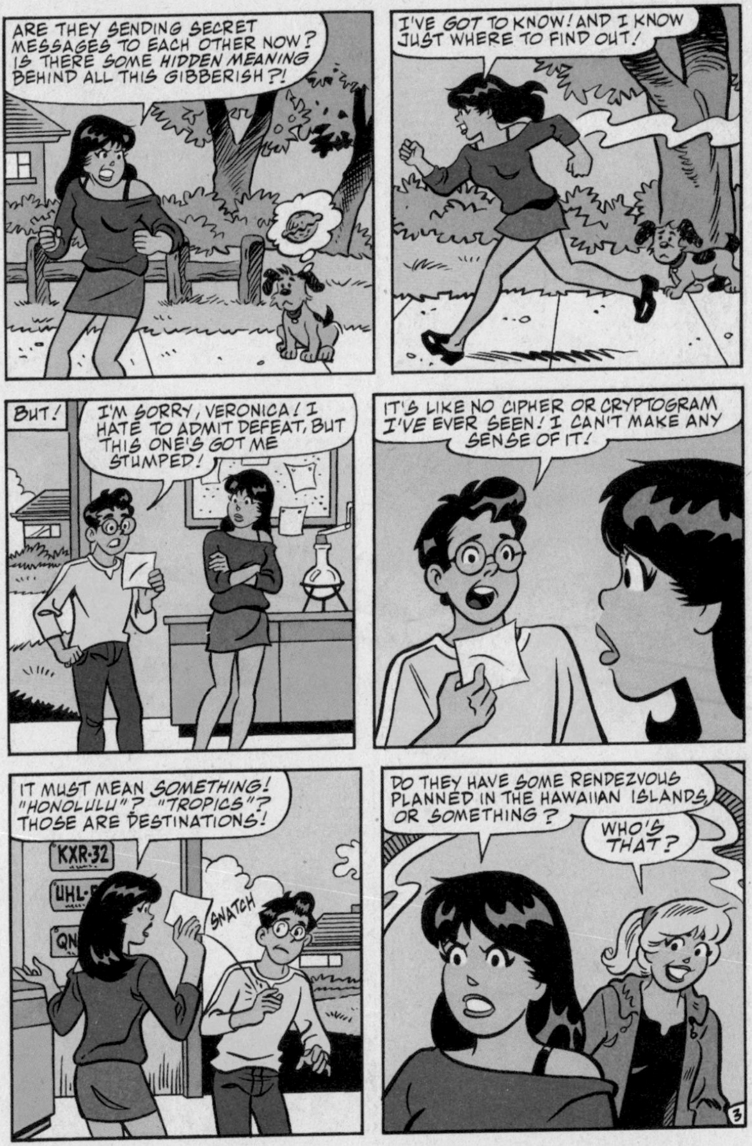
ARE THEY SENDING SECRET MESSAGES TO EACH OTHER NOW? IS THERE SOME HIDDEN MEANING BEHIND ALL THIS GIBBERISH?!
I'VE GOT TO KNOW! AND I KNOW JUST WHERE TO FIND OUT!
BUT!
I'M SORRY, VERONICA! I HATE TO ADMIT DEFEAT, BUT THIS ONE'S GOT ME STUMPED!
IT'S LIKE NO CIPHER OR CRYPTOGRAM I'VE EVER SEEN! I CAN'T MAKE ANY SENSE OF IT!
IT MUST MEAN SOMETHING! "HONOLULU"? "TROPICS"? THOSE ARE DESTINATIONS!
KXR-32
SNATCH
DO THEY HAVE SOME RENDEZVOUS PLANNED IN THE HAWAIIAN ISLANDS OR SOMETHING?
WHO'S THAT?
3

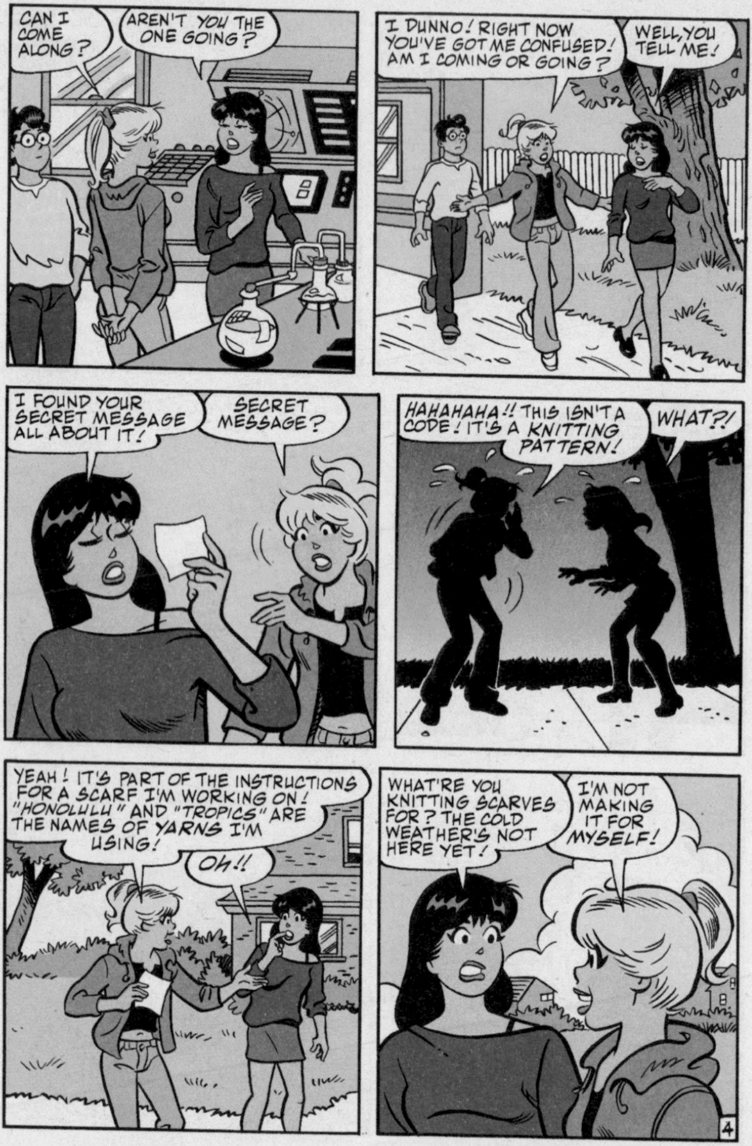
CAN I COME ALONG?
AREN'T YOU THE ONE GOING?
I DUNNO! RIGHT NOW YOU'VE GOT ME CONFUSED! AM I COMING OR GOING?
WELL, YOU TELL ME!
I FOUND YOUR SECRET MESSAGE ALL ABOUT IT!
SECRET MESSAGE?
HAHAHAHA!! THIS ISN'T A CODE! IT'S A KNITTING PATTERN!
WHAT?!
YEAH! IT'S PART OF THE INSTRUCTIONS FOR A SCARF I'M WORKING ON! "HONOLULU" AND "TROPICS" ARE THE NAMES OF YARNS I'M USING!
Oh!!
WHAT'RE YOU KNITTING SCARVES FOR? THE COLD WEATHER'S NOT HERE YET!
I'M NOT MAKING IT FOR MYSELF!
4

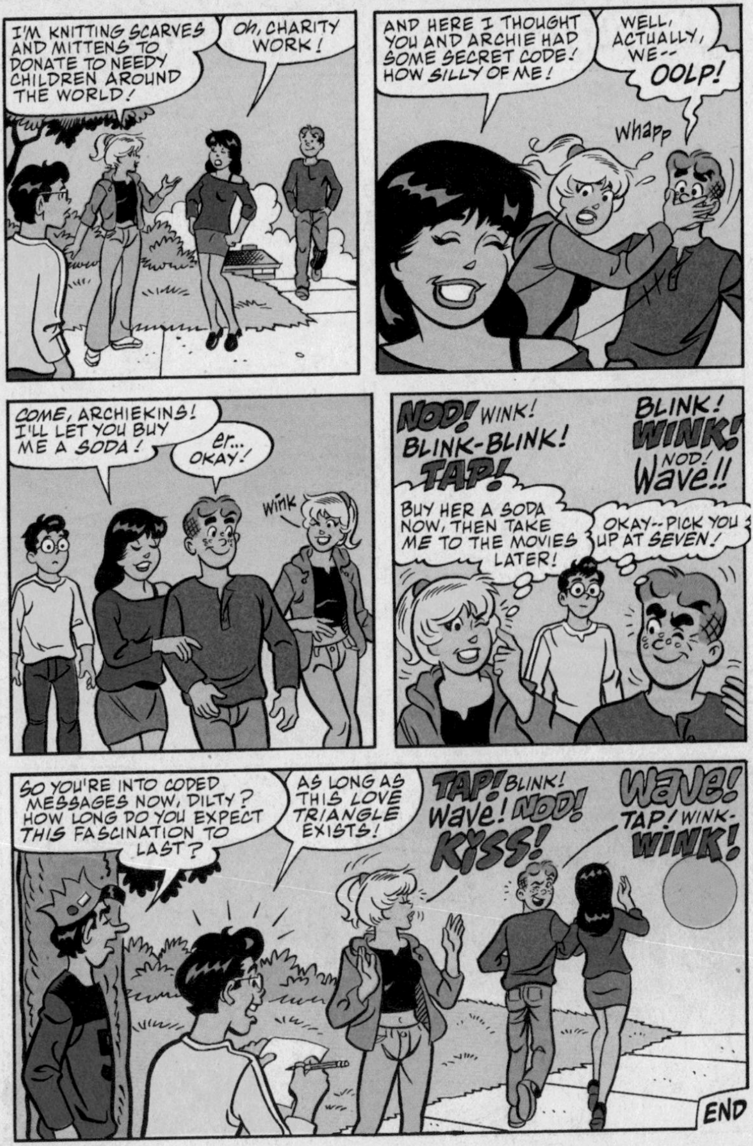
I'M KNITTING SCARVES AND MITTENS TO DONATE TO NEEDY CHILDREN AROUND THE WORLD!
Oh, CHARITY WORK!
AND HERE I THOUGHT YOU AND ARCHIE HAD SOME SECRET CODE! HOW SILLY OF ME!
WELL, ACTUALLY, WE--
OOLP!
Whapp
COME, ARCHIEKINS! I'LL LET YOU BUY ME A SODA!
er... OKAY!
wink
NOD! WINK! BLINK-BLINK! TAP!
BLINK! WINK! NOD! Wave!!
BUY HER A SODA NOW, THEN TAKE ME TO THE MOVIES LATER!
OKAY--PICK YOU UP AT SEVEN!
SO YOU'RE INTO CODED MESSAGES NOW, DILTY? HOW LONG DO YOU EXPECT THIS FASCINATION TO LAST?
AS LONG AS THIS LOVE TRIANGLE EXISTS!
TAP! BLINK! Wave! NOD! KISS!
Wave! TAP! WINK-WINK!
END

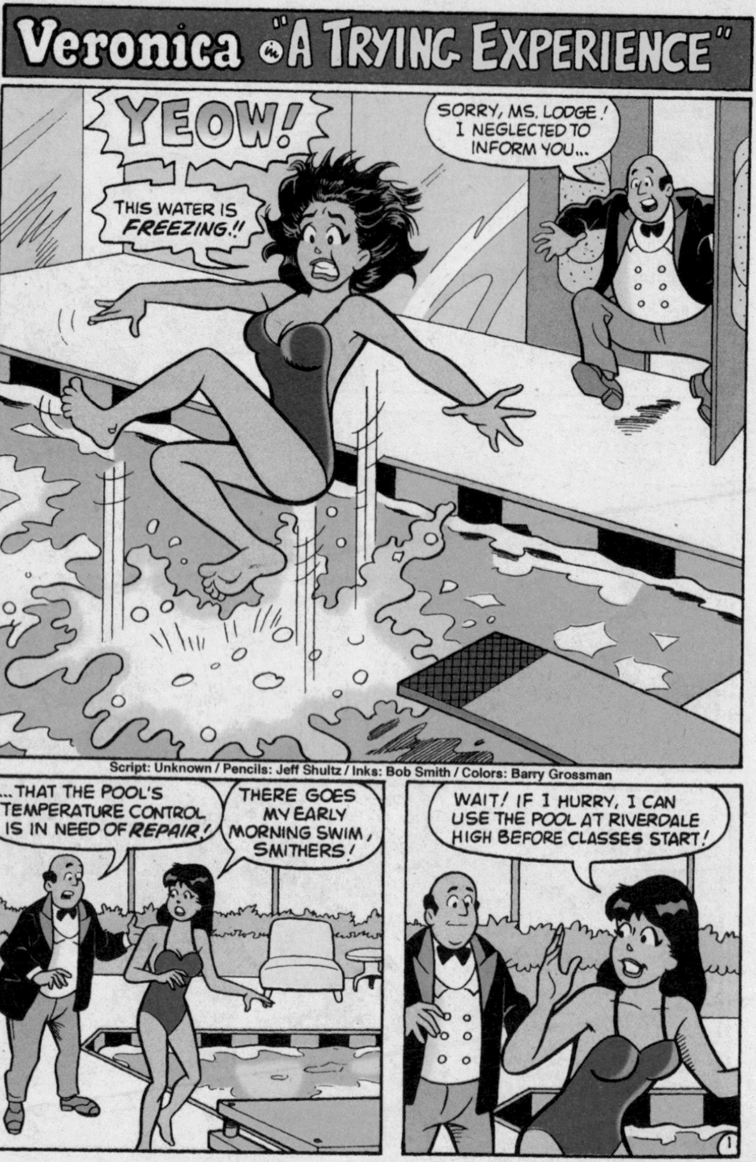
Veronica in "A TRYING EXPERIENCE"
YEOW!
THIS WATER IS FREEZING!!
SORRY, MS. LODGE! I NEGLECTED TO INFORM YOU...
Script: Unknown / Pencils: Jeff Shultz / Inks: Bob Smith / Colors: Barry Grossman
...THAT THE POOL'S TEMPERATURE CONTROL IS IN NEED OF REPAIR!
THERE GOES MY EARLY MORNING SWIM, SMITHERS!
WAIT! IF I HURRY, I CAN USE THE POOL AT RIVERDALE HIGH BEFORE CLASSES START!
1

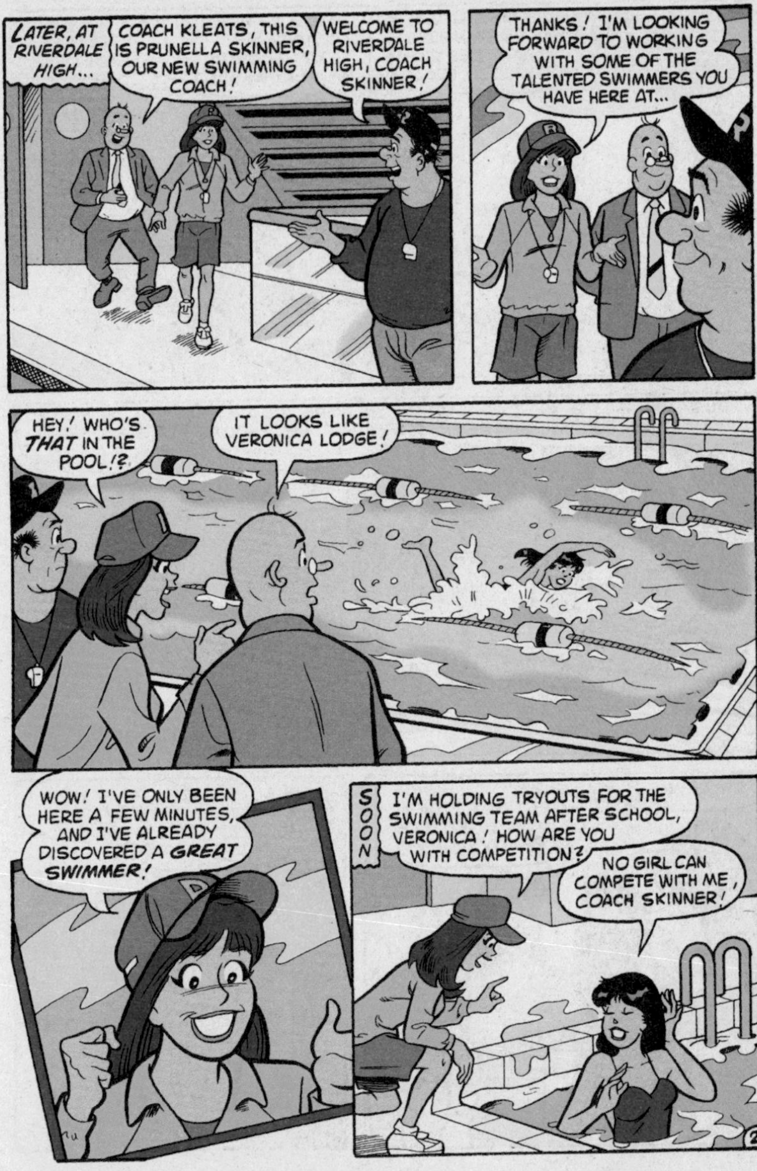
LATER, AT RIVERDALE HIGH...
COACH KLEATS, THIS IS PRUNELLA SKINNER, OUR NEW SWIMMING COACH!
WELCOME TO RIVERDALE HIGH, COACH SKINNER!
THANKS! I'M LOOKING FORWARD TO WORKING WITH SOME OF THE TALENTED SWIMMERS YOU HAVE HERE AT...
HEY! WHO'S *THAT* IN THE POOL!?
IT LOOKS LIKE VERONICA LODGE!
WOW! I'VE ONLY BEEN HERE A FEW MINUTES, AND I'VE ALREADY DISCOVERED A *GREAT SWIMMER!*
SOON
I'M HOLDING TRYOUTS FOR THE SWIMMING TEAM AFTER SCHOOL, VERONICA! HOW ARE YOU WITH COMPETITION?
NO GIRL CAN COMPETE WITH ME, COACH SKINNER!
2

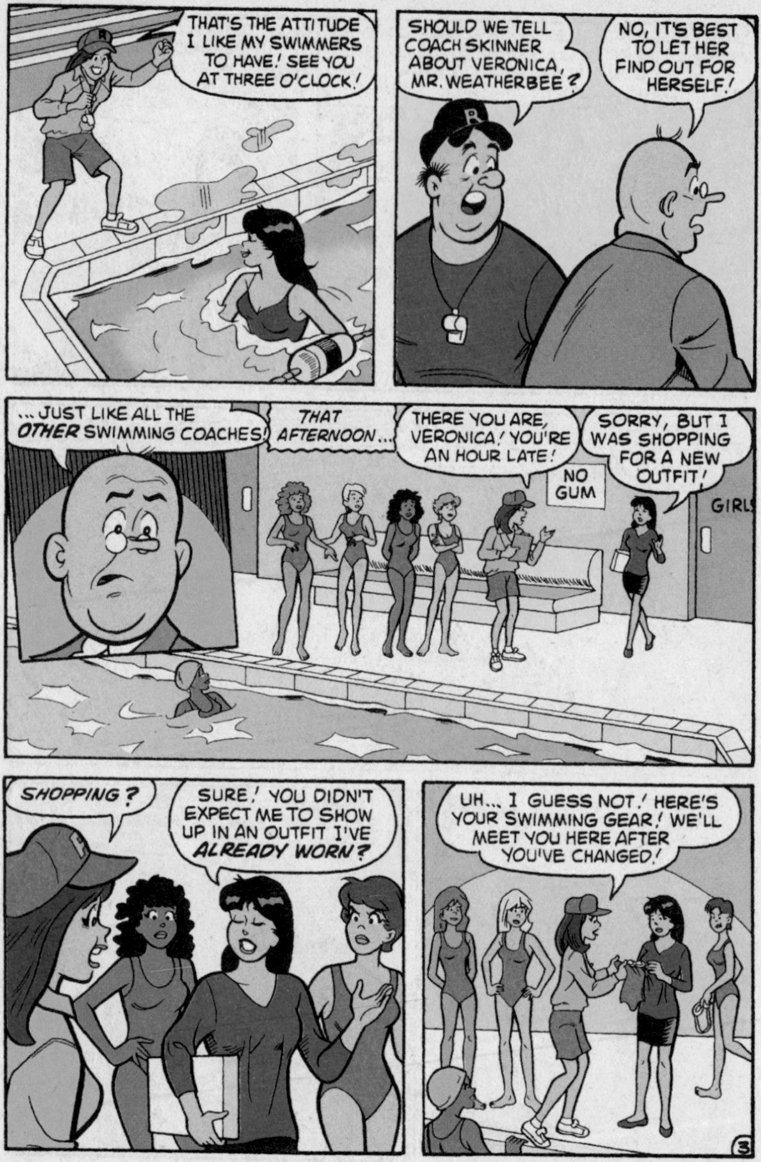
THAT'S THE ATTITUDE I LIKE MY SWIMMERS TO HAVE! SEE YOU AT THREE O'CLOCK!
SHOULD WE TELL COACH SKINNER ABOUT VERONICA, MR. WEATHERBEE?
NO, IT'S BEST TO LET HER FIND OUT FOR HERSELF!
...JUST LIKE ALL THE OTHER SWIMMING COACHES!
THAT AFTERNOON...
THERE YOU ARE, VERONICA! YOU'RE AN HOUR LATE!
NO GUM
SORRY, BUT I WAS SHOPPING FOR A NEW OUTFIT!
GIRLS
SHOPPING?
SURE! YOU DIDN'T EXPECT ME TO SHOW UP IN AN OUTFIT I'VE ALREADY WORN?
UH... I GUESS NOT! HERE'S YOUR SWIMMING GEAR! WE'LL MEET YOU HERE AFTER YOU'VE CHANGED!
3

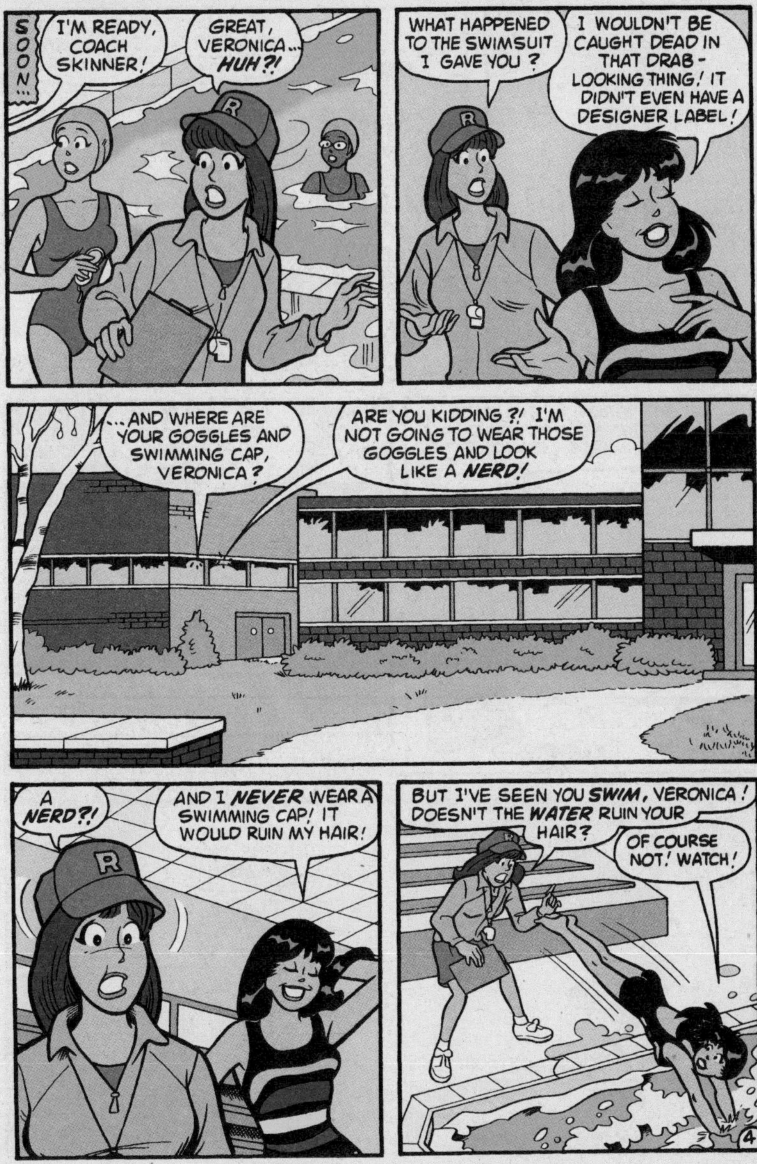

SOON...
I'M READY, COACH SKINNER!
GREAT, VERONICA... HUH?!
WHAT HAPPENED TO THE SWIMSUIT I GAVE YOU?
I WOULDN'T BE CAUGHT DEAD IN THAT DRAB-LOOKING THING! IT DIDN'T EVEN HAVE A DESIGNER LABEL!
...AND WHERE ARE YOUR GOGGLES AND SWIMMING CAP, VERONICA?
ARE YOU KIDDING?! I'M NOT GOING TO WEAR THOSE GOGGLES AND LOOK LIKE A NERD!
A NERD?!
AND I NEVER WEAR A SWIMMING CAP! IT WOULD RUIN MY HAIR!
BUT I'VE SEEN YOU SWIM, VERONICA! DOESN'T THE WATER RUIN YOUR HAIR?
OF COURSE NOT! WATCH!
4

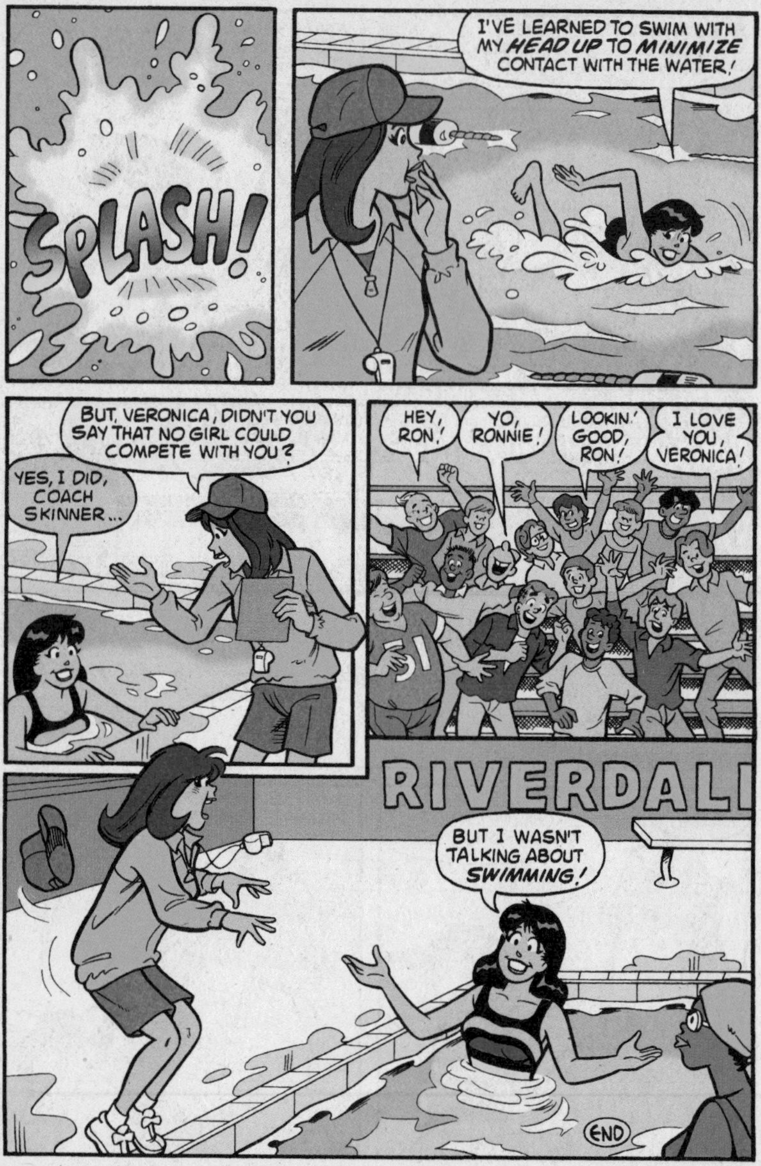
SPLASH!
I'VE LEARNED TO SWIM WITH MY HEAD UP TO MINIMIZE CONTACT WITH THE WATER!
BUT, VERONICA, DIDN'T YOU SAY THAT NO GIRL COULD COMPETE WITH YOU?
YES, I DID, COACH SKINNER...
HEY, RON!
YO, RONNIE!
LOOKIN' GOOD, RON!
I LOVE YOU, VERONICA!
RIVERDAL
BUT I WASN'T TALKING ABOUT SWIMMING!
END

Betty & Veronica's Princess Storybook Selection: Snow White & the Riverdale Dwarves
***Betty & Veronica* #266, 2013**
by Dan Parent, Jeff Shultz, Bob Smith, Jack Morelli and Digikore Studios

What is a "Betty"? She's someone who is the well-adjusted, pretty girl-next-door. She's the loyal friend who will always be there for you, who goes out of her way to do the right thing, to make her parents proud, to do well in school, to give back to her community, and to contribute to society with compassion. Maybe, unfortunately, she is too often overlooked or taken for granted. But that's okay for her. She nurtures and continues to put everyone else first.

What is a "Veronica"? She's beautiful, exotic, worldly, and comes from money. She's born with a silver spoon in her mouth. As a result, everything in life comes easy. She's flamboyant, talkative, and thrives on being the center of attention. She will go out of her way to do nice things for others, as long as it's good for her, too. She demands to be first and when her ego is properly catered to, she can be a great friend and captivating love interest.

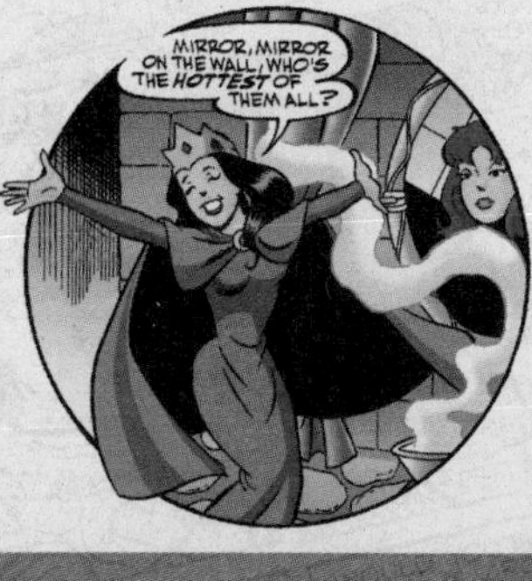
MIRROR, MIRROR ON THE WALL, WHO'S THE HOTTEST OF THEM ALL?

Michael Uslan
Executive Producer,
the **Batman** *movie series*

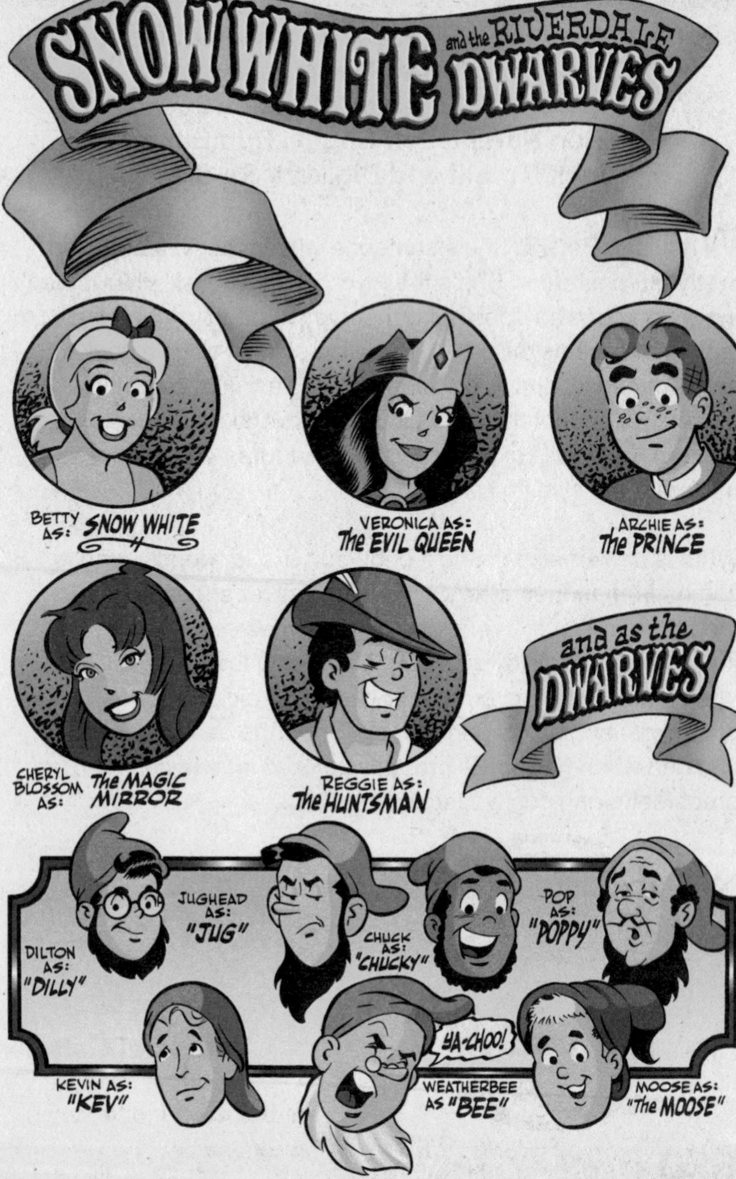
SNOW WHITE and the RIVERDALE DWARVES
BETTY AS: SNOW WHITE
VERONICA AS: The EVIL QUEEN
ARCHIE AS: The PRINCE
CHERYL BLOSSOM AS: The MAGIC MIRROR
REGGIE AS: The HUNTSMAN
and as the DWARVES
DILTON AS: "DILLY"
JUGHEAD AS: "JUG"
CHUCK AS: "CHUCKY"
POP AS: "POPPY"
KEVIN AS: "KEV"
YA-CHOO!
WEATHERBEE AS "BEE"
MOOSE AS: "The MOOSE"

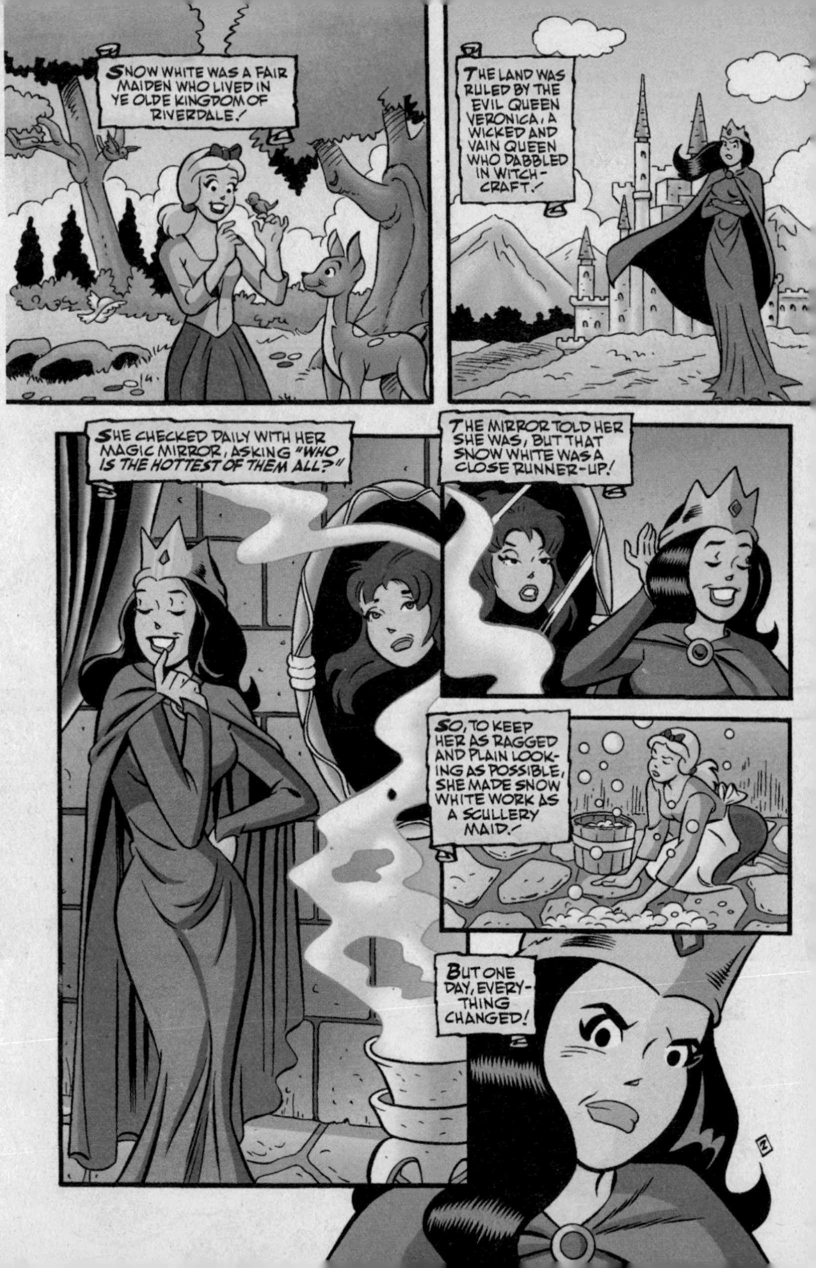
SNOW WHITE WAS A FAIR MAIDEN WHO LIVED IN YE OLDE KINGDOM OF RIVERDALE!
THE LAND WAS RULED BY THE EVIL QUEEN VERONICA, A WICKED AND VAIN QUEEN WHO DABBLED IN WITCH-CRAFT!
SHE CHECKED DAILY WITH HER MAGIC MIRROR, ASKING "WHO IS THE HOTTEST OF THEM ALL?"
THE MIRROR TOLD HER SHE WAS, BUT THAT SNOW WHITE WAS A CLOSE RUNNER-UP!
SO, TO KEEP HER AS RAGGED AND PLAIN LOOKING AS POSSIBLE, SHE MADE SNOW WHITE WORK AS A SCULLERY MAID!
BUT ONE DAY, EVERYTHING CHANGED!
2

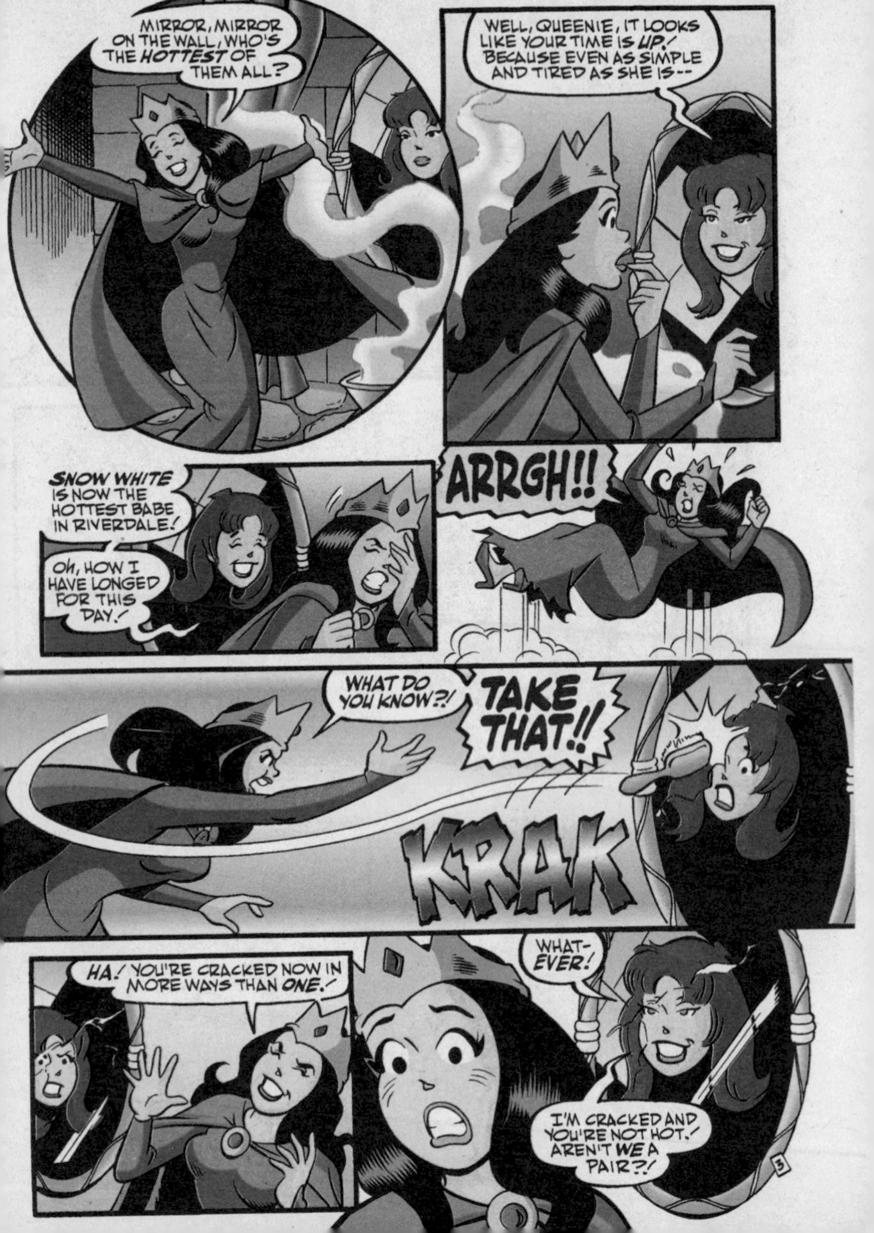
MIRROR, MIRROR ON THE WALL, WHO'S THE HOTTEST OF THEM ALL?
WELL, QUEENIE, IT LOOKS LIKE YOUR TIME IS UP! BECAUSE EVEN AS SIMPLE AND TIRED AS SHE IS--
SNOW WHITE IS NOW THE HOTTEST BABE IN RIVERDALE!
OH, HOW I HAVE LONGED FOR THIS DAY!
ARRGH!!
WHAT DO YOU KNOW?!
TAKE THAT!!
KRAK
HA! YOU'RE CRACKED NOW IN MORE WAYS THAN ONE!
WHAT-EVER!
I'M CRACKED AND YOU'RE NOT HOT! AREN'T WE A PAIR?!
3

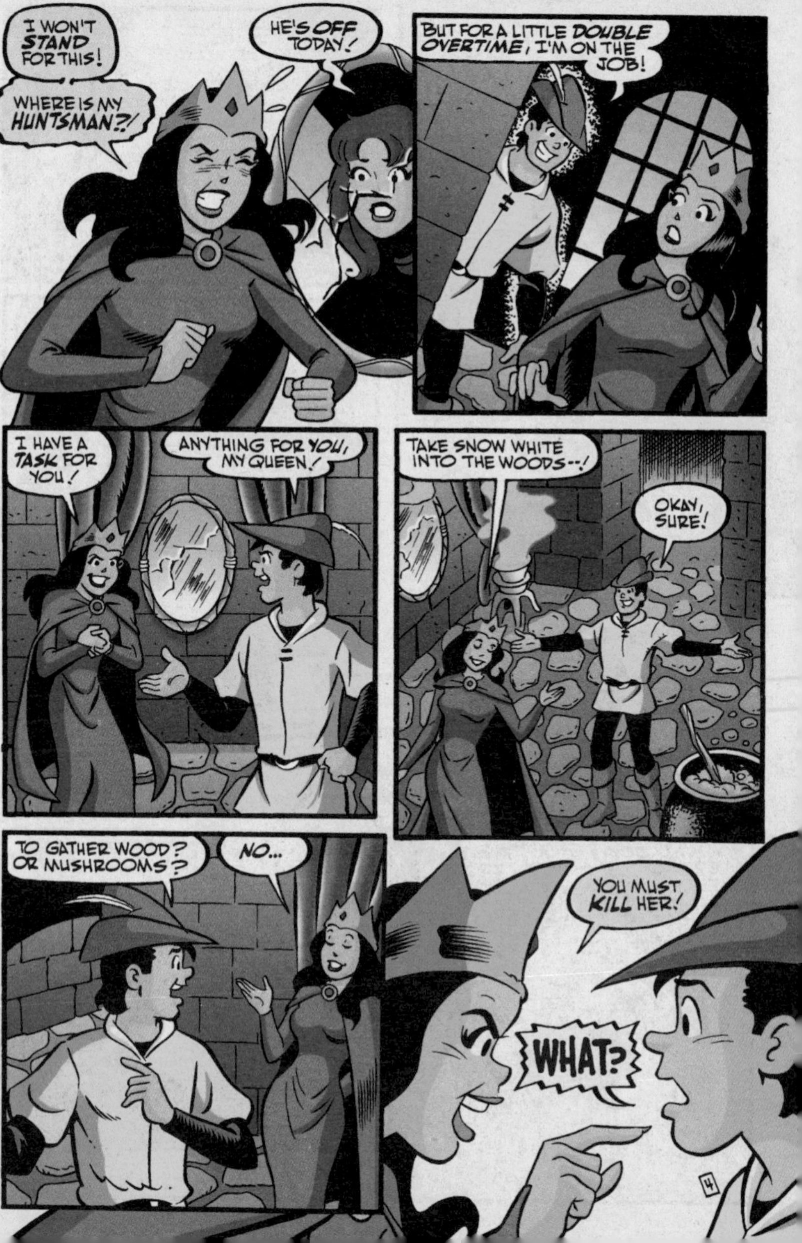

I WON'T STAND FOR THIS!
WHERE IS MY HUNTSMAN?!
HE'S OFF TODAY!
BUT FOR A LITTLE DOUBLE OVERTIME, I'M ON THE JOB!
I HAVE A TASK FOR YOU!
ANYTHING FOR YOU, MY QUEEN!
TAKE SNOW WHITE INTO THE WOODS--!
OKAY, SURE!
TO GATHER WOOD? OR MUSHROOMS?
NO...
YOU MUST KILL HER!
WHAT?
4

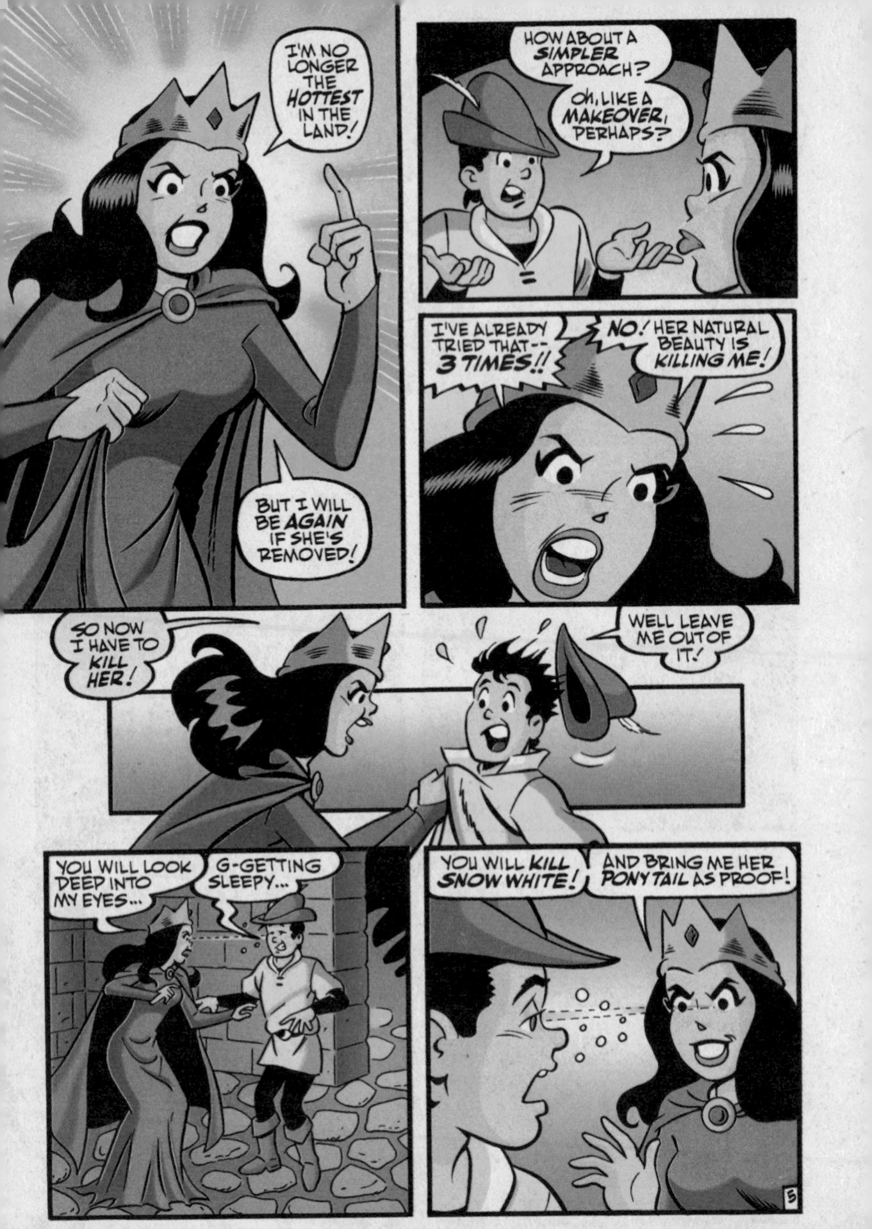
I'M NO LONGER THE HOTTEST IN THE LAND!
BUT I WILL BE AGAIN IF SHE'S REMOVED!
HOW ABOUT A SIMPLER APPROACH?
Oh, LIKE A MAKEOVER, PERHAPS?
I'VE ALREADY TRIED THAT-- 3 TIMES!!
NO! HER NATURAL BEAUTY IS KILLING ME!
SO NOW I HAVE TO KILL HER!
WELL LEAVE ME OUT OF IT!
YOU WILL LOOK DEEP INTO MY EYES...
G-GETTING SLEEPY...
YOU WILL KILL SNOW WHITE!
AND BRING ME HER PONY TAIL AS PROOF!
5

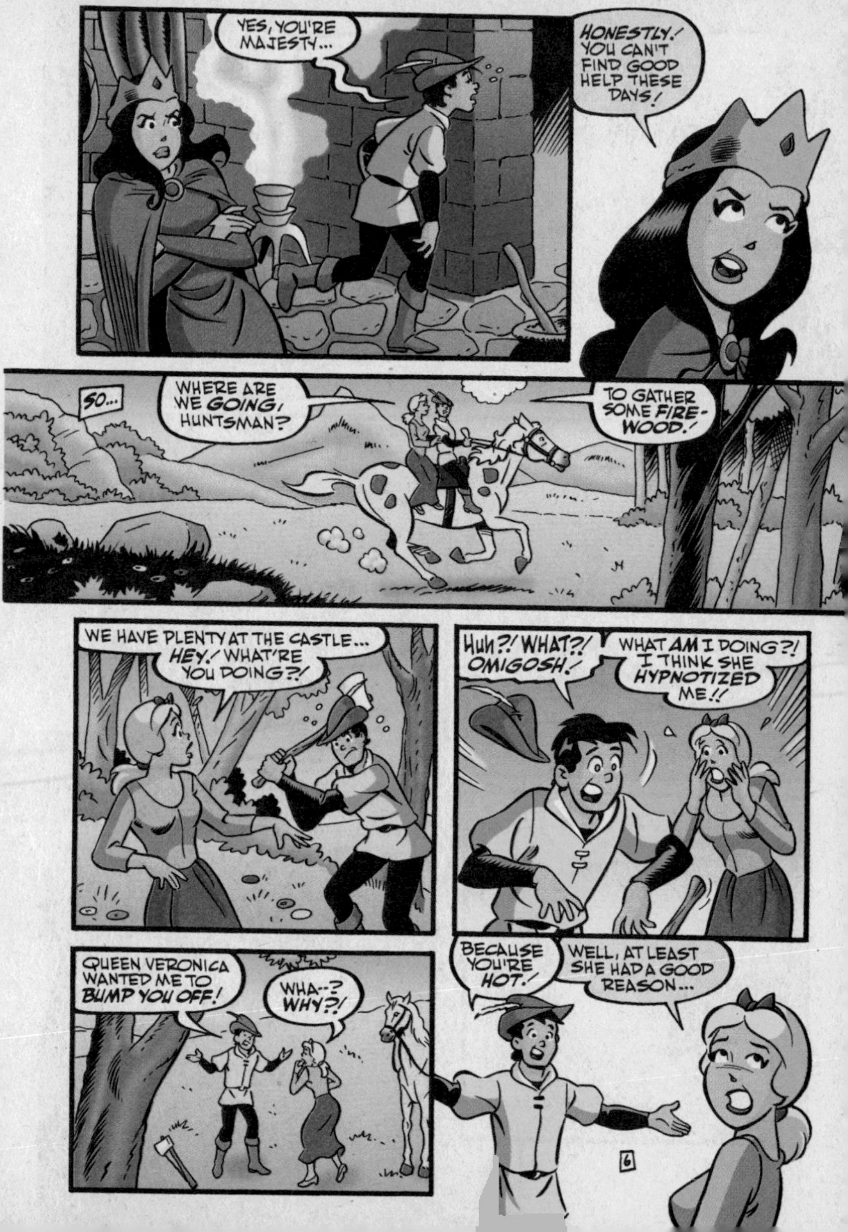

YES, YOU'RE MAJESTY...
HONESTLY! YOU CAN'T FIND GOOD HELP THESE DAYS!
SO...
WHERE ARE WE GOING, HUNTSMAN?
TO GATHER SOME FIRE-WOOD!
WE HAVE PLENTY AT THE CASTLE... HEY! WHAT'RE YOU DOING?!
Huh?! WHAT?! OMIGOSH!
WHAT AM I DOING?! I THINK SHE HYPNOTIZED ME!!
QUEEN VERONICA WANTED ME TO BUMP YOU OFF!
WHA--? WHY?!
BECAUSE YOU'RE HOT!
WELL, AT LEAST SHE HAD A GOOD REASON...
6

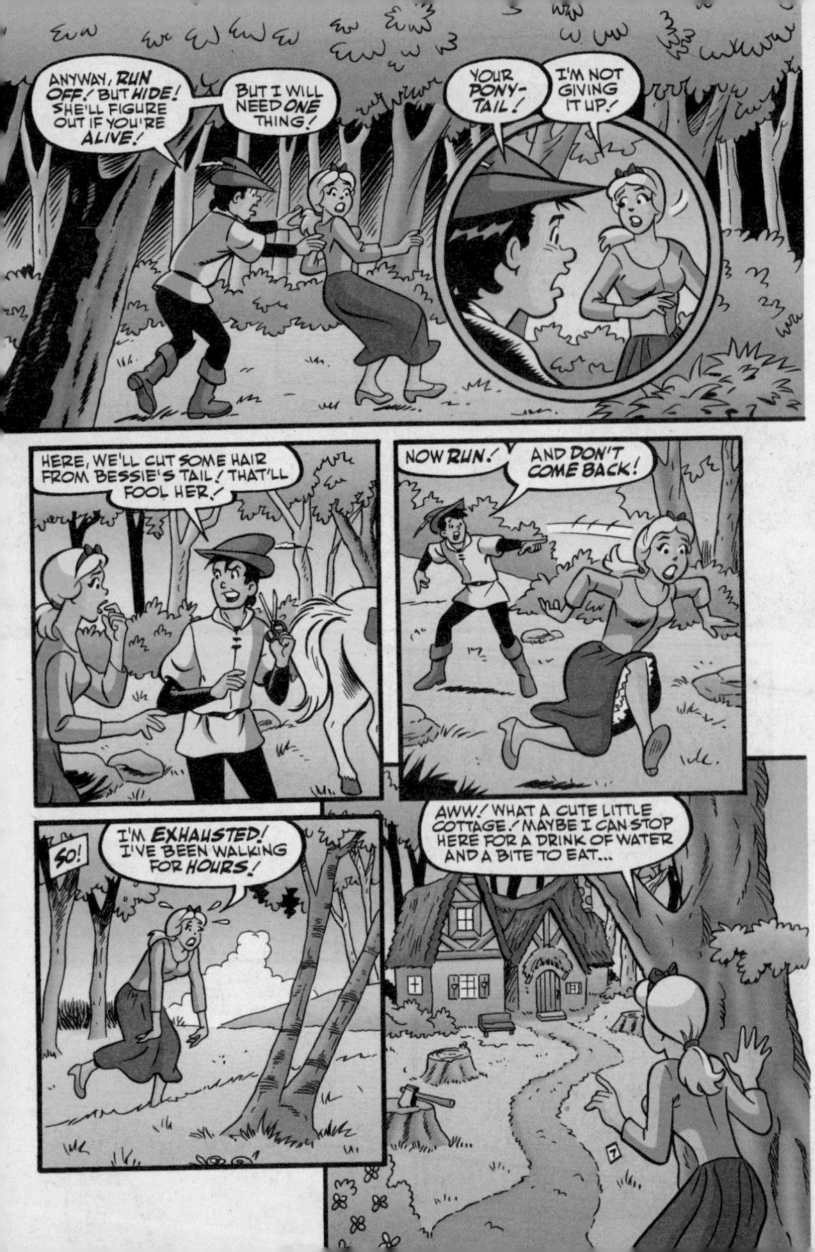
ANYWAY, RUN OFF! BUT HIDE! SHE'LL FIGURE OUT IF YOU'RE ALIVE!
BUT I WILL NEED ONE THING!
YOUR PONY-TAIL!
I'M NOT GIVING IT UP!
HERE, WE'LL CUT SOME HAIR FROM BESSIE'S TAIL! THAT'LL FOOL HER!
NOW RUN!
AND DON'T COME BACK!
SO!
I'M EXHAUSTED! I'VE BEEN WALKING FOR HOURS!
AWW! WHAT A CUTE LITTLE COTTAGE! MAYBE I CAN STOP HERE FOR A DRINK OF WATER AND A BITE TO EAT...
7

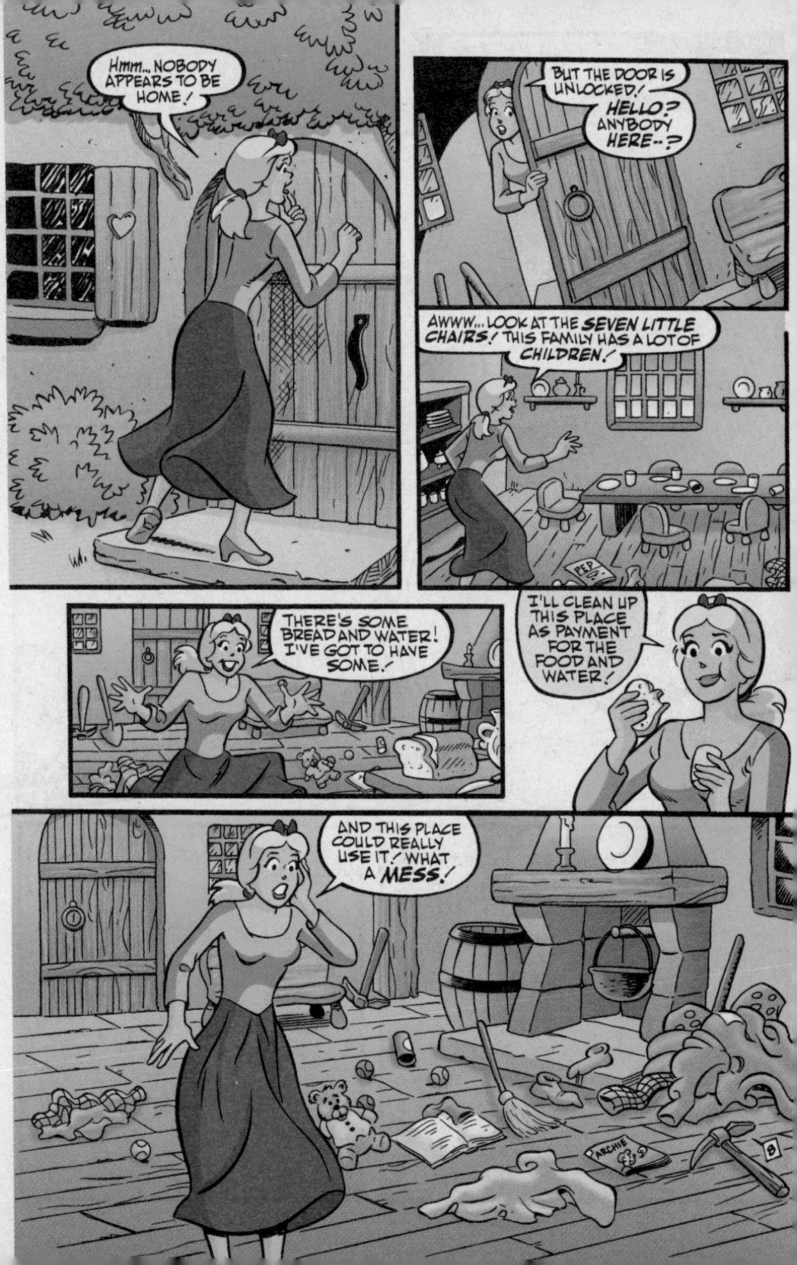

Hmm... NOBODY APPEARS TO BE HOME!
BUT THE DOOR IS UNLOCKED! HELLO? ANYBODY HERE--?
AWWW... LOOK AT THE SEVEN LITTLE CHAIRS! THIS FAMILY HAS A LOT OF CHILDREN!
PEP
THERE'S SOME BREAD AND WATER! I'VE GOT TO HAVE SOME!
I'LL CLEAN UP THIS PLACE AS PAYMENT FOR THE FOOD AND WATER!
AND THIS PLACE COULD REALLY USE IT! WHAT A MESS!
ARCHIE
8

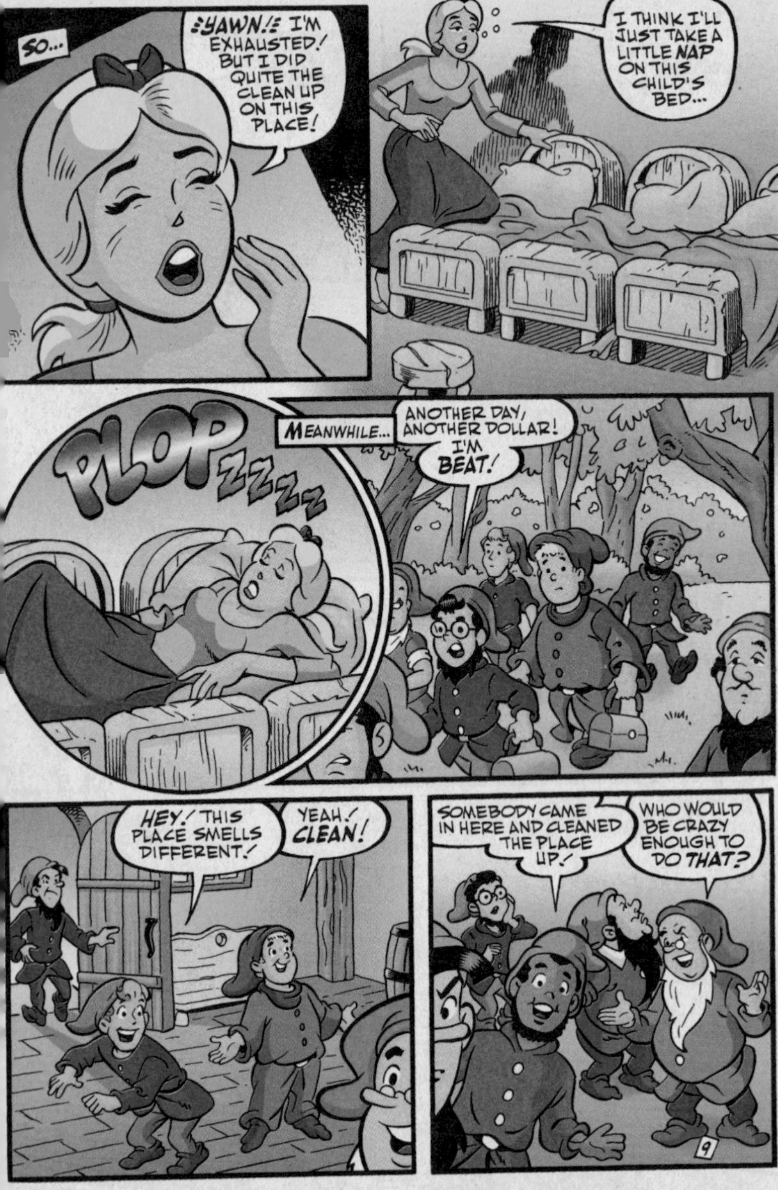
SO...
YAWN! I'M EXHAUSTED! BUT I DID QUITE THE CLEAN UP ON THIS PLACE!
I THINK I'LL JUST TAKE A LITTLE NAP ON THIS CHILD'S BED...
PLOP
ZZZZ
MEANWHILE...
ANOTHER DAY, ANOTHER DOLLAR!
I'M BEAT!
HEY! THIS PLACE SMELLS DIFFERENT!
YEAH! CLEAN!
SOMEBODY CAME IN HERE AND CLEANED THE PLACE UP!
WHO WOULD BE CRAZY ENOUGH TO DO THAT?
9

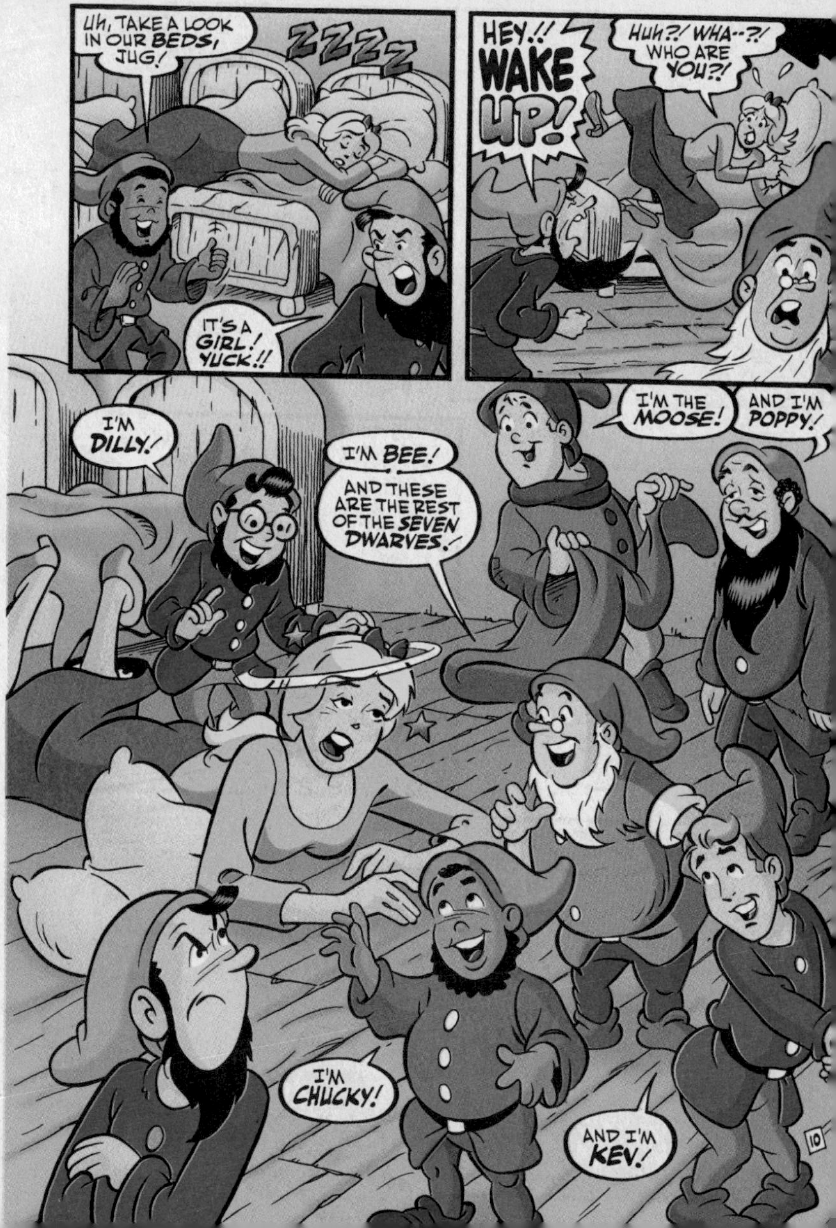
UH, TAKE A LOOK IN OUR BEDS, JUG!
ZZZZZ
IT'S A GIRL! YUCK!!
HEY!! WAKE UP!
HUH?! WHA--?! WHO ARE YOU?!
I'M DILLY!
I'M BEE!
AND THESE ARE THE REST OF THE SEVEN DWARVES.
I'M THE MOOSE!
AND I'M POPPY!
I'M CHUCKY!
AND I'M KEV!
10

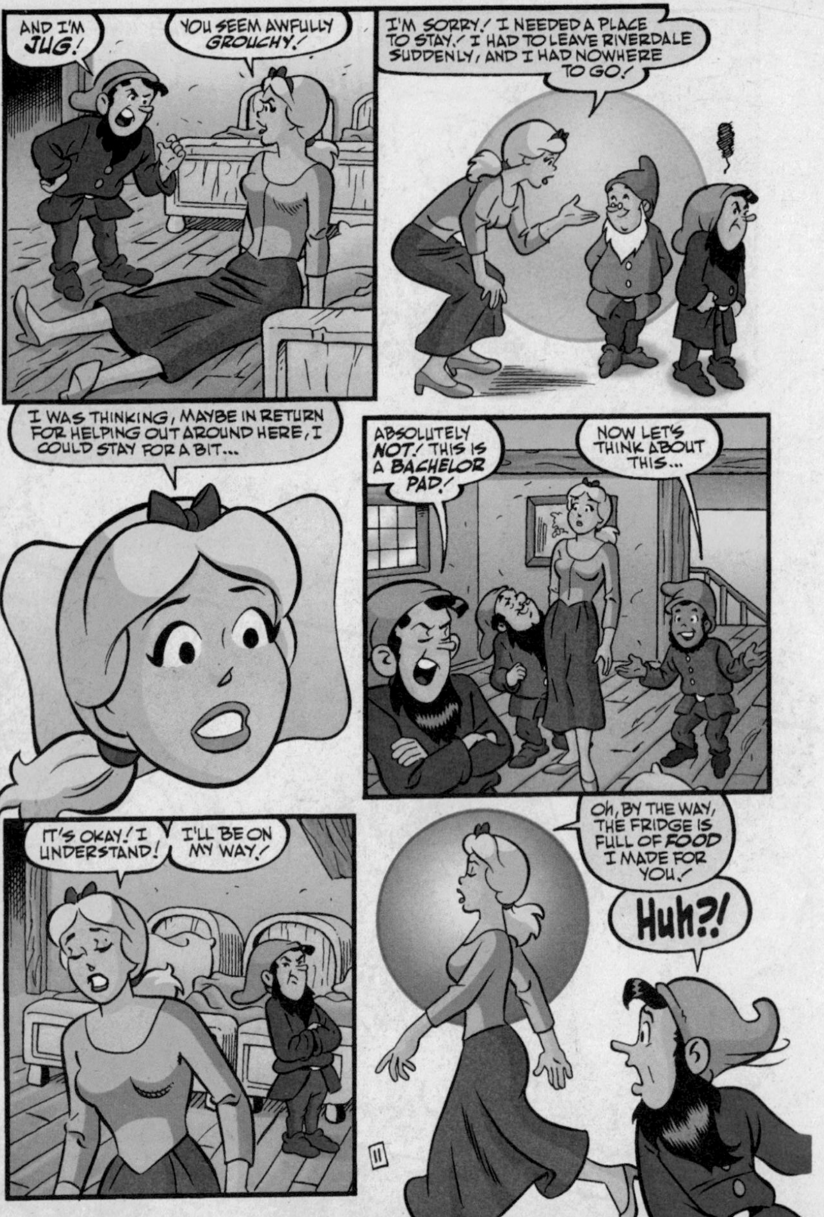

AND I'M JUG!
YOU SEEM AWFULLY GROUCHY!
I'M SORRY! I NEEDED A PLACE TO STAY! I HAD TO LEAVE RIVERDALE SUDDENLY, AND I HAD NOWHERE TO GO!
I WAS THINKING, MAYBE IN RETURN FOR HELPING OUT AROUND HERE, I COULD STAY FOR A BIT...
ABSOLUTELY NOT! THIS IS A BACHELOR PAD!
NOW LET'S THINK ABOUT THIS...
IT'S OKAY! I UNDERSTAND!
I'LL BE ON MY WAY!
Oh, BY THE WAY, THE FRIDGE IS FULL OF FOOD I MADE FOR YOU!
Huh?!
11

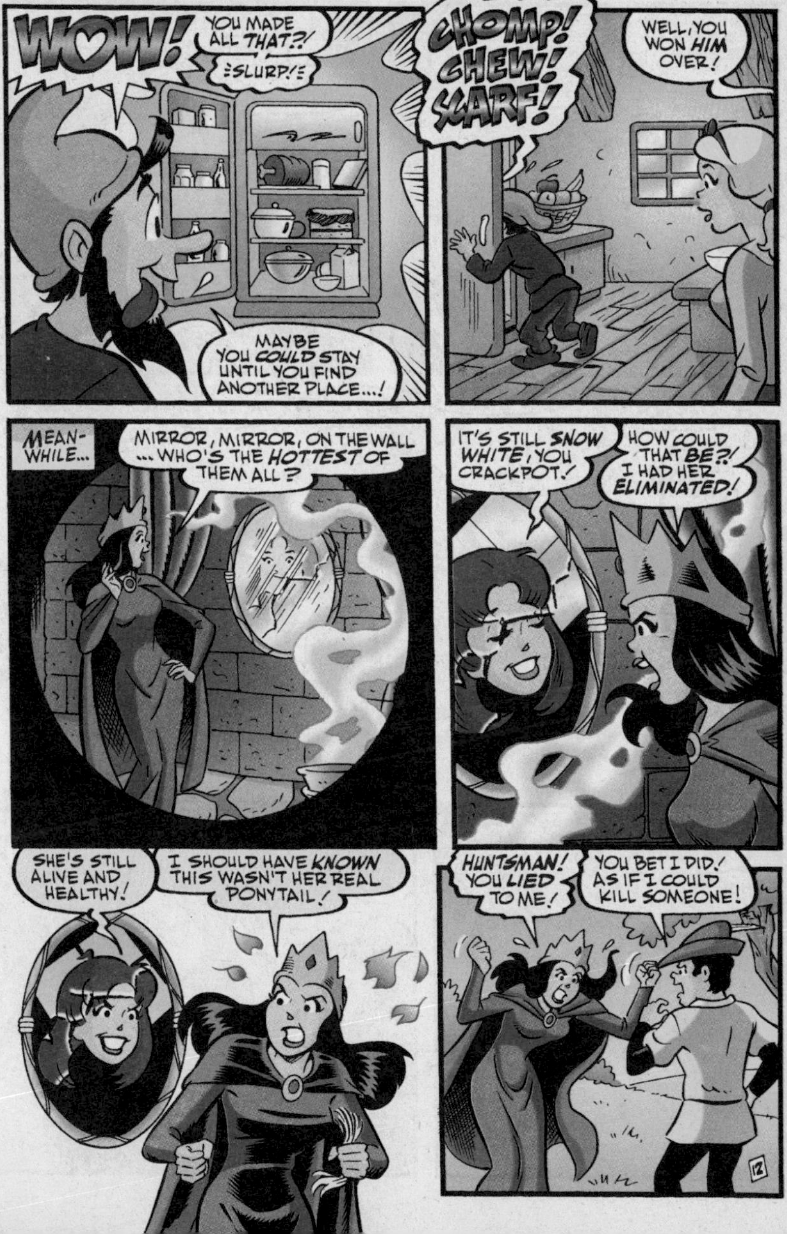
WOW!
YOU MADE ALL THAT?!
SLURP!
MAYBE YOU COULD STAY UNTIL YOU FIND ANOTHER PLACE...!
CHOMP! CHEW! SCARF!
WELL, YOU WON HIM OVER!
MEAN-WHILE...
MIRROR, MIRROR, ON THE WALL ... WHO'S THE HOTTEST OF THEM ALL?
IT'S STILL SNOW WHITE, YOU CRACKPOT!
HOW COULD THAT BE?! I HAD HER ELIMINATED!
SHE'S STILL ALIVE AND HEALTHY!
I SHOULD HAVE KNOWN THIS WASN'T HER REAL PONYTAIL!
HUNTSMAN! YOU LIED TO ME!
YOU BET I DID! AS IF I COULD KILL SOMEONE!
12

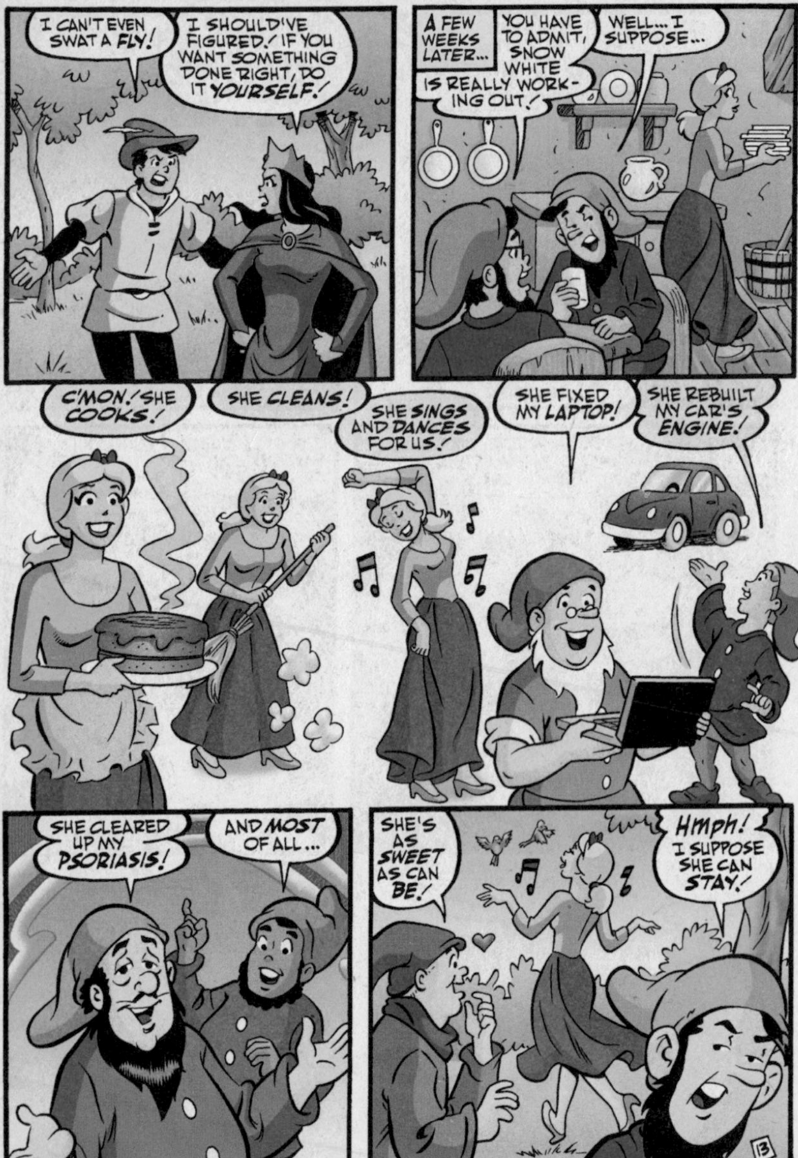

I CAN'T EVEN SWAT A FLY!
I SHOULD'VE FIGURED! IF YOU WANT SOMETHING DONE RIGHT, DO IT YOURSELF!
A FEW WEEKS LATER...
YOU HAVE TO ADMIT, SNOW WHITE IS REALLY WORKING OUT!
WELL... I SUPPOSE...
C'MON! SHE COOKS!
SHE CLEANS!
SHE SINGS AND DANCES FOR US!
SHE FIXED MY LAPTOP!
SHE REBUILT MY CAR'S ENGINE!
SHE CLEARED UP MY PSORIASIS!
AND MOST OF ALL...
SHE'S AS SWEET AS CAN BE!
Hmph! I SUPPOSE SHE CAN STAY!
13

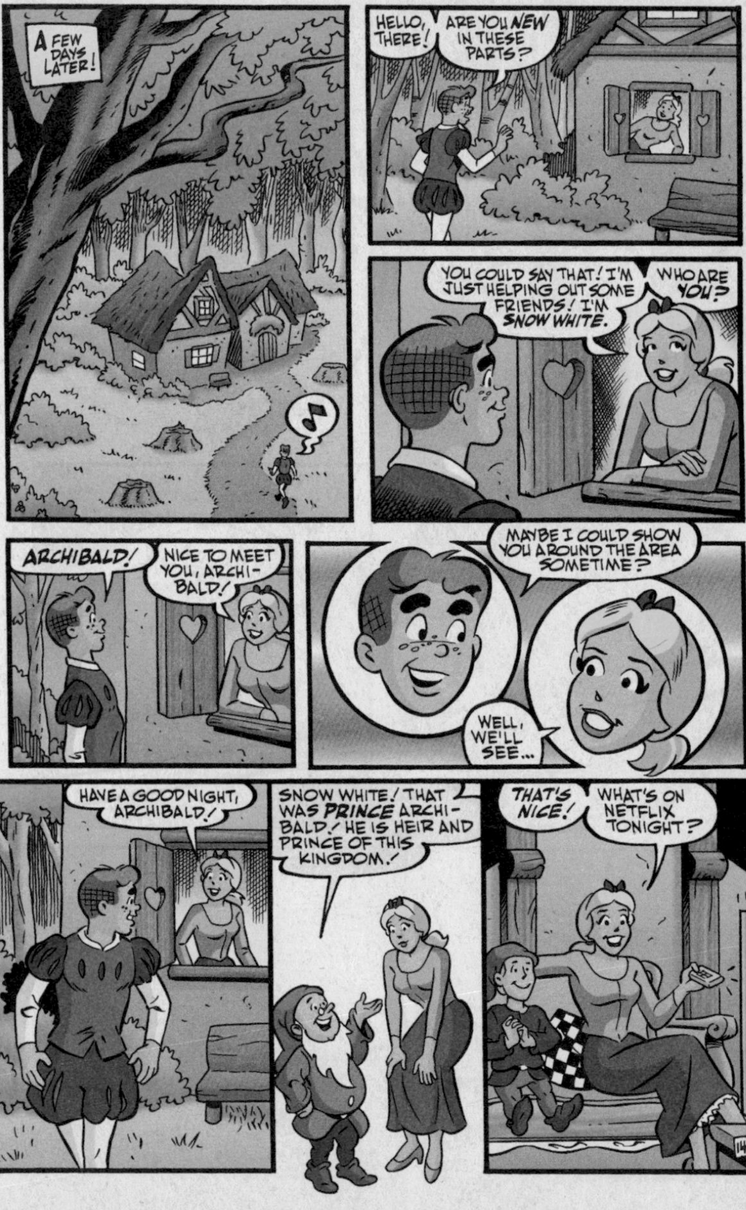
A FEW DAYS LATER!
HELLO, THERE!
ARE YOU NEW IN THESE PARTS?
YOU COULD SAY THAT! I'M JUST HELPING OUT SOME FRIENDS! I'M SNOW WHITE.
WHO ARE YOU?
ARCHIBALD!
NICE TO MEET YOU, ARCHI-BALD!
MAYBE I COULD SHOW YOU AROUND THE AREA SOMETIME?
WELL, WE'LL SEE...
HAVE A GOOD NIGHT, ARCHIBALD!
SNOW WHITE! THAT WAS PRINCE ARCHI-BALD! HE IS HEIR AND PRINCE OF THIS KINGDOM!
THAT'S NICE!
WHAT'S ON NETFLIX TONIGHT?
14

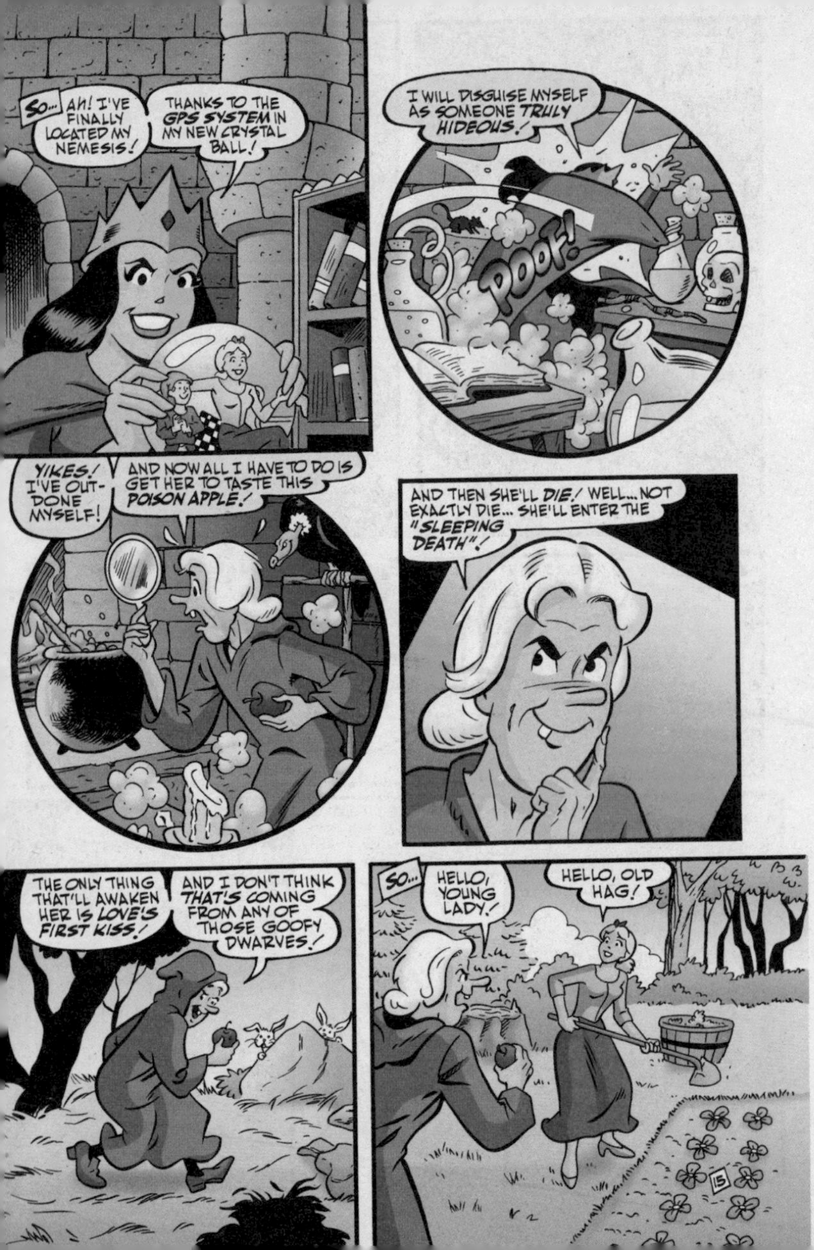
SO...
AH! I'VE FINALLY LOCATED MY NEMESIS!
THANKS TO THE GPS SYSTEM IN MY NEW CRYSTAL BALL!
I WILL DISGUISE MYSELF AS SOMEONE TRULY HIDEOUS!
POOF!
YIKES! I'VE OUT-DONE MYSELF!
AND NOW ALL I HAVE TO DO IS GET HER TO TASTE THIS POISON APPLE!
AND THEN SHE'LL DIE! WELL... NOT EXACTLY DIE... SHE'LL ENTER THE "SLEEPING DEATH"!
THE ONLY THING THAT'LL AWAKEN HER IS LOVE'S FIRST KISS!
AND I DON'T THINK THAT'S COMING FROM ANY OF THOSE GOOFY DWARVES!
SO...
HELLO, YOUNG LADY!
HELLO, OLD HAG!
15

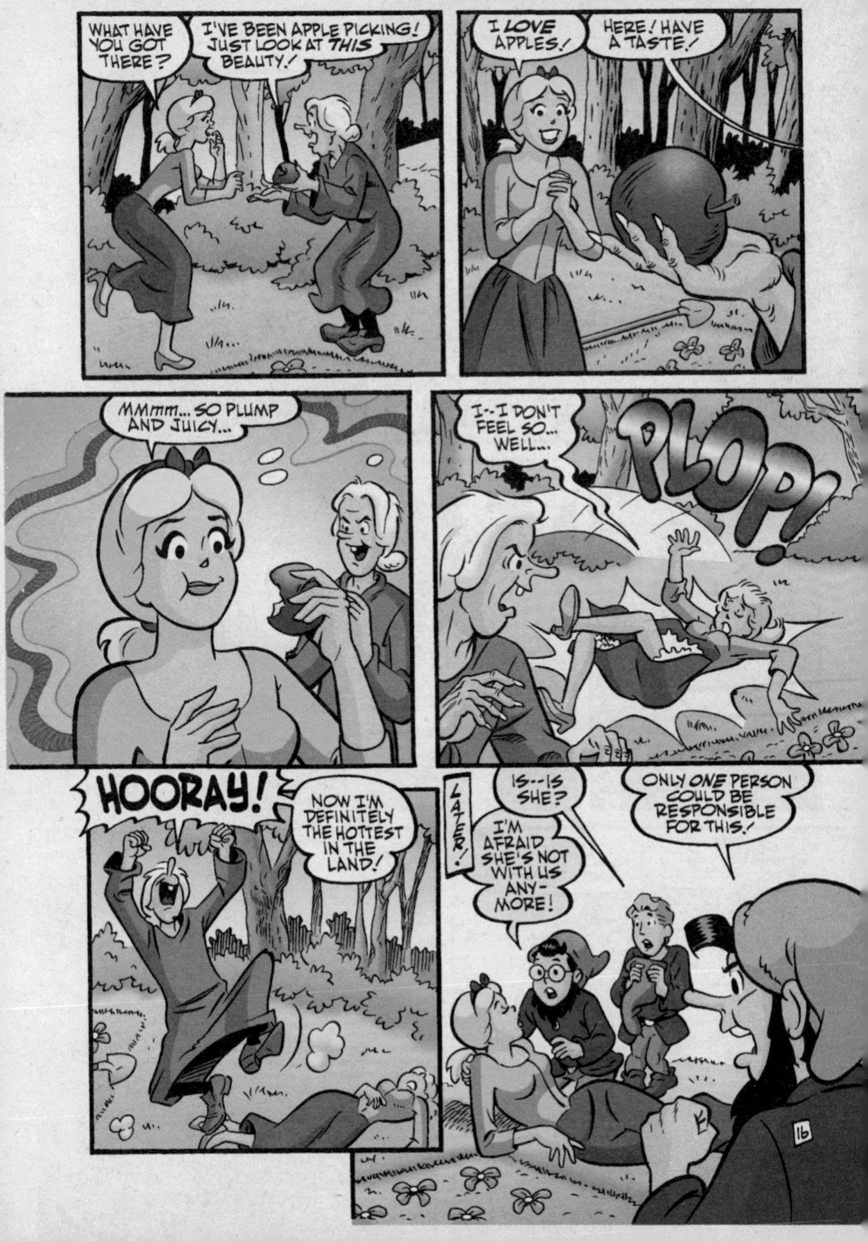
WHAT HAVE YOU GOT THERE?
I'VE BEEN APPLE PICKING! JUST LOOK AT *THIS* BEAUTY!
I *LOVE* APPLES!
HERE! HAVE A TASTE!
MMmmm... SO PLUMP AND JUICY...
I--I DON'T FEEL SO... WELL...
PLOP!
HOORAY!
NOW I'M DEFINITELY THE HOTTEST IN THE LAND!
LATER!
IS--IS SHE?
I'M AFRAID SHE'S NOT WITH US ANY-MORE!
ONLY *ONE* PERSON COULD BE RESPONSIBLE FOR THIS!
16

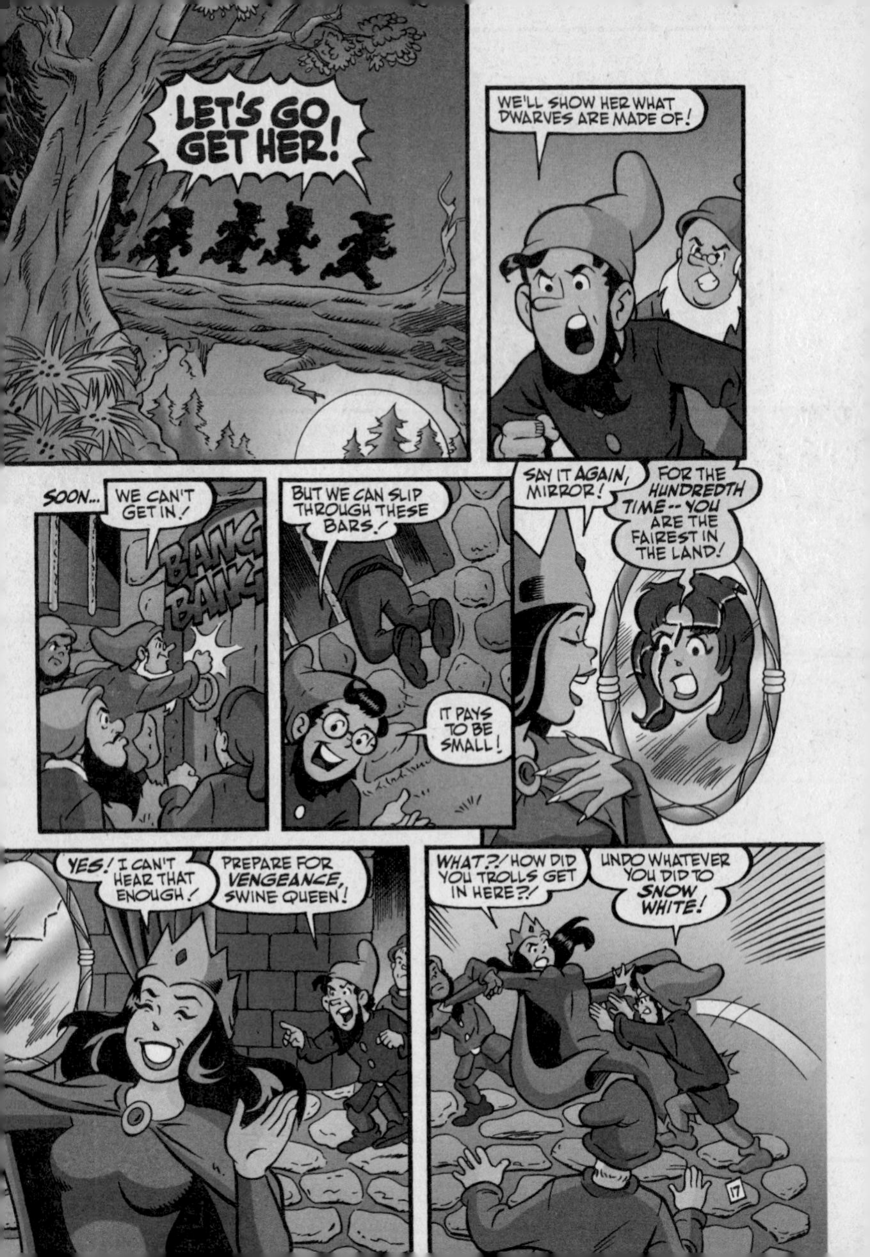
LET'S GO GET HER!
WE'LL SHOW HER WHAT DWARVES ARE MADE OF!
SOON...
WE CAN'T GET IN!
BANG BANG
BUT WE CAN SLIP THROUGH THESE BARS!
IT PAYS TO BE SMALL!
SAY IT AGAIN, MIRROR!
FOR THE HUNDREDTH TIME -- YOU ARE THE FAIREST IN THE LAND!
YES! I CAN'T HEAR THAT ENOUGH!
PREPARE FOR VENGEANCE, SWINE QUEEN!
WHAT?! HOW DID YOU TROLLS GET IN HERE?!
UNDO WHATEVER YOU DID TO SNOW WHITE!
17

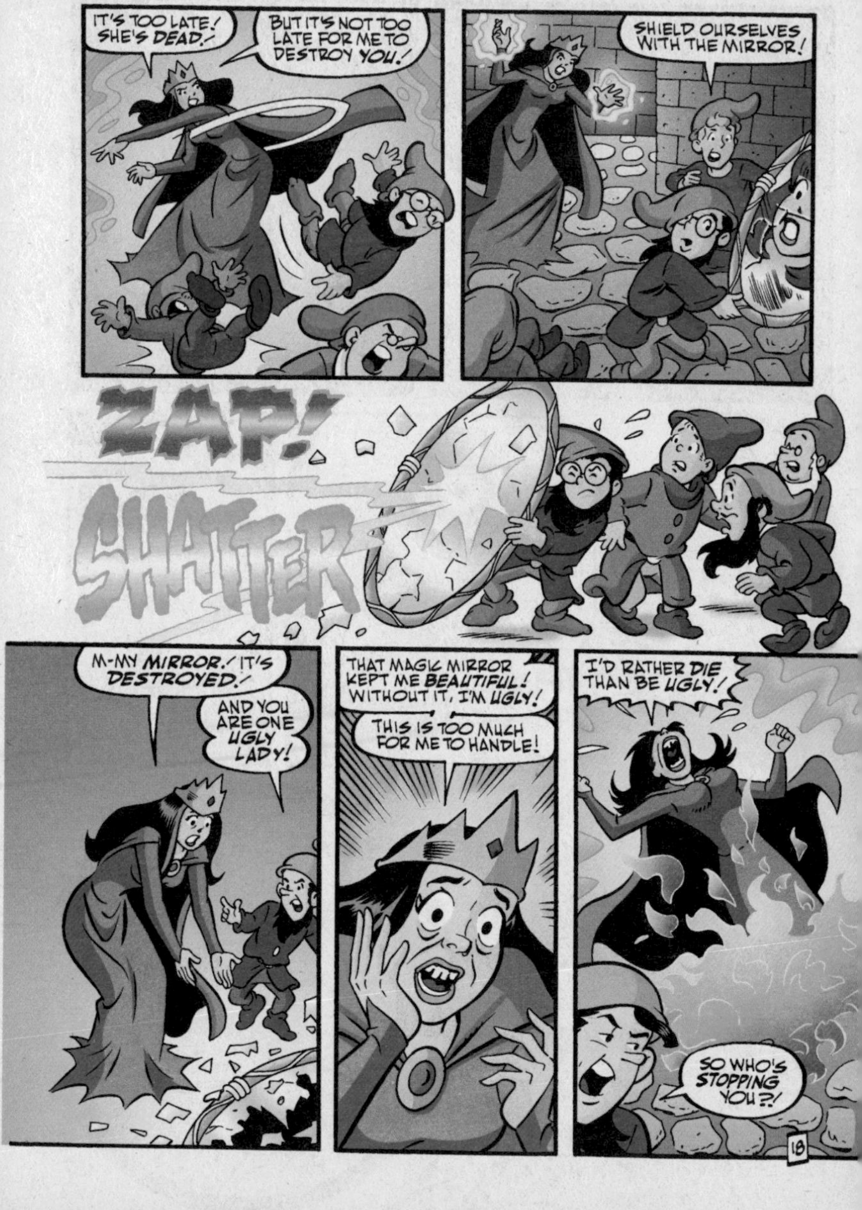
IT'S TOO LATE! SHE'S DEAD!
BUT IT'S NOT TOO LATE FOR ME TO DESTROY YOU!
SHIELD OURSELVES WITH THE MIRROR!
ZAP!
SHATTER
M-MY MIRROR! IT'S DESTROYED!
AND YOU ARE ONE UGLY LADY!
THAT MAGIC MIRROR KEPT ME BEAUTIFUL! WITHOUT IT, I'M UGLY!
THIS IS TOO MUCH FOR ME TO HANDLE!
I'D RATHER DIE THAN BE UGLY!
SO WHO'S STOPPING YOU?!

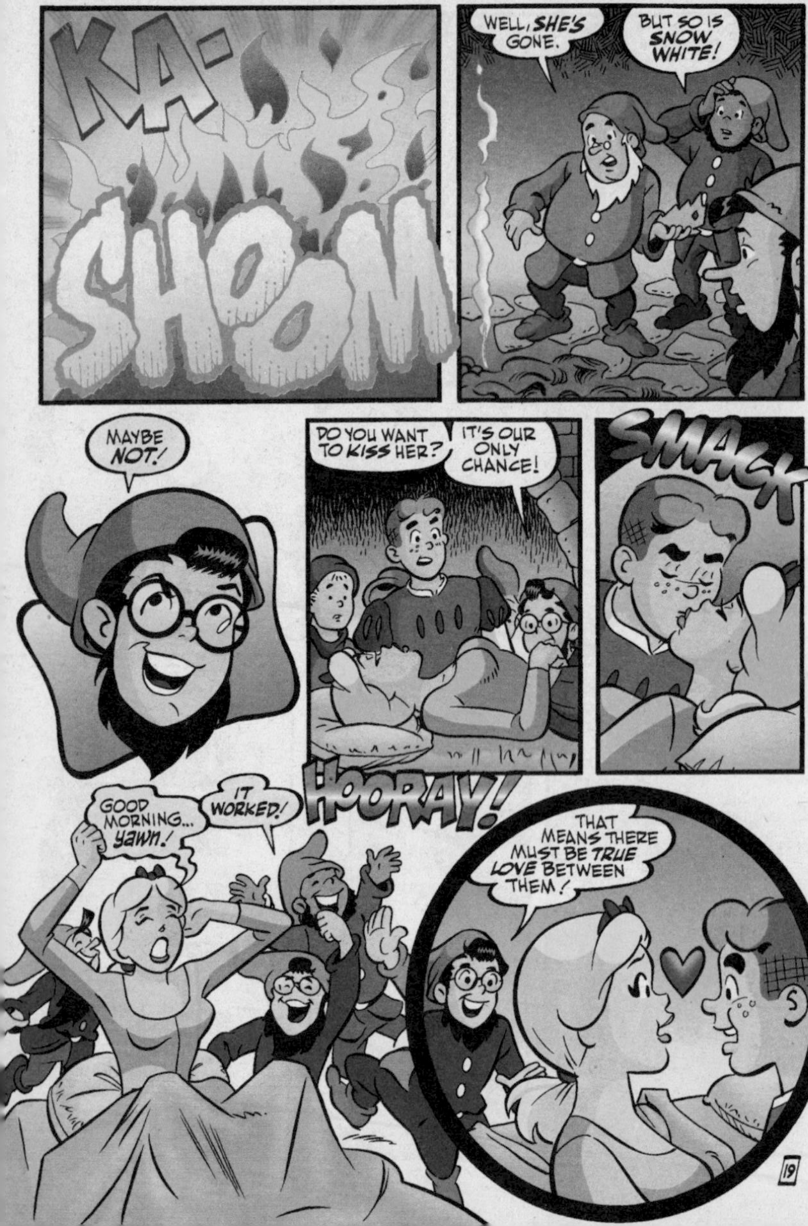
KA-SHOOM
WELL, SHE'S GONE.
BUT SO IS SNOW WHITE!
MAYBE NOT!
DO YOU WANT TO KISS HER?
IT'S OUR ONLY CHANCE!
SMACK
GOOD MORNING... yawn!
IT WORKED!
HOORAY!
THAT MEANS THERE MUST BE TRUE LOVE BETWEEN THEM!

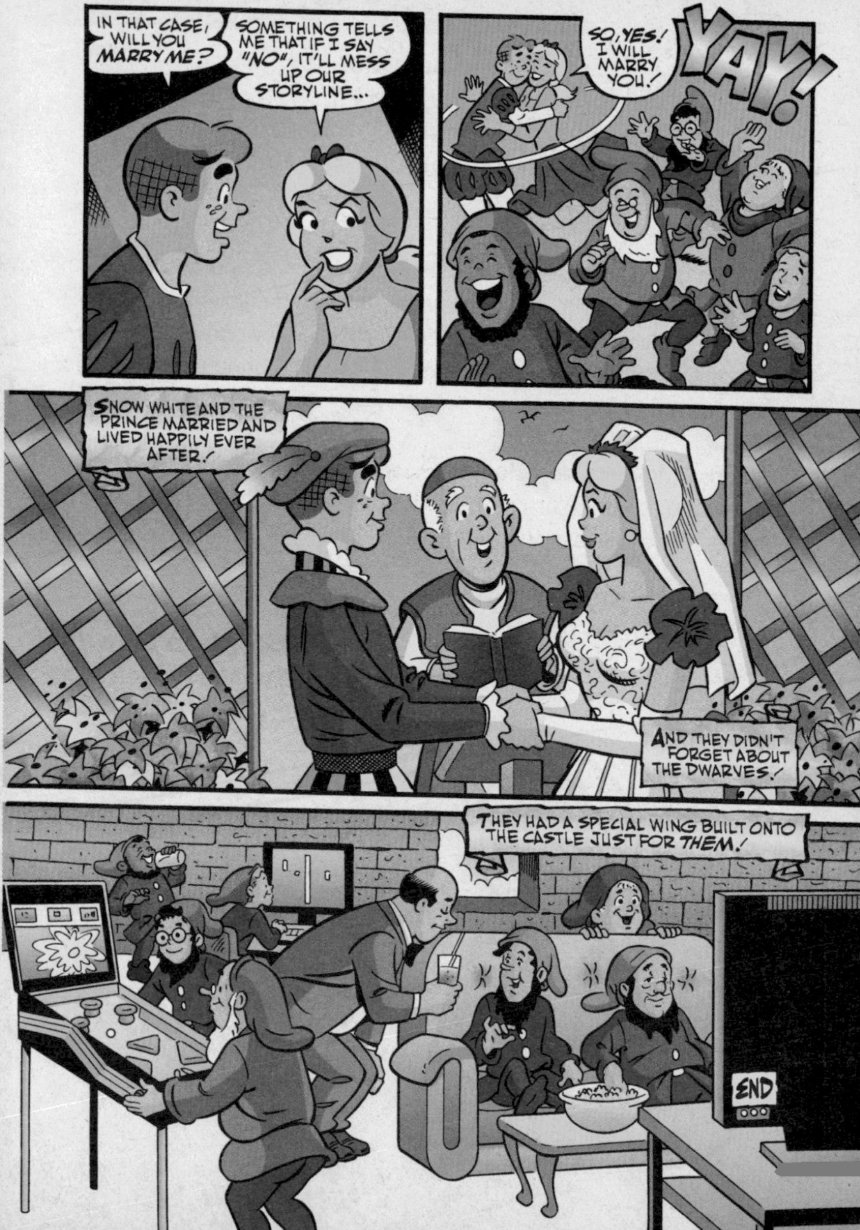
IN THAT CASE, WILL YOU MARRY ME?
SOMETHING TELLS ME THAT IF I SAY "NO", IT'LL MESS UP OUR STORYLINE...
SO, YES! I WILL MARRY YOU!
YAY!
SNOW WHITE AND THE PRINCE MARRIED AND LIVED HAPPILY EVER AFTER!
AND THEY DIDN'T FORGET ABOUT THE DWARVES!
THEY HAD A SPECIAL WING BUILT ONTO THE CASTLE JUST FOR THEM!
END

An Uncle's Monkey
Sabrina the Teenage Witch #1, 1971
by Frank Doyle, Dan DeCarlo,
Rudy Lapick, Bill Yoshida and Sal Contrera

With a script by the irrepressible Frank Doyle and art by the great Dan DeCarlo, "An Uncle's Monkey" is a hijinks-filled romp with that slinger of spells, Sabrina. I mean, how can it go wrong? It has the three M's that make for a classic Sabrina story—Magic, Mayhem and Monkeys!

"Magic, Mayhem and Monkeys"...what more can you ask for? I know... a rectangular-cut, peanut butter sandwich, no jelly. And that's all I have to say about that!

Stephen Oswald
Production Manager,
Archie Comics

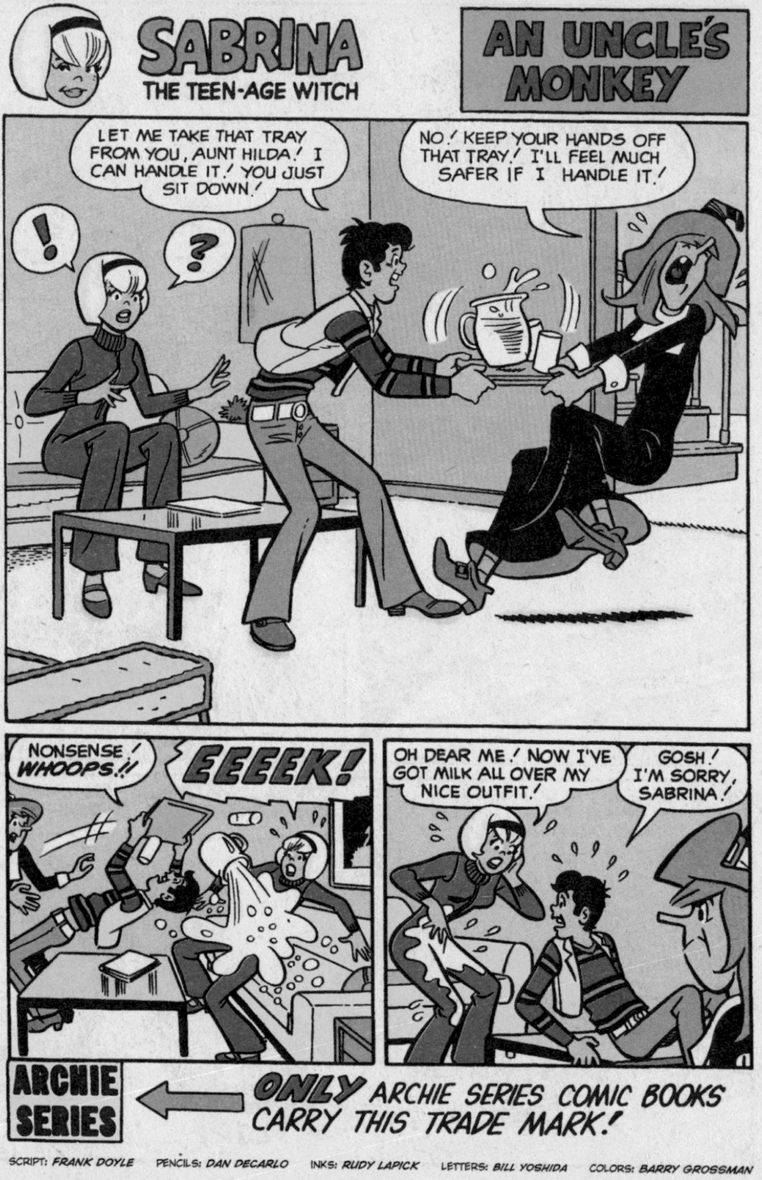
SABRINA
THE TEEN-AGE WITCH
AN UNCLE'S MONKEY
LET ME TAKE THAT TRAY FROM YOU, AUNT HILDA! I CAN HANDLE IT! YOU JUST SIT DOWN!
NO! KEEP YOUR HANDS OFF THAT TRAY! I'LL FEEL MUCH SAFER IF I HANDLE IT!
!
?
NONSENSE! WHOOPS!!!
EEEEK!
OH DEAR ME! NOW I'VE GOT MILK ALL OVER MY NICE OUTFIT!
GOSH! I'M SORRY, SABRINA!
ARCHIE SERIES
ONLY ARCHIE SERIES COMIC BOOKS CARRY THIS TRADE MARK!

SCRIPT: FRANK DOYLE PENCILS: DAN DECARLO INKS: RUDY LAPICK LETTERS: BILL YOSHIDA COLORS: BARRY GROSSMAN

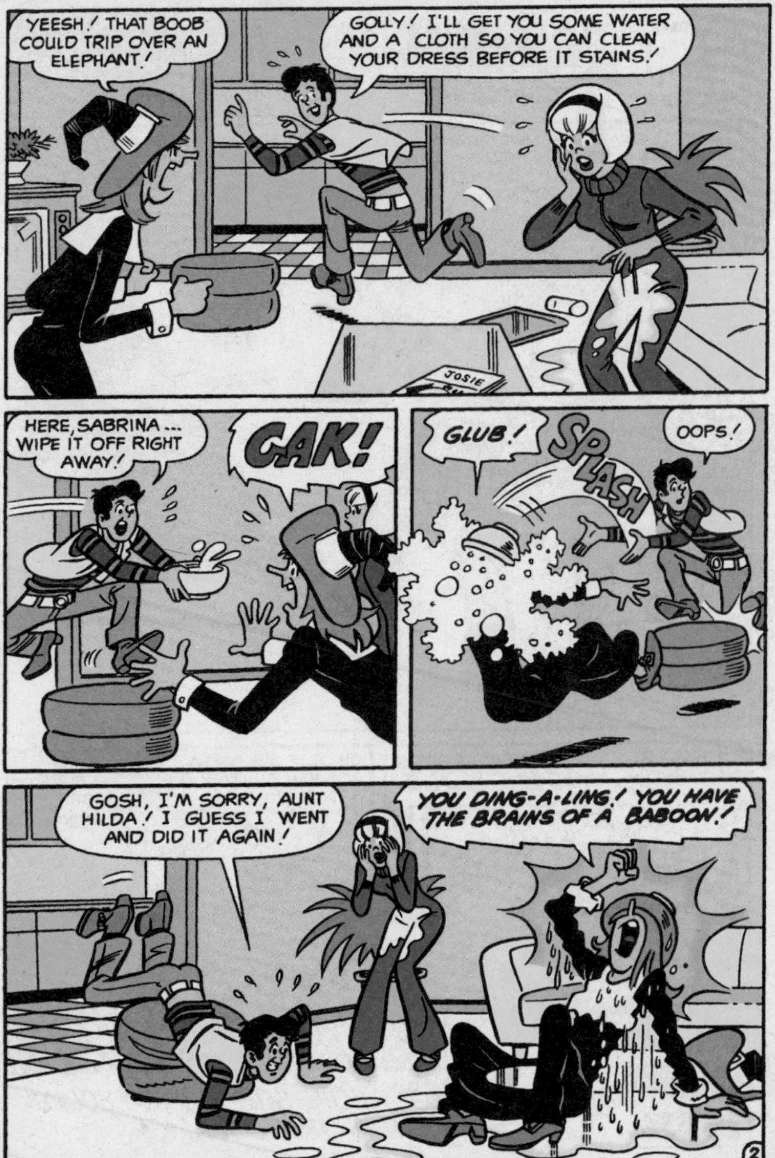
YEESH! THAT BOOB COULD TRIP OVER AN ELEPHANT!
GOLLY! I'LL GET YOU SOME WATER AND A CLOTH SO YOU CAN CLEAN YOUR DRESS BEFORE IT STAINS!
JOSIE
HERE, SABRINA... WIPE IT OFF RIGHT AWAY!
GAK!
GLUB!
SPLASH
OOPS!
GOSH, I'M SORRY, AUNT HILDA! I GUESS I WENT AND DID IT AGAIN!
YOU DING-A-LING! YOU HAVE THE BRAINS OF A BABOON!
2

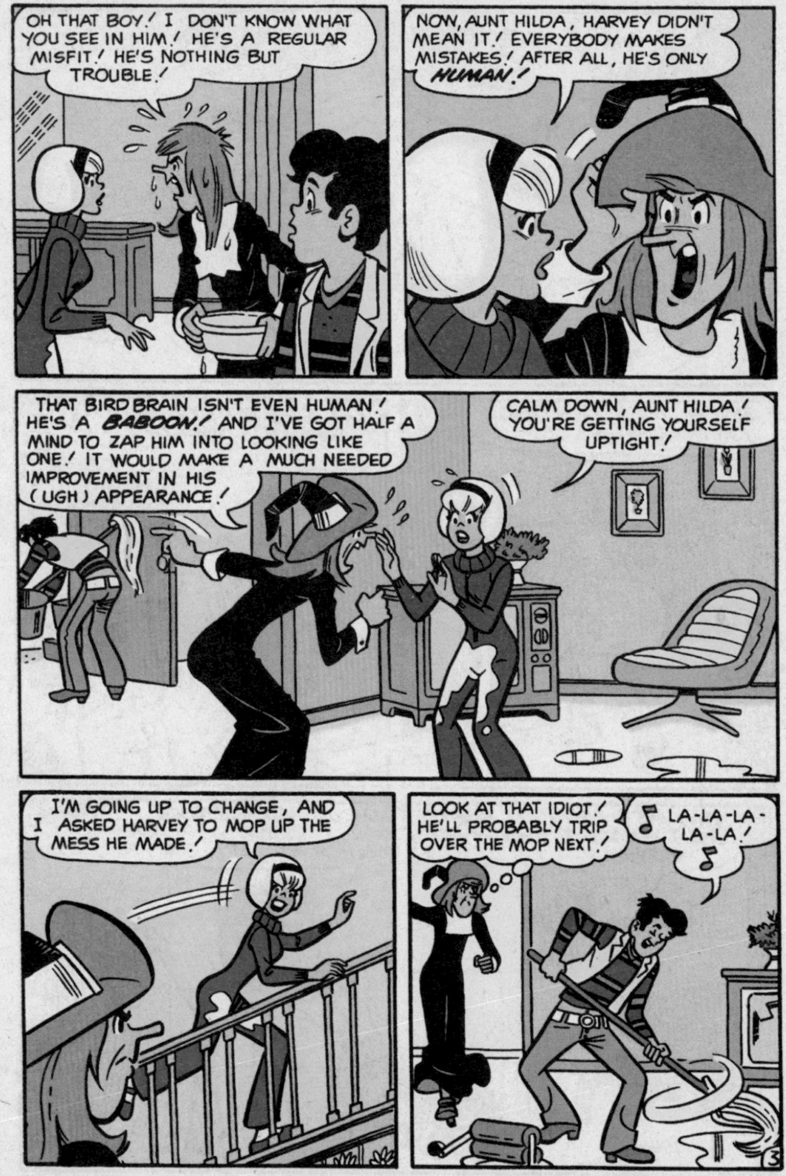
OH THAT BOY! I DON'T KNOW WHAT YOU SEE IN HIM! HE'S A REGULAR MISFIT! HE'S NOTHING BUT TROUBLE!
NOW, AUNT HILDA, HARVEY DIDN'T MEAN IT! EVERYBODY MAKES MISTAKES! AFTER ALL, HE'S ONLY HUMAN!
THAT BIRD BRAIN ISN'T EVEN HUMAN! HE'S A BABOON! AND I'VE GOT HALF A MIND TO ZAP HIM INTO LOOKING LIKE ONE! IT WOULD MAKE A MUCH NEEDED IMPROVEMENT IN HIS (UGH) APPEARANCE!
CALM DOWN, AUNT HILDA! YOU'RE GETTING YOURSELF UPTIGHT!
I'M GOING UP TO CHANGE, AND I ASKED HARVEY TO MOP UP THE MESS HE MADE!
LOOK AT THAT IDIOT! HE'LL PROBABLY TRIP OVER THE MOP NEXT!
LA-LA-LA-LA-LA!
3

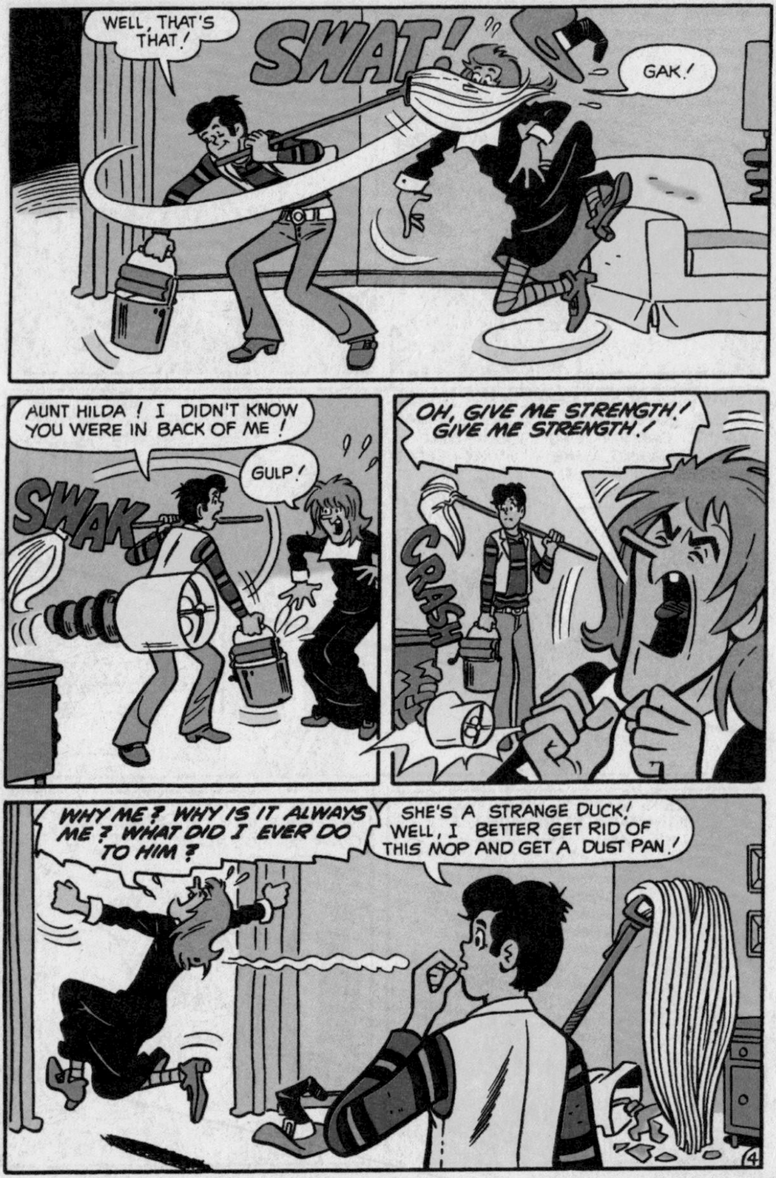
WELL, THAT'S THAT!
SWAT!
GAK!
AUNT HILDA! I DIDN'T KNOW YOU WERE IN BACK OF ME!
GULP!
SWAK
OH, GIVE ME STRENGTH! GIVE ME STRENGTH!
CRASH
WHY ME? WHY IS IT ALWAYS ME? WHAT DID I EVER DO TO HIM?
SHE'S A STRANGE DUCK! WELL, I BETTER GET RID OF THIS MOP AND GET A DUST PAN!
4

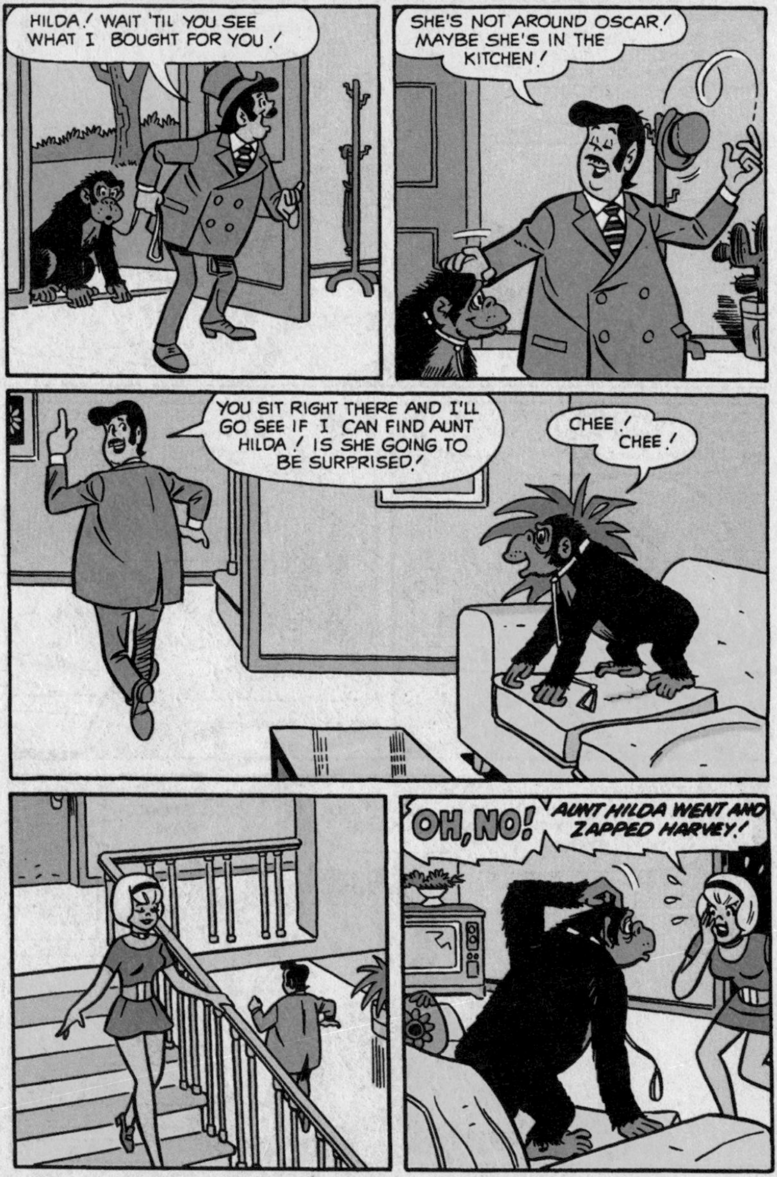
HILDA! WAIT 'TIL YOU SEE WHAT I BOUGHT FOR YOU!
SHE'S NOT AROUND OSCAR! MAYBE SHE'S IN THE KITCHEN!
YOU SIT RIGHT THERE AND I'LL GO SEE IF I CAN FIND AUNT HILDA! IS SHE GOING TO BE SURPRISED!
CHEE! CHEE!
OH, NO!
AUNT HILDA WENT AND ZAPPED HARVEY!

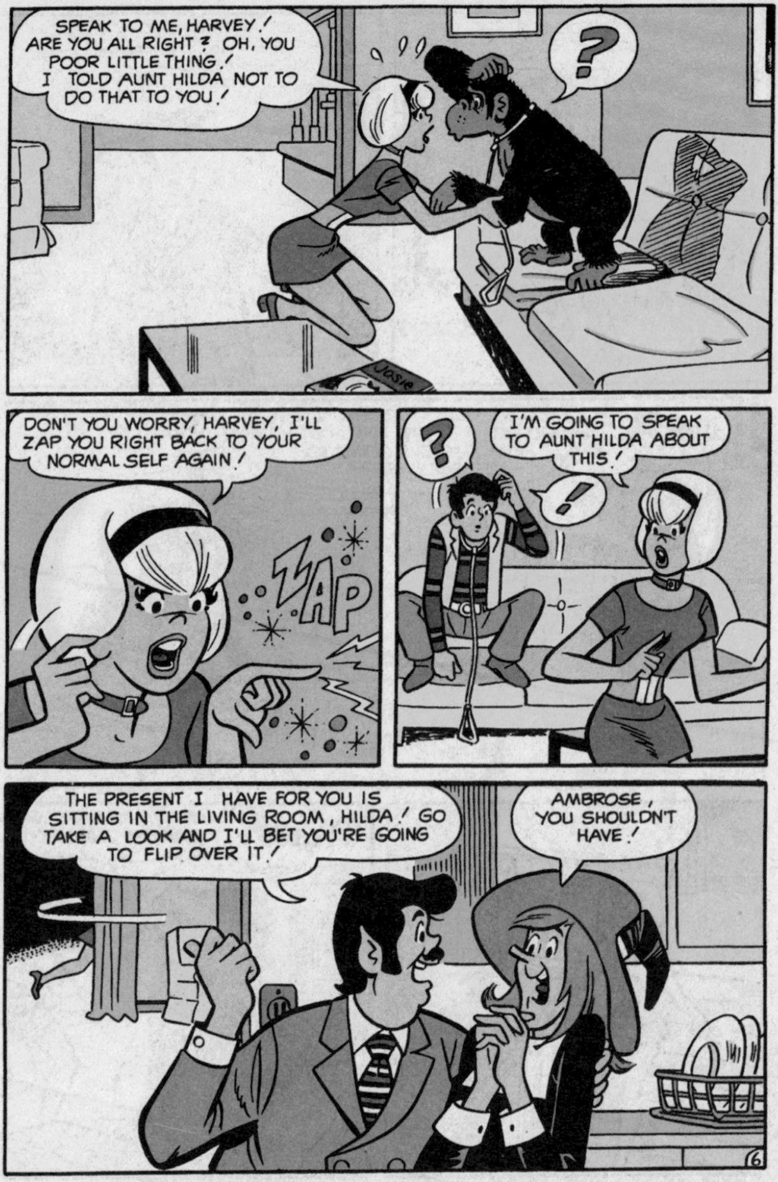
SPEAK TO ME, HARVEY! ARE YOU ALL RIGHT? OH, YOU POOR LITTLE THING! I TOLD AUNT HILDA NOT TO DO THAT TO YOU!
?
JOSIE
DON'T YOU WORRY, HARVEY, I'LL ZAP YOU RIGHT BACK TO YOUR NORMAL SELF AGAIN!
ZAP
?
I'M GOING TO SPEAK TO AUNT HILDA ABOUT THIS!
!
THE PRESENT I HAVE FOR YOU IS SITTING IN THE LIVING ROOM, HILDA! GO TAKE A LOOK AND I'LL BET YOU'RE GOING TO FLIP OVER IT!
AMBROSE, YOU SHOULDN'T HAVE!
6

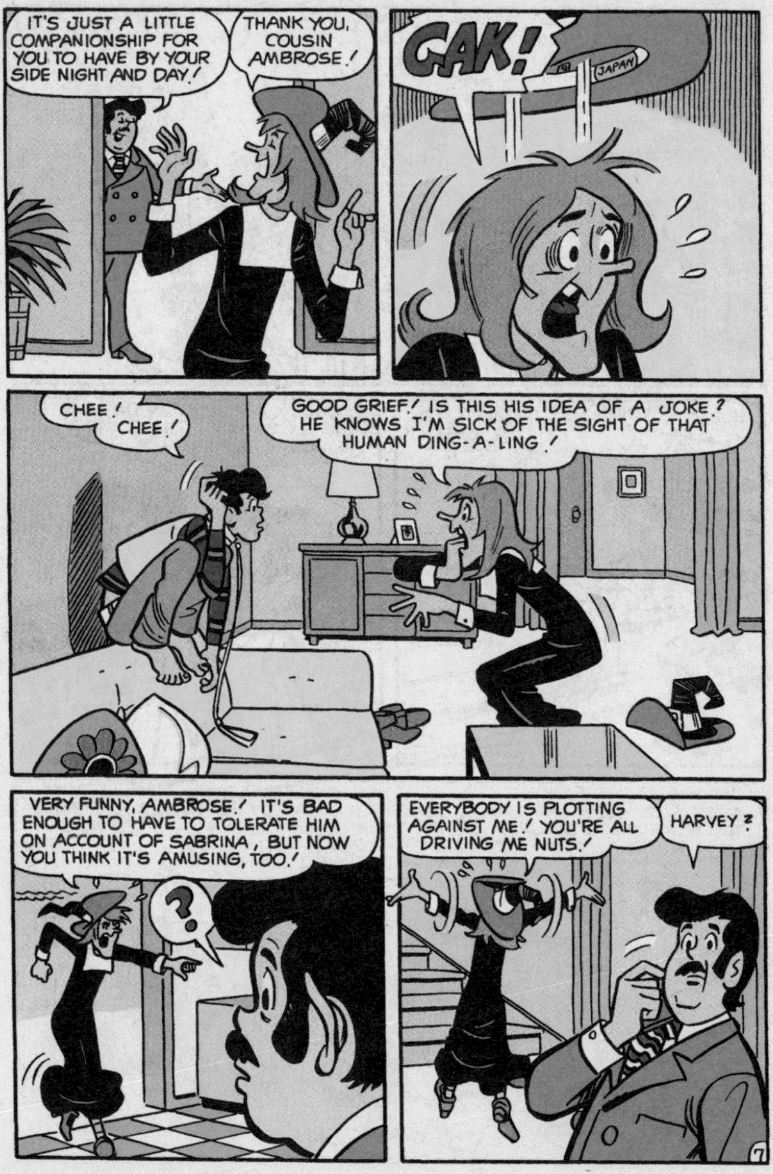
IT'S JUST A LITTLE COMPANIONSHIP FOR YOU TO HAVE BY YOUR SIDE NIGHT AND DAY!
THANK YOU, COUSIN AMBROSE!
GAK!
JAPAN
CHEE! CHEE!
GOOD GRIEF! IS THIS HIS IDEA OF A JOKE? HE KNOWS I'M SICK OF THE SIGHT OF THAT HUMAN DING-A-LING!
VERY FUNNY, AMBROSE! IT'S BAD ENOUGH TO HAVE TO TOLERATE HIM ON ACCOUNT OF SABRINA, BUT NOW YOU THINK IT'S AMUSING, TOO!
?
EVERYBODY IS PLOTTING AGAINST ME! YOU'RE ALL DRIVING ME NUTS!
HARVEY?

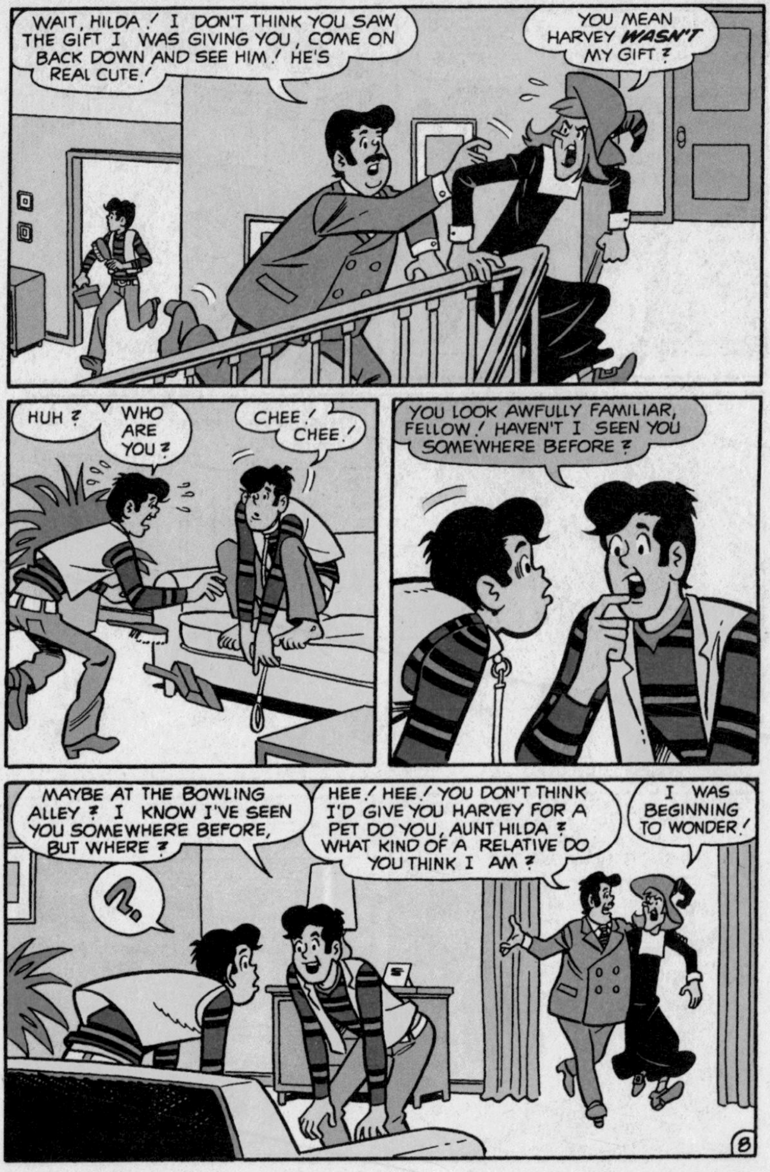
WAIT, HILDA! I DON'T THINK YOU SAW THE GIFT I WAS GIVING YOU, COME ON BACK DOWN AND SEE HIM! HE'S REAL CUTE!
YOU MEAN HARVEY **WASN'T** MY GIFT?
HUH?
WHO ARE YOU?
CHEE! CHEE!
YOU LOOK AWFULLY FAMILIAR, FELLOW! HAVEN'T I SEEN YOU SOMEWHERE BEFORE?
MAYBE AT THE BOWLING ALLEY? I KNOW I'VE SEEN YOU SOMEWHERE BEFORE, BUT WHERE?
HEE! HEE! YOU DON'T THINK I'D GIVE YOU HARVEY FOR A PET DO YOU, AUNT HILDA? WHAT KIND OF A RELATIVE DO YOU THINK I AM?
I WAS BEGINNING TO WONDER!
8

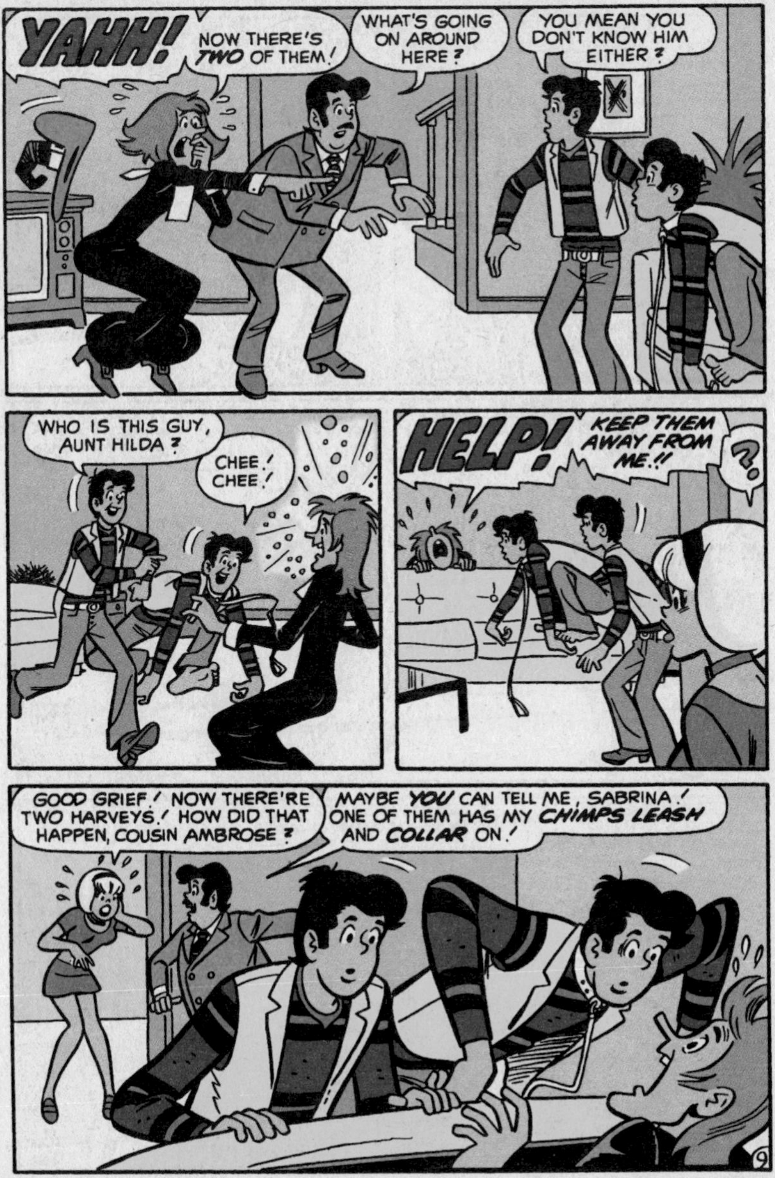
YAHH!
NOW THERE'S TWO OF THEM!
WHAT'S GOING ON AROUND HERE?
YOU MEAN YOU DON'T KNOW HIM EITHER?
WHO IS THIS GUY, AUNT HILDA?
CHEE! CHEE!
HELP!
KEEP THEM AWAY FROM ME.!!
?
GOOD GRIEF! NOW THERE'RE TWO HARVEYS! HOW DID THAT HAPPEN, COUSIN AMBROSE?
MAYBE YOU CAN TELL ME, SABRINA! ONE OF THEM HAS MY CHIMPS LEASH AND COLLAR ON!
9

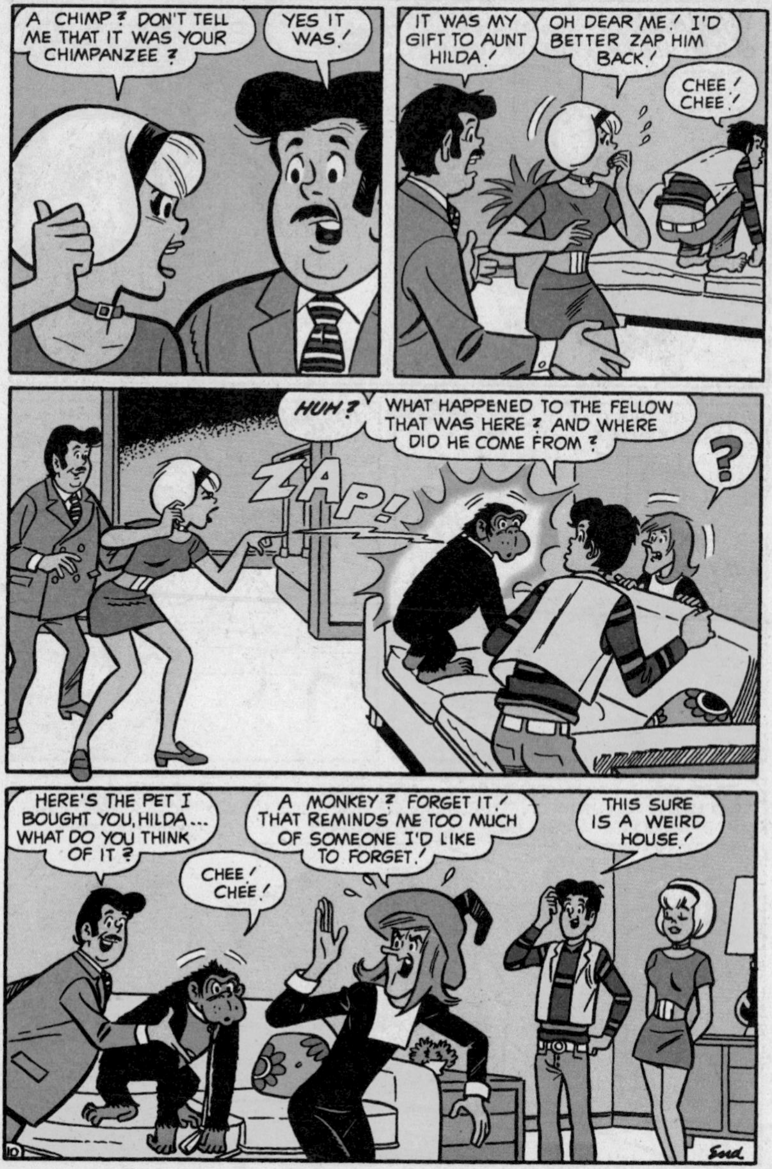
A CHIMP? DON'T TELL ME THAT IT WAS YOUR CHIMPANZEE?
YES IT WAS!
IT WAS MY GIFT TO AUNT HILDA!
OH DEAR ME! I'D BETTER ZAP HIM BACK!
CHEE! CHEE!
HUH?
WHAT HAPPENED TO THE FELLOW THAT WAS HERE? AND WHERE DID HE COME FROM?
ZAP!
?
HERE'S THE PET I BOUGHT YOU, HILDA... WHAT DO YOU THINK OF IT?
CHEE! CHEE!
A MONKEY? FORGET IT! THAT REMINDS ME TOO MUCH OF SOMEONE I'D LIKE TO FORGET!
THIS SURE IS A WEIRD HOUSE!
10
End

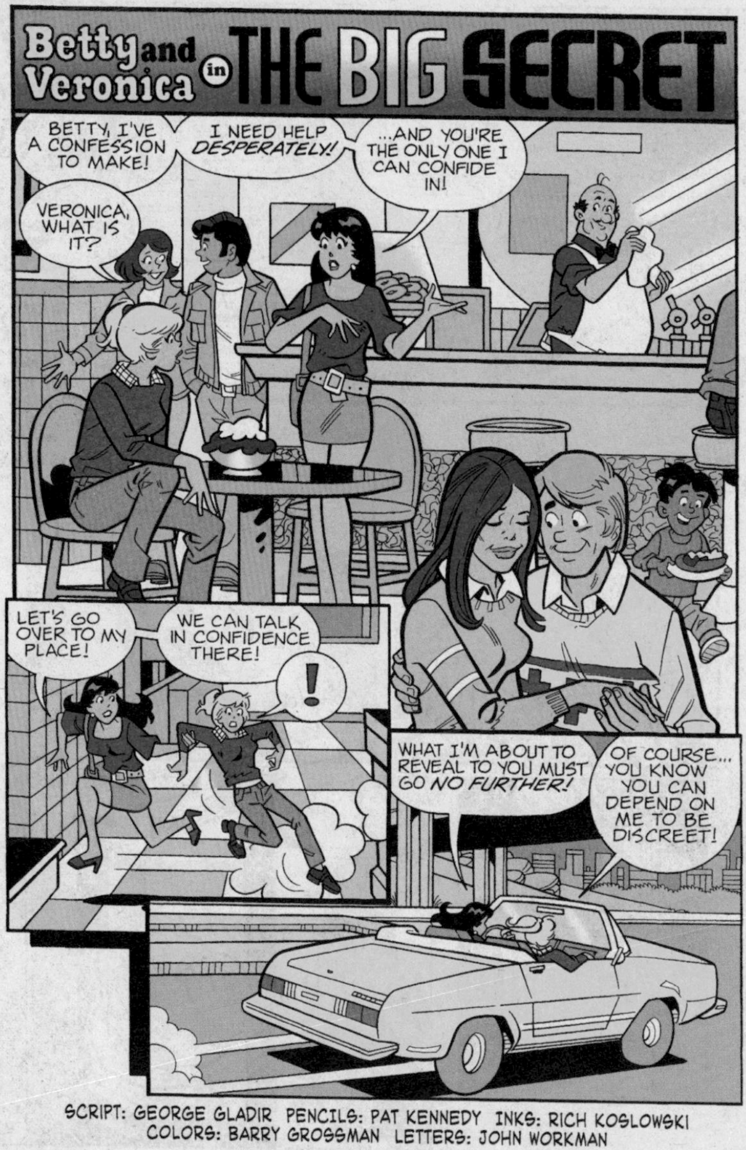
Betty and Veronica in THE BIG SECRET
BETTY, I'VE A CONFESSION TO MAKE!
I NEED HELP DESPERATELY!
...AND YOU'RE THE ONLY ONE I CAN CONFIDE IN!
VERONICA, WHAT IS IT?
LET'S GO OVER TO MY PLACE!
WE CAN TALK IN CONFIDENCE THERE!
!
WHAT I'M ABOUT TO REVEAL TO YOU MUST GO NO FURTHER!
OF COURSE... YOU KNOW YOU CAN DEPEND ON ME TO BE DISCREET!

SCRIPT: GEORGE GLADIR PENCILS: PAT KENNEDY INKS: RICH KOSLOWSKI
COLORS: BARRY GROSSMAN LETTERS: JOHN WORKMAN

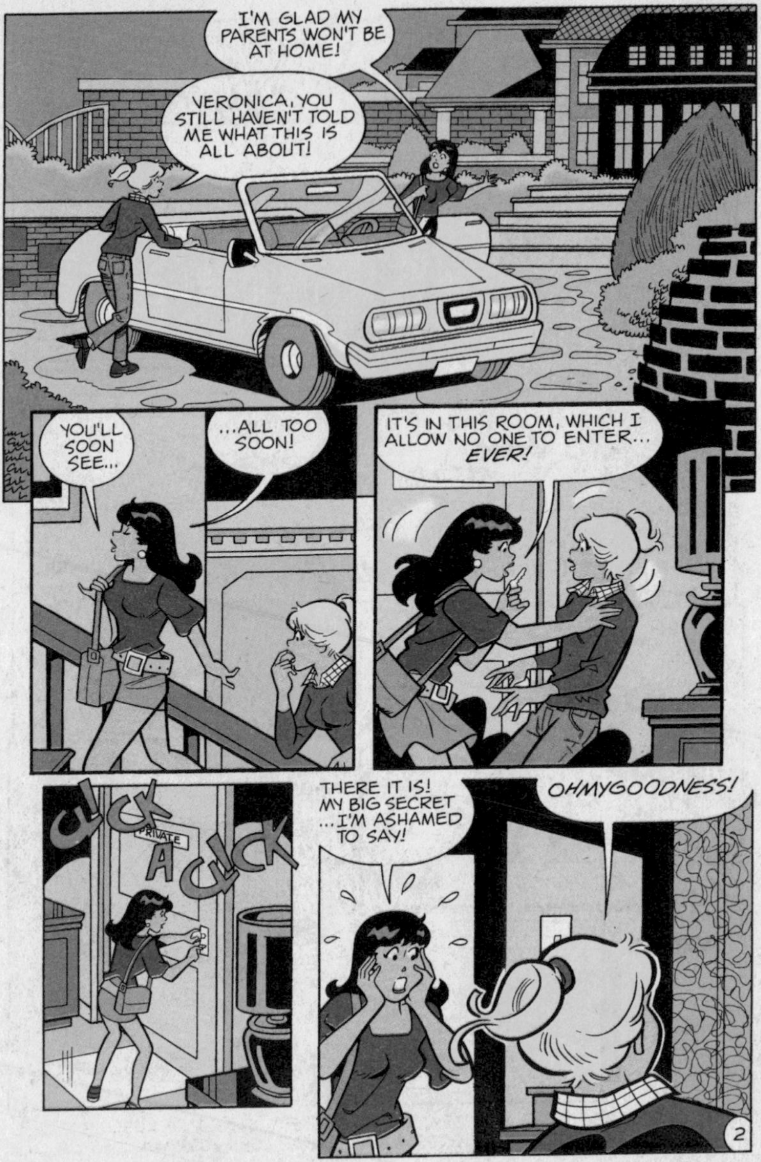
I'M GLAD MY PARENTS WON'T BE AT HOME!
VERONICA, YOU STILL HAVEN'T TOLD ME WHAT THIS IS ALL ABOUT!
YOU'LL SOON SEE...
...ALL TOO SOON!
IT'S IN THIS ROOM, WHICH I ALLOW NO ONE TO ENTER... *EVER!*
PRIVATE
CLICK
A
CLICK
THERE IT IS! MY BIG SECRET ...I'M ASHAMED TO SAY!
OHMYGOODNESS!

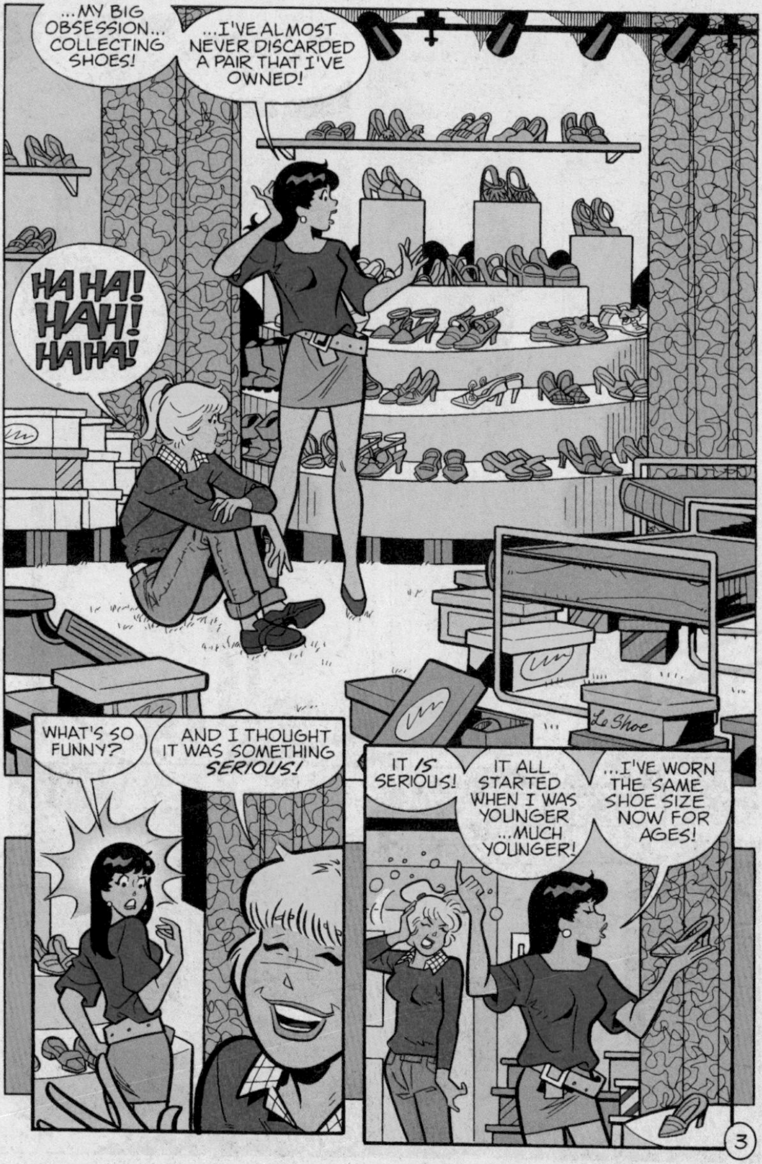
...MY BIG OBSESSION... COLLECTING SHOES!
...I'VE ALMOST NEVER DISCARDED A PAIR THAT I'VE OWNED!
HA HA! HAH! HAHA!
Le Shoe
WHAT'S SO FUNNY?
AND I THOUGHT IT WAS SOMETHING *SERIOUS!*
IT *IS* SERIOUS!
IT ALL STARTED WHEN I WAS YOUNGER ...MUCH YOUNGER!
...I'VE WORN THE SAME SHOE SIZE NOW FOR AGES!

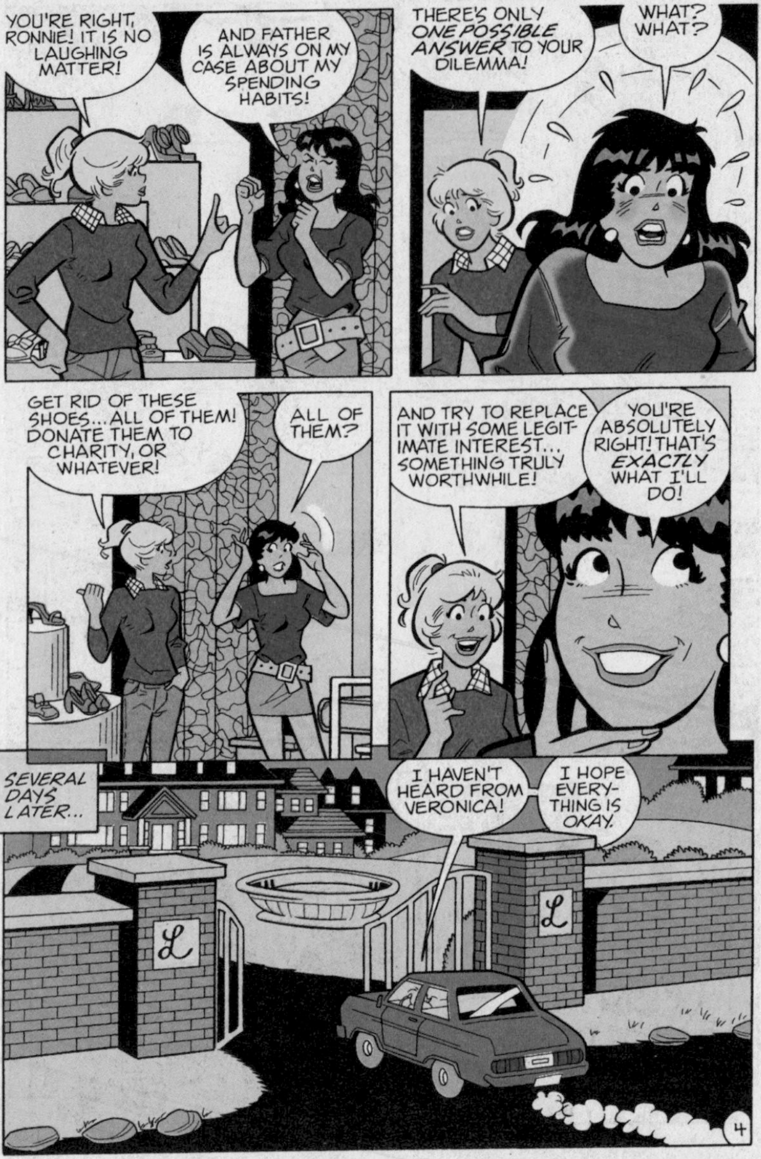
YOU'RE RIGHT, RONNIE! IT IS NO LAUGHING MATTER!
AND FATHER IS ALWAYS ON MY CASE ABOUT MY SPENDING HABITS!
THERE'S ONLY ONE POSSIBLE ANSWER TO YOUR DILEMMA!
WHAT? WHAT?
GET RID OF THESE SHOES... ALL OF THEM! DONATE THEM TO CHARITY, OR WHATEVER!
ALL OF THEM?
AND TRY TO REPLACE IT WITH SOME LEGIT-IMATE INTEREST... SOMETHING TRULY WORTHWHILE!
YOU'RE ABSOLUTELY RIGHT! THAT'S EXACTLY WHAT I'LL DO!
SEVERAL DAYS LATER...
I HAVEN'T HEARD FROM VERONICA!
I HOPE EVERY-THING IS OKAY.
L
L
4

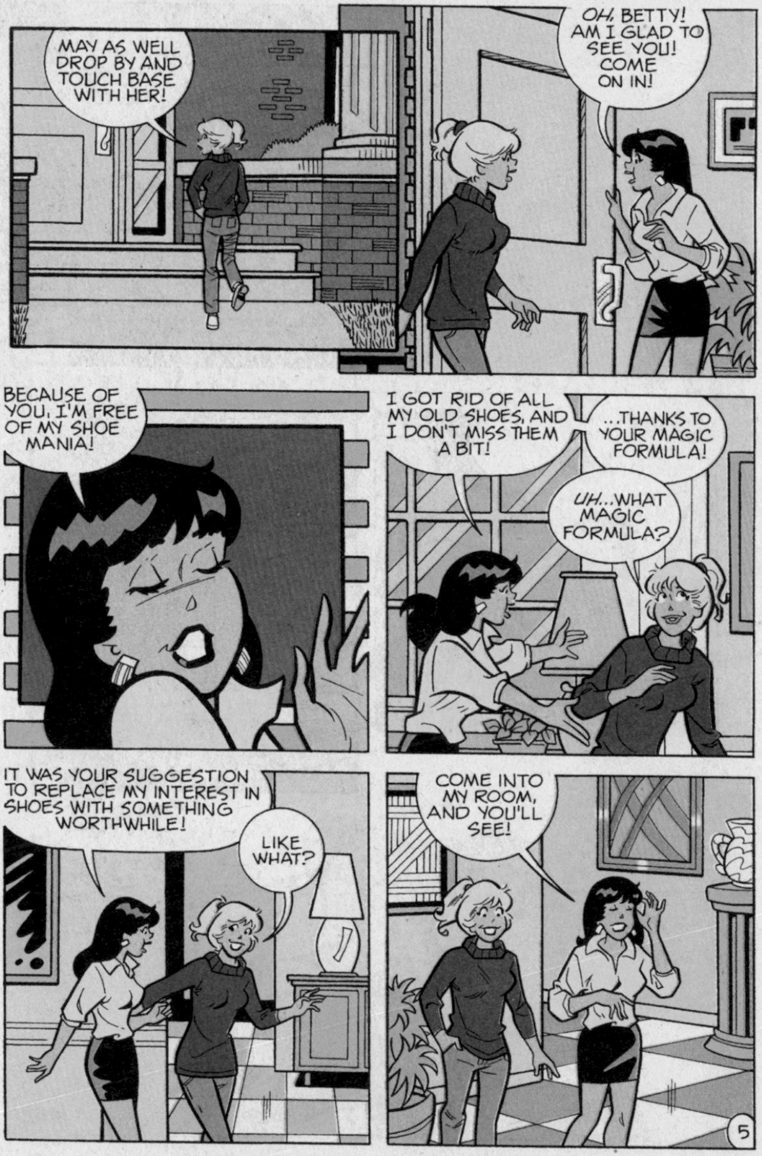
MAY AS WELL DROP BY AND TOUCH BASE WITH HER!
OH, BETTY! AM I GLAD TO SEE YOU! COME ON IN!
BECAUSE OF YOU, I'M FREE OF MY SHOE MANIA!
I GOT RID OF ALL MY OLD SHOES, AND I DON'T MISS THEM A BIT!
...THANKS TO YOUR MAGIC FORMULA!
UH...WHAT MAGIC FORMULA?
IT WAS YOUR SUGGESTION TO REPLACE MY INTEREST IN SHOES WITH SOMETHING WORTHWHILE!
LIKE WHAT?
COME INTO MY ROOM, AND YOU'LL SEE!

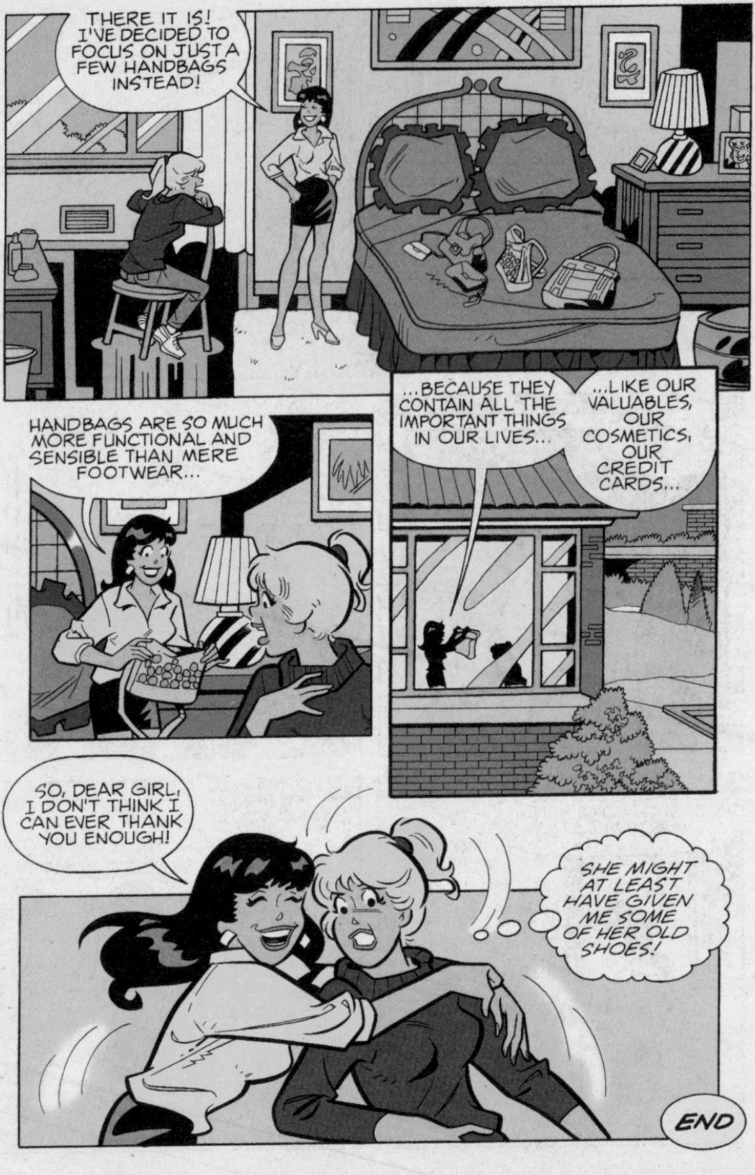
THERE IT IS! I'VE DECIDED TO FOCUS ON JUST A FEW HANDBAGS INSTEAD!
HANDBAGS ARE SO MUCH MORE FUNCTIONAL AND SENSIBLE THAN MERE FOOTWEAR...
...BECAUSE THEY CONTAIN ALL THE IMPORTANT THINGS IN OUR LIVES...
...LIKE OUR VALUABLES, OUR COSMETICS, OUR CREDIT CARDS...
SO, DEAR GIRL, I DON'T THINK I CAN EVER THANK YOU ENOUGH!
SHE MIGHT AT LEAST HAVE GIVEN ME SOME OF HER OLD SHOES!
END

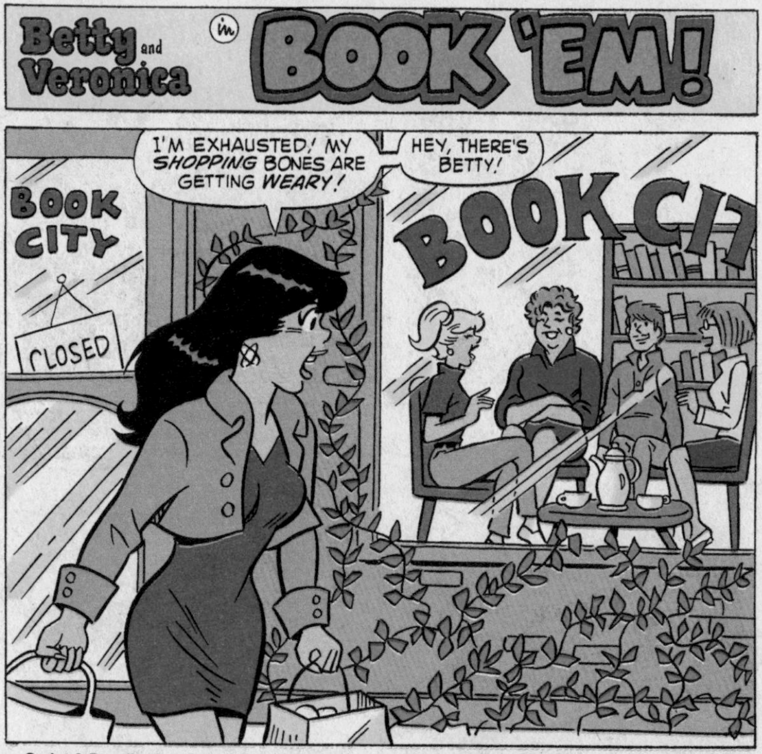
Betty and Veronica in
BOOK 'EM!
I'M EXHAUSTED! MY SHOPPING BONES ARE GETTING WEARY!
HEY, THERE'S BETTY!
BOOK CITY
CLOSED
BOOK CIT

Script & Pencils: Dan Parent / Inks: Rudy Lapick / Letters: Bill Yoshida / Colors: Barry Grossman

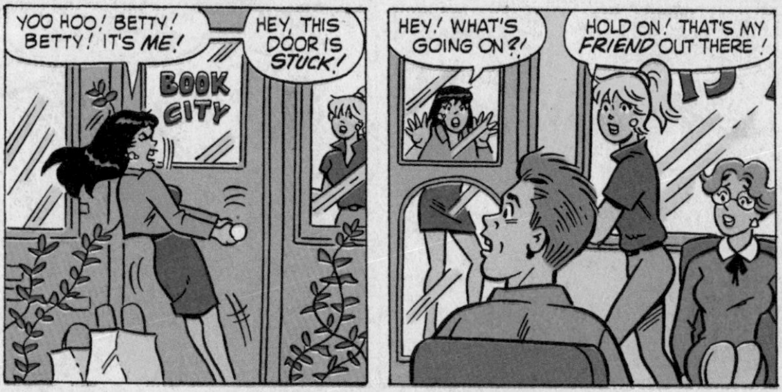
YOO HOO! BETTY! BETTY! IT'S ME!
HEY, THIS DOOR IS STUCK!
BOOK CITY
HEY! WHAT'S GOING ON?!
HOLD ON! THAT'S MY FRIEND OUT THERE!

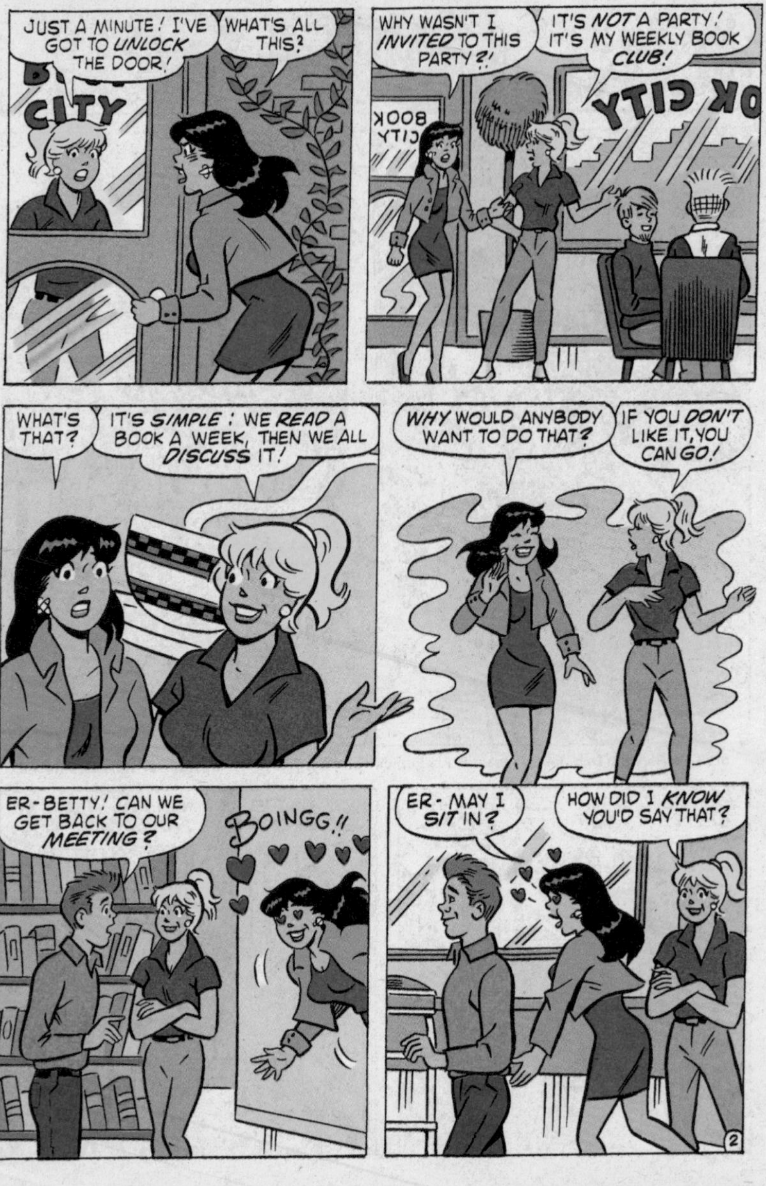
JUST A MINUTE! I'VE GOT TO UNLOCK THE DOOR!
WHAT'S ALL THIS?
CITY
WHY WASN'T I INVITED TO THIS PARTY?!
IT'S NOT A PARTY! IT'S MY WEEKLY BOOK CLUB!
BOOK CITY
WHAT'S THAT?
IT'S SIMPLE: WE READ A BOOK A WEEK, THEN WE ALL DISCUSS IT!
WHY WOULD ANYBODY WANT TO DO THAT?
IF YOU DON'T LIKE IT, YOU CAN GO!
ER-BETTY! CAN WE GET BACK TO OUR MEETING?
BOINGG!!
ER- MAY I SIT IN?
HOW DID I KNOW YOU'D SAY THAT?
2

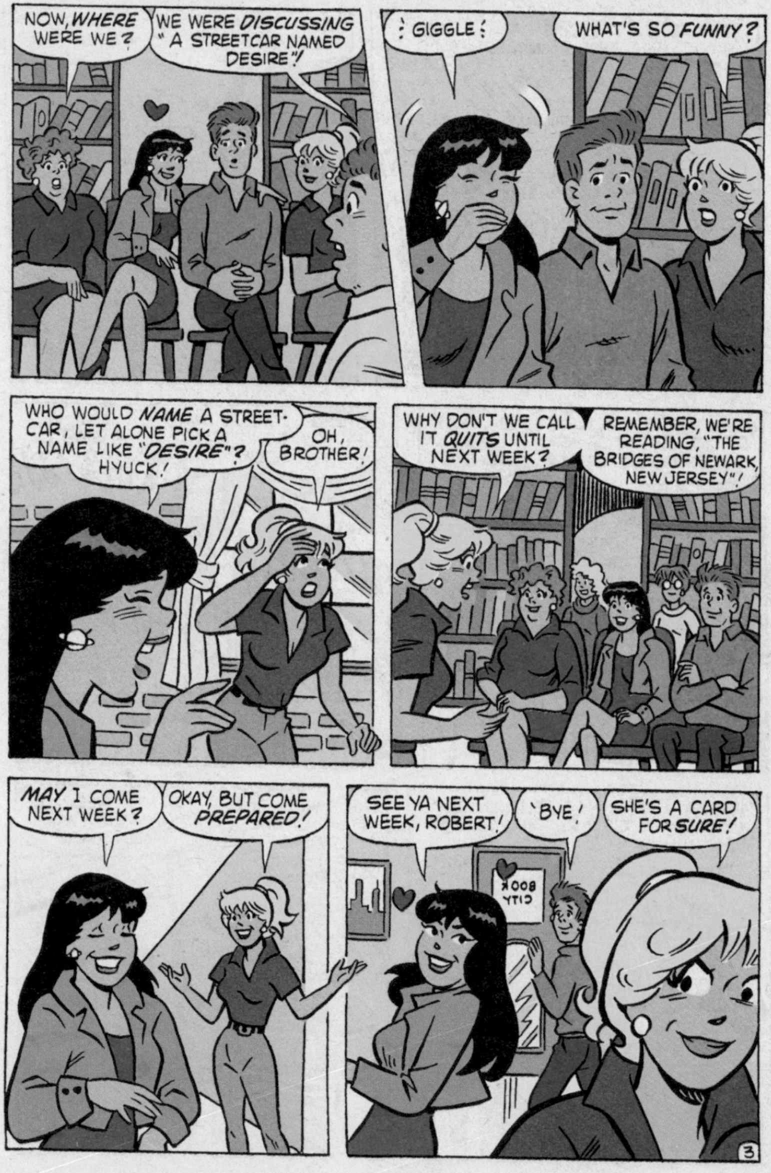

NOW, WHERE WERE WE?
WE WERE DISCUSSING "A STREETCAR NAMED DESIRE"!
GIGGLE
WHAT'S SO FUNNY?
WHO WOULD NAME A STREET-CAR, LET ALONE PICK A NAME LIKE "DESIRE"? HYUCK!
OH, BROTHER!
WHY DON'T WE CALL IT QUITS UNTIL NEXT WEEK?
REMEMBER, WE'RE READING, "THE BRIDGES OF NEWARK, NEW JERSEY"!
MAY I COME NEXT WEEK?
OKAY, BUT COME PREPARED!
SEE YA NEXT WEEK, ROBERT!
'BYE!
SHE'S A CARD FOR SURE!
3

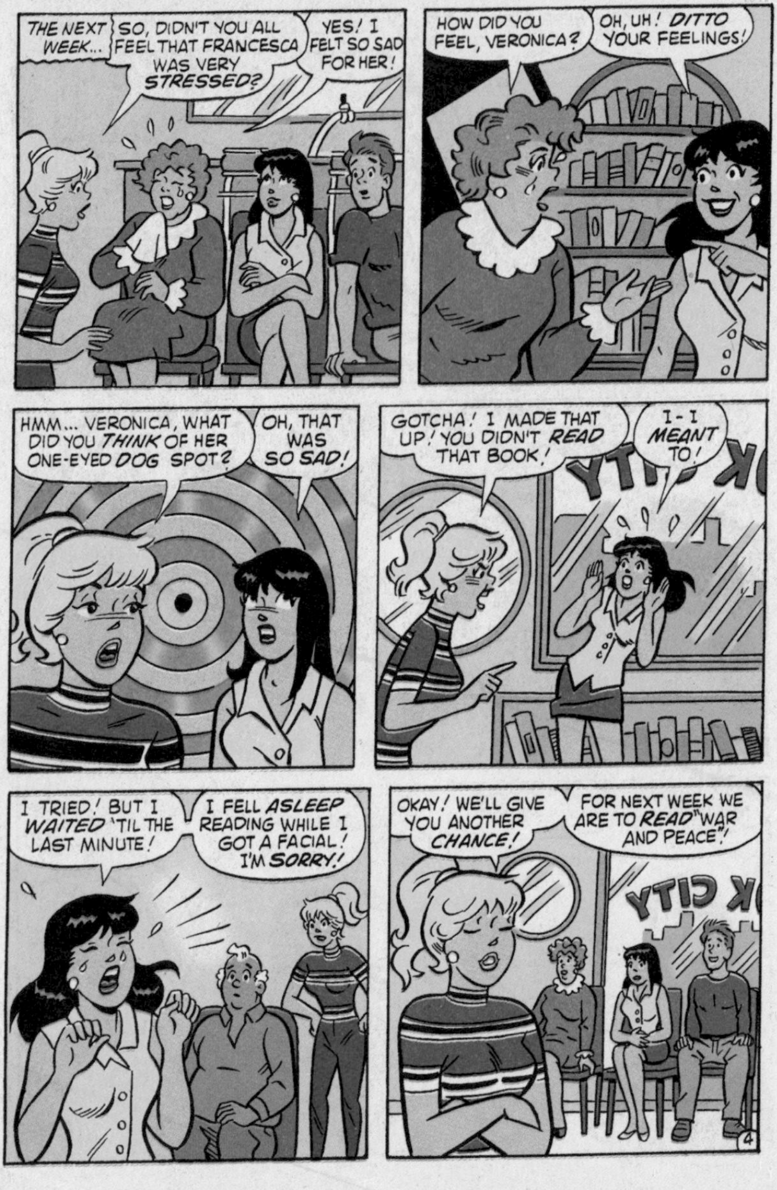
THE NEXT WEEK...
SO, DIDN'T YOU ALL FEEL THAT FRANCESCA WAS VERY STRESSED?
YES! I FELT SO SAD FOR HER!
HOW DID YOU FEEL, VERONICA?
OH, UH! DITTO YOUR FEELINGS!
HMM... VERONICA, WHAT DID YOU THINK OF HER ONE-EYED DOG SPOT?
OH, THAT WAS SO SAD!
GOTCHA! I MADE THAT UP! YOU DIDN'T READ THAT BOOK!
I-I MEANT TO!
I TRIED! BUT I WAITED 'TIL THE LAST MINUTE!
I FELL ASLEEP READING WHILE I GOT A FACIAL! I'M SORRY!
OKAY! WE'LL GIVE YOU ANOTHER CHANCE!
FOR NEXT WEEK WE ARE TO READ "WAR AND PEACE"!
4

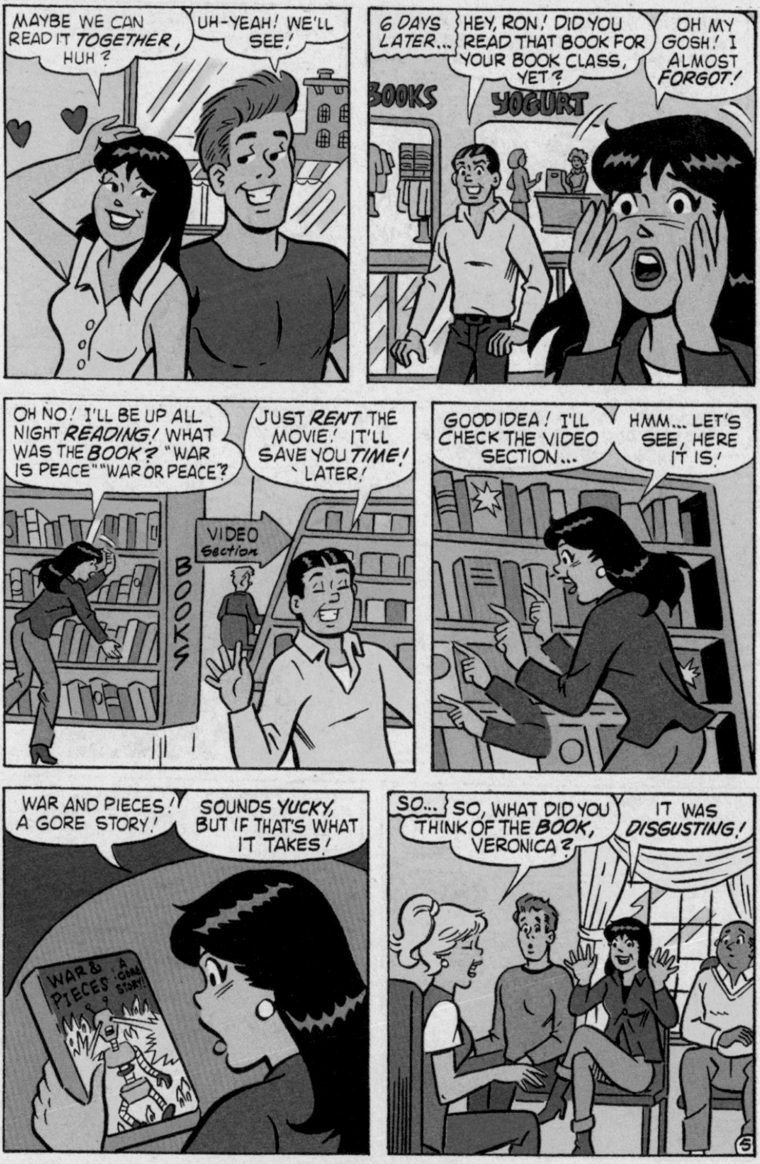

MAYBE WE CAN READ IT TOGETHER, HUH?
UH-YEAH! WE'LL SEE!
6 DAYS LATER...
HEY, RON! DID YOU READ THAT BOOK FOR YOUR BOOK CLASS, YET?
OH MY GOSH! I ALMOST FORGOT!
BOOKS
YOGURT
OH NO! I'LL BE UP ALL NIGHT READING! WHAT WAS THE BOOK? "WAR IS PEACE" "WAR OR PEACE"?
JUST RENT THE MOVIE! IT'LL SAVE YOU TIME! LATER!
VIDEO Section
BOOKS
GOOD IDEA! I'LL CHECK THE VIDEO SECTION...
HMM... LET'S SEE, HERE IT IS!
WAR AND PIECES! A GORE STORY!
SOUNDS YUCKY, BUT IF THAT'S WHAT IT TAKES!
WAR & PIECES
A GORE STORY!
SO...
SO, WHAT DID YOU THINK OF THE BOOK, VERONICA?
IT WAS DISGUSTING!
5

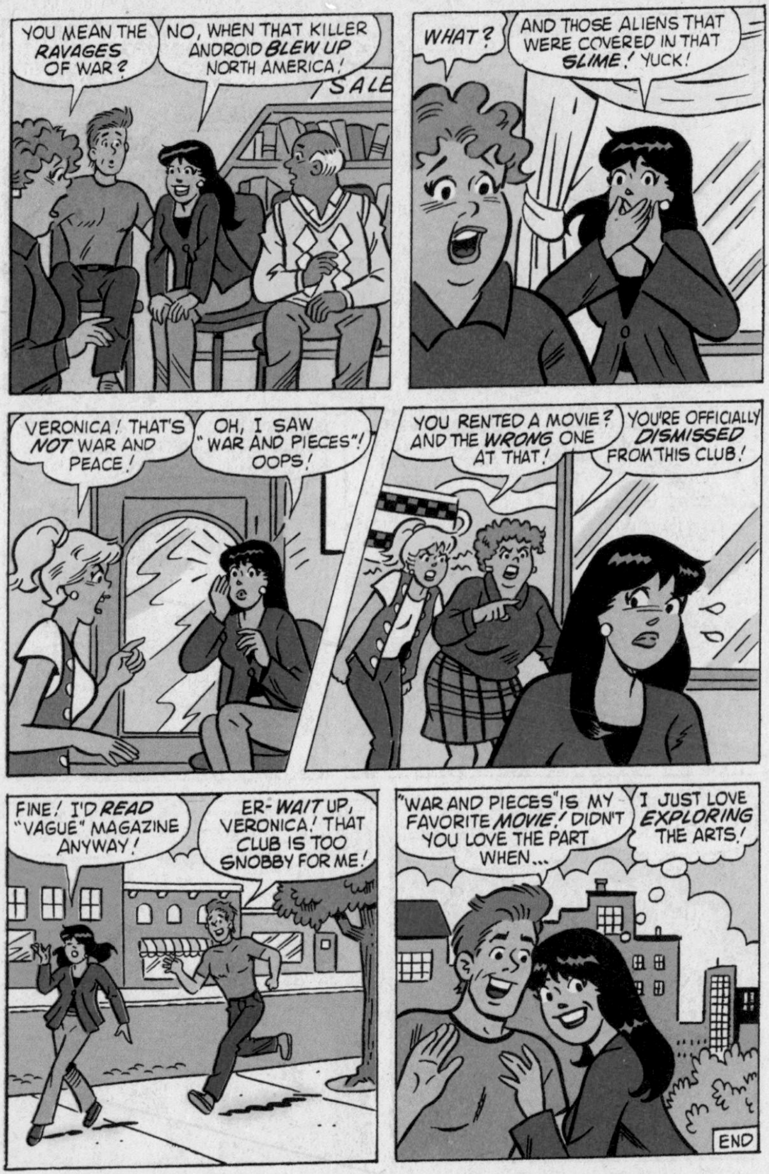
YOU MEAN THE RAVAGES OF WAR?
NO, WHEN THAT KILLER ANDROID BLEW UP NORTH AMERICA!
SALE
WHAT?
AND THOSE ALIENS THAT WERE COVERED IN THAT SLIME! YUCK!
VERONICA! THAT'S NOT WAR AND PEACE!
OH, I SAW "WAR AND PIECES"! OOPS!
YOU RENTED A MOVIE? AND THE WRONG ONE AT THAT!
YOU'RE OFFICIALLY DISMISSED FROM THIS CLUB!
FINE! I'D READ "VAGUE" MAGAZINE ANYWAY!
ER- WAIT UP, VERONICA! THAT CLUB IS TOO SNOBBY FOR ME!
"WAR AND PIECES" IS MY FAVORITE MOVIE! DIDN'T YOU LOVE THE PART WHEN...
I JUST LOVE EXPLORING THE ARTS!
END

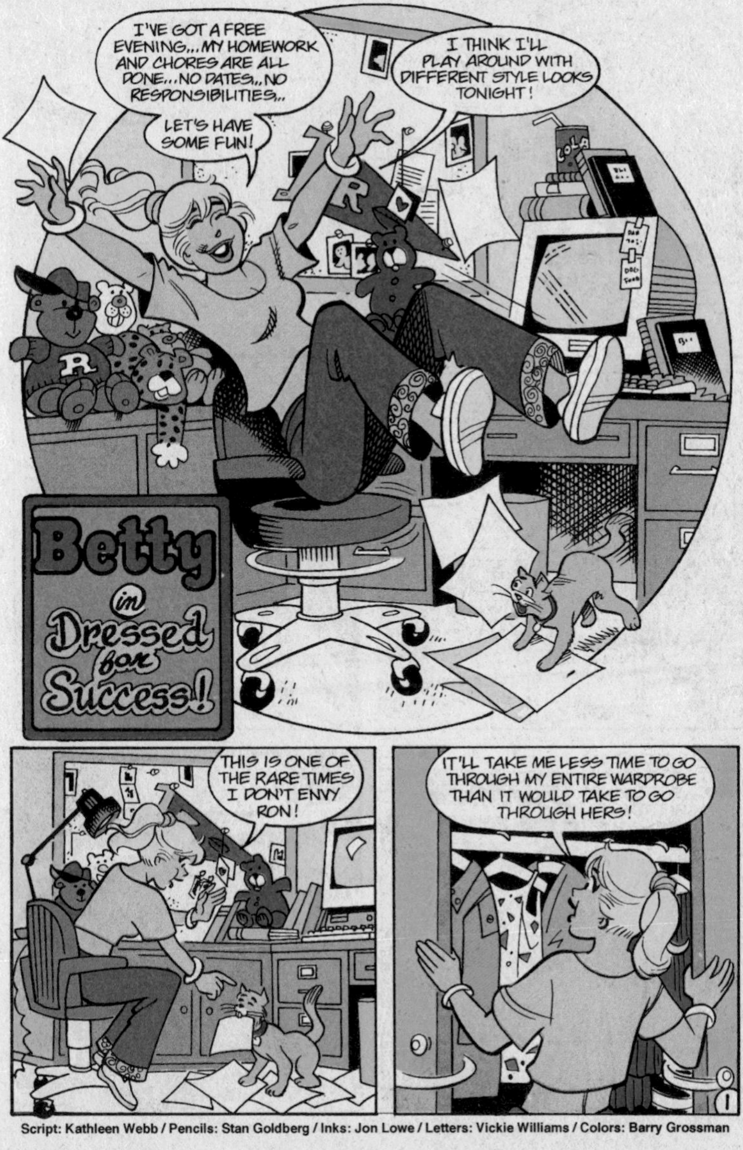

I'VE GOT A FREE EVENING... MY HOMEWORK AND CHORES ARE ALL DONE... NO DATES... NO RESPONSIBILITIES...
LET'S HAVE SOME FUN!
I THINK I'LL PLAY AROUND WITH DIFFERENT STYLE LOOKS TONIGHT!
Betty in Dressed for Success!
THIS IS ONE OF THE RARE TIMES I DON'T ENVY RON!
IT'LL TAKE ME LESS TIME TO GO THROUGH MY ENTIRE WARDROBE THAN IT WOULD TAKE TO GO THROUGH HERS!
1

Script: Kathleen Webb / Pencils: Stan Goldberg / Inks: Jon Lowe / Letters: Vickie Williams / Colors: Barry Grossman

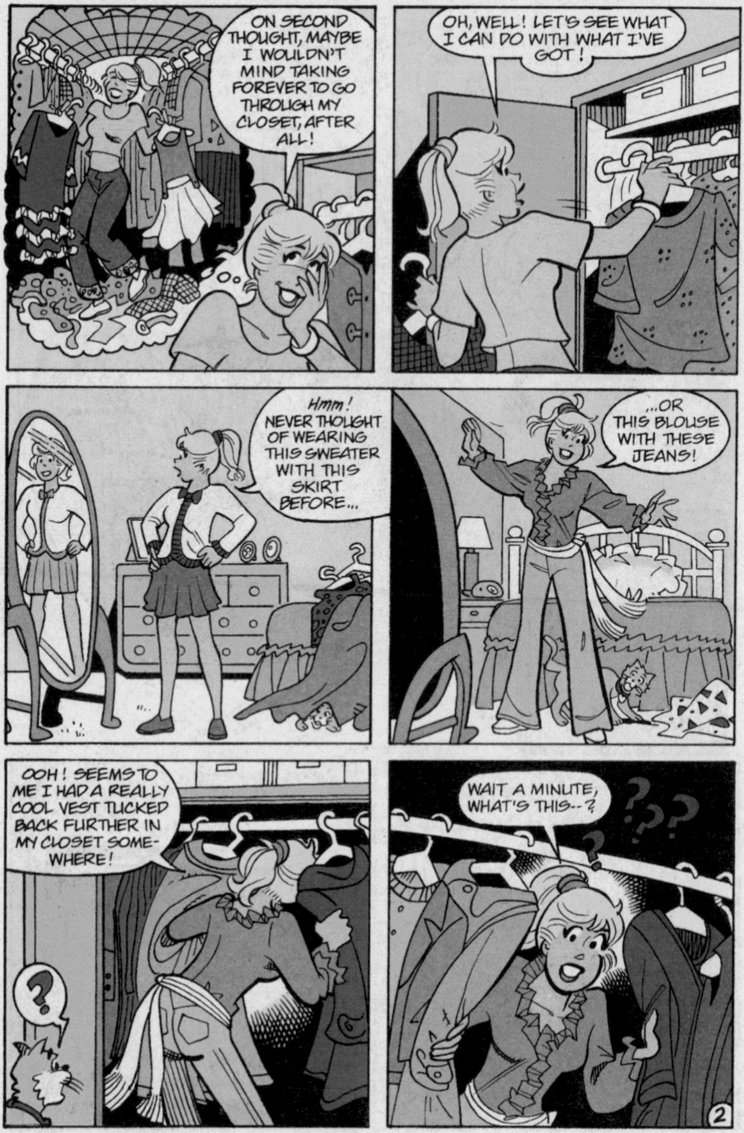
ON SECOND THOUGHT, MAYBE I WOULDN'T MIND TAKING FOREVER TO GO THROUGH MY CLOSET, AFTER ALL!
OH, WELL! LET'S SEE WHAT I CAN DO WITH WHAT I'VE GOT!
Hmm! NEVER THOUGHT OF WEARING THIS SWEATER WITH THIS SKIRT BEFORE...
...OR THIS BLOUSE WITH THESE JEANS!
OOH! SEEMS TO ME I HAD A REALLY COOL VEST TUCKED BACK FURTHER IN MY CLOSET SOME-WHERE!
?
WAIT A MINUTE, WHAT'S THIS--?
2

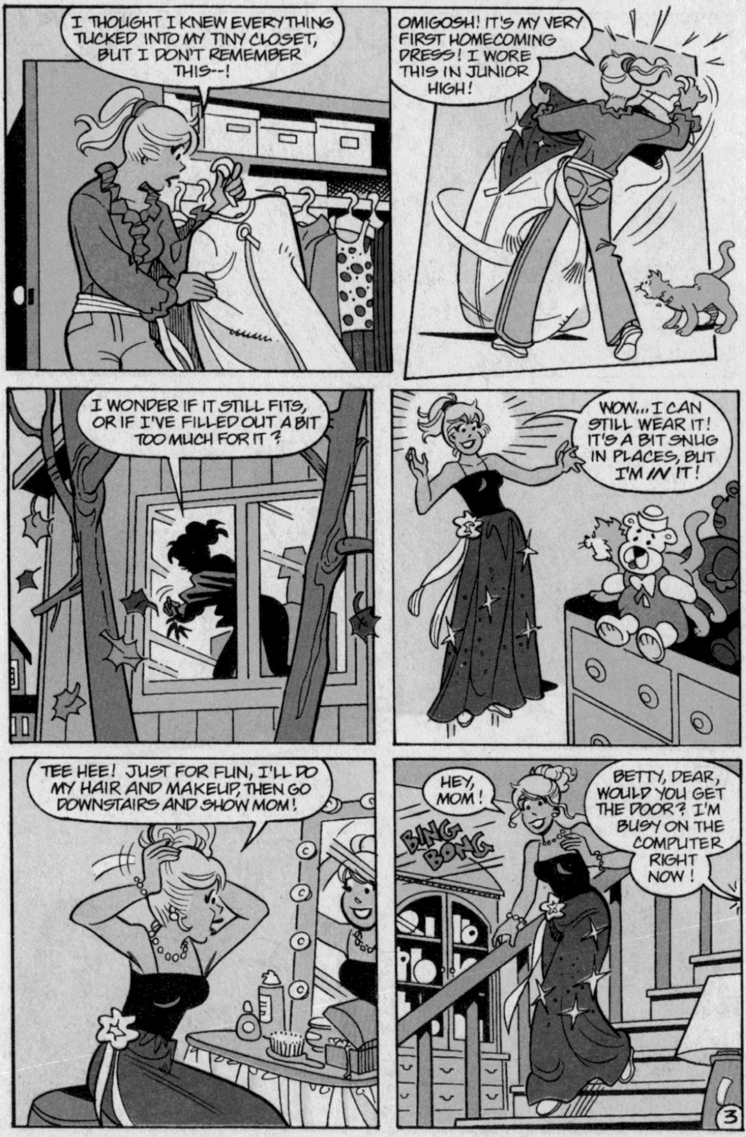
I THOUGHT I KNEW EVERYTHING TUCKED INTO MY TINY CLOSET, BUT I DON'T REMEMBER THIS--!
OMIGOSH! IT'S MY VERY FIRST HOMECOMING DRESS! I WORE THIS IN JUNIOR HIGH!
I WONDER IF IT STILL FITS, OR IF I'VE FILLED OUT A BIT TOO MUCH FOR IT?
WOW... I CAN STILL WEAR IT! IT'S A BIT SNUG IN PLACES, BUT I'M *IN* IT!
TEE HEE! JUST FOR FUN, I'LL DO MY HAIR AND MAKEUP, THEN GO DOWNSTAIRS AND SHOW MOM!
HEY, MOM!
BING BONG
BETTY, DEAR, WOULD YOU GET THE DOOR? I'M BUSY ON THE COMPUTER RIGHT NOW!
3

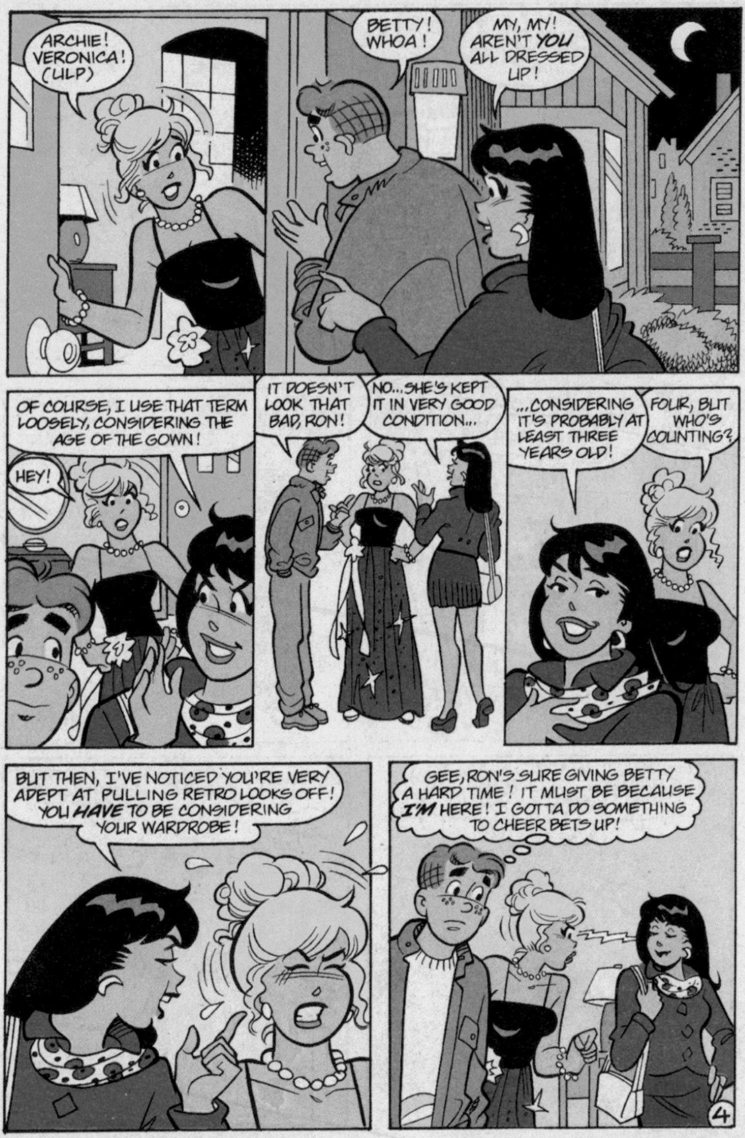
ARCHIE! VERONICA! (ULP)
BETTY! WHOA!
MY, MY! AREN'T YOU ALL DRESSED UP!
OF COURSE, I USE THAT TERM LOOSELY, CONSIDERING THE AGE OF THE GOWN!
HEY!
IT DOESN'T LOOK THAT BAD, RON!
NO... SHE'S KEPT IT IN VERY GOOD CONDITION...
...CONSIDERING IT'S PROBABLY AT LEAST THREE YEARS OLD!
FOUR, BUT WHO'S COUNTING?
BUT THEN, I'VE NOTICED YOU'RE VERY ADEPT AT PULLING RETRO LOOKS OFF! YOU HAVE TO BE CONSIDERING YOUR WARDROBE!
GEE, RON'S SURE GIVING BETTY A HARD TIME! IT MUST BE BECAUSE I'M HERE! I GOTTA DO SOMETHING TO CHEER BETS UP!
4

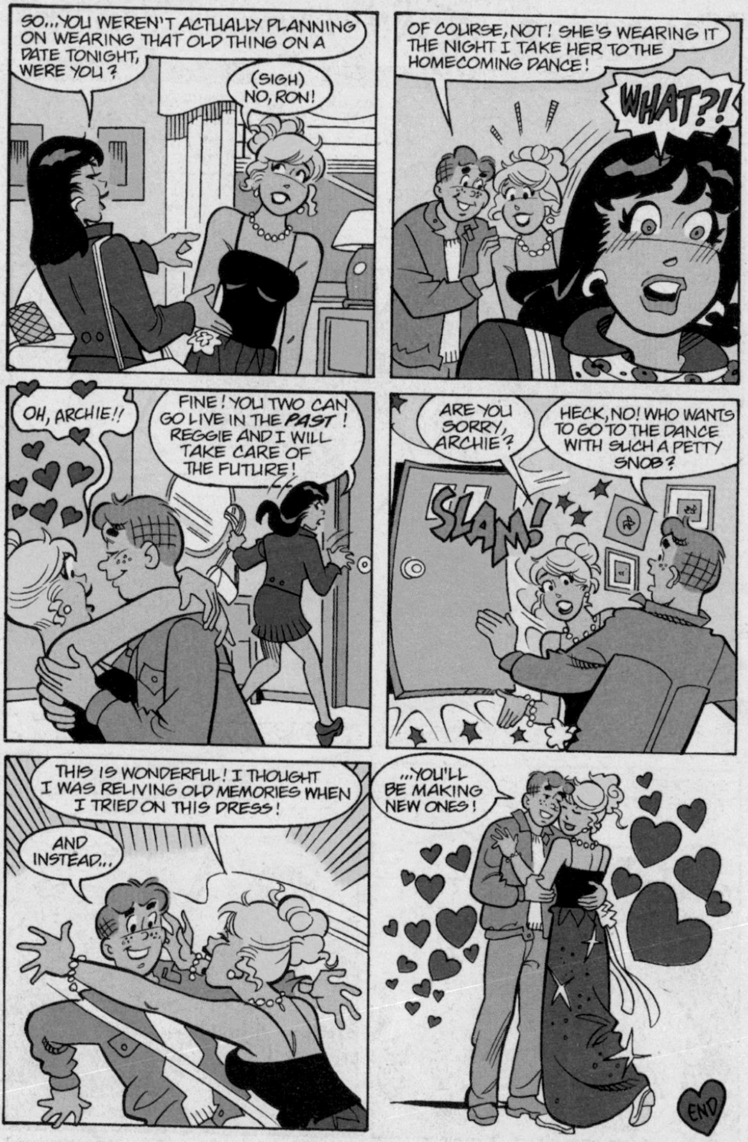
SO...YOU WEREN'T ACTUALLY PLANNING ON WEARING THAT OLD THING ON A DATE TONIGHT, WERE YOU?
(SIGH) NO, RON!
OF COURSE, NOT! SHE'S WEARING IT THE NIGHT I TAKE HER TO THE HOMECOMING DANCE!
WHAT?!
OH, ARCHIE!!
FINE! YOU TWO CAN GO LIVE IN THE PAST! REGGIE AND I WILL TAKE CARE OF THE FUTURE!
ARE YOU SORRY, ARCHIE?
HECK, NO! WHO WANTS TO GO TO THE DANCE WITH SUCH A PETTY SNOB?
SLAM!
THIS IS WONDERFUL! I THOUGHT I WAS RELIVING OLD MEMORIES WHEN I TRIED ON THIS DRESS!
AND INSTEAD...
...YOU'LL BE MAKING NEW ONES!
END

Veronica in "Taking the Initiative"

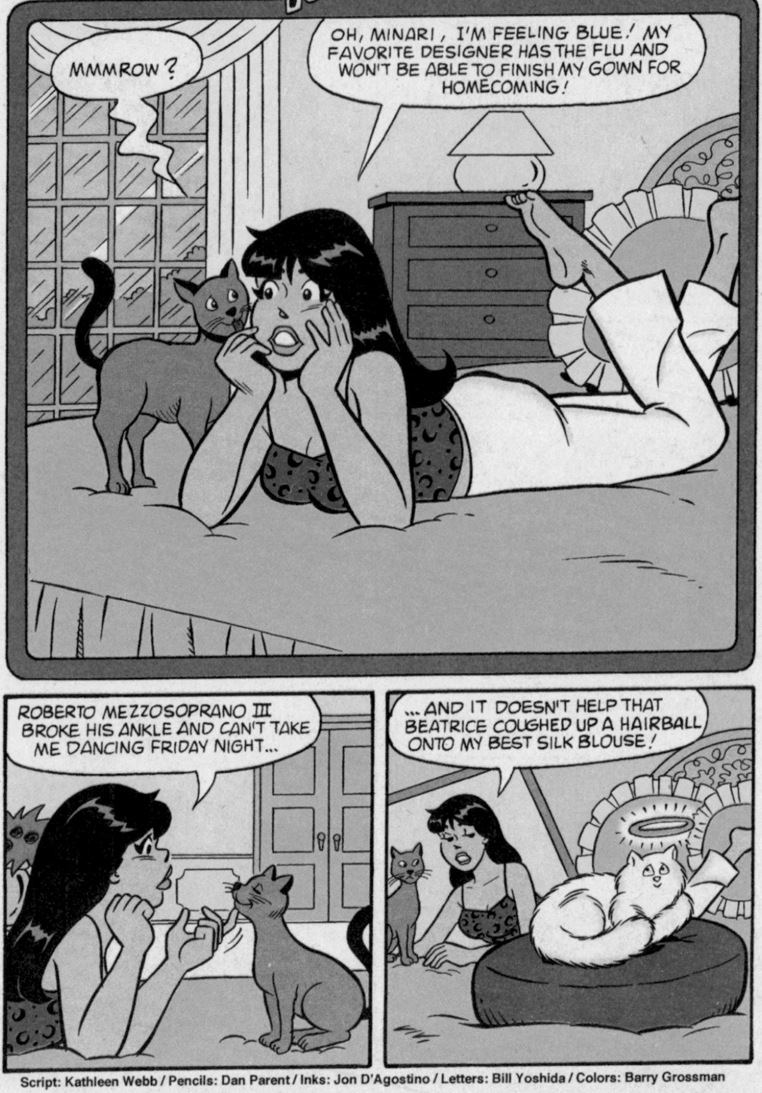
MMMROW?
OH, MINARI, I'M FEELING BLUE! MY FAVORITE DESIGNER HAS THE FLU AND WON'T BE ABLE TO FINISH MY GOWN FOR HOMECOMING!
ROBERTO MEZZOSOPRANO III BROKE HIS ANKLE AND CAN'T TAKE ME DANCING FRIDAY NIGHT...
...AND IT DOESN'T HELP THAT BEATRICE COUGHED UP A HAIRBALL ONTO MY BEST SILK BLOUSE!

Script: Kathleen Webb / Pencils: Dan Parent / Inks: Jon D'Agostino / Letters: Bill Yoshida / Colors: Barry Grossman

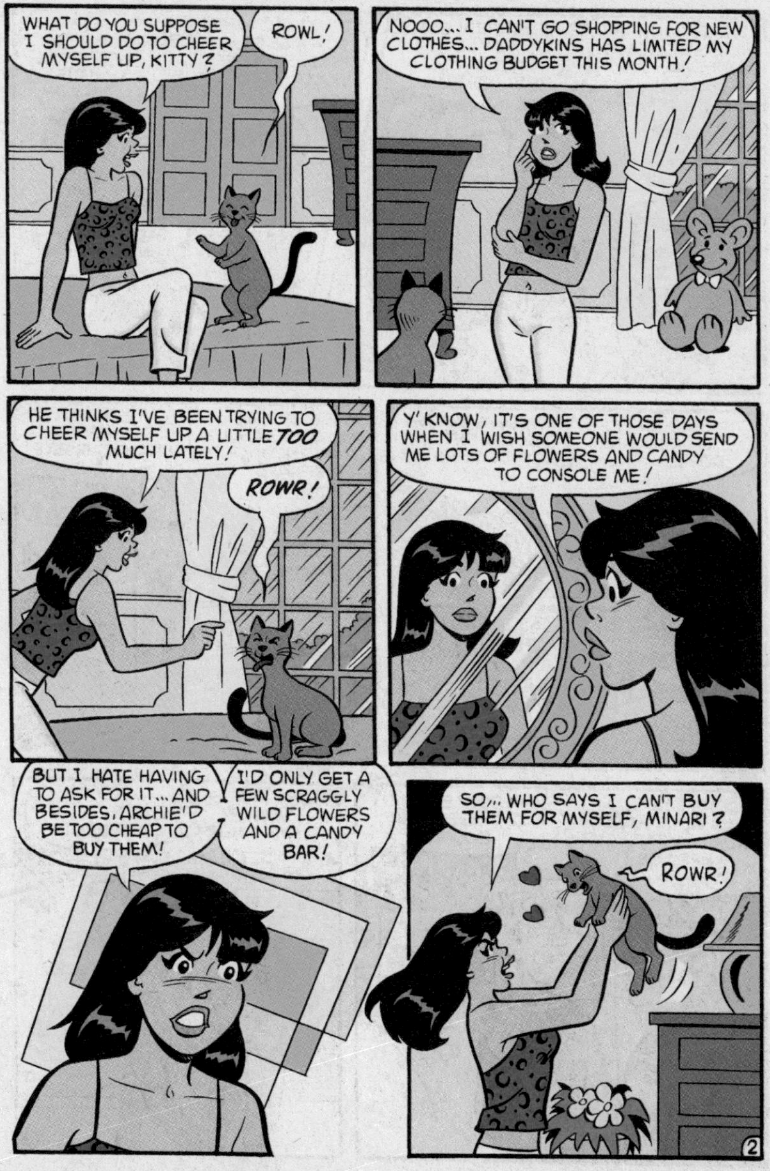
WHAT DO YOU SUPPOSE I SHOULD DO TO CHEER MYSELF UP, KITTY?
ROWL!
NOOO... I CAN'T GO SHOPPING FOR NEW CLOTHES... DADDYKINS HAS LIMITED MY CLOTHING BUDGET THIS MONTH!
HE THINKS I'VE BEEN TRYING TO CHEER MYSELF UP A LITTLE TOO MUCH LATELY!
ROWR!
Y' KNOW, IT'S ONE OF THOSE DAYS WHEN I WISH SOMEONE WOULD SEND ME LOTS OF FLOWERS AND CANDY TO CONSOLE ME!
BUT I HATE HAVING TO ASK FOR IT... AND BESIDES, ARCHIE'D BE TOO CHEAP TO BUY THEM!
I'D ONLY GET A FEW SCRAGGLY WILD FLOWERS AND A CANDY BAR!
SO,.. WHO SAYS I CAN'T BUY THEM FOR MYSELF, MINARI?
ROWR!
2

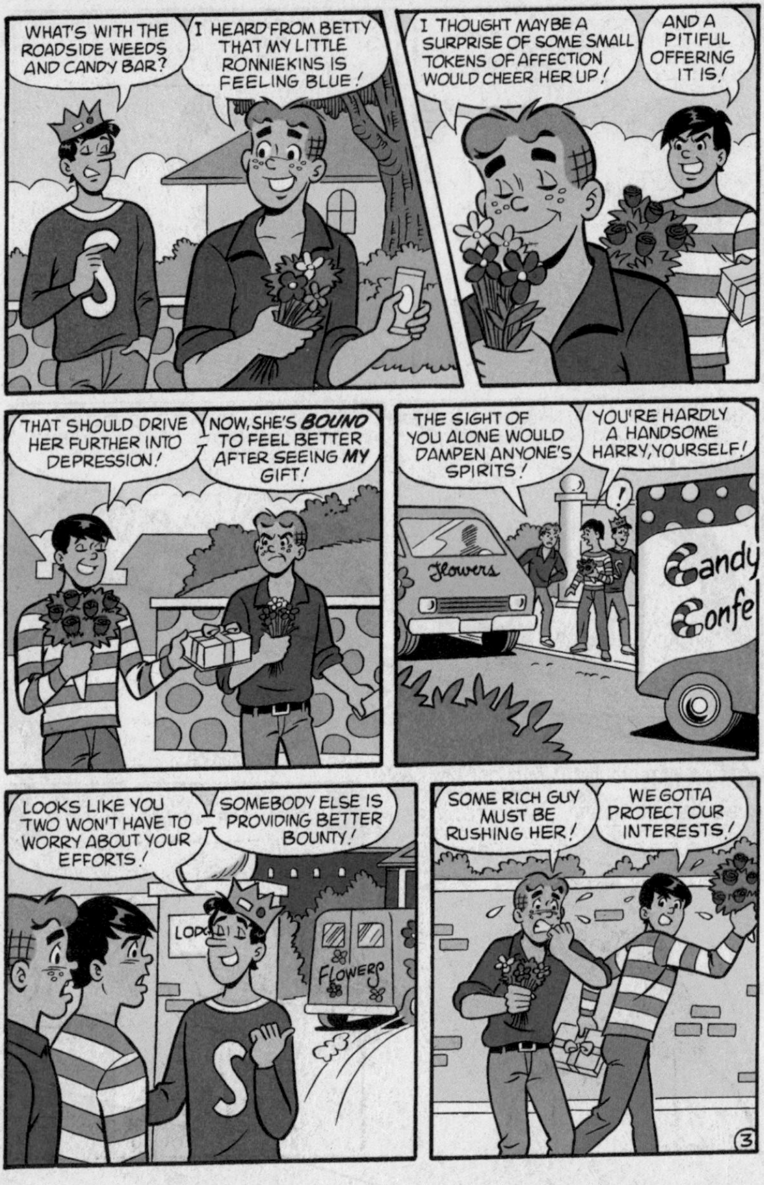
WHAT'S WITH THE ROADSIDE WEEDS AND CANDY BAR?
I HEARD FROM BETTY THAT MY LITTLE RONNIEKINS IS FEELING BLUE!
I THOUGHT MAYBE A SURPRISE OF SOME SMALL TOKENS OF AFFECTION WOULD CHEER HER UP!
AND A PITIFUL OFFERING IT IS!
THAT SHOULD DRIVE HER FURTHER INTO DEPRESSION!
NOW, SHE'S BOUND TO FEEL BETTER AFTER SEEING MY GIFT!
THE SIGHT OF YOU ALONE WOULD DAMPEN ANYONE'S SPIRITS!
YOU'RE HARDLY A HANDSOME HARRY, YOURSELF!
!
Flowers
Candy Confe
LOOKS LIKE YOU TWO WON'T HAVE TO WORRY ABOUT YOUR EFFORTS!
SOMEBODY ELSE IS PROVIDING BETTER BOUNTY!
FLOWERS
SOME RICH GUY MUST BE RUSHING HER!
WE GOTTA PROTECT OUR INTERESTS!
3

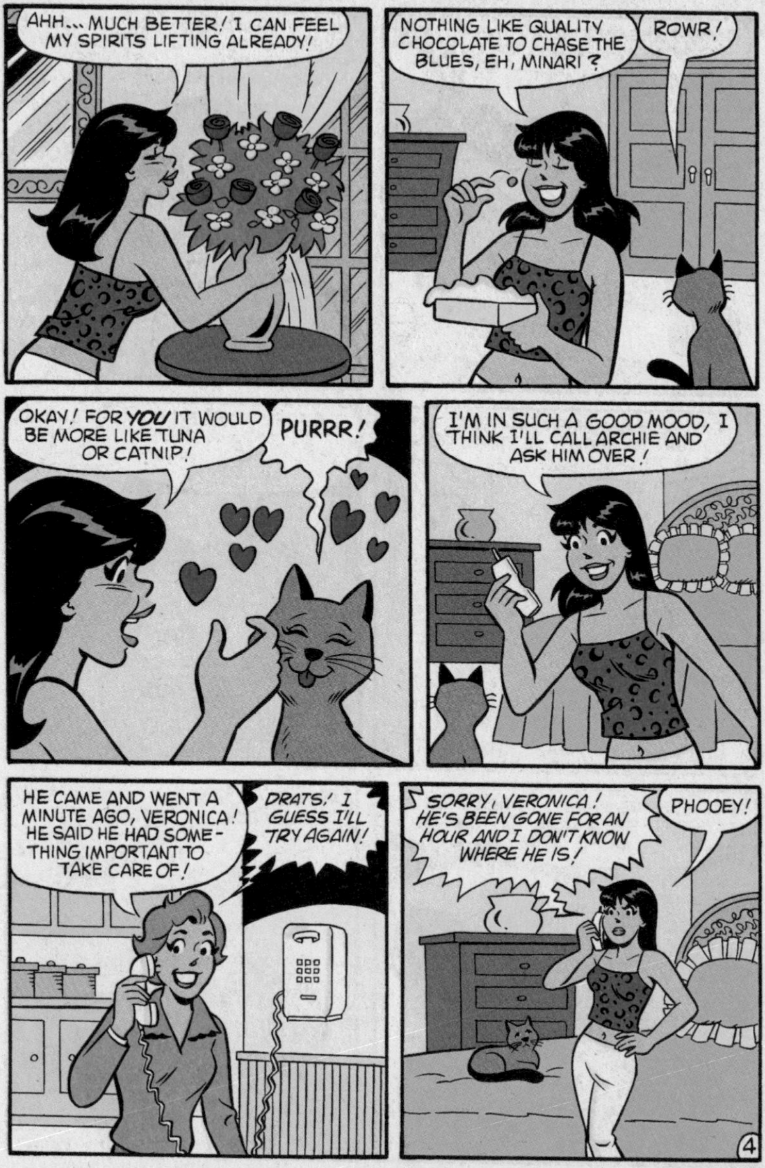
AHH... MUCH BETTER! I CAN FEEL MY SPIRITS LIFTING ALREADY!
NOTHING LIKE QUALITY CHOCOLATE TO CHASE THE BLUES, EH, MINARI ?
ROWR!
OKAY! FOR YOU IT WOULD BE MORE LIKE TUNA OR CATNIP!
PURRR!
I'M IN SUCH A GOOD MOOD, I THINK I'LL CALL ARCHIE AND ASK HIM OVER!
HE CAME AND WENT A MINUTE AGO, VERONICA! HE SAID HE HAD SOME-THING IMPORTANT TO TAKE CARE OF!
DRATS! I GUESS I'LL TRY AGAIN!
SORRY, VERONICA! HE'S BEEN GONE FOR AN HOUR AND I DON'T KNOW WHERE HE IS!
PHOOEY!
4

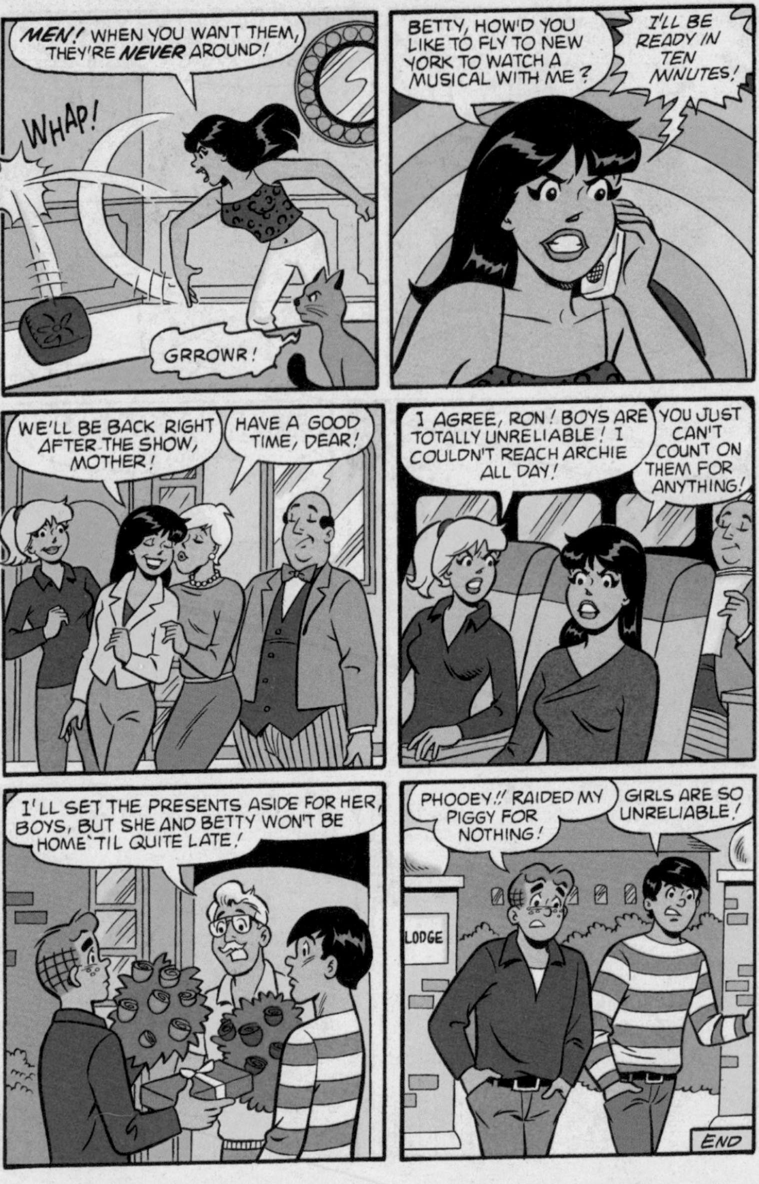
MEN! WHEN YOU WANT THEM, THEY'RE NEVER AROUND!
WHAP!
GRROWR!
BETTY, HOW'D YOU LIKE TO FLY TO NEW YORK TO WATCH A MUSICAL WITH ME?
I'LL BE READY IN TEN MINUTES!
WE'LL BE BACK RIGHT AFTER THE SHOW, MOTHER!
HAVE A GOOD TIME, DEAR!
I AGREE, RON! BOYS ARE TOTALLY UNRELIABLE! I COULDN'T REACH ARCHIE ALL DAY!
YOU JUST CAN'T COUNT ON THEM FOR ANYTHING!
I'LL SET THE PRESENTS ASIDE FOR HER, BOYS, BUT SHE AND BETTY WON'T BE HOME 'TIL QUITE LATE!
PHOOEY!! RAIDED MY PIGGY FOR NOTHING!
GIRLS ARE SO UNRELIABLE!
LODGE
END

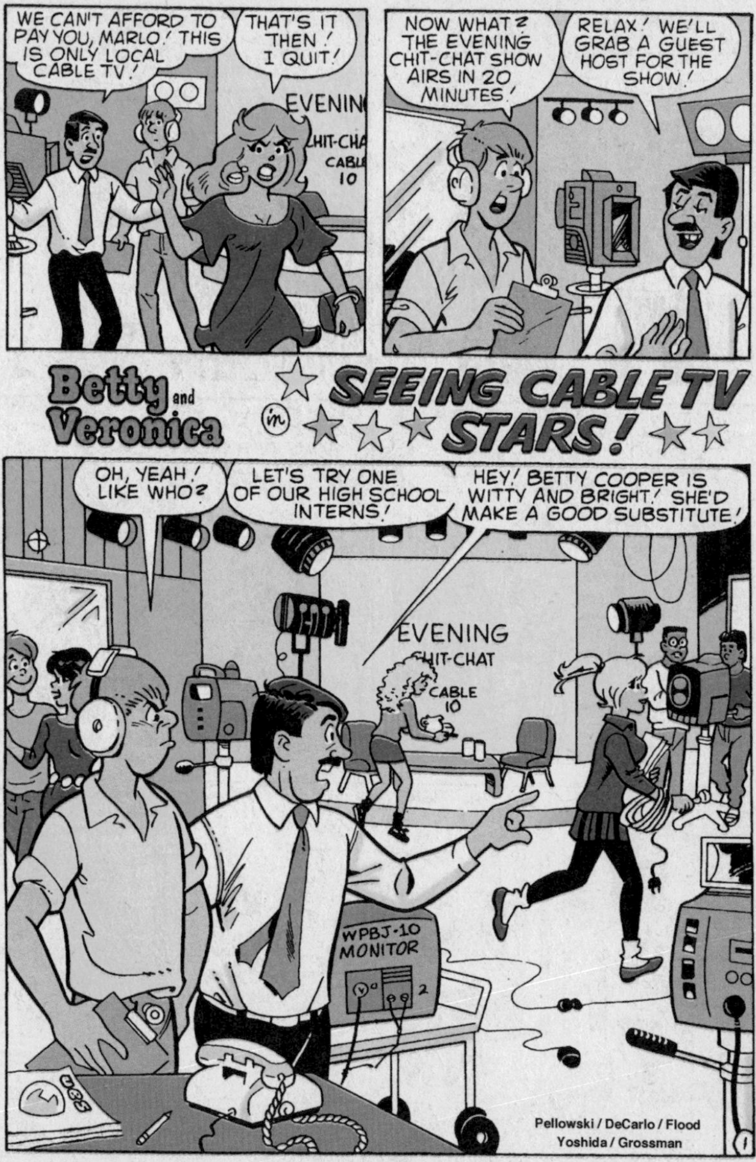
WE CAN'T AFFORD TO PAY YOU, MARLO! THIS IS ONLY LOCAL CABLE TV!
THAT'S IT THEN! I QUIT!
EVENING CHIT-CHA CABLE 10
NOW WHAT? THE EVENING CHIT-CHAT SHOW AIRS IN 20 MINUTES!
RELAX! WE'LL GRAB A GUEST HOST FOR THE SHOW!
Betty and Veronica in SEEING CABLE TV STARS!
OH, YEAH! LIKE WHO?
LET'S TRY ONE OF OUR HIGH SCHOOL INTERNS!
HEY! BETTY COOPER IS WITTY AND BRIGHT! SHE'D MAKE A GOOD SUBSTITUTE!
EVENING CHIT-CHAT CABLE 10
WPBJ-10 MONITOR
Pellowski / DeCarlo / Flood
Yoshida / Grossman
1

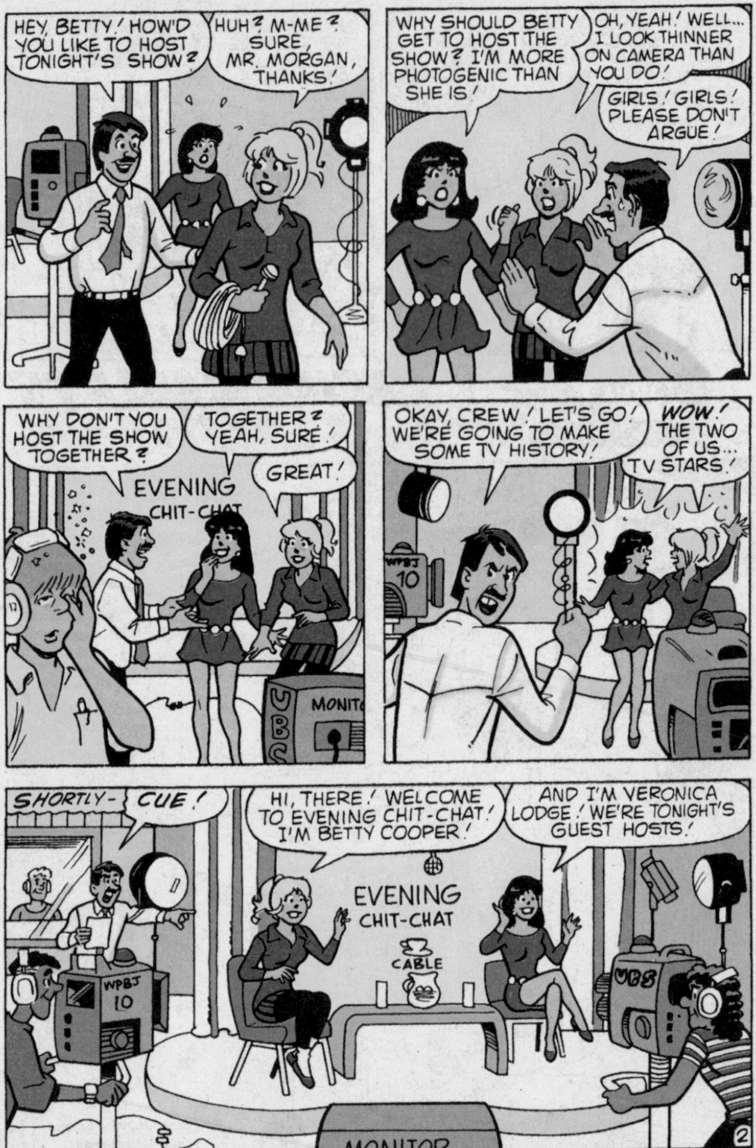

HEY, BETTY! HOW'D YOU LIKE TO HOST TONIGHT'S SHOW?
HUH? M-ME? SURE, MR. MORGAN, THANKS!
WHY SHOULD BETTY GET TO HOST THE SHOW? I'M MORE PHOTOGENIC THAN SHE IS!
OH, YEAH! WELL... I LOOK THINNER ON CAMERA THAN YOU DO!
GIRLS! GIRLS! PLEASE DON'T ARGUE!
WHY DON'T YOU HOST THE SHOW TOGETHER?
TOGETHER? YEAH, SURE!
GREAT!
EVENING CHIT-CHAT
MONITO
UBC
OKAY, CREW! LET'S GO! WE'RE GOING TO MAKE SOME TV HISTORY!
WOW! THE TWO OF US... TV STARS!
WPBJ 10
SHORTLY-
CUE!
HI, THERE! WELCOME TO EVENING CHIT-CHAT! I'M BETTY COOPER!
AND I'M VERONICA LODGE! WE'RE TONIGHT'S GUEST HOSTS!
EVENING CHIT-CHAT
CABLE
WPBJ 10
UBS
MONITOR
2

TONIGHT'S TOPIC IS... GULP! W-WHAT IS TONIGHT'S TOPIC, VERONICA?

HUH? DON'T ASK ME! I DON'T KNOW!

SOPHISTICATED CHIT-CHAT

OH, MY GOSH! THEY CAN'T THINK OF ANYTHING TO SAY!

PSSST! FAKE IT, GIRLS! TALK ABOUT ANYTHING THAT POPS INTO YOUR MIND! PRETEND THE CAMERAS AREN'T THERE!

SOPHISTICATED CHIT-CHAT

WPBJ 10

MONITO

AHH... SAY BETTY, DID YOU HEAR MIDGE WENT OUT WITH REGGIE MANTLE LAST SATURDAY?

NO! REALLY?

PHEW!

I BET THAT MADE BIG MOOSE REAL MAD!

MOOSE DOESN'T KNOW! HE THINKS MIDGE WENT TO VISIT A SICK FRIEND!

AFTERNOON CHIT-CHAT

THAT'S AS BAD AS CHUCK TELLING NANCY HE COULDN'T TAKE HER OUT BECAUSE HE HAD TO STUDY WITH DILTON!

DIDN'T THEY STUDY?

HA! I OVERHEARD DILTON TELL JUG THEY WENT TO A BEAUTY CONTEST TO STUDY THE CONTESTANTS!

CHUCK'S LUCKY NANCY DIDN'T FIND OUT!

3

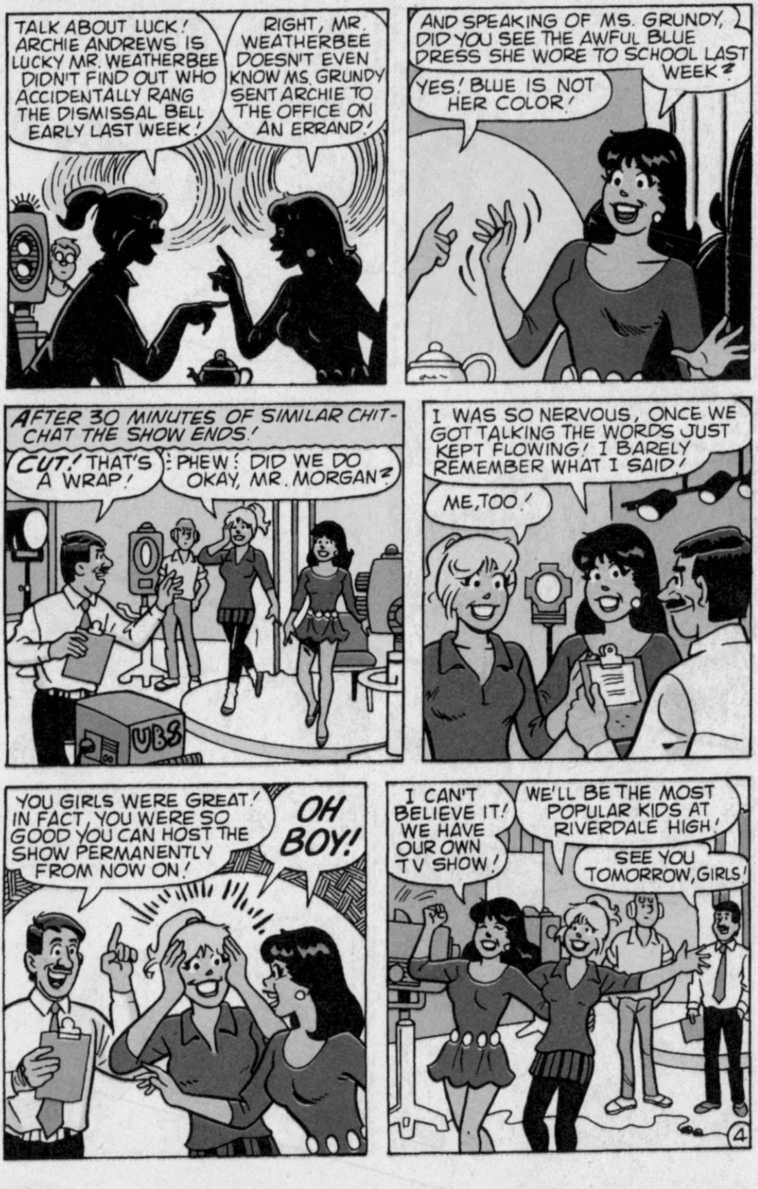
TALK ABOUT LUCK! ARCHIE ANDREWS IS LUCKY MR. WEATHERBEE DIDN'T FIND OUT WHO ACCIDENTALLY RANG THE DISMISSAL BELL EARLY LAST WEEK!
RIGHT, MR. WEATHERBEE DOESN'T EVEN KNOW MS. GRUNDY SENT ARCHIE TO THE OFFICE ON AN ERRAND!
AND SPEAKING OF MS. GRUNDY, DID YOU SEE THE AWFUL BLUE DRESS SHE WORE TO SCHOOL LAST WEEK?
YES! BLUE IS NOT HER COLOR!
AFTER 30 MINUTES OF SIMILAR CHIT-CHAT THE SHOW ENDS!
CUT! THAT'S A WRAP!
PHEW! DID WE DO OKAY, MR. MORGAN?
UBS
I WAS SO NERVOUS, ONCE WE GOT TALKING THE WORDS JUST KEPT FLOWING! I BARELY REMEMBER WHAT I SAID!
ME, TOO!
YOU GIRLS WERE GREAT! IN FACT, YOU WERE SO GOOD YOU CAN HOST THE SHOW PERMANENTLY FROM NOW ON!
OH BOY!
I CAN'T BELIEVE IT! WE HAVE OUR OWN TV SHOW!
WE'LL BE THE MOST POPULAR KIDS AT RIVERDALE HIGH!
SEE YOU TOMORROW, GIRLS!
4

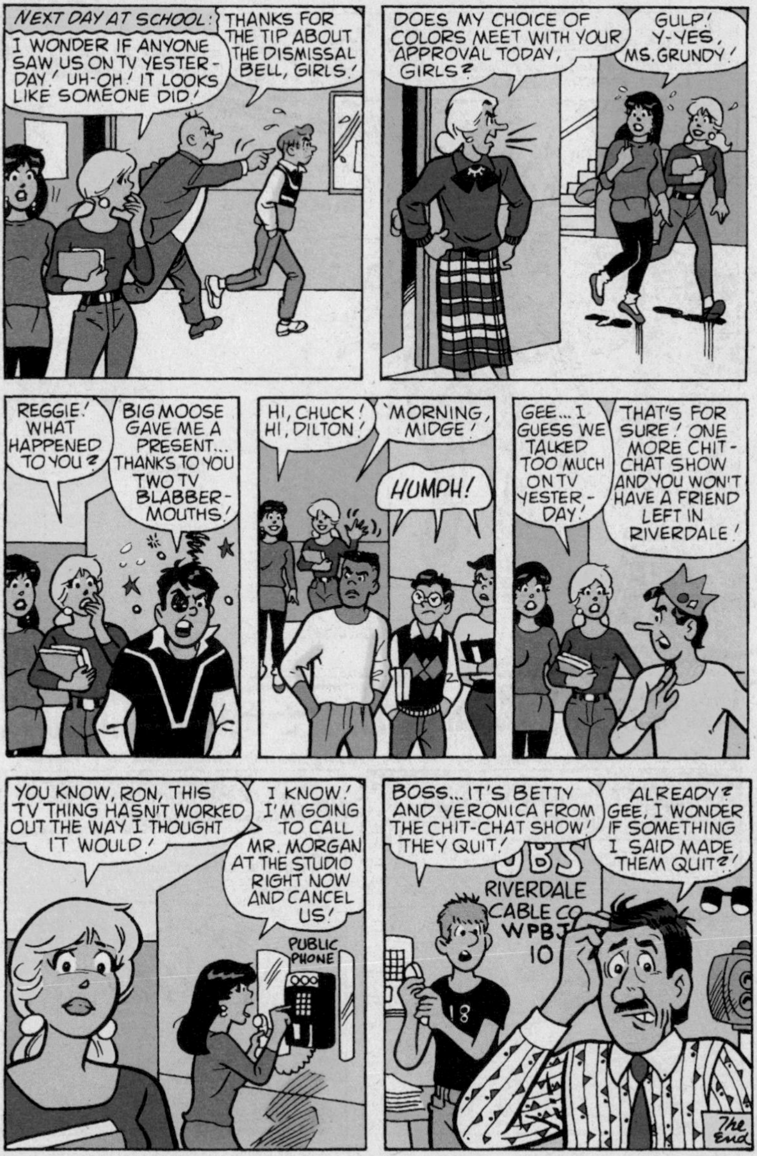
NEXT DAY AT SCHOOL:
I WONDER IF ANYONE SAW US ON TV YESTERDAY! UH-OH! IT LOOKS LIKE SOMEONE DID!
THANKS FOR THE TIP ABOUT THE DISMISSAL BELL, GIRLS!
DOES MY CHOICE OF COLORS MEET WITH YOUR APPROVAL TODAY, GIRLS?
GULP! Y-YES, MS. GRUNDY!
REGGIE! WHAT HAPPENED TO YOU?
BIG MOOSE GAVE ME A PRESENT... THANKS TO YOU TWO TV BLABBERMOUTHS!
HI, CHUCK! HI, DILTON!
'MORNING, MIDGE!
HUMPH!
GEE... I GUESS WE TALKED TOO MUCH ON TV YESTERDAY!
THAT'S FOR SURE! ONE MORE CHIT-CHAT SHOW AND YOU WON'T HAVE A FRIEND LEFT IN RIVERDALE!
YOU KNOW, RON, THIS TV THING HASN'T WORKED OUT THE WAY I THOUGHT IT WOULD!
I KNOW! I'M GOING TO CALL MR. MORGAN AT THE STUDIO RIGHT NOW AND CANCEL US!
PUBLIC PHONE
BOSS... IT'S BETTY AND VERONICA FROM THE CHIT-CHAT SHOW! THEY QUIT!
ALREADY? GEE, I WONDER IF SOMETHING I SAID MADE THEM QUIT?!
RIVERDALE CABLE CO WPBJ 10
The End

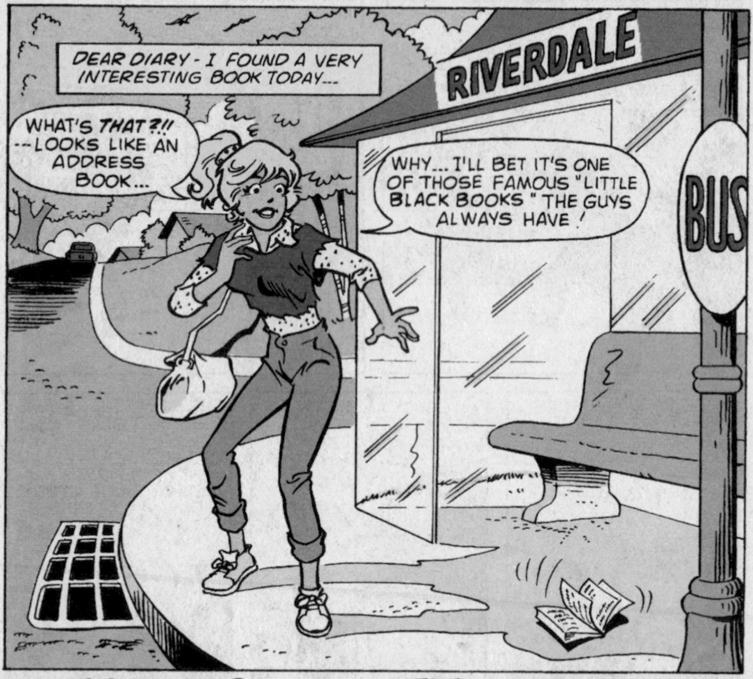
DEAR DIARY - I FOUND A VERY INTERESTING BOOK TODAY...
RIVERDALE
WHAT'S THAT?!! --LOOKS LIKE AN ADDRESS BOOK...
WHY... I'LL BET IT'S ONE OF THOSE FAMOUS "LITTLE BLACK BOOKS" THE GUYS ALWAYS HAVE!
BUS

Betty's Diary LITTLE BLACKMAIL BOOK

Script: Kathleen Webb / Pencils: Doug Crane / Inks: Mike Esposito / Letters: Bill Yoshida / Colors: Barry Grossman

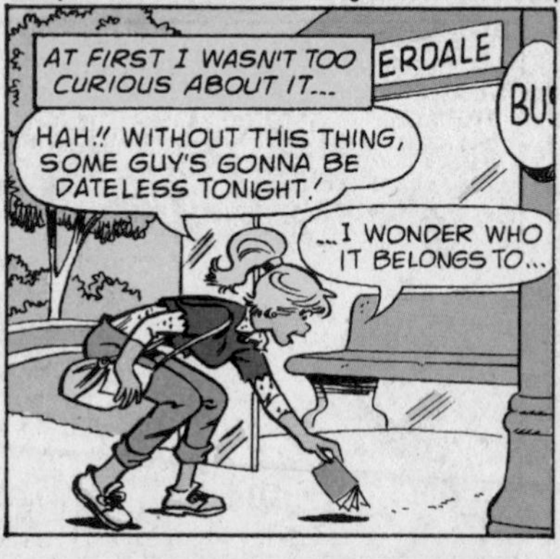
AT FIRST I WASN'T TOO CURIOUS ABOUT IT...
ERDALE
BUS
HAH!! WITHOUT THIS THING, SOME GUY'S GONNA BE DATELESS TONIGHT!
...I WONDER WHO IT BELONGS TO...

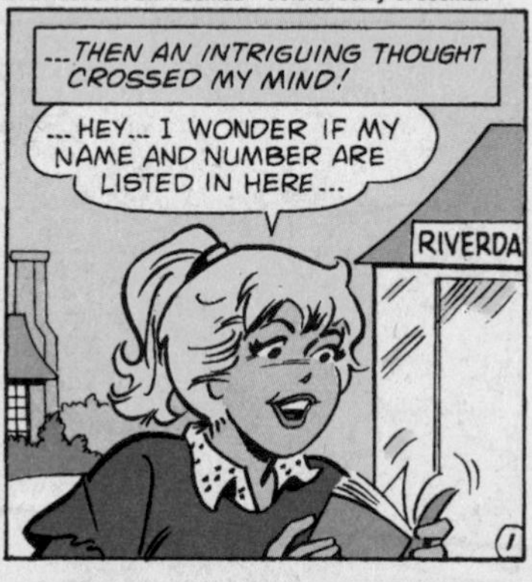
...THEN AN INTRIGUING THOUGHT CROSSED MY MIND!
...HEY... I WONDER IF MY NAME AND NUMBER ARE LISTED IN HERE...
RIVERDA
1

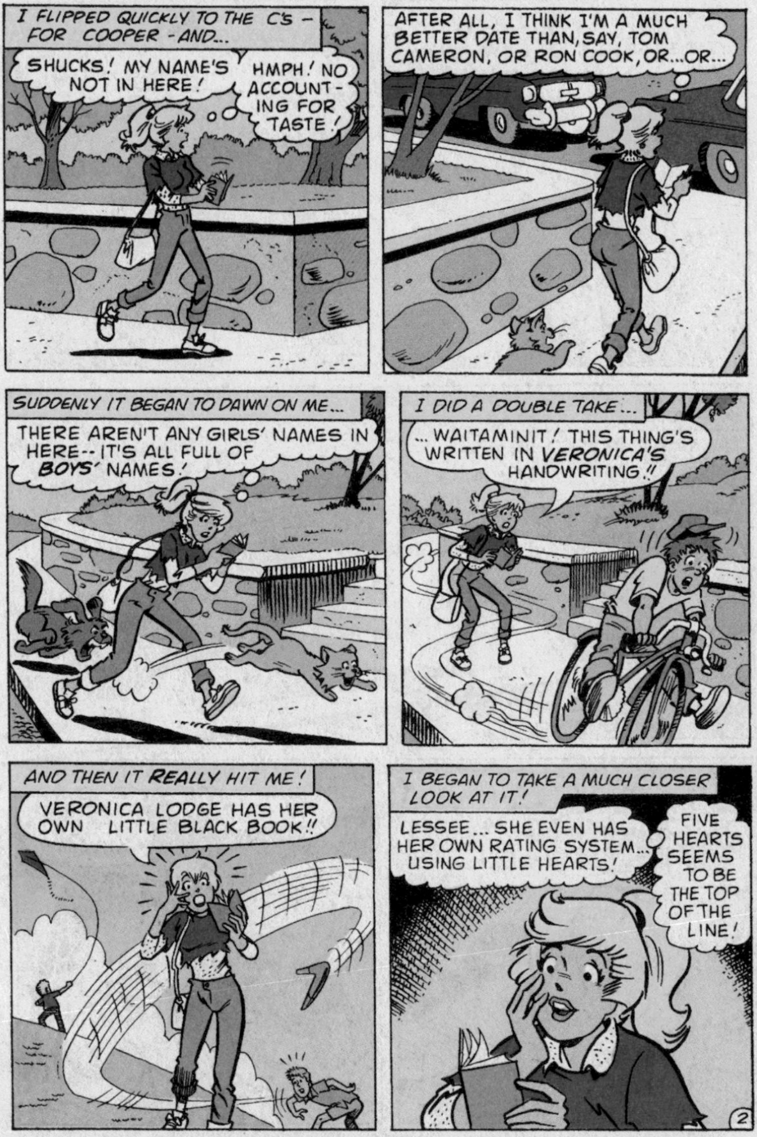
I FLIPPED QUICKLY TO THE C'S — FOR COOPER - AND...
SHUCKS! MY NAME'S NOT IN HERE!
HMPH! NO ACCOUNT-ING FOR TASTE!
AFTER ALL, I THINK I'M A MUCH BETTER DATE THAN, SAY, TOM CAMERON, OR RON COOK, OR...OR...
SUDDENLY IT BEGAN TO DAWN ON ME...
THERE AREN'T ANY GIRLS' NAMES IN HERE-- IT'S ALL FULL OF BOYS' NAMES!
I DID A DOUBLE TAKE...
...WAITAMINIT! THIS THING'S WRITTEN IN VERONICA'S HANDWRITING!!
AND THEN IT REALLY HIT ME!
VERONICA LODGE HAS HER OWN LITTLE BLACK BOOK!!
I BEGAN TO TAKE A MUCH CLOSER LOOK AT IT!
LESSEE... SHE EVEN HAS HER OWN RATING SYSTEM... USING LITTLE HEARTS!
FIVE HEARTS SEEMS TO BE THE TOP OF THE LINE!
2

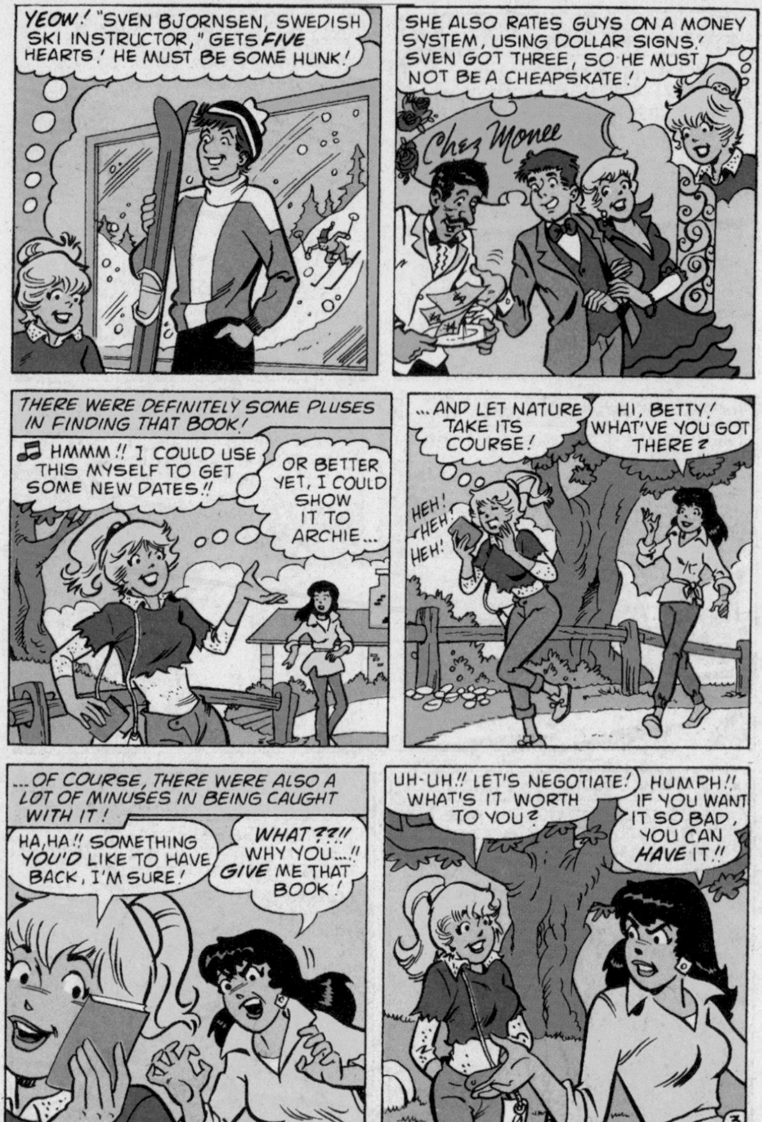
YEOW! "SVEN BJORNSEN, SWEDISH SKI INSTRUCTOR," GETS FIVE HEARTS! HE MUST BE SOME HUNK!
SHE ALSO RATES GUYS ON A MONEY SYSTEM, USING DOLLAR SIGNS! SVEN GOT THREE, SO HE MUST NOT BE A CHEAPSKATE!
Chez Monee
THERE WERE DEFINITELY SOME PLUSES IN FINDING THAT BOOK!
HMMM!! I COULD USE THIS MYSELF TO GET SOME NEW DATES!!
OR BETTER YET, I COULD SHOW IT TO ARCHIE...
...AND LET NATURE TAKE ITS COURSE!
HEH! HEH! HEH!
HI, BETTY! WHAT'VE YOU GOT THERE?
...OF COURSE, THERE WERE ALSO A LOT OF MINUSES IN BEING CAUGHT WITH IT!
HA,HA!! SOMETHING YOU'D LIKE TO HAVE BACK, I'M SURE!
WHAT??!! WHY YOU...!! GIVE ME THAT BOOK!
UH-UH!! LET'S NEGOTIATE! WHAT'S IT WORTH TO YOU?
HUMPH!! IF YOU WANT IT SO BAD, YOU CAN HAVE IT!!
3

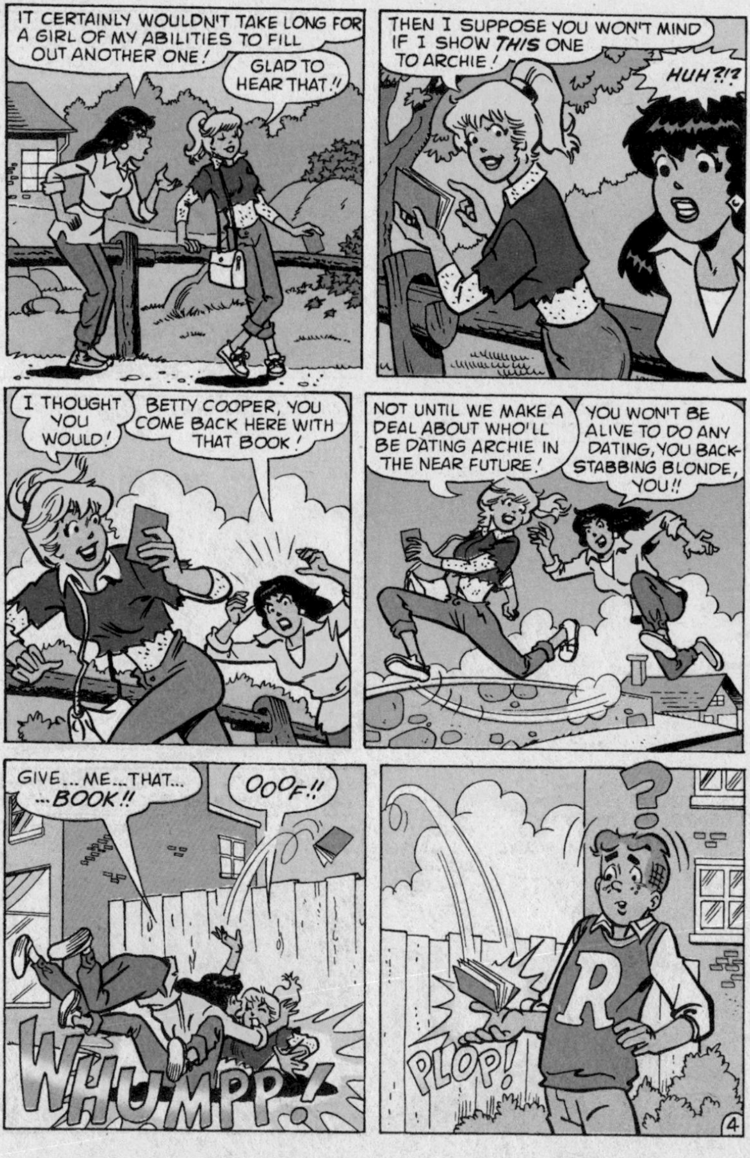
IT CERTAINLY WOULDN'T TAKE LONG FOR A GIRL OF MY ABILITIES TO FILL OUT ANOTHER ONE!
GLAD TO HEAR THAT!!
THEN I SUPPOSE YOU WON'T MIND IF I SHOW THIS ONE TO ARCHIE!
HUH?!?
I THOUGHT YOU WOULD!
BETTY COOPER, YOU COME BACK HERE WITH THAT BOOK!
NOT UNTIL WE MAKE A DEAL ABOUT WHO'LL BE DATING ARCHIE IN THE NEAR FUTURE!
YOU WON'T BE ALIVE TO DO ANY DATING, YOU BACK-STABBING BLONDE, YOU!!
GIVE... ME... THAT... ...BOOK!!
OOOF!!
WHUMPP!
?
PLOP!
4

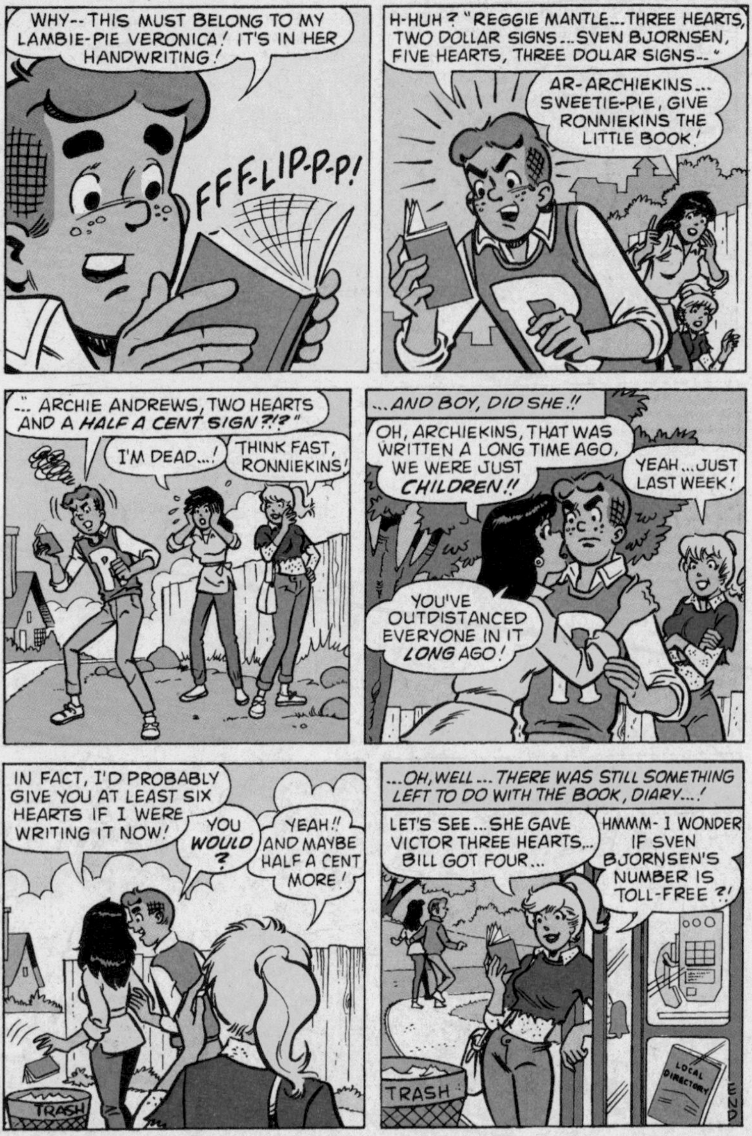

WHY-- THIS MUST BELONG TO MY LAMBIE-PIE VERONICA! IT'S IN HER HANDWRITING!
FFF-LIP-P-P!
H-HUH? "REGGIE MANTLE... THREE HEARTS, TWO DOLLAR SIGNS... SVEN BJORNSEN, FIVE HEARTS, THREE DOLLAR SIGNS--"
AR-ARCHIEKINS... SWEETIE-PIE, GIVE RONNIEKINS THE LITTLE BOOK!
"... ARCHIE ANDREWS, TWO HEARTS AND A HALF A CENT SIGN?!?"
I'M DEAD...!
THINK FAST, RONNIEKINS!
...AND BOY, DID SHE!!
OH, ARCHIEKINS, THAT WAS WRITTEN A LONG TIME AGO, WE WERE JUST CHILDREN!!
YEAH... JUST LAST WEEK!
YOU'VE OUTDISTANCED EVERYONE IN IT LONG AGO!
IN FACT, I'D PROBABLY GIVE YOU AT LEAST SIX HEARTS IF I WERE WRITING IT NOW!
YOU WOULD?
YEAH!! AND MAYBE HALF A CENT MORE!
TRASH
...OH, WELL... THERE WAS STILL SOMETHING LEFT TO DO WITH THE BOOK, DIARY...!
LET'S SEE... SHE GAVE VICTOR THREE HEARTS,... BILL GOT FOUR...
HMMM- I WONDER IF SVEN BJORNSEN'S NUMBER IS TOLL-FREE?!
TRASH
LOCAL DIRECTORY
END

Sight for Sore Eyes
Betty & Veronica #67, 1961
by Frank Doyle, Dan DeCarlo, Rudy Lapick and Vince DeCarlo

Comics are known for their entertainment value, but I've always found their abilities to be time capsules really fascinating. For example, this little tale has some of the wacky lingo and hairdos (or should I say, a particular hair-don't) found in the far-out '60s. The girls act as trendsetters, also acting as a microcosm for teenagers of that time. Now that this has become rather academic, let me just end with a traditional '60s sentence. Ahem. "Unless you're thicker than a $5 malt, you should start reading this outta sight story!"

Jonathan Betancourt
Director - Book Sales & Operations,
Archie Comics

Foul Bawl
Archie Giant Series #13, 1961
by Frank Doyle, Dan DeCarlo, Rudy Lapick, Vince DeCarlo and Barry Grossman

Betty, Veronica (and the rest of the Riverdale gang) taught me how to read... Three older sisters in the workforce when I was a wee lad meant paydays brought comics for their baby brother. It started out with them reading the words to me, and me following along in the pictures, but led me to teaching myself to read. I was always a Betty kinda guy… she was the girl next door… athletic, perky… and when I look at my wife, I can't help but think that Betty might have been an early influence for future decisions.

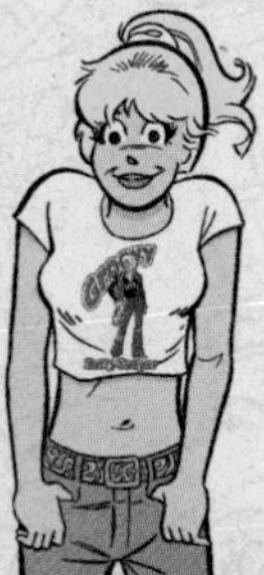

Howard Mackie
Renowned comic book Writer and Editor

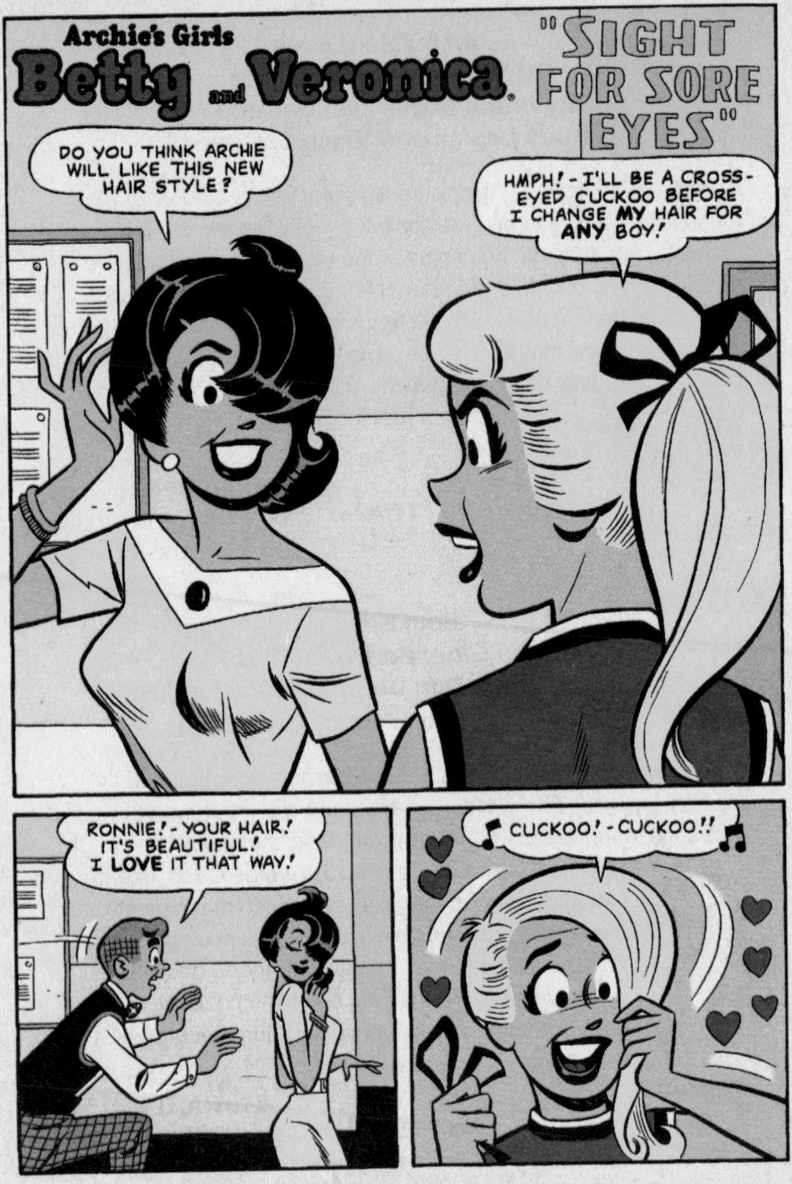
Archie's Girls
Betty and Veronica
"SIGHT FOR SORE EYES"
DO YOU THINK ARCHIE WILL LIKE THIS NEW HAIR STYLE?
HMPH! - I'LL BE A CROSS-EYED CUCKOO BEFORE I CHANGE MY HAIR FOR ANY BOY!
RONNIE! - YOUR HAIR! IT'S BEAUTIFUL! I LOVE IT THAT WAY!
CUCKOO! - CUCKOO!!

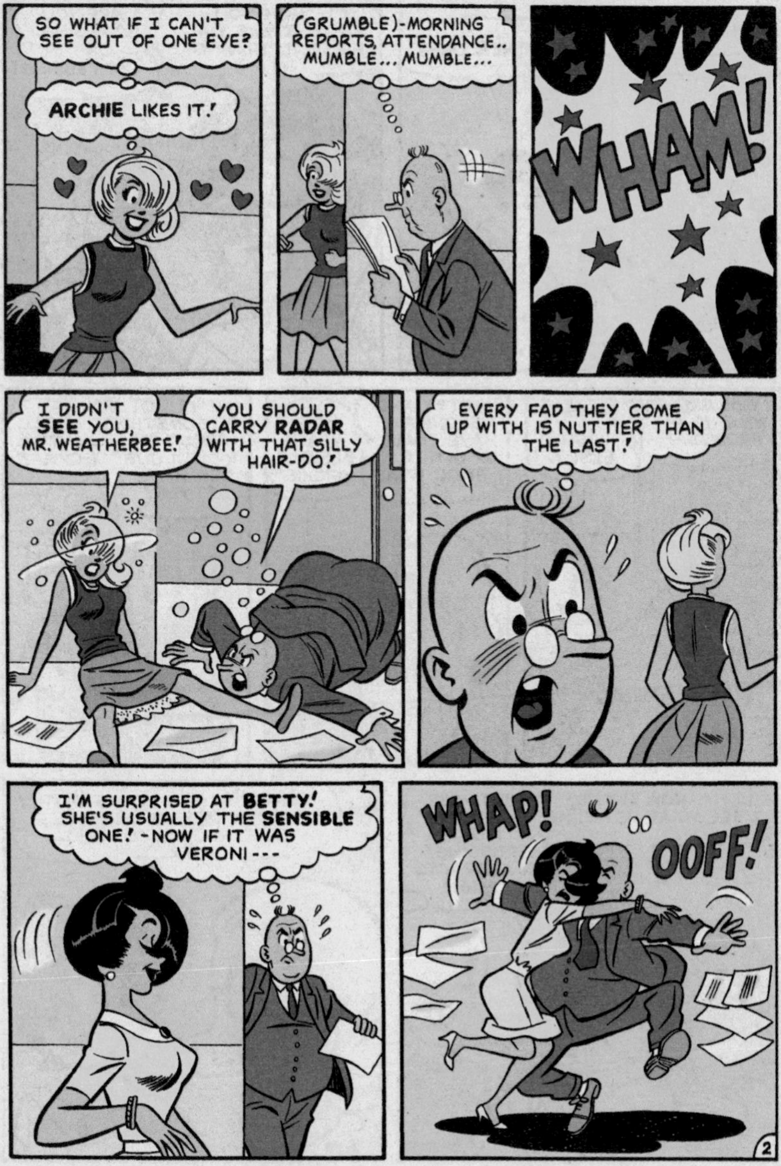

SO WHAT IF I CAN'T SEE OUT OF ONE EYE?
ARCHIE LIKES IT!
(GRUMBLE)-MORNING REPORTS, ATTENDANCE.. MUMBLE... MUMBLE...
WHAM!
I DIDN'T SEE YOU, MR. WEATHERBEE!
YOU SHOULD CARRY RADAR WITH THAT SILLY HAIR-DO!
EVERY FAD THEY COME UP WITH IS NUTTIER THAN THE LAST!
I'M SURPRISED AT BETTY! SHE'S USUALLY THE SENSIBLE ONE! -NOW IF IT WAS VERONI---
WHAP!
OOFF!

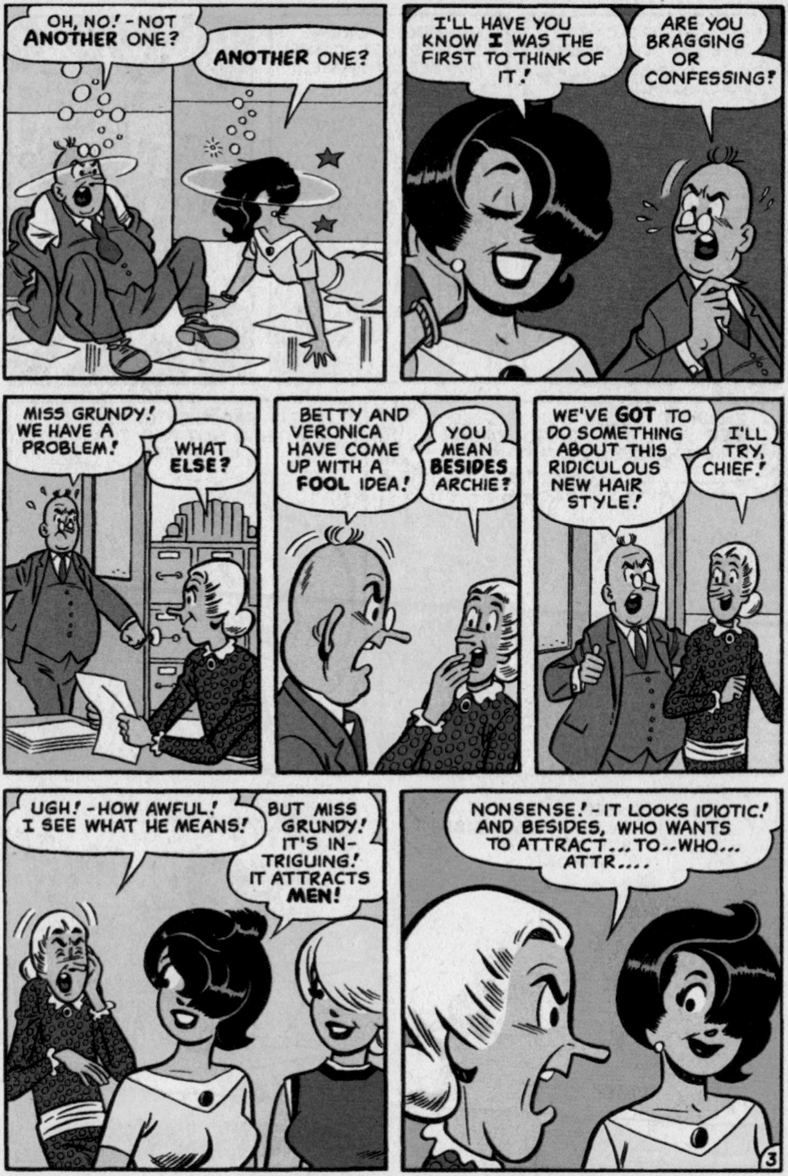

OH, NO! - NOT **ANOTHER** ONE?
ANOTHER ONE?
I'LL HAVE YOU KNOW **I** WAS THE FIRST TO THINK OF IT!
ARE YOU BRAGGING OR CONFESSING?
MISS GRUNDY! WE HAVE A PROBLEM!
WHAT **ELSE**?
BETTY AND VERONICA HAVE COME UP WITH A **FOOL** IDEA!
YOU MEAN **BESIDES** ARCHIE?
WE'VE **GOT** TO DO SOMETHING ABOUT THIS RIDICULOUS NEW HAIR STYLE!
I'LL TRY, CHIEF!
UGH! - HOW AWFUL! I SEE WHAT HE MEANS!
BUT MISS GRUNDY! IT'S IN-TRIGUING! IT ATTRACTS **MEN**!
NONSENSE! - IT LOOKS IDIOTIC! AND BESIDES, WHO WANTS TO ATTRACT... TO.. WHO... ATTR....
3

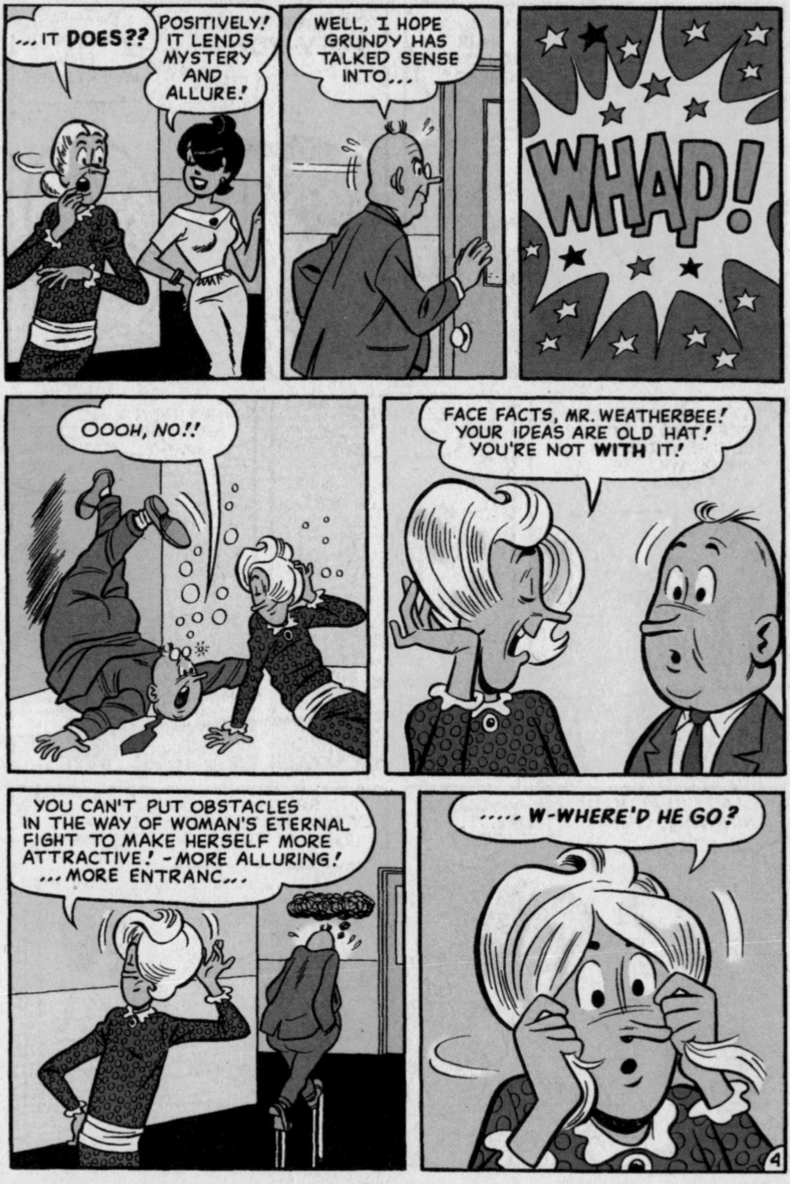
...IT DOES??
POSITIVELY! IT LENDS MYSTERY AND ALLURE!
WELL, I HOPE GRUNDY HAS TALKED SENSE INTO...
WHAP!
OOOH, NO!!
FACE FACTS, MR. WEATHERBEE! YOUR IDEAS ARE OLD HAT! YOU'RE NOT WITH IT!
YOU CAN'T PUT OBSTACLES IN THE WAY OF WOMAN'S ETERNAL FIGHT TO MAKE HERSELF MORE ATTRACTIVE! -MORE ALLURING! ...MORE ENTRANC...
..... W-WHERE'D HE GO?
4

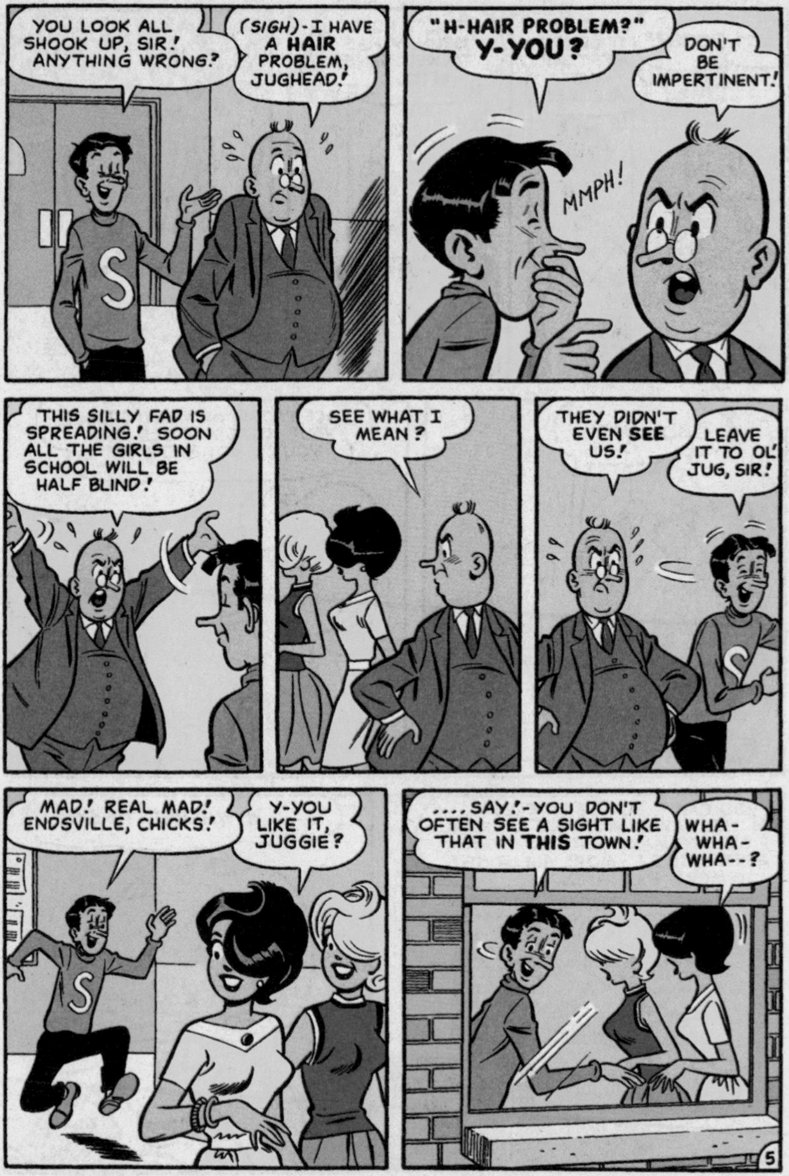
YOU LOOK ALL SHOOK UP, SIR! ANYTHING WRONG?
(SIGH)-I HAVE A HAIR PROBLEM, JUGHEAD!
"H-HAIR PROBLEM?" Y-YOU?
DON'T BE IMPERTINENT!
MMPH!
THIS SILLY FAD IS SPREADING! SOON ALL THE GIRLS IN SCHOOL WILL BE HALF BLIND!
SEE WHAT I MEAN?
THEY DIDN'T EVEN SEE US!
LEAVE IT TO OL' JUG, SIR!
MAD! REAL MAD! ENDSVILLE, CHICKS!
Y-YOU LIKE IT, JUGGIE?
....SAY!-YOU DON'T OFTEN SEE A SIGHT LIKE THAT IN THIS TOWN!
WHA-WHA-WHA--?

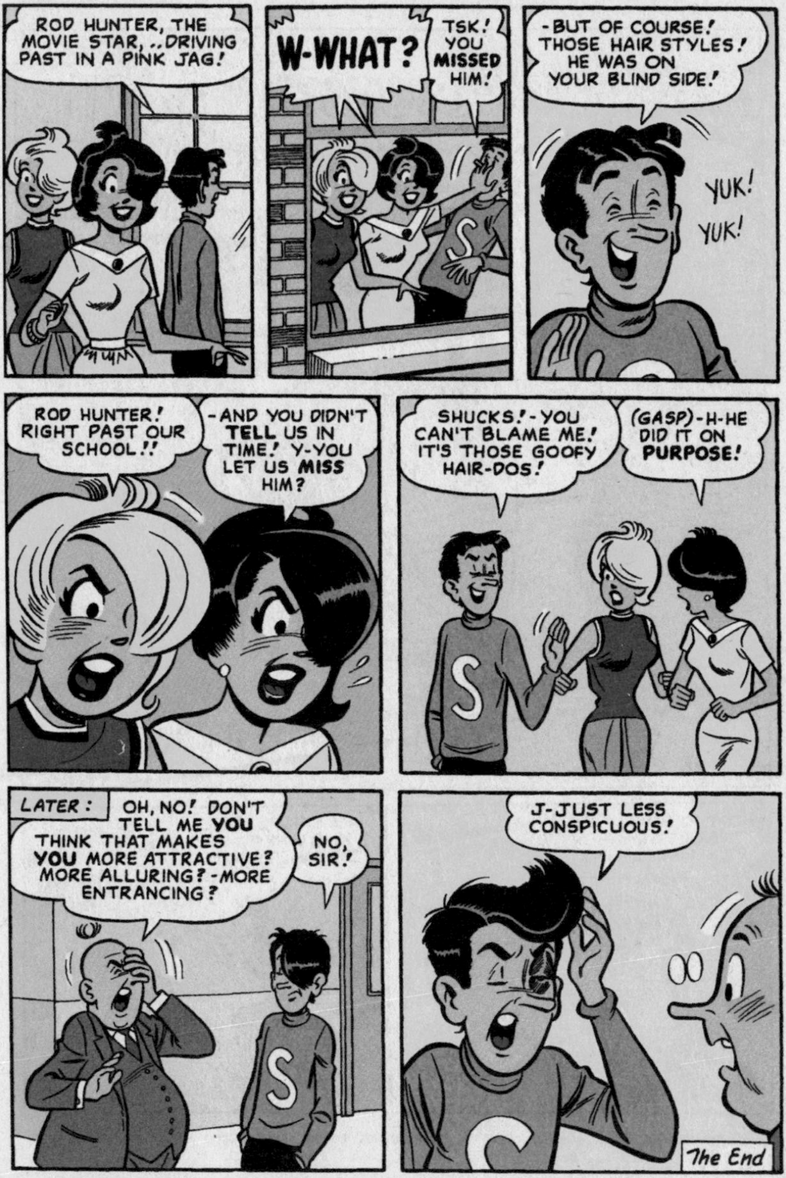
ROD HUNTER, THE MOVIE STAR, ..DRIVING PAST IN A PINK JAG!
W-WHAT?
TSK! YOU MISSED HIM!
-BUT OF COURSE! THOSE HAIR STYLES! HE WAS ON YOUR BLIND SIDE!
YUK! YUK!
ROD HUNTER! RIGHT PAST OUR SCHOOL!!
-AND YOU DIDN'T TELL US IN TIME! Y-YOU LET US MISS HIM?
SHUCKS! -YOU CAN'T BLAME ME! IT'S THOSE GOOFY HAIR-DOS!
(GASP)-H-HE DID IT ON PURPOSE!
LATER:
OH, NO! DON'T TELL ME YOU THINK THAT MAKES YOU MORE ATTRACTIVE? MORE ALLURING? -MORE ENTRANCING?
NO, SIR!
J-JUST LESS CONSPICUOUS!
The End

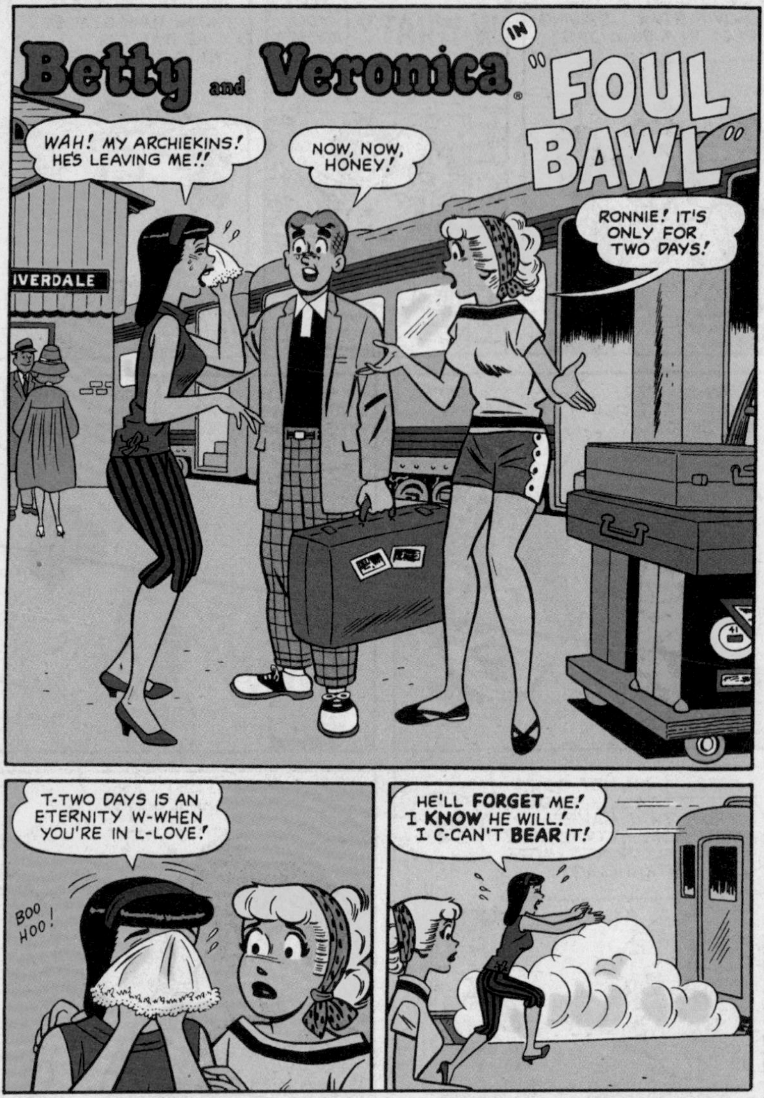
Betty and Veronica
IN
"FOUL BAWL"
WAH! MY ARCHIEKINS! HE'S LEAVING ME!!
NOW, NOW, HONEY!
RONNIE! IT'S ONLY FOR TWO DAYS!
IVERDALE
T-TWO DAYS IS AN ETERNITY W-WHEN YOU'RE IN L-LOVE!
BOO HOO!
HE'LL **FORGET** ME! I **KNOW** HE WILL! I C-CAN'T **BEAR** IT!

Script: **Frank Doyle** Pencils: **Dan DeCarlo** Inks: **Rudy Lapick** Letters: **Vince DeCarlo** Colors: **Barry Grossman**

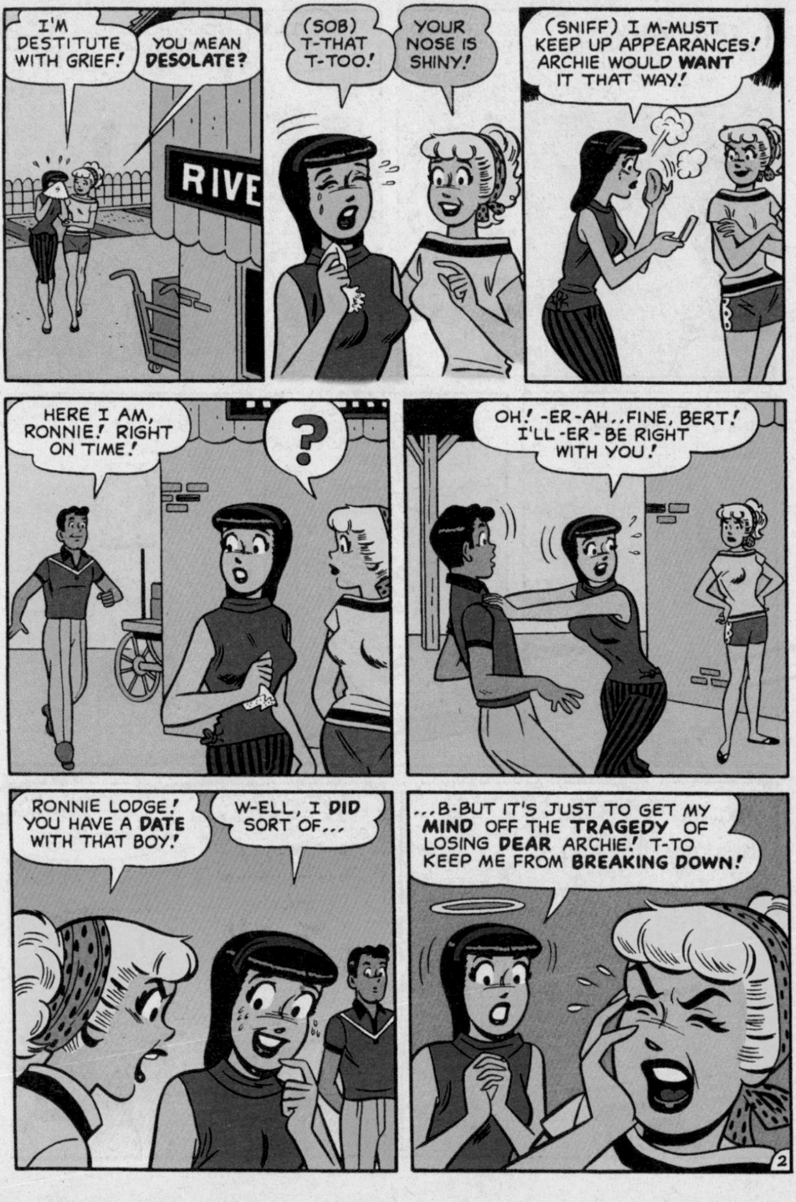
I'M DESTITUTE WITH GRIEF!
YOU MEAN DESOLATE?
RIVE
(SOB) T-THAT T-TOO!
YOUR NOSE IS SHINY!
(SNIFF) I M-MUST KEEP UP APPEARANCES! ARCHIE WOULD WANT IT THAT WAY!
HERE I AM, RONNIE! RIGHT ON TIME!
?
OH! -ER-AH..FINE, BERT! I'LL -ER - BE RIGHT WITH YOU!
RONNIE LODGE! YOU HAVE A DATE WITH THAT BOY!
W-ELL, I DID SORT OF...
...B-BUT IT'S JUST TO GET MY MIND OFF THE TRAGEDY OF LOSING DEAR ARCHIE! T-TO KEEP ME FROM BREAKING DOWN!
2

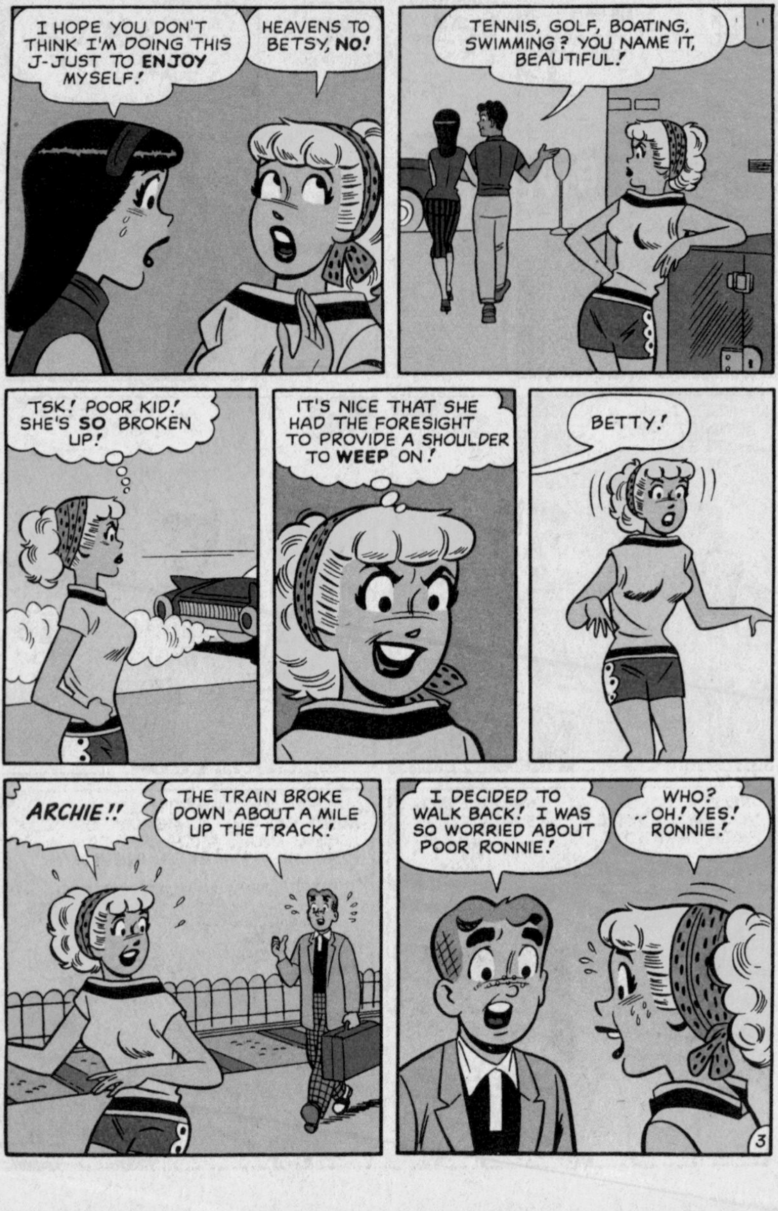
I HOPE YOU DON'T THINK I'M DOING THIS J-JUST TO ENJOY MYSELF!
HEAVENS TO BETSY, NO!
TENNIS, GOLF, BOATING, SWIMMING? YOU NAME IT, BEAUTIFUL!
TSK! POOR KID! SHE'S SO BROKEN UP!
IT'S NICE THAT SHE HAD THE FORESIGHT TO PROVIDE A SHOULDER TO WEEP ON!
BETTY!
ARCHIE!!
THE TRAIN BROKE DOWN ABOUT A MILE UP THE TRACK!
I DECIDED TO WALK BACK! I WAS SO WORRIED ABOUT POOR RONNIE!
WHO? ..OH! YES! RONNIE!
3

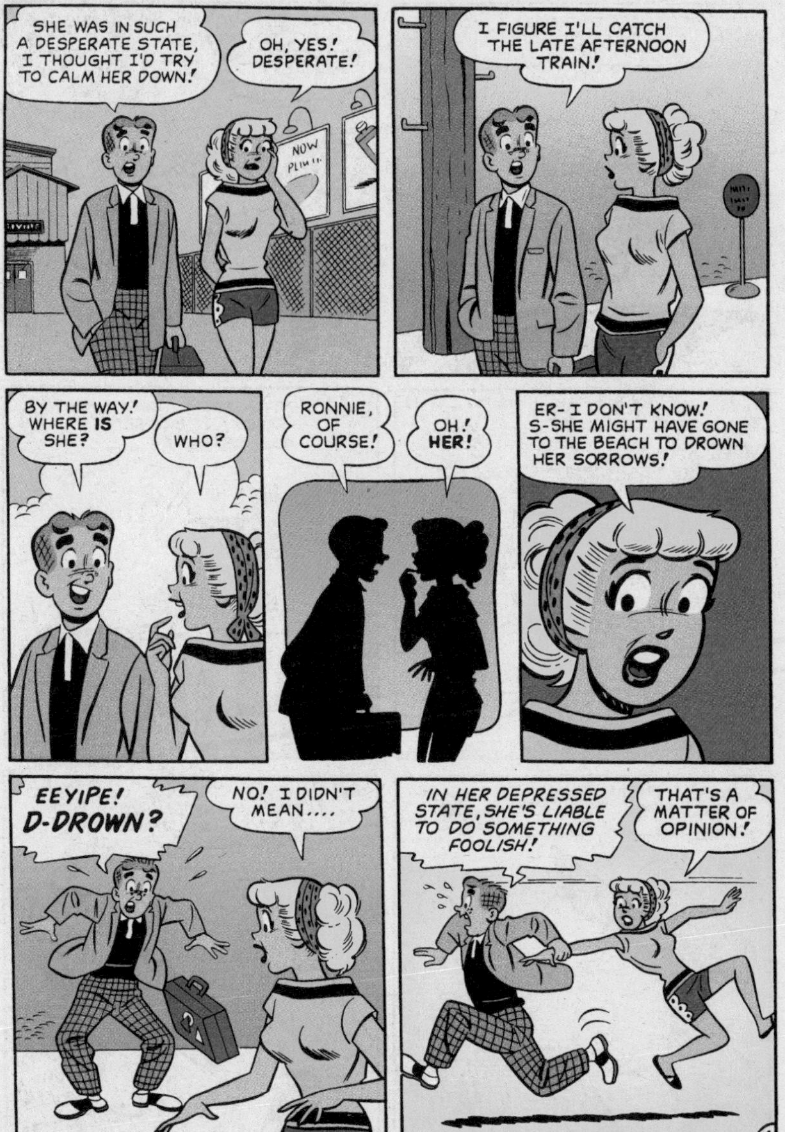
SHE WAS IN SUCH A DESPERATE STATE, I THOUGHT I'D TRY TO CALM HER DOWN!
OH, YES! DESPERATE!
I FIGURE I'LL CATCH THE LATE AFTERNOON TRAIN!
BY THE WAY! WHERE **IS** SHE?
WHO?
RONNIE, OF COURSE!
OH! **HER**!
ER- I DON'T KNOW! S-SHE MIGHT HAVE GONE TO THE BEACH TO DROWN HER SORROWS!
EEYIPE! D-DROWN?
NO! I DIDN'T MEAN....
IN HER DEPRESSED STATE, SHE'S LIABLE TO DO SOMETHING FOOLISH!
THAT'S A MATTER OF OPINION!
4

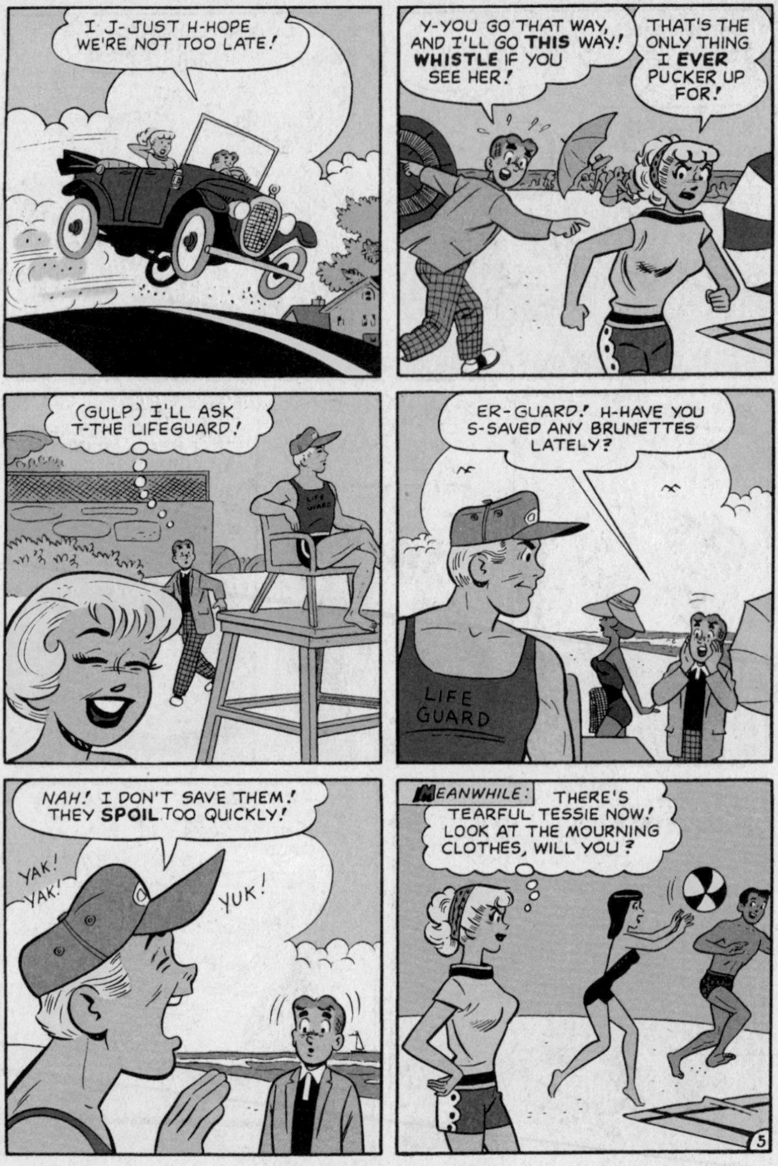
I J-JUST H-HOPE WE'RE NOT TOO LATE!
Y-YOU GO THAT WAY, AND I'LL GO THIS WAY! WHISTLE IF YOU SEE HER!
THAT'S THE ONLY THING I EVER PUCKER UP FOR!
(GULP) I'LL ASK T-THE LIFEGUARD!
LIFE GUARD
ER-GUARD! H-HAVE YOU S-SAVED ANY BRUNETTES LATELY?
LIFE GUARD
NAH! I DON'T SAVE THEM! THEY SPOIL TOO QUICKLY!
YAK! YAK!
YUK!
MEANWHILE:
THERE'S TEARFUL TESSIE NOW! LOOK AT THE MOURNING CLOTHES, WILL YOU?
5

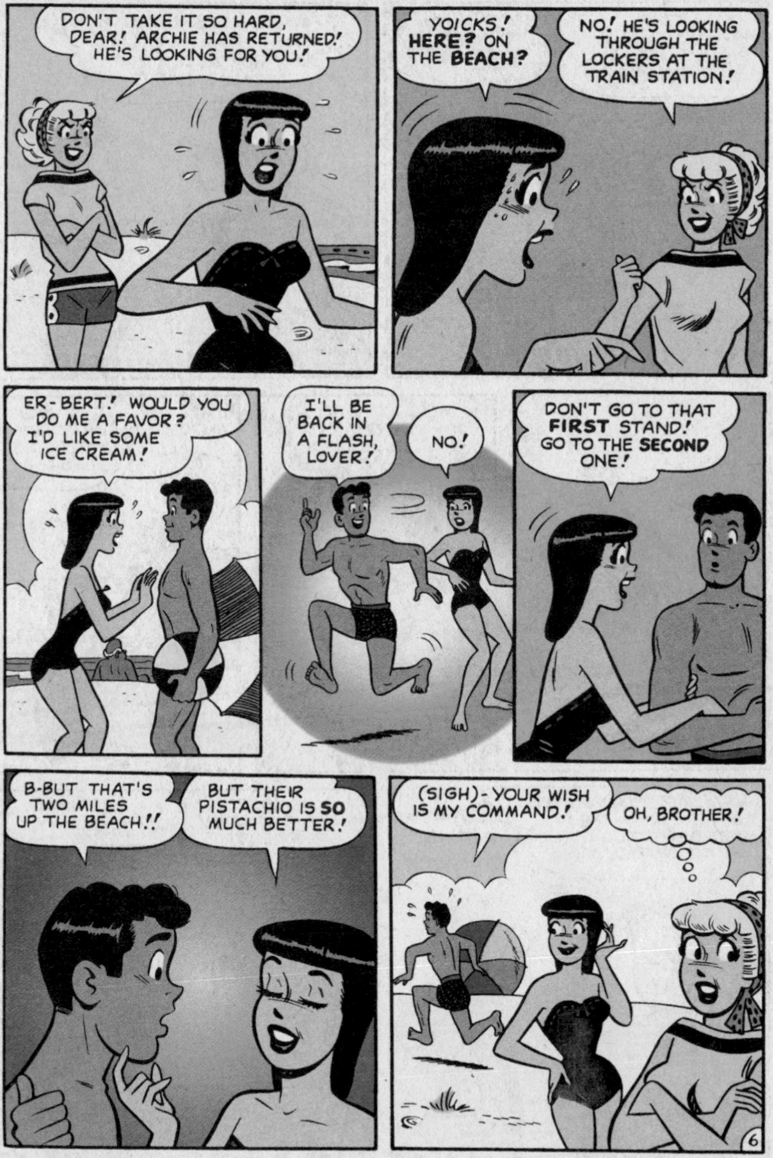
DON'T TAKE IT SO HARD, DEAR! ARCHIE HAS RETURNED! HE'S LOOKING FOR YOU!
YOICKS! HERE? ON THE BEACH?
NO! HE'S LOOKING THROUGH THE LOCKERS AT THE TRAIN STATION!
ER-BERT! WOULD YOU DO ME A FAVOR? I'D LIKE SOME ICE CREAM!
I'LL BE BACK IN A FLASH, LOVER!
NO!
DON'T GO TO THAT FIRST STAND! GO TO THE SECOND ONE!
B-BUT THAT'S TWO MILES UP THE BEACH!!
BUT THEIR PISTACHIO IS SO MUCH BETTER!
(SIGH)-YOUR WISH IS MY COMMAND!
OH, BROTHER!
6

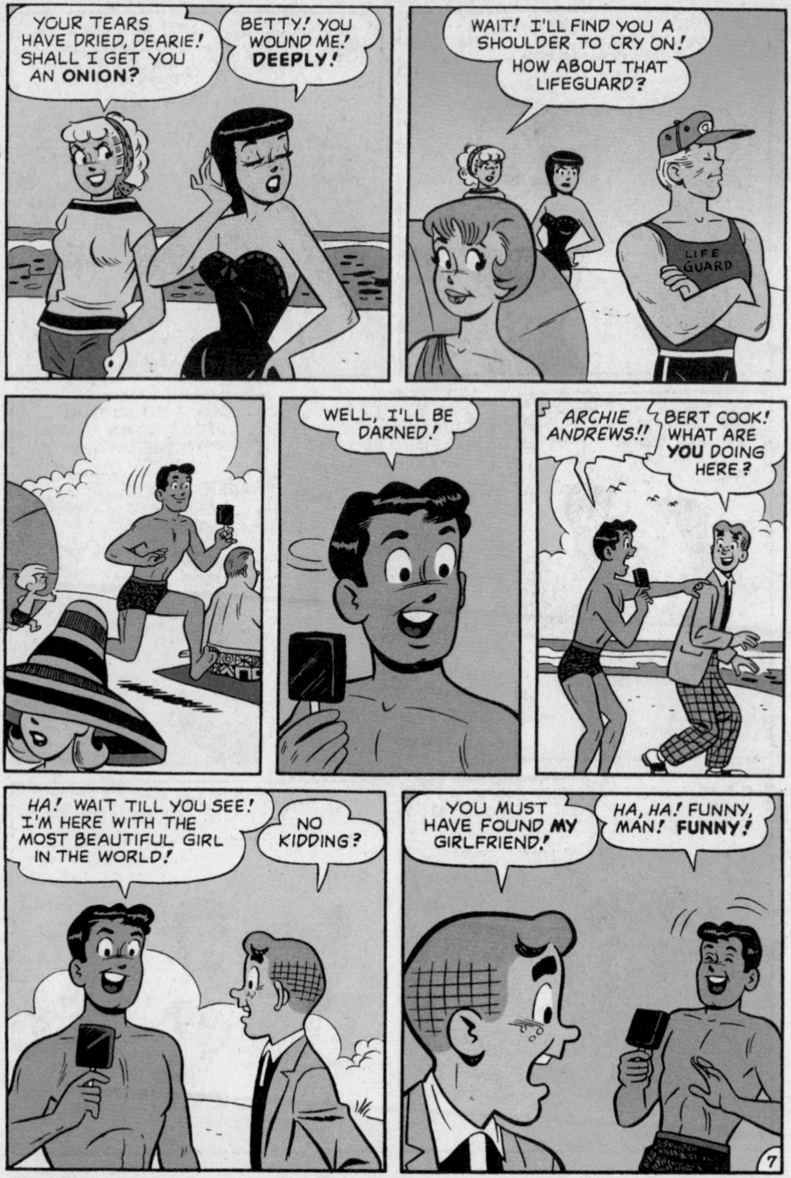
YOUR TEARS HAVE DRIED, DEARIE! SHALL I GET YOU AN **ONION**?
BETTY! YOU WOUND ME! **DEEPLY**!
WAIT! I'LL FIND YOU A SHOULDER TO CRY ON!
HOW ABOUT THAT LIFEGUARD?
LIFE GUARD
WELL, I'LL BE DARNED!
ARCHIE ANDREWS!!
BERT COOK! WHAT ARE **YOU** DOING HERE?
HA! WAIT TILL YOU SEE! I'M HERE WITH THE MOST BEAUTIFUL GIRL IN THE WORLD!
NO KIDDING?
YOU MUST HAVE FOUND **MY** GIRLFRIEND!
HA, HA! FUNNY, MAN! **FUNNY**!
7

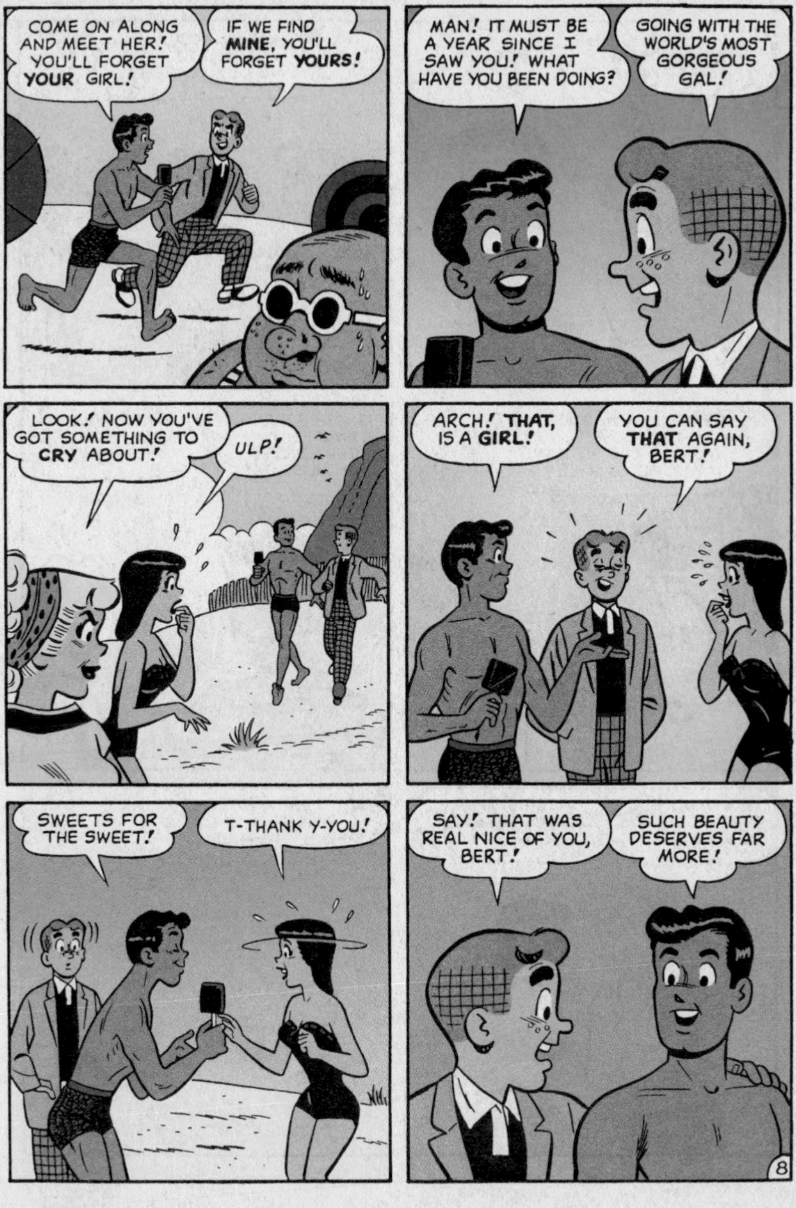
COME ON ALONG AND MEET HER! YOU'LL FORGET YOUR GIRL!
IF WE FIND MINE, YOU'LL FORGET YOURS!
MAN! IT MUST BE A YEAR SINCE I SAW YOU! WHAT HAVE YOU BEEN DOING?
GOING WITH THE WORLD'S MOST GORGEOUS GAL!
LOOK! NOW YOU'VE GOT SOMETHING TO CRY ABOUT!
ULP!
ARCH! THAT, IS A GIRL!
YOU CAN SAY THAT AGAIN, BERT!
SWEETS FOR THE SWEET!
T-THANK Y-YOU!
SAY! THAT WAS REAL NICE OF YOU, BERT!
SUCH BEAUTY DESERVES FAR MORE!
8

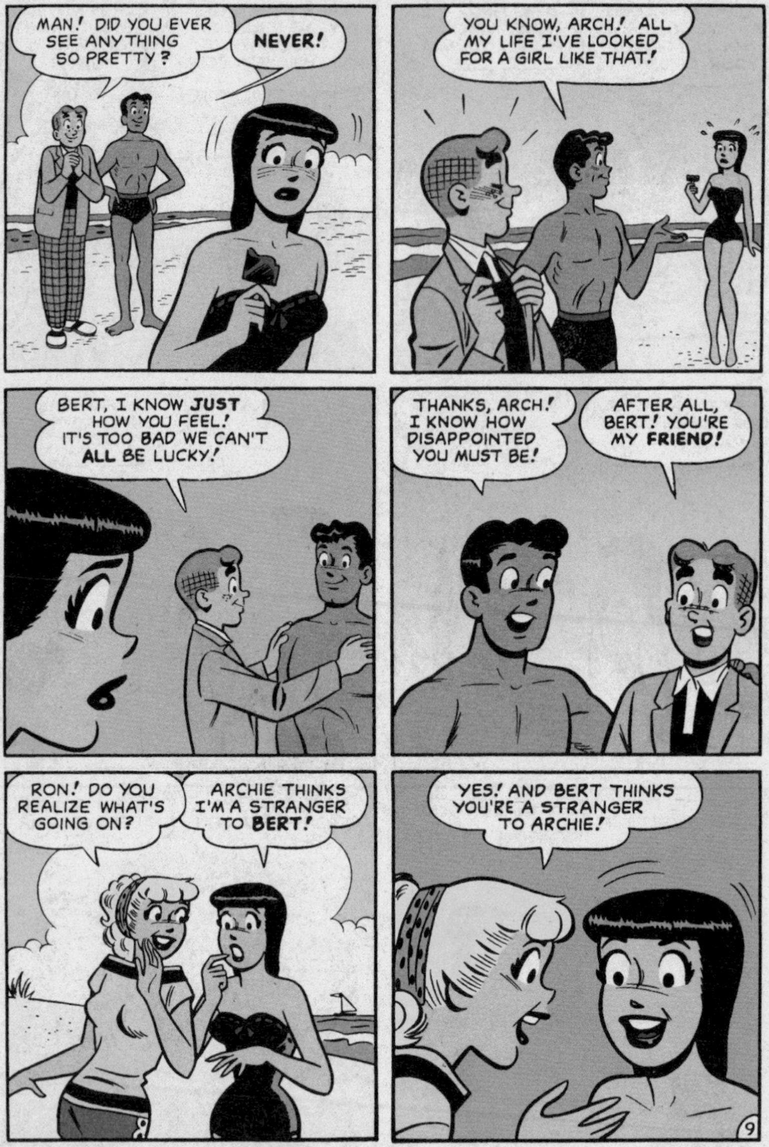
MAN! DID YOU EVER SEE ANYTHING SO PRETTY?
NEVER!
YOU KNOW, ARCH! ALL MY LIFE I'VE LOOKED FOR A GIRL LIKE THAT!
BERT, I KNOW JUST HOW YOU FEEL! IT'S TOO BAD WE CAN'T ALL BE LUCKY!
THANKS, ARCH! I KNOW HOW DISAPPOINTED YOU MUST BE!
AFTER ALL, BERT! YOU'RE MY FRIEND!
RON! DO YOU REALIZE WHAT'S GOING ON?
ARCHIE THINKS I'M A STRANGER TO BERT!
YES! AND BERT THINKS YOU'RE A STRANGER TO ARCHIE!
9

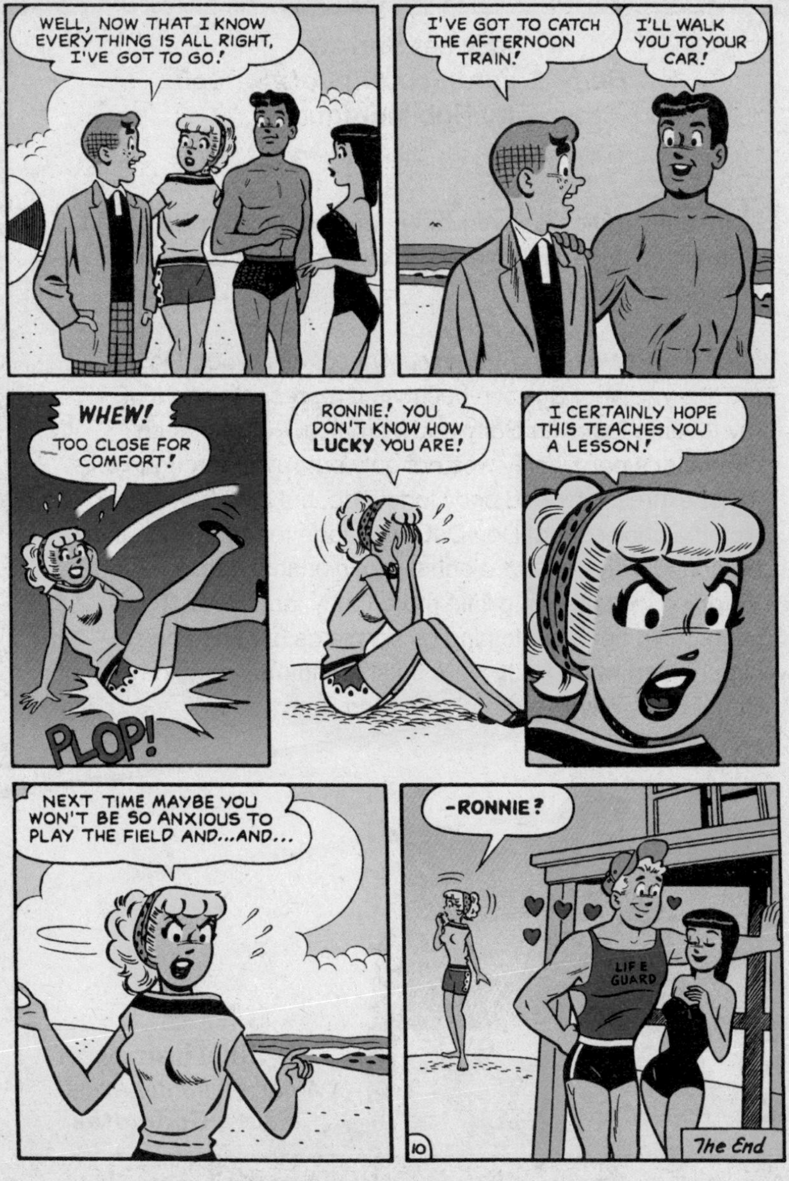
WELL, NOW THAT I KNOW EVERYTHING IS ALL RIGHT, I'VE GOT TO GO!
I'VE GOT TO CATCH THE AFTERNOON TRAIN!
I'LL WALK YOU TO YOUR CAR!
WHEW! —TOO CLOSE FOR COMFORT!
PLOP!
RONNIE! YOU DON'T KNOW HOW LUCKY YOU ARE!
I CERTAINLY HOPE THIS TEACHES YOU A LESSON!
NEXT TIME MAYBE YOU WON'T BE SO ANXIOUS TO PLAY THE FIELD AND...AND...
-RONNIE?
LIFE GUARD
10
The End

Sweet Sorrow
Betty & Veronica Annual #8, 1960
by Bob Montana

The early sixties is my favorite period of time for Betty and Veronica stories, with the late sixties and early seventies coming in second.

I can say in *Betty and Veronica Annual #8* (1960), I loved the story "Sweet Sorrow" because it represents some of my favorite looks for Betty and Veronica. For me, each character's personality was not only portrayed through their facial expressions and body language, but also from the clothing choices that Dan DeCarlo made for each character. Betty and Veronica were equally fashionable, but Veronica was always a little more fancy than Betty. That might have been something as simple as her shoes were high heeled when Betty wore flats, but to me that showed that Ronnie was driven more places than Betty.

Jill Thompson
Award-winning Artist,
Scary Godmother

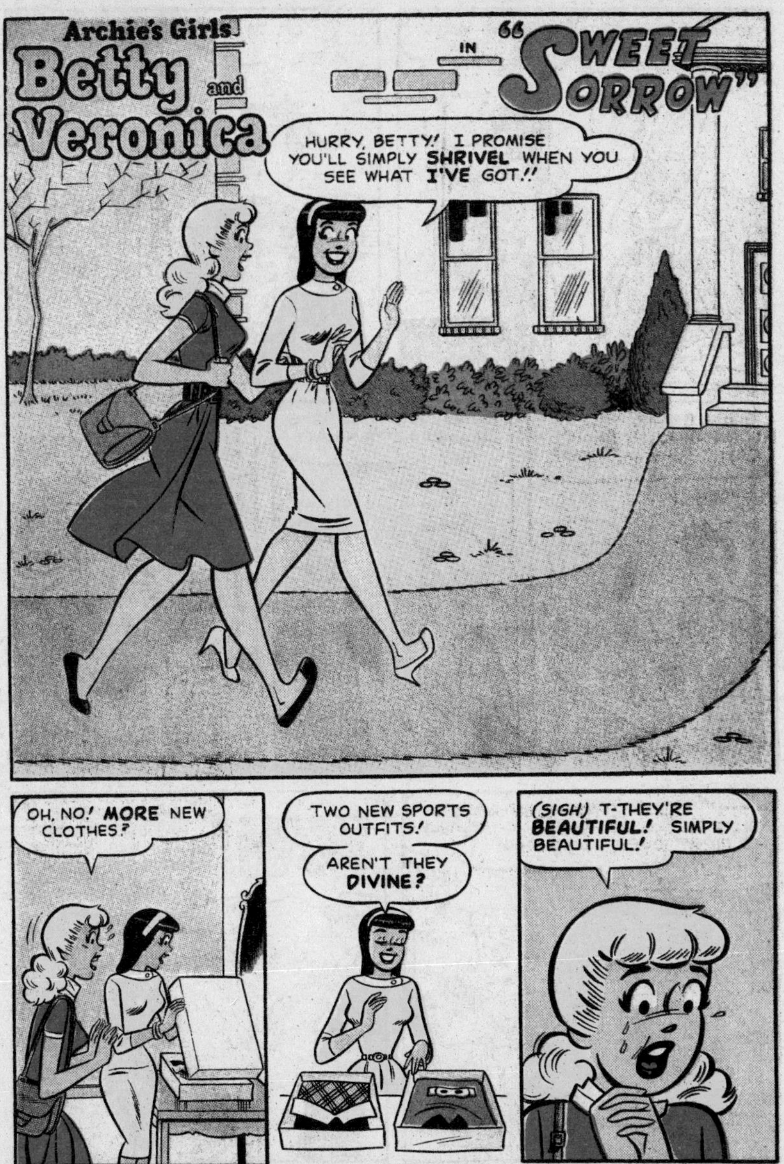
Archie's Girls
Betty and Veronica
IN "SWEET SORROW"
HURRY, BETTY! I PROMISE YOU'LL SIMPLY SHRIVEL WHEN YOU SEE WHAT I'VE GOT!!
OH, NO! MORE NEW CLOTHES?
TWO NEW SPORTS OUTFITS!
AREN'T THEY DIVINE?
(SIGH) T-THEY'RE BEAUTIFUL! SIMPLY BEAUTIFUL!

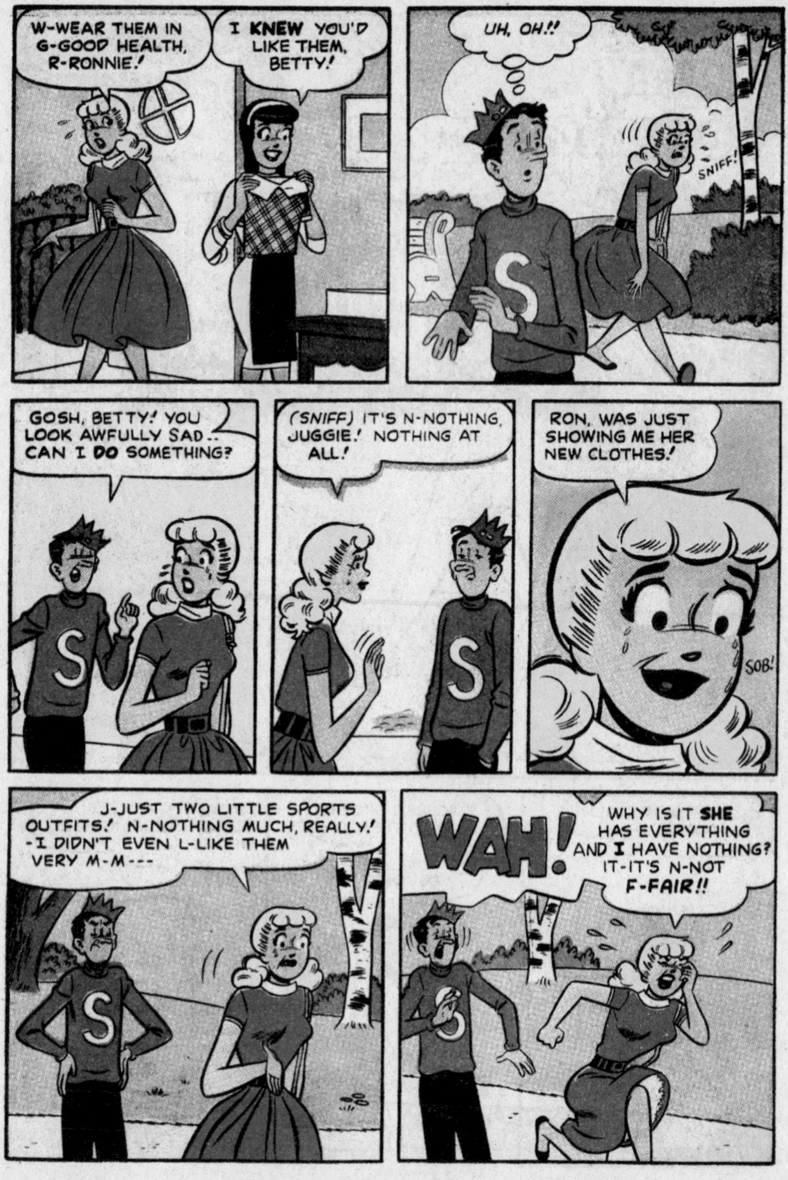

W-WEAR THEM IN G-GOOD HEALTH, R-RONNIE!
I KNEW YOU'D LIKE THEM, BETTY!
UH, OH!!
SNIFF!
GOSH, BETTY! YOU LOOK AWFULLY SAD.. CAN I DO SOMETHING?
(SNIFF) IT'S N-NOTHING, JUGGIE! NOTHING AT ALL!
RON, WAS JUST SHOWING ME HER NEW CLOTHES!
SOB!
J-JUST TWO LITTLE SPORTS OUTFITS! N-NOTHING MUCH, REALLY! -I DIDN'T EVEN L-LIKE THEM VERY M-M---
WAH!
WHY IS IT SHE HAS EVERYTHING AND I HAVE NOTHING? IT-IT'S N-NOT F-FAIR!!

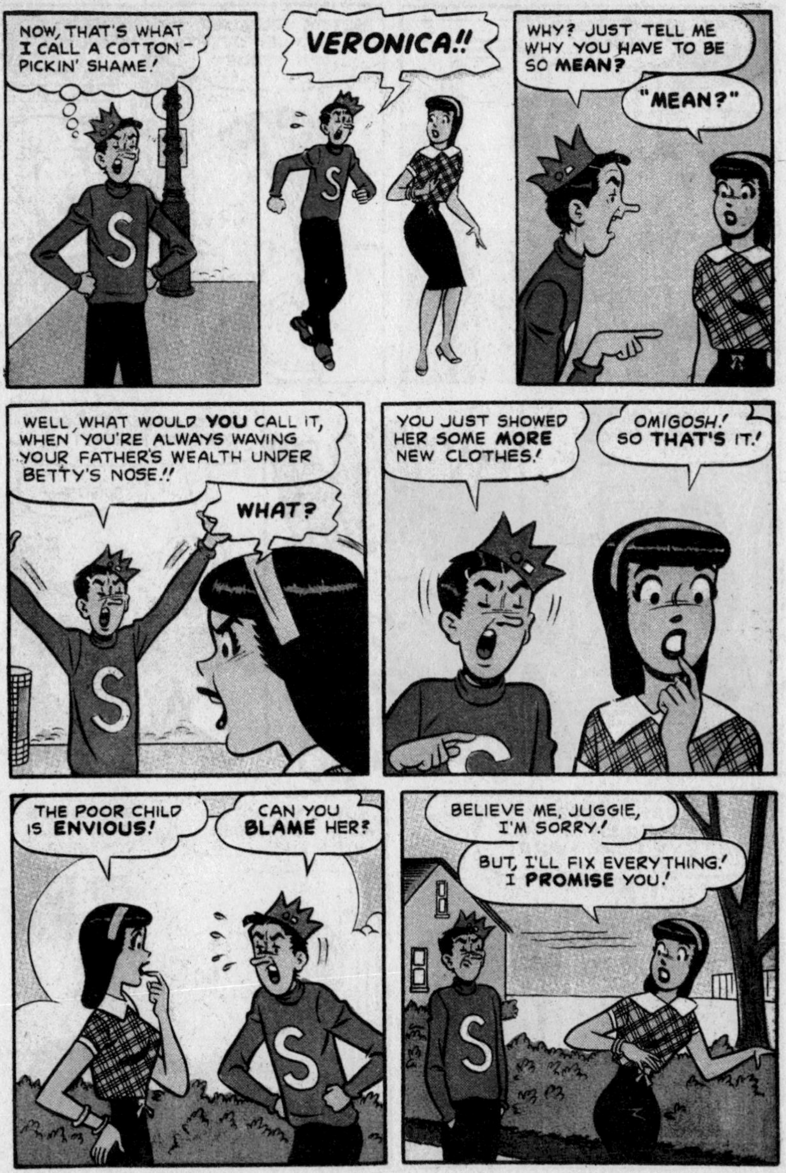
NOW, THAT'S WHAT I CALL A COTTON-PICKIN' SHAME!
VERONICA!!
WHY? JUST TELL ME WHY YOU HAVE TO BE SO MEAN?
"MEAN?"
WELL, WHAT WOULD YOU CALL IT, WHEN YOU'RE ALWAYS WAVING YOUR FATHER'S WEALTH UNDER BETTY'S NOSE!!
WHAT?
YOU JUST SHOWED HER SOME MORE NEW CLOTHES!
OMIGOSH! SO THAT'S IT!
THE POOR CHILD IS ENVIOUS!
CAN YOU BLAME HER?
BELIEVE ME, JUGGIE, I'M SORRY!
BUT, I'LL FIX EVERYTHING! I PROMISE YOU!

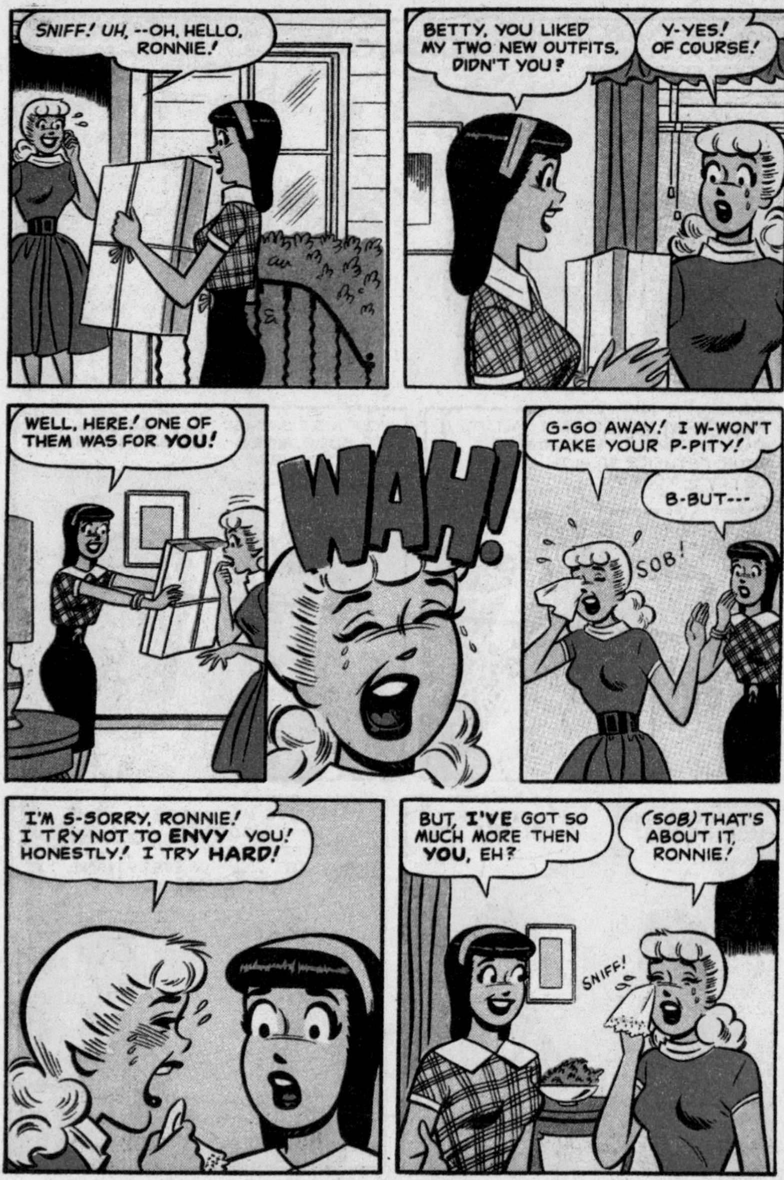
SNIFF! UH, --OH, HELLO, RONNIE!
BETTY, YOU LIKED MY TWO NEW OUTFITS, DIDN'T YOU?
Y-YES! OF COURSE!
WELL, HERE! ONE OF THEM WAS FOR YOU!
WAH!
G-GO AWAY! I W-WON'T TAKE YOUR P-PITY!
SOB!
B-BUT---
I'M S-SORRY, RONNIE! I TRY NOT TO ENVY YOU! HONESTLY! I TRY HARD!
BUT, I'VE GOT SO MUCH MORE THEN YOU, EH?
(SOB) THAT'S ABOUT IT, RONNIE!
SNIFF!

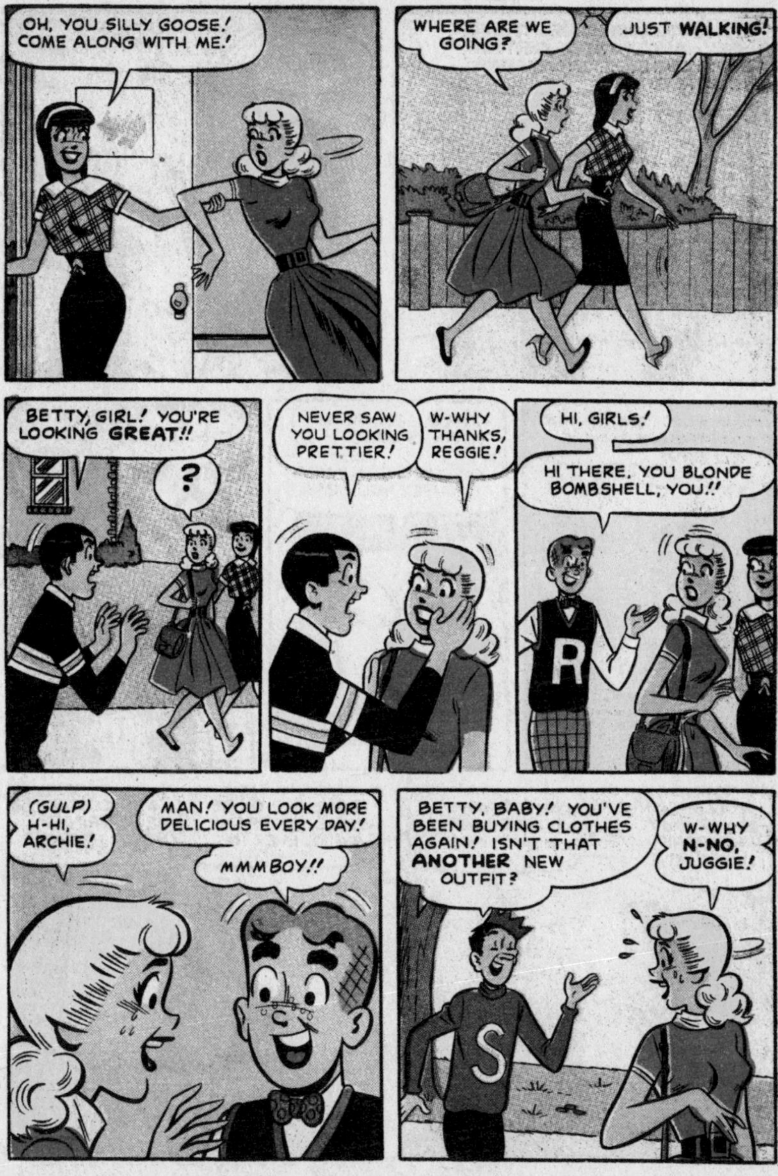
OH, YOU SILLY GOOSE! COME ALONG WITH ME!
WHERE ARE WE GOING?
JUST WALKING!
BETTY, GIRL! YOU'RE LOOKING GREAT!!
?
NEVER SAW YOU LOOKING PRETTIER!
W-WHY THANKS, REGGIE!
HI, GIRLS!
HI THERE, YOU BLONDE BOMBSHELL, YOU!!
(GULP) H-HI, ARCHIE!
MAN! YOU LOOK MORE DELICIOUS EVERY DAY!
MMMBOY!!
BETTY, BABY! YOU'VE BEEN BUYING CLOTHES AGAIN! ISN'T THAT ANOTHER NEW OUTFIT?
W-WHY N-NO, JUGGIE!
R
S

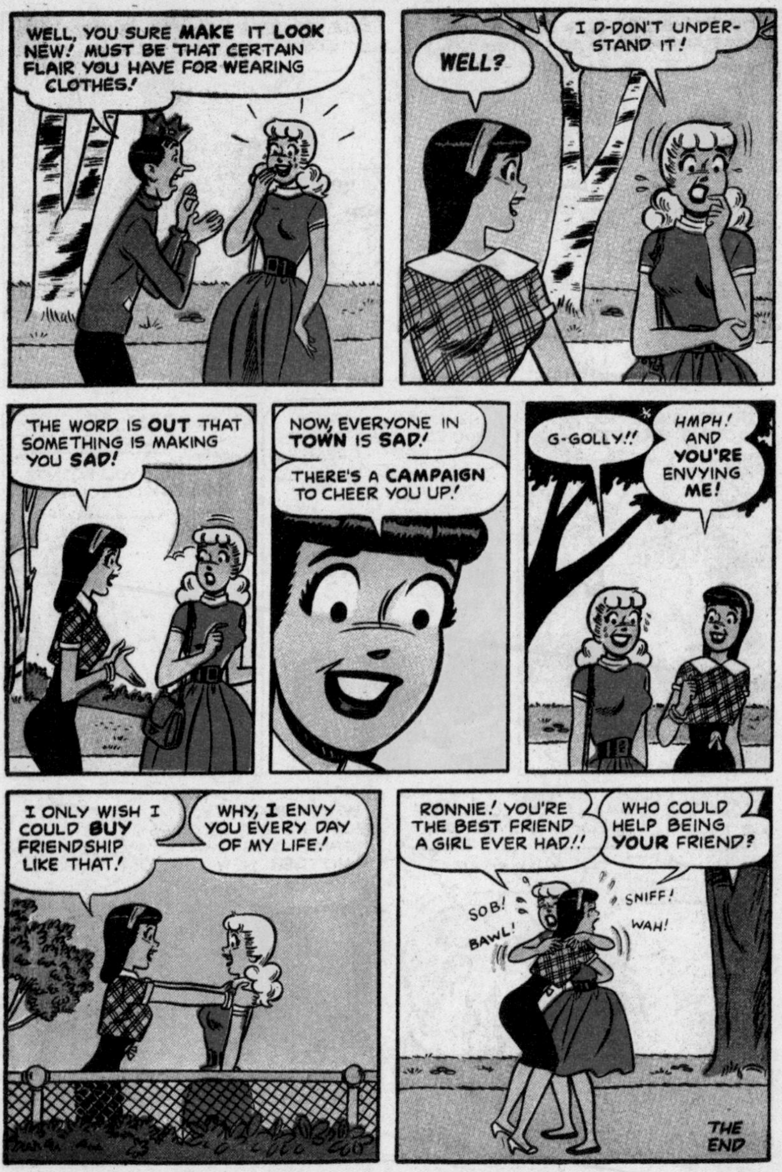
WELL, YOU SURE MAKE IT LOOK NEW! MUST BE THAT CERTAIN FLAIR YOU HAVE FOR WEARING CLOTHES!
WELL?
I D-DON'T UNDERSTAND IT!
THE WORD IS OUT THAT SOMETHING IS MAKING YOU SAD!
NOW, EVERYONE IN TOWN IS SAD!
THERE'S A CAMPAIGN TO CHEER YOU UP!
G-GOLLY!!
HMPH! AND YOU'RE ENVYING ME!
I ONLY WISH I COULD BUY FRIENDSHIP LIKE THAT!
WHY, I ENVY YOU EVERY DAY OF MY LIFE!
RONNIE! YOU'RE THE BEST FRIEND A GIRL EVER HAD!!
WHO COULD HELP BEING YOUR FRIEND?
SOB!
BAWL!
SNIFF!
WAH!
THE END

Archie Starring Betty and Veronica
Archie #5, 1943
by Harry Sahle and Janice Valleau (Ginger)

Betty and Veronica (as well as Archie, Jughead, and the gang) were everywhere when I was growing up in Tennessee. My mom would often get the comics for me at the local TG&Y, but I never really paid attention to particular stories. I guess my earliest memory of really noticing Betty and Veronica was the live-action variety show that came out in 1978.

I remember being really excited about a comic being on TV (*Legends of the Superheroes, Shazam* and *Wonder Woman* were already favorites) and eager to watch it. I think Veronica was the funniest one on the show, mostly because she got to play off Betty being so straight-laced, so I obviously took a shining to her. I was only five years old, so I wasn't as interested in the "girls" thing yet, so it was mostly all the humor and black hair of Veronica.

Mike Norton
Eisner Award-winning Artist,
Battlepug, Revival

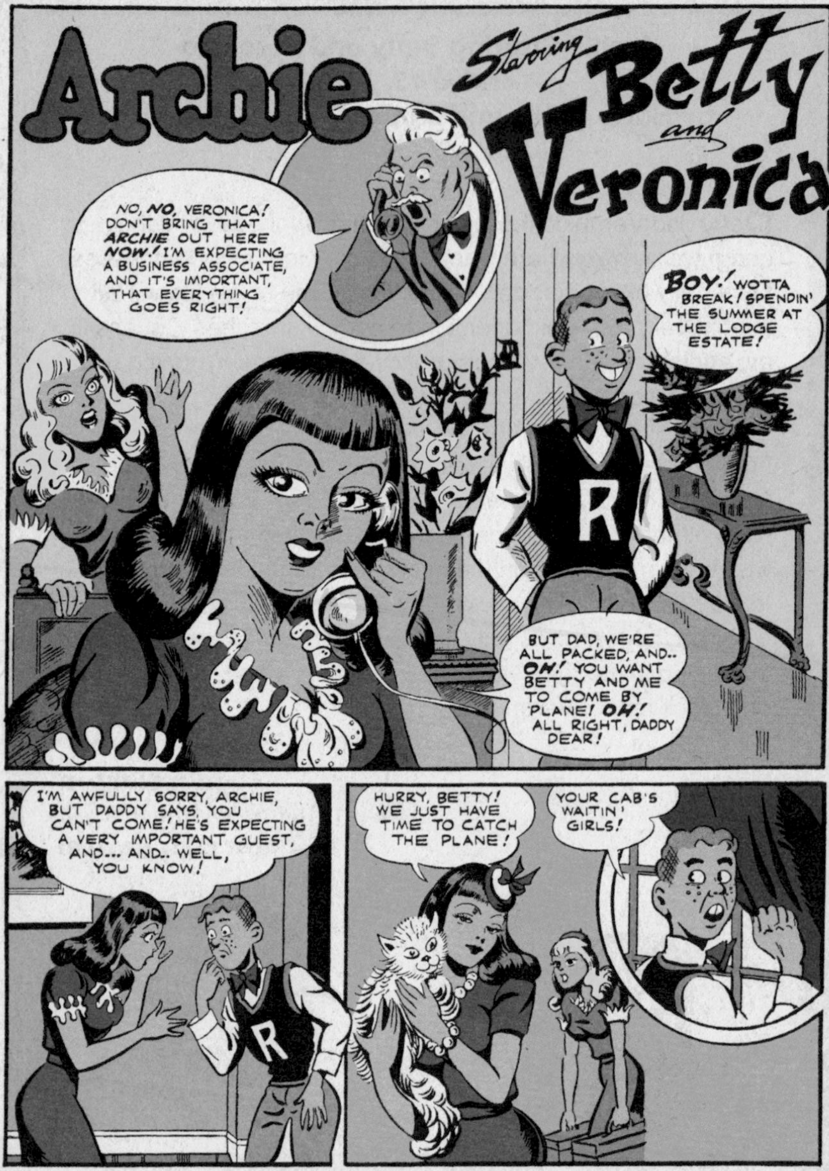
Archie
Starring Betty and Veronica
NO, NO, VERONICA! DON'T BRING THAT ARCHIE OUT HERE NOW! I'M EXPECTING A BUSINESS ASSOCIATE, AND IT'S IMPORTANT, THAT EVERYTHING GOES RIGHT!
BOY! WOTTA BREAK! SPENDIN' THE SUMMER AT THE LODGE ESTATE!
BUT DAD, WE'RE ALL PACKED, AND.. OH! YOU WANT BETTY AND ME TO COME BY PLANE! OH! ALL RIGHT, DADDY DEAR!
I'M AWFULLY SORRY, ARCHIE, BUT DADDY SAYS YOU CAN'T COME! HE'S EXPECTING A VERY IMPORTANT GUEST, AND... AND.. WELL, YOU KNOW!
HURRY, BETTY! WE JUST HAVE TIME TO CATCH THE PLANE!
YOUR CAB'S WAITIN' GIRLS!

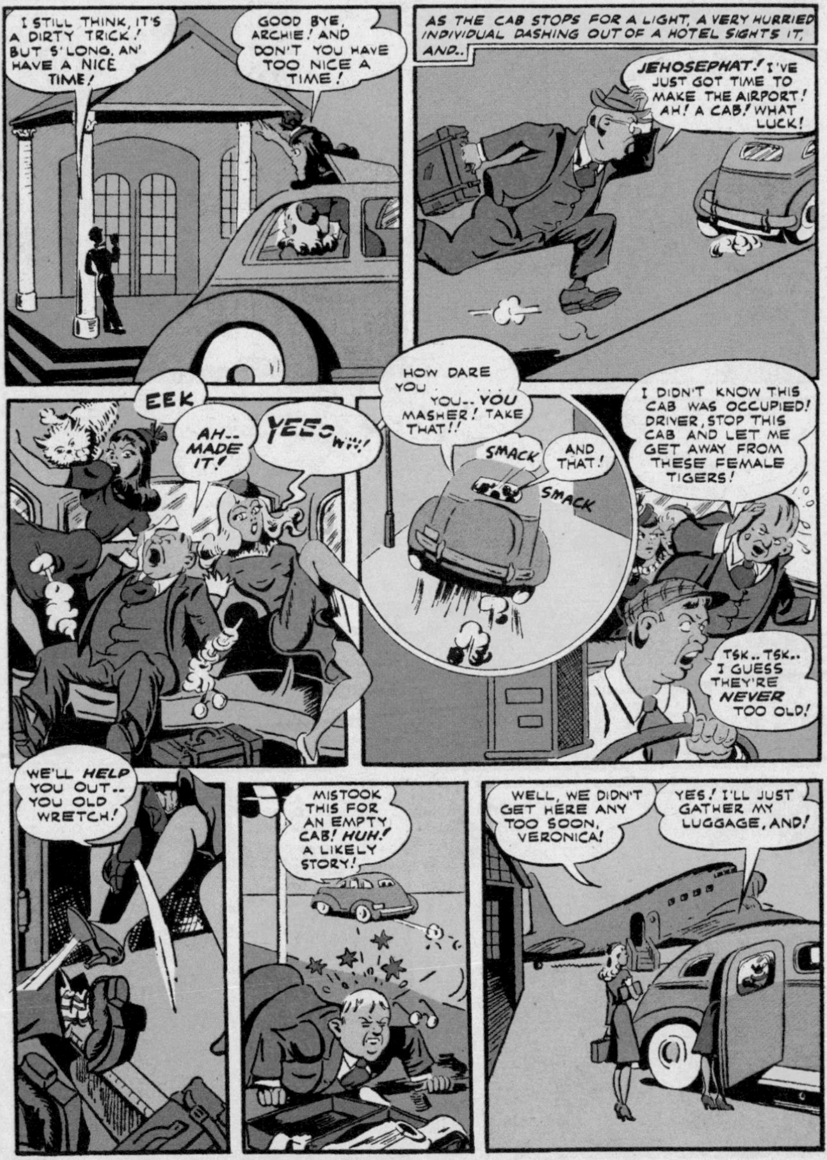
I STILL THINK, IT'S A DIRTY TRICK! BUT S'LONG, AN' HAVE A NICE TIME!
GOOD BYE, ARCHIE! AND DON'T YOU HAVE TOO NICE A TIME!
AS THE CAB STOPS FOR A LIGHT, A VERY HURRIED INDIVIDUAL DASHING OUT OF A HOTEL SIGHTS IT, AND..
JEHOSEPHAT! I'VE JUST GOT TIME TO MAKE THE AIRPORT! AH! A CAB! WHAT LUCK!
EEK
AH.. MADE IT!
YEEOWW!!
HOW DARE YOU YOU.. YOU MASHER! TAKE THAT!!
SMACK
AND THAT!
SMACK
I DIDN'T KNOW THIS CAB WAS OCCUPIED! DRIVER, STOP THIS CAB AND LET ME GET AWAY FROM THESE FEMALE TIGERS!
TSK.. TSK.. I GUESS THEY'RE NEVER TOO OLD!
WE'LL HELP YOU OUT.. YOU OLD WRETCH!
MISTOOK THIS FOR AN EMPTY CAB! HUH! A LIKELY STORY!
WELL, WE DIDN'T GET HERE ANY TOO SOON, VERONICA!
YES! I'LL JUST GATHER MY LUGGAGE, AND!

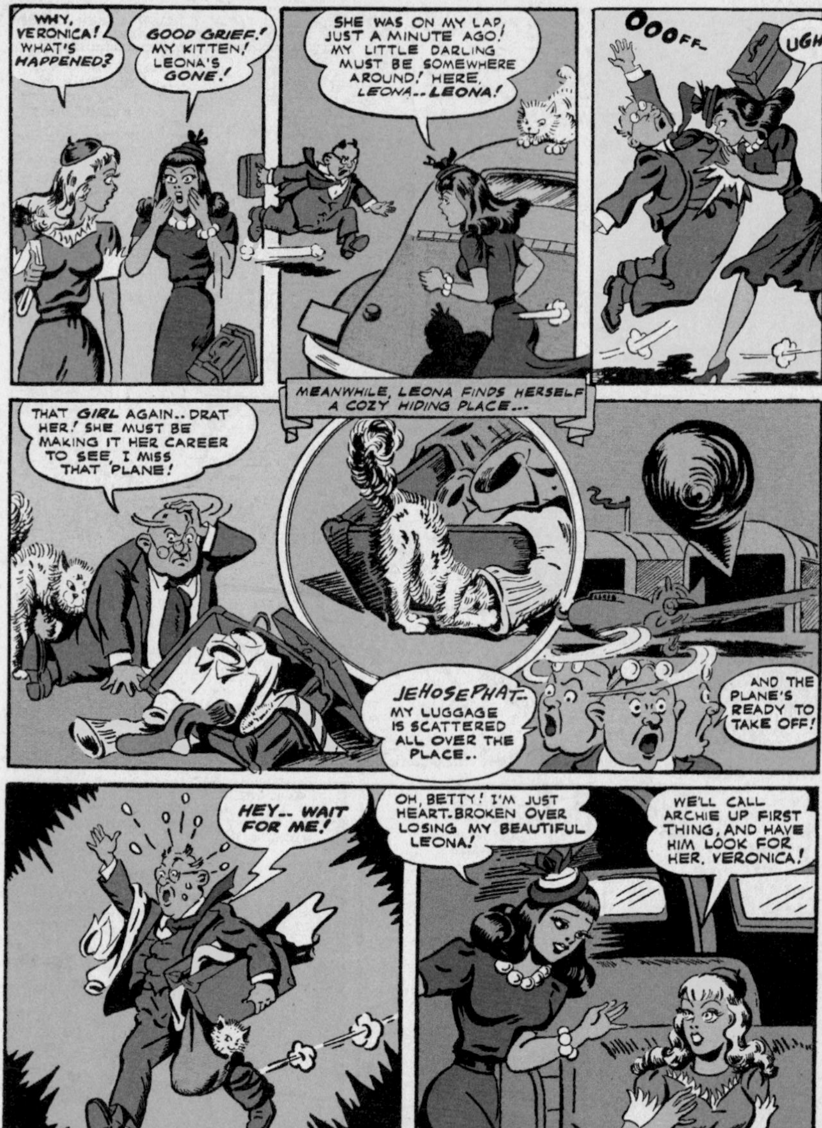
WHY, VERONICA! WHAT'S HAPPENED?
GOOD GRIEF! MY KITTEN! LEONA'S GONE!
SHE WAS ON MY LAP, JUST A MINUTE AGO! MY LITTLE DARLING MUST BE SOMEWHERE AROUND! HERE, LEONA.. LEONA!
OOOFF-
UGH!
MEANWHILE, LEONA FINDS HERSELF A COZY HIDING PLACE...
THAT GIRL AGAIN.. DRAT HER! SHE MUST BE MAKING IT HER CAREER TO SEE, I MISS THAT PLANE!
JEHOSEPHAT.. MY LUGGAGE IS SCATTERED ALL OVER THE PLACE..
AND THE PLANE'S READY TO TAKE OFF!
HEY.. WAIT FOR ME!
OH, BETTY! I'M JUST HEART-BROKEN OVER LOSING MY BEAUTIFUL LEONA!
WE'LL CALL ARCHIE UP FIRST THING, AND HAVE HIM LOOK FOR HER, VERONICA!

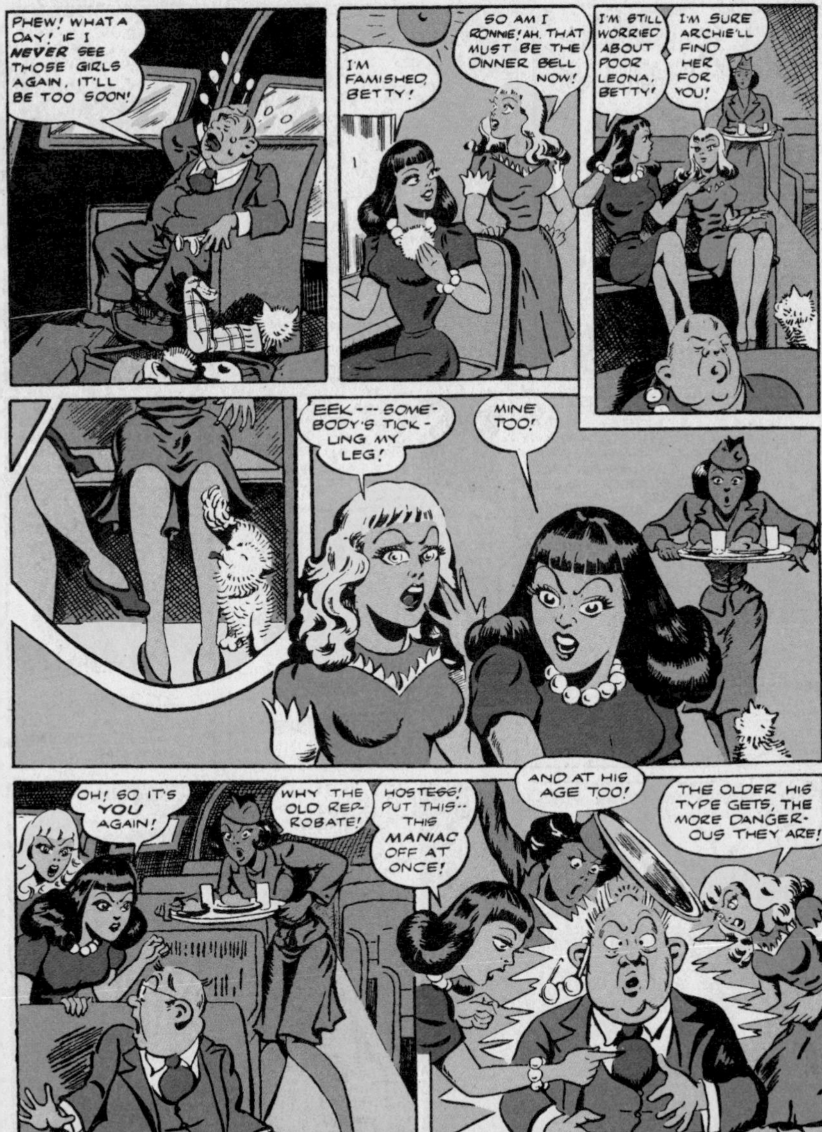
PHEW! WHAT A DAY! IF I NEVER SEE THOSE GIRLS AGAIN, IT'LL BE TOO SOON!
I'M FAMISHED, BETTY!
SO AM I RONNIE! AH. THAT MUST BE THE DINNER BELL NOW!
I'M STILL WORRIED ABOUT POOR LEONA, BETTY!
I'M SURE ARCHIE'LL FIND HER FOR YOU!
EEK---SOME-BODY'S TICK-LING MY LEG!
MINE TOO!
OH! SO IT'S YOU AGAIN!
WHY THE OLD REP-ROBATE!
HOSTESS! PUT THIS--THIS MANIAC OFF AT ONCE!
AND AT HIS AGE TOO!
THE OLDER HIS TYPE GETS, THE MORE DANGER-OUS THEY ARE!

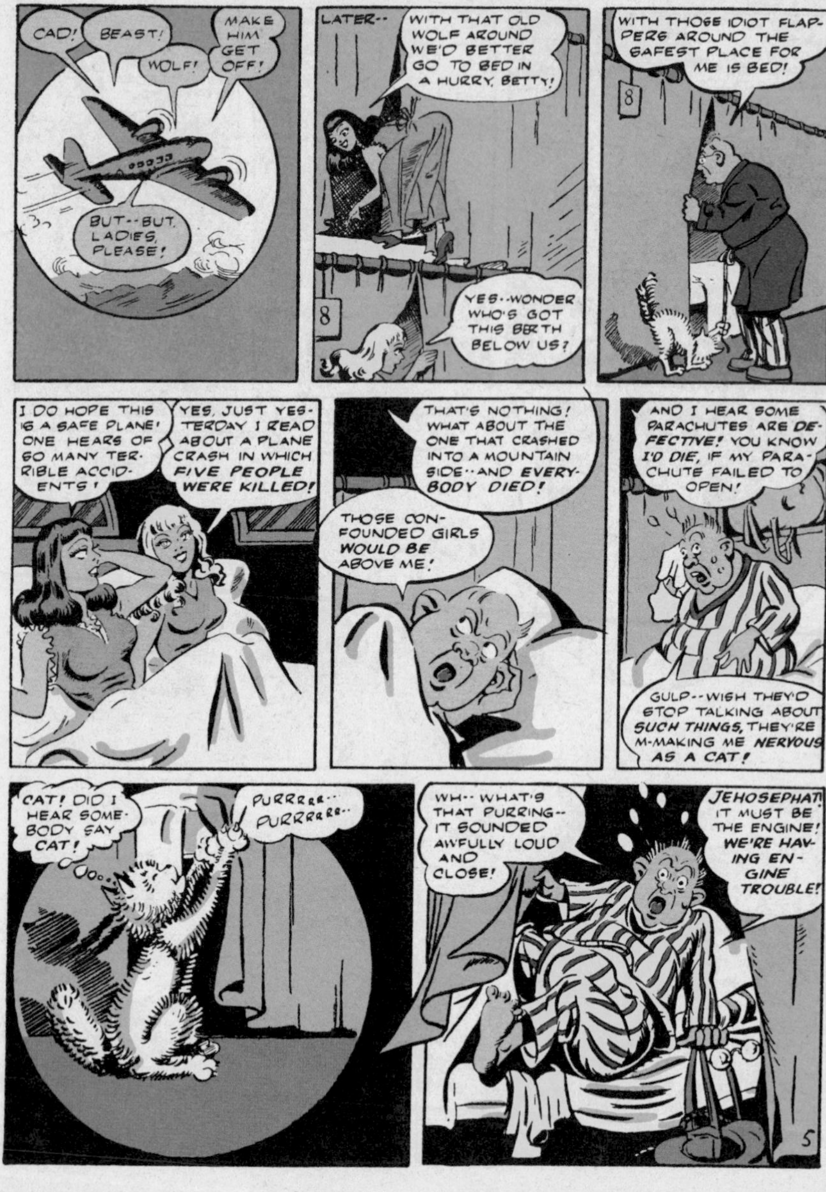
CAD!
BEAST!
WOLF!
MAKE HIM GET OFF!
BUT--BUT, LADIES, PLEASE!
LATER--
WITH THAT OLD WOLF AROUND WE'D BETTER GO TO BED IN A HURRY, BETTY!
YES--WONDER WHO'S GOT THIS BERTH BELOW US?
WITH THOSE IDIOT FLAPPERS AROUND THE SAFEST PLACE FOR ME IS BED!
I DO HOPE THIS IS A SAFE PLANE! ONE HEARS OF SO MANY TERRIBLE ACCIDENTS!
YES, JUST YESTERDAY I READ ABOUT A PLANE CRASH IN WHICH FIVE PEOPLE WERE KILLED!
THAT'S NOTHING! WHAT ABOUT THE ONE THAT CRASHED INTO A MOUNTAIN SIDE--AND EVERYBODY DIED!
THOSE CONFOUNDED GIRLS WOULD BE ABOVE ME!
AND I HEAR SOME PARACHUTES ARE DEFECTIVE! YOU KNOW I'D DIE, IF MY PARACHUTE FAILED TO OPEN!
GULP--WISH THEY'D STOP TALKING ABOUT SUCH THINGS, THEY'RE M-MAKING ME NERVOUS AS A CAT!
CAT! DID I HEAR SOMEBODY SAY CAT!
PURRRRRR-- PURRRRRR--
WH--WHAT'S THAT PURRING--IT SOUNDED AWFULLY LOUD AND CLOSE!
JEHOSEPHAT! IT MUST BE THE ENGINE! WE'RE HAVING ENGINE TROUBLE!
5

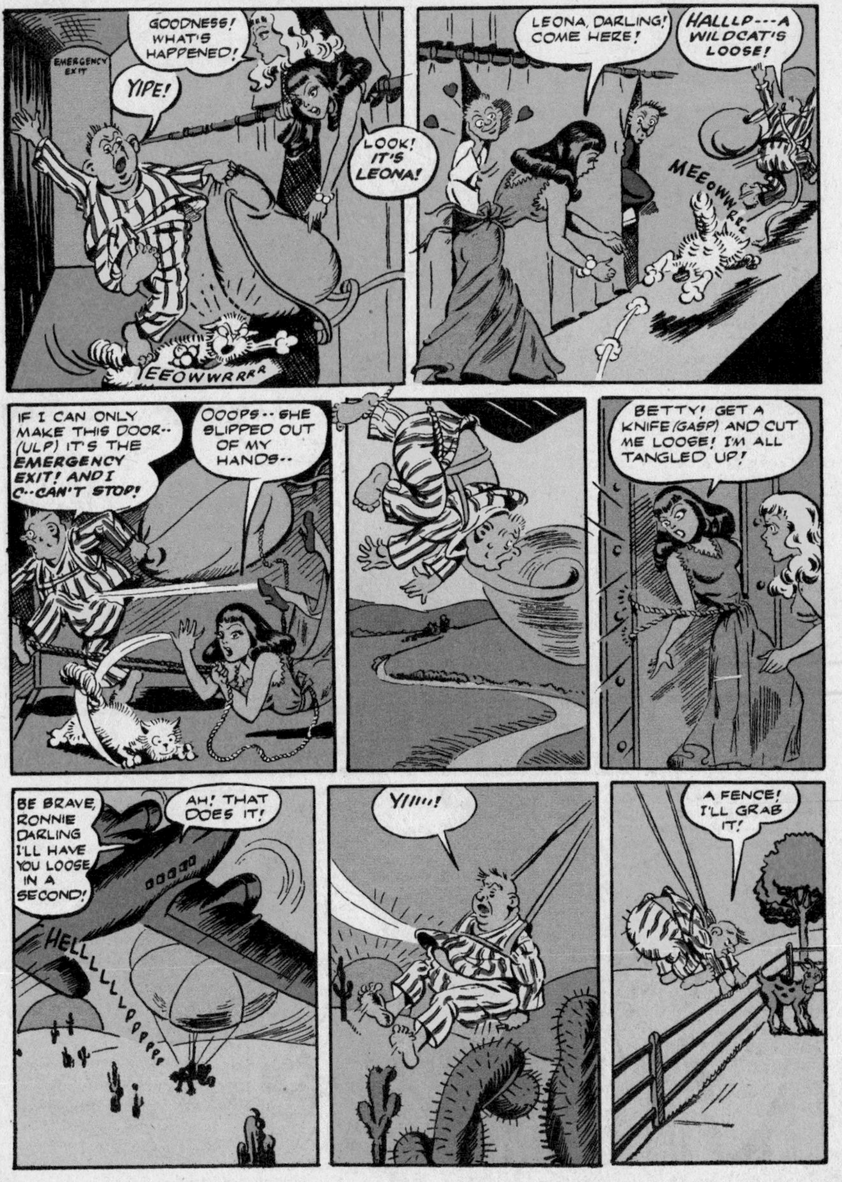
EMERGENCY EXIT
GOODNESS! WHAT'S HAPPENED!
YIPE!
LOOK! IT'S LEONA!
EEOWWRRRR
LEONA, DARLING! COME HERE!
HALLLP---A WILDCAT'S LOOSE!
MEEOWWRRR
IF I CAN ONLY MAKE THIS DOOR.. (ULP) IT'S THE EMERGENCY EXIT! AND I C--CAN'T STOP!
OOOPS -- SHE SLIPPED OUT OF MY HANDS..
BETTY! GET A KNIFE (GASP) AND CUT ME LOOSE! I'M ALL TANGLED UP!
BE BRAVE, RONNIE DARLING I'LL HAVE YOU LOOSE IN A SECOND!
AH! THAT DOES IT!
HELLLLLLLPPPPPP
YIIIII!
A FENCE! I'LL GRAB IT!

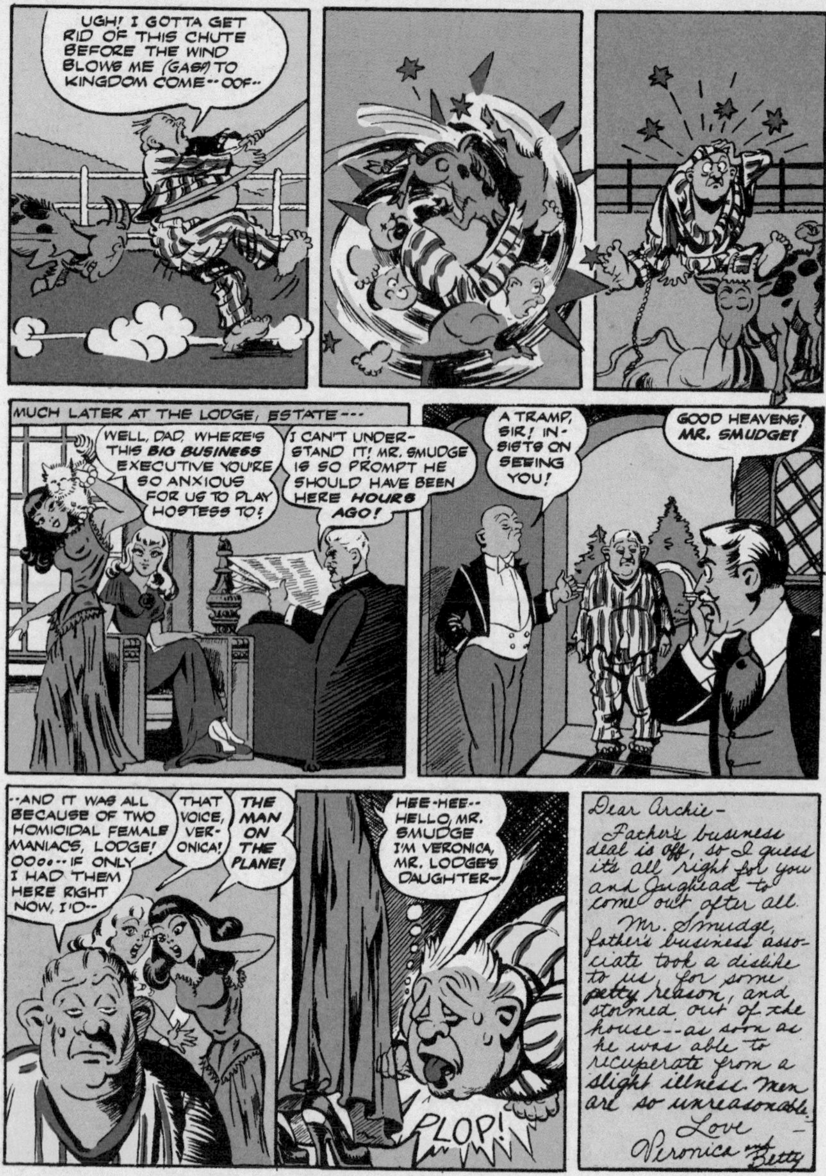
UGH! I GOTTA GET RID OF THIS CHUTE BEFORE THE WIND BLOWS ME (GASP) TO KINGDOM COME--OOF--
MUCH LATER AT THE LODGE ESTATE---
WELL, DAD, WHERE'S THIS BIG BUSINESS EXECUTIVE YOU'RE SO ANXIOUS FOR US TO PLAY HOSTESS TO!
I CAN'T UNDERSTAND IT! MR. SMUDGE IS SO PROMPT HE SHOULD HAVE BEEN HERE HOURS AGO!
A TRAMP, SIR! INSISTS ON SEEING YOU!
GOOD HEAVENS! MR. SMUDGE!
--AND IT WAS ALL BECAUSE OF TWO HOMICIDAL FEMALE MANIACS, LODGE! OOOo--IF ONLY I HAD THEM HERE RIGHT NOW, I'D--
THAT VOICE, VERONICA!
THE MAN ON THE PLANE!
HEE-HEE-- HELLO, MR. SMUDGE I'M VERONICA, MR. LODGE'S DAUGHTER--
PLOP!
Dear Archie-
Father's business deal is off, so I guess it's all right for you and Jughead to come out after all.
Mr. Smudge, father's business associate took a dislike to us for some petty reason, and stormed out of the house--as soon as he was able to recuperate from a slight illness. Men are so unreasonable!
Love
Veronica and Betty

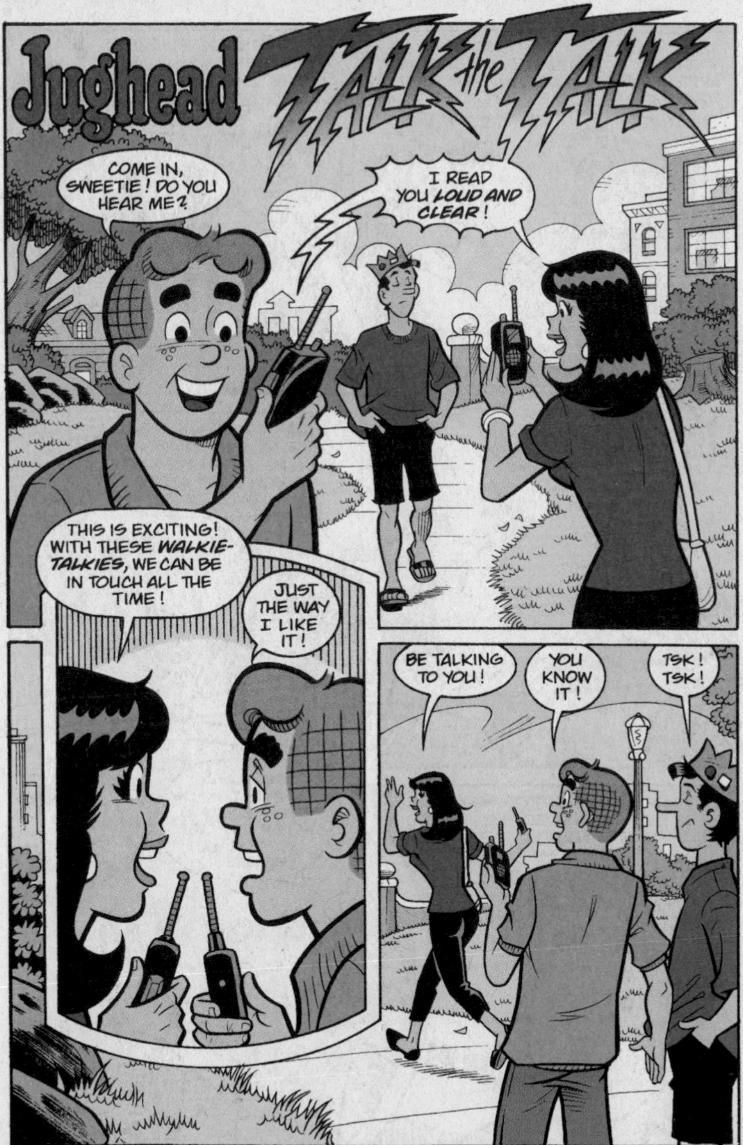

Jughead
TALK the TALK
COME IN, SWEETIE! DO YOU HEAR ME?
I READ YOU LOUD AND CLEAR!
THIS IS EXCITING! WITH THESE WALKIE-TALKIES, WE CAN BE IN TOUCH ALL THE TIME!
JUST THE WAY I LIKE IT!
BE TALKING TO YOU!
YOU KNOW IT!
TSK! TSK!

Script: Craig Boldman / Pencils: Rex Lindsey / Inks: Rich Koslowski / Letters: Vickie Williams / Colors: Barry Grossman

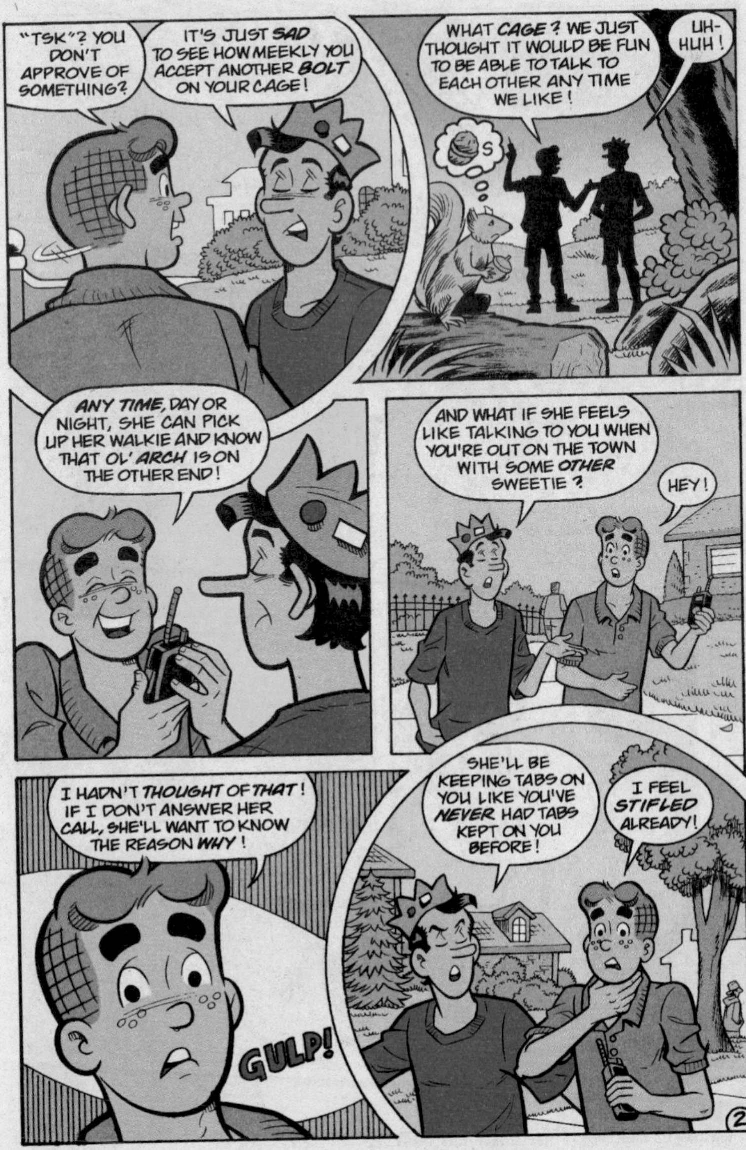
"TSK"? YOU DON'T APPROVE OF SOMETHING?
IT'S JUST SAD TO SEE HOW MEEKLY YOU ACCEPT ANOTHER BOLT ON YOUR CAGE!
WHAT CAGE? WE JUST THOUGHT IT WOULD BE FUN TO BE ABLE TO TALK TO EACH OTHER ANY TIME WE LIKE!
UH-HUH!
S
ANY TIME, DAY OR NIGHT, SHE CAN PICK UP HER WALKIE AND KNOW THAT OL' ARCH IS ON THE OTHER END!
AND WHAT IF SHE FEELS LIKE TALKING TO YOU WHEN YOU'RE OUT ON THE TOWN WITH SOME OTHER SWEETIE?
HEY!
I HADN'T THOUGHT OF THAT! IF I DON'T ANSWER HER CALL, SHE'LL WANT TO KNOW THE REASON WHY!
GULP!
SHE'LL BE KEEPING TABS ON YOU LIKE YOU'VE NEVER HAD TABS KEPT ON YOU BEFORE!
I FEEL STIFLED ALREADY!
2

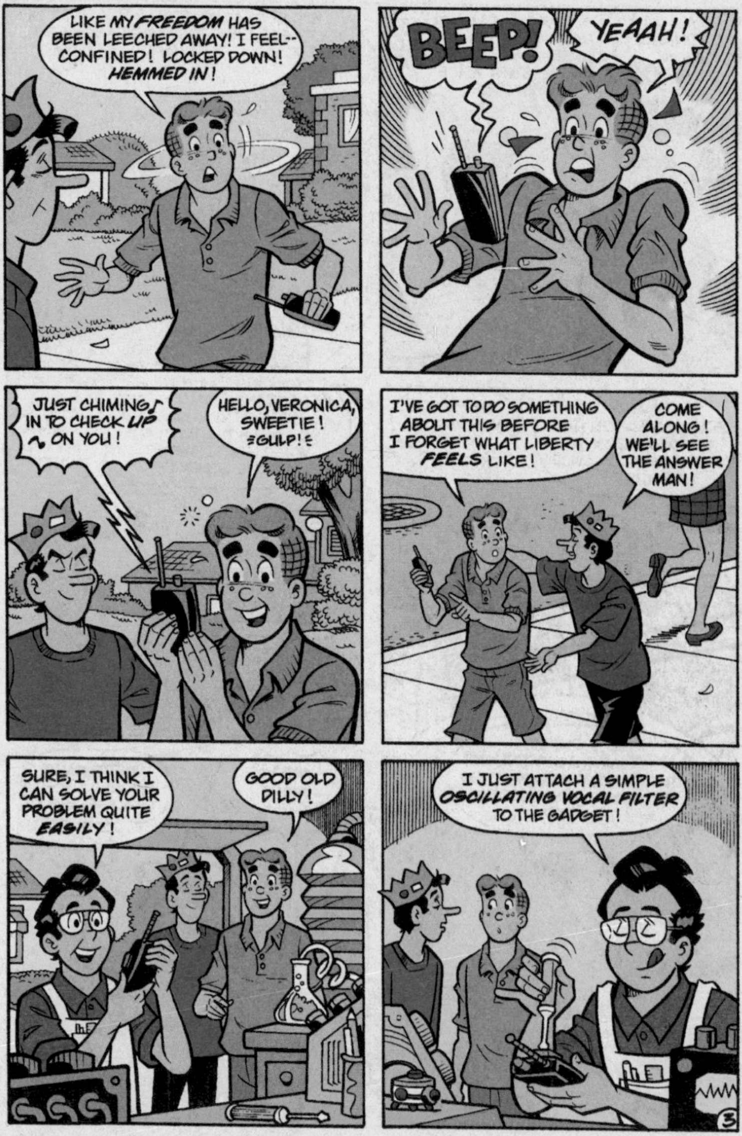
LIKE MY FREEDOM HAS BEEN LEECHED AWAY! I FEEL-- CONFINED! LOCKED DOWN! HEMMED IN!
BEEP!
YEAAH!
JUST CHIMING IN TO CHECK UP ON YOU!
HELLO, VERONICA, SWEETIE! GULP!
I'VE GOT TO DO SOMETHING ABOUT THIS BEFORE I FORGET WHAT LIBERTY FEELS LIKE!
COME ALONG! WE'LL SEE THE ANSWER MAN!
SURE, I THINK I CAN SOLVE YOUR PROBLEM QUITE EASILY!
GOOD OLD DILLY!
I JUST ATTACH A SIMPLE OSCILLATING VOCAL FILTER TO THE GADGET!
3

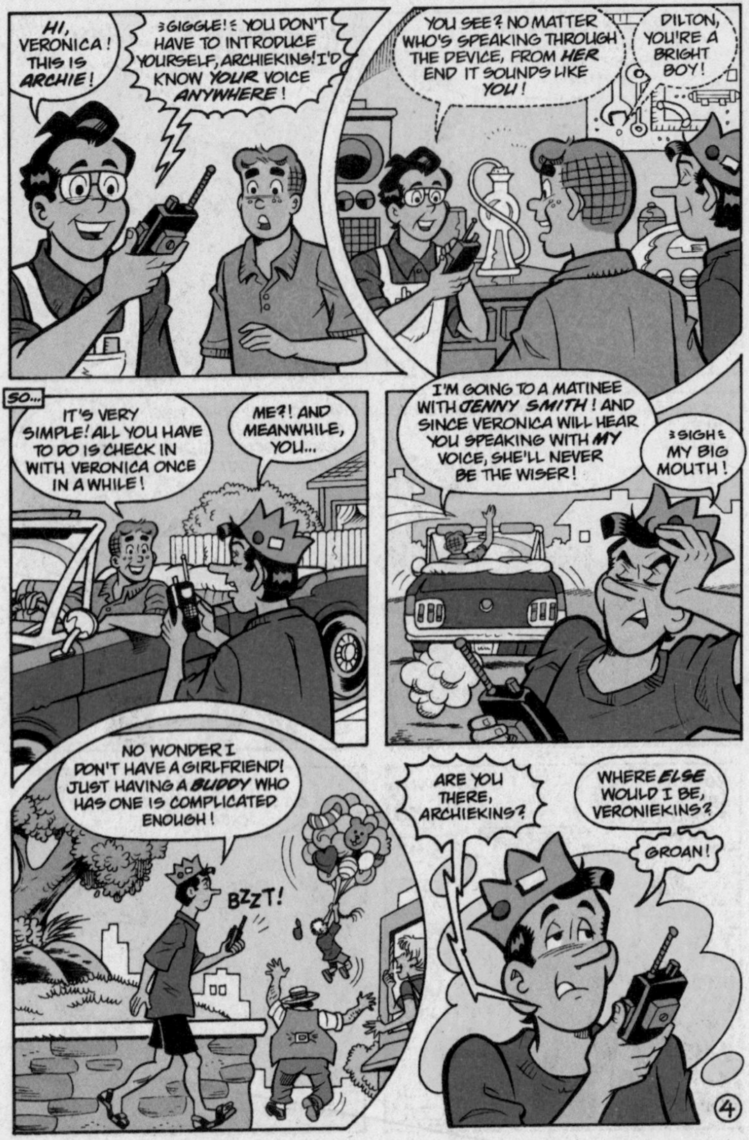
HI, VERONICA! THIS IS ARCHIE!
≋GIGGLE!≋ YOU DON'T HAVE TO INTRODUCE YOURSELF, ARCHIEKINS! I'D KNOW YOUR VOICE ANYWHERE!
YOU SEE? NO MATTER WHO'S SPEAKING THROUGH THE DEVICE, FROM HER END IT SOUNDS LIKE YOU!
DILTON, YOU'RE A BRIGHT BOY!
SO...
IT'S VERY SIMPLE! ALL YOU HAVE TO DO IS CHECK IN WITH VERONICA ONCE IN A WHILE!
ME?! AND MEANWHILE, YOU...
I'M GOING TO A MATINEE WITH JENNY SMITH! AND SINCE VERONICA WILL HEAR YOU SPEAKING WITH MY VOICE, SHE'LL NEVER BE THE WISER!
≋SIGH≋ MY BIG MOUTH!
NO WONDER I DON'T HAVE A GIRLFRIEND! JUST HAVING A BUDDY WHO HAS ONE IS COMPLICATED ENOUGH!
BZZT!
ARE YOU THERE, ARCHIEKINS?
WHERE ELSE WOULD I BE, VERONIEKINS?
GROAN!
4

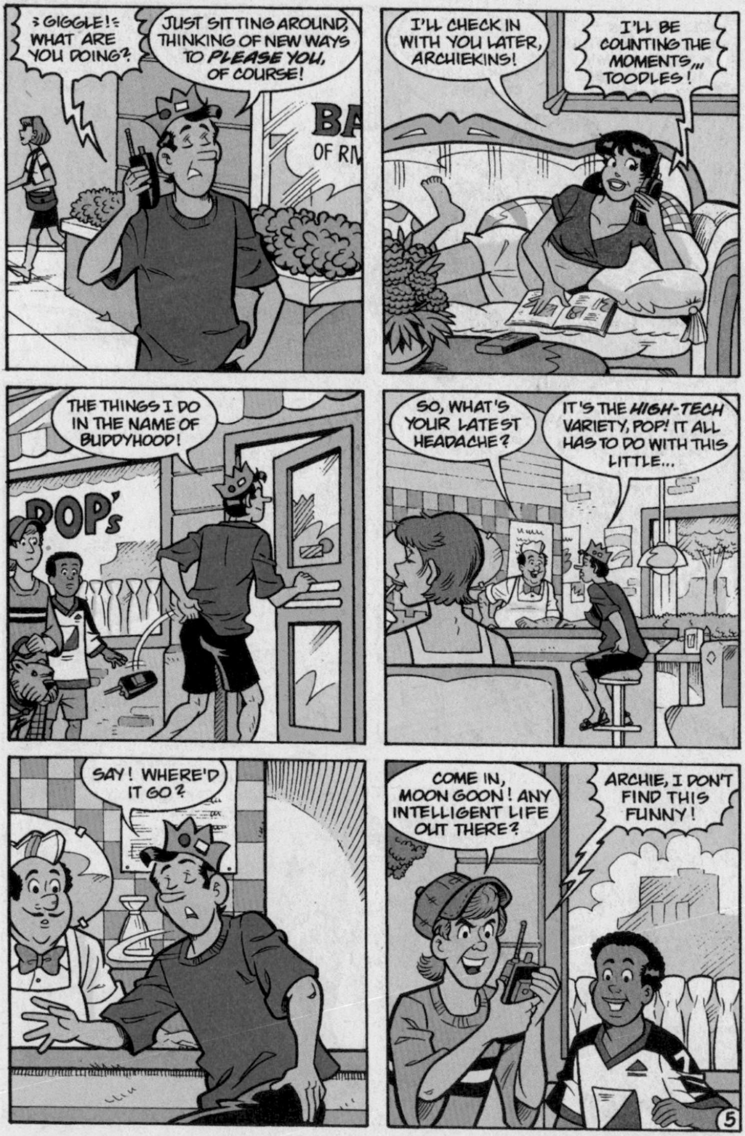

GIGGLE! WHAT ARE YOU DOING?
JUST SITTING AROUND, THINKING OF NEW WAYS TO PLEASE YOU, OF COURSE!
BA
OF RI
I'LL CHECK IN WITH YOU LATER, ARCHIEKINS!
I'LL BE COUNTING THE MOMENTS... TOODLES!
THE THINGS I DO IN THE NAME OF BUDDYHOOD!
POP's
SO, WHAT'S YOUR LATEST HEADACHE?
IT'S THE HIGH-TECH VARIETY, POP! IT ALL HAS TO DO WITH THIS LITTLE...
SAY! WHERE'D IT GO?
COME IN, MOON GOON! ANY INTELLIGENT LIFE OUT THERE?
ARCHIE, I DON'T FIND THIS FUNNY!
5

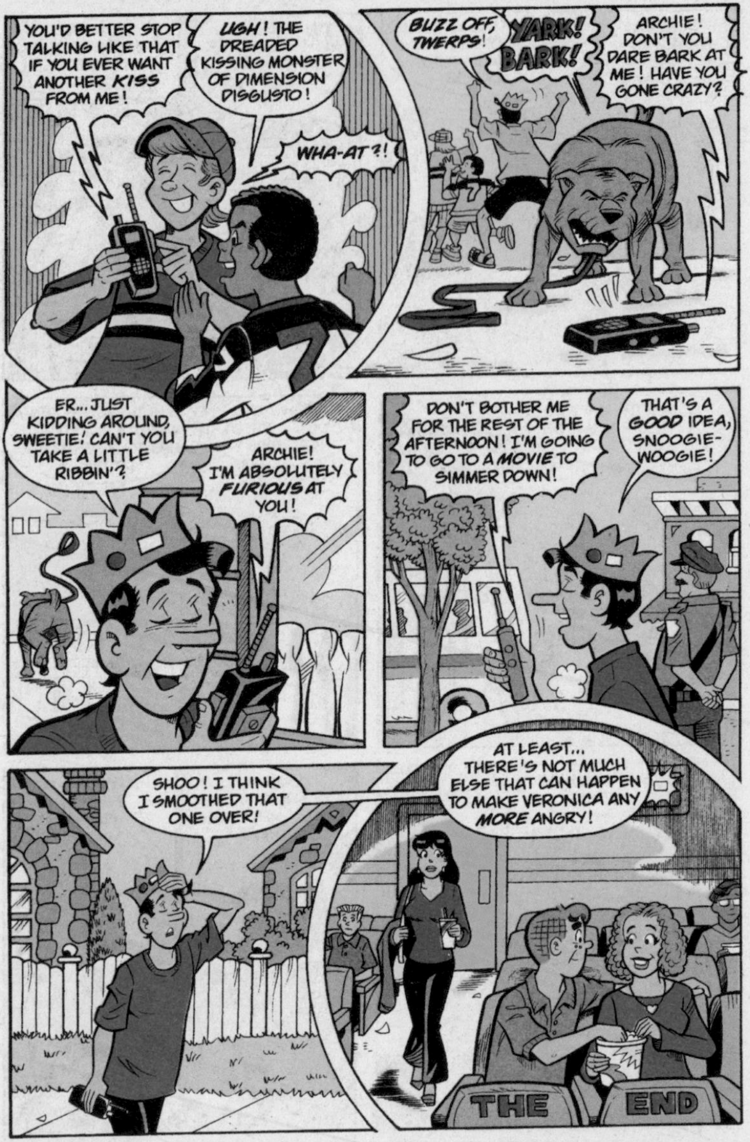
YOU'D BETTER STOP TALKING LIKE THAT IF YOU EVER WANT ANOTHER KISS FROM ME!
UGH! THE DREADED KISSING MONSTER OF DIMENSION DISGUSTO!
WHA-AT?!
BUZZ OFF, TWERPS!
YARK! BARK!
ARCHIE! DON'T YOU DARE BARK AT ME! HAVE YOU GONE CRAZY?
ER... JUST KIDDING AROUND, SWEETIE! CAN'T YOU TAKE A LITTLE RIBBIN'?
ARCHIE! I'M ABSOLUTELY FURIOUS AT YOU!
DON'T BOTHER ME FOR THE REST OF THE AFTERNOON! I'M GOING TO GO TO A MOVIE TO SIMMER DOWN!
THAT'S A GOOD IDEA, SNOOGIE-WOOGIE!
SHOO! I THINK I SMOOTHED THAT ONE OVER!
AT LEAST... THERE'S NOT MUCH ELSE THAT CAN HAPPEN TO MAKE VERONICA ANY MORE ANGRY!
THE END

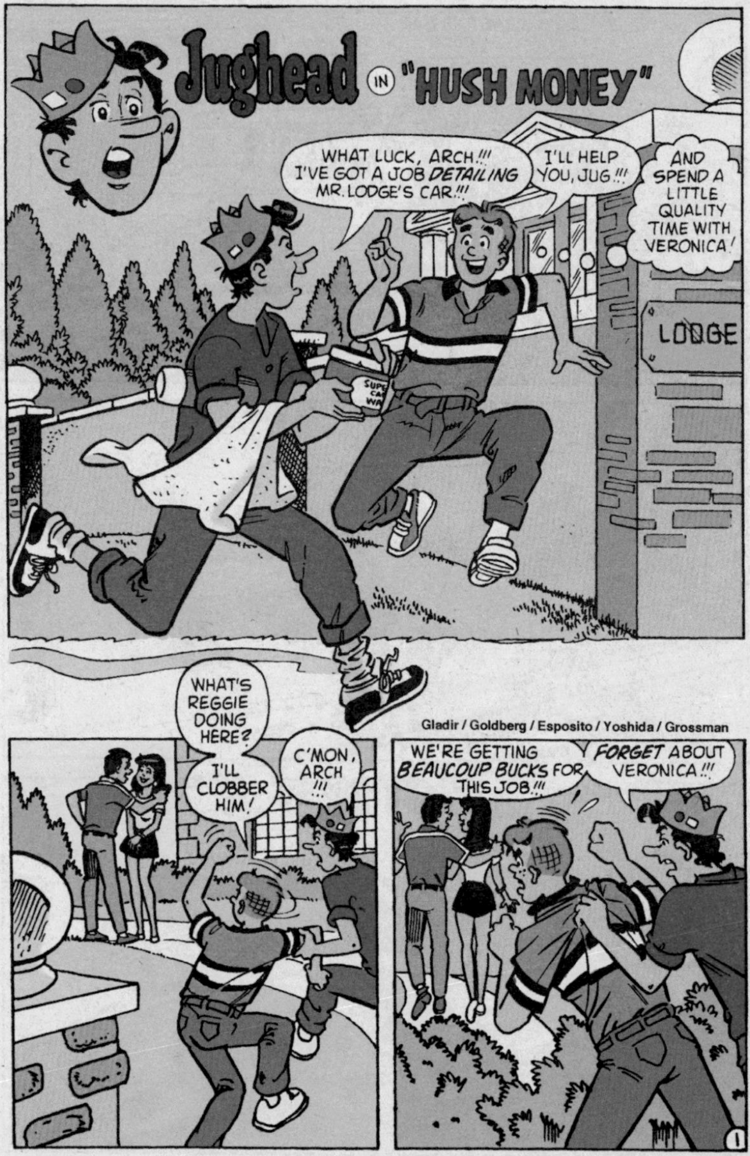
Jughead IN "HUSH MONEY"
WHAT LUCK, ARCH!!! I'VE GOT A JOB DETAILING MR. LODGE'S CAR!!!
I'LL HELP YOU, JUG!!!
AND SPEND A LITTLE QUALITY TIME WITH VERONICA!
LODGE
Gladir / Goldberg / Esposito / Yoshida / Grossman
WHAT'S REGGIE DOING HERE?
I'LL CLOBBER HIM!
C'MON, ARCH!!!
WE'RE GETTING BEAUCOUP BUCKS FOR THIS JOB!!!
FORGET ABOUT VERONICA!!!
1

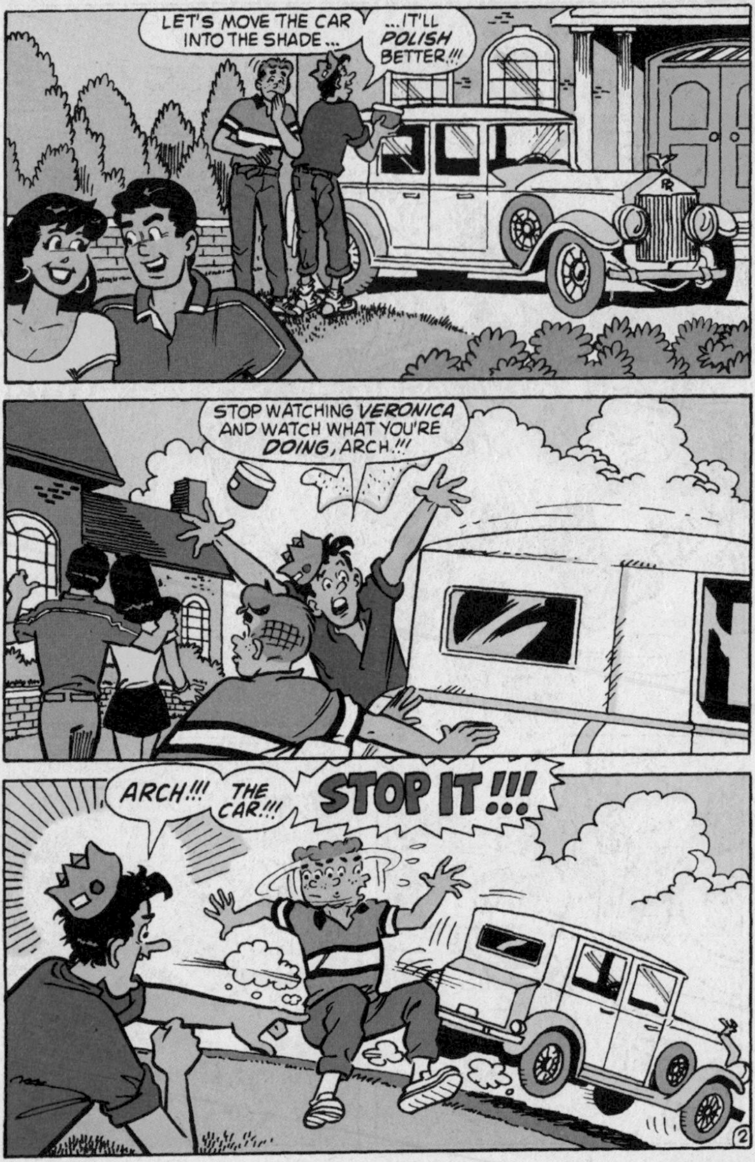
LET'S MOVE THE CAR INTO THE SHADE ...
...IT'LL POLISH BETTER!!!
STOP WATCHING VERONICA AND WATCH WHAT YOU'RE DOING, ARCH!!!
ARCH!!! THE CAR!!!
STOP IT!!!
2

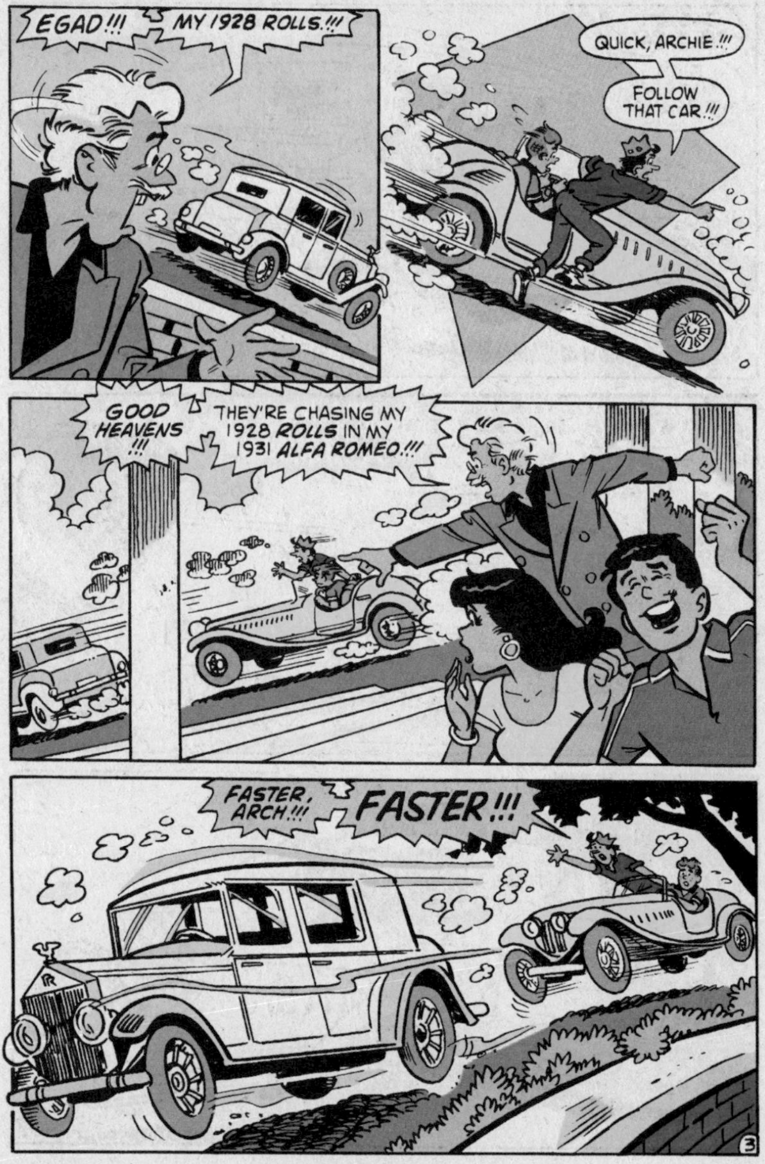

EGAD!!!
MY 1928 ROLLS!!!
QUICK, ARCHIE!!!
FOLLOW THAT CAR!!!
GOOD HEAVENS!!!
THEY'RE CHASING MY 1928 ROLLS IN MY 1931 ALFA ROMEO!!!
FASTER, ARCH!!!
FASTER!!!
3

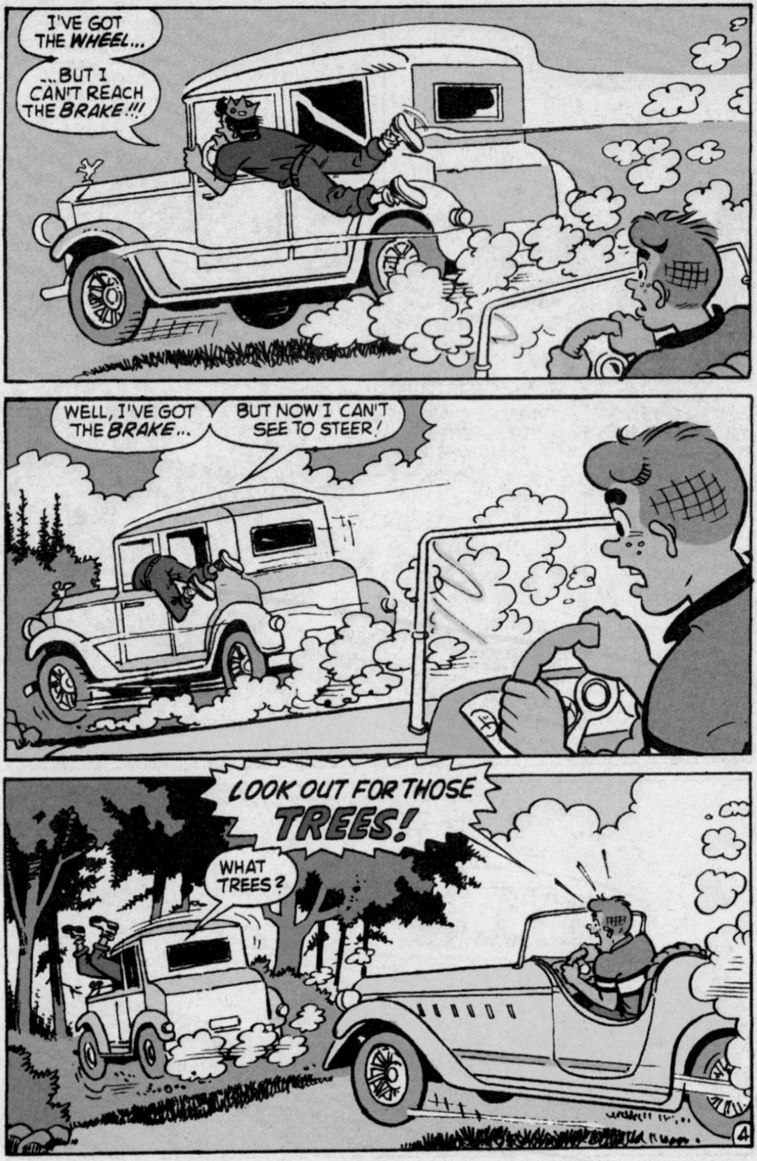
I'VE GOT THE WHEEL...
...BUT I CAN'T REACH THE BRAKE!!!
WELL, I'VE GOT THE BRAKE...
BUT NOW I CAN'T SEE TO STEER!
LOOK OUT FOR THOSE TREES!
WHAT TREES?
4

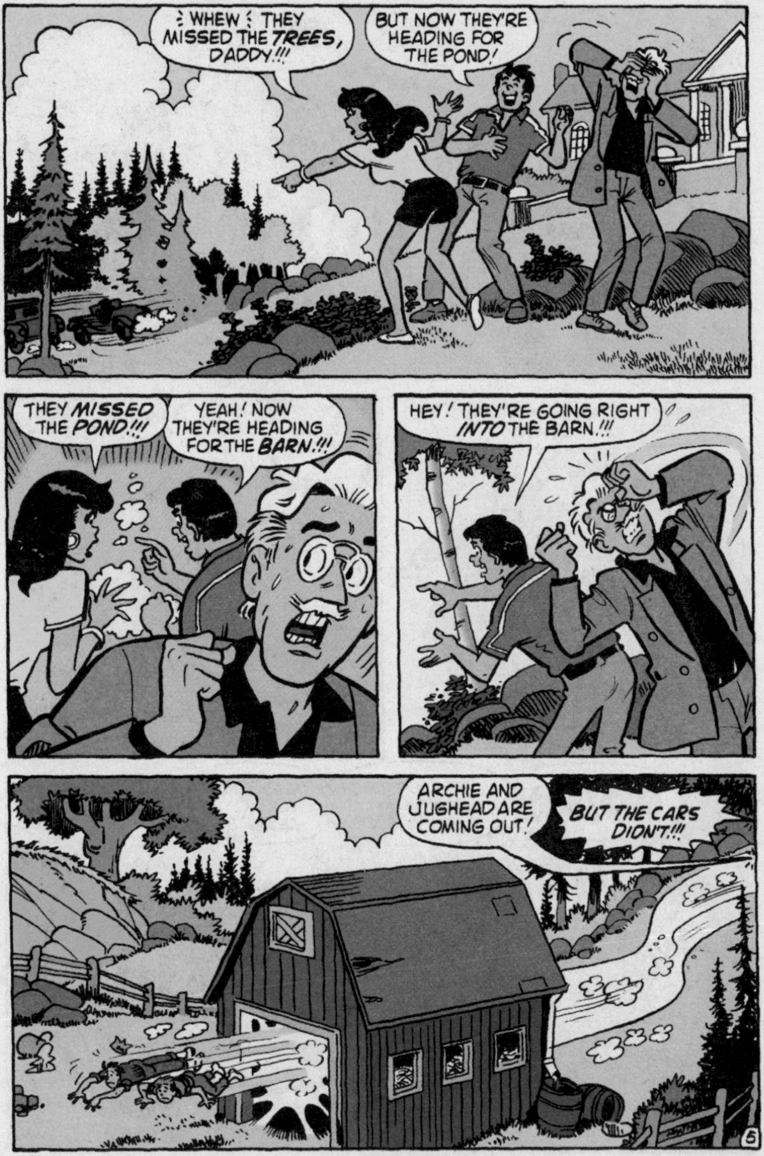

WHEW! THEY MISSED THE TREES, DADDY!!!
BUT NOW THEY'RE HEADING FOR THE POND!
THEY MISSED THE POND!!!
YEAH! NOW THEY'RE HEADING FOR THE BARN!!!
HEY! THEY'RE GOING RIGHT INTO THE BARN!!!
ARCHIE AND JUGHEAD ARE COMING OUT!
BUT THE CARS DIDN'T!!!
5

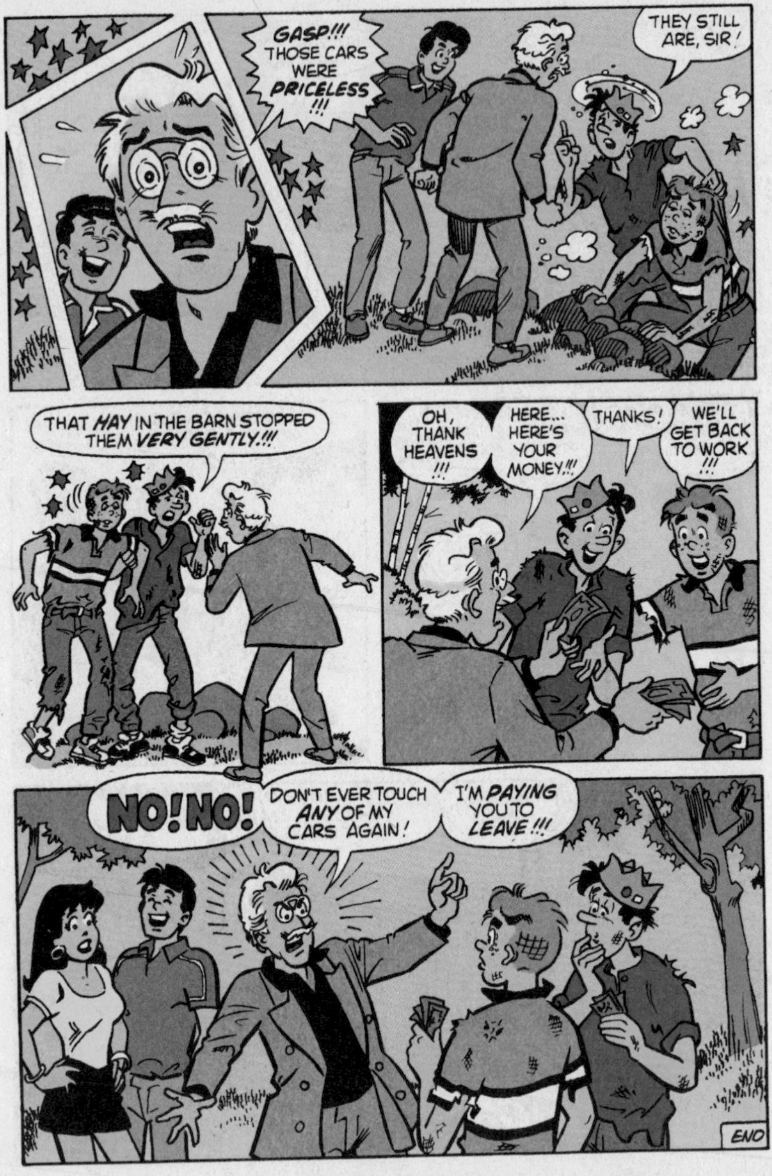
GASP!!! THOSE CARS WERE PRICELESS!!!
THEY STILL ARE, SIR!
THAT HAY IN THE BARN STOPPED THEM VERY GENTLY!!!
OH, THANK HEAVENS!!!
HERE... HERE'S YOUR MONEY!!!
THANKS!
WE'LL GET BACK TO WORK!!!
NO! NO!
DON'T EVER TOUCH ANY OF MY CARS AGAIN!
I'M PAYING YOU TO LEAVE!!!
END

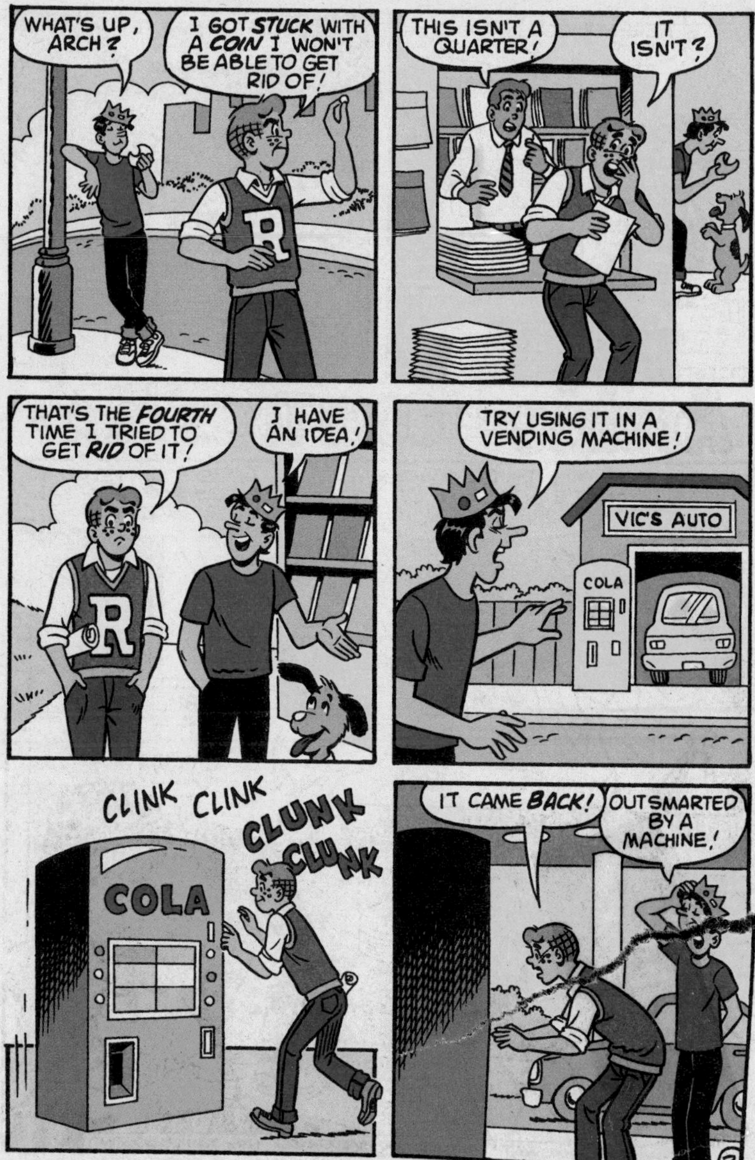
WHAT'S UP, ARCH?
I GOT STUCK WITH A COIN I WON'T BE ABLE TO GET RID OF!
THIS ISN'T A QUARTER!
IT ISN'T?
THAT'S THE FOURTH TIME I TRIED TO GET RID OF IT!
I HAVE AN IDEA!
TRY USING IT IN A VENDING MACHINE!
VIC'S AUTO
COLA
CLINK CLINK
CLUNK
CLUNK
COLA
IT CAME BACK!
OUTSMARTED BY A MACHINE!

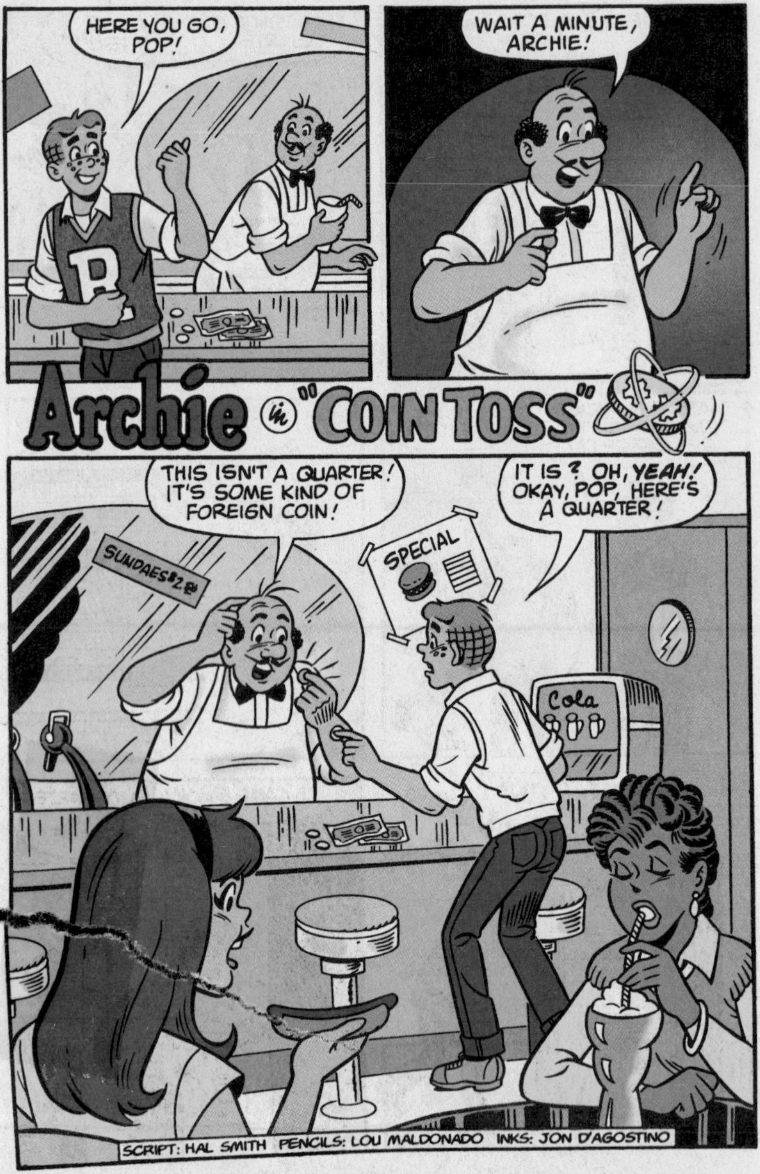
HERE YOU GO, POP!
WAIT A MINUTE, ARCHIE!
Archie in "COIN TOSS"
THIS ISN'T A QUARTER! IT'S SOME KIND OF FOREIGN COIN!
IT IS? OH, YEAH! OKAY, POP, HERE'S A QUARTER!
SUNDAES $2.00
SPECIAL
Cola
SCRIPT: HAL SMITH PENCILS: LOU MALDONADO INKS: JON D'AGOSTINO

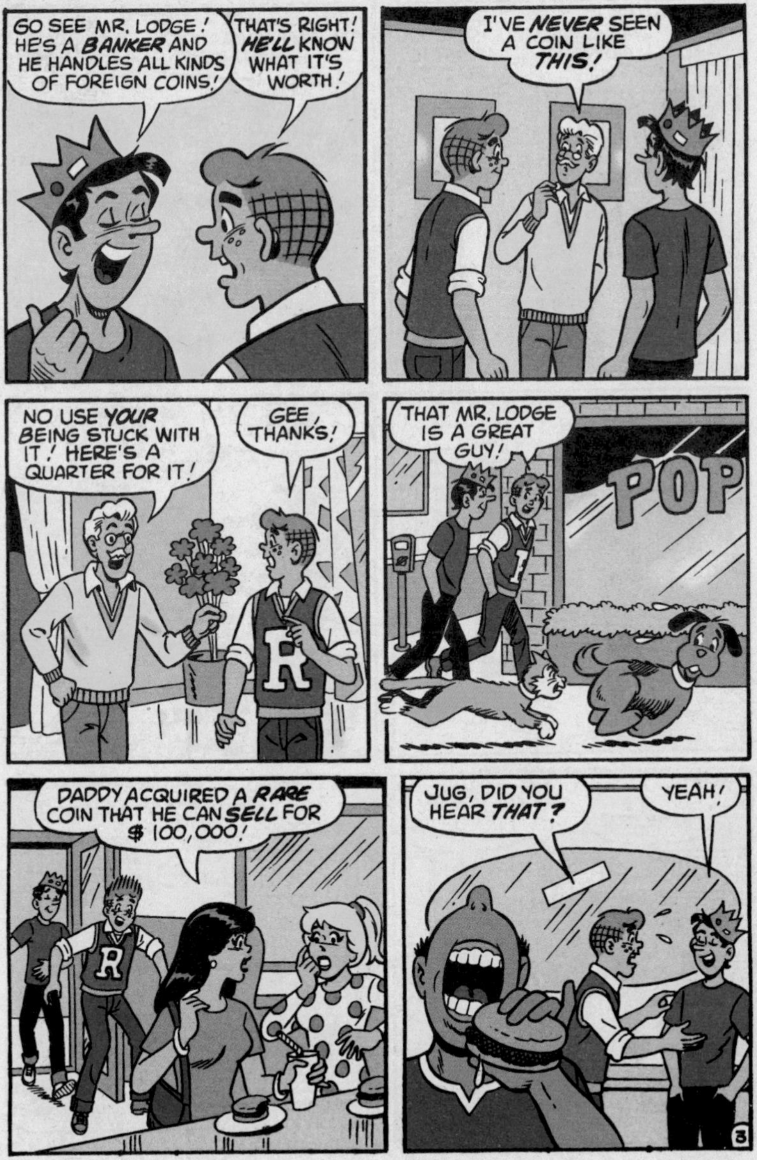
GO SEE MR. LODGE! HE'S A BANKER AND HE HANDLES ALL KINDS OF FOREIGN COINS!
THAT'S RIGHT! HE'LL KNOW WHAT IT'S WORTH!
I'VE NEVER SEEN A COIN LIKE THIS!
NO USE YOUR BEING STUCK WITH IT! HERE'S A QUARTER FOR IT!
GEE, THANKS!
THAT MR. LODGE IS A GREAT GUY!
POP
DADDY ACQUIRED A RARE COIN THAT HE CAN SELL FOR $ 100,000!
JUG, DID YOU HEAR THAT?
YEAH!
3

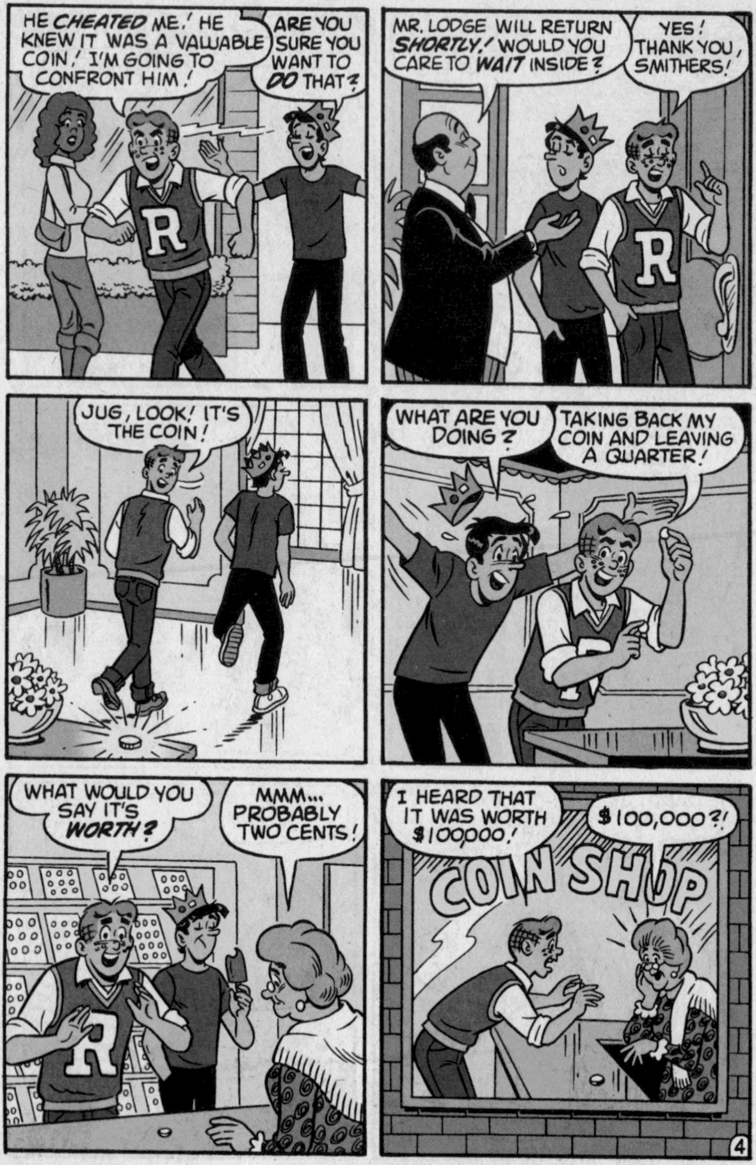
HE CHEATED ME! HE KNEW IT WAS A VALUABLE COIN! I'M GOING TO CONFRONT HIM!
ARE YOU SURE YOU WANT TO DO THAT?
MR. LODGE WILL RETURN SHORTLY! WOULD YOU CARE TO WAIT INSIDE?
YES! THANK YOU, SMITHERS!
JUG, LOOK! IT'S THE COIN!
WHAT ARE YOU DOING?
TAKING BACK MY COIN AND LEAVING A QUARTER!
WHAT WOULD YOU SAY IT'S WORTH?
MMM... PROBABLY TWO CENTS!
I HEARD THAT IT WAS WORTH $100,000!
$100,000?!
COIN SHOP
4

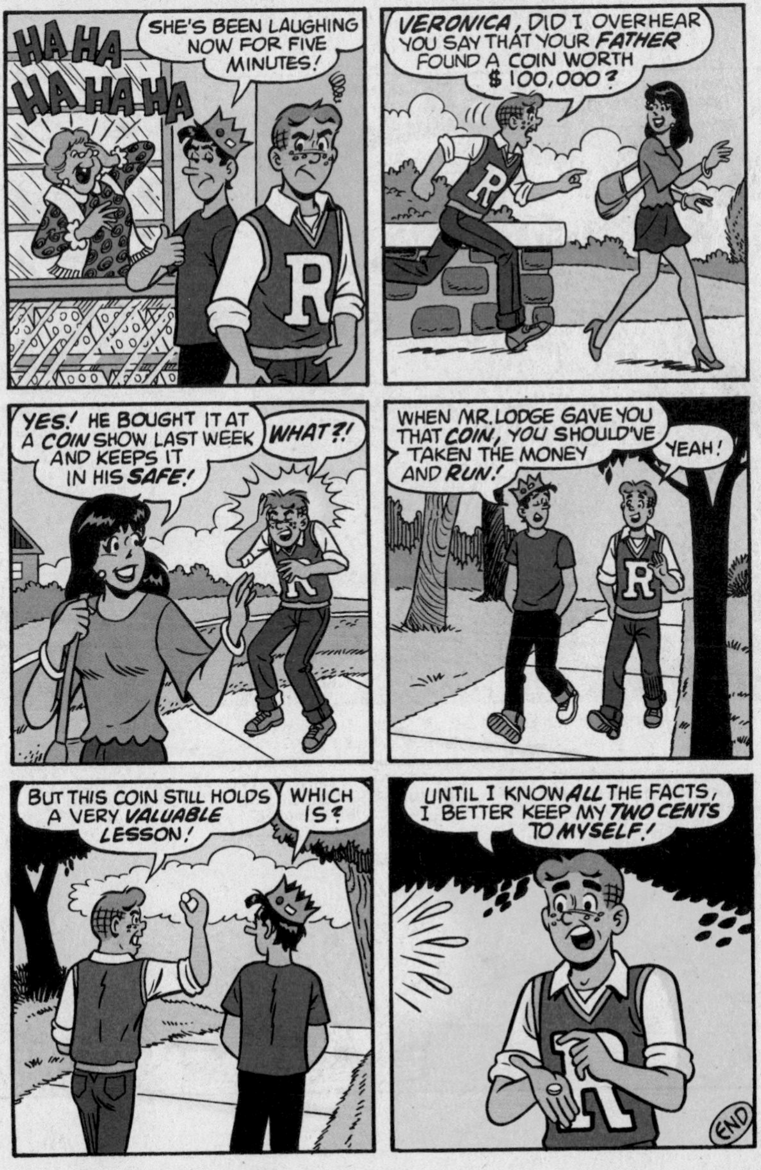
HA HA HA HA HA HA
SHE'S BEEN LAUGHING NOW FOR FIVE MINUTES!
VERONICA, DID I OVERHEAR YOU SAY THAT YOUR FATHER FOUND A COIN WORTH $ 100,000?
YES! HE BOUGHT IT AT A COIN SHOW LAST WEEK AND KEEPS IT IN HIS SAFE!
WHAT?!
WHEN MR. LODGE GAVE YOU THAT COIN, YOU SHOULD'VE TAKEN THE MONEY AND RUN!
YEAH!
BUT THIS COIN STILL HOLDS A VERY VALUABLE LESSON!
WHICH IS?
UNTIL I KNOW ALL THE FACTS, I BETTER KEEP MY TWO CENTS TO MYSELF!
END

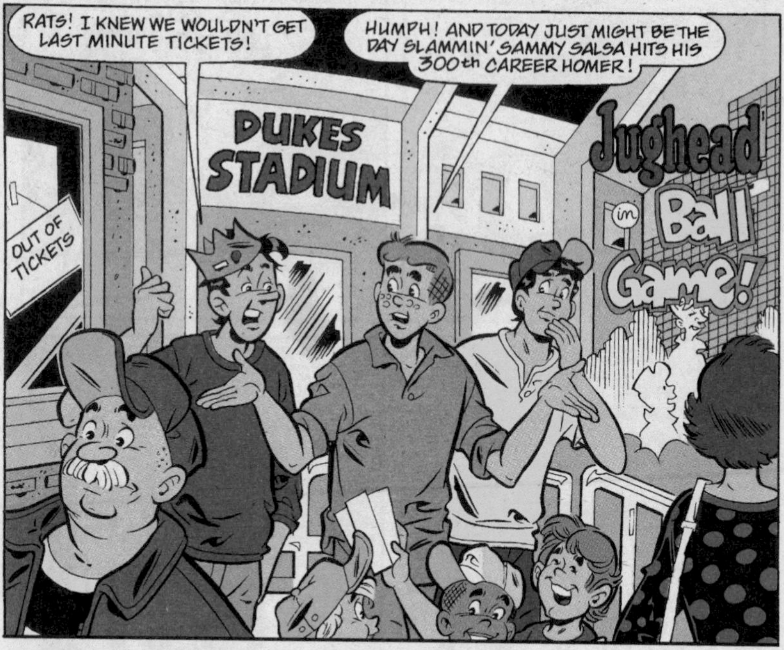
RATS! I KNEW WE WOULDN'T GET LAST MINUTE TICKETS!
HUMPH! AND TODAY JUST MIGHT BE THE DAY SLAMMIN' SAMMY SALSA HITS HIS 300th CAREER HOMER!
DUKES STADIUM
OUT OF TICKETS
Jughead in Ball Game!

SCRIPT: MIKE PELLOWSKI PENCILS: TIM KENNEDY INKS: KEN SELIG
COLORS: BARRY GROSSMAN LETTERS: VICKIE WILLIAMS

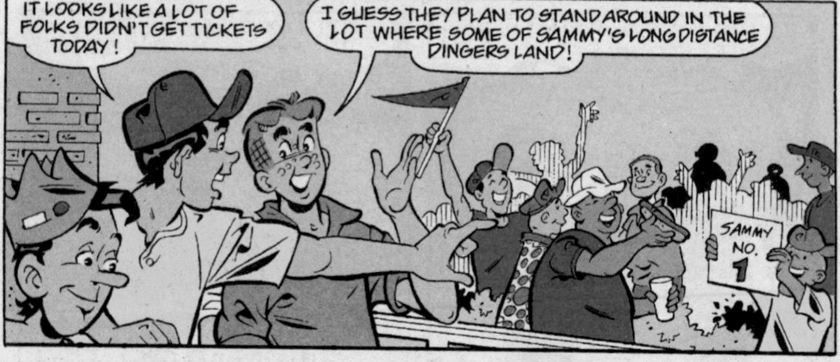
IT LOOKS LIKE A LOT OF FOLKS DIDN'T GET TICKETS TODAY!
I GUESS THEY PLAN TO STAND AROUND IN THE LOT WHERE SOME OF SAMMY'S LONG DISTANCE DINGERS LAND!
SAMMY NO. 1

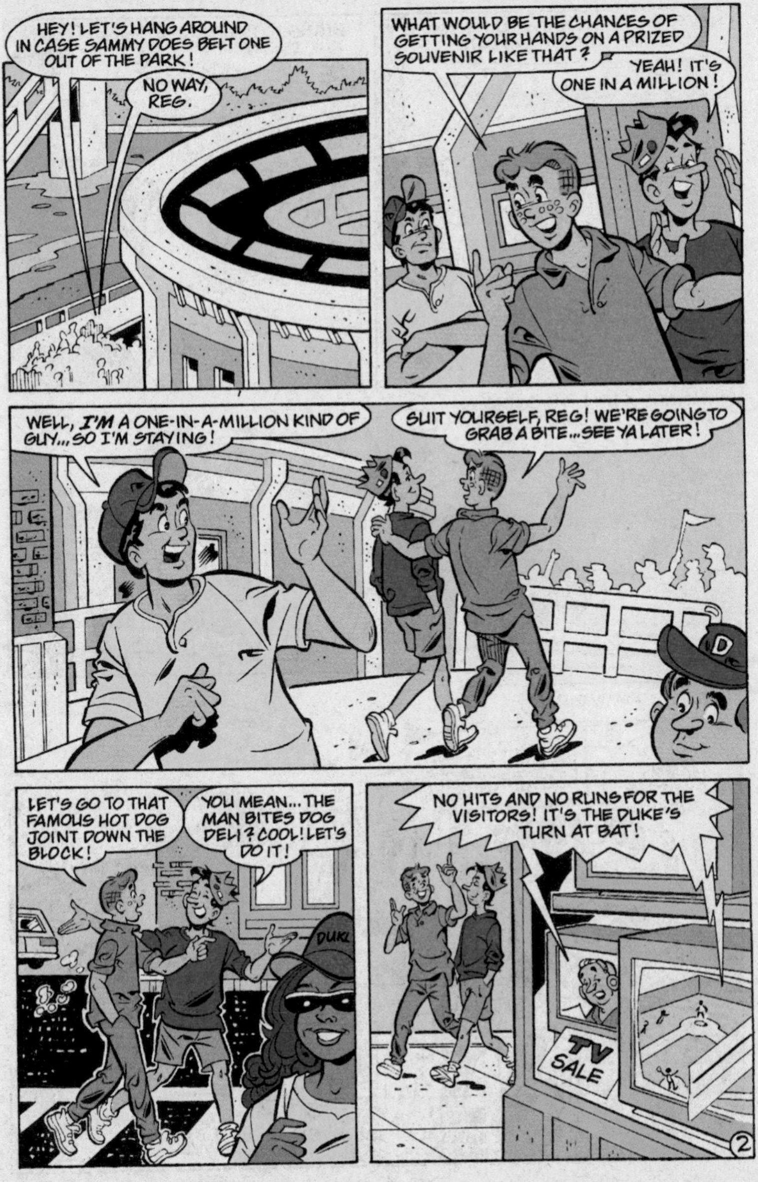
HEY! LET'S HANG AROUND IN CASE SAMMY DOES BELT ONE OUT OF THE PARK!
NO WAY, REG.
WHAT WOULD BE THE CHANCES OF GETTING YOUR HANDS ON A PRIZED SOUVENIR LIKE THAT?
YEAH! IT'S ONE IN A MILLION!
WELL, I'M A ONE-IN-A-MILLION KIND OF GUY... SO I'M STAYING!
SUIT YOURSELF, REG! WE'RE GOING TO GRAB A BITE... SEE YA LATER!
D
LET'S GO TO THAT FAMOUS HOT DOG JOINT DOWN THE BLOCK!
YOU MEAN... THE MAN BITES DOG DELI? COOL! LET'S DO IT!
DUKE
NO HITS AND NO RUNS FOR THE VISITORS! IT'S THE DUKE'S TURN AT BAT!
TV SALE
2

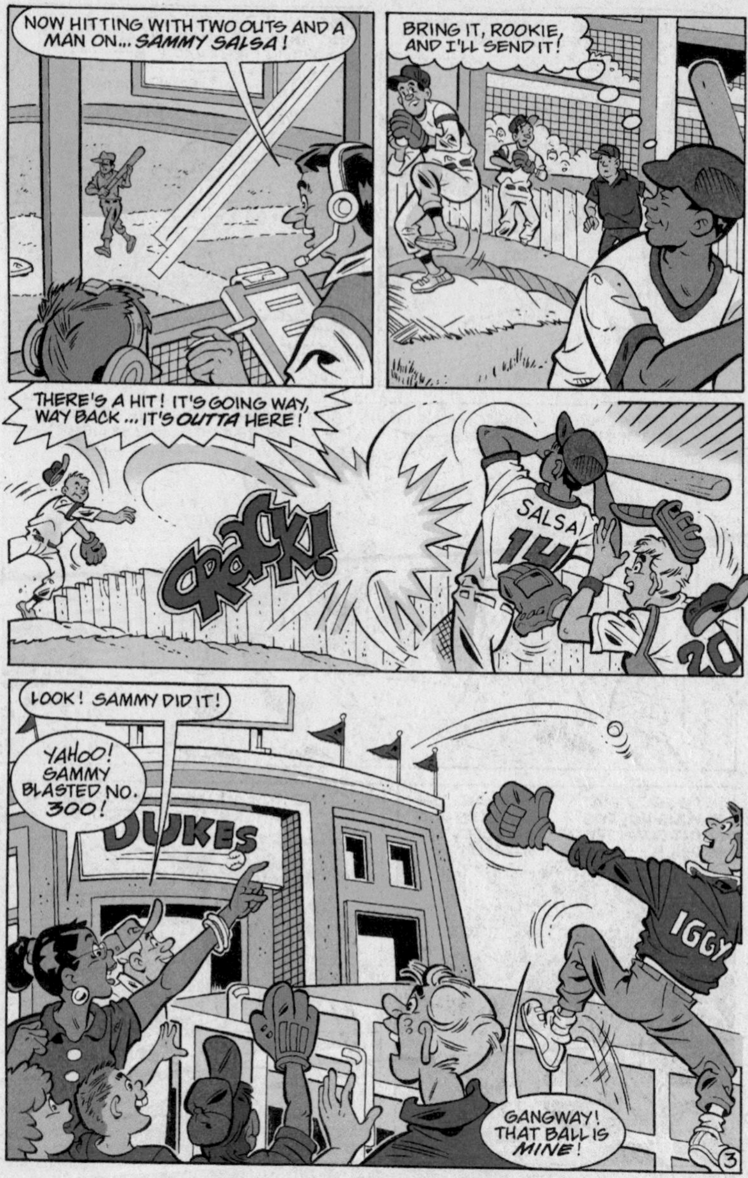

NOW HITTING WITH TWO OUTS AND A MAN ON... SAMMY SALSA!
BRING IT, ROOKIE, AND I'LL SEND IT!
THERE'S A HIT! IT'S GOING WAY, WAY BACK... IT'S OUTTA HERE!
CRACK!
SALSA 14
20
LOOK! SAMMY DID IT!
YAHOO! SAMMY BLASTED NO. 300!
DUKES
IGGY
GANGWAY! THAT BALL IS MINE!

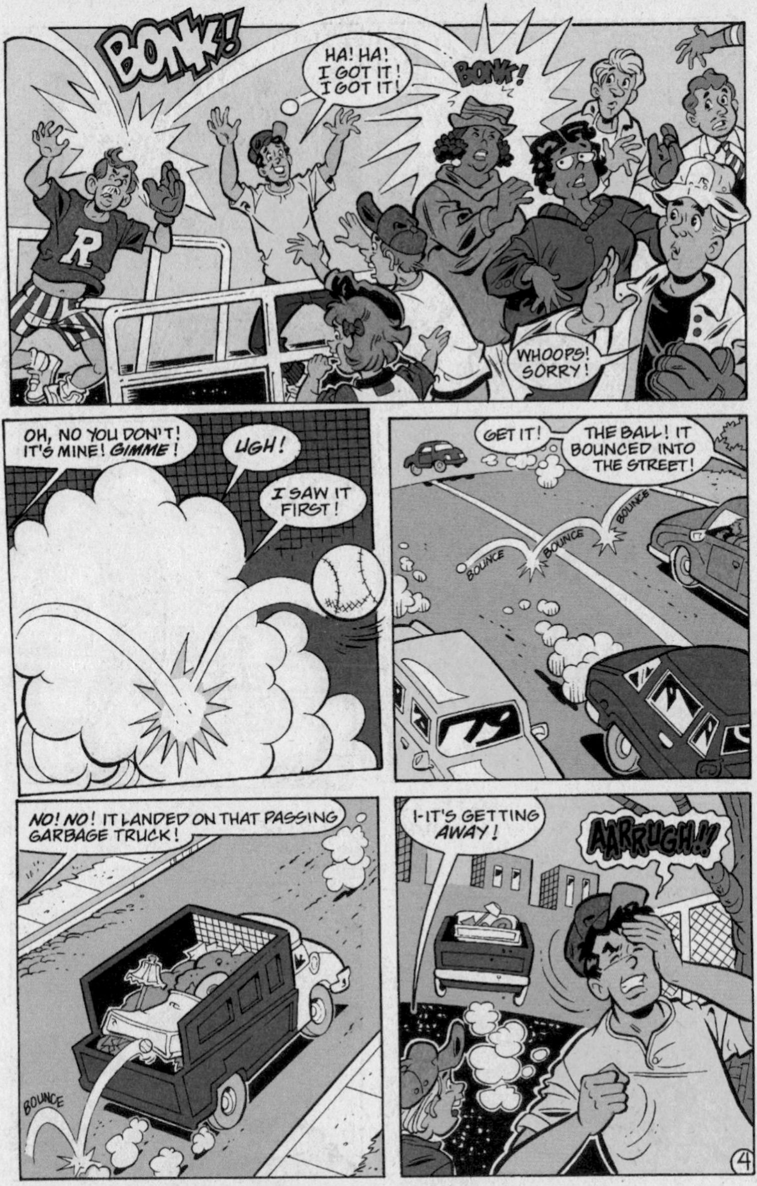
BONK!
HA! HA! I GOT IT! I GOT IT!
BONK!
WHOOPS! SORRY!
OH, NO YOU DON'T! IT'S MINE! GIMME!
UGH!
I SAW IT FIRST!
GET IT!
THE BALL! IT BOUNCED INTO THE STREET!
BOUNCE
BOUNCE
BOUNCE
NO! NO! IT LANDED ON THAT PASSING GARBAGE TRUCK!
BOUNCE
I-IT'S GETTING AWAY!
AARRUGH!!
4

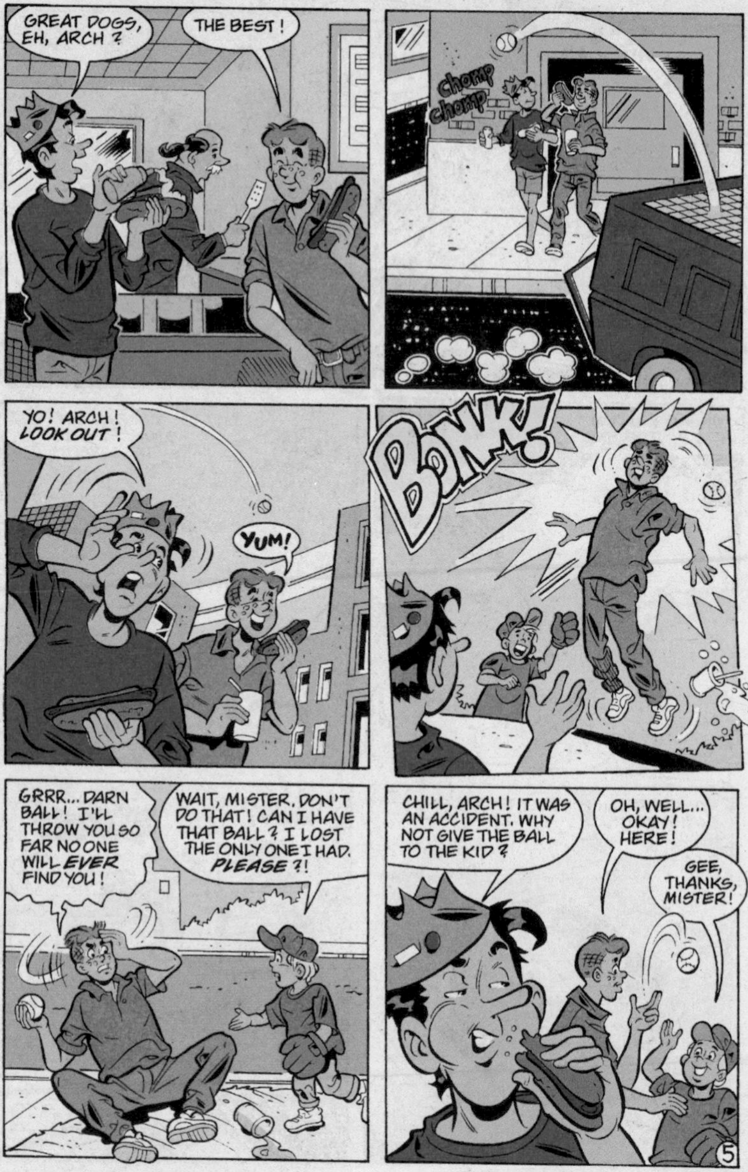
GREAT DOGS, EH, ARCH ?
THE BEST !
chomp chomp
YO! ARCH! LOOK OUT !
YUM!
BONK!
GRRR... DARN BALL! I'LL THROW YOU SO FAR NO ONE WILL EVER FIND YOU !
WAIT, MISTER. DON'T DO THAT! CAN I HAVE THAT BALL ? I LOST THE ONLY ONE I HAD. PLEASE ?!
CHILL, ARCH! IT WAS AN ACCIDENT. WHY NOT GIVE THE BALL TO THE KID ?
OH, WELL... OKAY! HERE!
GEE, THANKS, MISTER!

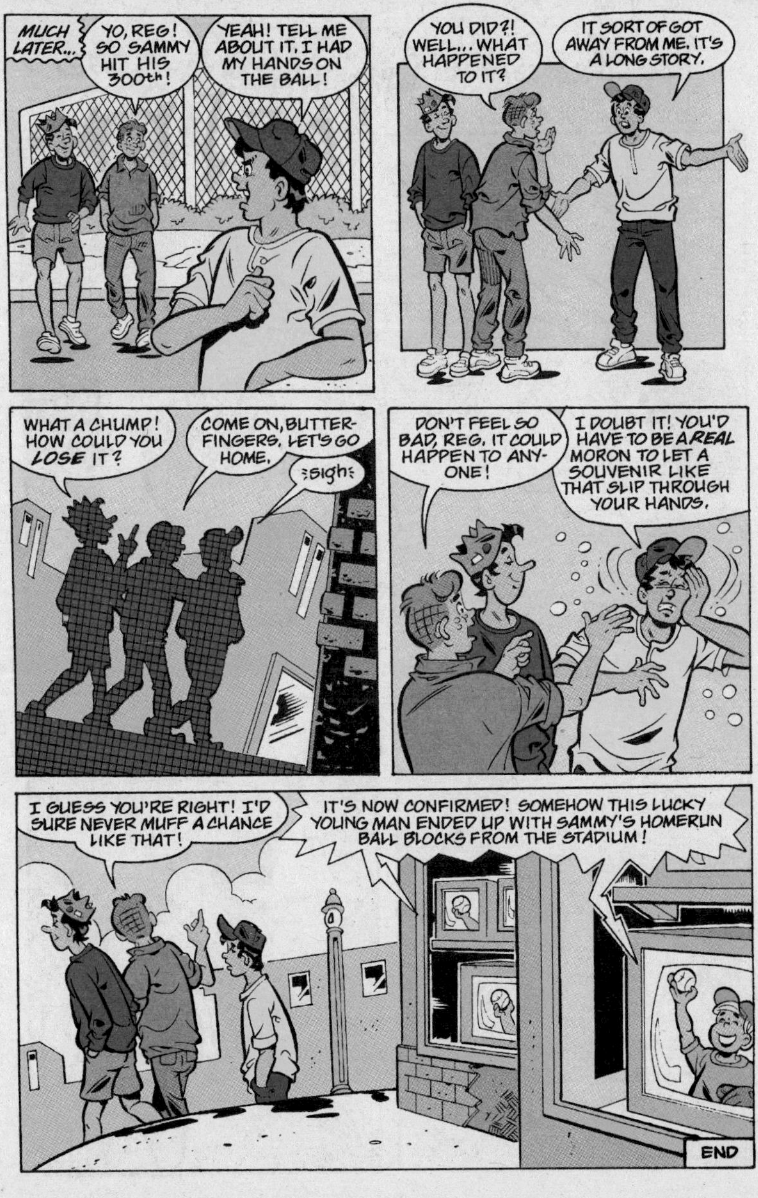
MUCH LATER...
YO, REG! SO SAMMY HIT HIS 300th!
YEAH! TELL ME ABOUT IT. I HAD MY HANDS ON THE BALL!
YOU DID?! WELL... WHAT HAPPENED TO IT?
IT SORT OF GOT AWAY FROM ME. IT'S A LONG STORY.
WHAT A CHUMP! HOW COULD YOU LOSE IT?
COME ON, BUTTER-FINGERS. LET'S GO HOME.
sigh
DON'T FEEL SO BAD, REG. IT COULD HAPPEN TO ANY-ONE!
I DOUBT IT! YOU'D HAVE TO BE A REAL MORON TO LET A SOUVENIR LIKE THAT SLIP THROUGH YOUR HANDS.
I GUESS YOU'RE RIGHT! I'D SURE NEVER MUFF A CHANCE LIKE THAT!
IT'S NOW CONFIRMED! SOMEHOW THIS LUCKY YOUNG MAN ENDED UP WITH SAMMY'S HOMERUN BALL BLOCKS FROM THE STADIUM!
END

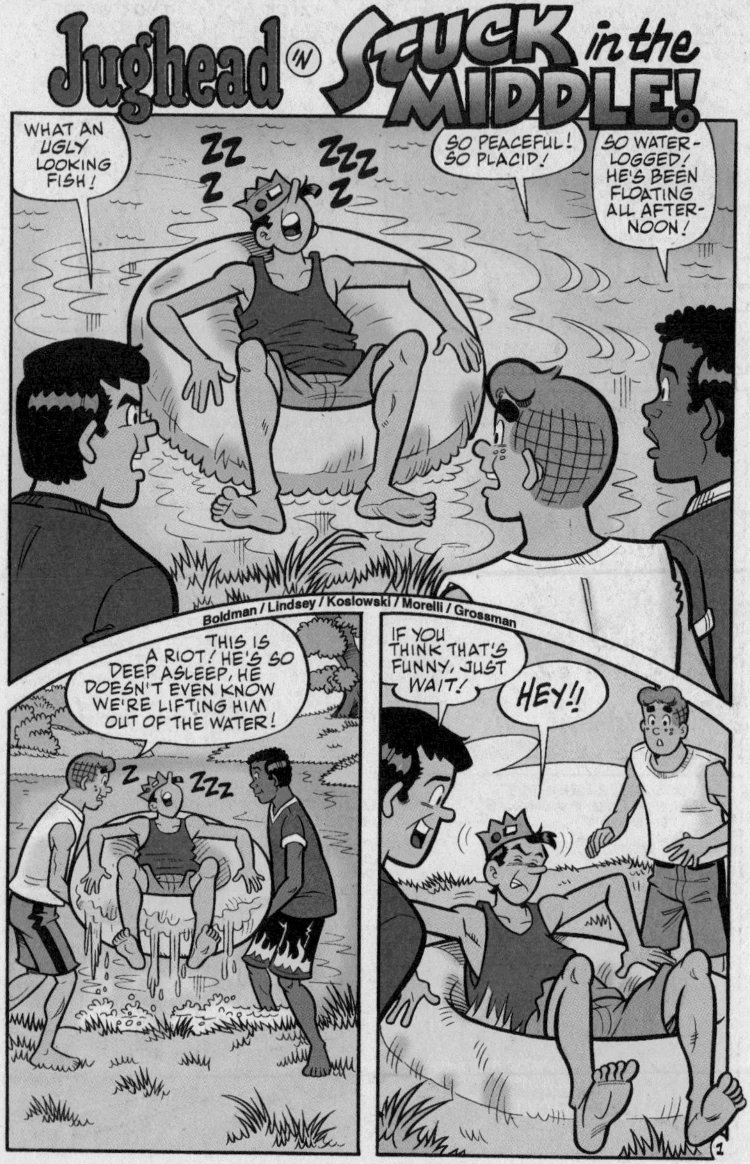
Jughead in Stuck in the MIDDLE!
WHAT AN UGLY LOOKING FISH!
ZZ Z
ZZZ Z
SO PEACEFUL! SO PLACID!
SO WATER-LOGGED! HE'S BEEN FLOATING ALL AFTER-NOON!
Boldman / Lindsey / Koslowski / Morelli / Grossman
THIS IS A RIOT! HE'S SO DEEP ASLEEP, HE DOESN'T EVEN KNOW WE'RE LIFTING HIM OUT OF THE WATER!
Z ZZZ
IF YOU THINK THAT'S FUNNY, JUST WAIT!
HEY!!
1

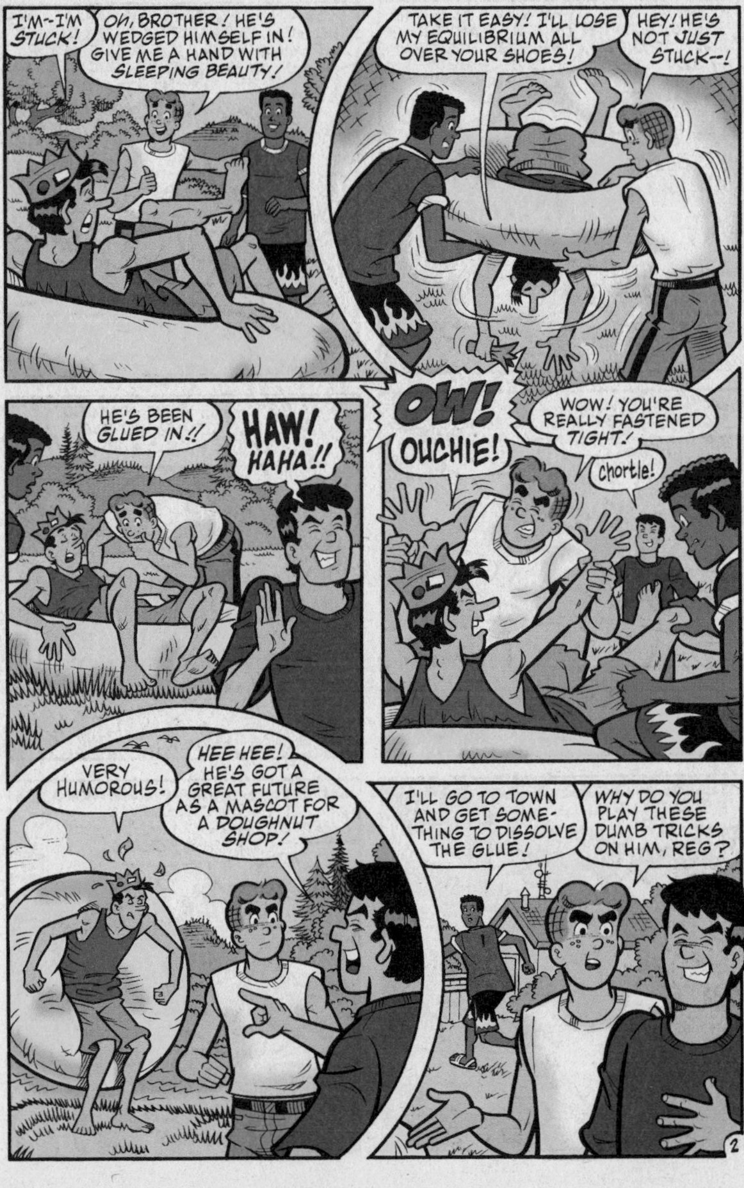

I'M--I'M STUCK!
OH, BROTHER! HE'S WEDGED HIMSELF IN! GIVE ME A HAND WITH SLEEPING BEAUTY!
TAKE IT EASY! I'LL LOSE MY EQUILIBRIUM ALL OVER YOUR SHOES!
HEY! HE'S NOT JUST STUCK--!
OW!
HE'S BEEN GLUED IN!!
HAW! HAHA!!
OUCHIE!
WOW! YOU'RE REALLY FASTENED TIGHT!
chortle!
VERY HUMOROUS!
HEE HEE! HE'S GOT A GREAT FUTURE AS A MASCOT FOR A DOUGHNUT SHOP!
I'LL GO TO TOWN AND GET SOME-THING TO DISSOLVE THE GLUE!
WHY DO YOU PLAY THESE DUMB TRICKS ON HIM, REG?
2

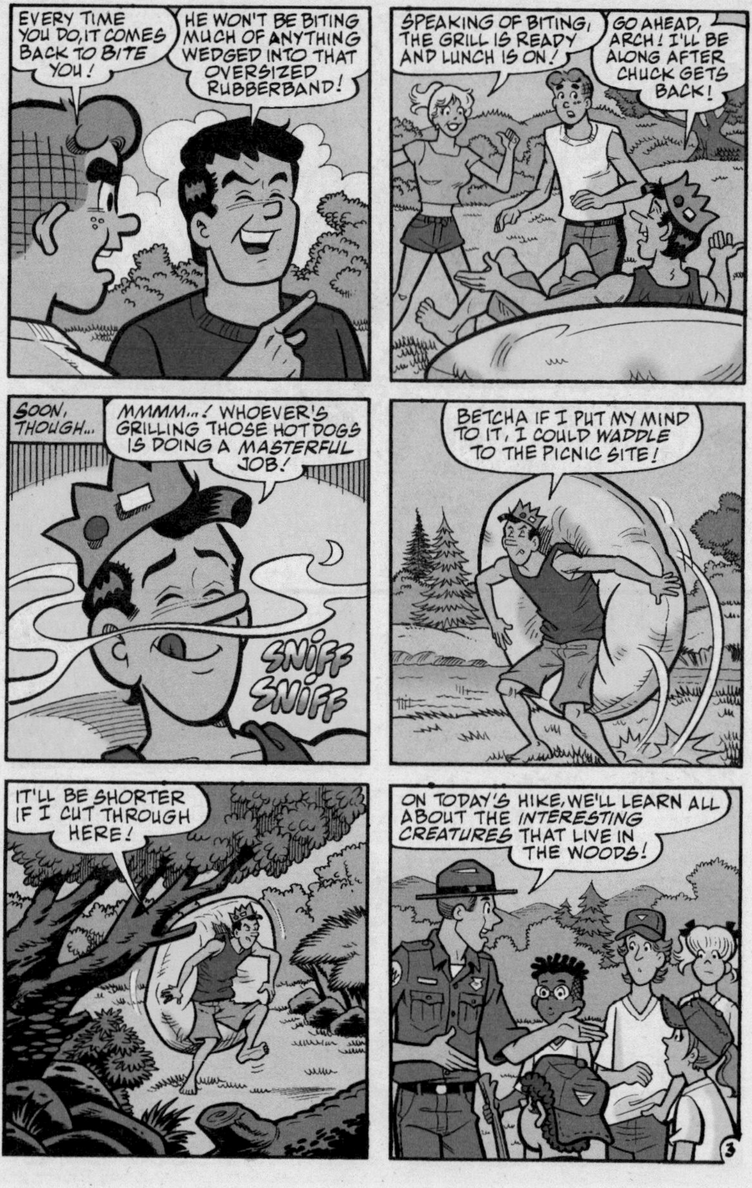
EVERY TIME YOU DO, IT COMES BACK TO BITE YOU!
HE WON'T BE BITING MUCH OF ANYTHING WEDGED INTO THAT OVERSIZED RUBBERBAND!
SPEAKING OF BITING, THE GRILL IS READY AND LUNCH IS ON!
GO AHEAD, ARCH! I'LL BE ALONG AFTER CHUCK GETS BACK!
SOON, THOUGH...
MMMM...! WHOEVER'S GRILLING THOSE HOT DOGS IS DOING A MASTERFUL JOB!
SNIFF SNIFF
BETCHA IF I PUT MY MIND TO IT, I COULD WADDLE TO THE PICNIC SITE!
IT'LL BE SHORTER IF I CUT THROUGH HERE!
ON TODAY'S HIKE, WE'LL LEARN ALL ABOUT THE INTERESTING CREATURES THAT LIVE IN THE WOODS!
3

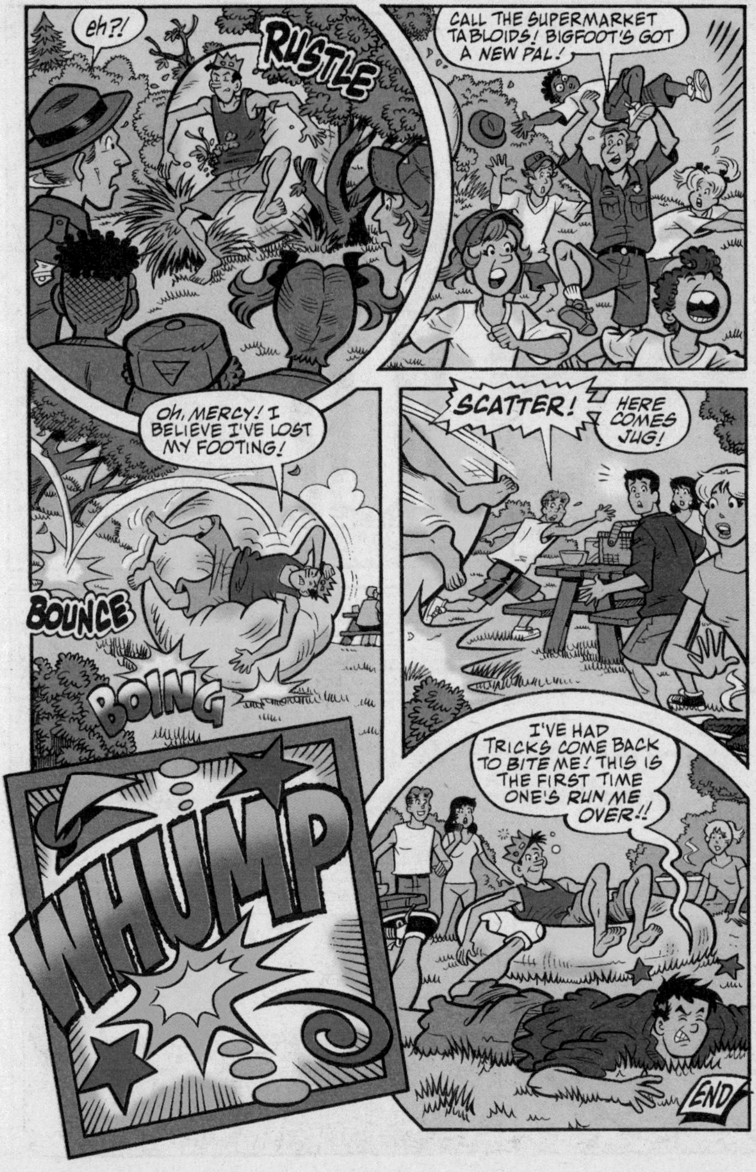
eh?!
RUSTLE
CALL THE SUPERMARKET TABLOIDS! BIGFOOT'S GOT A NEW PAL!
OH, MERCY! I BELIEVE I'VE LOST MY FOOTING!
BOUNCE
BOING
SCATTER!
HERE COMES JUG!
WHUMP
I'VE HAD TRICKS COME BACK TO BITE ME! THIS IS THE FIRST TIME ONE'S RUN ME OVER!!
END

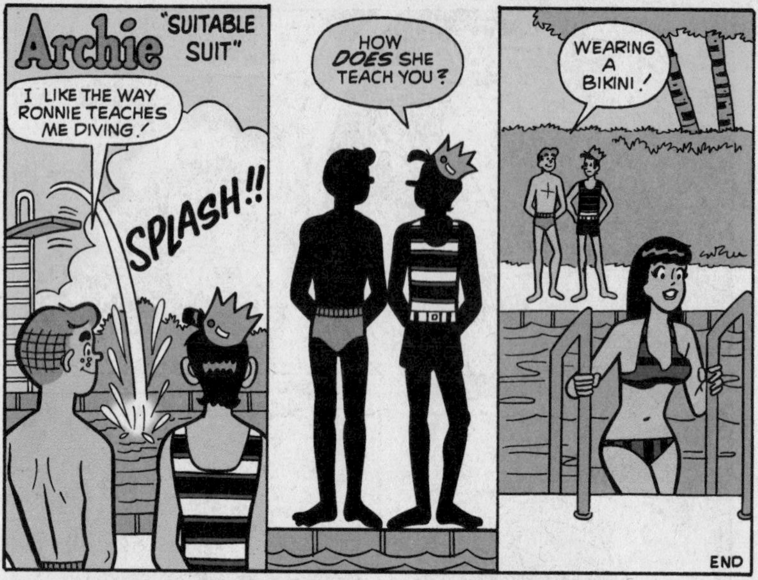
Archie
"SUITABLE SUIT"
I LIKE THE WAY RONNIE TEACHES ME DIVING!
SPLASH!!
HOW DOES SHE TEACH YOU?
WEARING A BIKINI!
END

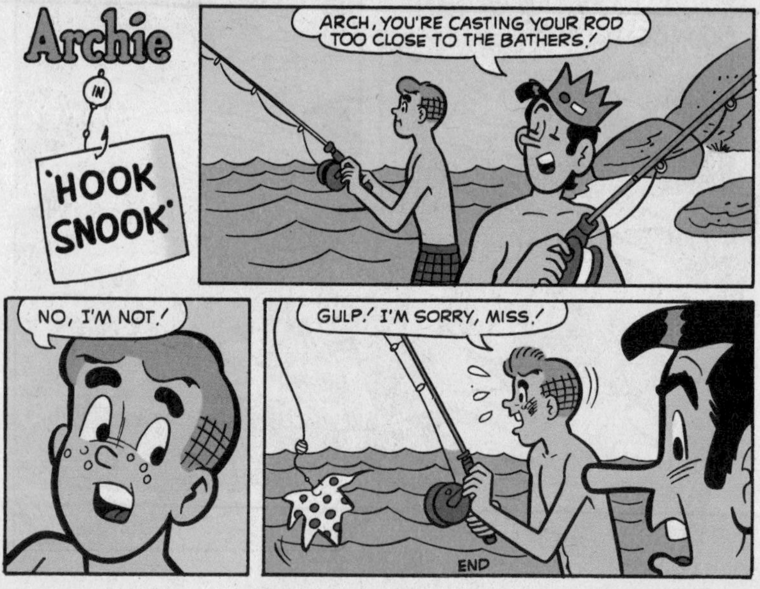
Archie
IN
"HOOK SNOOK"
ARCH, YOU'RE CASTING YOUR ROD TOO CLOSE TO THE BATHERS!
NO, I'M NOT!
GULP! I'M SORRY, MISS!
END

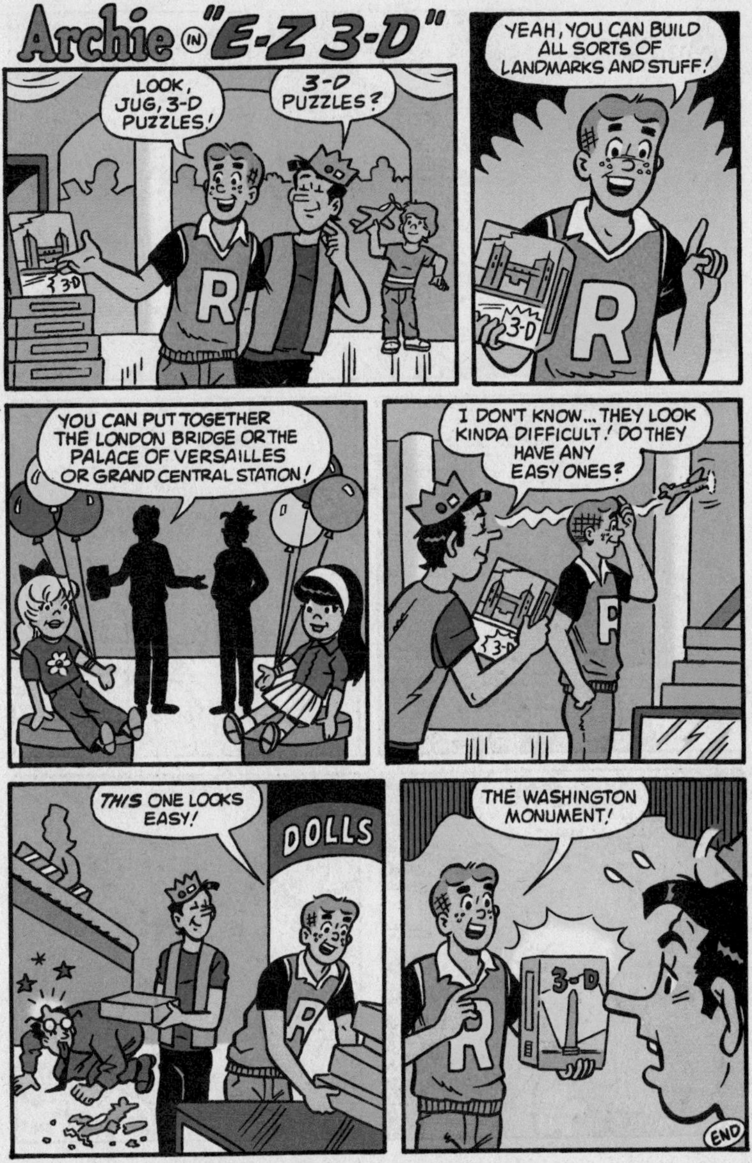
Archie in "E-Z 3-D"
LOOK, JUG, 3-D PUZZLES!
3-D PUZZLES?
3-D
YEAH, YOU CAN BUILD ALL SORTS OF LANDMARKS AND STUFF!
3-D
YOU CAN PUT TOGETHER THE LONDON BRIDGE OR THE PALACE OF VERSAILLES OR GRAND CENTRAL STATION!
I DON'T KNOW... THEY LOOK KINDA DIFFICULT! DO THEY HAVE ANY EASY ONES?
THIS ONE LOOKS EASY!
DOLLS
THE WASHINGTON MONUMENT!
3-D
END

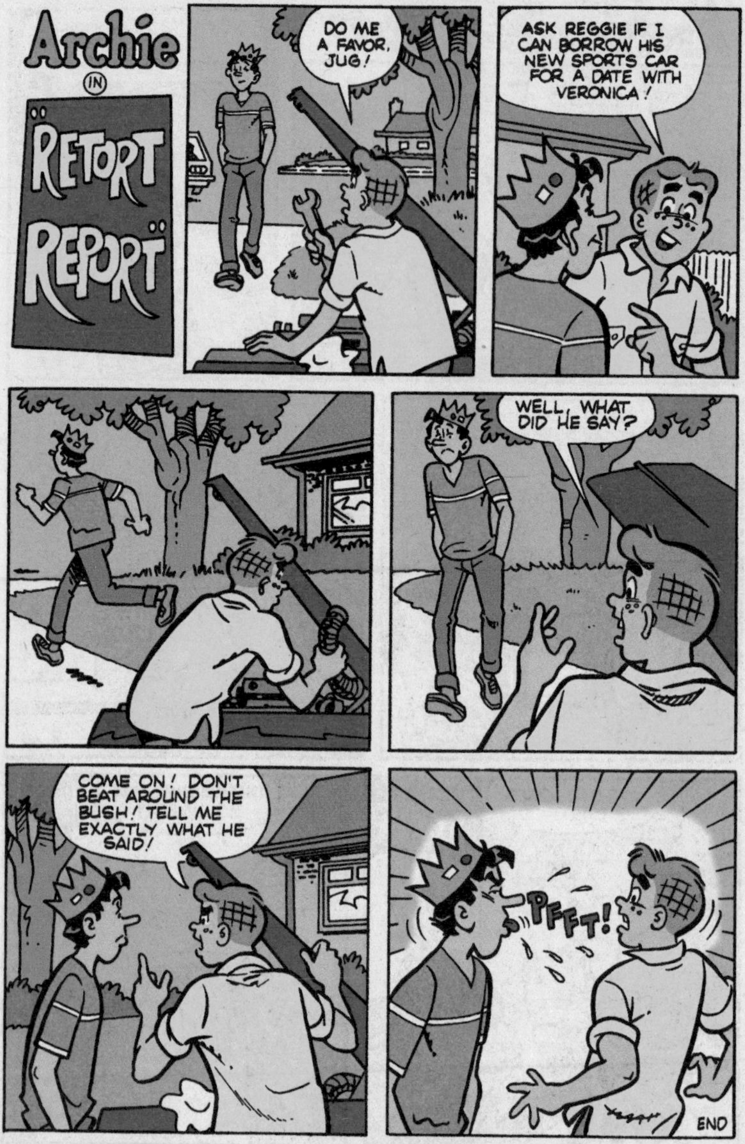
Archie
IN
RETORT REPORT
DO ME A FAVOR, JUG!
ASK REGGIE IF I CAN BORROW HIS NEW SPORTS CAR FOR A DATE WITH VERONICA!
WELL, WHAT DID HE SAY?
COME ON! DON'T BEAT AROUND THE BUSH! TELL ME EXACTLY WHAT HE SAID!
PFFFT!
END

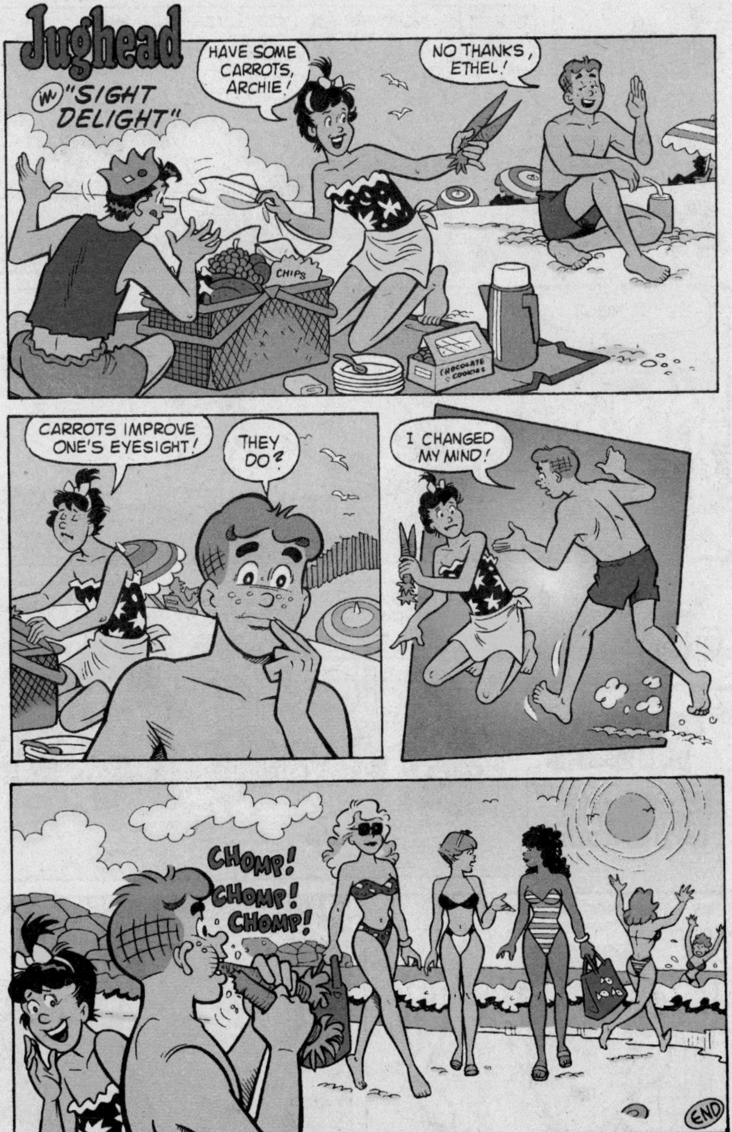
Jughead
in "SIGHT DELIGHT"
HAVE SOME CARROTS, ARCHIE!
NO THANKS, ETHEL!
CHIPS
CHOCOLATE COOKIES
CARROTS IMPROVE ONE'S EYESIGHT!
THEY DO?
I CHANGED MY MIND!
CHOMP! CHOMP! CHOMP!
END

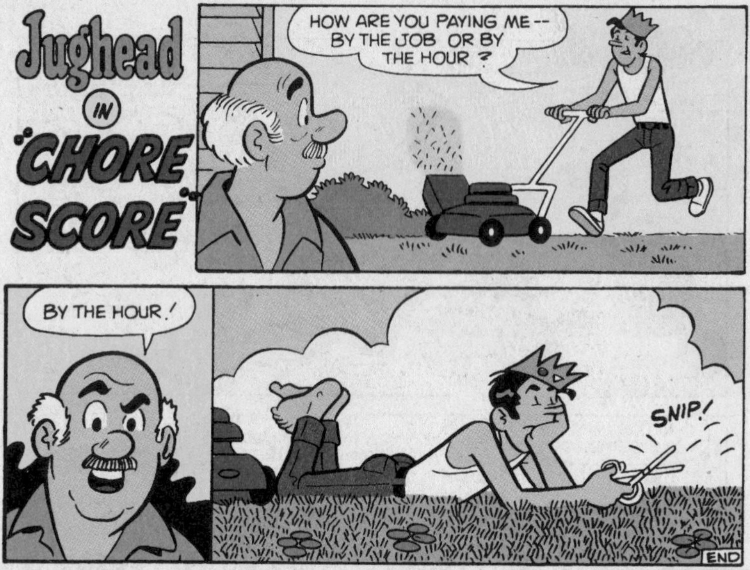
Jughead
IN
"CHORE SCORE"
HOW ARE YOU PAYING ME -- BY THE JOB OR BY THE HOUR ?
BY THE HOUR!
SNIP!
END

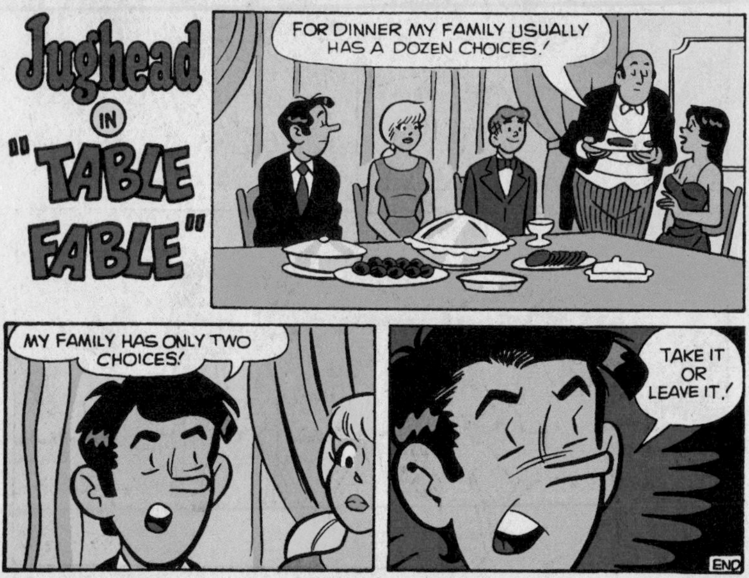
Jughead
IN
"TABLE FABLE"
FOR DINNER MY FAMILY USUALLY HAS A DOZEN CHOICES!
MY FAMILY HAS ONLY TWO CHOICES!
TAKE IT OR LEAVE IT!
END

Spell It Out
Sabrina #70, 2005
by Tania del Rio, Jim Amash, Jeff Powell,
Ridge Rooms and Jason Jensen

"Spell It Out" was one of my favorite Sabrina stories to write and draw. It has it all: romantic drama surrounding a classic love triangle, a new twist on the pun behind the word "spelling" (it has a very different meaning in the Magic Realm vs. the mortal world), and intense competition with fierce rivals! Sabrina also had a chance to show off her unique magical abilities, which doubly served to advance the overall plot further by revealing more clues to the mystery behind her heightened powers.

However, what I love best about this story is that, throughout it all, Sabrina is still just an average teenage girl, getting herself into ridiculous situations in order to impress her ex-boyfriend, Harvey. I think we can all relate to that feeling of rejection and wanting to get back in the game. It doesn't matter that she's one of the most skilled witches of her time—she's more concerned about her social life than about saving the world at this point!

Tania del Rio
Writer and Artist,
Archie Comics

Mr. Marvelous
Archie's Pals 'n' Gals #173, 1985
by George Gladir and Samm Schwartz

In this bittersweet effort from veteran Archie writer George Gladir and illustrator Samm Schwartz, Big Ethel finds the man of her dreams... only to discover that he's part fish! With the help of her new merman friend, she makes a big splash at Riverdale High's formal dance.

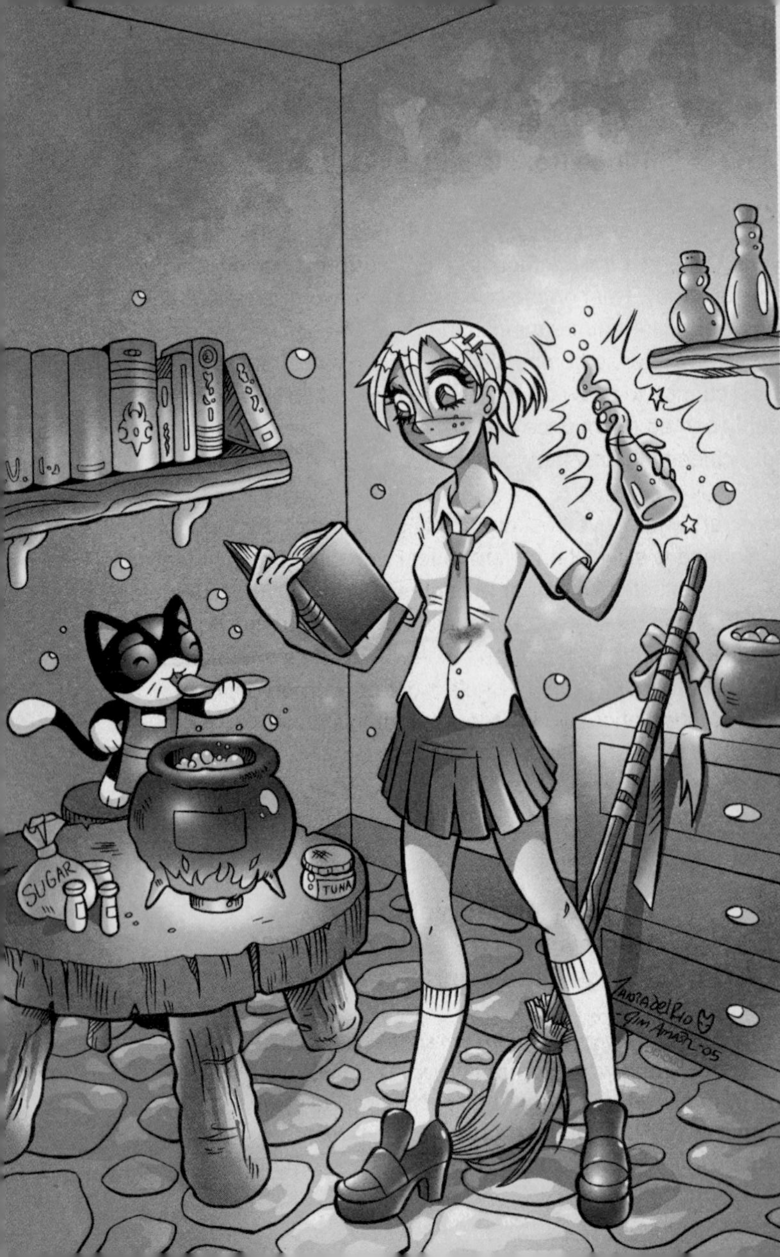
SUGAR
TUNA

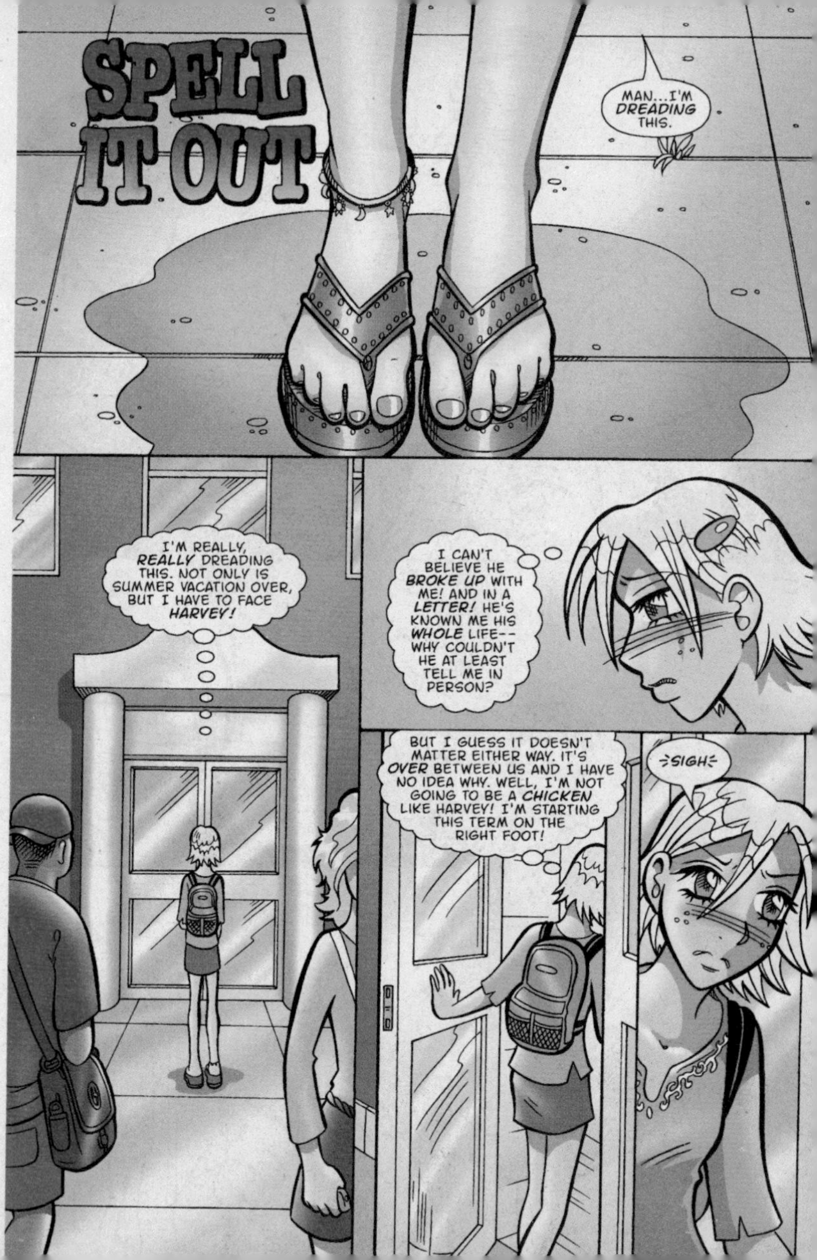
SPELL IT OUT
MAN... I'M DREADING THIS.
I'M REALLY, REALLY DREADING THIS. NOT ONLY IS SUMMER VACATION OVER, BUT I HAVE TO FACE HARVEY!
I CAN'T BELIEVE HE BROKE UP WITH ME! AND IN A LETTER! HE'S KNOWN ME HIS WHOLE LIFE-- WHY COULDN'T HE AT LEAST TELL ME IN PERSON?
BUT I GUESS IT DOESN'T MATTER EITHER WAY. IT'S OVER BETWEEN US AND I HAVE NO IDEA WHY. WELL, I'M NOT GOING TO BE A CHICKEN LIKE HARVEY! I'M STARTING THIS TERM ON THE RIGHT FOOT!
SIGH

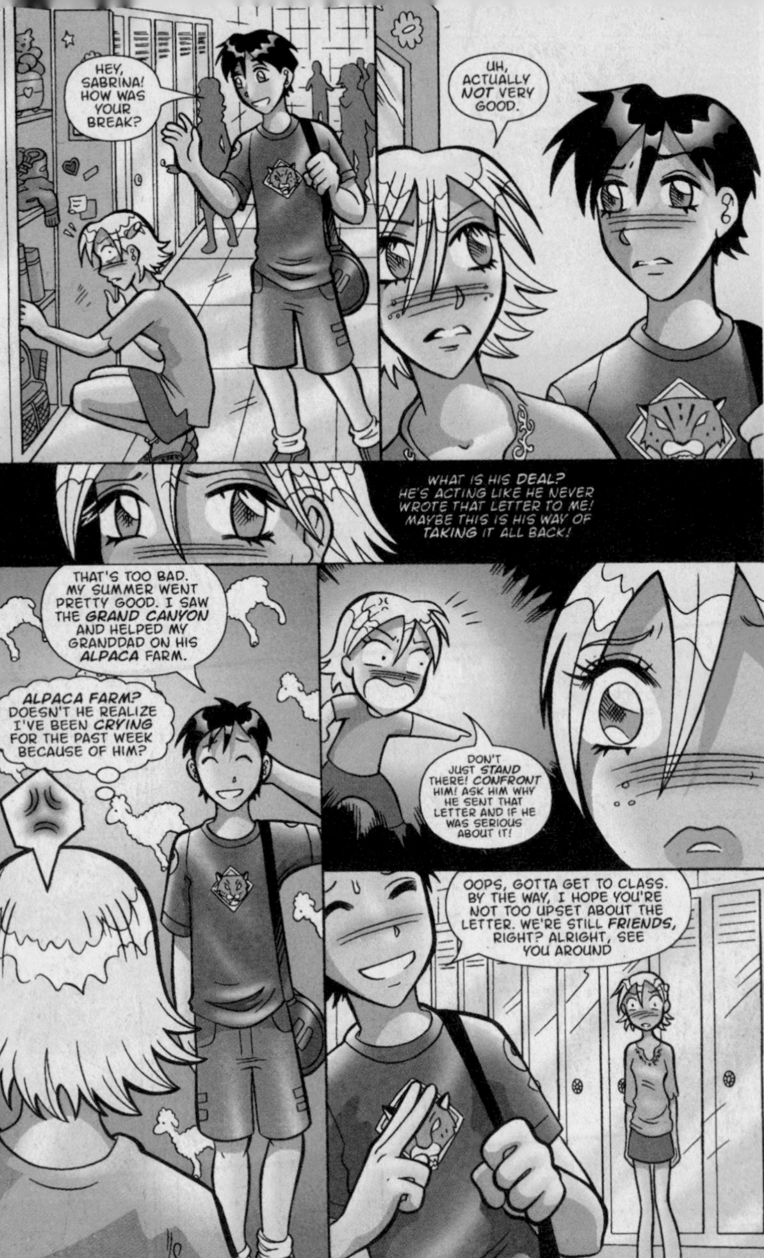

HEY, SABRINA! HOW WAS YOUR BREAK?
UH, ACTUALLY *NOT* VERY GOOD.
WHAT IS HIS *DEAL*? HE'S ACTING LIKE HE NEVER WROTE THAT LETTER TO ME! MAYBE THIS IS HIS WAY OF *TAKING* IT ALL BACK!
THAT'S TOO BAD. MY SUMMER WENT PRETTY GOOD. I SAW THE *GRAND CANYON* AND HELPED MY GRANDDAD ON HIS *ALPACA* FARM.
ALPACA FARM? DOESN'T HE REALIZE I'VE BEEN *CRYING* FOR THE PAST WEEK BECAUSE OF HIM?
DON'T JUST *STAND* THERE! *CONFRONT* HIM! ASK HIM WHY HE SENT THAT LETTER AND IF HE WAS SERIOUS ABOUT IT!
OOPS, GOTTA GET TO CLASS. BY THE WAY, I HOPE YOU'RE NOT TOO UPSET ABOUT THE LETTER. WE'RE STILL *FRIENDS*, RIGHT? ALRIGHT, SEE YOU AROUND

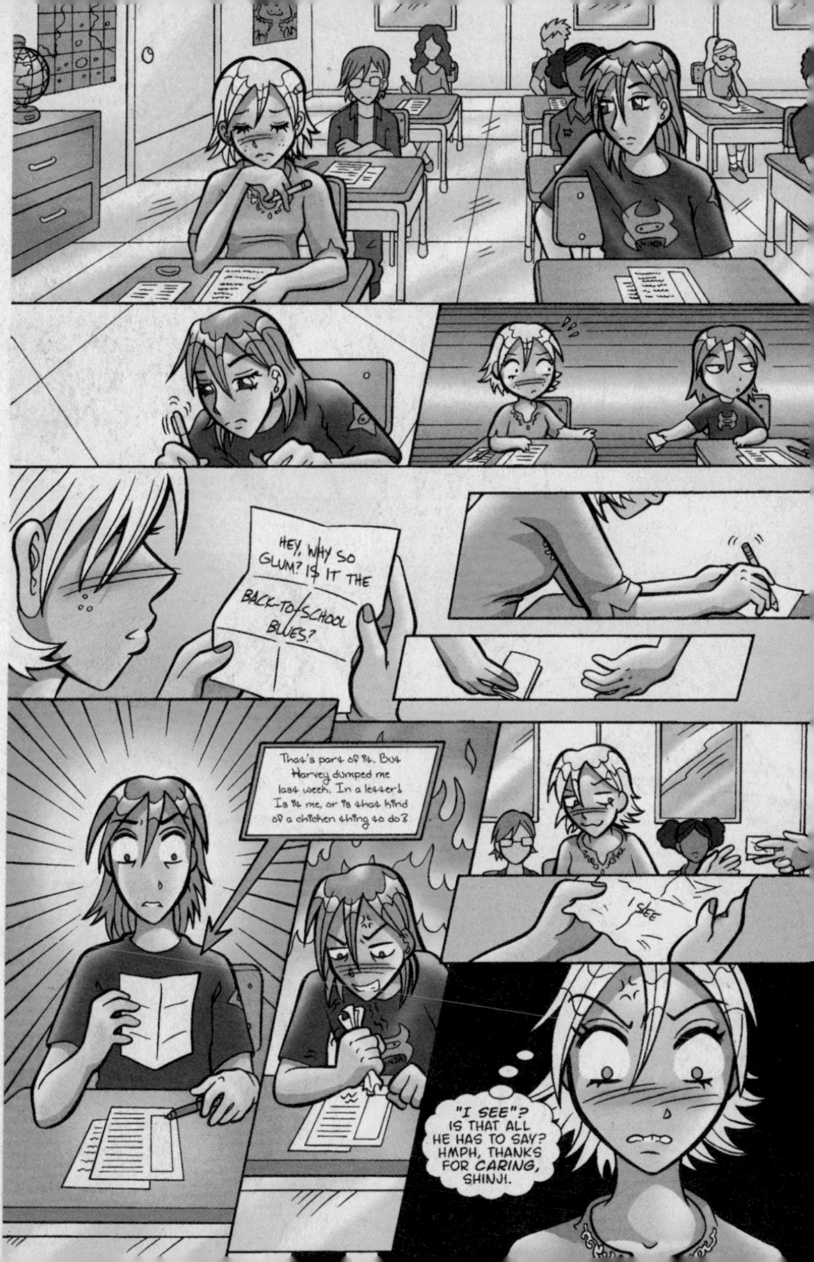
HEY, WHY SO GLUM? IS IT THE BACK-TO-SCHOOL BLUES?
That's part of it. But Harvey dumped me last week. In a letter! Is it me, or is that kind of a chicken thing to do?
I SEE
"I SEE"? IS THAT ALL HE HAS TO SAY? HMPH, THANKS FOR CARING, SHINJI.

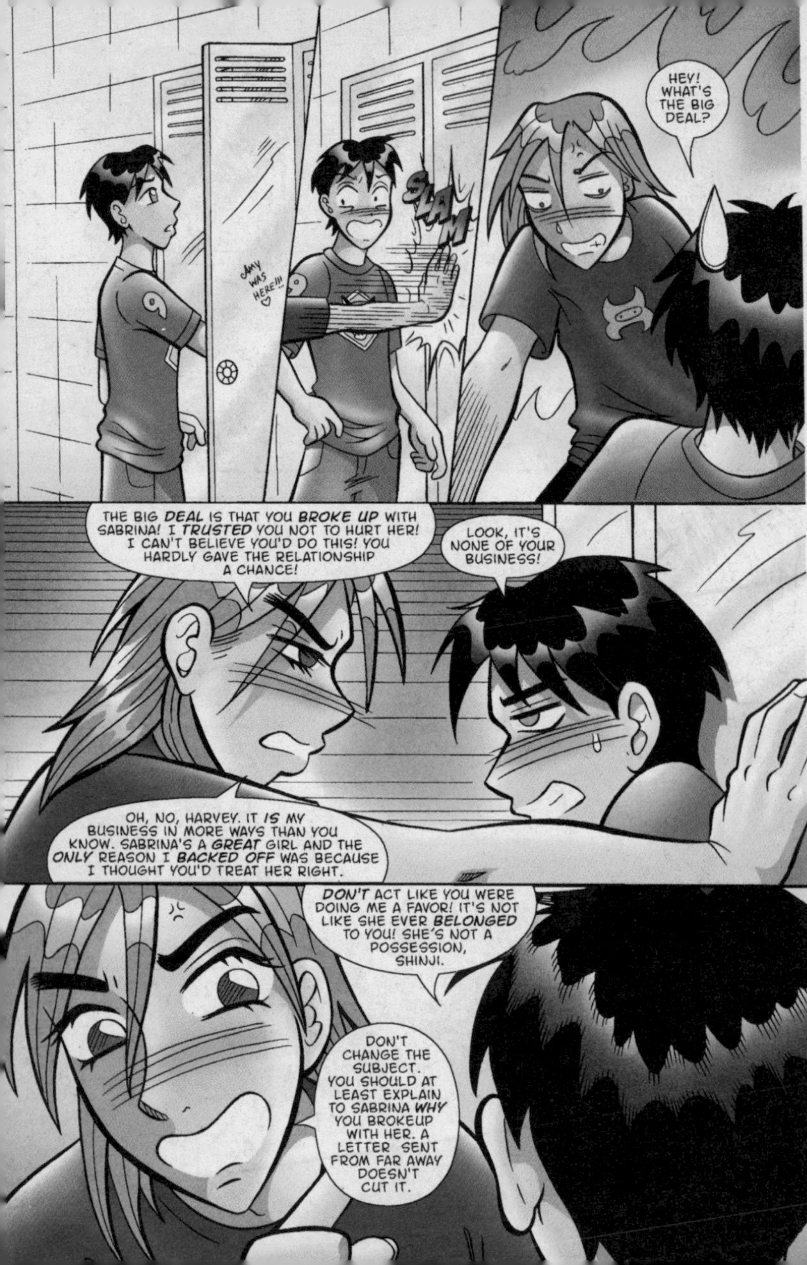

AMY WAS HERE!!!
SLAM
HEY! WHAT'S THE BIG DEAL?
THE BIG DEAL IS THAT YOU BROKE UP WITH SABRINA! I TRUSTED YOU NOT TO HURT HER! I CAN'T BELIEVE YOU'D DO THIS! YOU HARDLY GAVE THE RELATIONSHIP A CHANCE!
LOOK, IT'S NONE OF YOUR BUSINESS!
OH, NO, HARVEY. IT IS MY BUSINESS IN MORE WAYS THAN YOU KNOW. SABRINA'S A GREAT GIRL AND THE ONLY REASON I BACKED OFF WAS BECAUSE I THOUGHT YOU'D TREAT HER RIGHT.
DON'T ACT LIKE YOU WERE DOING ME A FAVOR! IT'S NOT LIKE SHE EVER BELONGED TO YOU! SHE'S NOT A POSSESSION, SHINJI.
DON'T CHANGE THE SUBJECT. YOU SHOULD AT LEAST EXPLAIN TO SABRINA WHY YOU BROKEUP WITH HER. A LETTER SENT FROM FAR AWAY DOESN'T CUT IT.

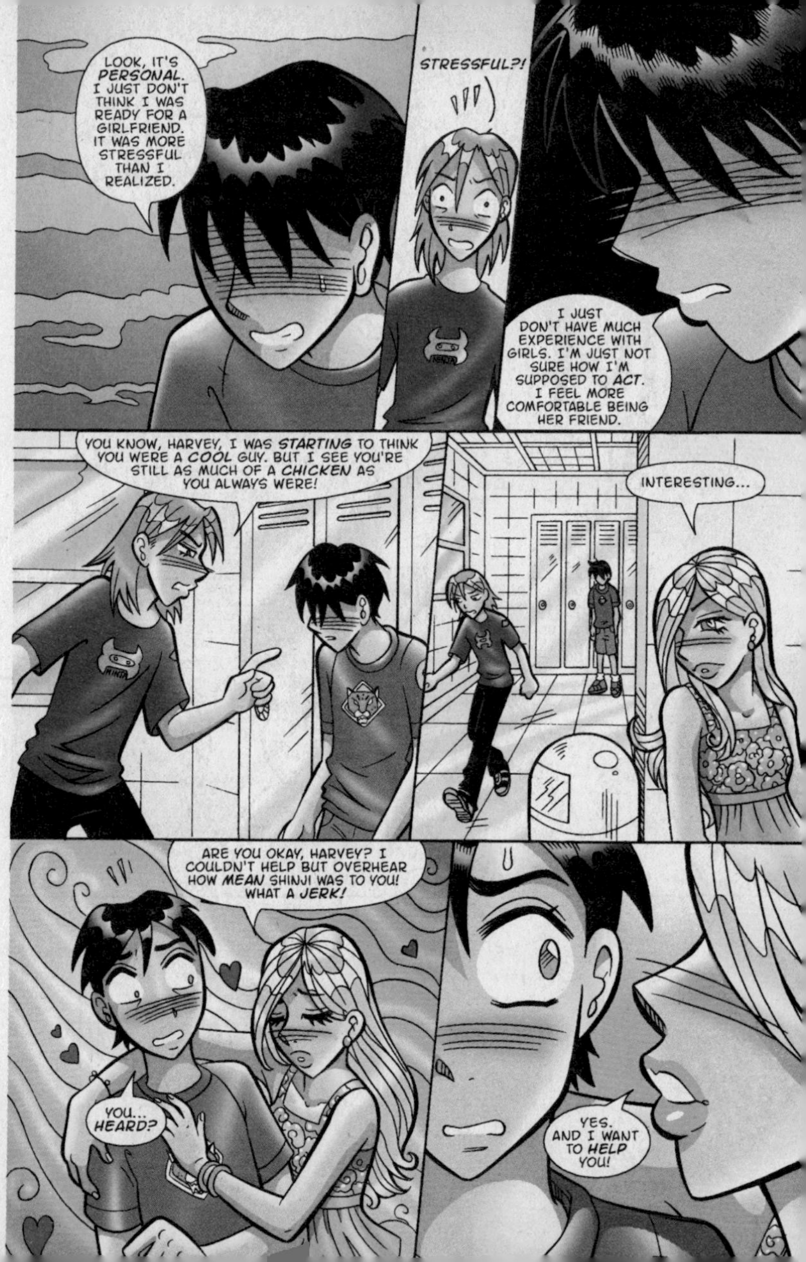
LOOK, IT'S PERSONAL. I JUST DON'T THINK I WAS READY FOR A GIRLFRIEND. IT WAS MORE STRESSFUL THAN I REALIZED.
STRESSFUL?!
I JUST DON'T HAVE MUCH EXPERIENCE WITH GIRLS. I'M JUST NOT SURE HOW I'M SUPPOSED TO ACT. I FEEL MORE COMFORTABLE BEING HER FRIEND.
YOU KNOW, HARVEY, I WAS STARTING TO THINK YOU WERE A COOL GUY. BUT I SEE YOU'RE STILL AS MUCH OF A CHICKEN AS YOU ALWAYS WERE!
INTERESTING...
ARE YOU OKAY, HARVEY? I COULDN'T HELP BUT OVERHEAR HOW MEAN SHINJI WAS TO YOU! WHAT A JERK!
YOU... HEARD?
YES. AND I WANT TO HELP YOU!

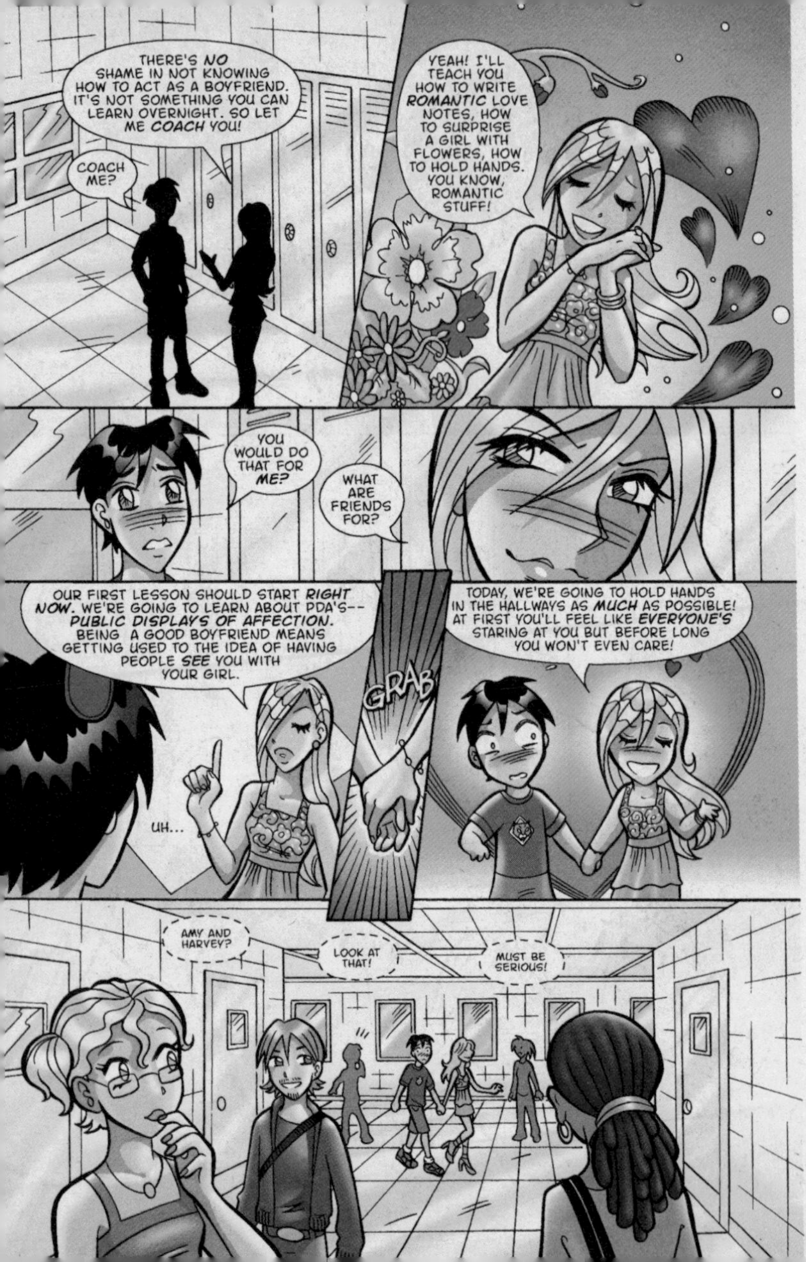
THERE'S NO SHAME IN NOT KNOWING HOW TO ACT AS A BOYFRIEND. IT'S NOT SOMETHING YOU CAN LEARN OVERNIGHT. SO LET ME COACH YOU!
COACH ME?
YEAH! I'LL TEACH YOU HOW TO WRITE ROMANTIC LOVE NOTES, HOW TO SURPRISE A GIRL WITH FLOWERS, HOW TO HOLD HANDS. YOU KNOW, ROMANTIC STUFF!
YOU WOULD DO THAT FOR ME?
WHAT ARE FRIENDS FOR?
OUR FIRST LESSON SHOULD START RIGHT NOW. WE'RE GOING TO LEARN ABOUT PDA'S-- PUBLIC DISPLAYS OF AFFECTION. BEING A GOOD BOYFRIEND MEANS GETTING USED TO THE IDEA OF HAVING PEOPLE SEE YOU WITH YOUR GIRL.
UH...
GRAB
TODAY, WE'RE GOING TO HOLD HANDS IN THE HALLWAYS AS MUCH AS POSSIBLE! AT FIRST YOU'LL FEEL LIKE EVERYONE'S STARING AT YOU BUT BEFORE LONG YOU WON'T EVEN CARE!
AMY AND HARVEY?
LOOK AT THAT!
MUST BE SERIOUS!

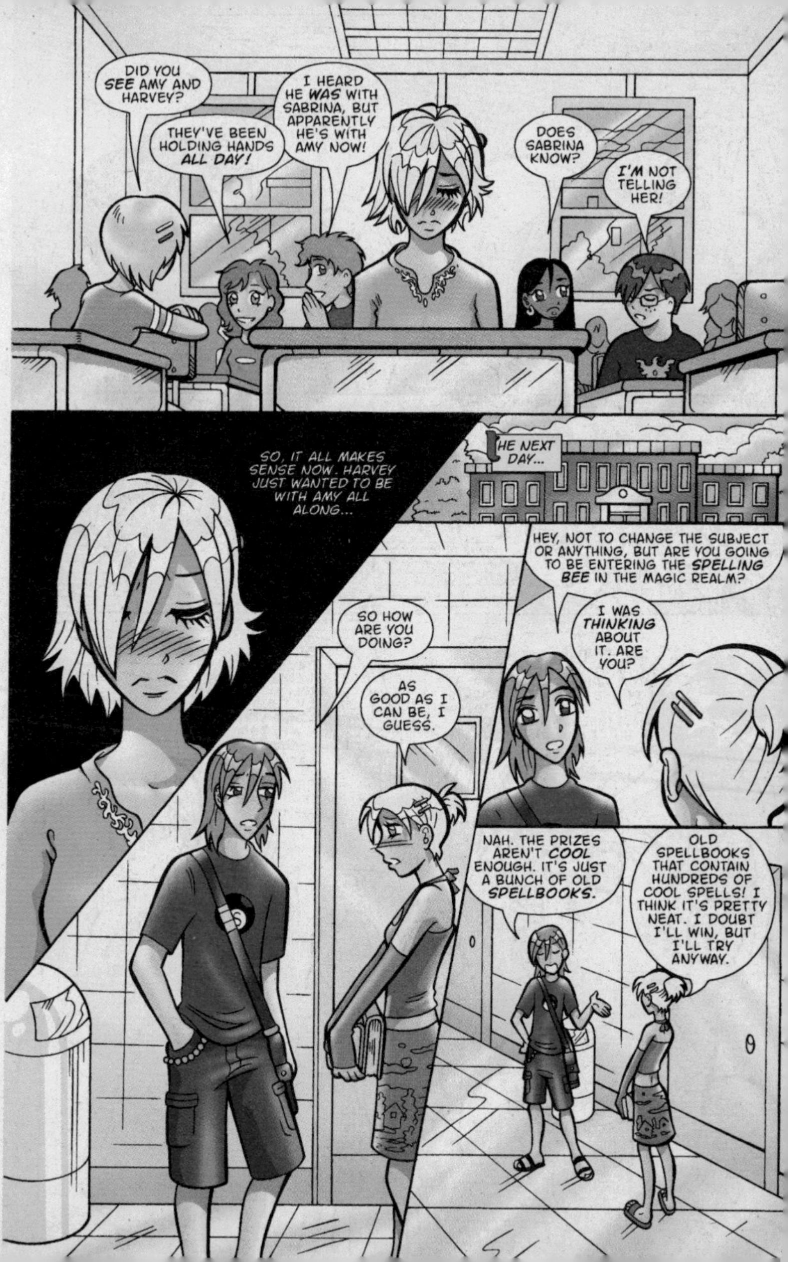
DID YOU SEE AMY AND HARVEY?
THEY'VE BEEN HOLDING HANDS ALL DAY!
I HEARD HE WAS WITH SABRINA, BUT APPARENTLY HE'S WITH AMY NOW!
DOES SABRINA KNOW?
I'M NOT TELLING HER!
SO, IT ALL MAKES SENSE NOW. HARVEY JUST WANTED TO BE WITH AMY ALL ALONG...
THE NEXT DAY...
SO HOW ARE YOU DOING?
AS GOOD AS I CAN BE, I GUESS.
HEY, NOT TO CHANGE THE SUBJECT OR ANYTHING, BUT ARE YOU GOING TO BE ENTERING THE SPELLING BEE IN THE MAGIC REALM?
I WAS THINKING ABOUT IT. ARE YOU?
NAH. THE PRIZES AREN'T COOL ENOUGH. IT'S JUST A BUNCH OF OLD SPELLBOOKS.
OLD SPELLBOOKS THAT CONTAIN HUNDREDS OF COOL SPELLS! I THINK IT'S PRETTY NEAT. I DOUBT I'LL WIN, BUT I'LL TRY ANYWAY.

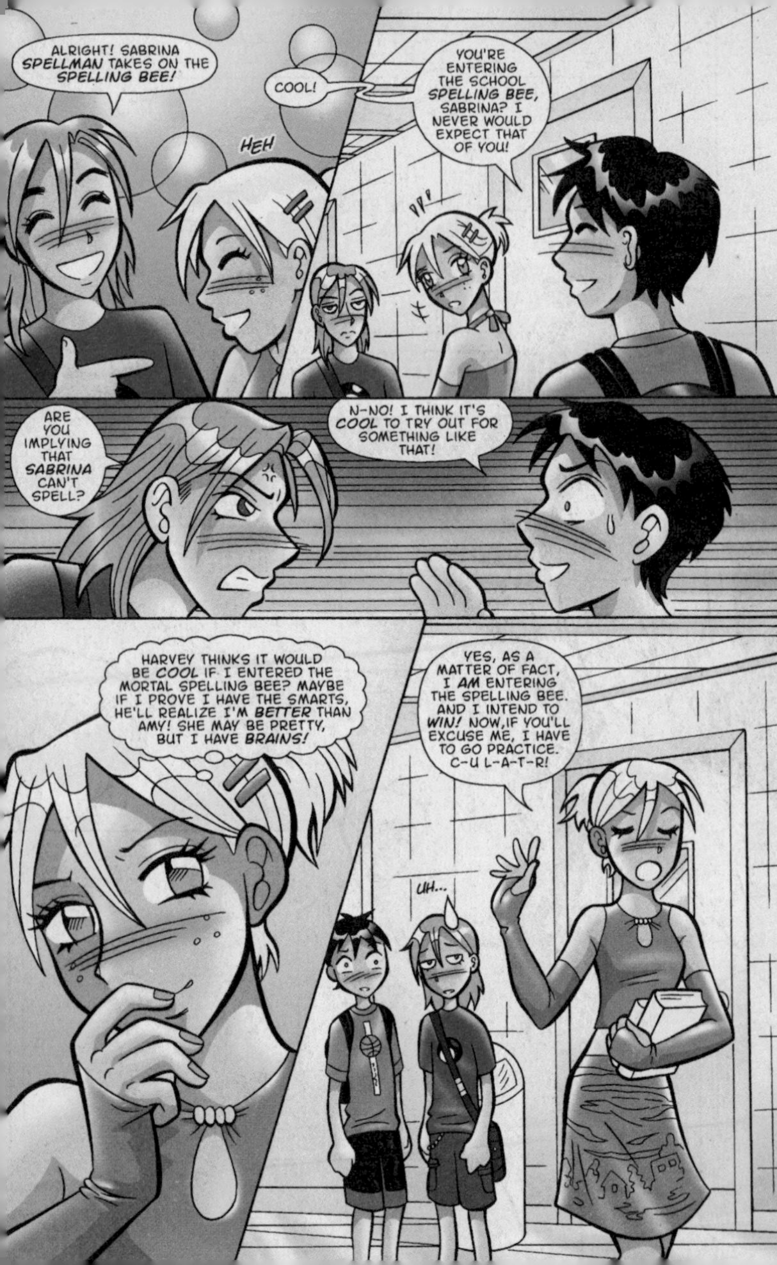
ALRIGHT! SABRINA SPELLMAN TAKES ON THE SPELLING BEE!
COOL!
HEH
YOU'RE ENTERING THE SCHOOL SPELLING BEE, SABRINA? I NEVER WOULD EXPECT THAT OF YOU!
ARE YOU IMPLYING THAT SABRINA CAN'T SPELL?
N-NO! I THINK IT'S COOL TO TRY OUT FOR SOMETHING LIKE THAT!
HARVEY THINKS IT WOULD BE COOL IF I ENTERED THE MORTAL SPELLING BEE? MAYBE IF I PROVE I HAVE THE SMARTS, HE'LL REALIZE I'M BETTER THAN AMY! SHE MAY BE PRETTY, BUT I HAVE BRAINS!
YES, AS A MATTER OF FACT, I AM ENTERING THE SPELLING BEE. AND I INTEND TO WIN! NOW, IF YOU'LL EXCUSE ME, I HAVE TO GO PRACTICE. C-U L-A-T-R!
UH...

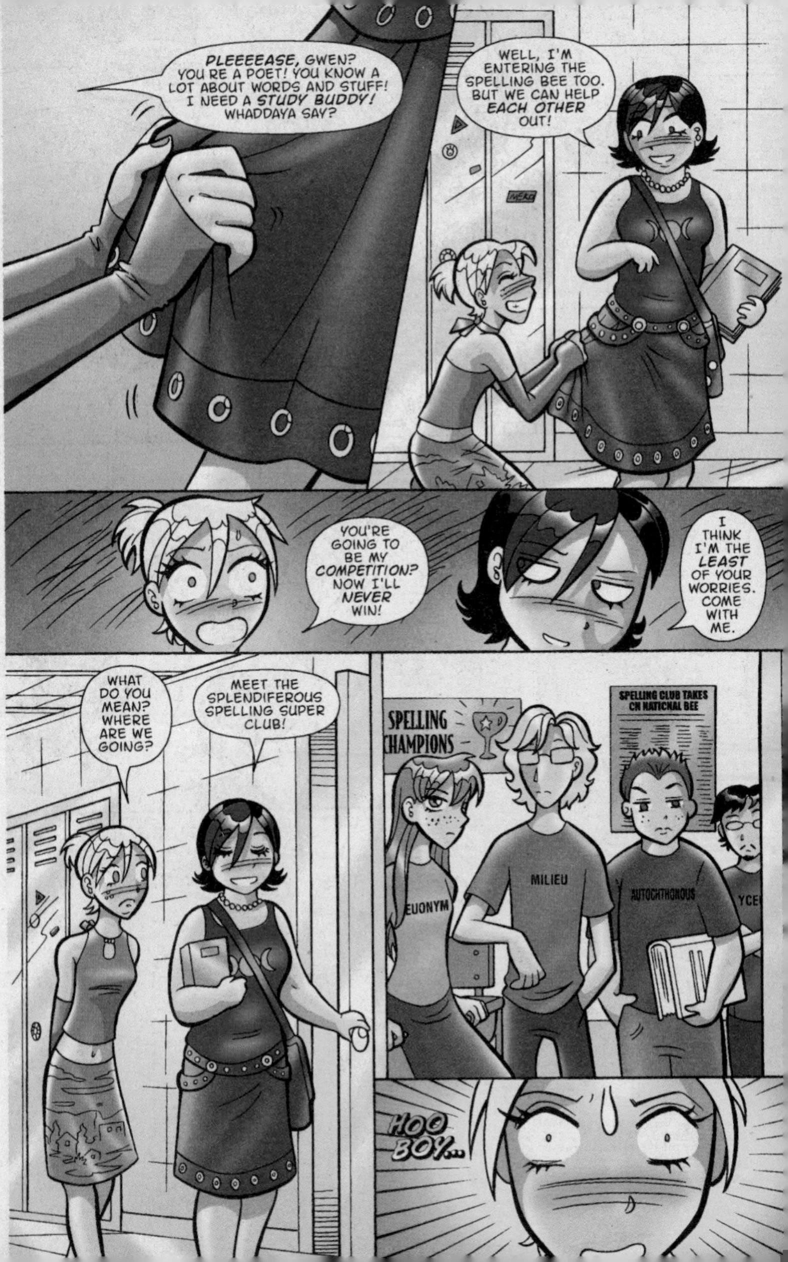
PLEEEEASE, GWEN? YOU'RE A POET! YOU KNOW A LOT ABOUT WORDS AND STUFF! I NEED A STUDY BUDDY! WHADDAYA SAY?
WELL, I'M ENTERING THE SPELLING BEE TOO. BUT WE CAN HELP EACH OTHER OUT!
YOU'RE GOING TO BE MY COMPETITION? NOW I'LL NEVER WIN!
I THINK I'M THE LEAST OF YOUR WORRIES. COME WITH ME.
WHAT DO YOU MEAN? WHERE ARE WE GOING?
MEET THE SPLENDIFEROUS SPELLING SUPER CLUB!
SPELLING CHAMPIONS
SPELLING CLUB TAKES ON NATIONAL BEE
EUONYM
MILIEU
AUTOCHTHONOUS
HOO BOY...

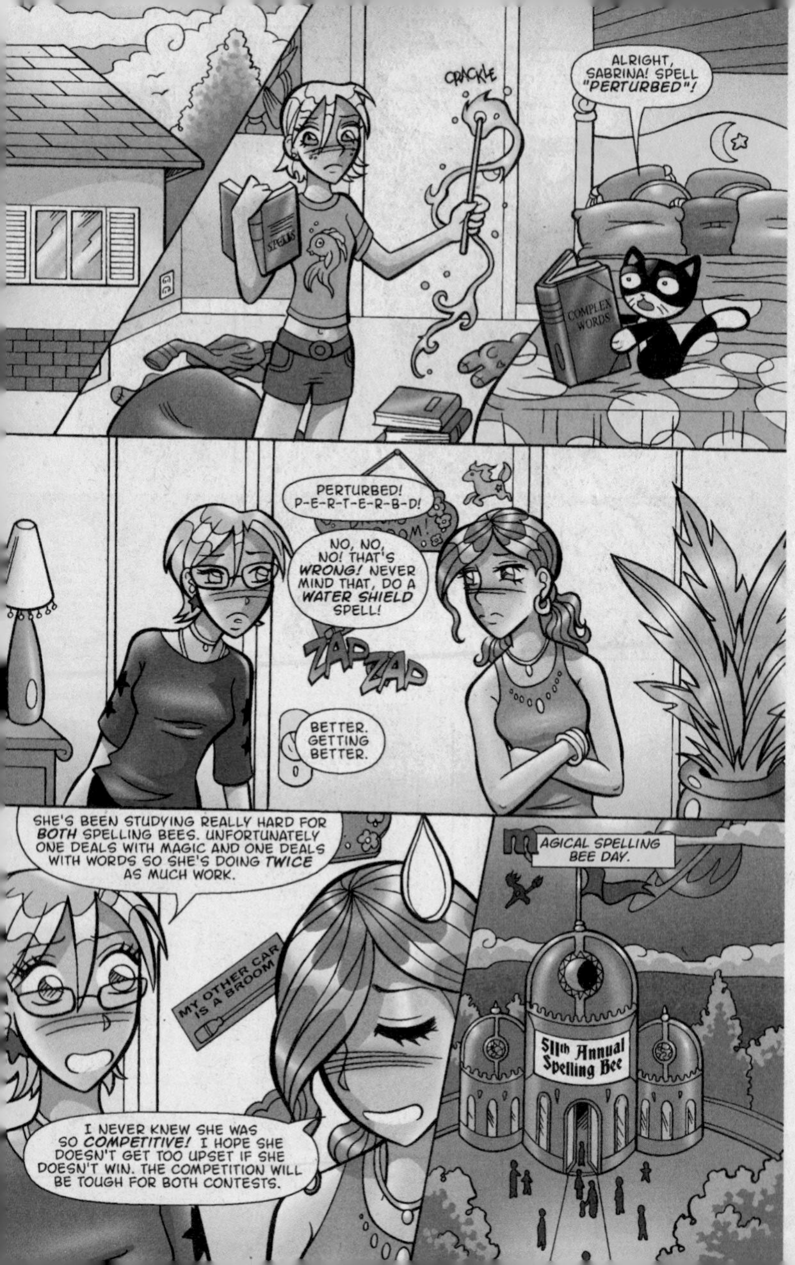

CRACKLE
SPELLS
ALRIGHT, SABRINA! SPELL "PERTURBED"!
COMPLEX WORDS
PERTURBED! P-E-R-T-E-R-B-D!
NO, NO, NO! THAT'S WRONG! NEVER MIND THAT, DO A WATER SHIELD SPELL!
ZAP ZAP
BETTER. GETTING BETTER.
SHE'S BEEN STUDYING REALLY HARD FOR BOTH SPELLING BEES. UNFORTUNATELY ONE DEALS WITH MAGIC AND ONE DEALS WITH WORDS SO SHE'S DOING TWICE AS MUCH WORK.
MY OTHER CAR IS A BROOM
I NEVER KNEW SHE WAS SO COMPETITIVE! I HOPE SHE DOESN'T GET TOO UPSET IF SHE DOESN'T WIN. THE COMPETITION WILL BE TOUGH FOR BOTH CONTESTS.
MAGICAL SPELLING BEE DAY.
511th Annual Spelling Bee

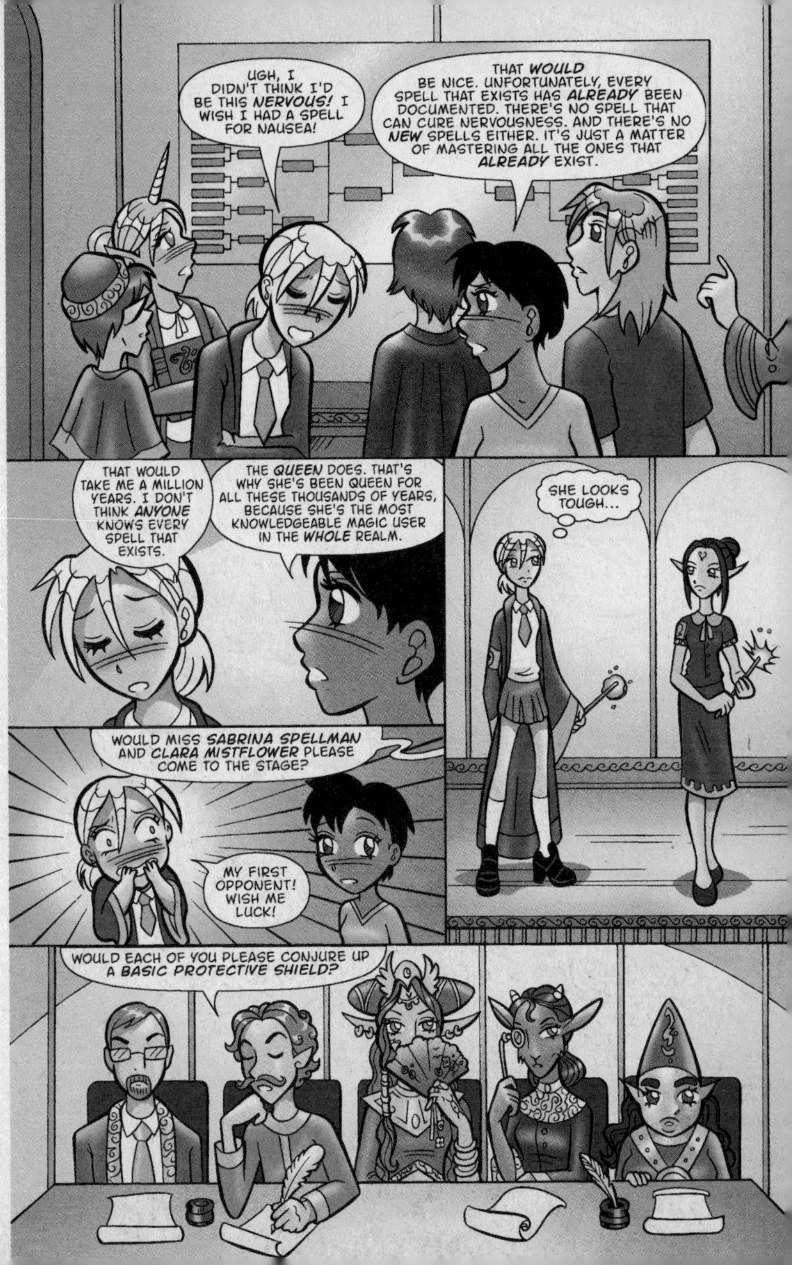
UGH, I DIDN'T THINK I'D BE THIS *NERVOUS!* I WISH I HAD A SPELL FOR NAUSEA!
THAT *WOULD* BE NICE. UNFORTUNATELY, EVERY SPELL THAT EXISTS HAS *ALREADY* BEEN DOCUMENTED. THERE'S NO SPELL THAT CAN CURE NERVOUSNESS. AND THERE'S NO *NEW* SPELLS EITHER. IT'S JUST A MATTER OF MASTERING ALL THE ONES THAT *ALREADY* EXIST.
THAT WOULD TAKE ME A MILLION YEARS. I DON'T THINK *ANYONE* KNOWS EVERY SPELL THAT EXISTS.
THE *QUEEN* DOES. THAT'S WHY SHE'S BEEN QUEEN FOR ALL THESE THOUSANDS OF YEARS, BECAUSE SHE'S THE MOST KNOWLEDGEABLE MAGIC USER IN THE *WHOLE* REALM.
WOULD MISS *SABRINA SPELLMAN* AND *CLARA MISTFLOWER* PLEASE COME TO THE STAGE?
MY FIRST OPPONENT! WISH ME LUCK!
SHE LOOKS TOUGH...
WOULD EACH OF YOU PLEASE CONJURE UP A *BASIC PROTECTIVE SHIELD?*

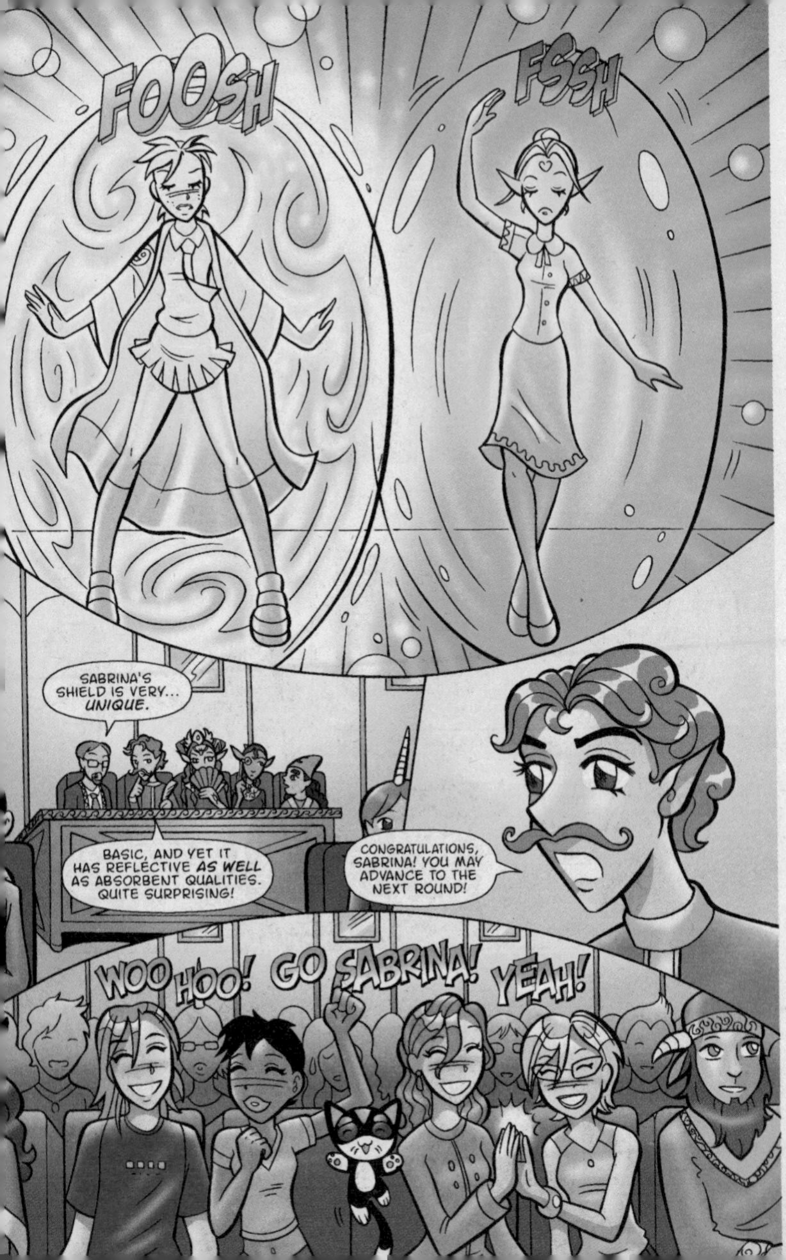
FOOSH
FSSH
SABRINA'S SHIELD IS VERY... UNIQUE.
BASIC, AND YET IT HAS REFLECTIVE AS WELL AS ABSORBENT QUALITIES. QUITE SURPRISING!
CONGRATULATIONS, SABRINA! YOU MAY ADVANCE TO THE NEXT ROUND!
WOO HOO! GO SABRINA! YEAH!

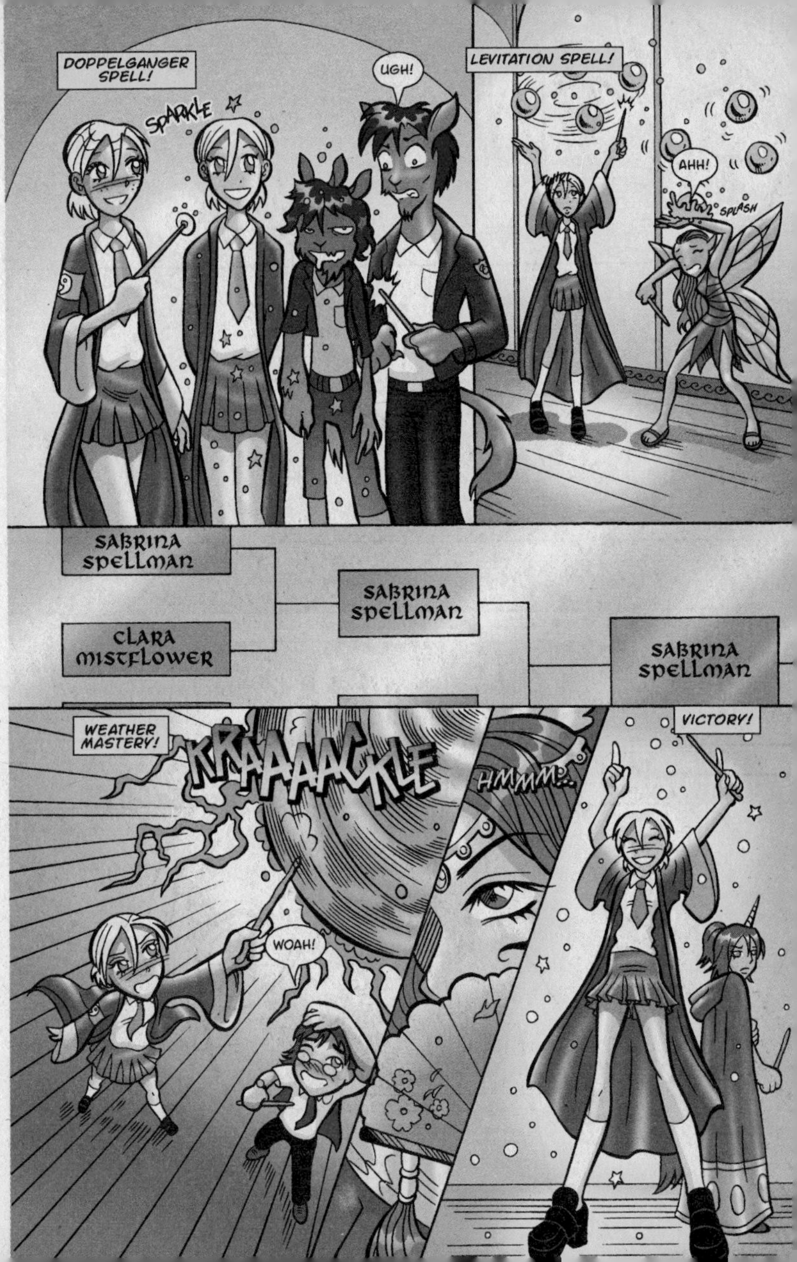
DOPPELGANGER SPELL!
SPARKLE
UGH!
LEVITATION SPELL!
AHH!
SPLASH
SABRINA SPELLMAN
CLARA MISTFLOWER
SABRINA SPELLMAN
SABRINA SPELLMAN
WEATHER MASTERY!
KRAAAACKLE
HMMM...
WOAH!
VICTORY!

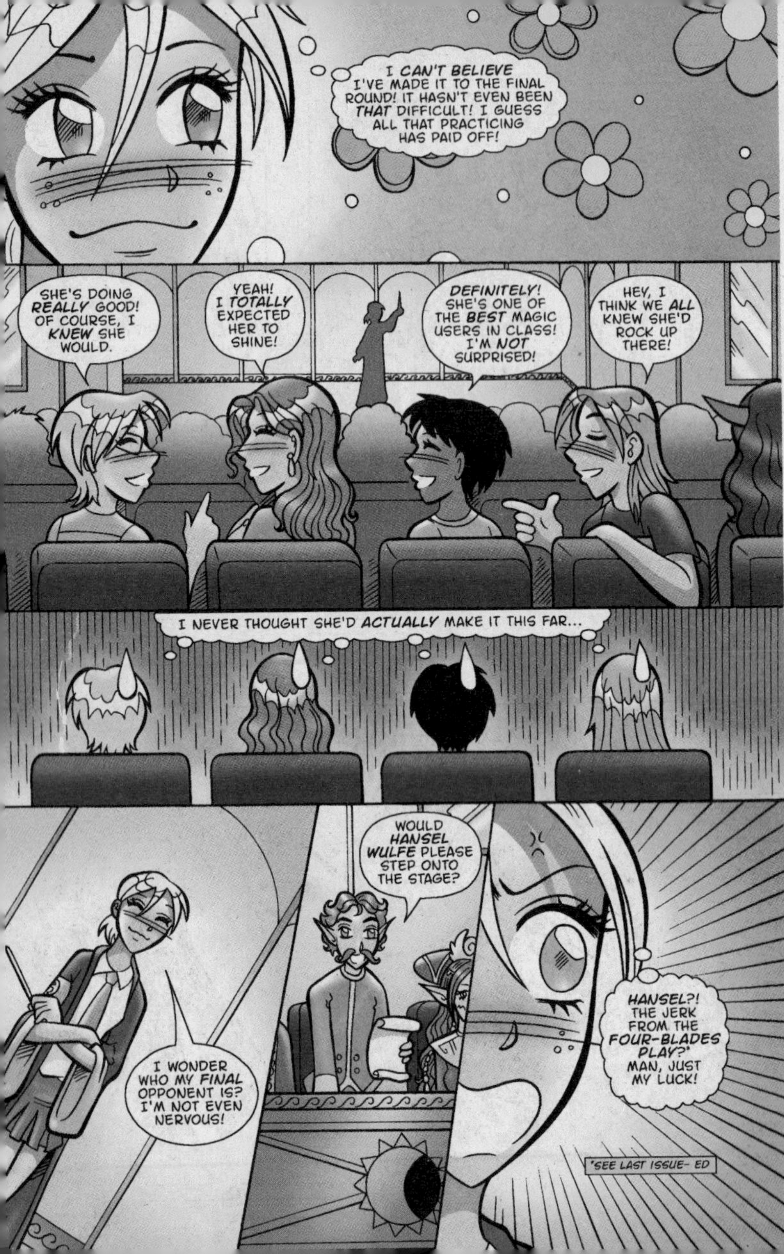
I CAN'T BELIEVE I'VE MADE IT TO THE FINAL ROUND! IT HASN'T EVEN BEEN THAT DIFFICULT! I GUESS ALL THAT PRACTICING HAS PAID OFF!
SHE'S DOING REALLY GOOD! OF COURSE, I KNEW SHE WOULD.
YEAH! I TOTALLY EXPECTED HER TO SHINE!
DEFINITELY! SHE'S ONE OF THE BEST MAGIC USERS IN CLASS! I'M NOT SURPRISED!
HEY, I THINK WE ALL KNEW SHE'D ROCK UP THERE!
I NEVER THOUGHT SHE'D ACTUALLY MAKE IT THIS FAR...
I WONDER WHO MY FINAL OPPONENT IS? I'M NOT EVEN NERVOUS!
WOULD HANSEL WULFE PLEASE STEP ONTO THE STAGE?
HANSEL?! THE JERK FROM THE FOUR-BLADES PLAY?* MAN, JUST MY LUCK!
*SEE LAST ISSUE- ED

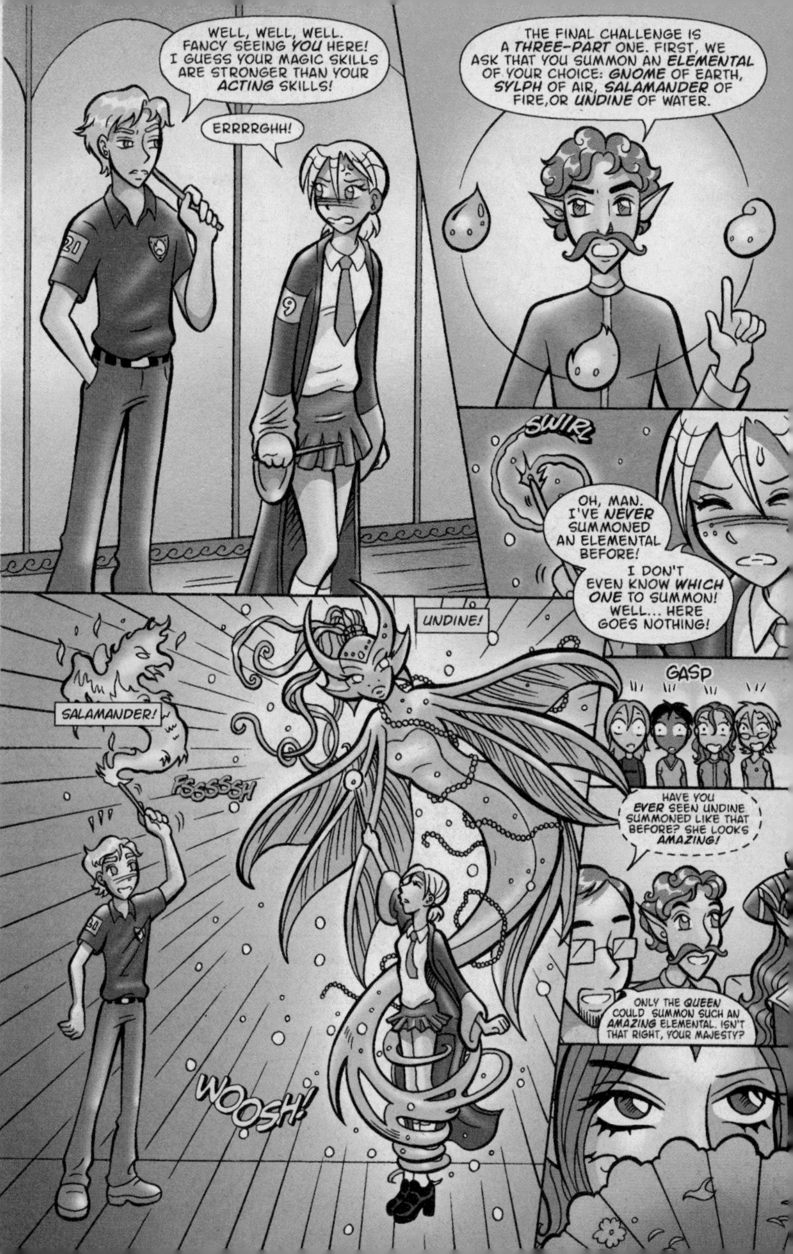

WELL, WELL, WELL. FANCY SEEING YOU HERE! I GUESS YOUR MAGIC SKILLS ARE STRONGER THAN YOUR ACTING SKILLS!
ERRRRGHH!
THE FINAL CHALLENGE IS A THREE-PART ONE. FIRST, WE ASK THAT YOU SUMMON AN ELEMENTAL OF YOUR CHOICE: GNOME OF EARTH, SYLPH OF AIR, SALAMANDER OF FIRE, OR UNDINE OF WATER.
SWIRL
OH, MAN. I'VE NEVER SUMMONED AN ELEMENTAL BEFORE!
I DON'T EVEN KNOW WHICH ONE TO SUMMON! WELL... HERE GOES NOTHING!
SALAMANDER!
FSSSSSH
UNDINE!
WOOSH!
GASP
HAVE YOU EVER SEEN UNDINE SUMMONED LIKE THAT BEFORE? SHE LOOKS AMAZING!
ONLY THE QUEEN COULD SUMMON SUCH AN AMAZING ELEMENTAL. ISN'T THAT RIGHT, YOUR MAJESTY?

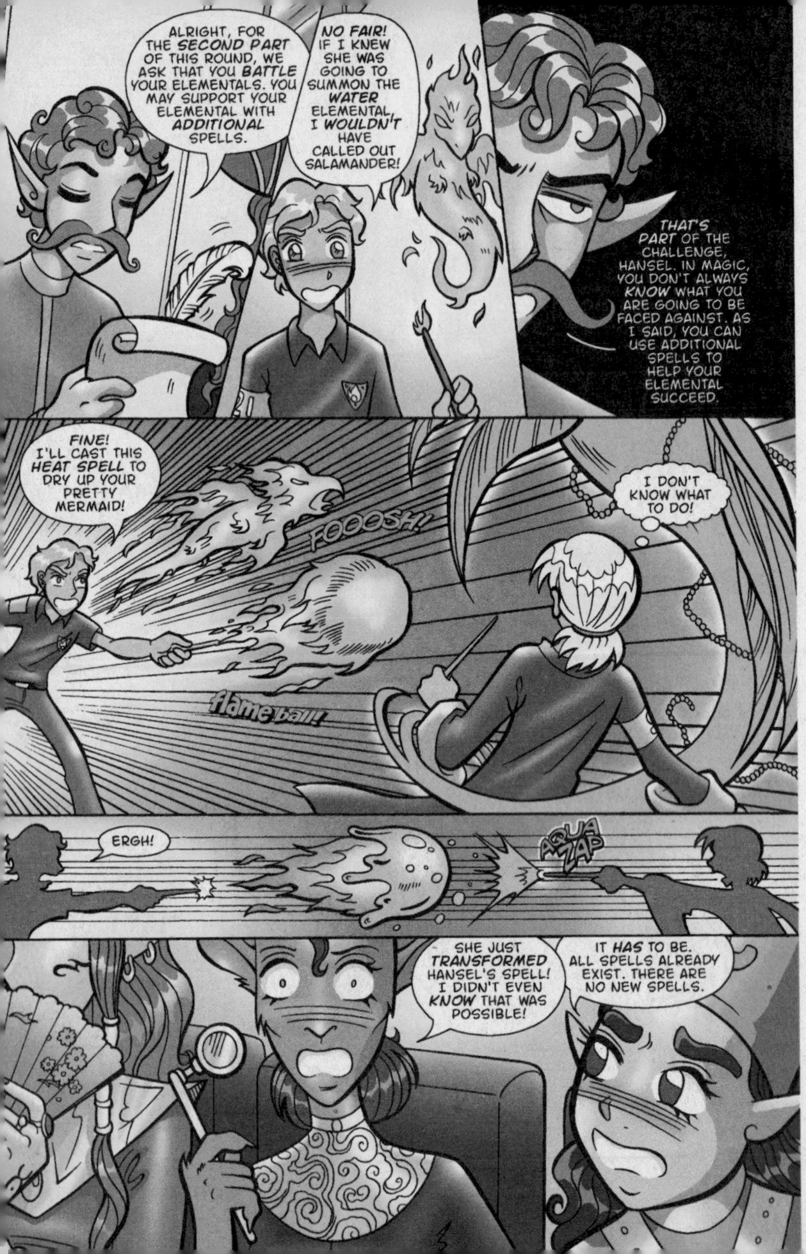

ALRIGHT, FOR THE SECOND PART OF THIS ROUND, WE ASK THAT YOU BATTLE YOUR ELEMENTALS. YOU MAY SUPPORT YOUR ELEMENTAL WITH ADDITIONAL SPELLS.
NO FAIR! IF I KNEW SHE WAS GOING TO SUMMON THE WATER ELEMENTAL, I WOULDN'T HAVE CALLED OUT SALAMANDER!
THAT'S PART OF THE CHALLENGE, HANSEL. IN MAGIC, YOU DON'T ALWAYS KNOW WHAT YOU ARE GOING TO BE FACED AGAINST. AS I SAID, YOU CAN USE ADDITIONAL SPELLS TO HELP YOUR ELEMENTAL SUCCEED.
FINE! I'LL CAST THIS HEAT SPELL TO DRY UP YOUR PRETTY MERMAID!
FOOOSH!
I DON'T KNOW WHAT TO DO!
flame ball!
ERGH!
AQUA ZAP
SHE JUST TRANSFORMED HANSEL'S SPELL! I DIDN'T EVEN KNOW THAT WAS POSSIBLE!
IT HAS TO BE. ALL SPELLS ALREADY EXIST. THERE ARE NO NEW SPELLS.

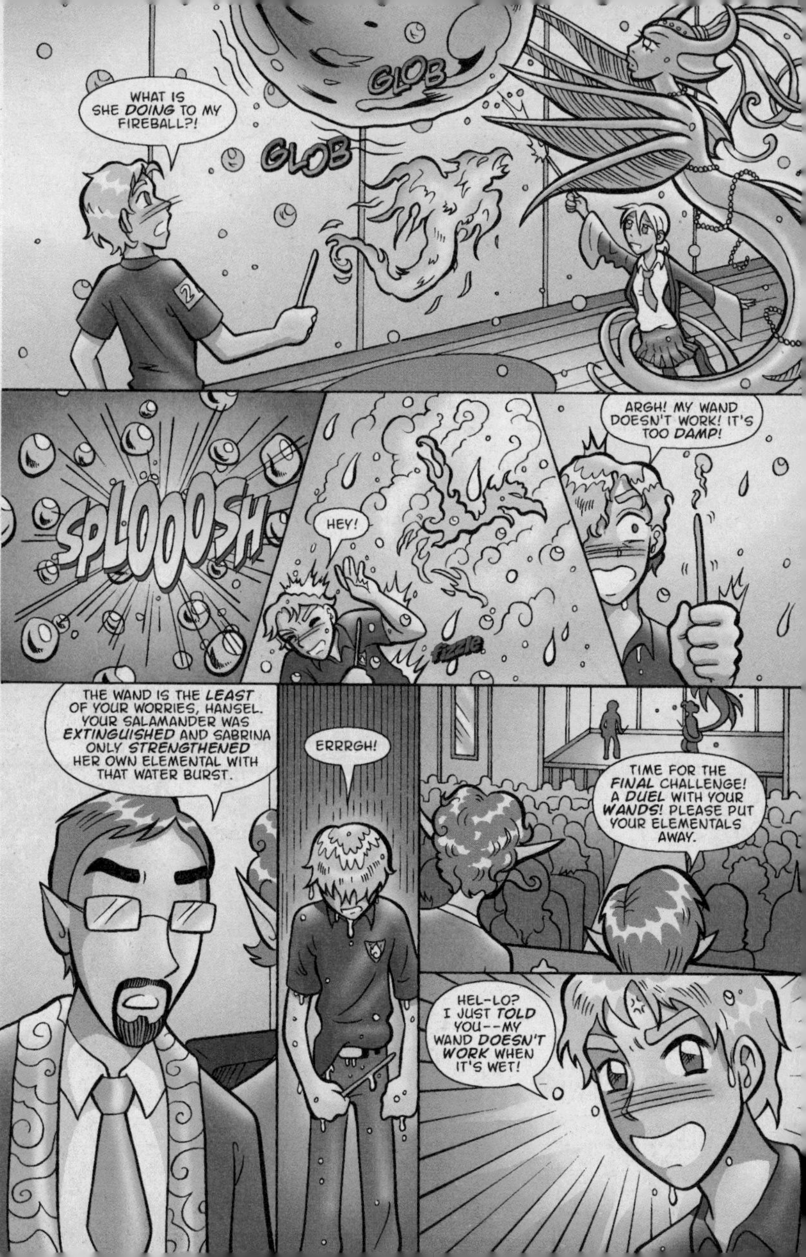

GLOB
WHAT IS SHE DOING TO MY FIREBALL?!
GLOB
SPLOOOSH
HEY!
fizzle
ARGH! MY WAND DOESN'T WORK! IT'S TOO DAMP!
THE WAND IS THE LEAST OF YOUR WORRIES, HANSEL. YOUR SALAMANDER WAS EXTINGUISHED AND SABRINA ONLY STRENGTHENED HER OWN ELEMENTAL WITH THAT WATER BURST.
ERRRGH!
TIME FOR THE FINAL CHALLENGE! A DUEL WITH YOUR WANDS! PLEASE PUT YOUR ELEMENTALS AWAY.
HEL-LO? I JUST TOLD YOU--MY WAND DOESN'T WORK WHEN IT'S WET!

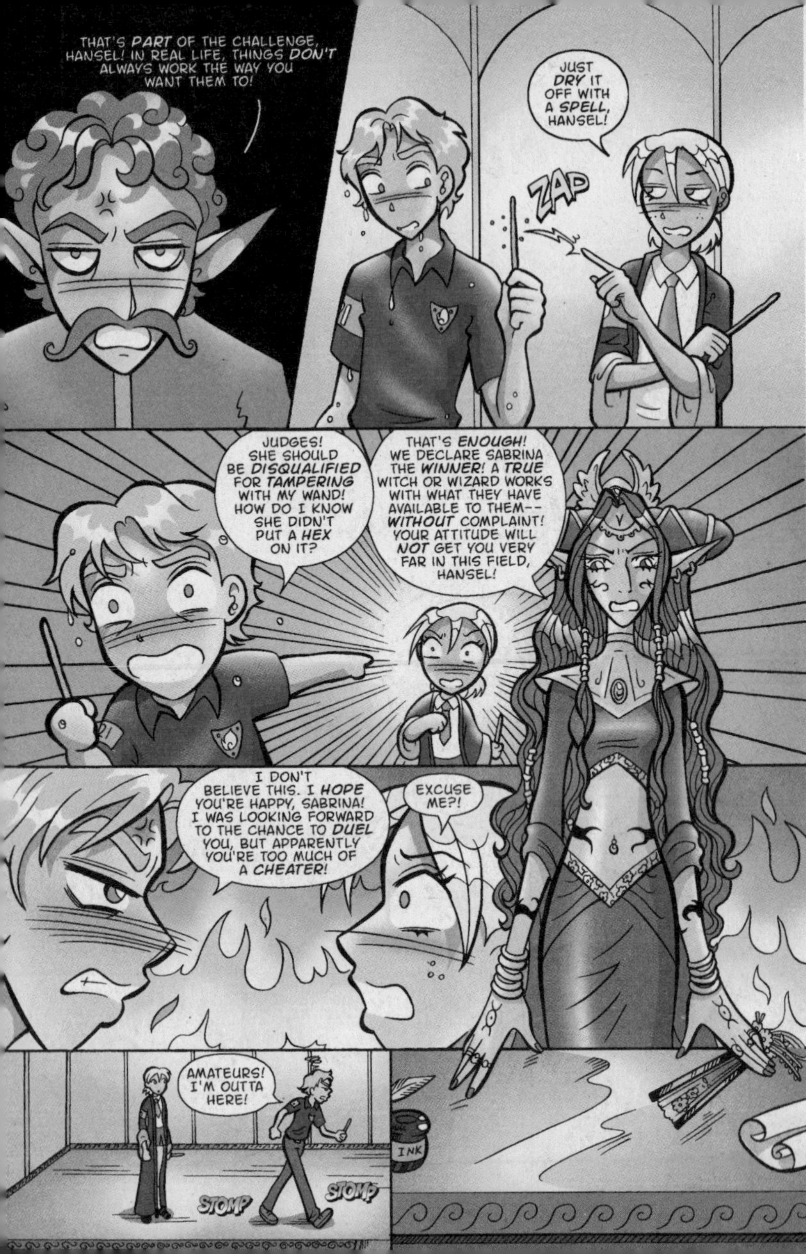

THAT'S PART OF THE CHALLENGE, HANSEL! IN REAL LIFE, THINGS DON'T ALWAYS WORK THE WAY YOU WANT THEM TO!
JUST DRY IT OFF WITH A SPELL, HANSEL!
ZAP
JUDGES! SHE SHOULD BE DISQUALIFIED FOR TAMPERING WITH MY WAND! HOW DO I KNOW SHE DIDN'T PUT A HEX ON IT?
THAT'S ENOUGH! WE DECLARE SABRINA THE WINNER! A TRUE WITCH OR WIZARD WORKS WITH WHAT THEY HAVE AVAILABLE TO THEM-- WITHOUT COMPLAINT! YOUR ATTITUDE WILL NOT GET YOU VERY FAR IN THIS FIELD, HANSEL!
I DON'T BELIEVE THIS. I HOPE YOU'RE HAPPY, SABRINA! I WAS LOOKING FORWARD TO THE CHANCE TO DUEL YOU, BUT APPARENTLY YOU'RE TOO MUCH OF A CHEATER!
EXCUSE ME?!
AMATEURS! I'M OUTTA HERE!
STOMP
STOMP
INK

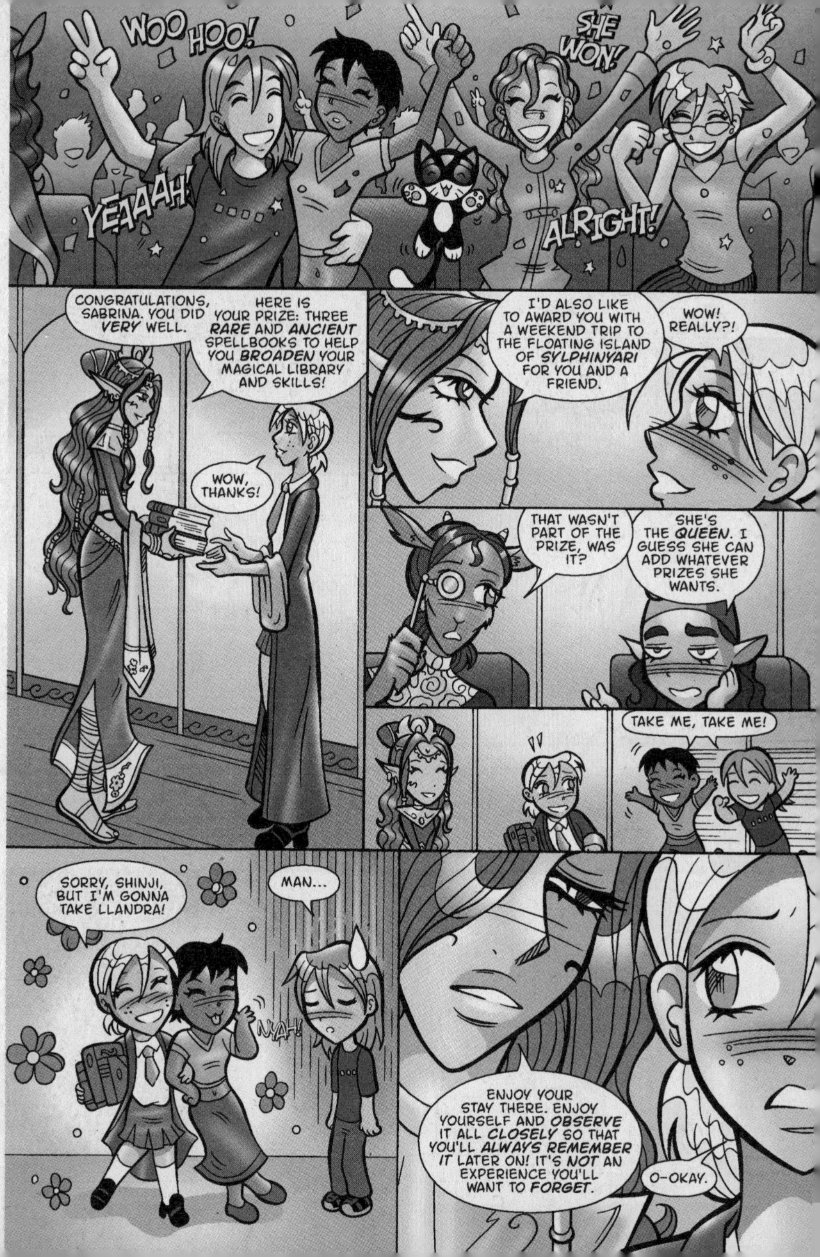

WOO HOO!
SHE WON!
YEAAAH!
ALRIGHT!
CONGRATULATIONS, SABRINA. YOU DID VERY WELL.
HERE IS YOUR PRIZE: THREE RARE AND ANCIENT SPELLBOOKS TO HELP YOU BROADEN YOUR MAGICAL LIBRARY AND SKILLS!
WOW, THANKS!
I'D ALSO LIKE TO AWARD YOU WITH A WEEKEND TRIP TO THE FLOATING ISLAND OF SYLPHINYARI FOR YOU AND A FRIEND.
WOW! REALLY?!
THAT WASN'T PART OF THE PRIZE, WAS IT?
SHE'S THE QUEEN. I GUESS SHE CAN ADD WHATEVER PRIZES SHE WANTS.
TAKE ME, TAKE ME!
SORRY, SHINJI, BUT I'M GONNA TAKE LLANDRA!
MAN...
NYAH!
ENJOY YOUR STAY THERE. ENJOY YOURSELF AND OBSERVE IT ALL CLOSELY SO THAT YOU'LL ALWAYS REMEMBER IT LATER ON! IT'S NOT AN EXPERIENCE YOU'LL WANT TO FORGET.
O-OKAY.

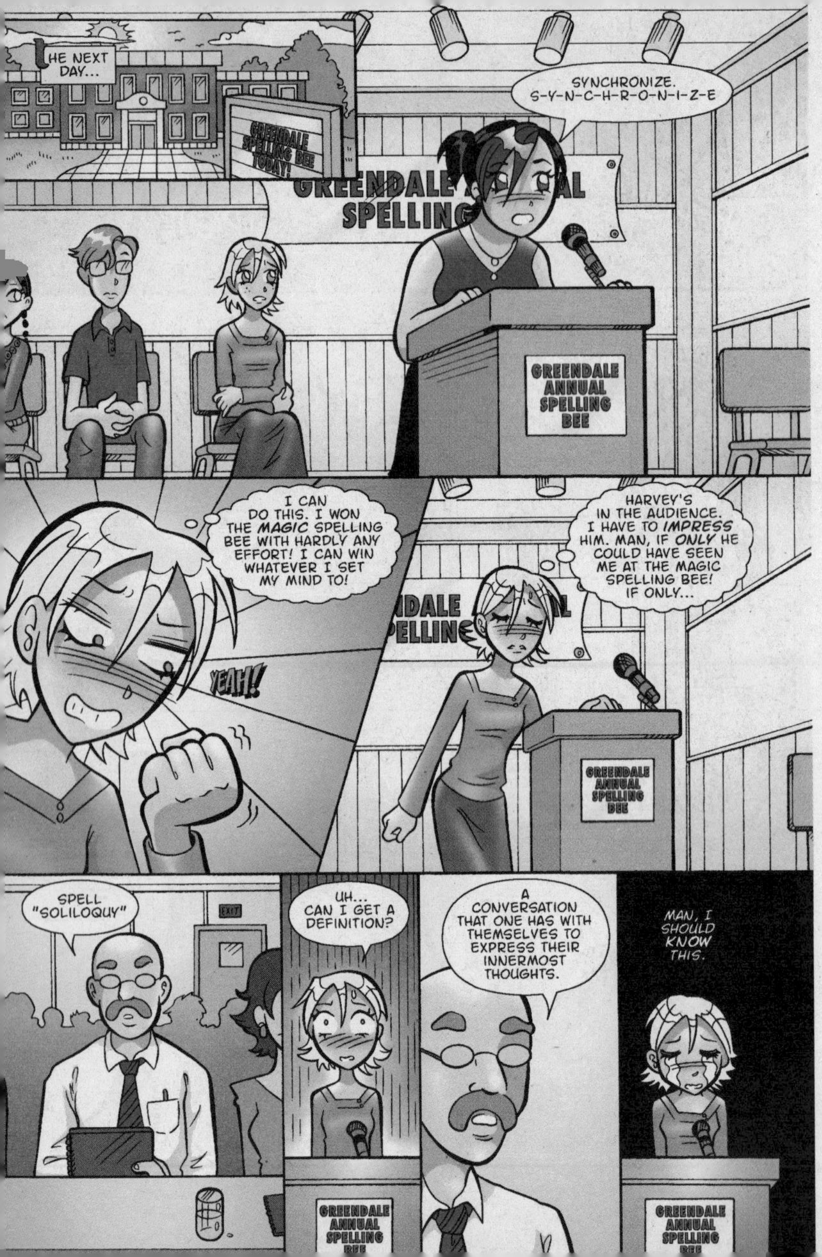

THE NEXT DAY...
GREENDALE SPELLING BEE TODAY!
SYNCHRONIZE. S-Y-N-C-H-R-O-N-I-Z-E
GREENDALE ANNUAL SPELLING BEE
I CAN DO THIS. I WON THE MAGIC SPELLING BEE WITH HARDLY ANY EFFORT! I CAN WIN WHATEVER I SET MY MIND TO!
YEAH!!
HARVEY'S IN THE AUDIENCE. I HAVE TO IMPRESS HIM. MAN, IF ONLY HE COULD HAVE SEEN ME AT THE MAGIC SPELLING BEE! IF ONLY...
GREENDALE ANNUAL SPELLING BEE
SPELL "SOLILOQUY"
EXIT
UH... CAN I GET A DEFINITION?
A CONVERSATION THAT ONE HAS WITH THEMSELVES TO EXPRESS THEIR INNERMOST THOUGHTS.
MAN, I SHOULD KNOW THIS.

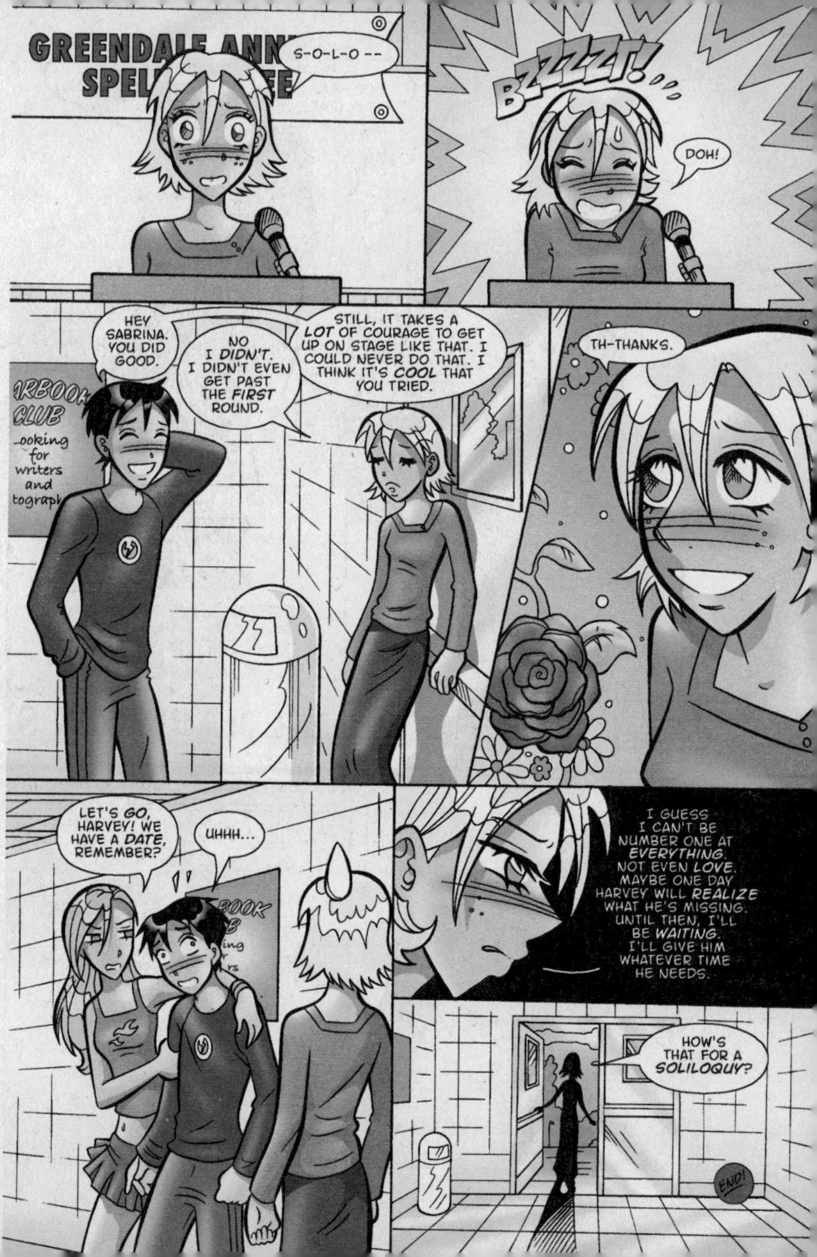
GREENDALE ANN
SPEL EE
S-O-L-O --
BZZZZT!
DOH!
HEY SABRINA. YOU DID GOOD.
NO I DIDN'T. I DIDN'T EVEN GET PAST THE FIRST ROUND.
STILL, IT TAKES A LOT OF COURAGE TO GET UP ON STAGE LIKE THAT. I COULD NEVER DO THAT. I THINK IT'S COOL THAT YOU TRIED.
RBOOK CLUB -ooking for writers and tograph
TH-THANKS.
LET'S GO, HARVEY! WE HAVE A DATE, REMEMBER?
UHHH...
I GUESS I CAN'T BE NUMBER ONE AT EVERYTHING. NOT EVEN LOVE. MAYBE ONE DAY HARVEY WILL REALIZE WHAT HE'S MISSING. UNTIL THEN, I'LL BE WAITING. I'LL GIVE HIM WHATEVER TIME HE NEEDS.
HOW'S THAT FOR A SOLILOQUY?
END!

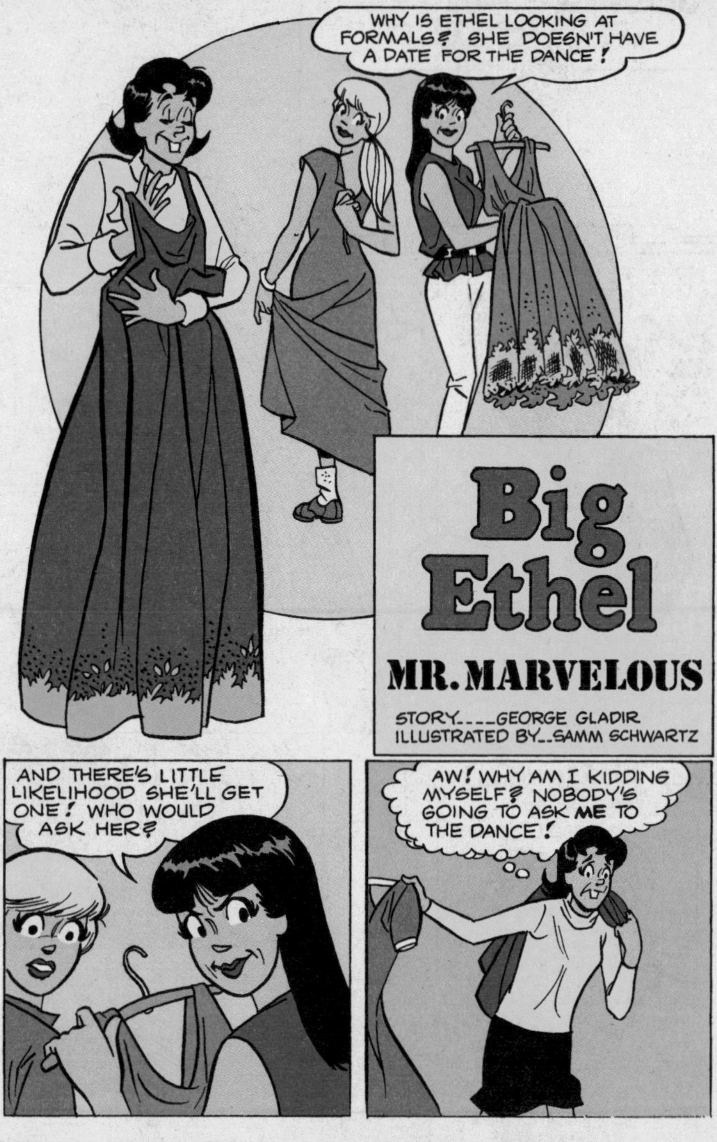
WHY IS ETHEL LOOKING AT FORMALS? SHE DOESN'T HAVE A DATE FOR THE DANCE!
Big Ethel
MR. MARVELOUS
STORY----GEORGE GLADIR
ILLUSTRATED BY--SAMM SCHWARTZ
AND THERE'S LITTLE LIKELIHOOD SHE'LL GET ONE! WHO WOULD ASK HER?
AW! WHY AM I KIDDING MYSELF? NOBODY'S GOING TO ASK ME TO THE DANCE!

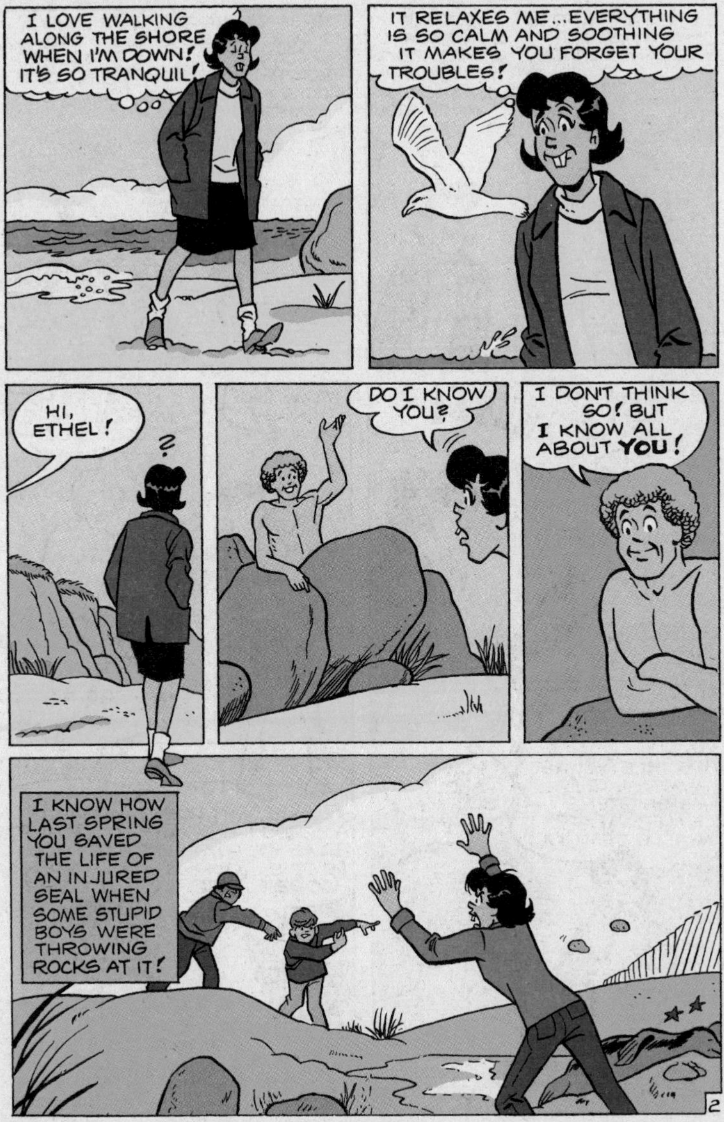
I LOVE WALKING ALONG THE SHORE WHEN I'M DOWN! IT'S SO TRANQUIL!
IT RELAXES ME...EVERYTHING IS SO CALM AND SOOTHING IT MAKES YOU FORGET YOUR TROUBLES!
HI, ETHEL!
?
DO I KNOW YOU?
I DON'T THINK SO! BUT I KNOW ALL ABOUT **YOU**!
I KNOW HOW LAST SPRING YOU SAVED THE LIFE OF AN INJURED SEAL WHEN SOME STUPID BOYS WERE THROWING ROCKS AT IT!
2

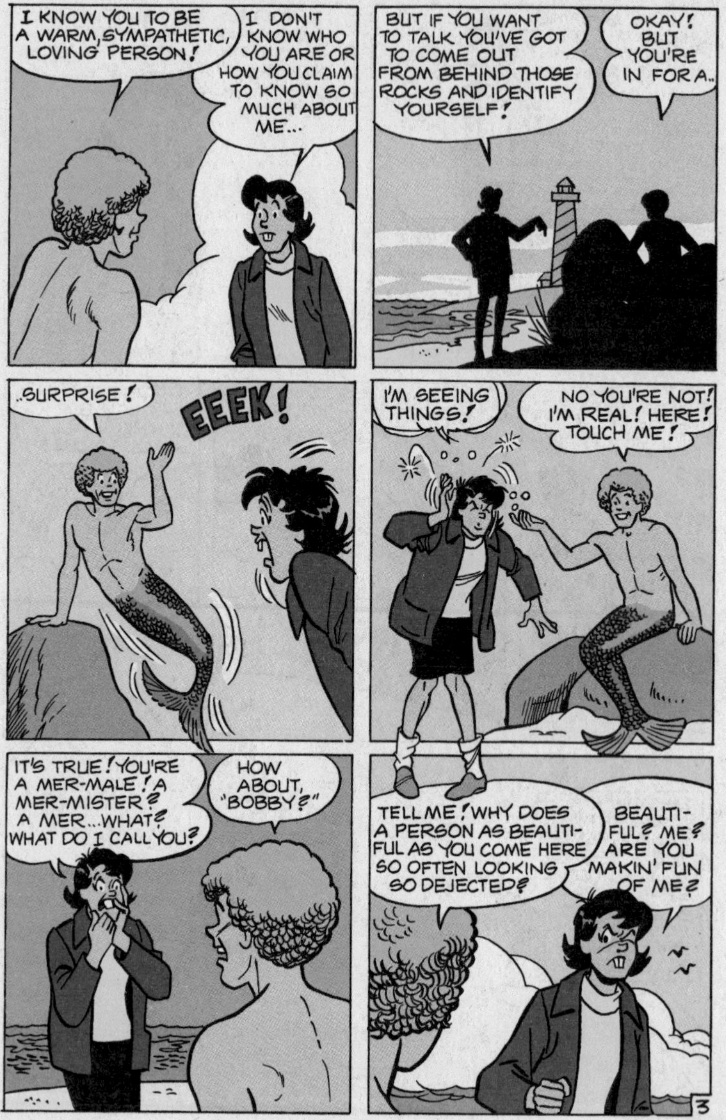
I KNOW YOU TO BE A WARM, SYMPATHETIC, LOVING PERSON!
I DON'T KNOW WHO YOU ARE OR HOW YOU CLAIM TO KNOW SO MUCH ABOUT ME...
BUT IF YOU WANT TO TALK YOU'VE GOT TO COME OUT FROM BEHIND THOSE ROCKS AND IDENTIFY YOURSELF!
OKAY! BUT YOU'RE IN FOR A..
..SURPRISE!
EEEK!
I'M SEEING THINGS!
NO YOU'RE NOT! I'M REAL! HERE! TOUCH ME!
IT'S TRUE! YOU'RE A MER-MALE! A MER-MISTER? A MER...WHAT? WHAT DO I CALL YOU?
HOW ABOUT, "BOBBY?"
TELL ME! WHY DOES A PERSON AS BEAUTIFUL AS YOU COME HERE SO OFTEN LOOKING SO DEJECTED?
BEAUTIFUL? ME? ARE YOU MAKIN' FUN OF ME?
3

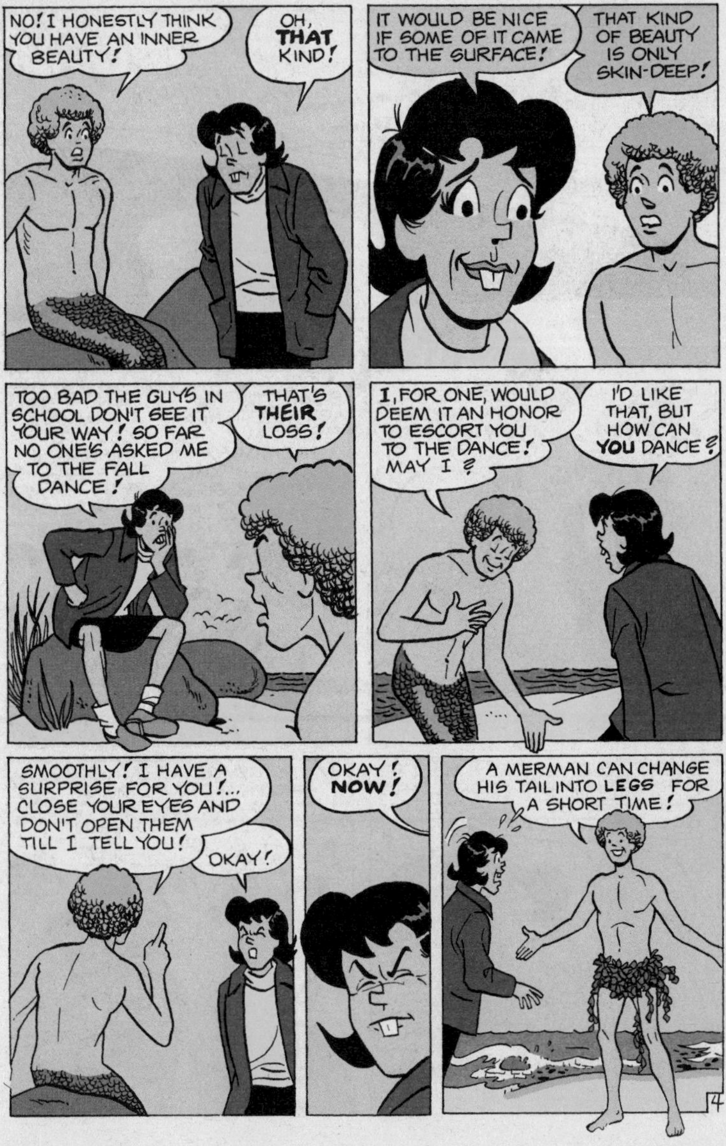
NO! I HONESTLY THINK YOU HAVE AN INNER BEAUTY!
OH, **THAT** KIND!
IT WOULD BE NICE IF SOME OF IT CAME TO THE SURFACE!
THAT KIND OF BEAUTY IS ONLY SKIN-DEEP!
TOO BAD THE GUYS IN SCHOOL DON'T SEE IT YOUR WAY! SO FAR NO ONE'S ASKED ME TO THE FALL DANCE!
THAT'S **THEIR** LOSS!
I, FOR ONE, WOULD DEEM IT AN HONOR TO ESCORT YOU TO THE DANCE! MAY I?
I'D LIKE THAT, BUT HOW CAN **YOU** DANCE?
SMOOTHLY! I HAVE A SURPRISE FOR YOU!... CLOSE YOUR EYES AND DON'T OPEN THEM TILL I TELL YOU!
OKAY!
OKAY! **NOW**!
A MERMAN CAN CHANGE HIS TAIL INTO **LEGS** FOR A SHORT TIME!
4

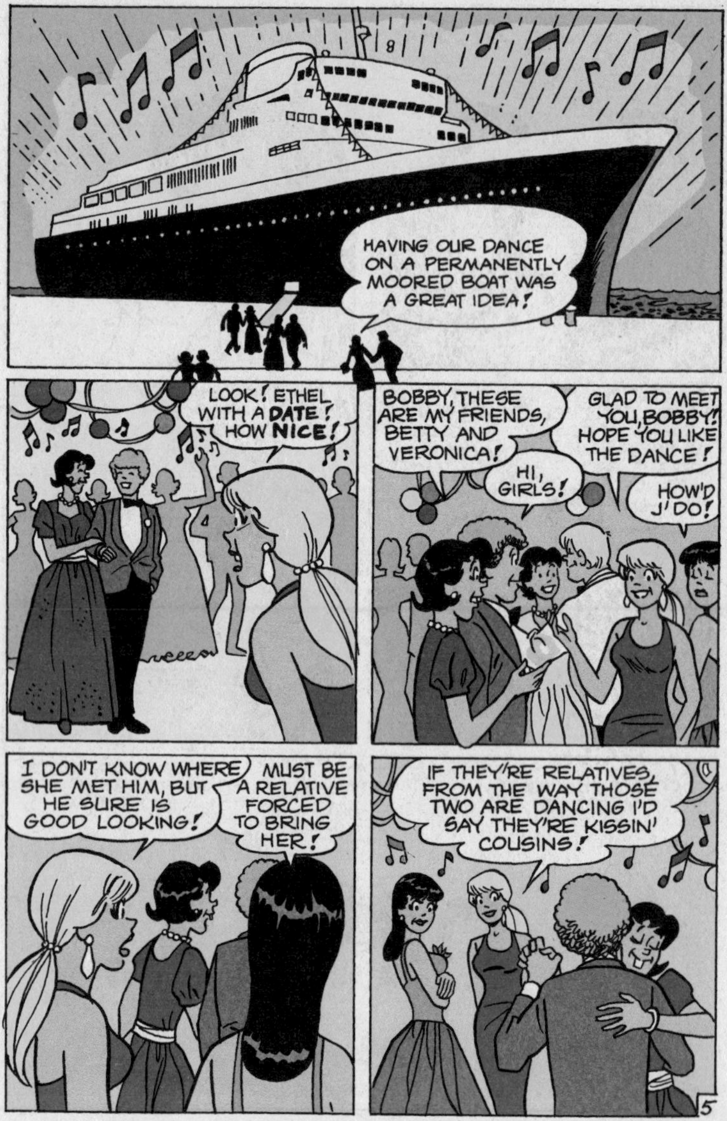
HAVING OUR DANCE ON A PERMANENTLY MOORED BOAT WAS A GREAT IDEA!
LOOK! ETHEL WITH A DATE! HOW NICE!
BOBBY, THESE ARE MY FRIENDS, BETTY AND VERONICA!
HI, GIRLS!
GLAD TO MEET YOU, BOBBY! HOPE YOU LIKE THE DANCE!
HOW'D J'DO!
I DON'T KNOW WHERE SHE MET HIM, BUT HE SURE IS GOOD LOOKING!
MUST BE A RELATIVE FORCED TO BRING HER!
IF THEY'RE RELATIVES, FROM THE WAY THOSE TWO ARE DANCING I'D SAY THEY'RE KISSIN' COUSINS!

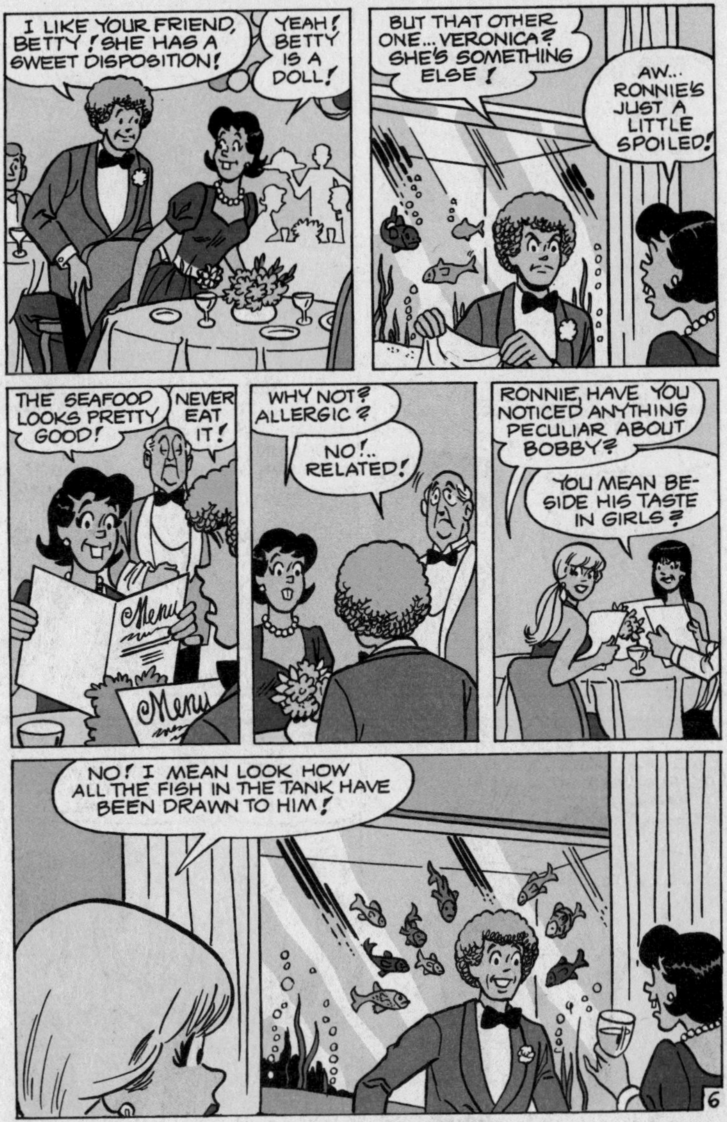

I LIKE YOUR FRIEND, BETTY! SHE HAS A SWEET DISPOSITION!
YEAH! BETTY IS A DOLL!
BUT THAT OTHER ONE... VERONICA? SHE'S SOMETHING ELSE!
AW... RONNIE'S JUST A LITTLE SPOILED!
THE SEAFOOD LOOKS PRETTY GOOD!
NEVER EAT IT!
WHY NOT? ALLERGIC?
NO!.. RELATED!
RONNIE, HAVE YOU NOTICED ANYTHING PECULIAR ABOUT BOBBY?
YOU MEAN BE-SIDE HIS TASTE IN GIRLS?
NO! I MEAN LOOK HOW ALL THE FISH IN THE TANK HAVE BEEN DRAWN TO HIM!
6

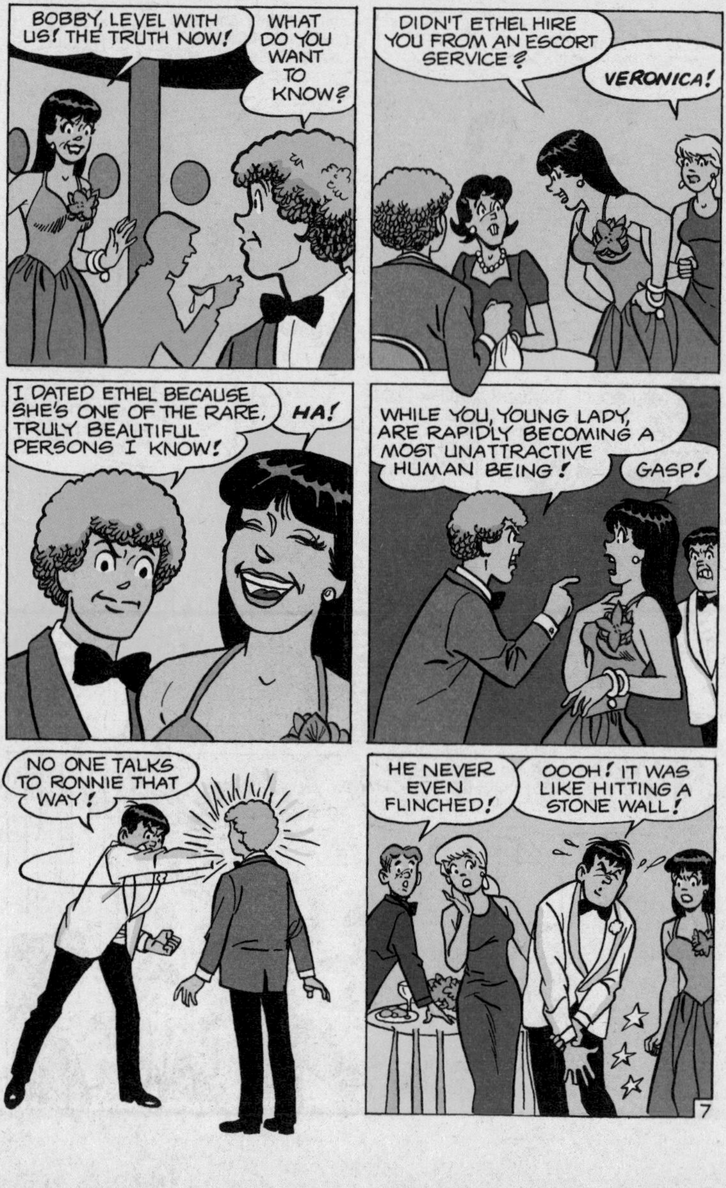

BOBBY, LEVEL WITH US! THE TRUTH NOW!
WHAT DO YOU WANT TO KNOW?
DIDN'T ETHEL HIRE YOU FROM AN ESCORT SERVICE?
VERONICA!
I DATED ETHEL BECAUSE SHE'S ONE OF THE RARE, TRULY BEAUTIFUL PERSONS I KNOW!
HA!
WHILE YOU, YOUNG LADY, ARE RAPIDLY BECOMING A MOST UNATTRACTIVE HUMAN BEING!
GASP!
NO ONE TALKS TO RONNIE THAT WAY!
HE NEVER EVEN FLINCHED!
OOOH! IT WAS LIKE HITTING A STONE WALL!

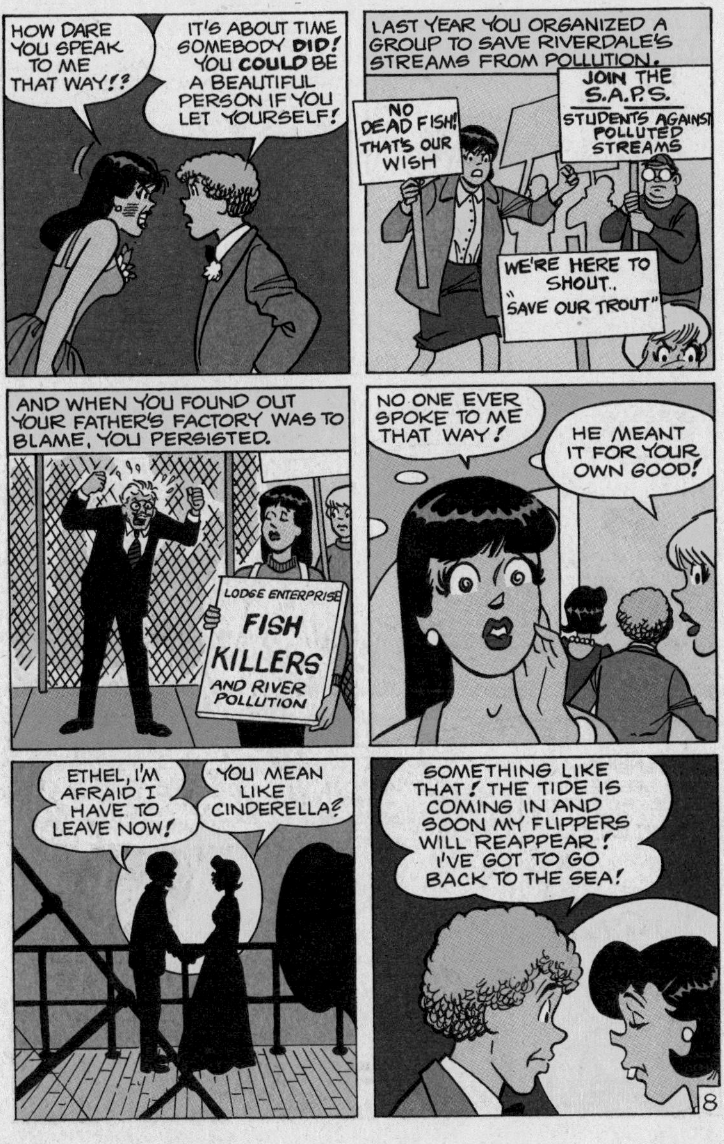
HOW DARE YOU SPEAK TO ME THAT WAY!?
IT'S ABOUT TIME SOMEBODY DID! YOU COULD BE A BEAUTIFUL PERSON IF YOU LET YOURSELF!
LAST YEAR YOU ORGANIZED A GROUP TO SAVE RIVERDALE'S STREAMS FROM POLLUTION.
NO DEAD FISH! THAT'S OUR WISH
JOIN THE S.A.P.S. STUDENTS AGAINST POLLUTED STREAMS
WE'RE HERE TO SHOUT.. "SAVE OUR TROUT"
AND WHEN YOU FOUND OUT YOUR FATHER'S FACTORY WAS TO BLAME, YOU PERSISTED.
LODGE ENTERPRISE FISH KILLERS AND RIVER POLLUTION
NO ONE EVER SPOKE TO ME THAT WAY!
HE MEANT IT FOR YOUR OWN GOOD!
ETHEL, I'M AFRAID I HAVE TO LEAVE NOW!
YOU MEAN LIKE CINDERELLA?
SOMETHING LIKE THAT! THE TIDE IS COMING IN AND SOON MY FLIPPERS WILL REAPPEAR! I'VE GOT TO GO BACK TO THE SEA!
8

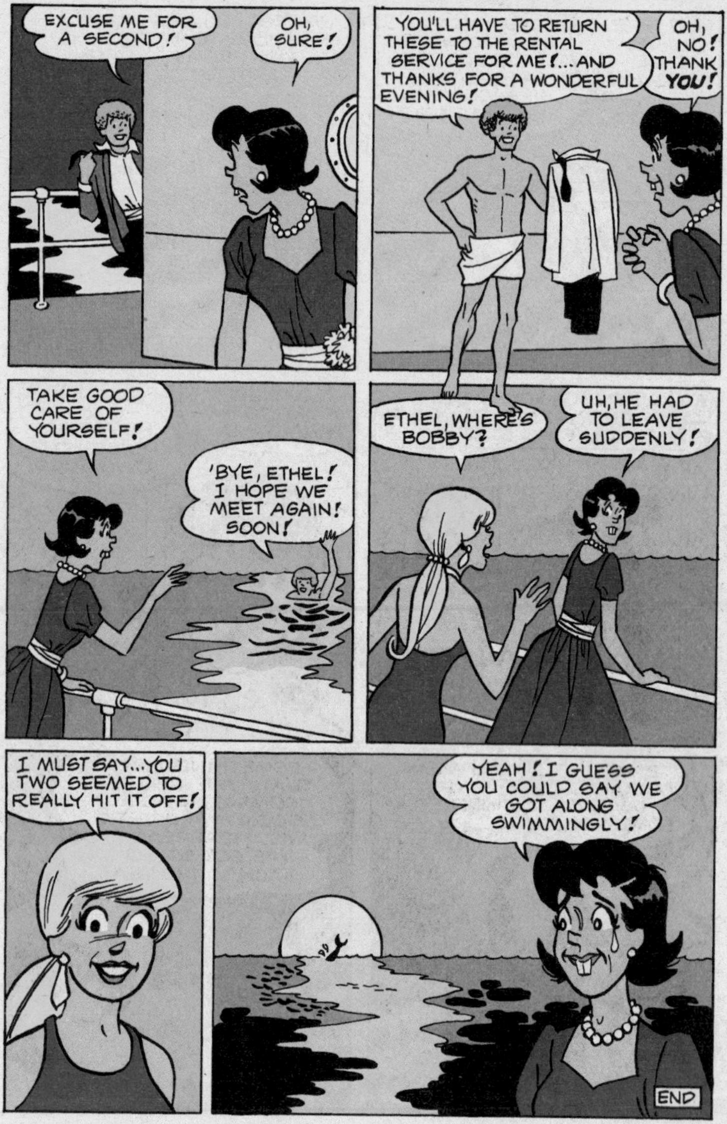
EXCUSE ME FOR A SECOND!
OH, SURE!
YOU'LL HAVE TO RETURN THESE TO THE RENTAL SERVICE FOR ME!... AND THANKS FOR A WONDERFUL EVENING!
OH, NO! THANK YOU!
TAKE GOOD CARE OF YOURSELF!
'BYE, ETHEL! I HOPE WE MEET AGAIN! SOON!
ETHEL, WHERE'S BOBBY?
UH, HE HAD TO LEAVE SUDDENLY!
I MUST SAY... YOU TWO SEEMED TO REALLY HIT IT OFF!
YEAH! I GUESS YOU COULD SAY WE GOT ALONG SWIMMINGLY!
END

Archie's Girls Betty and Veronica

From the Vault of Archie Comics!

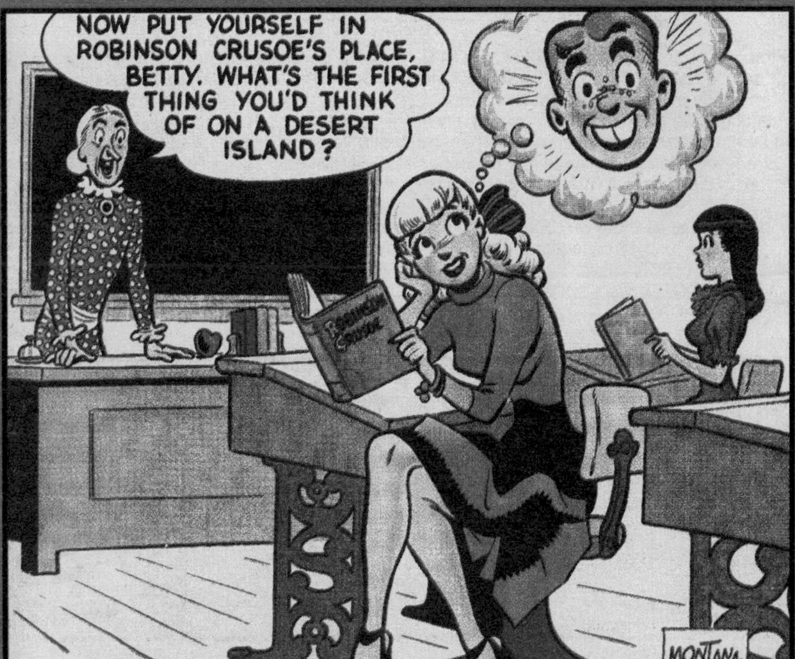
NOW PUT YOURSELF IN ROBINSON CRUSOE'S PLACE, BETTY. WHAT'S THE FIRST THING YOU'D THINK OF ON A DESERT ISLAND?
MONTANA

From the Vault of Archie Comics!

VERONICA

ARCHIE

BETTY

It's time to open up the famed Archie Vault once again! These classic stories from the 1940s are sure to give you a lesson in history, an insight on the fashions of the time and some just downright good fun! Let's not hesitate any further...!

First, in this story from **ARCHIE #10 (1944)**, Veronica becomes jealous when Betty gets a little too neighborly with the attractive boy next door, leading to a little *friendly fire*! Next, in a particularly historic story from **ARCHIE #14 (1945)**, the girls do their part for the war efforts by signing up to be waitresses in the faculty lunchroom. But what they end up *serving up* proves to be more than anyone can chew! Then, Betty and Veronica's decision to try out the new trend of making "life masks," ends in a plaster disaster in this story from **ARCHIE #15 (1945)**! Next up, in a tale from **ARCHIE #19 (1946)**, Mr. Weatherbee starts an aviation training class at Riverdale High—but only for male students! Can the girls prove that they're just as worthy to be airborne as the boys? Finally, in a story from **ARCHIE #20 (1946)**, Betty's banned from cheerleading—but will she get the last *hoo'rah* in the end?

ARCHIE COMICS are not only comical comics; they also serve as an important look back at our cultural history! Come back again next time for even more hilarious history courtesy of **THE ARCHIE VAULT!**

JUGHEAD

APPROVED
AN
Archie
MAGAZINE
· READING ·

REGGIE

The following stories are reprinted without alteration for historical reference.

Archie - AMERICA'S TOP TEEN-AGER

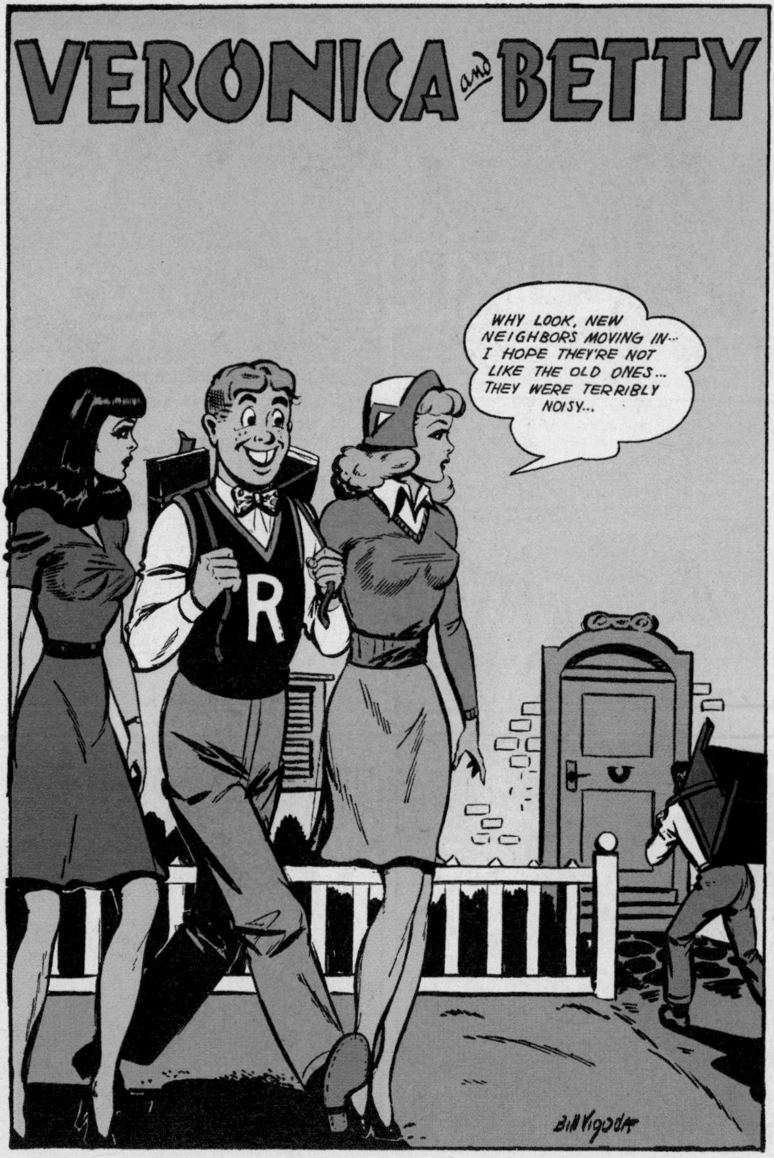
VERONICA and BETTY
WHY LOOK, NEW NEIGHBORS MOVING IN... I HOPE THEY'RE NOT LIKE THE OLD ONES... THEY WERE TERRIBLY NOISY...
R
Bill Vigoda

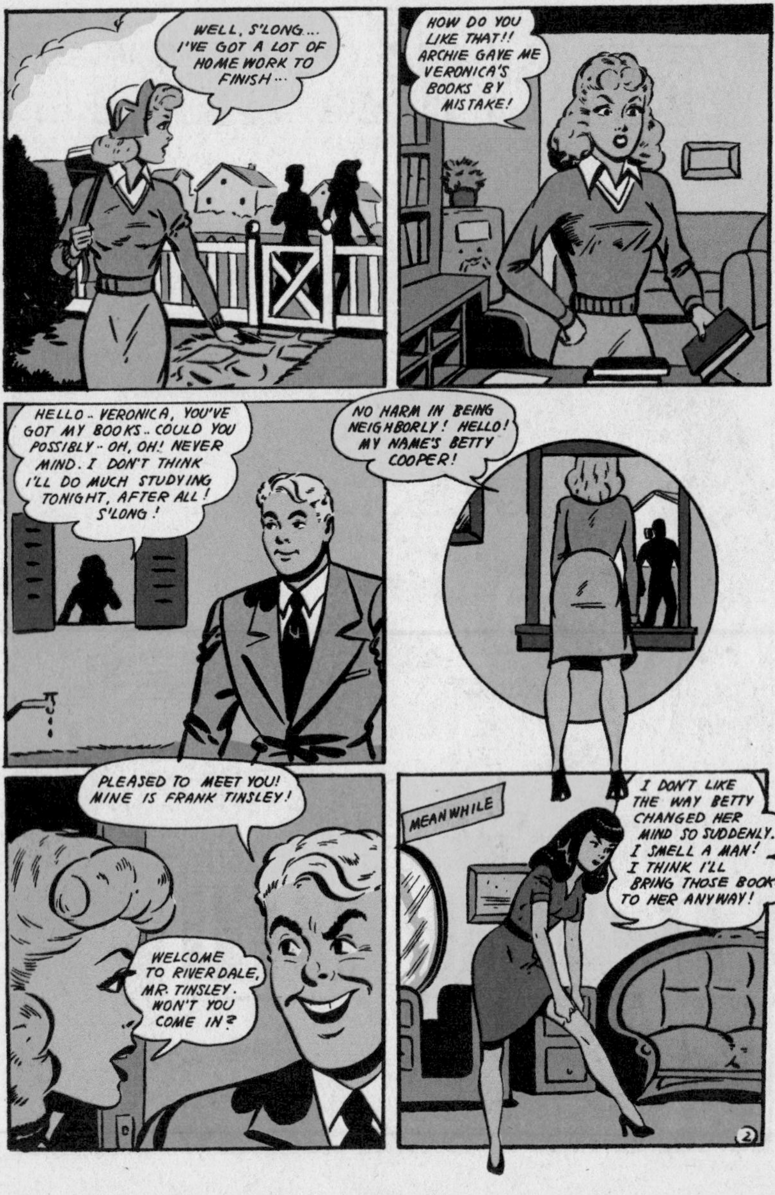
WELL, S'LONG... I'VE GOT A LOT OF HOME WORK TO FINISH...
HOW DO YOU LIKE THAT!! ARCHIE GAVE ME VERONICA'S BOOKS BY MISTAKE!
HELLO.. VERONICA, YOU'VE GOT MY BOOKS.. COULD YOU POSSIBLY.. OH, OH! NEVER MIND. I DON'T THINK I'LL DO MUCH STUDYING TONIGHT, AFTER ALL! S'LONG!
NO HARM IN BEING NEIGHBORLY! HELLO! MY NAME'S BETTY COOPER!
PLEASED TO MEET YOU! MINE IS FRANK TINSLEY!
WELCOME TO RIVERDALE, MR. TINSLEY. WON'T YOU COME IN?
MEANWHILE
I DON'T LIKE THE WAY BETTY CHANGED HER MIND SO SUDDENLY. I SMELL A MAN! I THINK I'LL BRING THOSE BOOKS TO HER ANYWAY!
2

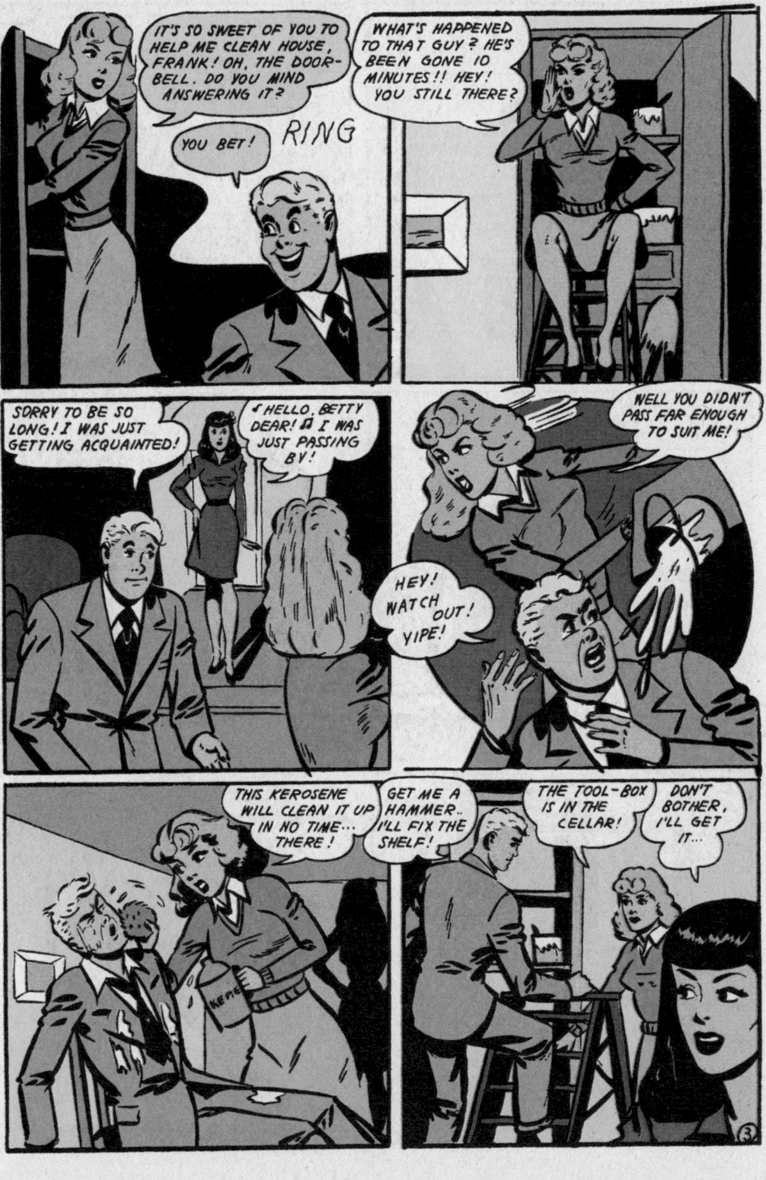

IT'S SO SWEET OF YOU TO HELP ME CLEAN HOUSE, FRANK! OH, THE DOOR-BELL. DO YOU MIND ANSWERING IT?
YOU BET!
RING
WHAT'S HAPPENED TO THAT GUY? HE'S BEEN GONE 10 MINUTES!! HEY! YOU STILL THERE?
SORRY TO BE SO LONG! I WAS JUST GETTING ACQUAINTED!
HELLO, BETTY DEAR! I WAS JUST PASSING BY!
WELL YOU DIDN'T PASS FAR ENOUGH TO SUIT ME!
HEY! WATCH OUT! YIPE!
THIS KEROSENE WILL CLEAN IT UP IN NO TIME... THERE!
GET ME A HAMMER.. I'LL FIX THE SHELF!
THE TOOL-BOX IS IN THE CELLAR!
DON'T BOTHER, I'LL GET IT...
3

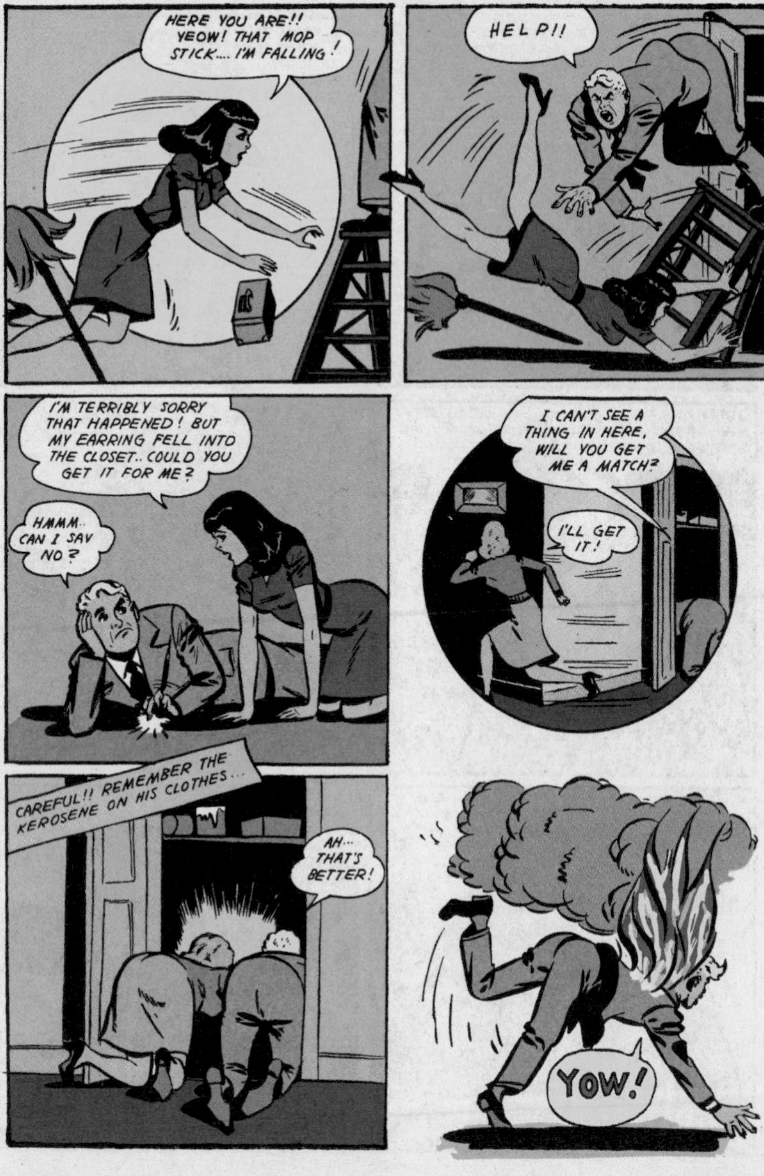
HERE YOU ARE!! YEOW! THAT MOP STICK.... I'M FALLING!
HELP!!
I'M TERRIBLY SORRY THAT HAPPENED! BUT MY EARRING FELL INTO THE CLOSET.. COULD YOU GET IT FOR ME?
HMMM.. CAN I SAY NO?
I CAN'T SEE A THING IN HERE, WILL YOU GET ME A MATCH?
I'LL GET IT!
CAREFUL!! REMEMBER THE KEROSENE ON HIS CLOTHES...
AH... THAT'S BETTER!
YOW!

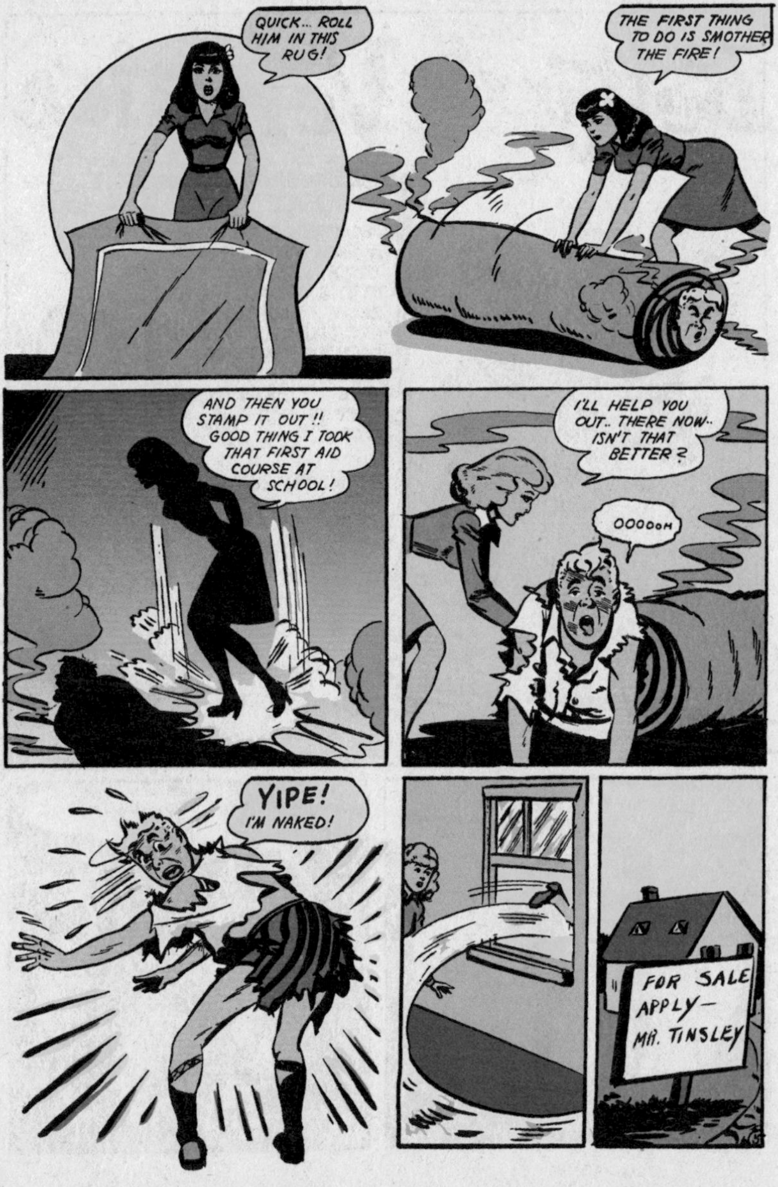
QUICK... ROLL HIM IN THIS RUG!
THE FIRST THING TO DO IS SMOTHER THE FIRE!
AND THEN YOU STAMP IT OUT!! GOOD THING I TOOK THAT FIRST AID COURSE AT SCHOOL!
I'LL HELP YOU OUT.. THERE NOW.. ISN'T THAT BETTER?
OOOOoH
YIPE! I'M NAKED!
FOR SALE APPLY— MR. TINSLEY

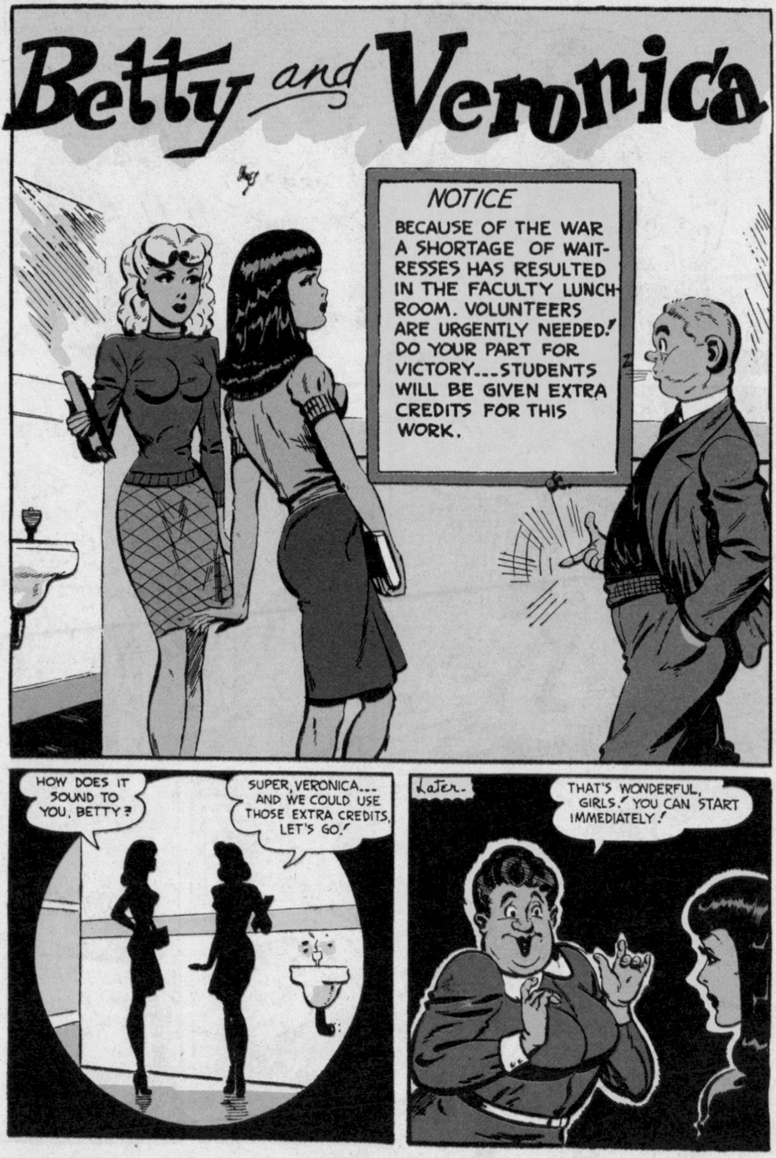
Betty and Veronica
NOTICE
BECAUSE OF THE WAR A SHORTAGE OF WAITRESSES HAS RESULTED IN THE FACULTY LUNCHROOM. VOLUNTEERS ARE URGENTLY NEEDED! DO YOUR PART FOR VICTORY...STUDENTS WILL BE GIVEN EXTRA CREDITS FOR THIS WORK.
HOW DOES IT SOUND TO YOU, BETTY?
SUPER, VERONICA... AND WE COULD USE THOSE EXTRA CREDITS. LET'S GO!
Later.
THAT'S WONDERFUL, GIRLS! YOU CAN START IMMEDIATELY!

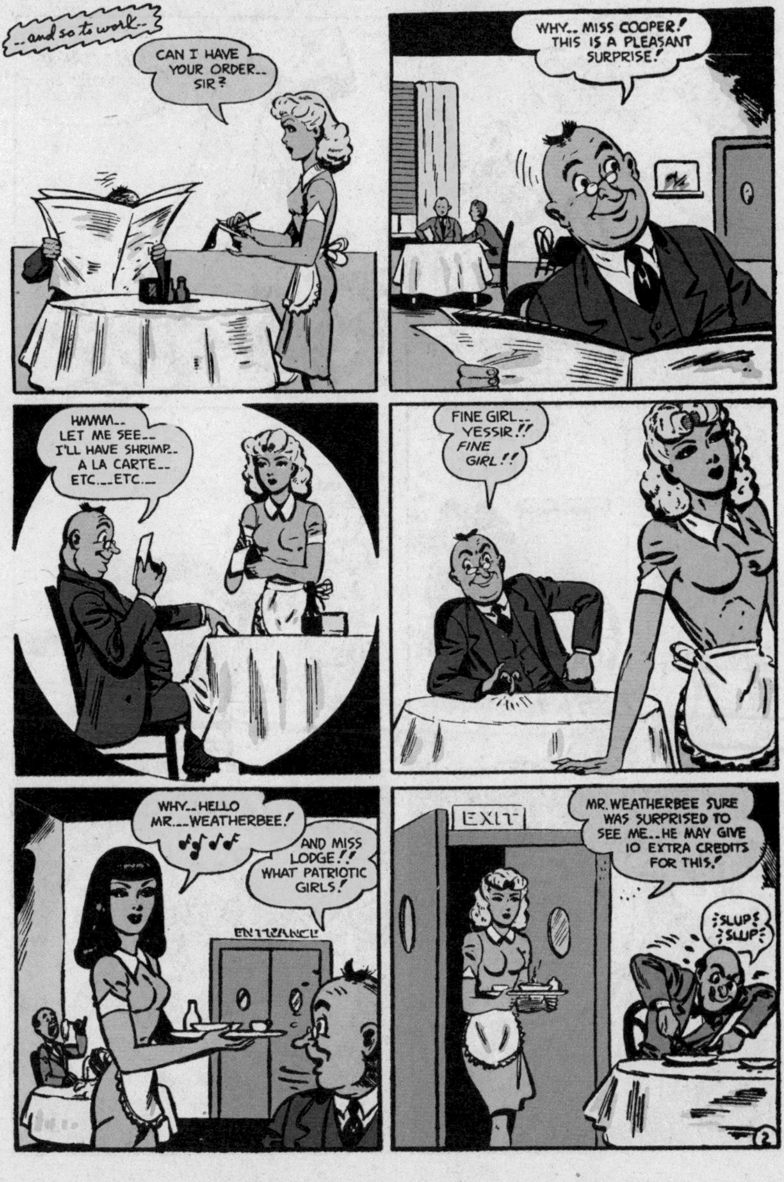

..and so to work..
CAN I HAVE YOUR ORDER.. SIR?
WHY.. MISS COOPER! THIS IS A PLEASANT SURPRISE!
HMMM.. LET ME SEE.. I'LL HAVE SHRIMP.. A LA CARTE.. ETC...ETC...
FINE GIRL.. YESSIR!! FINE GIRL!!
WHY..HELLO MR...WEATHERBEE!
AND MISS LODGE!! WHAT PATRIOTIC GIRLS!
ENTRANCE
EXIT
MR.WEATHERBEE SURE WAS SURPRISED TO SEE ME..HE MAY GIVE 10 EXTRA CREDITS FOR THIS!
SLUP SLUP
2

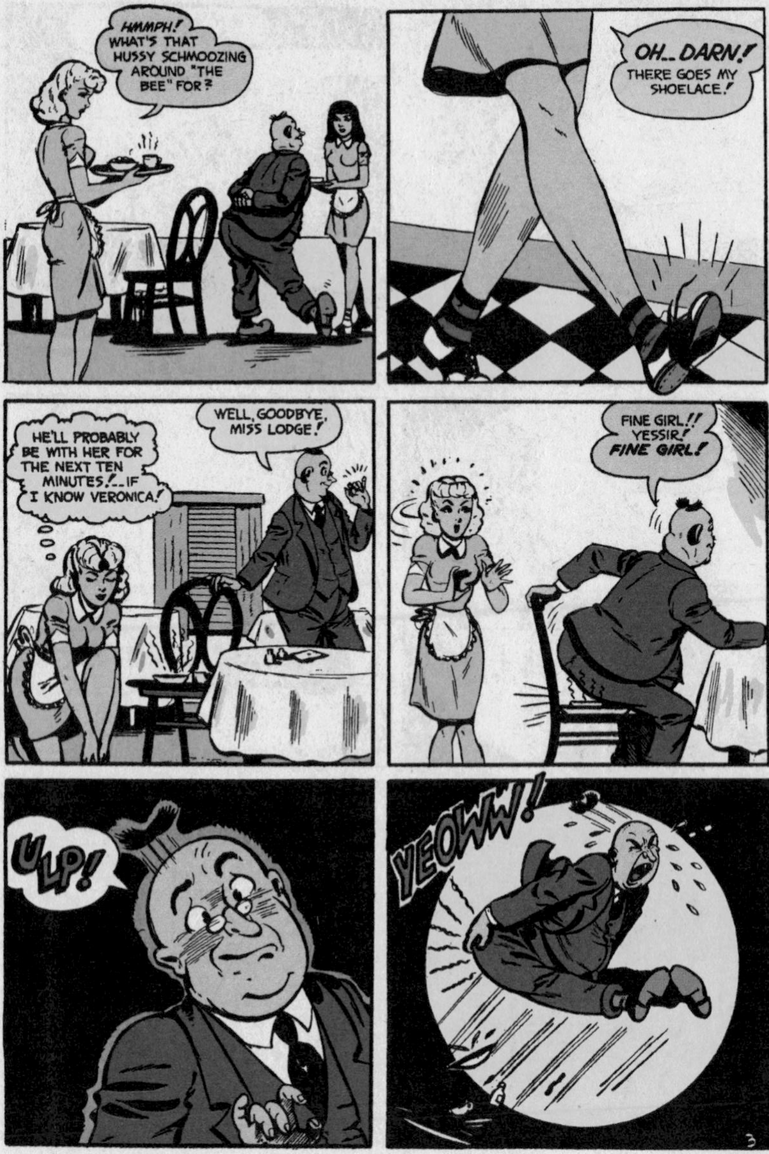
HMMPH! WHAT'S THAT HUSSY SCHMOOZING AROUND "THE BEE" FOR?
OH...DARN! THERE GOES MY SHOELACE!
HE'LL PROBABLY BE WITH HER FOR THE NEXT TEN MINUTES!...IF I KNOW VERONICA!
WELL, GOODBYE, MISS LODGE!
FINE GIRL!! YESSIR! FINE GIRL!
ULP!
YEOWW!

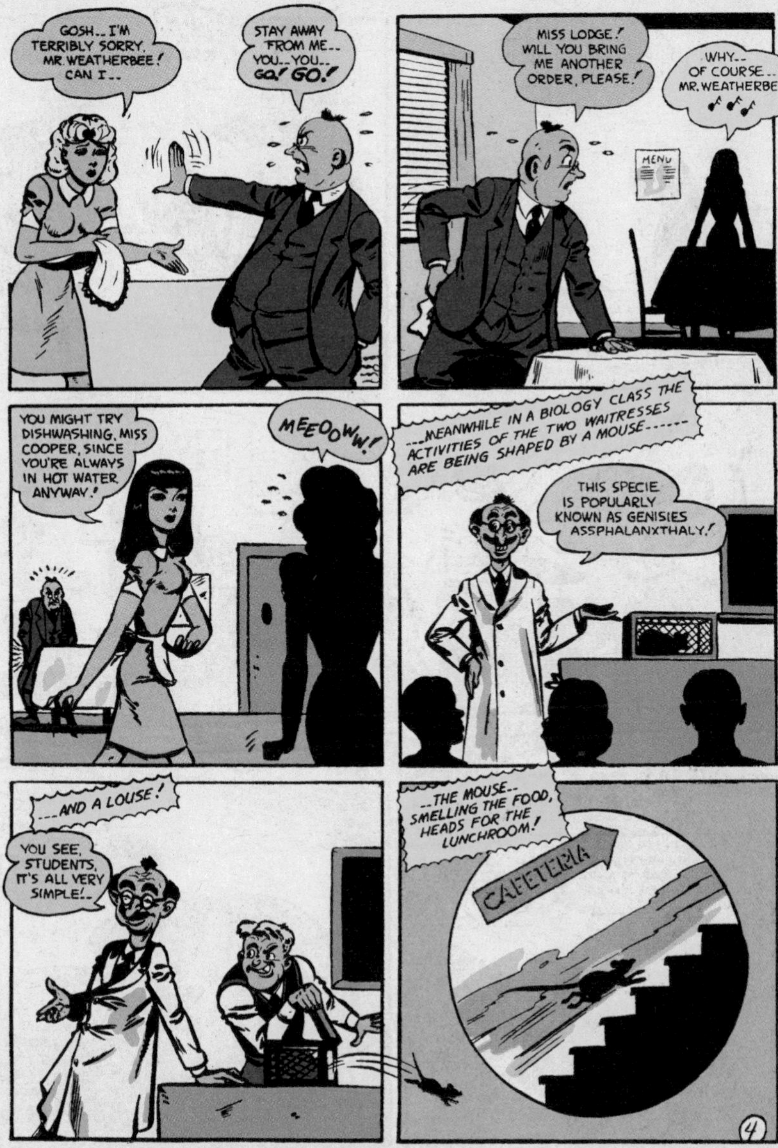

GOSH.. I'M TERRIBLY SORRY, MR. WEATHERBEE! CAN I..
STAY AWAY FROM ME.. YOU.. YOU.. GO! GO!
MISS LODGE! WILL YOU BRING ME ANOTHER ORDER, PLEASE!
WHY.. OF COURSE.. MR. WEATHERBEE
MENU
YOU MIGHT TRY DISHWASHING, MISS COOPER, SINCE YOU'RE ALWAYS IN HOT WATER ANYWAY!
MEEOOWW!
...MEANWHILE IN A BIOLOGY CLASS THE ACTIVITIES OF THE TWO WAITRESSES ARE BEING SHAPED BY A MOUSE......
THIS SPECIE IS POPULARLY KNOWN AS GENISIES ASSPHALANXTHALY!
...AND A LOUSE!
YOU SEE, STUDENTS, IT'S ALL VERY SIMPLE!..
..THE MOUSE.. SMELLING THE FOOD, HEADS FOR THE LUNCHROOM!
CAFETERIA

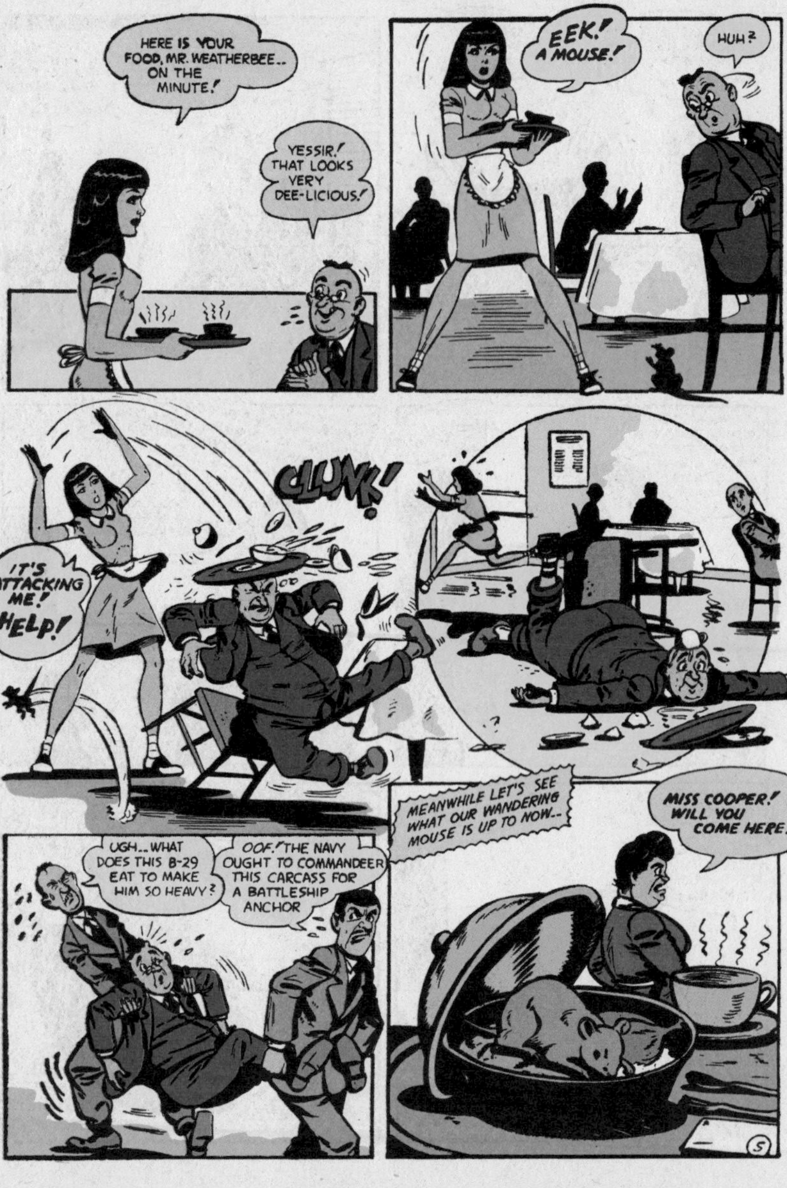
HERE IS YOUR FOOD, MR. WEATHERBEE.. ON THE MINUTE!
YESSIR! THAT LOOKS VERY DEE-LICIOUS!
EEK! A MOUSE!
HUH?
CLUNK!
IT'S ATTACKING ME! HELP!
MEANWHILE LET'S SEE WHAT OUR WANDERING MOUSE IS UP TO NOW..
UGH.. WHAT DOES THIS B-29 EAT TO MAKE HIM SO HEAVY?
OOF! THE NAVY OUGHT TO COMMANDEER THIS CARCASS FOR A BATTLESHIP ANCHOR
MISS COOPER! WILL YOU COME HERE!
5

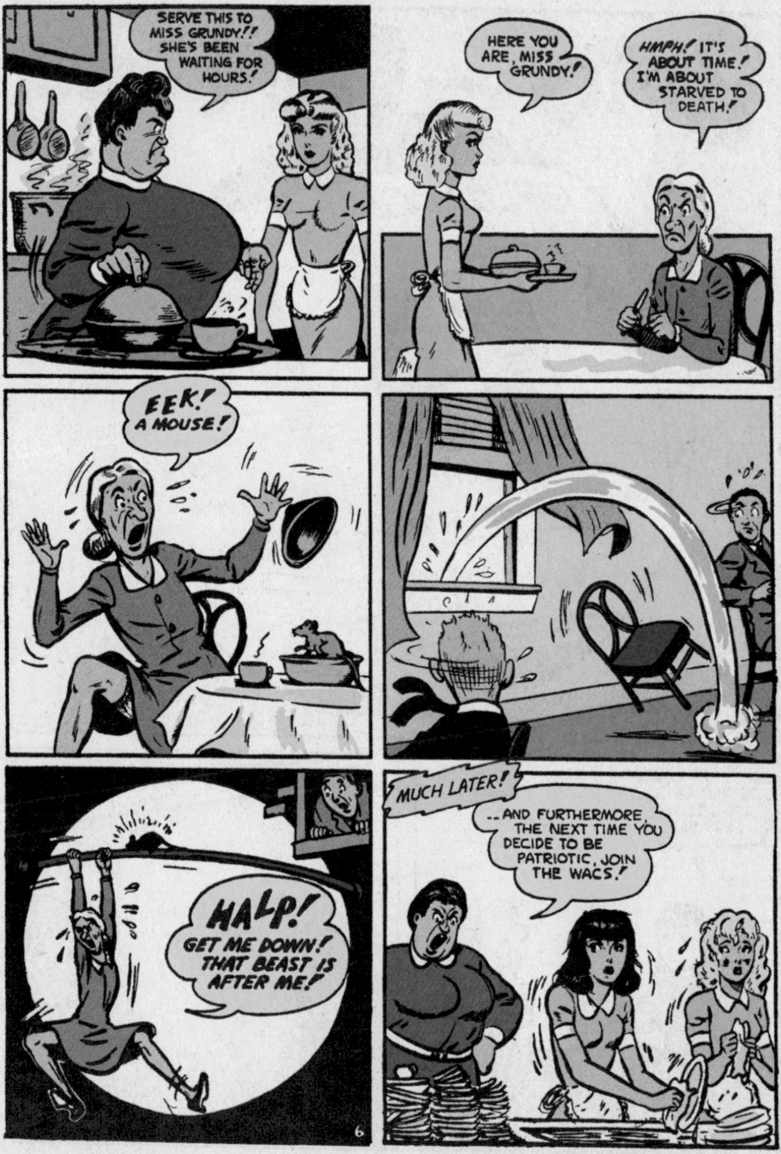
SERVE THIS TO MISS GRUNDY!! SHE'S BEEN WAITING FOR HOURS!
HERE YOU ARE, MISS GRUNDY!
HMPH! IT'S ABOUT TIME! I'M ABOUT STARVED TO DEATH!
EEK! A MOUSE!
HALP! GET ME DOWN! THAT BEAST IS AFTER ME!
MUCH LATER!
..AND FURTHERMORE, THE NEXT TIME YOU DECIDE TO BE PATRIOTIC, JOIN THE WACS!
6

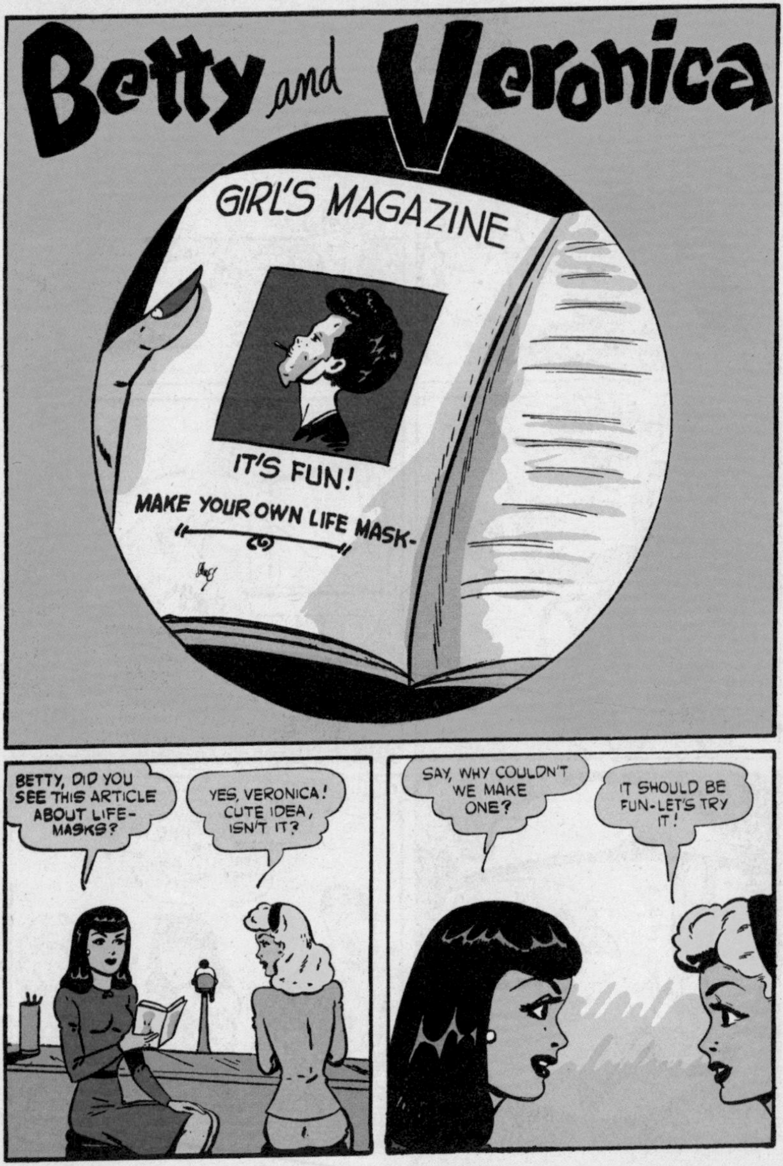

Betty and Veronica
GIRL'S MAGAZINE
IT'S FUN!
MAKE YOUR OWN LIFE MASK-
BETTY, DID YOU SEE THIS ARTICLE ABOUT LIFE-MASKS?
YES, VERONICA! CUTE IDEA, ISN'T IT?
SAY, WHY COULDN'T WE MAKE ONE?
IT SHOULD BE FUN-LET'S TRY IT!

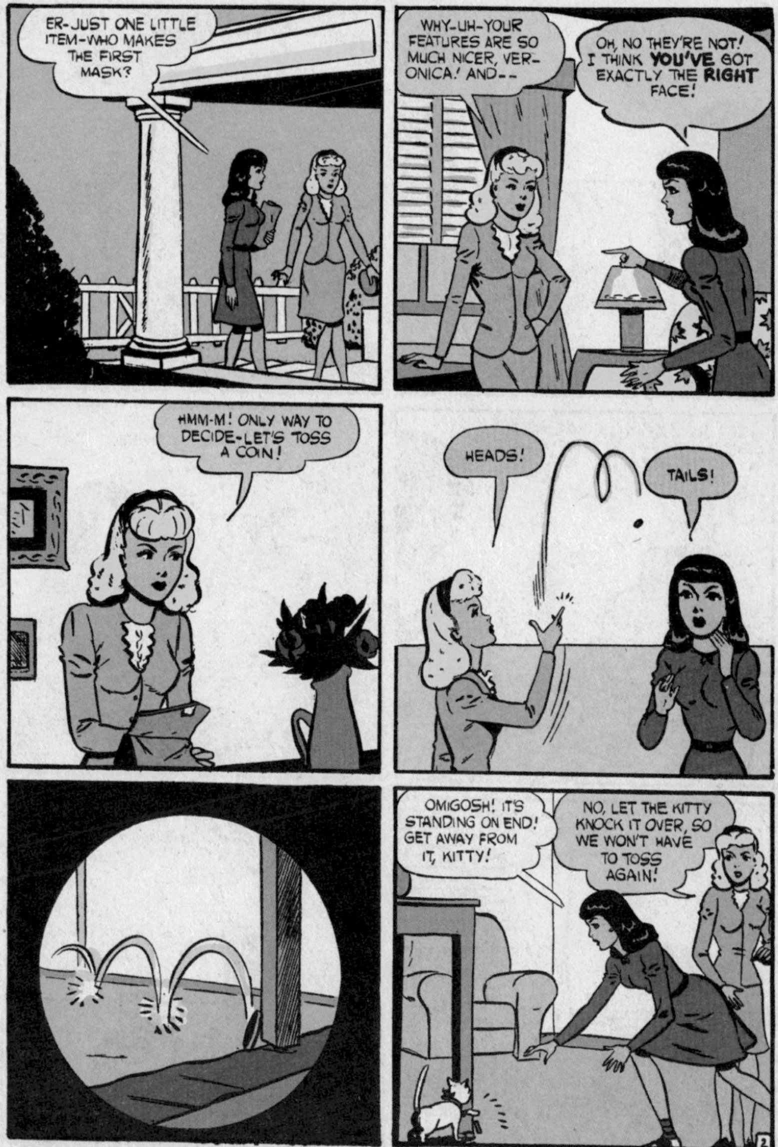

ER-JUST ONE LITTLE ITEM-WHO MAKES THE FIRST MASK?
WHY-UH-YOUR FEATURES ARE SO MUCH NICER, VERONICA! AND--
OH, NO THEY'RE NOT! I THINK **YOU'VE** GOT EXACTLY THE **RIGHT** FACE!
HMM-M! ONLY WAY TO DECIDE-LET'S TOSS A COIN!
HEADS!
TAILS!
OMIGOSH! IT'S STANDING ON END! GET AWAY FROM IT, KITTY!
NO, LET THE KITTY KNOCK IT OVER, SO WE WON'T HAVE TO TOSS AGAIN!
2

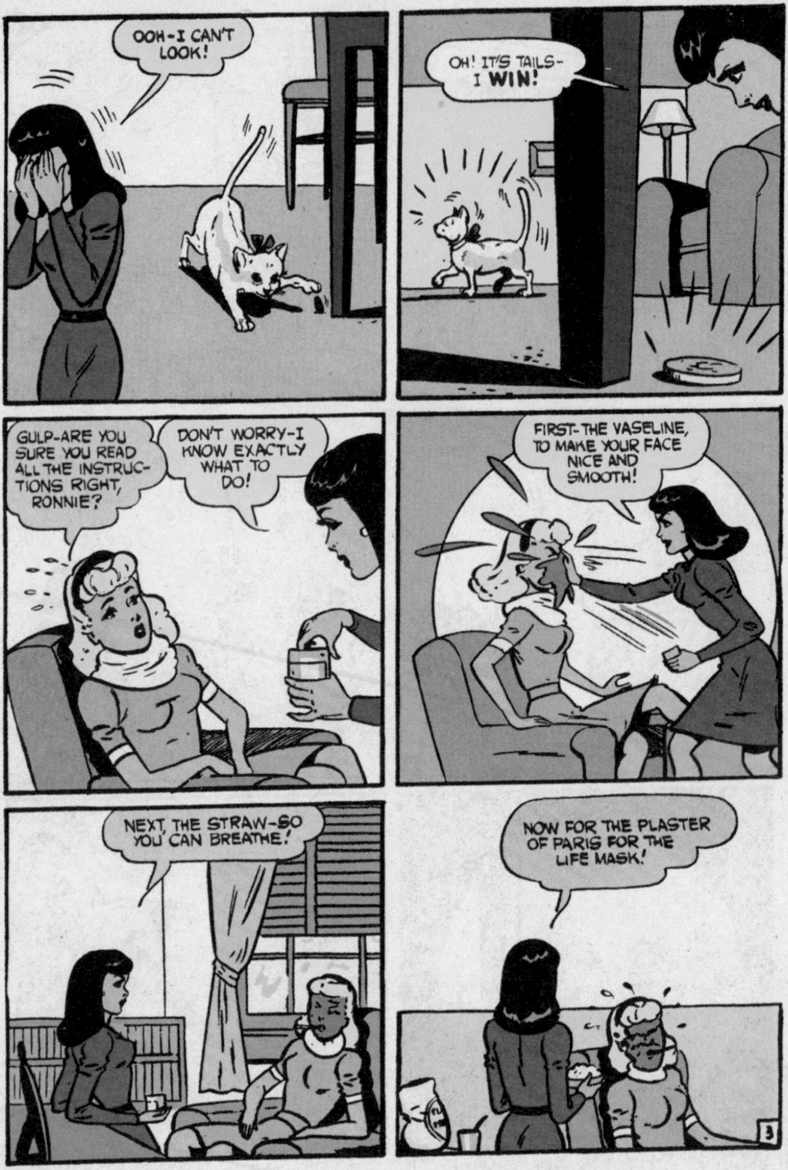
OOH-I CAN'T LOOK!
OH! IT'S TAILS-I **WIN**!
GULP-ARE YOU SURE YOU READ ALL THE INSTRUCTIONS RIGHT, RONNIE?
DON'T WORRY-I KNOW EXACTLY WHAT TO DO!
FIRST-THE VASELINE, TO MAKE YOUR FACE NICE AND SMOOTH!
NEXT, THE STRAW-SO YOU CAN BREATHE!
NOW FOR THE PLASTER OF PARIS FOR THE LIFE MASK!
3

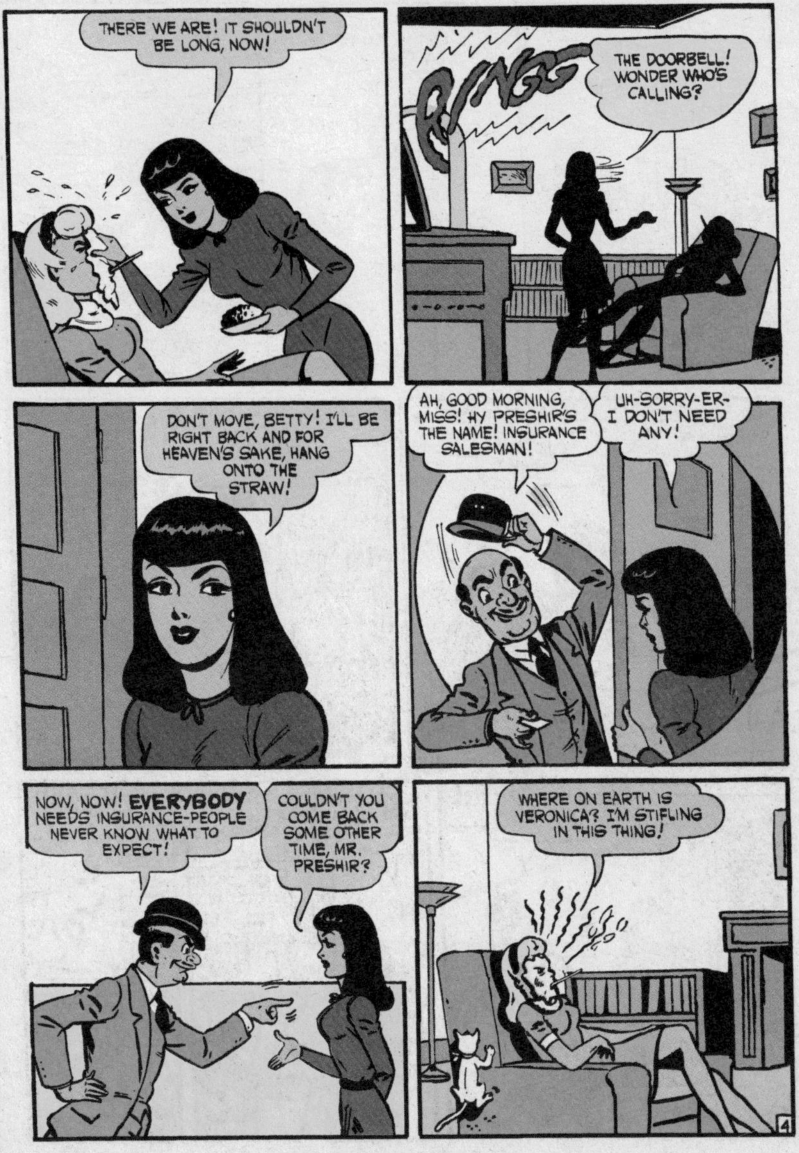
THERE WE ARE! IT SHOULDN'T BE LONG, NOW!
RINGG
THE DOORBELL! WONDER WHO'S CALLING?
DON'T MOVE, BETTY! I'LL BE RIGHT BACK AND FOR HEAVEN'S SAKE, HANG ONTO THE STRAW!
AH, GOOD MORNING, MISS! HY PRESHIR'S THE NAME! INSURANCE SALESMAN!
UH-SORRY-ER- I DON'T NEED ANY!
NOW, NOW! EVERYBODY NEEDS INSURANCE-PEOPLE NEVER KNOW WHAT TO EXPECT!
COULDN'T YOU COME BACK SOME OTHER TIME, MR. PRESHIR?
WHERE ON EARTH IS VERONICA? I'M STIFLING IN THIS THING!
4

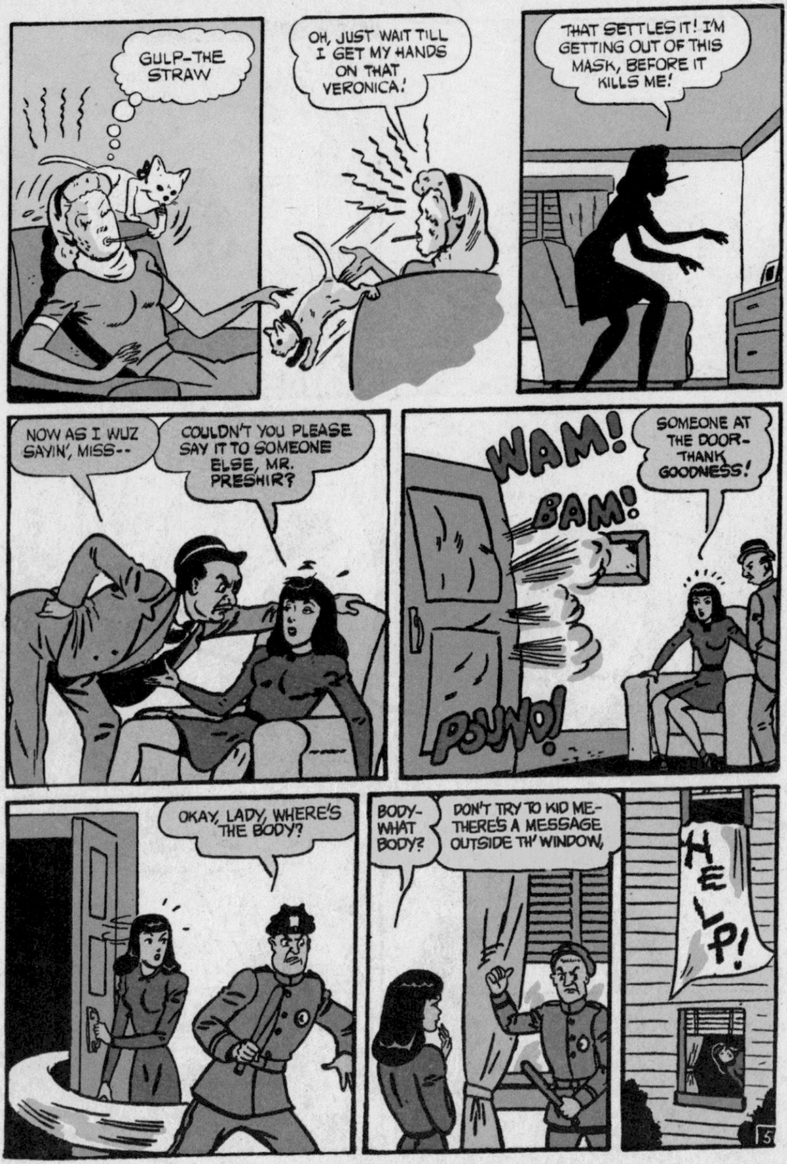
GULP-THE STRAW
OH, JUST WAIT TILL I GET MY HANDS ON THAT VERONICA!
THAT SETTLES IT! I'M GETTING OUT OF THIS MASK, BEFORE IT KILLS ME!
NOW AS I WUZ SAYIN', MISS--
COULDN'T YOU PLEASE SAY IT TO SOMEONE ELSE, MR. PRESHIR?
WAM!
BAM!
POUND!
SOMEONE AT THE DOOR-THANK GOODNESS!
OKAY, LADY, WHERE'S THE BODY?
BODY-WHAT BODY?
DON'T TRY TO KID ME-THERE'S A MESSAGE OUTSIDE TH' WINDOW,
HELP!
5

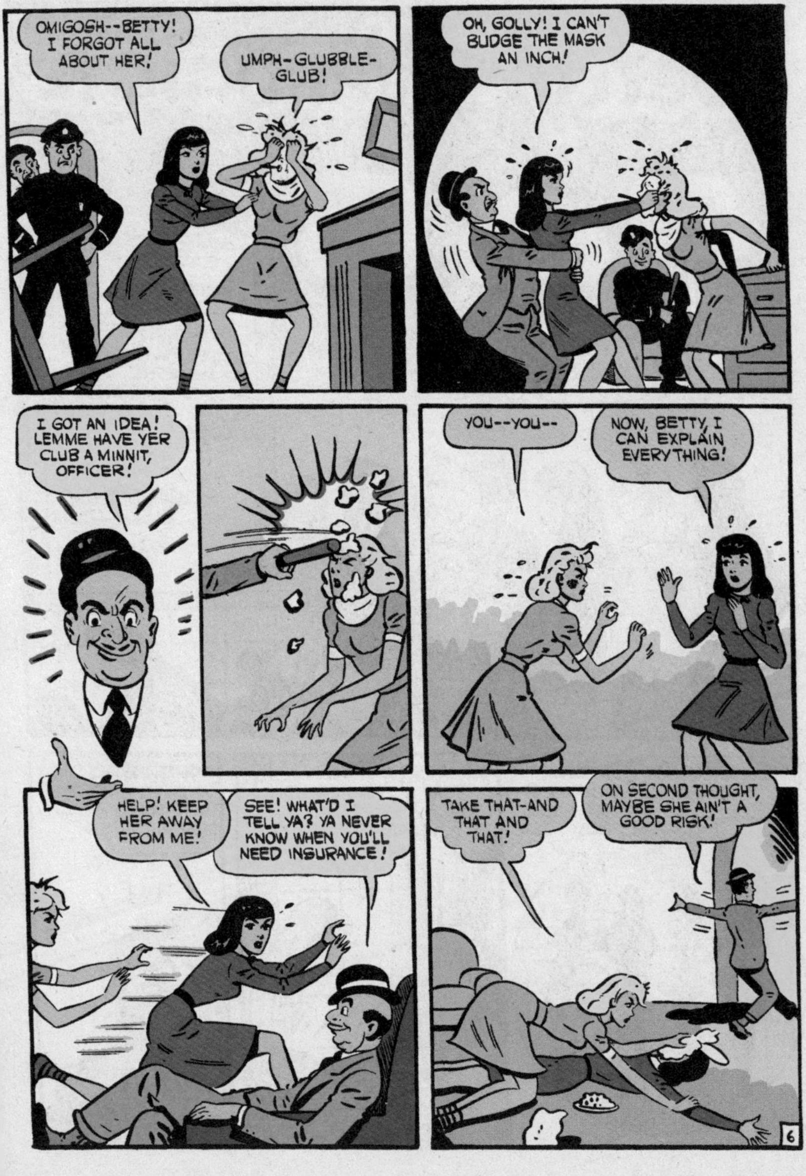
OMIGOSH--BETTY! I FORGOT ALL ABOUT HER!
UMPH-GLUBBLE-GLUB!
OH, GOLLY! I CAN'T BUDGE THE MASK AN INCH!
I GOT AN IDEA! LEMME HAVE YER CLUB A MINNIT, OFFICER!
YOU--YOU--
NOW, BETTY, I CAN EXPLAIN EVERYTHING!
HELP! KEEP HER AWAY FROM ME!
SEE! WHAT'D I TELL YA? YA NEVER KNOW WHEN YOU'LL NEED INSURANCE!
TAKE THAT-AND THAT AND THAT!
ON SECOND THOUGHT, MAYBE SHE AIN'T A GOOD RISK!
6

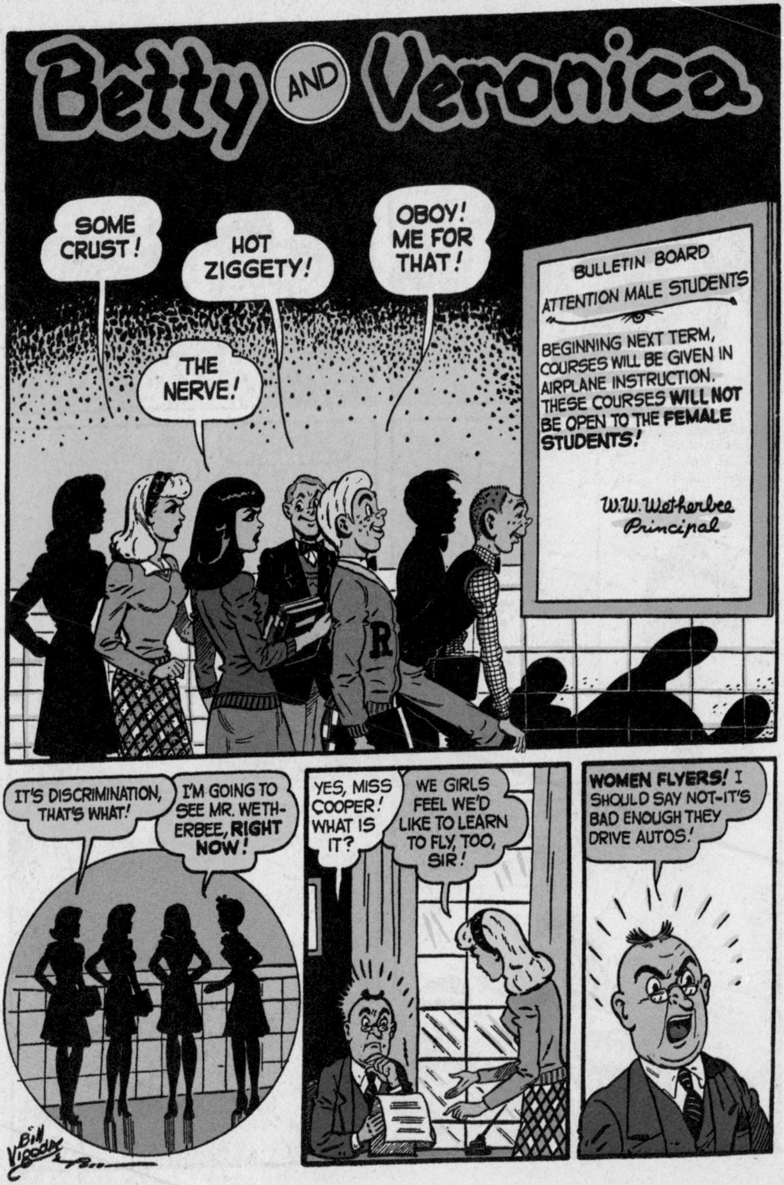
Betty AND Veronica
SOME CRUST!
HOT ZIGGETY!
OBOY! ME FOR THAT!
THE NERVE!
BULLETIN BOARD
ATTENTION MALE STUDENTS
BEGINNING NEXT TERM, COURSES WILL BE GIVEN IN AIRPLANE INSTRUCTION. THESE COURSES WILL NOT BE OPEN TO THE FEMALE STUDENTS!
W.W. Wetherbee Principal
R
IT'S DISCRIMINATION, THAT'S WHAT!
I'M GOING TO SEE MR. WETH-ERBEE, RIGHT NOW!
YES, MISS COOPER! WHAT IS IT?
WE GIRLS FEEL WE'D LIKE TO LEARN TO FLY, TOO, SIR!
WOMEN FLYERS! I SHOULD SAY NOT-IT'S BAD ENOUGH THEY DRIVE AUTOS!
Bill Vigoda

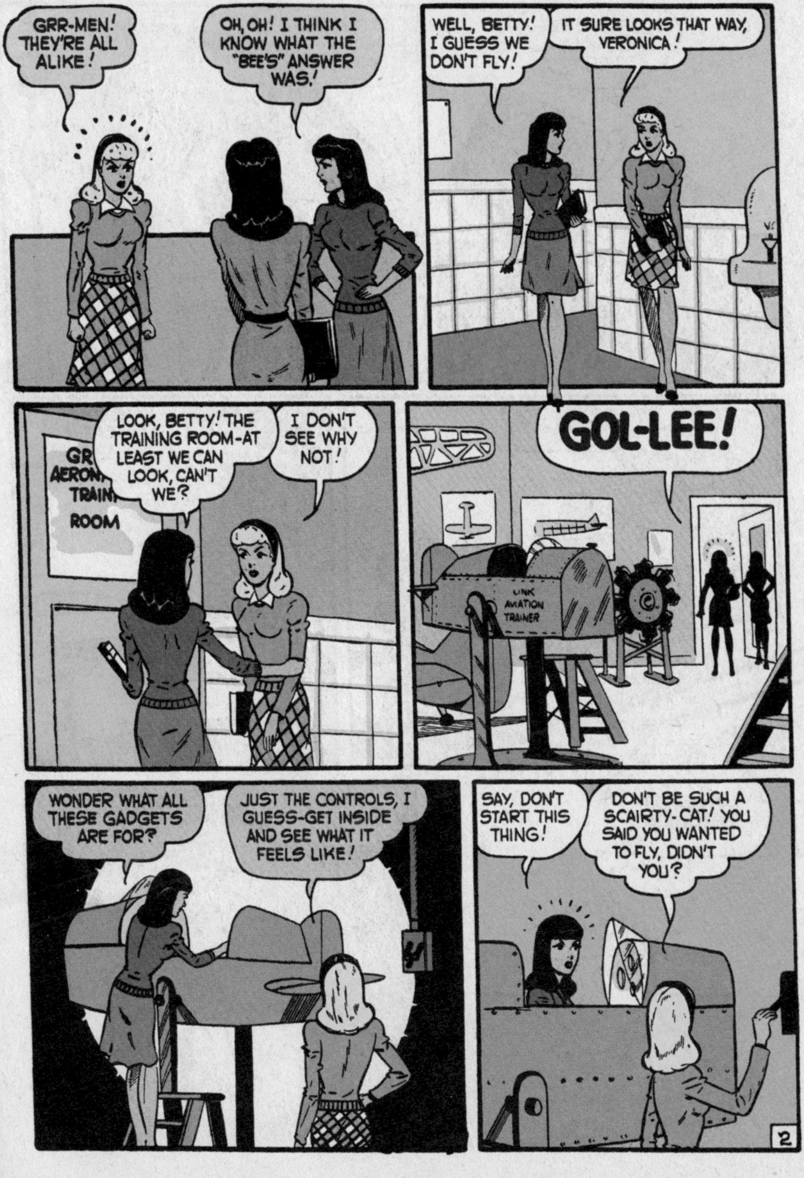
GRR-MEN! THEY'RE ALL ALIKE!
OH, OH! I THINK I KNOW WHAT THE "BEE'S" ANSWER WAS!
WELL, BETTY! I GUESS WE DON'T FLY!
IT SURE LOOKS THAT WAY, VERONICA!
GR AERON TRAIN ROOM
LOOK, BETTY! THE TRAINING ROOM-AT LEAST WE CAN LOOK, CAN'T WE?
I DON'T SEE WHY NOT!
GOL-LEE!
LINK AVIATION TRAINER
WONDER WHAT ALL THESE GADGETS ARE FOR?
JUST THE CONTROLS, I GUESS-GET INSIDE AND SEE WHAT IT FEELS LIKE!
SAY, DON'T START THIS THING!
DON'T BE SUCH A SCAIRTY-CAT! YOU SAID YOU WANTED TO FLY, DIDN'T YOU?
2

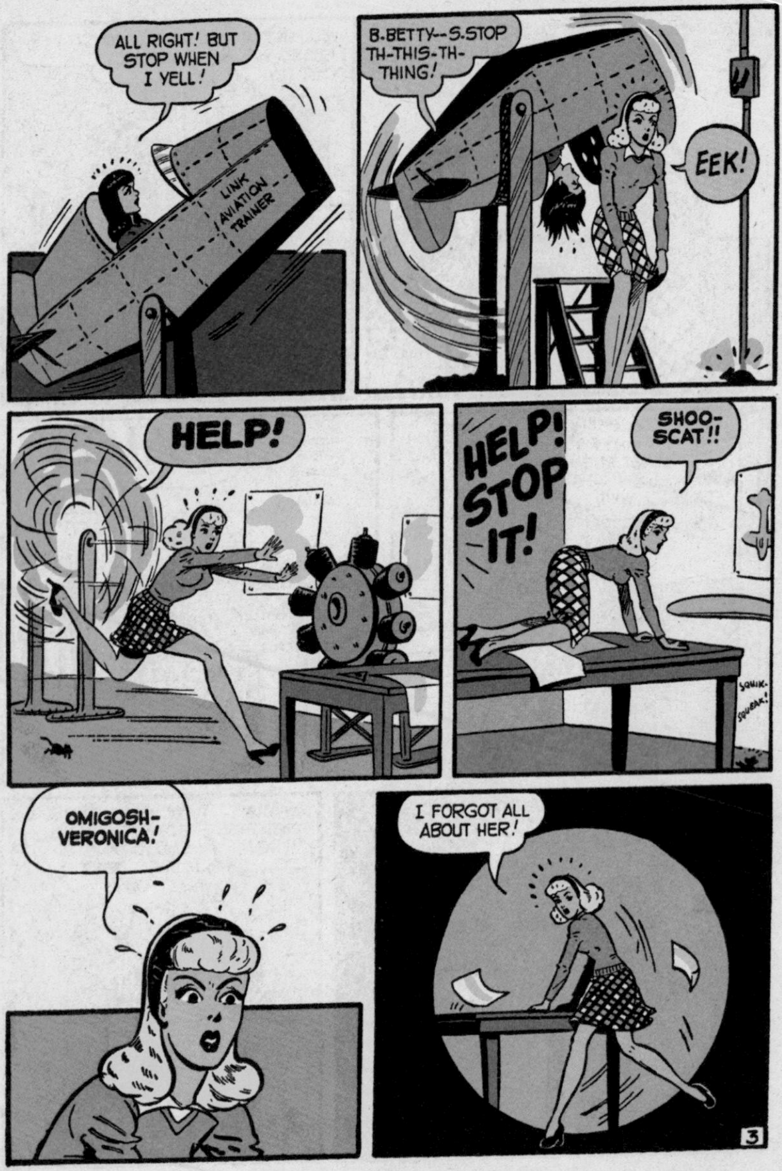
ALL RIGHT! BUT STOP WHEN I YELL!
LINK AVIATION TRAINER
B-BETTY--S-STOP TH-THIS-TH-THING!
EEK!
HELP!
HELP! STOP IT!
SHOO-SCAT!!
SQUIK-SQUEAK!
OMIGOSH-VERONICA!
I FORGOT ALL ABOUT HER!
3

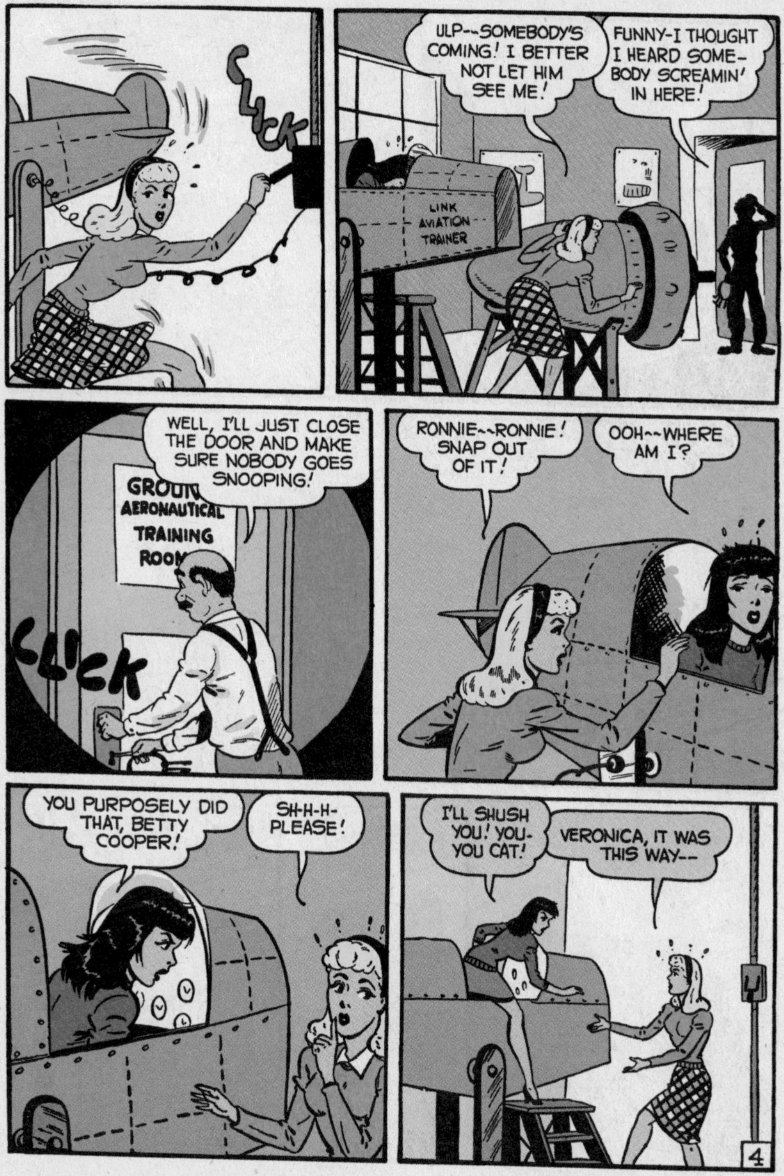
CLICK
ULP--SOMEBODY'S COMING! I BETTER NOT LET HIM SEE ME!
FUNNY-I THOUGHT I HEARD SOME-BODY SCREAMIN' IN HERE!
LINK AVIATION TRAINER
WELL, I'LL JUST CLOSE THE DOOR AND MAKE SURE NOBODY GOES SNOOPING!
AERONAUTICAL TRAINING
CLICK
RONNIE--RONNIE! SNAP OUT OF IT!
OOH--WHERE AM I?
YOU PURPOSELY DID THAT, BETTY COOPER!
SH-H-H-PLEASE!
I'LL SHUSH YOU! YOU-YOU CAT!
VERONICA, IT WAS THIS WAY--
4

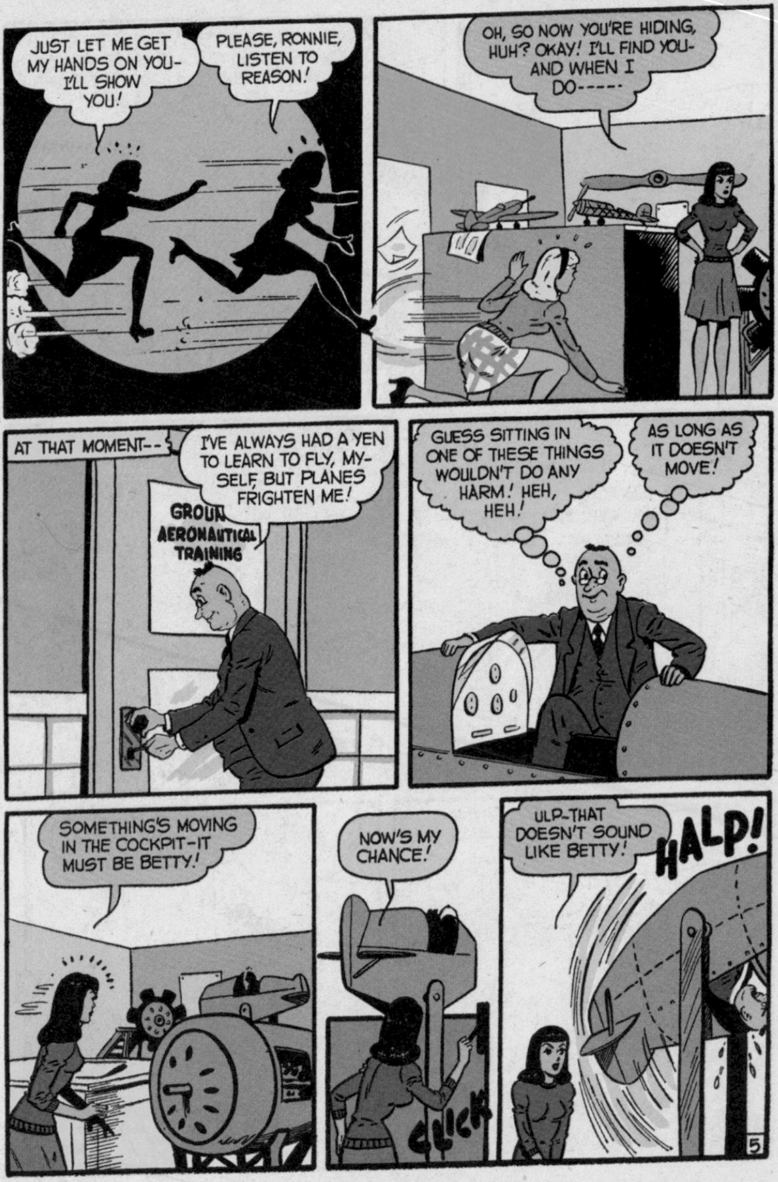
JUST LET ME GET MY HANDS ON YOU- I'LL SHOW YOU!
PLEASE, RONNIE, LISTEN TO REASON!
OH, SO NOW YOU'RE HIDING, HUH? OKAY! I'LL FIND YOU- AND WHEN I DO-----
AT THAT MOMENT--
I'VE ALWAYS HAD A YEN TO LEARN TO FLY, MYSELF, BUT PLANES FRIGHTEN ME!
GROUN
AERONAUTICAL
TRAINING
GUESS SITTING IN ONE OF THESE THINGS WOULDN'T DO ANY HARM! HEH, HEH!
AS LONG AS IT DOESN'T MOVE!
SOMETHING'S MOVING IN THE COCKPIT-IT MUST BE BETTY!
NOW'S MY CHANCE!
CLICK
ULP-THAT DOESN'T SOUND LIKE BETTY!
HALP!
5

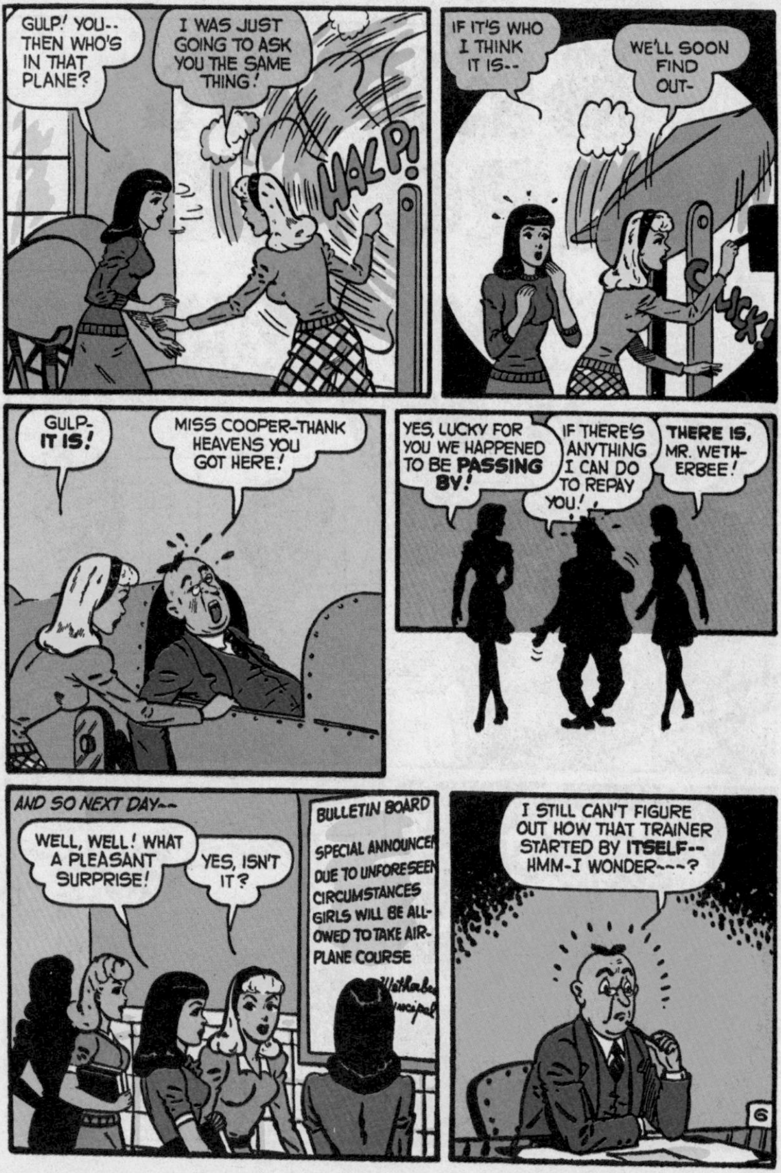
GULP! YOU-- THEN WHO'S IN THAT PLANE?
I WAS JUST GOING TO ASK YOU THE SAME THING!
HALP!
IF IT'S WHO I THINK IT IS--
WE'LL SOON FIND OUT-
CLICK!
GULP- IT IS!
MISS COOPER-THANK HEAVENS YOU GOT HERE!
YES, LUCKY FOR YOU WE HAPPENED TO BE PASSING BY!
IF THERE'S ANYTHING I CAN DO TO REPAY YOU!
THERE IS, MR. WETH-ERBEE!
AND SO NEXT DAY--
WELL, WELL! WHAT A PLEASANT SURPRISE!
YES, ISN'T IT?
BULLETIN BOARD
SPECIAL ANNOUNCE
DUE TO UNFORESEEN
CIRCUMSTANCES
GIRLS WILL BE ALL-
OWED TO TAKE AIR-
PLANE COURSE
I STILL CAN'T FIGURE OUT HOW THAT TRAINER STARTED BY ITSELF-- HMM-I WONDER---?
6

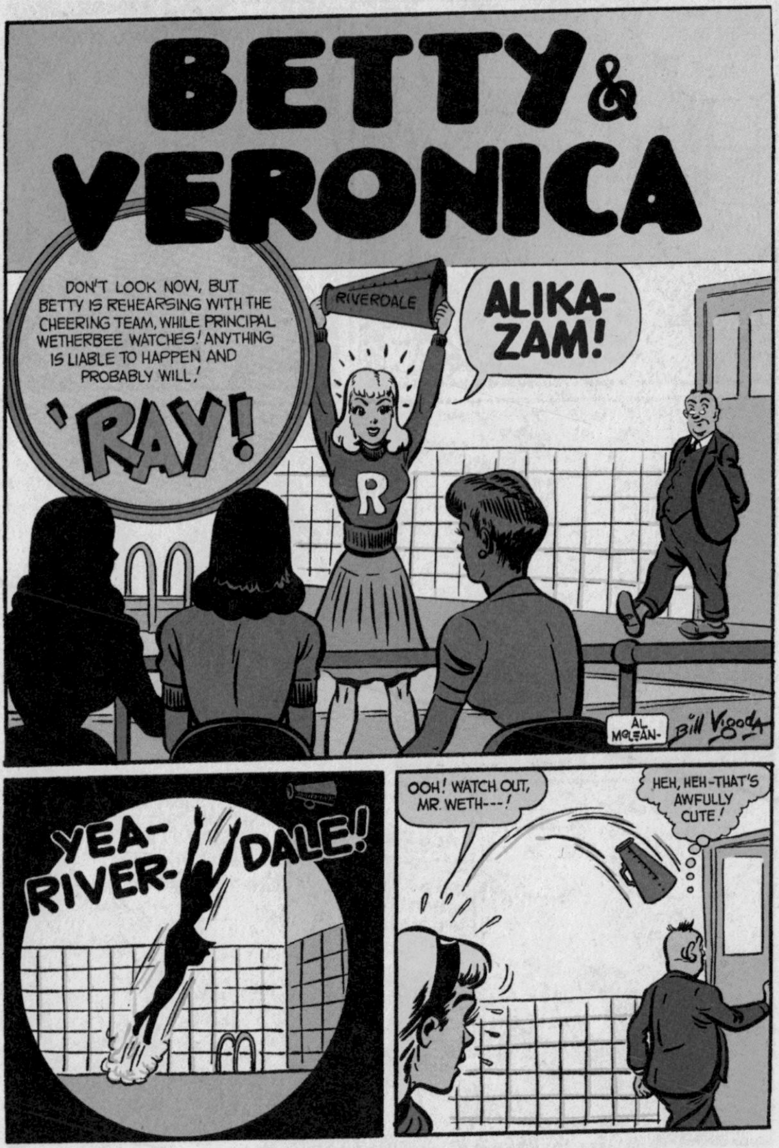
BETTY & VERONICA
DON'T LOOK NOW, BUT BETTY IS REHEARSING WITH THE CHEERING TEAM, WHILE PRINCIPAL WETHERBEE WATCHES! ANYTHING IS LIABLE TO HAPPEN AND PROBABLY WILL!
'RAY!
RIVERDALE
ALIKA-ZAM!
AL McLEAN-
Bill Vigoda
YEA-RIVER-DALE!
OOH! WATCH OUT, MR. WETH---!
HEH, HEH-THAT'S AWFULLY CUTE!

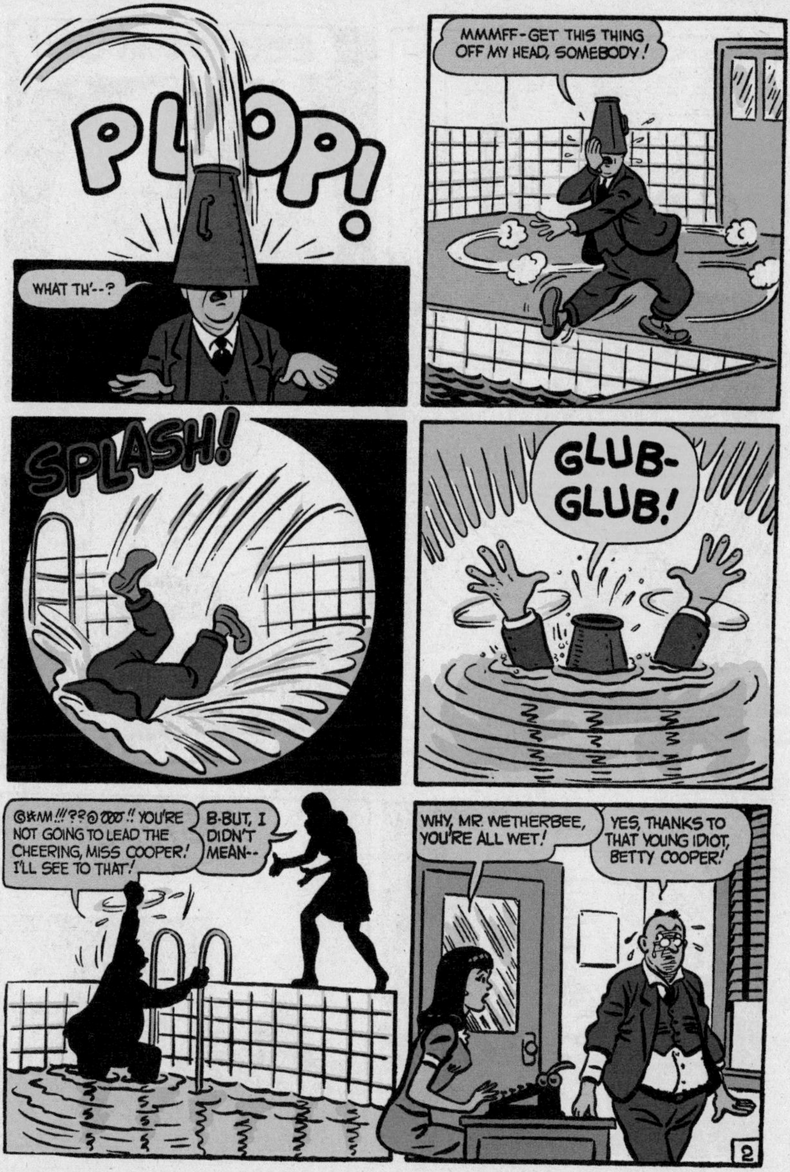
PLOP!
WHAT TH'--?
MMMFF-GET THIS THING OFF MY HEAD, SOMEBODY!
SPLASH!
GLUB-GLUB!
@%M!!!??@ơơơ!! YOU'RE NOT GOING TO LEAD THE CHEERING, MISS COOPER! I'LL SEE TO THAT!
B-BUT, I DIDN'T MEAN--
WHY, MR. WETHERBEE, YOU'RE ALL WET!
YES, THANKS TO THAT YOUNG IDIOT, BETTY COOPER!
2

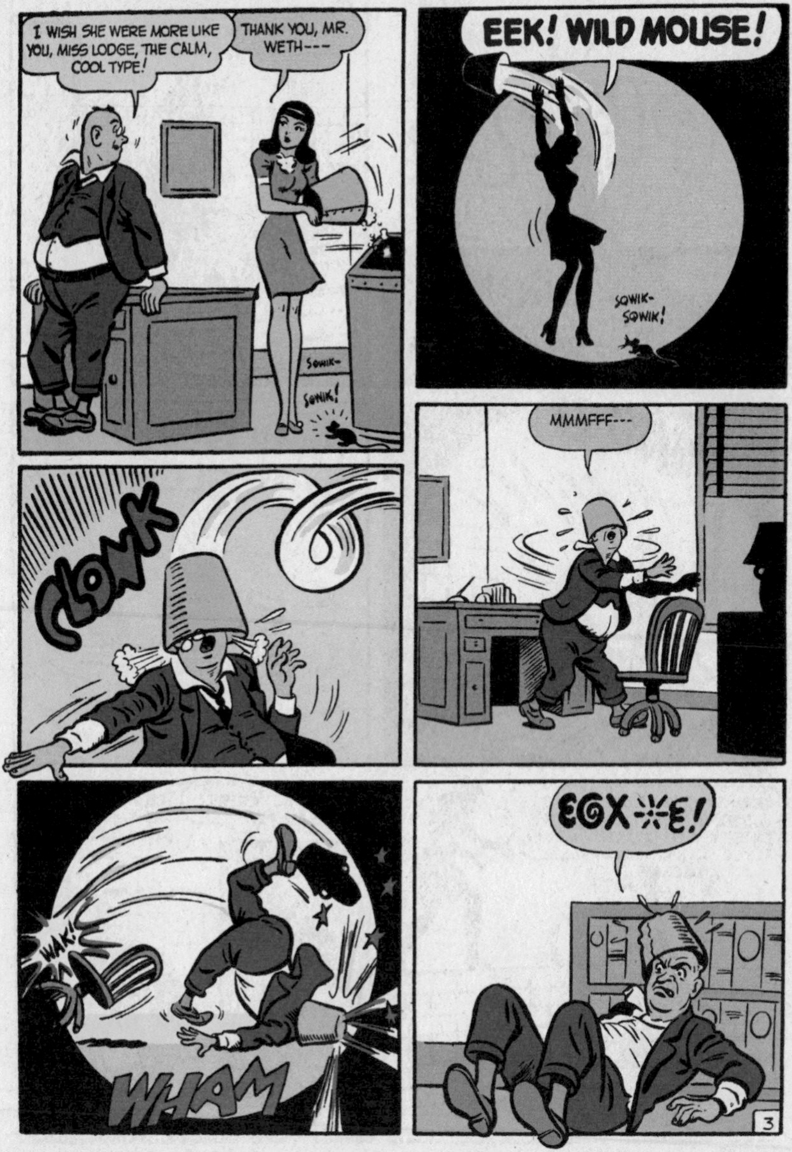

I WISH SHE WERE MORE LIKE YOU, MISS LODGE, THE CALM, COOL TYPE!
THANK YOU, MR. WETH---
SQWIK-
SQWIK!
EEK! WILD MOUSE!
SQWIK-
SQWIK!
CLONK
MMMFFF---
WAK!
WHAM
3

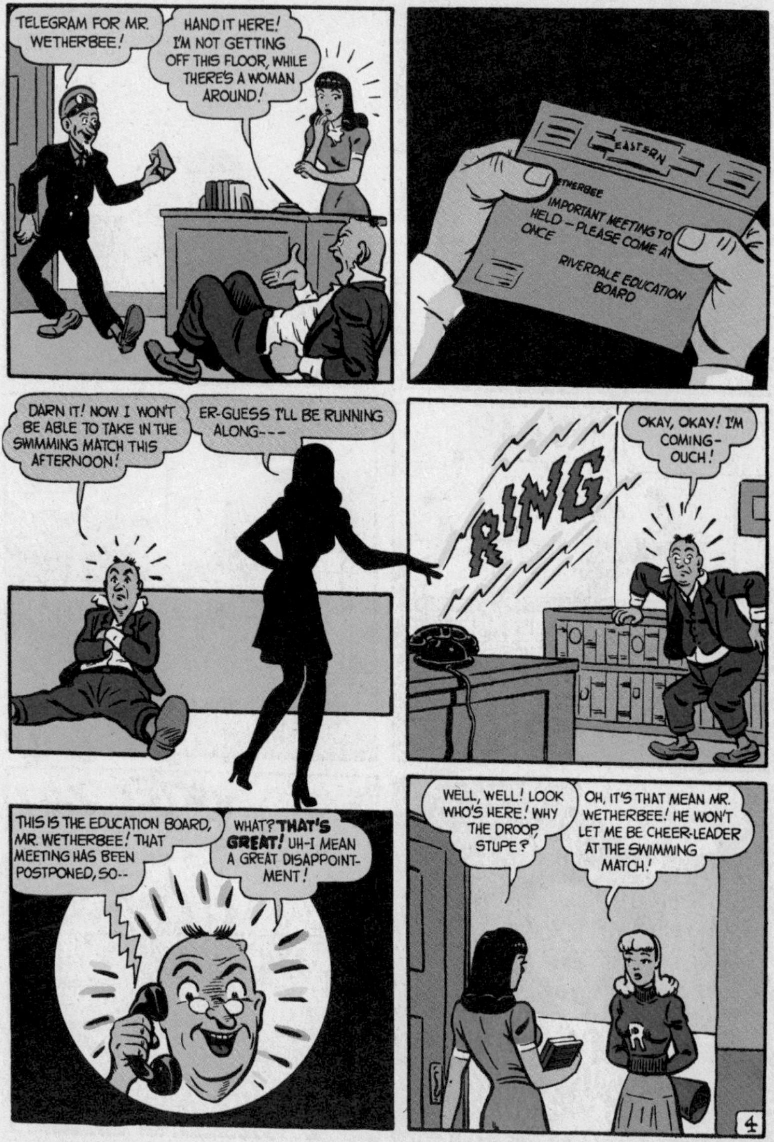
TELEGRAM FOR MR. WETHERBEE!
HAND IT HERE! I'M NOT GETTING OFF THIS FLOOR, WHILE THERE'S A WOMAN AROUND!
EASTERN
WETHERBEE
IMPORTANT MEETING TO HELD — PLEASE COME AT ONCE
RIVERDALE EDUCATION BOARD
DARN IT! NOW I WON'T BE ABLE TO TAKE IN THE SWIMMING MATCH THIS AFTERNOON!
ER-GUESS I'LL BE RUNNING ALONG---
RING
OKAY, OKAY! I'M COMING- OUCH!
THIS IS THE EDUCATION BOARD, MR. WETHERBEE! THAT MEETING HAS BEEN POSTPONED, SO--
WHAT? THAT'S GREAT! UH-I MEAN A GREAT DISAPPOINT-MENT!
WELL, WELL! LOOK WHO'S HERE! WHY THE DROOP, STUPE?
OH, IT'S THAT MEAN MR. WETHERBEE! HE WON'T LET ME BE CHEER-LEADER AT THE SWIMMING MATCH!
R
4

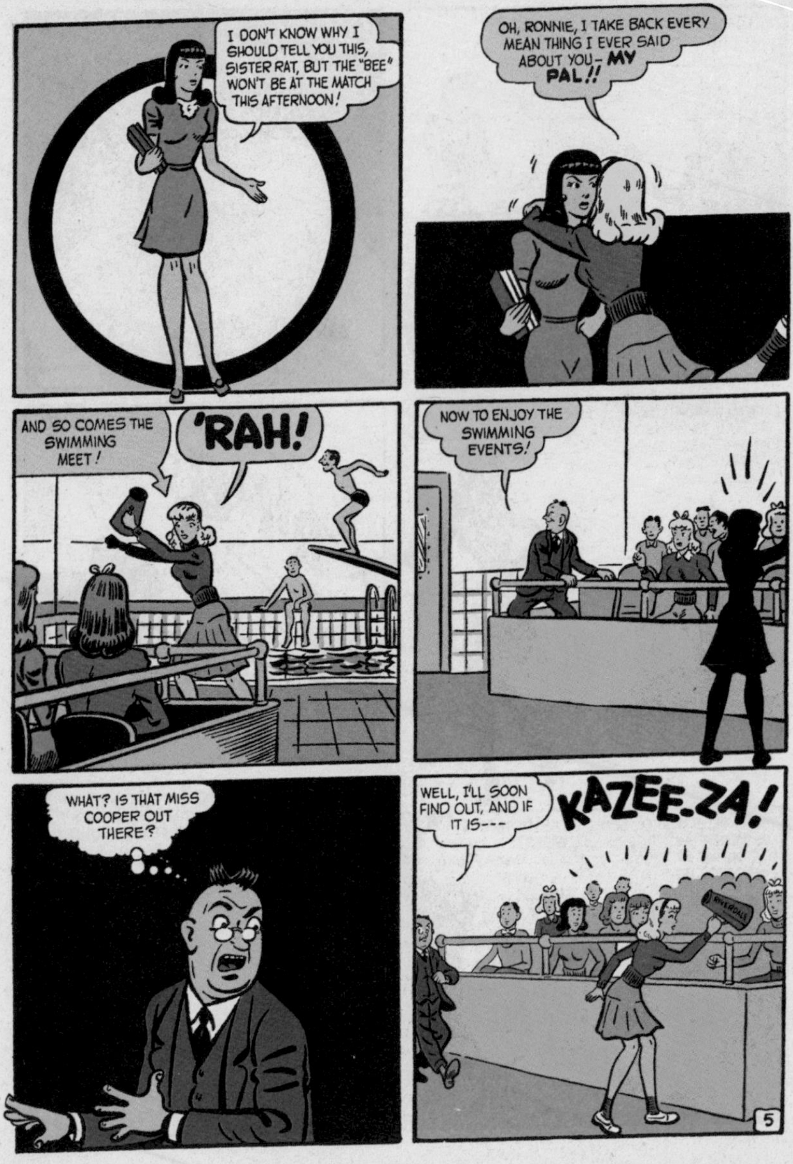
I DON'T KNOW WHY I SHOULD TELL YOU THIS, SISTER RAT, BUT THE "BEE" WON'T BE AT THE MATCH THIS AFTERNOON!
OH, RONNIE, I TAKE BACK EVERY MEAN THING I EVER SAID ABOUT YOU– MY PAL!!
AND SO COMES THE SWIMMING MEET!
'RAH!
NOW TO ENJOY THE SWIMMING EVENTS!
WHAT? IS THAT MISS COOPER OUT THERE?
WELL, I'LL SOON FIND OUT, AND IF IT IS---
KAZEE-ZA!
5

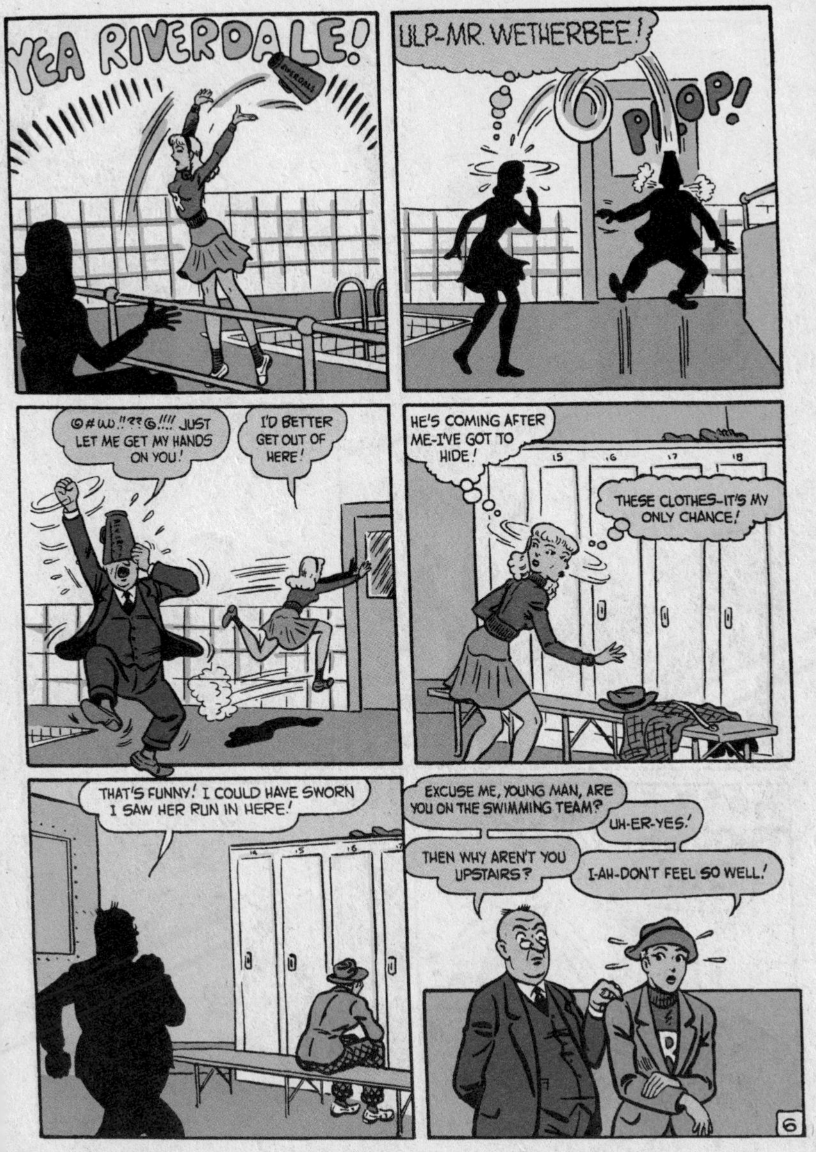
YEA RIVERDALE!
RIVERDALE
ULP-MR. WETHERBEE!
PLOP!
©#ω!!??©!!!! JUST LET ME GET MY HANDS ON YOU!
I'D BETTER GET OUT OF HERE!
HE'S COMING AFTER ME-I'VE GOT TO HIDE!
THESE CLOTHES-IT'S MY ONLY CHANCE!
THAT'S FUNNY! I COULD HAVE SWORN I SAW HER RUN IN HERE!
EXCUSE ME, YOUNG MAN, ARE YOU ON THE SWIMMING TEAM?
UH-ER-YES!
THEN WHY AREN'T YOU UPSTAIRS?
I-AH-DON'T FEEL SO WELL!
6

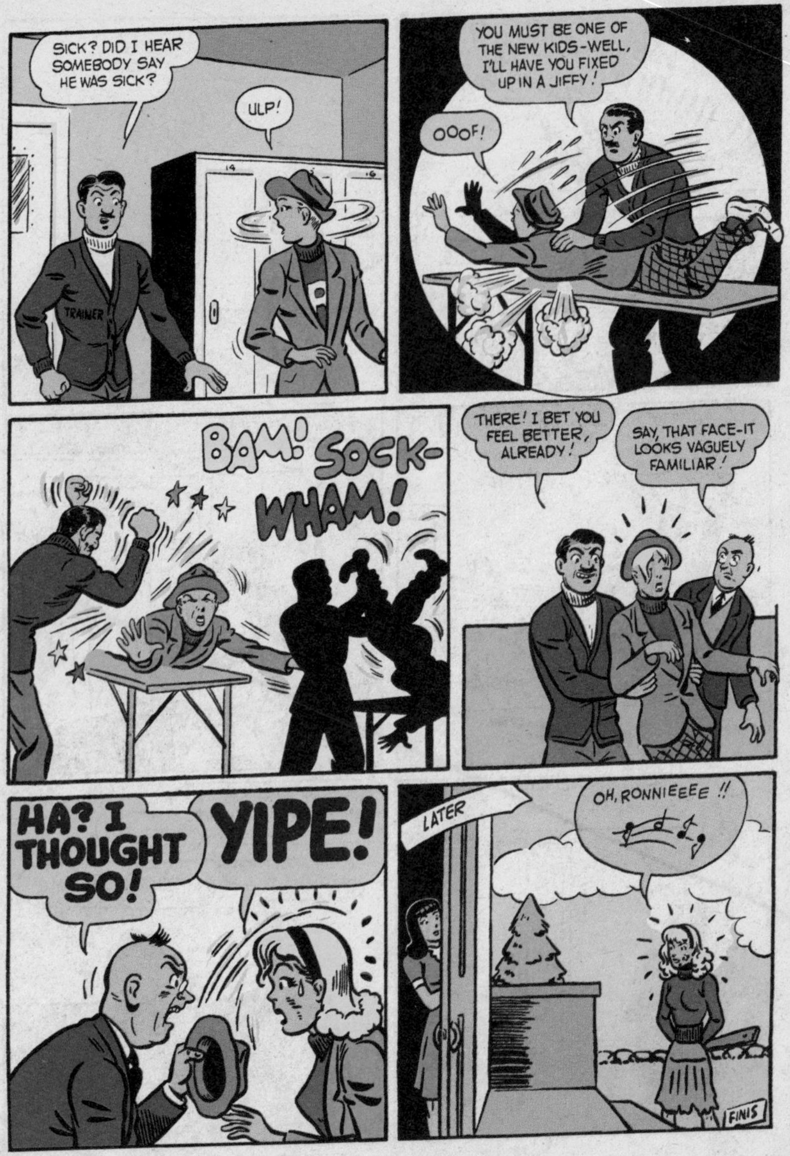

SICK? DID I HEAR SOMEBODY SAY HE WAS SICK?
ULP!
TRAINER
YOU MUST BE ONE OF THE NEW KIDS-WELL, I'LL HAVE YOU FIXED UP IN A JIFFY!
OOOF!
BAM! SOCK-WHAM!
THERE! I BET YOU FEEL BETTER, ALREADY!
SAY, THAT FACE-IT LOOKS VAGUELY FAMILIAR!
HA? I THOUGHT SO!
YIPE!
LATER
OH, RONNIEEEE !!
FINIS

Glamour in White
Archie #4, 1943
by Harry Sahle and Janice Valleau (Ginger)

The early Betty & Veronica stories are very interesting because the dynamic between the girls was so drastically different. The two girls, though from different backgrounds, treated each other as equals who weren't afraid to step up to each other when the time came—and they were both so sassy! How often now do you see Betty spending all day in a beauty parlor to get ready then complaining about doing volunteer work? Actually, I have to admit... I think of the two girls of this era, I prefer Veronica! Even if her motivations were occasionally self-serving, she still went out of her way to help others. Plus, her fashion was fab and she had a great Bettie Page-esque hairstyle!

Jamie Lee Rotante
Proofreader, Archie Comics

Of Men and Mermaids!
Archie #17, 1945
by Bill Vigoda and Al McLean

Great classic stories. They have all the elements that you don't see often nowadays. Betty and Veronica really go at each other both verbally and physically with a lot of fun slapstick bits that makes this a great read. My favorite part is Archie pretending to drown, then getting knocked out by Betty in "Of Men and Mermaids!" I mean, honestly, how often have you seen Betty socking people in the jaw recently? It really shows off her early feisty side.

Stephen Oswald
Production Manager, Archie Comics

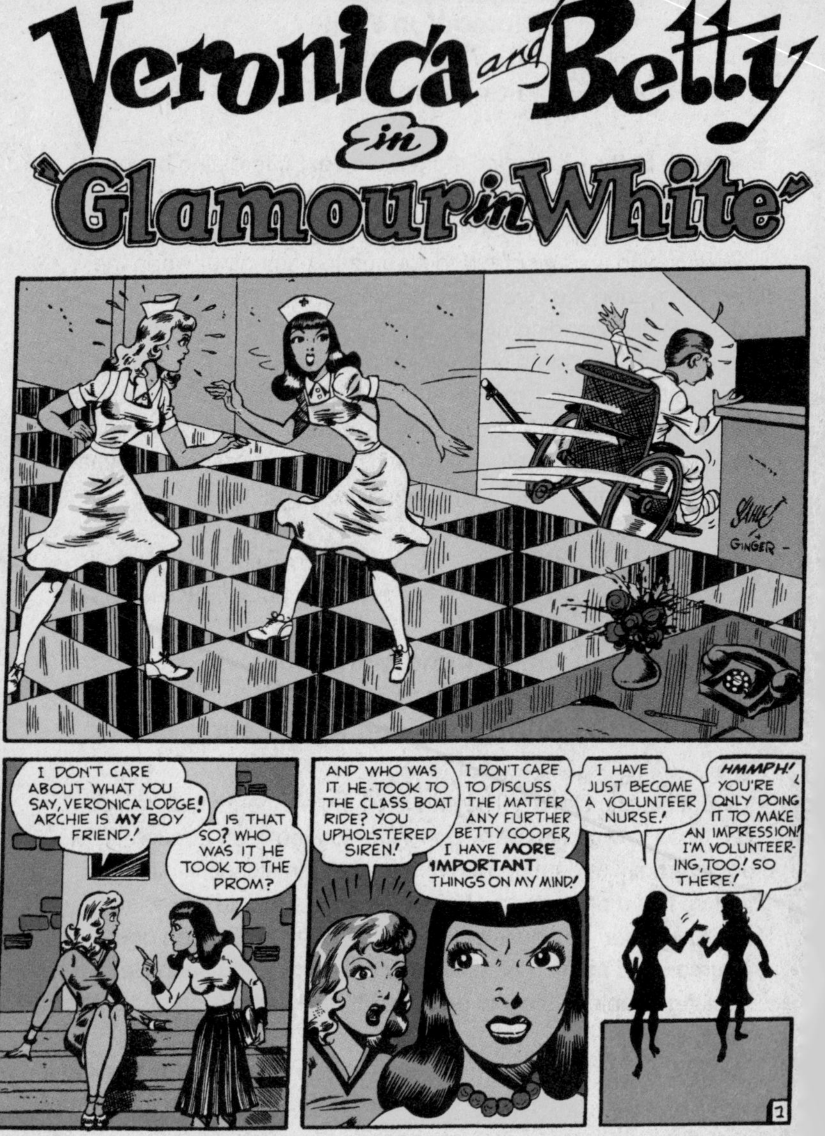
Veronica and Betty
in
"Glamour in White"
SAHLE & GINGER
I DON'T CARE ABOUT WHAT YOU SAY, VERONICA LODGE! ARCHIE IS MY BOY FRIEND!
IS THAT SO? WHO WAS IT HE TOOK TO THE PROM?
AND WHO WAS IT HE TOOK TO THE CLASS BOAT RIDE? YOU UPHOLSTERED SIREN!
I DON'T CARE TO DISCUSS THE MATTER ANY FURTHER BETTY COOPER, I HAVE MORE IMPORTANT THINGS ON MY MIND!
I HAVE JUST BECOME A VOLUNTEER NURSE!
HMMPH! YOU'RE ONLY DOING IT TO MAKE AN IMPRESSION! I'M VOLUNTEERING, TOO! SO THERE!
1

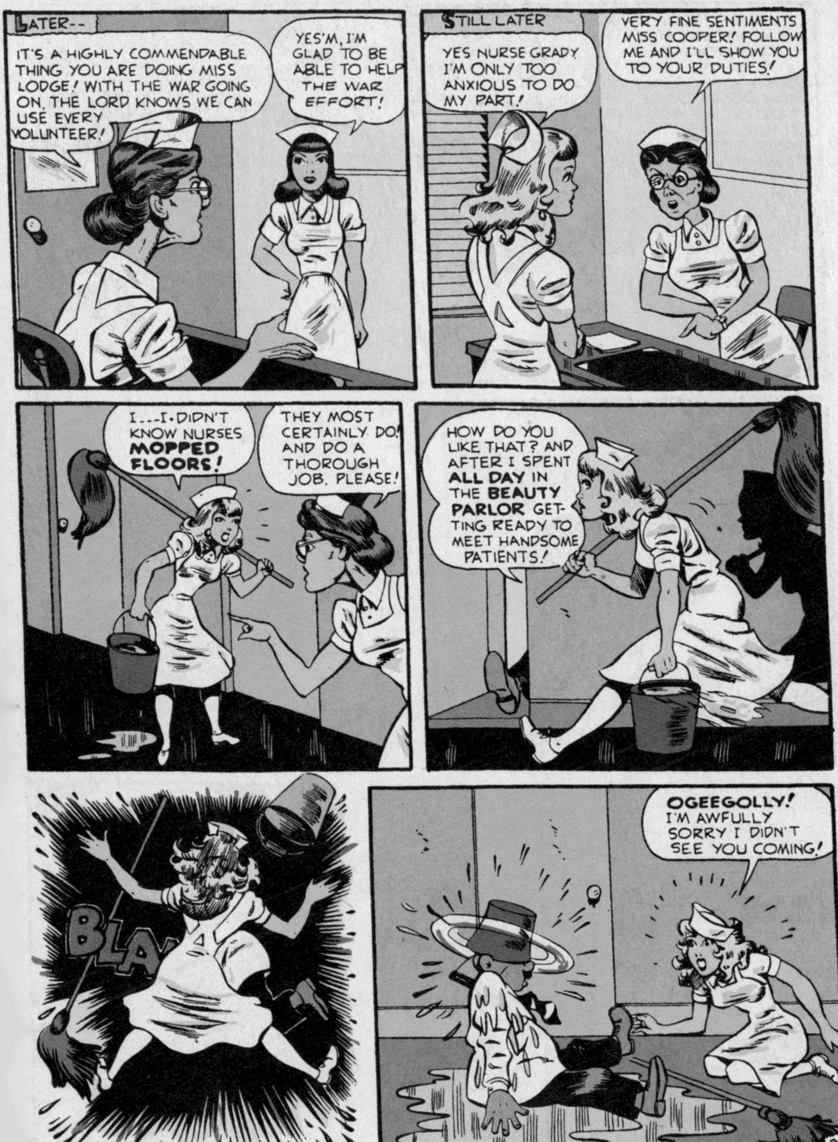
LATER--
IT'S A HIGHLY COMMENDABLE THING YOU ARE DOING MISS LODGE! WITH THE WAR GOING ON, THE LORD KNOWS WE CAN USE EVERY VOLUNTEER!
YES'M, I'M GLAD TO BE ABLE TO HELP THE WAR EFFORT!
STILL LATER
YES NURSE GRADY. I'M ONLY TOO ANXIOUS TO DO MY PART!
VERY FINE SENTIMENTS MISS COOPER! FOLLOW ME AND I'LL SHOW YOU TO YOUR DUTIES!
I---I-DIDN'T KNOW NURSES MOPPED FLOORS!
THEY MOST CERTAINLY DO! AND DO A THOROUGH JOB, PLEASE!
HOW DO YOU LIKE THAT? AND AFTER I SPENT ALL DAY IN THE BEAUTY PARLOR GETTING READY TO MEET HANDSOME PATIENTS!
BLAM
OGEEGOLLY! I'M AWFULLY SORRY I DIDN'T SEE YOU COMING!
2

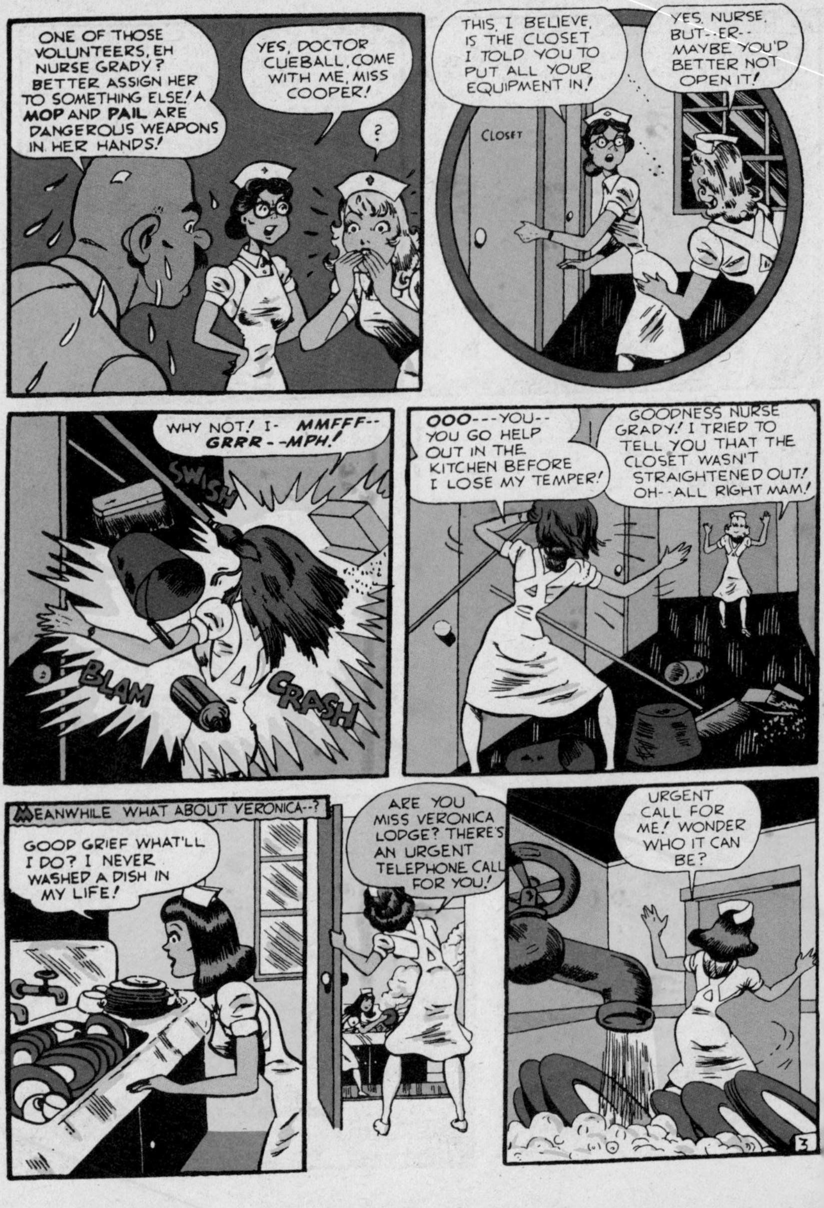

ONE OF THOSE VOLUNTEERS, EH NURSE GRADY? BETTER ASSIGN HER TO SOMETHING ELSE! A MOP AND PAIL ARE DANGEROUS WEAPONS IN HER HANDS!
YES, DOCTOR CUEBALL, COME WITH ME, MISS COOPER!
?
THIS, I BELIEVE, IS THE CLOSET I TOLD YOU TO PUT ALL YOUR EQUIPMENT IN!
YES, NURSE, BUT--ER--MAYBE YOU'D BETTER NOT OPEN IT!
CLOSET
WHY NOT! I- MMFFF--GRRR--MPH!
SWISH
BLAM
CRASH
OOO---YOU--YOU GO HELP OUT IN THE KITCHEN BEFORE I LOSE MY TEMPER!
GOODNESS NURSE GRADY! I TRIED TO TELL YOU THAT THE CLOSET WASN'T STRAIGHTENED OUT! OH--ALL RIGHT MAM!
MEANWHILE WHAT ABOUT VERONICA--?
GOOD GRIEF WHAT'LL I DO? I NEVER WASHED A DISH IN MY LIFE!
ARE YOU MISS VERONICA LODGE? THERE'S AN URGENT TELEPHONE CALL FOR YOU!
URGENT CALL FOR ME! WONDER WHO IT CAN BE?
3

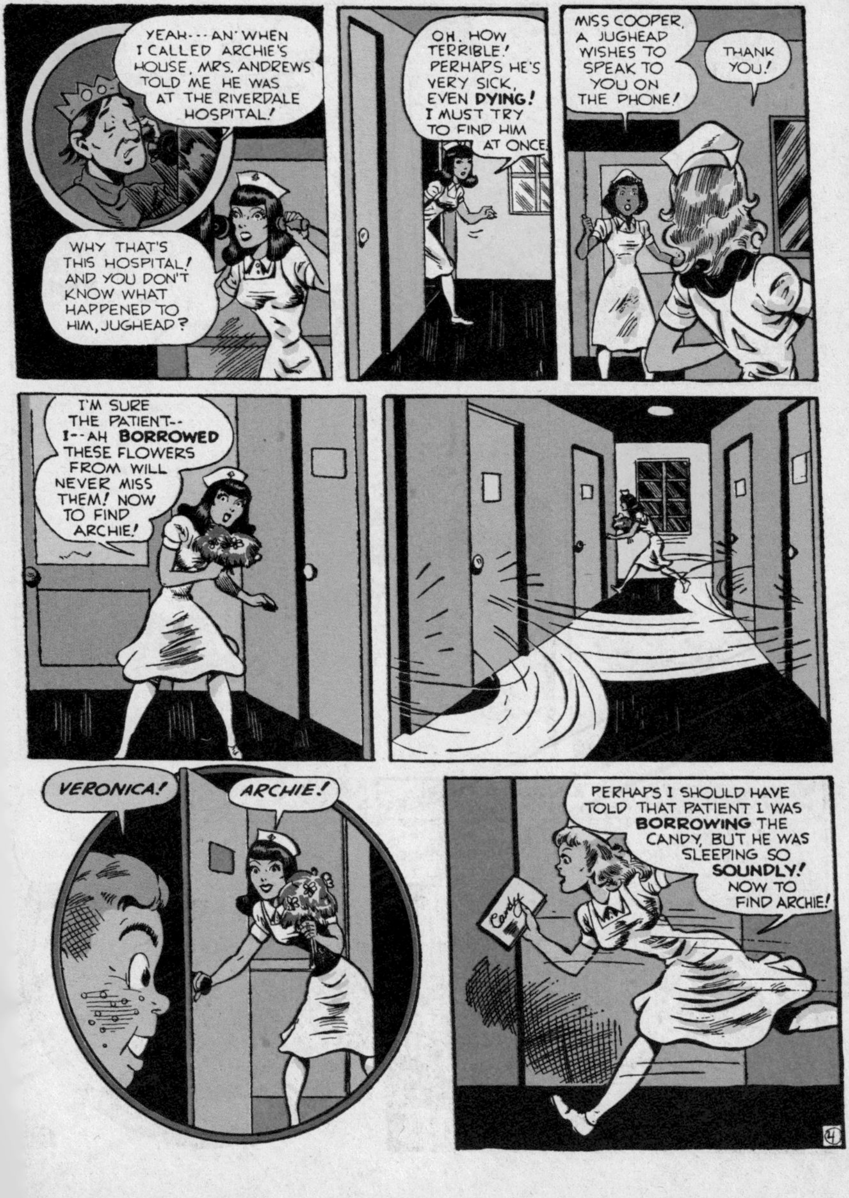
YEAH--- AN' WHEN I CALLED ARCHIE'S HOUSE, MRS. ANDREWS TOLD ME HE WAS AT THE RIVERDALE HOSPITAL!
WHY THAT'S THIS HOSPITAL! AND YOU DON'T KNOW WHAT HAPPENED TO HIM, JUGHEAD?
OH, HOW TERRIBLE! PERHAPS HE'S VERY SICK, EVEN DYING! I MUST TRY TO FIND HIM AT ONCE!
MISS COOPER, A JUGHEAD WISHES TO SPEAK TO YOU ON THE PHONE!
THANK YOU!
I'M SURE THE PATIENT-- I--AH BORROWED THESE FLOWERS FROM WILL NEVER MISS THEM! NOW TO FIND ARCHIE!
VERONICA!
ARCHIE!
PERHAPS I SHOULD HAVE TOLD THAT PATIENT I WAS BORROWING THE CANDY, BUT HE WAS SLEEPING SO SOUNDLY! NOW TO FIND ARCHIE!
Candy
4

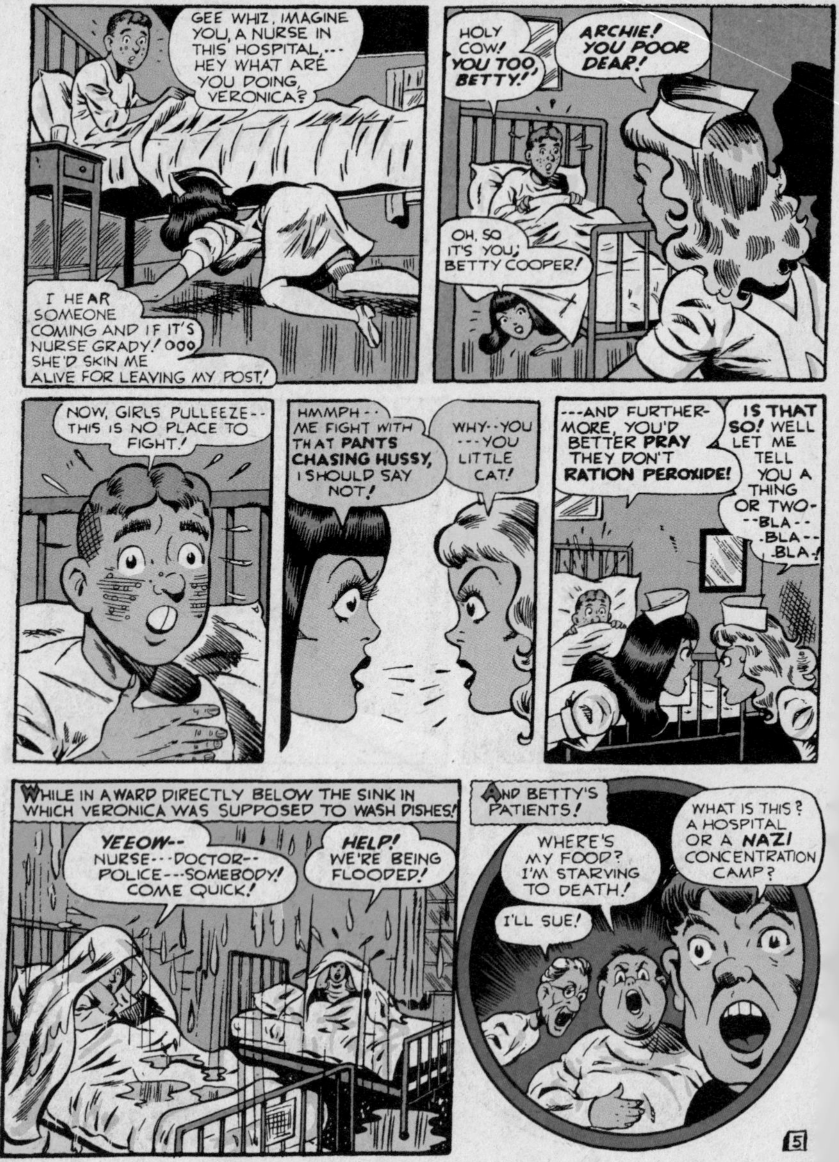

GEE WHIZ, IMAGINE YOU, A NURSE IN THIS HOSPITAL,--- HEY WHAT ARE YOU DOING, VERONICA?
I HEAR SOMEONE COMING AND IF IT'S NURSE GRADY! OOO SHE'D SKIN ME ALIVE FOR LEAVING MY POST!
HOLY COW! YOU TOO, BETTY!
ARCHIE! YOU POOR DEAR!
OH, SO IT'S YOU; BETTY COOPER!
NOW, GIRLS PULLEEZE-- THIS IS NO PLACE TO FIGHT!
HMMPH-- ME FIGHT WITH THAT PANTS CHASING HUSSY, I SHOULD SAY NOT!
WHY--YOU ---YOU LITTLE CAT!
---AND FURTHER-MORE, YOU'D BETTER PRAY THEY DON'T RATION PEROXIDE!
IS THAT SO! WELL LET ME TELL YOU A THING OR TWO- --BLA-- -BLA-- -BLA-!
WHILE IN A WARD DIRECTLY BELOW THE SINK IN WHICH VERONICA WAS SUPPOSED TO WASH DISHES!
YEEOW-- NURSE---DOCTOR-- POLICE---SOMEBODY! COME QUICK!
HELP! WE'RE BEING FLOODED!
AND BETTY'S PATIENTS!
WHAT IS THIS? A HOSPITAL OR A NAZI CONCENTRATION CAMP?
WHERE'S MY FOOD? I'M STARVING TO DEATH!
I'LL SUE!

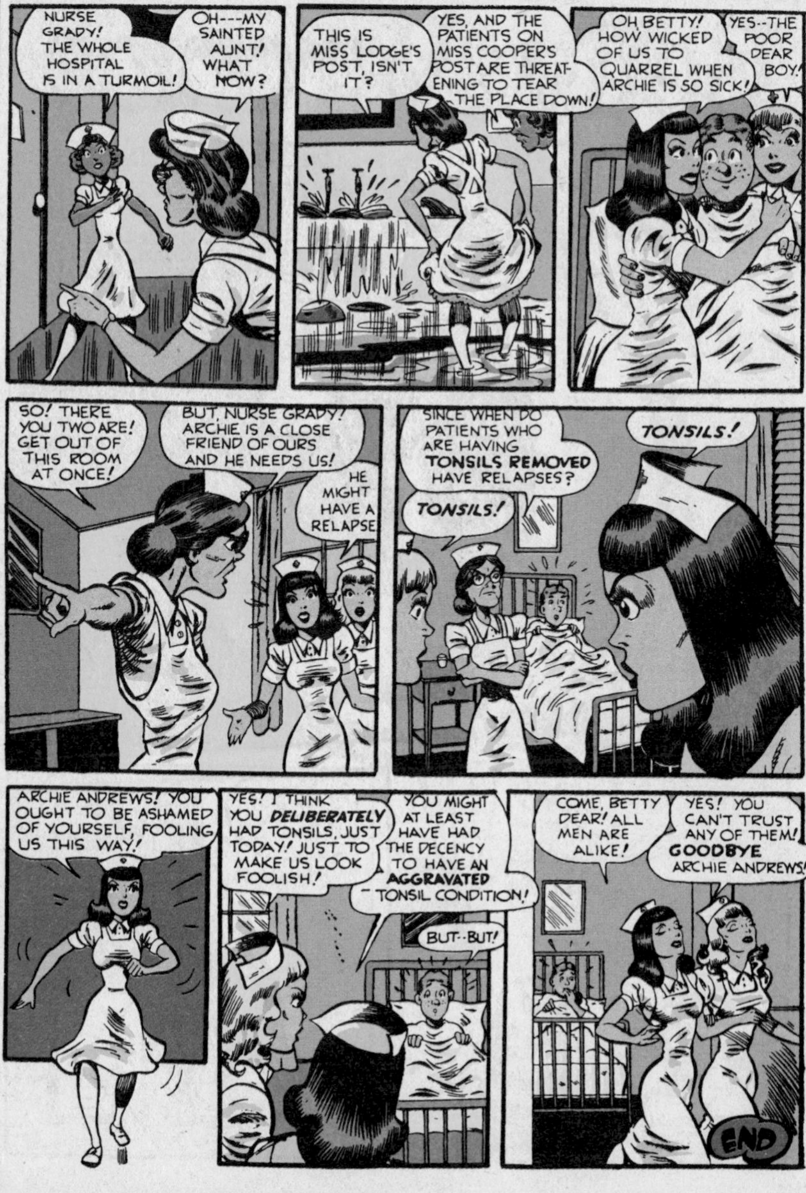
NURSE GRADY! THE WHOLE HOSPITAL IS IN A TURMOIL!
OH---MY SAINTED AUNT! WHAT NOW?
THIS IS MISS LODGE'S POST, ISN'T IT?
YES, AND THE PATIENTS ON MISS COOPER'S POST ARE THREATENING TO TEAR THE PLACE DOWN!
OH BETTY! HOW WICKED OF US TO QUARREL WHEN ARCHIE IS SO SICK!
YES--THE POOR DEAR BOY!
SO! THERE YOU TWO ARE! GET OUT OF THIS ROOM AT ONCE!
BUT, NURSE GRADY! ARCHIE IS A CLOSE FRIEND OF OURS AND HE NEEDS US!
HE MIGHT HAVE A RELAPSE
SINCE WHEN DO PATIENTS WHO ARE HAVING TONSILS REMOVED HAVE RELAPSES?
TONSILS!
TONSILS!
ARCHIE ANDREWS! YOU OUGHT TO BE ASHAMED OF YOURSELF, FOOLING US THIS WAY!
YES! I THINK YOU DELIBERATELY HAD TONSILS, JUST TODAY! JUST TO MAKE US LOOK FOOLISH!
YOU MIGHT AT LEAST HAVE HAD THE DECENCY TO HAVE AN AGGRAVATED TONSIL CONDITION!
BUT--BUT!
COME, BETTY DEAR! ALL MEN ARE ALIKE!
YES! YOU CAN'T TRUST ANY OF THEM! GOODBYE ARCHIE ANDREWS!
END

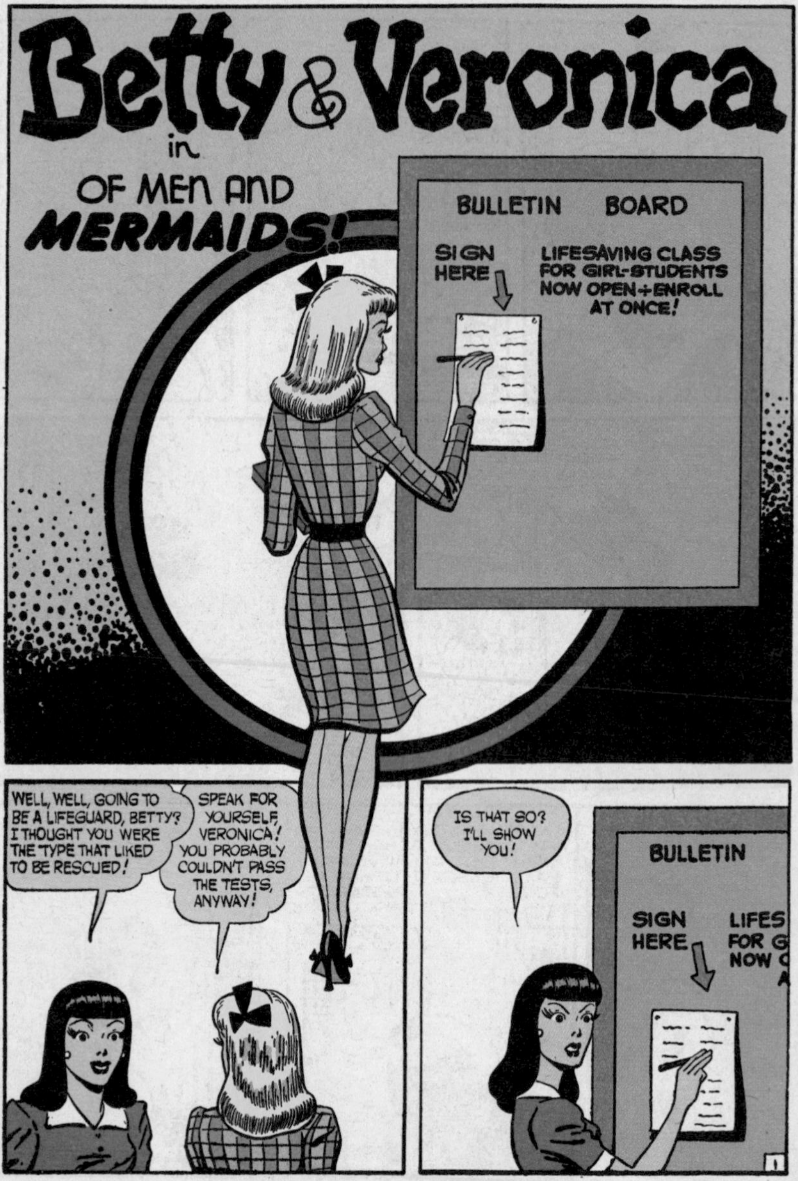

Betty & Veronica
in
OF MEN AND MERMAIDS!
BULLETIN BOARD
SIGN HERE
LIFESAVING CLASS FOR GIRL-STUDENTS NOW OPEN + ENROLL AT ONCE!
WELL, WELL, GOING TO BE A LIFEGUARD, BETTY? I THOUGHT YOU WERE THE TYPE THAT LIKED TO BE RESCUED!
SPEAK FOR YOURSELF, VERONICA! YOU PROBABLY COULDN'T PASS THE TESTS, ANYWAY!
IS THAT SO? I'LL SHOW YOU!
BULLETIN
SIGN HERE
1

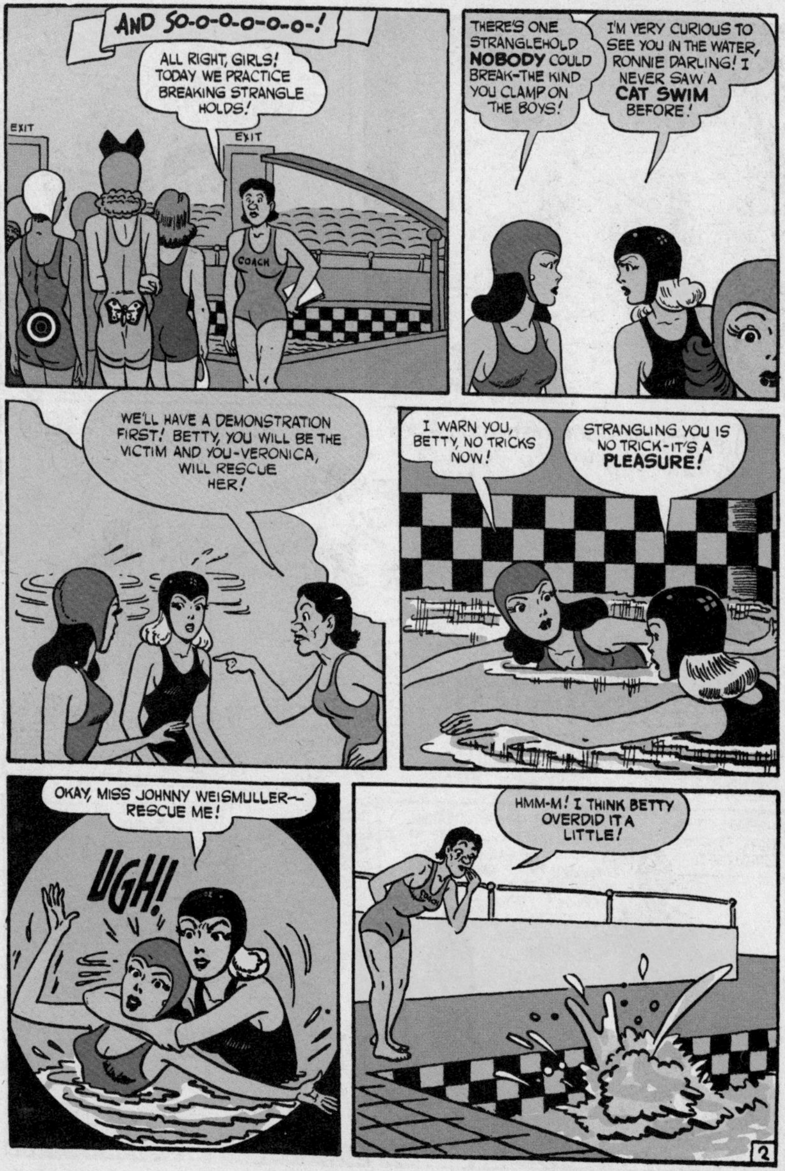

AND SO-O-O-O-O-O-O-!
ALL RIGHT, GIRLS! TODAY WE PRACTICE BREAKING STRANGLE HOLDS!
EXIT
EXIT
COACH
THERE'S ONE STRANGLEHOLD NOBODY COULD BREAK-THE KIND YOU CLAMP ON THE BOYS!
I'M VERY CURIOUS TO SEE YOU IN THE WATER, RONNIE DARLING! I NEVER SAW A CAT SWIM BEFORE!
WE'LL HAVE A DEMONSTRATION FIRST! BETTY, YOU WILL BE THE VICTIM AND YOU-VERONICA, WILL RESCUE HER!
I WARN YOU, BETTY, NO TRICKS NOW!
STRANGLING YOU IS NO TRICK-IT'S A PLEASURE!
OKAY, MISS JOHNNY WEISMULLER-- RESCUE ME!
UGH!
HMM-M! I THINK BETTY OVERDID IT A LITTLE!
COACH
2

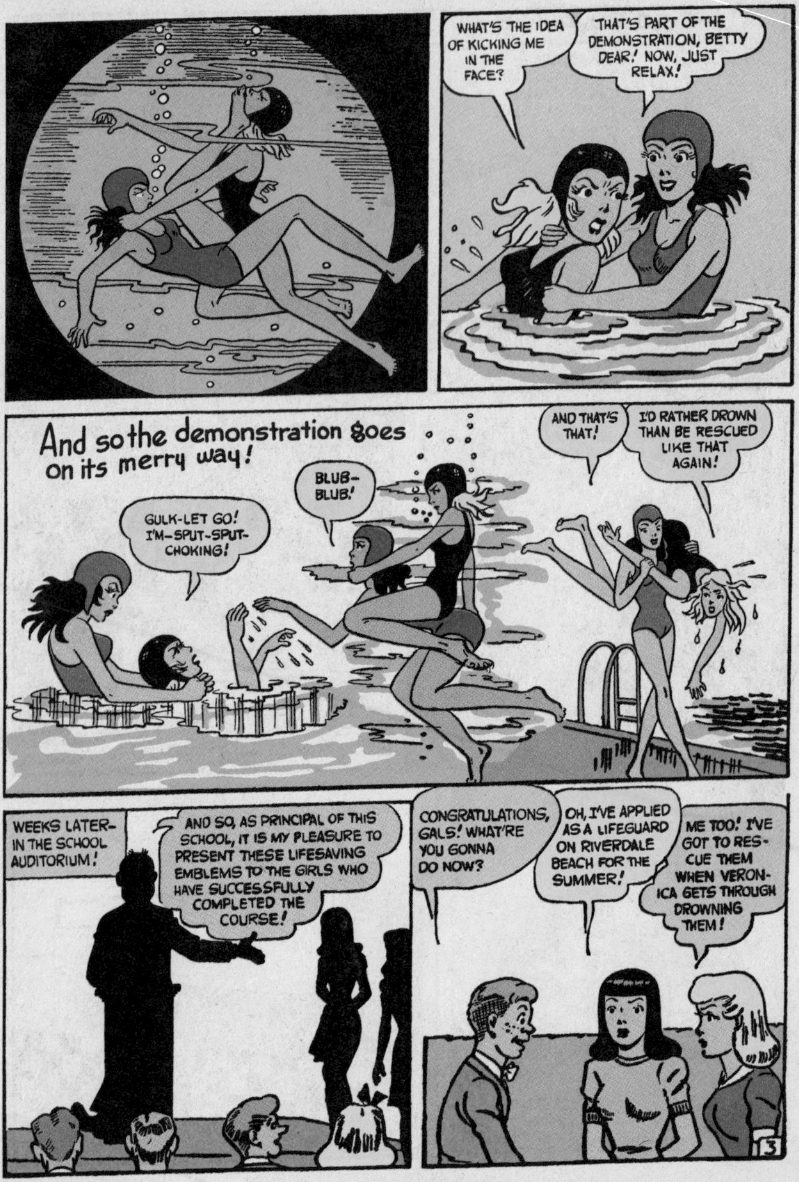

WHAT'S THE IDEA OF KICKING ME IN THE FACE?
THAT'S PART OF THE DEMONSTRATION, BETTY DEAR! NOW, JUST RELAX!
And so the demonstration goes on its merry way!
GULK-LET GO! I'M-SPUT-SPUT-CHOKING!
BLUB-BLUB!
AND THAT'S THAT!
I'D RATHER DROWN THAN BE RESCUED LIKE THAT AGAIN!
WEEKS LATER-IN THE SCHOOL AUDITORIUM!
AND SO, AS PRINCIPAL OF THIS SCHOOL, IT IS MY PLEASURE TO PRESENT THESE LIFESAVING EMBLEMS TO THE GIRLS WHO HAVE SUCCESSFULLY COMPLETED THE COURSE!
CONGRATULATIONS, GALS! WHAT'RE YOU GONNA DO NOW?
OH, I'VE APPLIED AS A LIFEGUARD ON RIVERDALE BEACH FOR THE SUMMER!
ME TOO! I'VE GOT TO RESCUE THEM WHEN VERONICA GETS THROUGH DROWNING THEM!
3

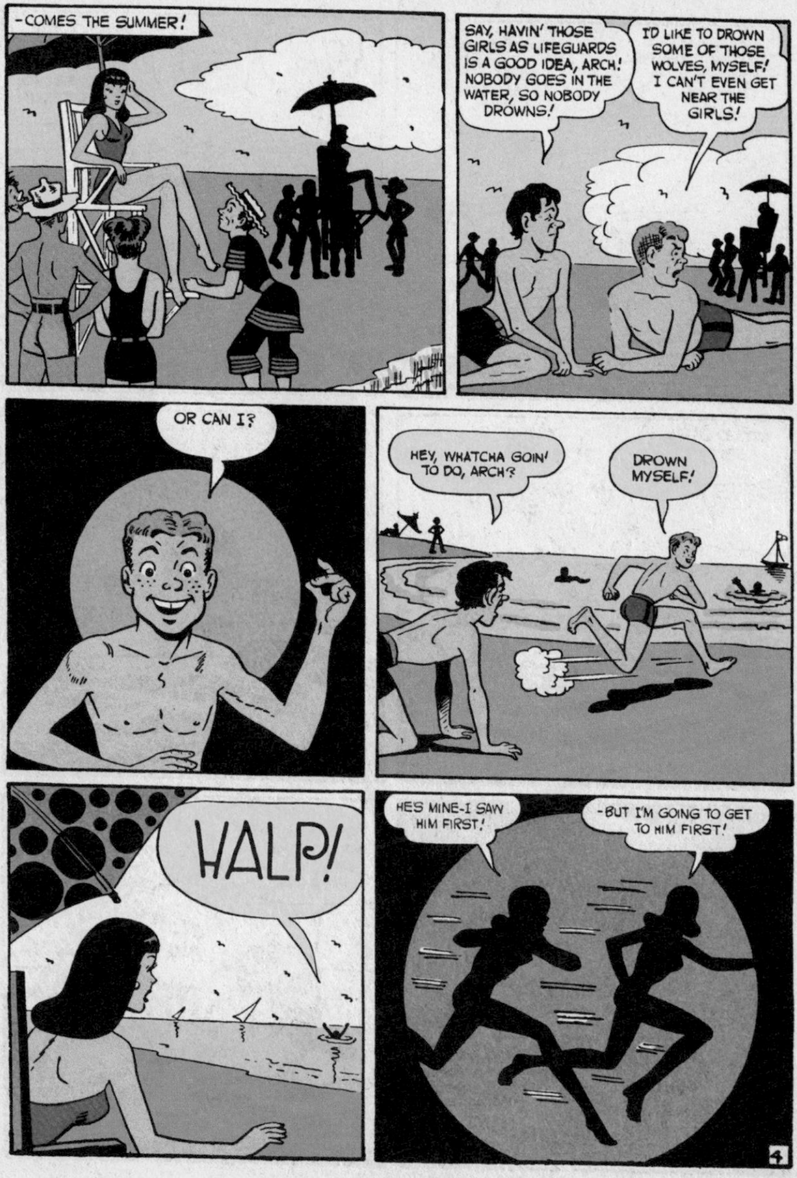

-COMES THE SUMMER!
SAY, HAVIN' THOSE GIRLS AS LIFEGUARDS IS A GOOD IDEA, ARCH! NOBODY GOES IN THE WATER, SO NOBODY DROWNS!
I'D LIKE TO DROWN SOME OF THOSE WOLVES, MYSELF! I CAN'T EVEN GET NEAR THE GIRLS!
OR CAN I?
HEY, WHATCHA GOIN' TO DO, ARCH?
DROWN MYSELF!
HALP!
HE'S MINE-I SAW HIM FIRST!
-BUT I'M GOING TO GET TO HIM FIRST!
4

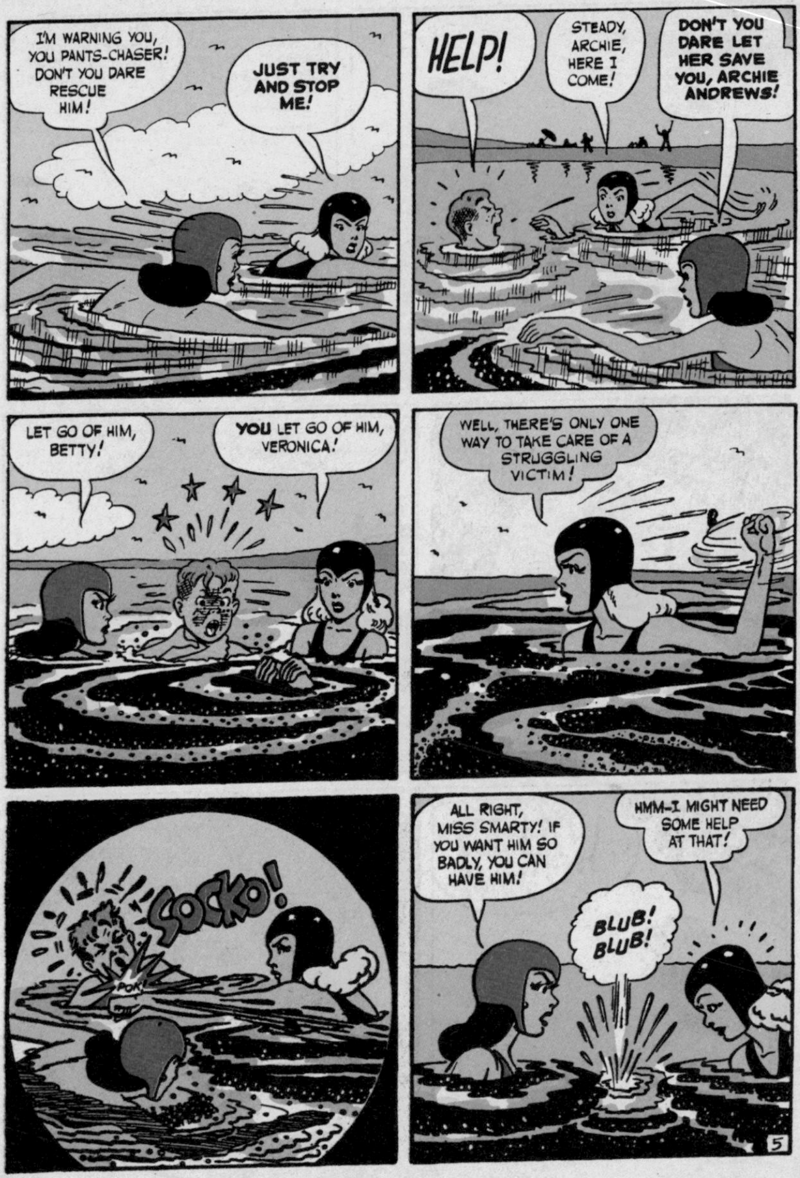

I'M WARNING YOU, YOU PANTS-CHASER! DON'T YOU DARE RESCUE HIM!
JUST TRY AND STOP ME!
HELP!
STEADY, ARCHIE, HERE I COME!
DON'T YOU DARE LET HER SAVE YOU, ARCHIE ANDREWS!
LET GO OF HIM, BETTY!
YOU LET GO OF HIM, VERONICA!
WELL, THERE'S ONLY ONE WAY TO TAKE CARE OF A STRUGGLING VICTIM!
SOCKO!
POK
ALL RIGHT, MISS SMARTY! IF YOU WANT HIM SO BADLY, YOU CAN HAVE HIM!
HMM-I MIGHT NEED SOME HELP AT THAT!
BLUB! BLUB!
5

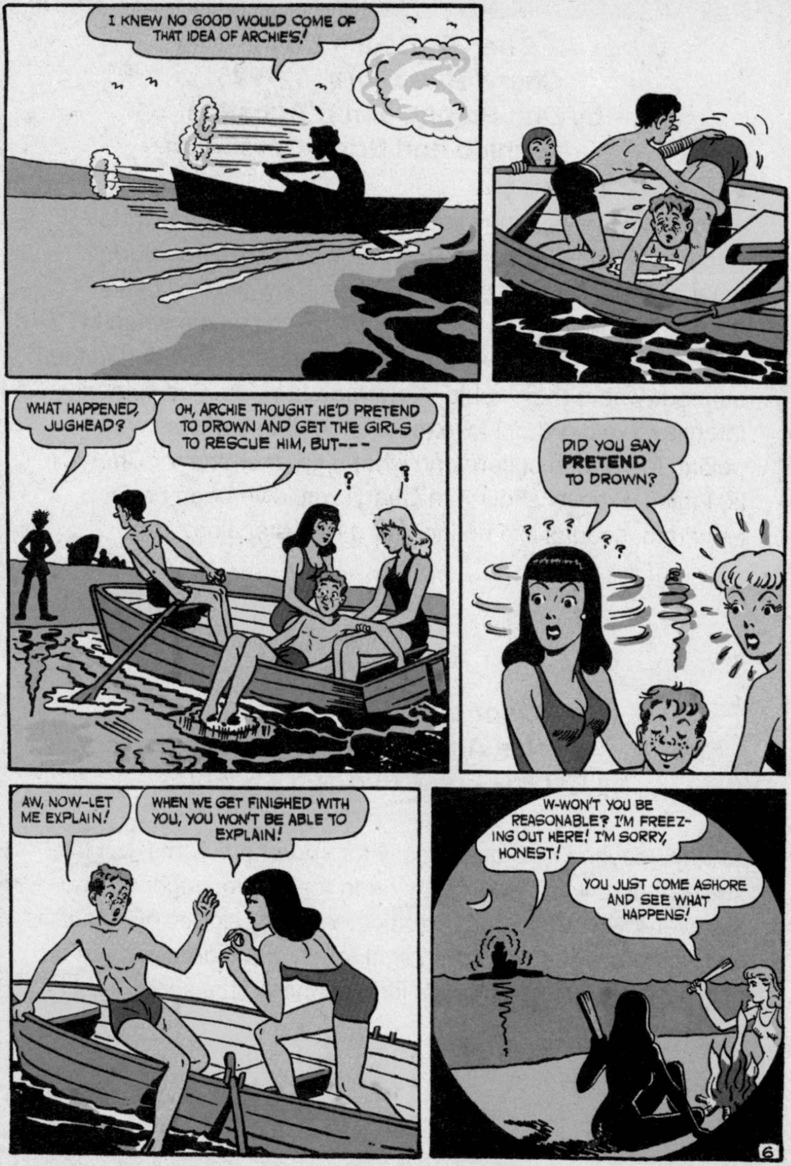
I KNEW NO GOOD WOULD COME OF THAT IDEA OF ARCHIE'S!
WHAT HAPPENED, JUGHEAD?
OH, ARCHIE THOUGHT HE'D PRETEND TO DROWN AND GET THE GIRLS TO RESCUE HIM, BUT---
DID YOU SAY **PRETEND** TO DROWN?
AW, NOW-LET ME EXPLAIN!
WHEN WE GET FINISHED WITH YOU, YOU WON'T BE ABLE TO EXPLAIN!
W-WON'T YOU BE REASONABLE? I'M FREEZ-ING OUT HERE! I'M SORRY, HONEST!
YOU JUST COME ASHORE AND SEE WHAT HAPPENS!
6

Cheryl's Beach Bash!
Cheryl Blossom #15, 1995
by Dan Parent, Jon D'Agostino,
Bill Yoshida and Barry Grossman

I can't believe so many years have passed since I wrote and drew "Cheryl's Beach Bash!" It was a fun three-parter where Cheryl has her own MTV-style show set in a beach house. For all you kids out there, there was a time when MTV showed videos, and they had a beach house show during the summer where they would show various videos, do celebrity interviews, etc. What I love most about these stories was poking fun at pop culture and what a great character Cheryl is. I think a reality show with Cheryl would've been perfect. Hmmmm, sounds like an idea for a new storyline.

Dan Parent
Writer and Artist, Archie Comics

Poor Little Rich Whirl
Archie Annual #8, 1956-1957
by George Frese and Terry Szenics

Okay, maybe I'm known mostly for superhero yarns, but I've always had a warm spot in my heart for Archie, Jughead and the ever-lovely Betty and Veronica. Youthful stories of humor and romance, handled with a light touch, have always been popular and always will be as long as the Archie series is here to entertain us.

Stan Lee
Creator of Spider-Man

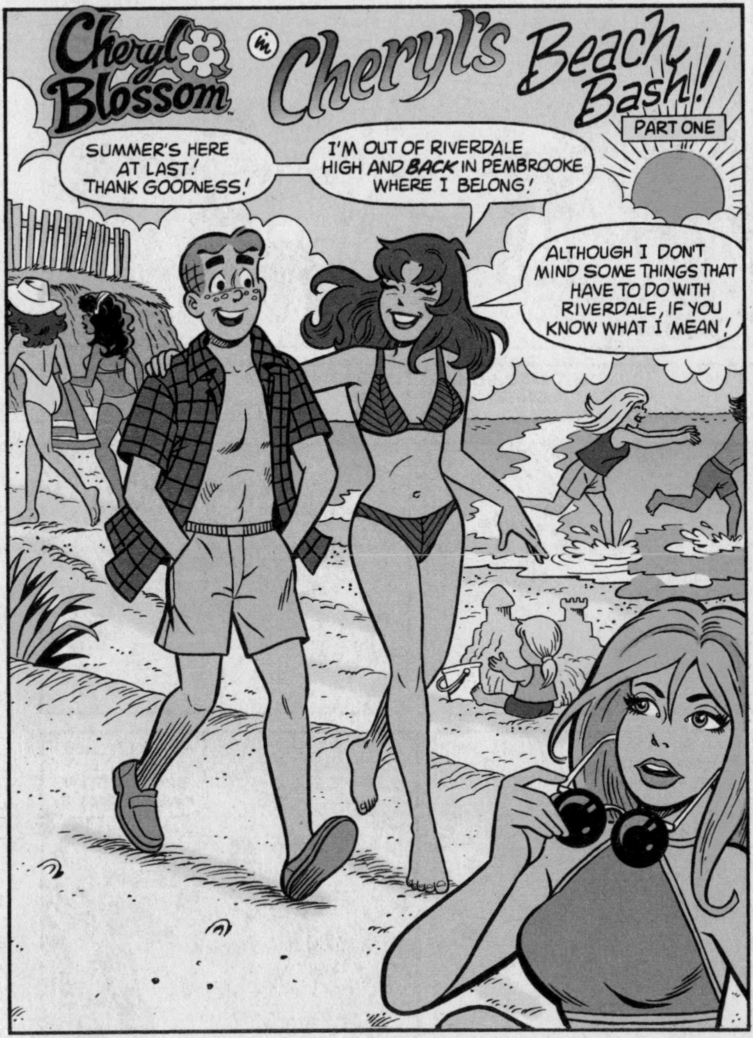
Cheryl Blossom
in
Cheryl's Beach Bash!
PART ONE
SUMMER'S HERE AT LAST! THANK GOODNESS!
I'M OUT OF RIVERDALE HIGH AND BACK IN PEMBROOKE WHERE I BELONG!
ALTHOUGH I DON'T MIND SOME THINGS THAT HAVE TO DO WITH RIVERDALE, IF YOU KNOW WHAT I MEAN!

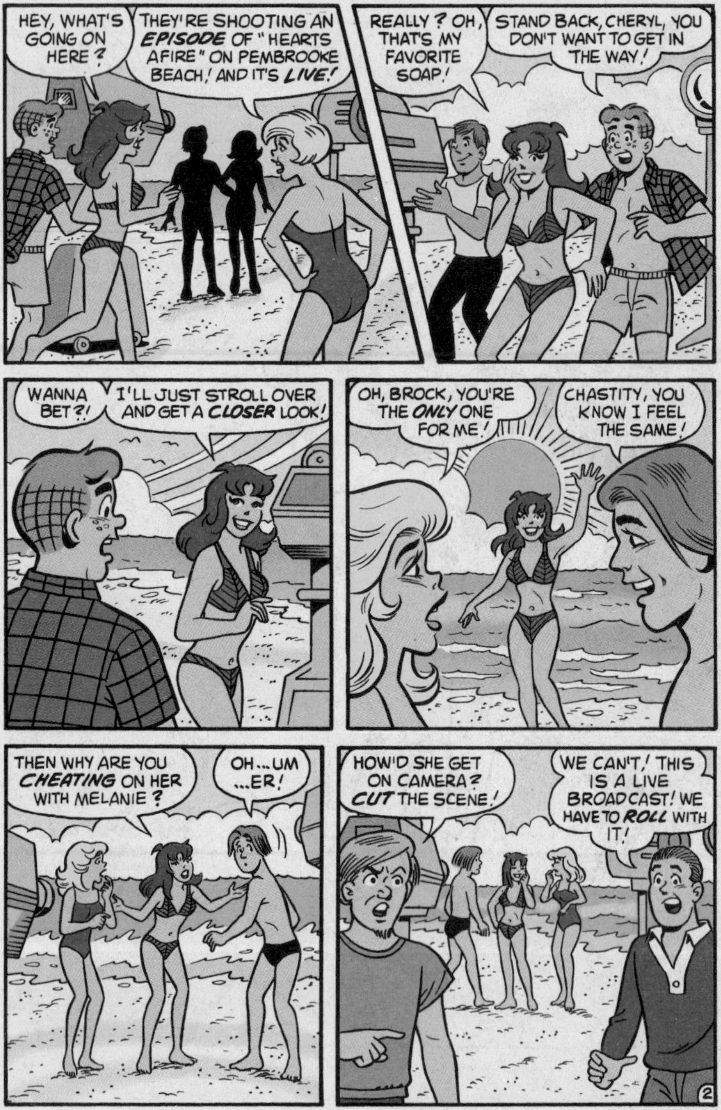
HEY, WHAT'S GOING ON HERE?
THEY'RE SHOOTING AN EPISODE OF "HEARTS AFIRE" ON PEMBROOKE BEACH! AND IT'S LIVE!
REALLY? OH, THAT'S MY FAVORITE SOAP!
STAND BACK, CHERYL, YOU DON'T WANT TO GET IN THE WAY!
WANNA BET?!
I'LL JUST STROLL OVER AND GET A CLOSER LOOK!
OH, BROCK, YOU'RE THE ONLY ONE FOR ME!
CHASTITY, YOU KNOW I FEEL THE SAME!
THEN WHY ARE YOU CHEATING ON HER WITH MELANIE?
OH...UM ...ER!
HOW'D SHE GET ON CAMERA? CUT THE SCENE!
WE CAN'T! THIS IS A LIVE BROADCAST! WE HAVE TO ROLL WITH IT!
2

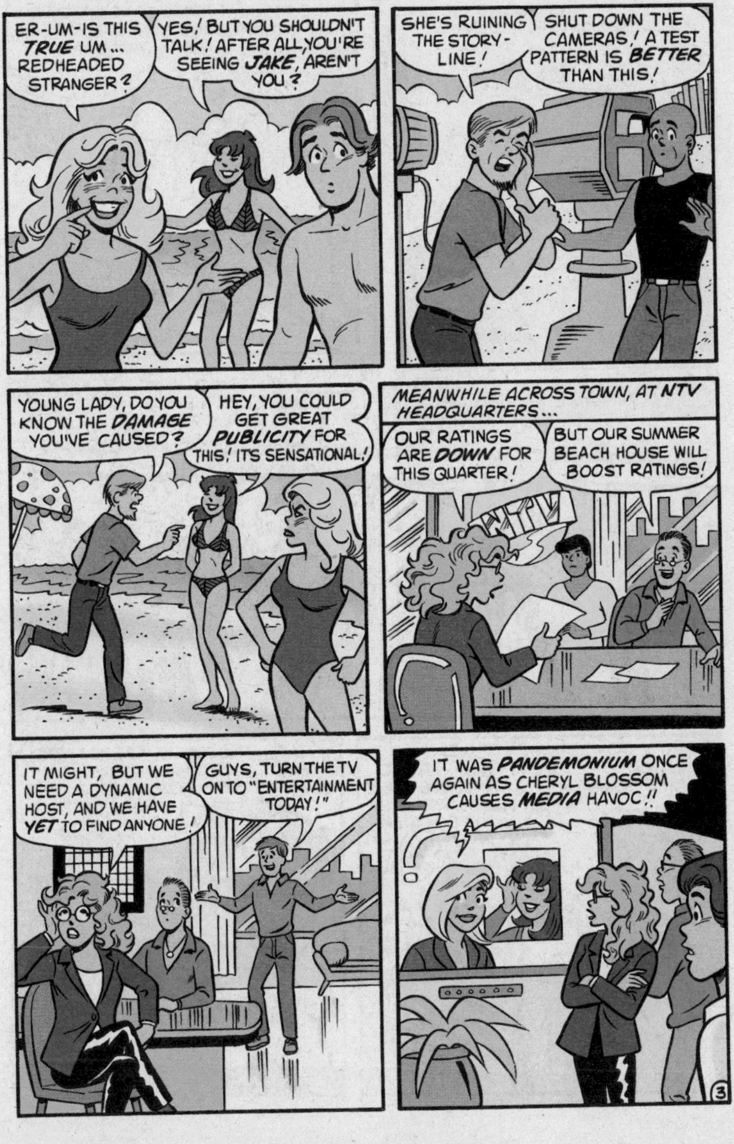

ER-UM-IS THIS TRUE UM... REDHEADED STRANGER?
YES! BUT YOU SHOULDN'T TALK! AFTER ALL, YOU'RE SEEING JAKE, AREN'T YOU?
SHE'S RUINING THE STORY-LINE!
SHUT DOWN THE CAMERAS! A TEST PATTERN IS BETTER THAN THIS!
YOUNG LADY, DO YOU KNOW THE DAMAGE YOU'VE CAUSED?
HEY, YOU COULD GET GREAT PUBLICITY FOR THIS! IT'S SENSATIONAL!
MEANWHILE ACROSS TOWN, AT NTV HEADQUARTERS...
OUR RATINGS ARE DOWN FOR THIS QUARTER!
BUT OUR SUMMER BEACH HOUSE WILL BOOST RATINGS!
NTV
IT MIGHT, BUT WE NEED A DYNAMIC HOST, AND WE HAVE YET TO FIND ANYONE!
GUYS, TURN THE TV ON TO "ENTERTAINMENT TODAY!"
IT WAS PANDEMONIUM ONCE AGAIN AS CHERYL BLOSSOM CAUSES MEDIA HAVOC!!
3

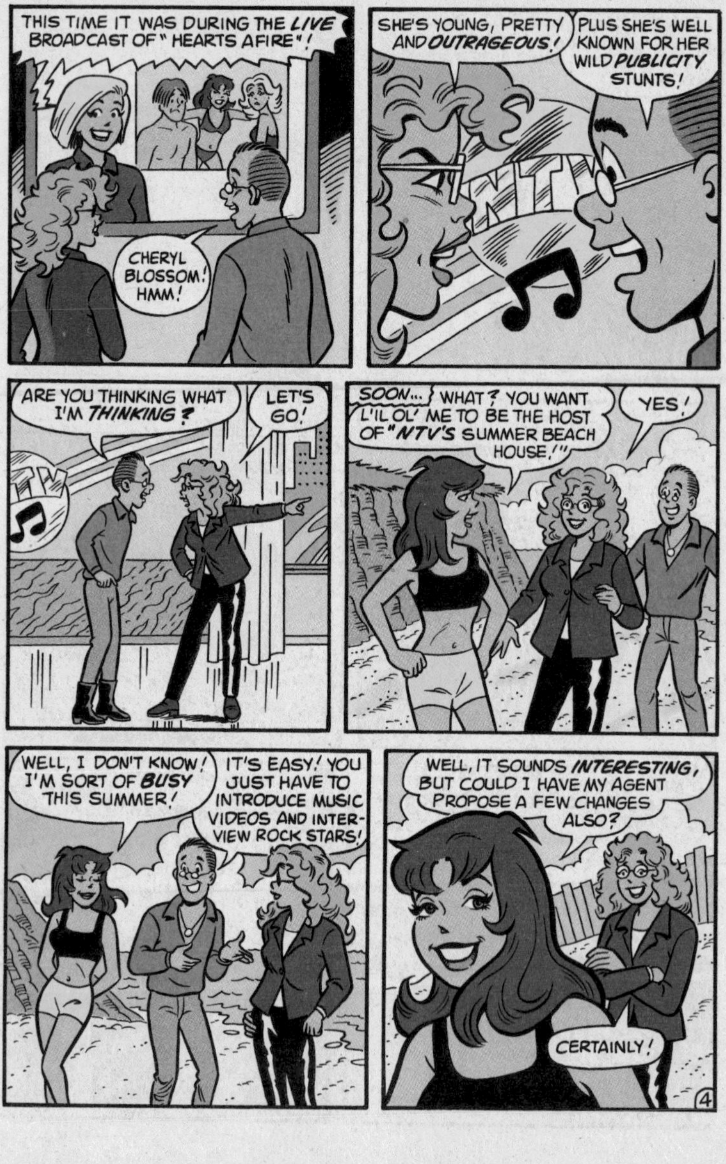
THIS TIME IT WAS DURING THE LIVE BROADCAST OF "HEARTS AFIRE"!
CHERYL BLOSSOM! HMM!
SHE'S YOUNG, PRETTY AND OUTRAGEOUS!
PLUS SHE'S WELL KNOWN FOR HER WILD PUBLICITY STUNTS!
NTV
ARE YOU THINKING WHAT I'M THINKING?
LET'S GO!
SOON...
WHAT? YOU WANT L'IL OL' ME TO BE THE HOST OF "NTV'S SUMMER BEACH HOUSE!"
YES!
WELL, I DON'T KNOW! I'M SORT OF BUSY THIS SUMMER!
IT'S EASY! YOU JUST HAVE TO INTRODUCE MUSIC VIDEOS AND INTER-VIEW ROCK STARS!
WELL, IT SOUNDS INTERESTING, BUT COULD I HAVE MY AGENT PROPOSE A FEW CHANGES ALSO?
CERTAINLY!
4

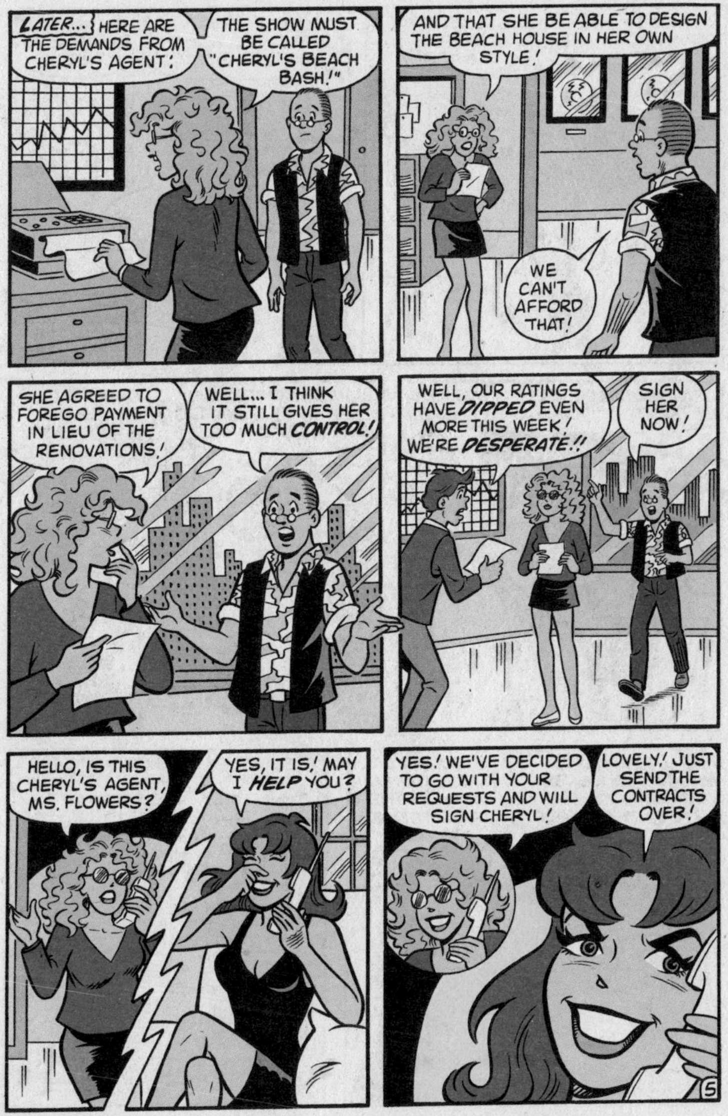
LATER...
HERE ARE THE DEMANDS FROM CHERYL'S AGENT:
THE SHOW MUST BE CALLED "CHERYL'S BEACH BASH!"
AND THAT SHE BE ABLE TO DESIGN THE BEACH HOUSE IN HER OWN STYLE!
WE CAN'T AFFORD THAT!
SHE AGREED TO FOREGO PAYMENT IN LIEU OF THE RENOVATIONS!
WELL... I THINK IT STILL GIVES HER TOO MUCH CONTROL!
WELL, OUR RATINGS HAVE DIPPED EVEN MORE THIS WEEK! WE'RE DESPERATE!!
SIGN HER NOW!
HELLO, IS THIS CHERYL'S AGENT, MS. FLOWERS?
YES, IT IS! MAY I HELP YOU?
YES! WE'VE DECIDED TO GO WITH YOUR REQUESTS AND WILL SIGN CHERYL!
LOVELY! JUST SEND THE CONTRACTS OVER!
5

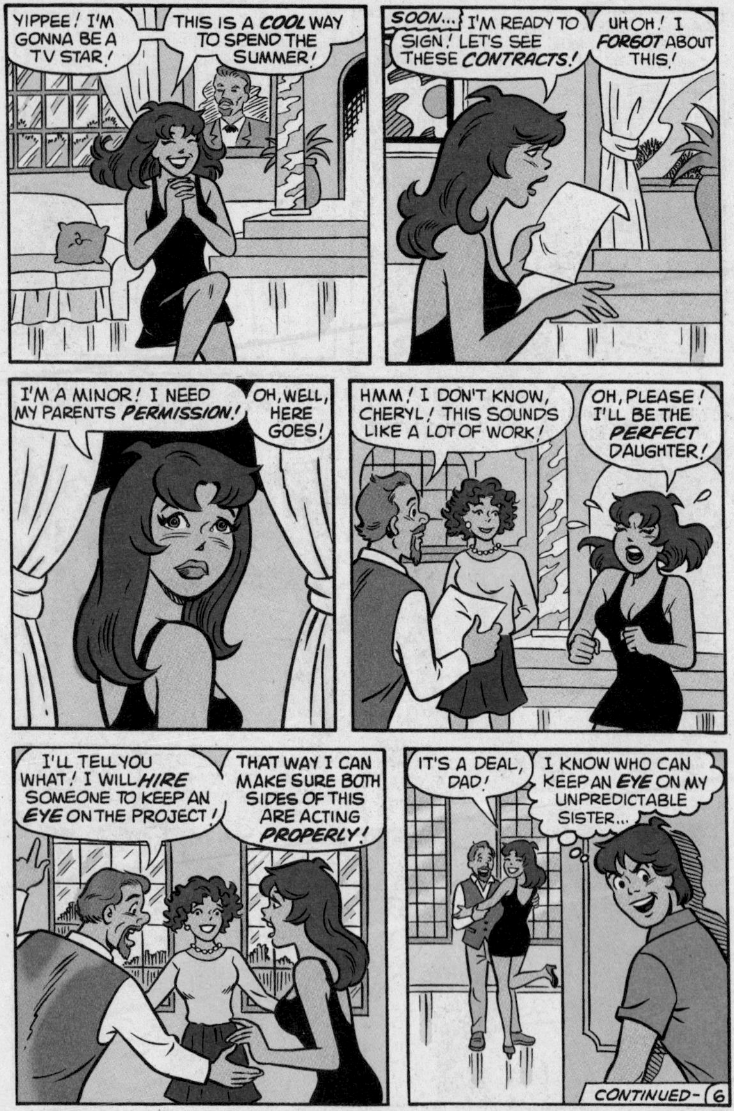

YIPPEE! I'M GONNA BE A TV STAR!
THIS IS A COOL WAY TO SPEND THE SUMMER!
SOON...
I'M READY TO SIGN! LET'S SEE THESE CONTRACTS!
UH OH! I FORGOT ABOUT THIS!
I'M A MINOR! I NEED MY PARENTS PERMISSION!
OH, WELL, HERE GOES!
HMM! I DON'T KNOW, CHERYL! THIS SOUNDS LIKE A LOT OF WORK!
OH, PLEASE! I'LL BE THE PERFECT DAUGHTER!
I'LL TELL YOU WHAT! I WILL HIRE SOMEONE TO KEEP AN EYE ON THE PROJECT!
THAT WAY I CAN MAKE SURE BOTH SIDES OF THIS ARE ACTING PROPERLY!
IT'S A DEAL, DAD!
I KNOW WHO CAN KEEP AN EYE ON MY UNPREDICTABLE SISTER...
CONTINUED-
6

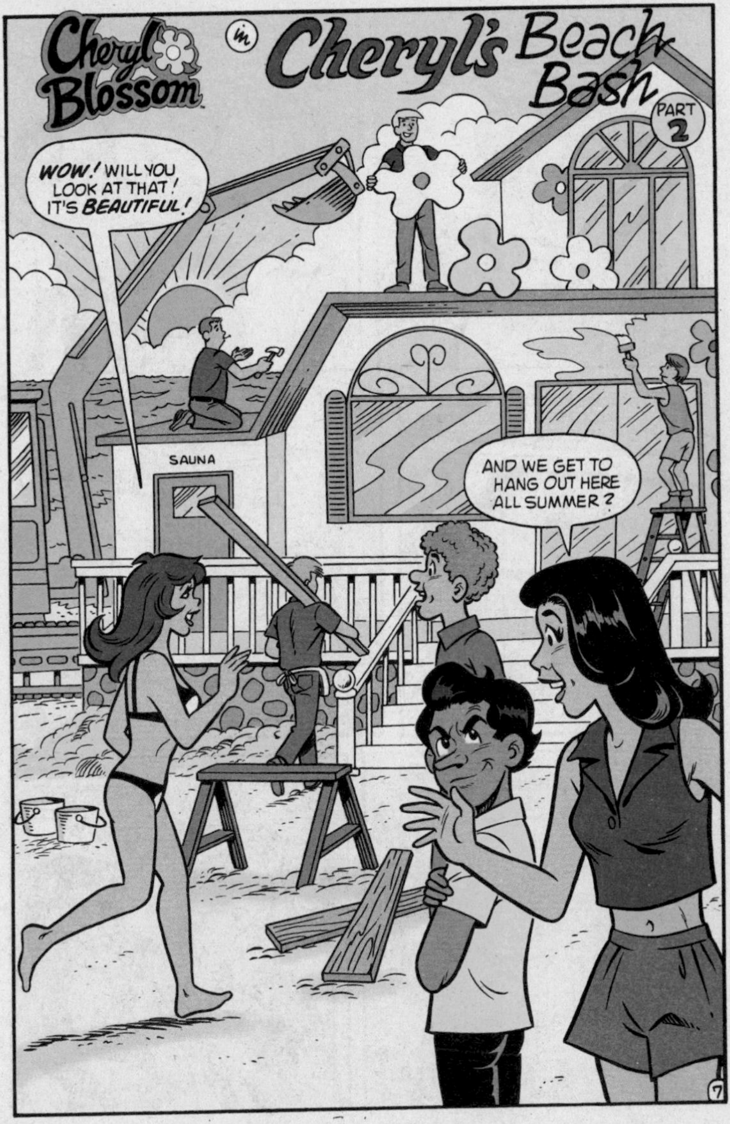
Cheryl Blossom
in
Cheryl's Beach Bash
PART 2
WOW! WILL YOU LOOK AT THAT! IT'S BEAUTIFUL!
SAUNA
AND WE GET TO HANG OUT HERE ALL SUMMER?
7

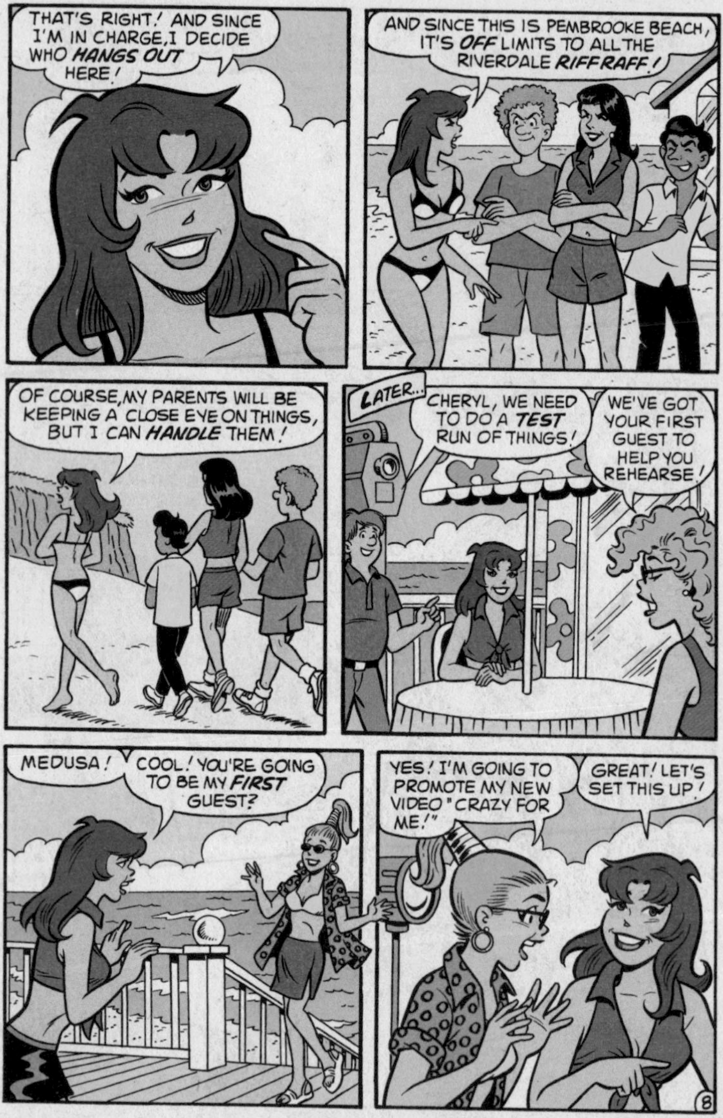
THAT'S RIGHT! AND SINCE I'M IN CHARGE, I DECIDE WHO HANGS OUT HERE!
AND SINCE THIS IS PEMBROOKE BEACH, IT'S OFF LIMITS TO ALL THE RIVERDALE RIFFRAFF!
OF COURSE, MY PARENTS WILL BE KEEPING A CLOSE EYE ON THINGS, BUT I CAN HANDLE THEM!
LATER...
CHERYL, WE NEED TO DO A TEST RUN OF THINGS!
WE'VE GOT YOUR FIRST GUEST TO HELP YOU REHEARSE!
MEDUSA!
COOL! YOU'RE GOING TO BE MY FIRST GUEST?
YES! I'M GOING TO PROMOTE MY NEW VIDEO "CRAZY FOR ME!"
GREAT! LET'S SET THIS UP!
8

THAT'S ME IN MY NEW VIDEO!
HONK! HONK!
NTV
WHAT'S ALL THE RACKET?
IT LOOKS LIKE A YACHT!
IT IS! IT'S MY BROTHER'S YACHT!
DON'T WORRY! I'LL DEAL WITH THIS QUICKLY!
HI, SIS! I'M HAVING A PARTY! WANNA JOIN US?
NO, I DON'T! STOP THIS NONSENSE NOW!
WHAT DO YOU MEAN?
YOU'RE HAVING A LOUD, OBNOXIOUS PARTY JUST TO ANNOY ME!
AS MUCH AS I'D LIKE THAT TO BE TRUE, IT'S NOT!
THEN LEAVE!
9

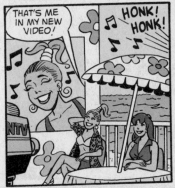

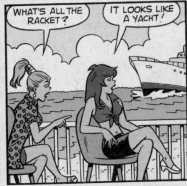

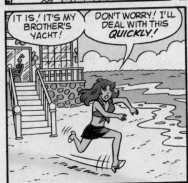

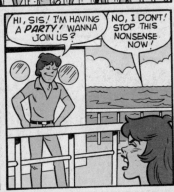

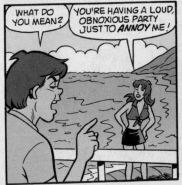

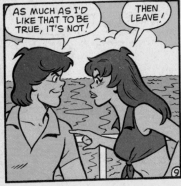

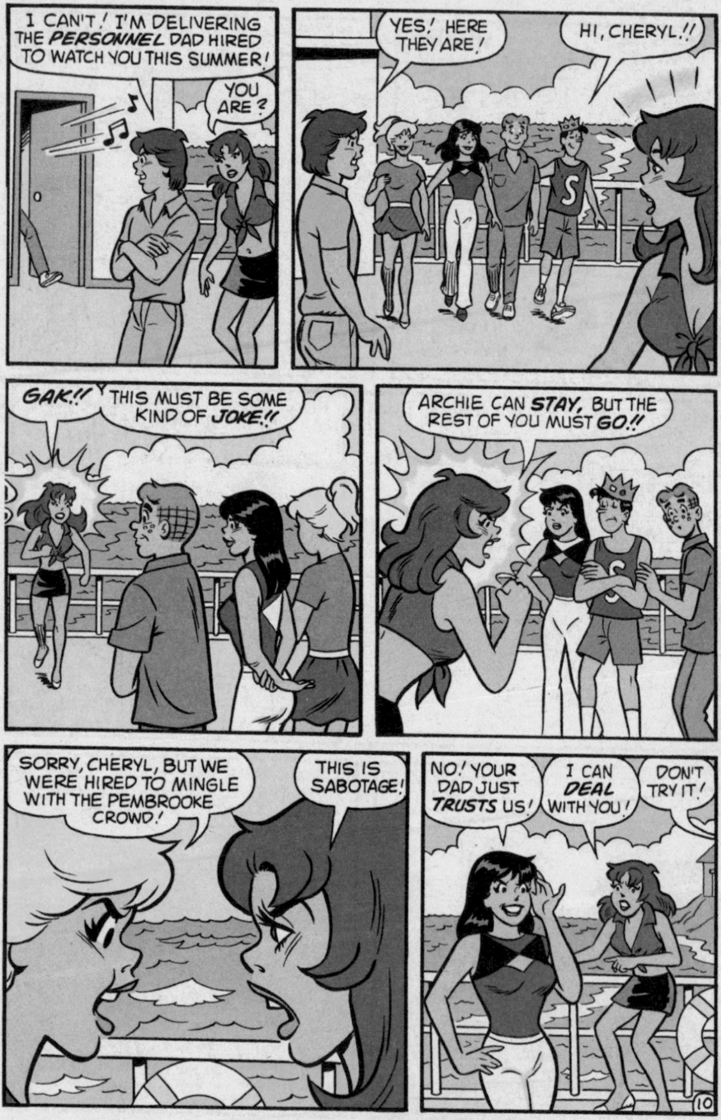
I CAN'T! I'M DELIVERING THE PERSONNEL DAD HIRED TO WATCH YOU THIS SUMMER!
YOU ARE?
YES! HERE THEY ARE!
HI, CHERYL!!
GAK!!
THIS MUST BE SOME KIND OF JOKE!!
ARCHIE CAN STAY, BUT THE REST OF YOU MUST GO!!
SORRY, CHERYL, BUT WE WERE HIRED TO MINGLE WITH THE PEMBROOKE CROWD!
THIS IS SABOTAGE!
NO! YOUR DAD JUST TRUSTS US!
I CAN DEAL WITH YOU!
DON'T TRY IT!
10

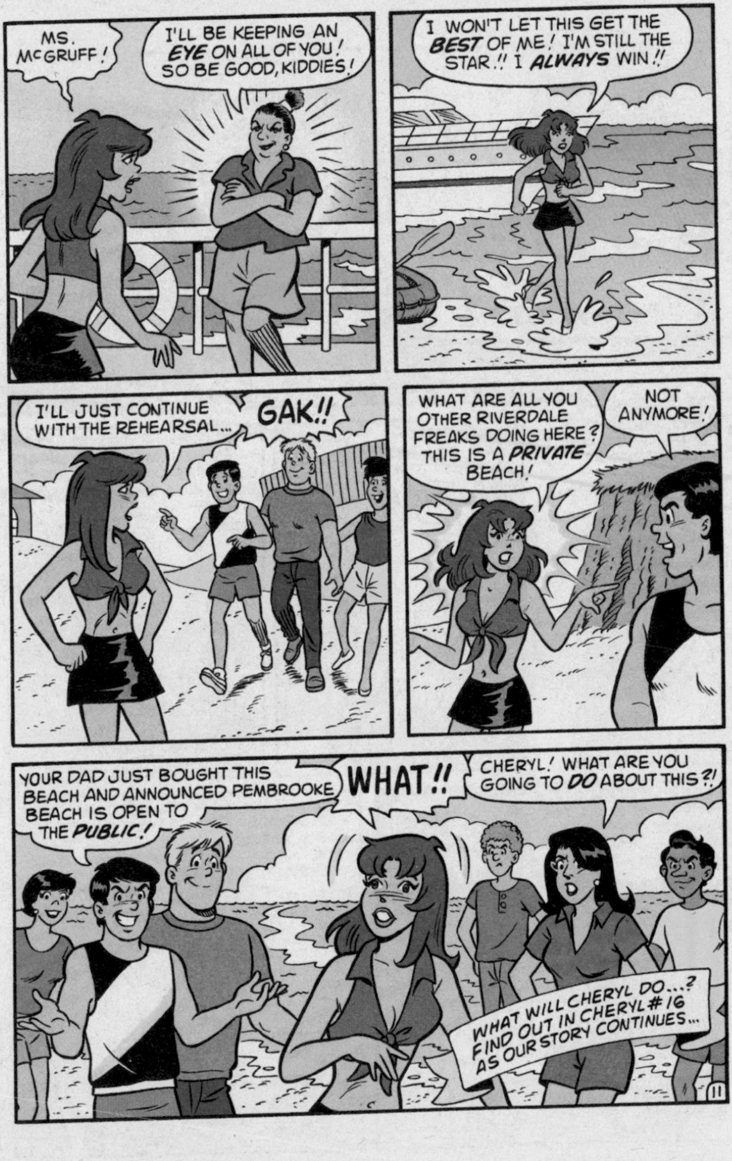
MS. McGRUFF!
I'LL BE KEEPING AN EYE ON ALL OF YOU! SO BE GOOD, KIDDIES!
I WON'T LET THIS GET THE BEST OF ME! I'M STILL THE STAR!! I ALWAYS WIN!!
I'LL JUST CONTINUE WITH THE REHEARSAL...
GAK!!
WHAT ARE ALL YOU OTHER RIVERDALE FREAKS DOING HERE? THIS IS A PRIVATE BEACH!
NOT ANYMORE!
YOUR DAD JUST BOUGHT THIS BEACH AND ANNOUNCED PEMBROOKE BEACH IS OPEN TO THE PUBLIC!
WHAT!!
CHERYL! WHAT ARE YOU GOING TO DO ABOUT THIS?!
WHAT WILL CHERYL DO...? FIND OUT IN CHERYL #16 AS OUR STORY CONTINUES...
11

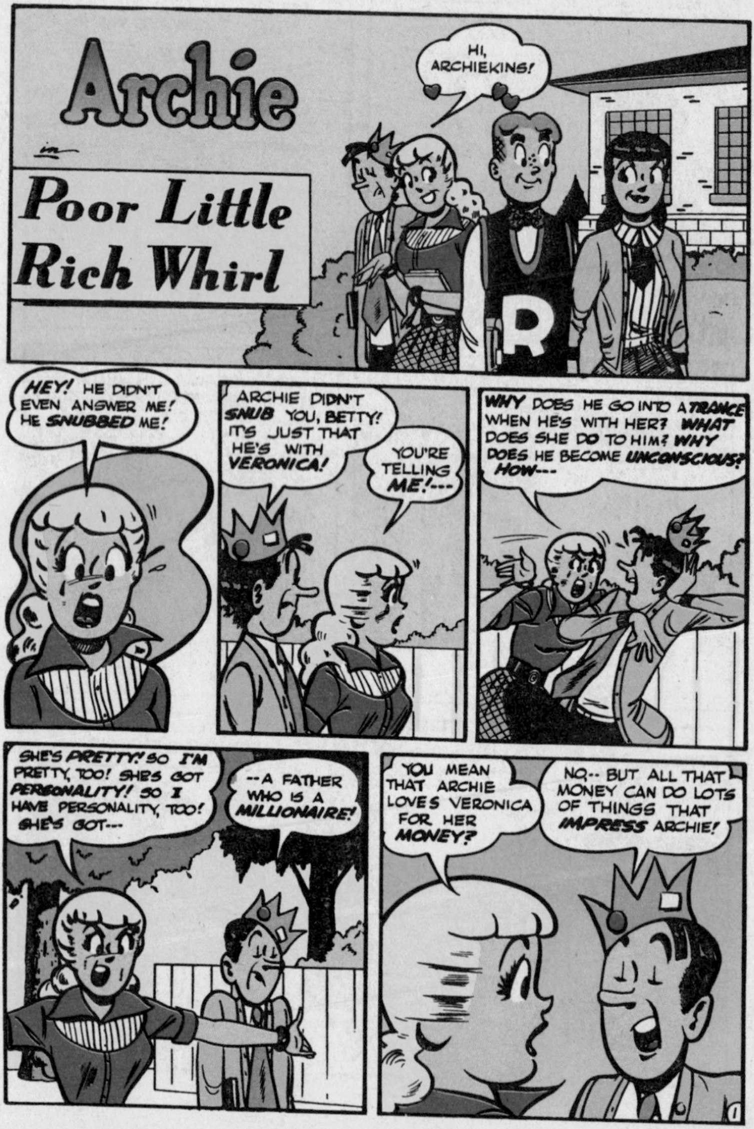
Archie
in
Poor Little Rich Whirl
HI, ARCHIEKINS!
HEY! HE DIDN'T EVEN ANSWER ME! HE SNUBBED ME!
ARCHIE DIDN'T SNUB YOU, BETTY! IT'S JUST THAT HE'S WITH VERONICA!
YOU'RE TELLING ME!---
WHY DOES HE GO INTO A TRANCE WHEN HE'S WITH HER? WHAT DOES SHE DO TO HIM? WHY DOES HE BECOME UNCONSCIOUS? HOW---
SHE'S PRETTY! SO I'M PRETTY, TOO! SHE'S GOT PERSONALITY! SO I HAVE PERSONALITY, TOO! SHE'S GOT---
--A FATHER WHO IS A MILLIONAIRE!
YOU MEAN THAT ARCHIE LOVES VERONICA FOR HER MONEY?
NO-- BUT ALL THAT MONEY CAN DO LOTS OF THINGS THAT IMPRESS ARCHIE!
1

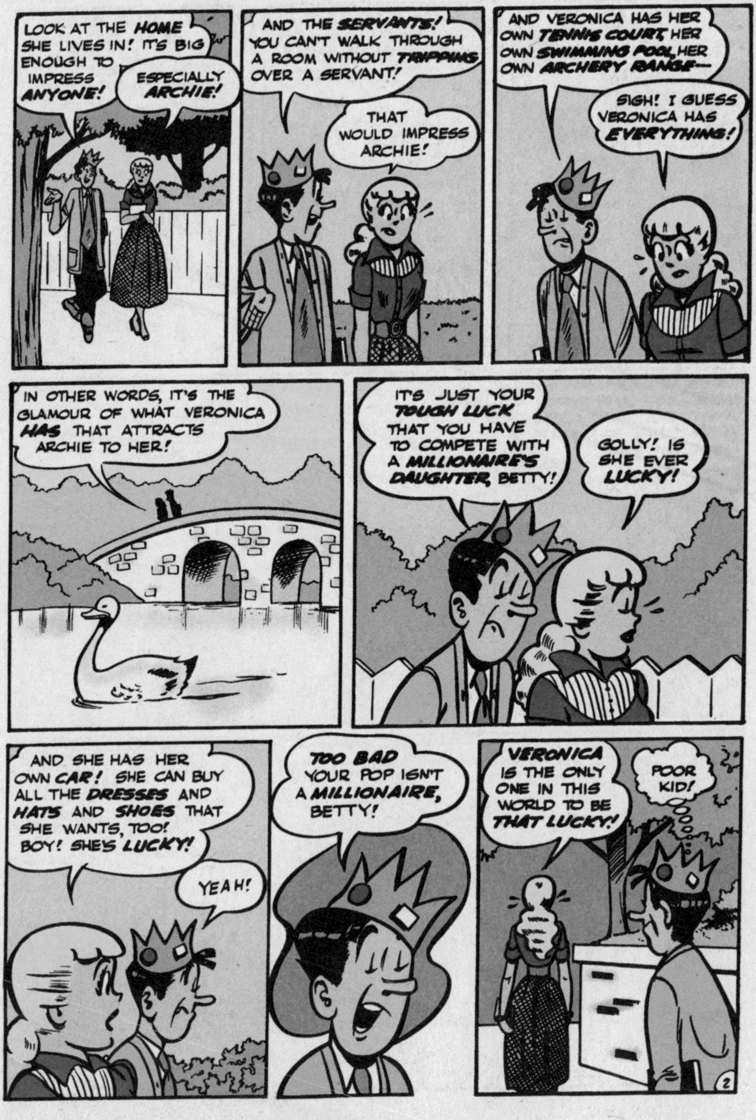

LOOK AT THE HOME SHE LIVES IN! IT'S BIG ENOUGH TO IMPRESS ANYONE!
ESPECIALLY ARCHIE!
AND THE SERVANTS! YOU CAN'T WALK THROUGH A ROOM WITHOUT TRIPPING OVER A SERVANT!
THAT WOULD IMPRESS ARCHIE!
AND VERONICA HAS HER OWN TENNIS COURT, HER OWN SWIMMING POOL, HER OWN ARCHERY RANGE--
SIGH! I GUESS VERONICA HAS EVERYTHING!
IN OTHER WORDS, IT'S THE GLAMOUR OF WHAT VERONICA HAS THAT ATTRACTS ARCHIE TO HER!
IT'S JUST YOUR TOUGH LUCK THAT YOU HAVE TO COMPETE WITH A MILLIONAIRE'S DAUGHTER, BETTY!
GOLLY! IS SHE EVER LUCKY!
AND SHE HAS HER OWN CAR! SHE CAN BUY ALL THE DRESSES AND HATS AND SHOES THAT SHE WANTS, TOO! BOY! SHE'S LUCKY!
YEAH!
TOO BAD YOUR POP ISN'T A MILLIONAIRE, BETTY!
VERONICA IS THE ONLY ONE IN THIS WORLD TO BE THAT LUCKY!
POOR KID!

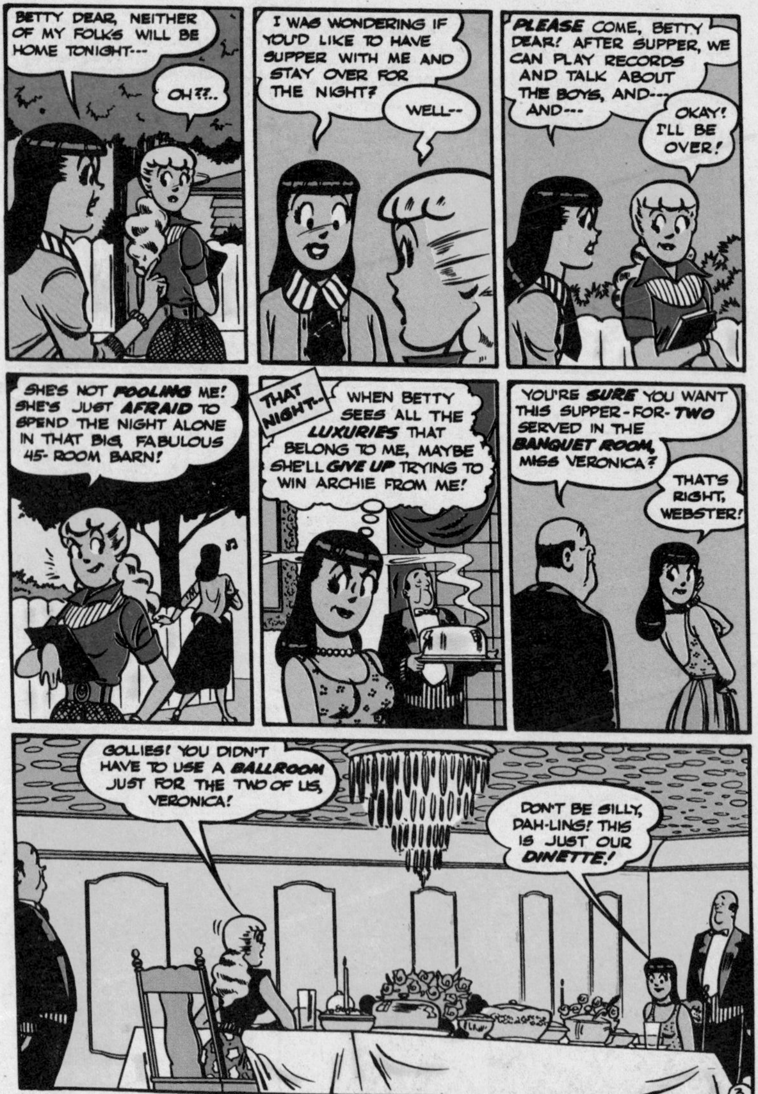
BETTY DEAR, NEITHER OF MY FOLKS WILL BE HOME TONIGHT---
OH??..
I WAS WONDERING IF YOU'D LIKE TO HAVE SUPPER WITH ME AND STAY OVER FOR THE NIGHT?
WELL--
PLEASE COME, BETTY DEAR! AFTER SUPPER, WE CAN PLAY RECORDS AND TALK ABOUT THE BOYS, AND--- AND---
OKAY! I'LL BE OVER!
SHE'S NOT FOOLING ME! SHE'S JUST AFRAID TO SPEND THE NIGHT ALONE IN THAT BIG, FABULOUS 45- ROOM BARN!
THAT NIGHT--
WHEN BETTY SEES ALL THE LUXURIES THAT BELONG TO ME, MAYBE SHE'LL GIVE UP TRYING TO WIN ARCHIE FROM ME!
YOU'RE SURE YOU WANT THIS SUPPER-FOR-TWO SERVED IN THE BANQUET ROOM, MISS VERONICA?
THAT'S RIGHT, WEBSTER!
GOLLIES! YOU DIDN'T HAVE TO USE A BALLROOM JUST FOR THE TWO OF US, VERONICA!
DON'T BE SILLY, DAH-LING! THIS IS JUST OUR DINETTE!
3

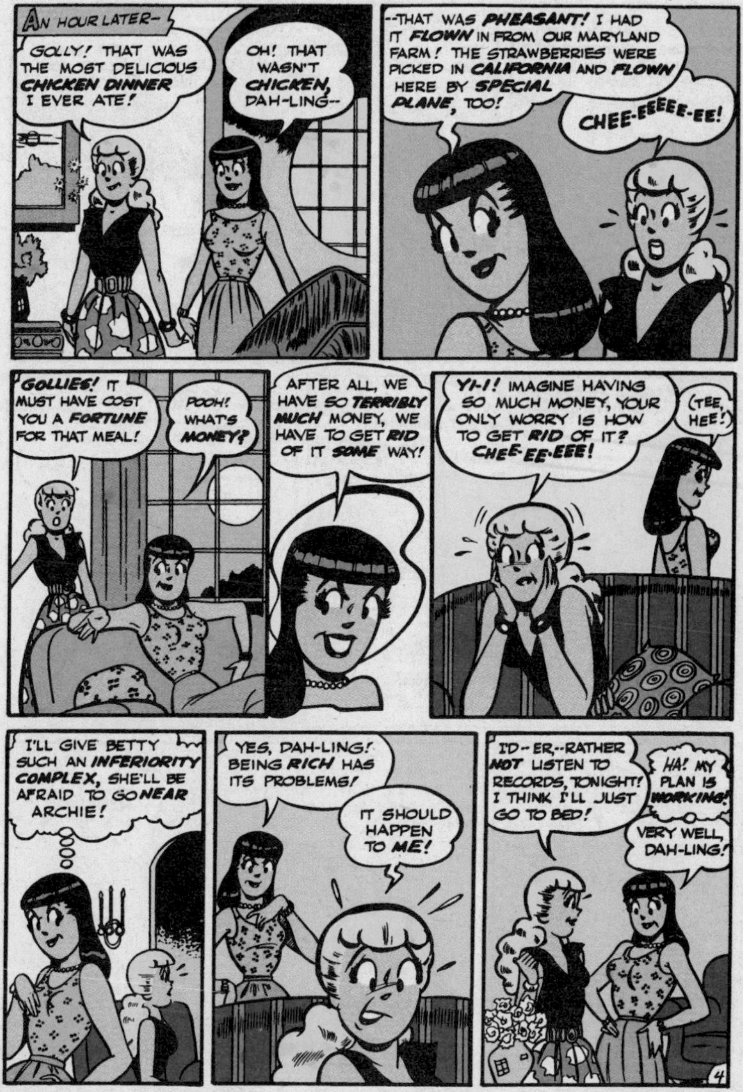
AN HOUR LATER—
GOLLY! THAT WAS THE MOST DELICIOUS CHICKEN DINNER I EVER ATE!
OH! THAT WASN'T CHICKEN, DAH-LING--
--THAT WAS PHEASANT! I HAD IT FLOWN IN FROM OUR MARYLAND FARM! THE STRAWBERRIES WERE PICKED IN CALIFORNIA AND FLOWN HERE BY SPECIAL PLANE, TOO!
CHEE-EEEEE-EE!
GOLLIES! IT MUST HAVE COST YOU A FORTUNE FOR THAT MEAL!
POOH! WHAT'S MONEY?
AFTER ALL, WE HAVE SO TERRIBLY MUCH MONEY, WE HAVE TO GET RID OF IT SOME WAY!
YI-I! IMAGINE HAVING SO MUCH MONEY, YOUR ONLY WORRY IS HOW TO GET RID OF IT? CHEE-EE-EEE!
(TEE, HEE!)
I'LL GIVE BETTY SUCH AN INFERIORITY COMPLEX, SHE'LL BE AFRAID TO GO NEAR ARCHIE!
YES, DAH-LING! BEING RICH HAS ITS PROBLEMS!
IT SHOULD HAPPEN TO ME!
I'D--ER,--RATHER NOT LISTEN TO RECORDS, TONIGHT! I THINK I'LL JUST GO TO BED!
HA! MY PLAN IS WORKING!
VERY WELL, DAH-LING!
4

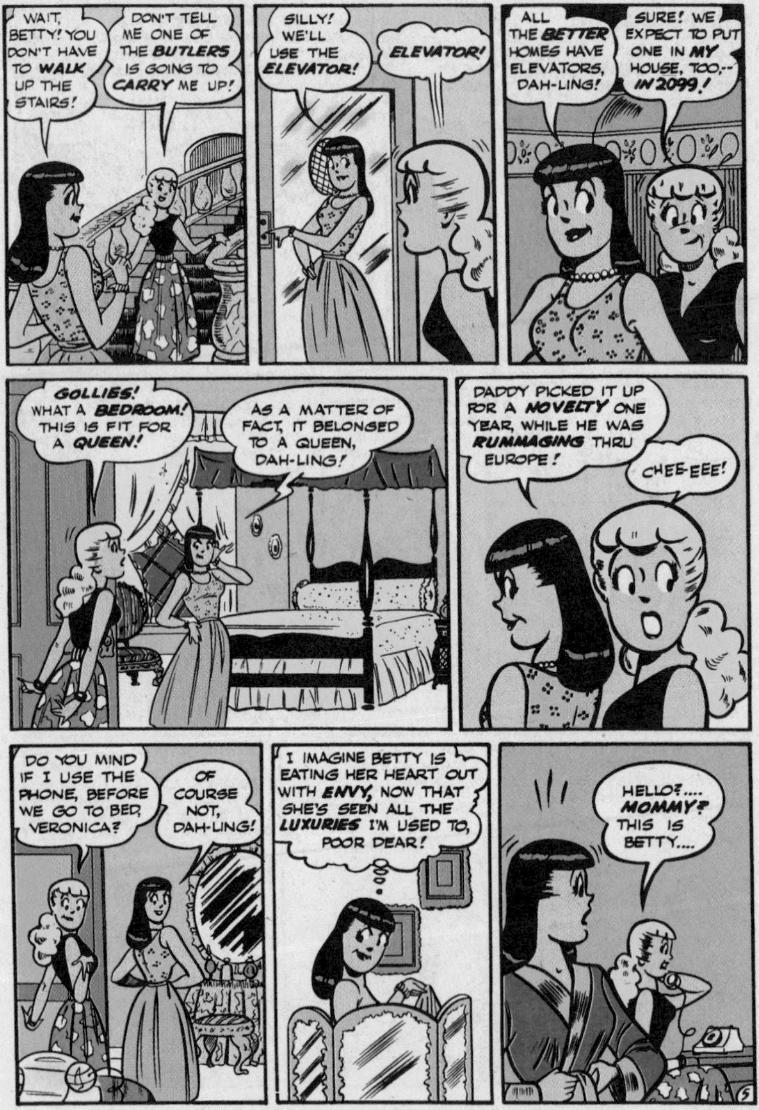
WAIT, BETTY! YOU DON'T HAVE TO WALK UP THE STAIRS!
DON'T TELL ME ONE OF THE BUTLERS IS GOING TO CARRY ME UP!
SILLY! WE'LL USE THE ELEVATOR!
ELEVATOR!
ALL THE BETTER HOMES HAVE ELEVATORS, DAH-LING!
SURE! WE EXPECT TO PUT ONE IN MY HOUSE, TOO,-- IN 2099!
GOLLIES! WHAT A BEDROOM! THIS IS FIT FOR A QUEEN!
AS A MATTER OF FACT, IT BELONGED TO A QUEEN, DAH-LING!
DADDY PICKED IT UP FOR A NOVELTY ONE YEAR, WHILE HE WAS RUMMAGING THRU EUROPE!
CHEE-EEE!
DO YOU MIND IF I USE THE PHONE, BEFORE WE GO TO BED, VERONICA?
OF COURSE NOT, DAH-LING!
I IMAGINE BETTY IS EATING HER HEART OUT WITH ENVY, NOW THAT SHE'S SEEN ALL THE LUXURIES I'M USED TO, POOR DEAR!
HELLO?.... MOMMY? THIS IS BETTY....
5

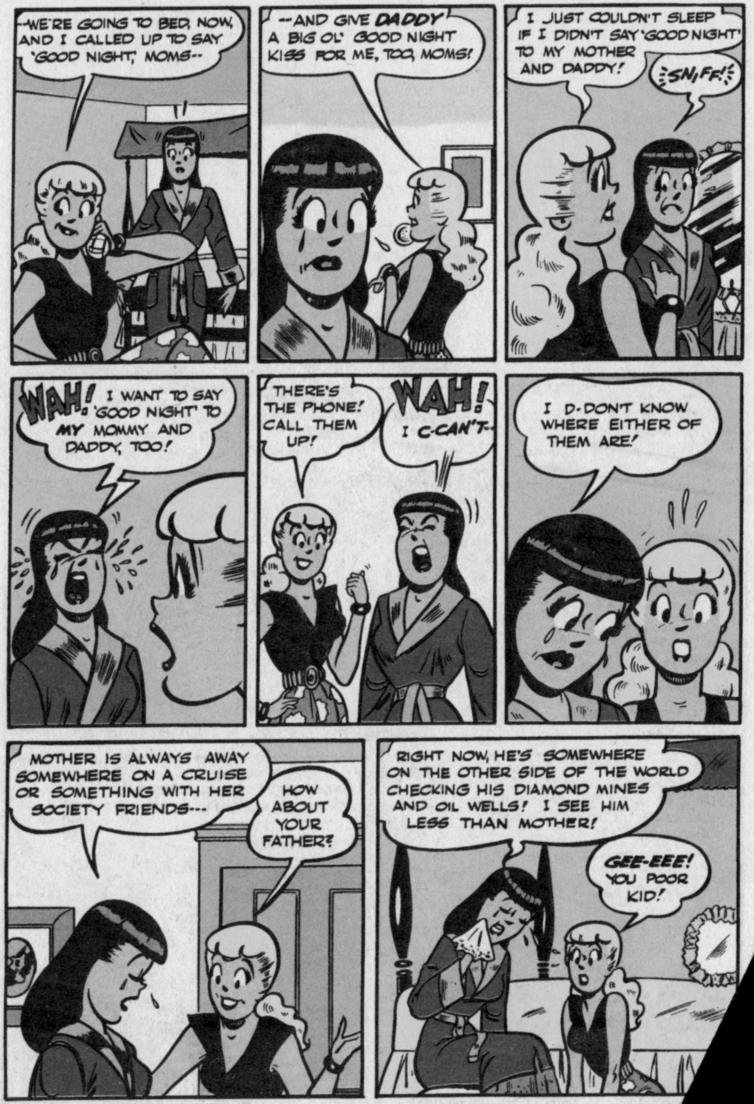
--WE'RE GOING TO BED, NOW, AND I CALLED UP TO SAY 'GOOD NIGHT,' MOMS--
--AND GIVE DADDY A BIG OL' GOOD NIGHT KISS FOR ME, TOO, MOMS!
I JUST COULDN'T SLEEP IF I DIDN'T SAY 'GOOD NIGHT' TO MY MOTHER AND DADDY!
SNIFF!
WAH! I WANT TO SAY 'GOOD NIGHT' TO MY MOMMY AND DADDY, TOO!
THERE'S THE PHONE! CALL THEM UP!
WAH! I C-CAN'T--
I D-DON'T KNOW WHERE EITHER OF THEM ARE!
MOTHER IS ALWAYS AWAY SOMEWHERE ON A CRUISE OR SOMETHING WITH HER SOCIETY FRIENDS---
HOW ABOUT YOUR FATHER?
RIGHT NOW, HE'S SOMEWHERE ON THE OTHER SIDE OF THE WORLD CHECKING HIS DIAMOND MINES AND OIL WELLS! I SEE HIM LESS THAN MOTHER!
GEE-EEE! YOU POOR KID!

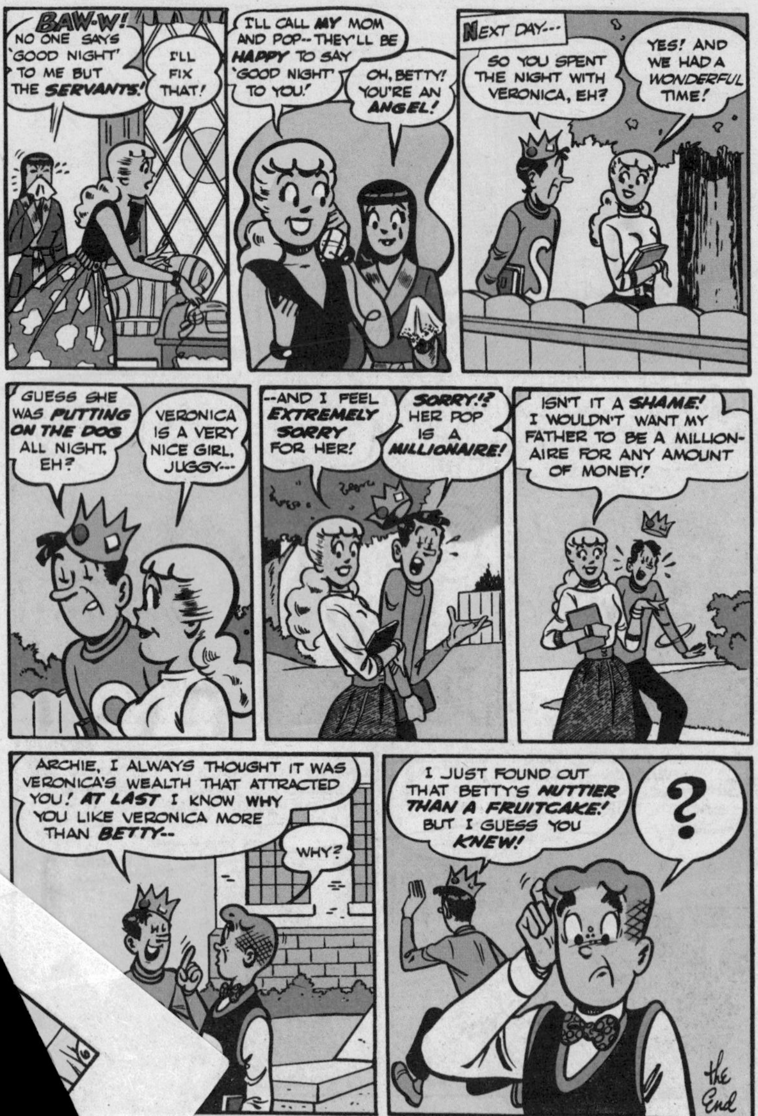
BAW-W! NO ONE SAYS 'GOOD NIGHT' TO ME BUT THE SERVANTS!
I'LL FIX THAT!
I'LL CALL MY MOM AND POP-- THEY'LL BE HAPPY TO SAY 'GOOD NIGHT' TO YOU!
OH, BETTY! YOU'RE AN ANGEL!
NEXT DAY---
SO YOU SPENT THE NIGHT WITH VERONICA, EH?
YES! AND WE HAD A WONDERFUL TIME!
GUESS SHE WAS PUTTING ON THE DOG ALL NIGHT, EH?
VERONICA IS A VERY NICE GIRL, JUGGY---
--AND I FEEL EXTREMELY SORRY FOR HER!
SORRY!? HER POP IS A MILLIONAIRE!
ISN'T IT A SHAME! I WOULDN'T WANT MY FATHER TO BE A MILLIONAIRE FOR ANY AMOUNT OF MONEY!
ARCHIE, I ALWAYS THOUGHT IT WAS VERONICA'S WEALTH THAT ATTRACTED YOU! AT LAST I KNOW WHY YOU LIKE VERONICA MORE THAN BETTY--
WHY?
I JUST FOUND OUT THAT BETTY'S NUTTIER THAN A FRUITCAKE! BUT I GUESS YOU KNEW!
?
The End